THE LIAR KING

Also by Greg Ke...

GREG KEYES

THE BRIAR KING

The Kingdoms of
Thorn and Bone: Book One

TOR

First published 2003 by The Ballantine Publishing Group, New York

First published in Great Britian 2003 by Tor

This edition published 2004 by Tor
an imprint of Pan Macmillan Ltd
Pan Macmillan, 20 New Wharf Road, London N1 9RR
Basingstoke and Oxford
Associated companies throughout the world
www.panmacmillan.com
www.toruk.com

ISBN 0 330 41945 5

9 8 7 6 5 4 3 2 1

A CIP catalogue record for this book is available from
the British Library.

Printed and bound in Australia
by McPherson's Printing Group

All Pan Macmillan titles are available from www.panmacmillan.com
or from Bookpost by telephoning 01624 677237.

For my brother,
Timothy Howard Keyes

Know, O Proud Heart of Fear, that in those days there were no kings and queens, no lords and vassals. In the countless millennia before Everon, known also as the Age of Man, there were only masters and slaves. The masters were ancient, as practiced at cruelty as the stars at shining. They were more powerful than gods, and they were not men.

Their slaves were innumerable, but all of our mothers and fathers were among them. Humans were their cattle and their playthings. But even slaves of a thousand generations may be born with hearts bright enough to hope and dark enough to do what must be done. Even a slave may rise from the dust, and whet his gaze into a knife, and tell his master, "You will never own me."

—THE TESTIMONY OF SAINT ANEMLEN AT THE COURT OF THE BLACK JESTER,
SHORTLY BEFORE THE COMMENCEMENT OF HIS TORTURES

THE BORN QUEEN

T HE SKY CRACKED AND LIGHTNING fell through its crooked
seams. With it came a black sleet tasting of smoke, copper, and
brimstone. With it came a howling like a gale from hell.

Carsek drew himself up, clutching his bloody bandages, hoping they
would keep his guts in until he saw the end of this, one way or another.

"She must order the charge soon," he grunted, pushing himself to
his feet with the butt of his spear.

A hand jerked at Carsek's ankle. "Get back down, you fool, if you
want to live until the charge."

Carsek spared a glance at his companion, a man in torn chain mail
and no helm, blue eyes pleading through the dark mat of his wet hair.

"*You* crouch, Thaniel," Carsek muttered. "I've done enough crouching. Fourteen days we've been squatting in these pig holes, sleeping in
our own shit and blood. Can't you hear? They're fighting up front, and
I'll see it, I will." He peered through the driving rain, trying to make out
what was happening.

"You'll see death waving hello," Thaniel said. "That's what you'll see.
Our time will come soon enough."

"I'm sick of crawling on my belly in this filth. I was trained to fight
on my feet. I want an opponent, one with blood I can spill, with bones I
can break. I'm a warrior, by Taranos! I was promised a war, not this

slaughter, not wounds given by specters we never see, by ghost-needles and winds of iron."

"Wish you may and might. I wish for a plump girl named Alis or Favor or How-May-I-Please-You to sit on my lap and feed me plums. I wish for ten pints of ale. I wish for a bed stuffed with swandown. Yet here I am still stuck in the mud, with *you*. What's your wishing getting you? Do you see your enemy?"

"I see fields smoking to the horizon, even in this pissing rain. I see these trench graves we dug for ourselves. I see the damned keep, as big as a mountain. I see—" He saw a wall of black, growing larger with impossible speed.

"Slitwind!" he shouted, hurling himself back into the trench. In his haste he landed face first in mud that reeked of ammonia and gangrene.

"What?" Thaniel said, but then even the smoke-gray sun above them was gone, and a sound like a thousand thousand swords on a thousand thousand whetstones scraped at the insides of their skulls. Two men who hadn't ducked swiftly enough flopped into the mud, headless, blood jetting from their necks.

"Another damned Skasloi magick," Thaniel said. "I told you."

Carsek howled in rage and frustration, and the rain fell even harder. Thaniel gripped his arm. "Hold on, Carsek. Wait. It won't be long, now. When *she* comes, the magicks of the Skasloi will be as nothing."

"So you say. I've seen nothing to prove it."

"She has the power."

Carsek brushed Thaniel's hand from his shoulder. "You're one of her own, a Bornman. She's your queen, your witch. Of course you believe in her."

"Oh, of course," Thaniel said. "We believe whatever we're told, we Bornmen. We're stupid like that. But you believe in her, too, Carsek, or you wouldn't be here."

"She had all the right words. But where is the steel? Your Born Queen has talked us all right into death."

"Wouldn't death be better than slavery?"

Carsek tasted blood in his mouth. He spit, and saw that his spittle was black. "Seven sevens of the generations of my fathers have lived and died slaved to the Skasloi lords," he sneered. "I don't even know all of their names. You Bornmen have been here for only twenty years. Most of you were whelped otherwhere, without the whip, without the masters. What do you know of slavery? You or your redheaded witch?"

Thaniel didn't answer for a moment, and when he did, it was without his usual bantering tone. "Carsek, I've not known you long, but together we slaughtered the Vhomar giants at the Ford of Silence. We killed so many we made a bridge of their bodies. You and I, we marched across the Gorgon plain, where a quarter of our company fell to dust. I've seen you fight. I know your passion. You can't fool me. Your people have been slaves longer, yes, but it's all the same. A slave is a slave. And we *will* win, Carsek, you bloody-handed monster. So drink this, and count your blessings we got this far."

He passed Carsek a flask. It had something in it that tasted like fire, but it dulled the pain.

"Thanks," Carsek grunted, handing it back. He paused, then went on. "I'm sorry. It's just the damned waiting. It's like being in my cage, before the master sent me out to fight."

Thaniel nodded, took a swig from the flask himself, then stoppered it. Nearby, Findos the Half-Handed, deep in a fever, shrieked at some memory or nightmare.

"I've always wondered, but never asked," Thaniel said pensively. "Why do you *Vhiri Croatani* call us the Bornmen, anyway?"

Carsek wiped the rain from his eyes with the back of his hand. "That's a strange question. It's what you call yourselves, isn't it? *Vhiri Genian*, yes? And your queen, the firstborn of your people in this place, isn't she named Genia, 'the Born'?"

Thaniel blinked at him, then threw back his head and laughed.

"What's so funny?"

Thaniel shook his head. "I see now. In your language that's how it sounds. But really—" He stopped, for a sudden exclamation had gone up among the men, a mass cry of fear and horror that moved down from the front.

Carsek put his hand down to push himself up, and found the mud strangely warm. A viscous, sweet-smelling fluid was flowing down the trench, two fingers deep.

"By all that's holy," Thaniel swore.

It was blood, a river of it.

With an inarticulate cry, Carsek came back to his feet.

"No more of this. No more!"

He started to clamber out of the trench.

"Stop, warrior," a voice commanded.

A woman's voice, and it halted him as certainly as the spectral whip of a master.

He turned and saw *her*.

She wore black mail, and her face above it was whiter than bone. Her long auburn hair hung lank, soaked by the pestilent rain, but she was beautiful as no earthly woman could be. Her eyes sparked like lightning in the heart of a black cloud.

Behind her stood her champions, clad much as she, bared fey-swords gleaming like hot brass. Tall and unafraid, they stood. They looked like gods.

"Great queen!" Carsek stammered.

"You are ready to fight, warrior?" she asked.

"I am, Majesty. By Taranos, I am!"

"Pick fifty men and follow me."

The forward trenches were filled with milled meat, with few pieces still recognizable as human. Carsek tried to ignore the sucking his feet made, somehow different from walking in ordinary mud. He had less success ignoring the stench of opened bowels and fresh offal. What had killed them? A demon? A spell? He didn't care. They were gone, but he was going to *fight*, by the Twin and the Bull.

When they halted in the foremost trench, which was half again as deep as Carsek was tall, he could see the black walls of the fortress looming above. This was what nearly a month and two thousand or more sacrifices had gained them—a hole at the foot of the fortress.

"Now it's just a brisk walk to the wall that can't be broken and the gate that can't be breached," Thaniel said. "The battle's nearly won!"

"Now who's the skeptic? Here's a chance for glory, and to die on my feet," Carsek said. "It's all I ask."

"Hah," Thaniel said. "Myself, I intend not only to cover myself in glory, but to have a drink when it's all done." He held out his palm.

"Take my hand, Carsek. Let's agree—we'll meet for a drink when it's over. Overlooking the arena where once you fought. And there we shall account who has more glory. And it shall be me!"

Carsek took his hand. "In the very seat of the master." The two men clenched a mutual fist.

"It's done, then," Thaniel said. "You won't break a promise, and I won't, so surely we'll both live."

"Surely," Carsek said.

Planks were brought and laid so they might scale their own trench. Then Genia Dare, the queen, gave them all a fierce smile.

"When this sun sets we shall all be free or all dead," she said. "I do not intend to die." With that, she drew her feysword and turned to Carsek. "I must reach the gate. Do you understand? Until the gate falls, five thousand is no better than fifty, for I can protect no greater number than two score and ten from Skasloi slaughter-spelling if they have us 'neath their fatal eyes, and if we can do naught but stand in their gaze. Once the gate is sundered, we can sweep through too quickly for them to strike down. This will be a hard charge, my heroes—but no spell will touch you, that I swear. It's only sword and shaft, flesh and bone you must fight."

"Flesh and bone are grass, and I am a sickle," Carsek said. "I will get you to the gate, Majesty."

"Then go and do it."

Carsek hardly felt his wounds anymore. His belly was light and his head full of fire. He was the first up the plank, first to set his feet on the black soil.

Lightning wrenched at him, and slitwinds, but this time they parted, passed to left and right of him, Thaniel, and all his men. He heard Thaniel hoot with joy as the deadly magicks passed them by, impotent as a eunuch's ghost.

They charged across the smoking earth, howling, and Carsek saw, through rage-reddened vision, that he at last had a real enemy in front of his spear.

"It's Vhomar, lads!" he shouted. "Nothing but Vhomar!"

Thaniel laughed. "And just a few of them!" he added.

A few, indeed. A few hundred, ranged six ranks deep before the gate. Each stood head and shoulders taller than the tallest man in Carsek's band. Carsek had fought many a Vhomar in the arena, and respected them there, as much as any worthy foe deserved. Now he hated them as he hated nothing mortal. Of all of the slaves of the Skasloi, only the Vhomar had chosen to remain slaves, to fight those who rose against the masters.

A hundred Vhomar bows thrummed together, and black-winged shafts hummed and thudded amongst his men, so that every third one of them fell.

A second flight melted in the rain and did not touch them at all, and then Carsek was at the front rank of the enemy, facing a wall of giants in iron cuirasses, shouting up at their brutish, unhuman faces.

The moment stretched out, slow and silent in Carsek's mind. Plenty of time to notice details, the spears and shields bossed with spikes, the very grain of the wood, black rain dripping from the brows of the creature looming in front of him, the scar on its cheek, its one blue eye and one black eye, the mole above the black one . . .

Then sound came back, a hammer strike as Carsek feinted. He made as if to thrust his spear into the giant's face but dropped instead, coming up beneath the huge shield as it lifted, driving his manslayer under the overlapping plates of the armor, skirling at the top of his lungs as leather and fabric and flesh parted. He wrenched at his weapon as the warrior toppled, but the haft snapped.

Carsek drew his ax. The press of bodies closed as the Vhomar surged forward, and Carsek's own men, eager for killing, slammed into him from behind. He found himself suffocating in the sweaty stench, caught between shield and armored belly, and no room to swing his ax. Something hit his helm so hard it rang, and then the steel cap was torn from his head. Thick fingers knotted in Carsek's hair, and suddenly his feet were no longer on the ground.

He kicked in the air as the monster drew him up by the scalp, dangled him so it was staring into his eyes. The Vhomar drew back the massive sword it gripped in its other hand, bent on decapitating him.

"You damned fool!" Carsek shouted at it, shattering the giant's teeth with the edge of his ax, then savaged its neck with his second blow. Bellowing, the Vhomar dropped him, trying to staunch its lifeblood with its own hands. Carsek hamstrung it and went on.

The work stayed close and bloody, he knew not for how long. For each Vhomar Carsek killed, there was always another, if not two or three. He had actually forgotten his goal was the gate, when there it was before him. Through the press he saw feyswords glittering, glimpsed auburn hair and sparks of pale viridian. Then he was pushed back, until the gate receded from view and thought.

The rain stopped, but the sky grew darker. All Carsek could hear was his own wheezing breath; all he could see was blood and the rise and fall of iron, like the lips of sea waves breaking above him. His arm could hardly hold itself up for more killing, and of his fifty men he now stood in a circle with the eight who remained, Thaniel among them. And still the giants came on, wave on wave of them.

But then there was a sound like all the gods screaming. A new tide swept up from behind him, a wall of shouting men, hundreds pouring out of the trenches, crushing into the ranks of their enemies, and for the first time Carsek looked up from death and witnessed the impossible.

The massive steel portals of the citadel hung from their hinges, twisted almost beyond recognizing, and below them, white light blazed.

The battle swept past them, and as Carsek's legs gave way, Thaniel caught him.

"She's done it," Carsek said. "Your Born Witch has done it!"

"I told you she would," Thaniel said. "I told you."

Carsek wasn't there when the inner keep fell. His wounds had reopened and had to be bound again. But as the clouds broke, and the dying sun hemorrhaged across the horizon, Thaniel came for him.

"She wants you there," Thaniel said. "You deserve it."

"We all do," Carsek managed.

With Thaniel under one shoulder, he climbed the bloody steps of the massive central tower, remembering when he trod it last, in chains, on his way to fight in the arena, how the gilded balustrades and strange statues had glimmered in Skasloi witchlight. It had been beautiful and terrible.

Even now, shattered, blackened, it still brought fear. Fear from childhood and beyond, of the master's power, of the lash that could not be seen but that burned to the soul.

Even now it seemed it must all be a trick, another elaborate game, another way for the masters to extract pleasure from the pain and hopelessness of their slaves.

But when they came to the great hall, and Carsek saw Genia Dare standing with her boot on the master's throat, he knew in his heart they had won.

The Skasloi lord still wore shadow. Carsek had never seen his face, and did not now. But he knew the sound of the master's laughter as it rose up from beneath the queen's heel. For as long as he lived, Carsek would not forget that mocking, spectral, dying laugh.

Genia Dare's voice rang above that laughter. "We have torn open your keep, scattered your powers and armies, and now you will die," she said. "If this amuses you, you could have obtained your amusement much more easily. We would have been happy to kill you long ago."

The master broke off his cackling. He spoke words like spiders crawling from the mouth of a corpse, delicate, deadly. The sound that catches you unaware and wrenches your heart into your throat.

"I am *amused*," he said, "because you think you have won something. You have won nothing but decay. You have used the *sedos* power, foolish children.

"Did you think we knew nothing of the sedos? Fools. We had good reasons for avoiding the paths of its fell might. You have cursed yourselves. You have cursed your generations to come. In the final days, the end of my world will have been cleaner than the end of yours. You have no idea what you have done."

The Born Queen spat down upon him. "That for your curse," she snapped.

"It is not my curse, slave," the master said. "It is your own."

"We are not your slaves."

"You were born slaves. You will die slaves. You have merely summoned a new master. The daughters of your seed will face what you have wrought, and it will obliterate them."

Between one blink and the other, a flash like heat lightning erupted behind Carsek's eyes, then *vision*. He saw green forests rot into putrid heaths, a poison sun sinking into a bleak, sterile sea. He walked through castles and cities carpeted in human bones, felt them crack beneath his heels. And he saw, standing over it all, the Born Queen, Genia Dare, laughing as if it brought her joy.

Then it was over, and he was on the floor, as was almost everyone else in the room, clutching their heads, moaning, weeping. Only the queen still stood, white fire dripping from her hands. The master was silent.

"We do not fear your curse!" Genia said. "We are no longer your slaves. There is no fear in us. Your world, your curses, your power are all now gone. It is our world now, a human one."

The master only twitched in response. He did not speak again.

"A slow death for him," Carsek heard the queen say, in a lower voice. "A very, very slow death."

And for Carsek, that was the end of it. They took the master away, and he never saw him again.

The Born Queen, chin held high, turned to regard them all, and Carsek felt her gaze touch his for just an instant. Again he felt a flash, like fire, and for a moment he almost fell to his knees before her.

But he was never going down on his knees again, not for anyone.

"Today, we start counting the days and seasons again," she said. "To-day is the Day of the Valiant; it is the *Vhasris Slanon*! From this instant, day, month, season, and year, we reckon our own time!"

Despite their wounds and fatigue, the shouts that filled the hall were almost deafening.

Carsek and Thaniel went back down, to where the celebrations were beginning. Carsek, for his part, wanted only to sleep, to forget, and to never dream again. But Thaniel reminded him of their oath.

And so it was, as his wounds stiffened, they drank Thaniel's brandy, and Carsek sat on a throne of chalcedony and looked down upon the arena where he had fought and killed so many fellow slaves.

"I killed a hundred, before the gate," Thaniel asserted.

"I killed a hundred and five," Carsek replied.

"You can't count to a hundred and five," Thaniel retorted.

"Aye, I can. It's how many times I've had your sister."

"Well," Thaniel mused, "then my sister had to have been counting *for* you. I know that after two hands and two feet, I had to start counting for your mother."

At that, both men paused.

"We are very funny men, aren't we?" Carsek grunted.

"We are men," Thaniel said, more soberly. "And alive, and free. And that is enough." He scratched his head. "I didn't understand that last thing she said. The name we're to reckon our years by?"

"She does us a great honor," Carsek said. "It is the old tongue of the *Vhiri Croatani*, the language of my fathers. *Vhasris* means *dawn*. *Slanon* means . . . Hmm, I don't think I know your word for that."

"Use several, then."

"It means beautiful, and whole, and healthy. Like a newborn baby, perfect, with no blemishes."

"You sound like a poet, Carsek."

Carsek felt his face redden. To change the subject, he pointed at the arena. "I've never seen it from up here," he murmured.

"Does it look different?"

"Very. Smaller. I think I like it."

"We made it, Carsek." Thaniel sighed. "As the queen said, the world is ours now. What shall we do with it?"

"The gods know. I've never even thought about it." He winced at a sudden pain in his belly.

"Carsek?" Thaniel asked, concerned.

"I'll heal." Carsek downed another swallow of the liquid fire. "Tell me," he said. "As long as we're giving lessons in language. What were you saying back there, in the trench? About you people not being the Bornmen?"

Thaniel chuckled again. "I always thought you called us that because we are so recent to this land, because we were the last that the Skasloi captured to be their slaves. But it's just that you *misheard* us."

"You aren't being clear," Carsek told him. "I might be dying. Shouldn't you be clear?"

"You aren't dying, you rancid beast, but I'll try to be clear anyway. When my people first came here, we thought we were in a place called

Virginia. It was named for a queen, I think, in the old country; I don't know, I was born here. But our queen is named after her, too—Virginia Elizabeth Dare—that's her real name. When we said Virginia you dumb Croatani thought we were speaking your language, calling ourselves *Vhiri Genian*—Born Men. It was a confusion of tongues, you see."

"Oh," Carsek said, and then he collapsed.

When he woke, four days later, he was pleased that at least he hadn't dreamed.

That was the fourth day of the epoch known as *Eberon Vhasris Slanon*.

PROLOGUE

The day the last Skasloi stronghold fell began the age known as
Eberon Vhasris Slanon *in the language of the elder Cavarum.*
When the language itself was forgotten by all but a few cloistered
scholars in the church the name for the age persisted in the
tongues of men as Everon, *just as* Slanon *remained attached to the*
place of the victory itself in the Lierish form Eslen.

    Everon was an age of human beings in all their glories and
failings. The children of the rebellion multiplied and covered the
land with their kingdoms.

    In the year 2,223 E. the age of Everon came to an abrupt and
terrible end.

    It may be that I am the last to remember it.

    —*The Codex Tereminnam,* AUTHOR ANON.

IN THE MONTH OF ETRAMEN, in the year twenty-two fifteen of
Everon, two girls crouched in the darkest tangles of a sacred garden
in the city of the dead, praying not to be seen.

Anne, who at eight was the eldest, peered cautiously through the thickly woven branches and creepers enclosing them.

"Is it really a Scaos?" Austra, a year younger, asked.

"Hush!" Anne whispered. "Yes, it's a Scaos, and a monstrous one, so keep low or he'll see your hair. It's too yellow."

"Yours is too red," Austra replied. "Fastia says it's rust because you don't use your head enough."

"Figs for Fastia. Keep quiet, and go that way."

"It's darker that way."

"I know. But we can't let him see us. He'll kill us, but not fast. He'll eat us a bit at a time. But he's too big to follow us back in there."

"He could use an ax, or a sword, and cut the branches."

"No," Anne said. "Don't you know *anything*? This is a *horz,* not just any old garden. That's why everything is so wild here. No one is allowed to cut it, not even *him*. If he cuts it, Saint Fessa and Saint Selfan will curse him."

"Won't they curse us for hiding here?"

"We aren't cutting anything," Anne said reasonably. "We're just hiding. Anyhow, if the Scaos catches us, we'll be worse than cursed, won't we? We'll be dead."

"You're scaring me."

"I just saw him move!" Anne squeaked. "He's right over there! For the saints and love of your life, go!"

Austra moaned and lurched forward, pushing through twining roots of ancient oaks, through vines of thorn, primrose, and wild grape so ancient they were thicker than Anne's legs. The smell was earth and leaves and a faint, sweet corruption. Grayish green light was all that the layers of leaves and boughs allowed them of the sun's bright lamp. Out there, in the broad, lead-paved streets of the city of ghosts, it was noon. Here, it was twilight.

They came into a small space where nothing grew, though vegetation arched over it, like a little room built by the Phay, and there crouched together for a moment.

"He's still after us," Anne panted. "Do you hear?"

"Yes. What shall we do?"

"We'll—"

She never got to finish. Something cracked with a sound like a dish breaking, and then they were sliding into the open mouth of the earth. They landed with a thump on a hard stone surface.

For several moments, Anne lay on her back, blinking up at the dim light above, spitting dust from her mouth. Austra was just breathing fast, making funny little noises.

"Are you well?" Anne asked the other girl.

Austra nodded. "Uh-huh. But what happened? Where are we?" Then her eyes went huge. "We're buried! The dead have taken us!"

"No!" Anne said, her own terror receding. "No, look, we've just fallen into an older tomb. Very old, because the horz has been here for four hundred years, and this is *under* it." She pointed to the light falling down the same dirt slope they had come down. "The ground must have been thin there. But see, we can go back out."

"Let's go, then," Austra said. "Quickly."

Anne tossed her red locks. "Let's look around first. I'll bet no one has been here for a thousand years."

"I don't think it's a tomb," Austra said. "Tombs look just like houses. This doesn't."

Austra was right, it didn't. They had fallen at the edge of a big, round room. Seven huge stones set like pillars held up an even bigger flat rock like a roof, and smaller stones had been fitted around to keep the dirt out.

"Maybe this is what houses looked like a thousand years ago," Anne suggested.

"Maybe it's a Scaosen tomb!" Austra exclaimed. "Maybe it's *his* tomb."

"They didn't have tombs," Anne said. "They thought they were immortal. Come on, I want to see that."

"What is it?"

Anne stood and made her way to a box of stone, longer than it was tall or wide.

"I think it's a sarcophagus," she said. "It's not all ornamented like the ones we use now, but it's the same shape."

"You mean there's a dead person in there."

"Uh-huh." She brushed her hand across the lid and felt incisions in the stone. "There's something written here."

"What?"

"It's just letters. *V, I, D, A*. It doesn't make a word."

"Maybe it's another language."

"Or an abbreviation. *V*—" She stopped, transfixed by a sudden thought. "Austra. Virgenya Dare! *V-I* for Virgenya and *D-A* for Dare."

"That can't be right," Austra said.

"No," Anne whispered. "It must be. Look how old this tomb is. Virgenya Dare was the first of my family born in the world. This *has* to be her."

"I thought your family had ruled Crotheny for only a hundred years," Austra said.

"It's true," Anne replied. "But she could have come here, during the time of the first kingdoms. No one knows where she went, after the wars, or where she was buried. This *is* her. I know it, somehow. It must be. Help me get the lid off, so I can see her."

"Anne! No!"

"Come on, Austra. She's my ancestor. She won't mind." Anne strained at the lid, but it wouldn't move. When she finally cajoled the reluctant Austra into helping her, it still didn't move at first; but as the two girls strained, the heavy stone lid shifted a fingersbreadth.

"That's it! It's moving!"

But try as they might, they couldn't budge it more.

Anne tried to look into the crack. She saw nothing, but the smell was funny. Not bad, just strange, like the old place under a bed that hasn't been cleaned for a very long time.

"Lady Virgenya?" she whispered into the box, hearing her voice hum around inside. "My name is Anne. My father is William, the king of Crotheny. I'm pleased to meet you."

No answer came, but Anne was sure the spirit had heard. After all, sleeping for this long, she was probably slow to wake. "I'll bring candles to burn for you," Anne promised. "And gifts."

"Please, let's go," Austra pleaded.

"Yes, very well," Anne agreed. "Mother or Fastia will miss us pretty soon, anyway."

"Are we still hiding from the Scaos?"

"No, I'm tired of that game," Anne replied. "This is better. This is *real*. And it's our secret. I don't want anyone else to find it. So we have to go, now, before they look this far. Fastia might be small enough to squeeze through."

"Why does it have to be secret?"

"It just does. Come on."

They managed to scramble back up through the hole and the tangled vegetation, until at last they emerged near the crumbly stone wall of the horz. Fastia was standing there, her back to them, long brown hair flowing down her green gown. She turned as she heard them approach.

"Where have you—" She broke off and vented an outraged laugh. "Ah! Just *look* at you two. Filthy! What in the name of the saints have you been into?"

"Sorry!" Anne said. "We were just pretending a Scaos was after us."

"You'll wish it was only a Scaos when Mother sees you. Anne, these are our revered ancestors all around us. We're supposed to honor Aunt Fiene, to put her body in the afterhouse. It's a very solemn business, and you're supposed to *be* there, not playing games in the horz."

"We were bored," Anne said. "Aunt Fiene wouldn't care."

"It's not Aunt Fiene you have to worry about—it's Mother and Father." She brushed at the grime staining Anne's white gown. "There's no way to get you clean, either," Fastia replied, "not before Mother sees."

"*You* used to play here," Anne said. "You told me so."

"Maybe I did," her older sister replied, "but I'm fifteen now and about to be married. I'm not allowed to play anymore. And I'm not allowed to let you play, either, at least not right now. I was supposed to watch you. Now you've gotten me in trouble."

"We're sorry, Fastia."

Her older sister smiled and pushed back her dark hair, so like their mother's, so *unlike* Anne's strawberry mop. "It's all right, little sister. This time I'll take the blame. But when I'm married, I'll be governing you younger children, so you'd better get used to paying attention to me. Practice. Try minding me at least half the time, please? You, too, Austra."

"Yes, Archgreffess," Austra mumbled, curtseying.

"Thank you, Fastia," Anne added. For an instant, Anne almost told her older sister what they had found. But she didn't. Fastia had become strange lately. Not as much fun, more serious. More grown-up. Anne loved her, but she wasn't sure she could trust her anymore.

That night, after the scolding, when the candles went dark and she and Austra lay on their broad feather bed, Anne pinched Austra's arm. Not hard enough to hurt, but almost.

"Ow!" Austra complained. "Why did you do that?"

"If you ever tell what we found today," Anne warned, "I'll pinch you harder!"

"I said I wouldn't tell."

"Swear it. Swear it by your mother and father."

Austra was quiet for a moment. "They're dead," she whispered.

"All the better. The dead are better at hearing promises than the living, my father always says."

"Don't make me," Austra pleaded. She sounded sad, almost as if she was going to start crying.

"Never mind," Anne said. "I'm sorry. I'll think of something else for you to swear by tomorrow. All right?"

"All right," Austra said.

"Good night, Austra. May the Black Mary stay away."

"Good night," Austra replied. And soon her breathing indicated she was asleep.

But Anne couldn't sleep. Her head filled with stories, heroic tales of the great war with the Scaosen, demons, and of Virgenya Dare. And she thought of that dark crack in the coffin, the faint sigh she was sure she had heard. She nursed her secret, her prize, and finally, smiling, drifted into dreams of darkling fields and brooding forests.

PART I

THE COMING
OF THE GREFFYN

The Year 2,223 of Everon

The Month of Terthmen

O what has form like to the lion
Yet visage and an eagle's mien
And what has venom for its blood
And eyes no living man hath seen?

—*From a riddle song of eastern Crotheny*

The blood of regals shall run like a river.
So drowndeth the world.

—*Translated from the Tafles Taceis, or Book of Murmurs*

CHAPTER ONE

THE HOLTER

Aspar White smelled murder. Its scent was like a handful of autumn leaves, crisped by the first frost and crushed in the palm.

Dirty Jesp, the Sefry woman who had raised him, told him once that his peculiar sense came from having been born of a dying mother below the gallows where the Raver took his sacrifices. But Jesp made her living as a liar, and the why didn't matter anyway. All Aspar cared about was that his nose was usually right. Someone was about to kill someone else, or try.

Aspar had just walked into the Sow's Teat after a week of hard going in the Walham Foothills. His muscles burned with fatigue, his mouth was grittier than sand, and for days he had been dreaming of the cool, dark, honeyed sweetness of stout. He'd had just one sip, one moment of it dancing on his tongue, one kiss of foam on his lips, when the scent came and ruined the taste.

With a sigh, he set the grainy earthenware mug on the pitted oak of his table and looked around the dark, crowded interior of the tavern, one hand straying to the planished bone grip of his dirk, wondering where death was coming from and where it was going.

He saw only the usual crowd—charcoal burners mostly, their faces smudged black by their trade, joking and laughing as they drank away the taste of soot on their tongues. Nearer the door, which had been propped open to let in the evening air, Loh—the miller's boy, in his clean, lace-trimmed shirt—gestured grandly with his mug, and his friends hooted as he drained the whole thing in one long draught. Four Hornladh merchants in checkered doublets and red hose stood near the hearth, where a spitted boar dripped sizzling into the coals, and around them gathered a clump of youths, faces eager and ruddy in the firelight, begging stories about the wide world beyond their tiny village of Colbaely.

Nothing that even looked like a brawl about to start. Aspar picked up his mug again. Maybe the beer was a little off, today.

But then he saw where murder was coming from. It came in through the open door, along with the first tentative trilling of whippoorwills and a faint, damp promise of rain.

He was just a boy, maybe fifteen. Not from Colbaely, Aspar knew for sure, and probably not even from the Greffy of Holtmarh. The newcomer swept a desperate, hurried gaze around the room, squinting, trying to adjust his eyes to the light, clearly searching for someone.

Then he saw Aspar, alone at his table, and lurched toward him. The young fellow was clad in brain-tanned elkskin breeches and a shirt of homespun that had seen better days. His brown hair was matted, caked with mud, and full of leaves. Aspar saw the apple in his throat bobble convulsively as he pulled a rather large sword from a sheath on his back and quickened his pace.

Aspar took another pull on his beer and sighed. It tasted worse than the last. In the sudden silence, the boy's buskins *swish-swish*ed on the slate-tiled floor.

"You're the holter," the boy said in a thick Almannish accent. "The kongsman."

"I'm the king's forester," Aspar agreed. "It's easily known, for I wear his colors. I'll be Aspar White. And you'd be? . . ."

"H'am the man is going to slooter you," the boy said.

Aspar lifted his head just slightly, so he was looking at the lad with one eye. He held the sword clumsily. "Why?" he asked.

"You know why."

"No. If I knew why, I never would have asked."

"You know saint-buggering well—*tho ya theen manns slootered meen kon*—"

"Speak the king's tongue, boy."

"*Grim* take the king!" the boy shouted. "It's not *his* forest!"

"Well, you'll have to take that up with him. He thinks it is, you know, and he's the king."

"I mean to. Right after I take it up with you. This goes all the way back to Eslen before h'am done. But it starts here with you, murtherer."

Aspar sighed. He could hear it in the young man's voice, see it in the set of his shoulders. No use talking anymore. He stood quickly, stepped inside the sword point, and slammed his beer mug against the side of the boy's head. The kiln-fired clay cracked and the fellow screamed, dropping his weapon and clutching his split ear. Aspar calmly yanked out his long dirk, grabbed the boy by the collar, hauled him up easily with one large, callused hand, and pushed him down roughly onto the bench across the table from where he had been sitting.

The boy stared defiantly at him through a mask of pain and blood. The hand holding the side of his head was shiny and dark in the dim light.

"You all see!" the boy croaked. "Witness, all! He'll murther me like he slootered mine fam'ly."

"Boy, just calm down," Aspar snapped. He picked up the sword and set it next to him on his bench, with the table between it and the boy. He kept his own dirk out.

"Armann, bring me another beer."

"Y'just busted one of my mugs!" the hostler shouted, his nearly round face beet-red.

"Bring it or I'll bust something else."

Some of the charmen laughed at that, and then most of the rest of them joined in. The chatter started up again.

Aspar watched the boy while he waited for the beer. The lad's fingers were trembling, and he couldn't look up. His courage seemed to be leaking out of him with his blood.

That was often the case, Aspar found. Bleed a man a little, and he grew less heroic.

"What happened to your family, boy?"

"As eft you don't know."

"You want another cuff? Grim eat you, but I'll beat you till you come out with it. I don't take to threats, and I don't take to being called a killer unless I did the killing. And in the end I don't care what did 'r didn't happen to a bunch of squatters—except that if something ill happened in the forest, that's my *job*, to know about it, y'see? Because if I don't care about you, I care about the forest, and about the king's justice. So spell me it!"

"I just—I—they're dead!" And suddenly he burst out crying. As tears ran through the blood on his face and trailed down his chin, Aspar realized that even fifteen had been an overestimate. The lad was probably no more than thirteen, just big for his age.

"Sceat on this," Aspar grumbled.

"Aspar White!" He looked up to see Winna Rufoote, the hostler's daughter. She was less than half his age, just nineteen, pretty with her oval face, green eyes, and flaxen hair. Strong willed. Trouble looking for lodging. Aspar avoided her when he could.

"Winna—"

"Don't 'Winna' me. You burst this poor boy's brains all over—and one of our mugs—and now you're just going to sit here and drink beer while he bleeds on everything?"

"Look—"

"I won't hear a word of it. Not from you, s'posed to be the king's man. First you'll help me get this boy to a room so I can clean him up. Then you'll put your mark on one o' them royal notes or else pay good copper for our mug. After that, y'can have another beer, and not before."

"If this weren't the only hostel in town—"

"But it *is*, isn't it? And if you want to stay welcome here—"

"You know you can't turn me out."

"No. Turn out the king's man? Sure I can't. But you might start finding your beer tasting like piss, if you understand me."

"It already tastes like piss," Aspar grumbled.

She put her hands on her hips and glared at him. He suddenly felt a little weak in the knees. In twenty-five years as a holter, he had faced bears, lions, more outlaws than he could even count. But he had never learned how to handle a pretty woman.

"He *did* come in here to kill me, the little sceat," Aspar reminded her sheepishly.

"An' how is that such a strange thing? I've been tempted myself." She pulled out a rag and handed it to the boy. "What's your name?" she asked.

"Uscaor," he mumbled. "Uscaor Fraletson."

"Your ear's just a bit cut, Uscaor. It'll be okay."

Aspar blew out a long breath and stood back up. "Come on, boy. Let's get you cleaned up, hey? So you'll look nice when you come to murther me in my bed."

But as the boy swayed to his feet, Aspar caught the scent of death again and noticed, for the first time, the boy's right hand. It was bruised purple and black, and the sight of it sent a tingle up his spine.

"What happened there, boy?" Aspar asked.

"I don't know," Uscaor said softly. "I don't remember."

"Come on, Uscaor," Winna said. "Let's find you a bed."

Aspar watched him go, frowning. The boy had meant to kill him, all right, though he hadn't come very close. But that hand—maybe that was the thing his nose was trying tell him about all along.

Uneasily, he waited for another beer.

"He's asleep," Winna told Aspar some time later, after she'd been alone with the boy for a while. "I don't think he's eaten or slept for two or three days. And that hand—it's so swollen and hot. Not like any sort of wound I've seen before."

"Yah," Aspar said. "Me either. Maybe I ought to cut it off of 'im and take it for the apothecary in Eslen to have a look at."

"You can't fool me, Asp," Winna said. "You're rougher than an elm at the skin, but in your heart there's softer stuff."

"Don't convince yourself of that, Winn. Did he spell why he wants me dead?"

"Same as he told you. He thinks you killed his family."

"Why would he think that?"

"Hey, Winna!" someone yelled, from across the room. "Leave off the king's bear and come wet me!" He banged an empty mug on the table.

"Do as you usually do, Banf—wet yourself. You know where the tap is. I'll know what to charge you by how much you throw up later."

That got a burst of jeers at the fellow's expense as Winna sat down across from Aspar.

"He and his family put up a camp down near Taff Creek," she continued, "a few leagues from where it meets the Warlock—"

"Right. Squatters, as I reckoned."

"So they squatted in the royal forest. Lots do that. Does that mean they deserve to die?"

"I didn't kill them for that. Raver's teeth! I didn't kill them at all."

"Uscaor says he saw the king's colors on the men who did it."

"No. I don't know what he saw, but he never saw that. None of my woodsmen are within thirty leagues of here."

"You sure?"

"Damned sure."

"Then who killed them?"

"I wat not. There's plenty of room in the King's Forest for all manner of outlaws. But I suppose I'll be finding out." He took another drink of his beer. "By the Taff, you say? That's about two days. I'll be leaving at first light, so tell Paet to have my horses ready." He finished the beer in a single long swallow and rose from the table. "See you."

"Wait. Don't you want to talk to the boy some more?"

"What for? He doesn't know what happened. He probably didn't even *see* anybody. I'll bet the part about the king's colors is a lie."

"How do you reckon that?"

"Maunt my words, Winn. Squatters live in terror of the king's justice. They all reckon they're going to be hanged or beheaded or hunted down, and they think I'm a two-headed uttin. I don't discourage stories like that. I spread 'em, in fact. Somebody killed this boy's kin, and he didn't see who. He reckoned it was me. The rest he made up when he started feeling foolish."

"But someone killed them," she said.

"Yah. That much of his story I believe." He sighed and stood. "Night, Winn."

"You aren't going by yourself?"

"All of my men are too far away. I have to go while the trail is still warm."

"Wait for some of your men. Send word to Dongal."

"No time. Why so nervous, Winn? I know what I'm doing."

She nodded. "Just a feeling. That something's different this time. People coming up out of the forest have been . . . different."

"I know the forest better than anyone. It's the same as it's always been."

She nodded reluctantly.

"Well, as I said, good night."

Her hand caught his. "Be careful, you," she murmured, and gave it a little squeeze.

"Certain," he said, hoping he turned quickly enough that she couldn't see him blush.

Aspar rose at first cockcrow, when the light out his window was still mostly starborn. By the time he'd splashed water from a crockery basin in his face and shaved the gray stubble sprouting there, cinched on his elkskin breeches and padded cotton gambeson, the east was primrose.

He considered his boiled-leather cuirass; that was going to be hot today.

He put it on anyway. Better hot than dead.

He strapped on his bone-handled dirk and settled his throwing ax into its loop on the same belt. He took his bow from its oilskin case, checked the wood and extra strings, counted his arrows. Then he re-cased the bow, slipped on his high boots, and went downstairs.

"First light, eh?" Winna said, as he passed through the common room.

"Getting old," Aspar grumbled.

"Well, have some breakfast as you're not too early for it."

"That reminds me. I need to buy—"

"I've packed you a week's worth of food. Paetur is loading it up for you."

"Oh. Thanks."

"Sit."

She brought him a trencher of black bread with garlic sausage and fried apples. He ate every bit of it. When he was finished, Winna wasn't in sight, but he could hear her knocking about in the kitchen. For an instant, he remembered having a woman knocking about his own kitchen, in his own house.

A long time ago, and the pain was still there. Winna was young enough to be his daughter. He left quietly, so as not to attract her attention, feeling faintly cowardly. Once outside he made straight for the stables.

Paetur, Winna's younger brother, was busy with Angel and Ogre. Paet was tall, blond, and gangly. He was—what?—thirteen?

"Morning, sir," Paet said, when he saw Aspar.

"I'm not a knight, boy."

"Yah, but you're the closest we have hereabouts, except old Sir Symen."

"A knight's a knight. Sir Symen is one; I'm not." He nodded at his mounts. "They ready to go?"

"Ogre says yah, Angel says ney. I think you ought to leave Angel with me." He patted the roan on the neck.

"She said that, did she?" Aspar grunted. "Could be she's tired from the running you gave her yesterday?"

"I never—"

"Lie to me and I'll whip you good, and your father will thank me for it."

Paet reddened and studied his shoes. "Well . . . she needed a stretch."

"Next time ask, you hear? And for pity's sake, *don't* try to ride Ogre."

The barred bay chose that moment to snort, as if in agreement. Paet laughed.

"What's so funny?"

"Tom tried, yesterday. To ride Ogre."

"When do they bury him?"

"He lost two front teeth, is all."

"Lucky. The boy's lucky."

"Yes, Master White."

Aspar patted Ogre's muzzle. "Looks like you packed them well. You want to arrange my quiver and bow?"

"Could I?" The boy's eyes sparkled eagerly.

"I reckon." He handed the weapon over.

"Is it true you've killed six uttins with this?"

"There's no such thing as uttins, boy. Nor greffyns, nor alvs, nor basil-nix, nor tax-counters with hearts."

"That's what I told my friths. But Rink says his uncle saw an uttin himself—"

"Got drunk and saw his own reflection, more likely."

"But you did kill the Black Wargh and his bandits, didn't you? All ten of them."

"Yah," Aspar said curtly.

"I'm going to do something like that someday."

"It's not all it's made out to be," Aspar replied. With that, he mounted up on Ogre and started off. Angel followed obediently. So did Paet.

"Where do you think you're going?" Aspar demanded.

"Down by the Warlock. A Sefry caravan came in last night. I want to get my fortune told."

"You'd be better off staying away from them," Aspar advised.

"Weren't you raised Sefry, Master White? Didn't Dirty Jesp raise you?"

"Yah. So I know what I'm talking about."

The Sefry had chosen a nice spot, a violet-embroidered meadow over-looking the river and embraced on all sides by thick-limbed wateroaks. They were still setting their tents. A big one of faded crimson and gold was fully erected, the clan crest—three eyes and a crescent moon—waving in a diffident zephyr. Hobbled horses grazed in the meadow, where ten men and twice that many children hammered stakes, uncoiled lines, and unrolled canvas. Most were stripped to the waist, for the sun wasn't yet high enough to sear their milk-white skin. Unlike most folk, the Sefry never darkened from the sun. In full light, they went swaddled head to toe.

"Hallo, there," one of the men called, a narrow-shouldered fellow with features that suggested thirty years but that Aspar knew were lying by at least fifteen. He had known Afas when they were both children, and Afas was the older. "Do I see Dirt's Bastard, there?" The Sefry straightened, hammer swinging at his side.

Aspar dismounted. *Dirt's Bastard.* Not a nickname he'd ever cared for.

"Hallo, Afas," he replied, refusing to let his annoyance show. "Nice to see you, too."

"Come to run us off?"

"What's the point? I'd just be wishing you on a different town, probably another in or around my jurisdiction. Besides, I'm on my way out."

"Well, that's generous." The Sefry tilted his head. "*She* said you'd be here. She was almost wrong, ney?"

"Who's 'she'?"

"Mother Cilth."

"Grim! She still alive?"

"They rarely die, these old women."

Aspar stopped a few paces from Afas. The two men were of a height, but there the resemblance stopped. Aspar had weight to go with his altitude, an oak to Afas' willow. Close up, Afas' skin was a map, the blue rivers, streams, rills, and rinns of his veins plainly visible. He had six pale nipples, set like a cat's on his lithe, wiry torso. His hair was midnight dark, tied back with a gold ribbon.

"Where'd you just come from?" Aspar asked.

"South."

"Come through the forest?"

Afas' indigo eyes went wide and guileless. "You know better than that, Holter. We wouldn't travel in King Randolf's forest without permission."

"King Randolf died thirteen years ago. It's William, now."

"Nevertheless."

"Well. I'm going to Taff Creek. A boy came in last night saying his kin were murdered down there. I'd be grateful if you've heard anything worth repeating. I wouldn't ask too close where you heard it."

"Decent of you. But I wat nothing about that. But I'll tell you this— if I *had* been in the forest, I'd be out of there now. I'd be going far away from it."

"Where *are* you going?"

"We'll tinker here for a few days, to earn for supplies. After that? Far away. Tero Gallé, maybe, or Virgenya."

"Why?"

Afas jerked his head toward the largest tent, the one already set up. "Because *she* says so. I don't know more than that, nor do I want to. But you can ask her. In fact, she said you'd want to ask her."

"Hmm. Well. I suppose I ought to, then."

"Might be healthiest."

"Right. Stay out of trouble, hey? I've got enough to worry about without having to track you down later."

"Sure. Anything for you, Dirt."

Mother Cilth had been old when Aspar was a boy. Now she might have been a ghost looking across the chasm of death. She sat on a pile of cushions, robed in black, coifed in black. Only her face was visible, an ivory mask spidered with sapphire. Her eyes, palest gold, watched his every movement. Jesp's eyes had been that color. And Qerla's.

"There you are," Mother Cilth rasped. "Jesperedh said you would be here."

Aspar bit back telling her how long Jesp had been dead. It wouldn't matter. Whether it was all pretense or whether the Sefry had come to believe their own lies, he had never really known. It didn't matter, because either way their constant talk of speaking with the dead was so much annoying sceat. The dead were dead; they did not speak.

"You wanted to see me?" He made a small attempt to keep the irritation from his voice, but it wasn't something he was good at.

"I see you already. I want to talk to you."

"I'm here, Mother. I'm listening."

"Still rude. Still impatient. I thought my sister taught you better."

"Maybe her lessons would have taken better if she had had a little help from the rest of you," Aspar replied, unable to keep the bitterness from his voice. "Take me as you find me or not at all. It wasn't me wanted to talk to you."

"Yes, it was."

That was true, sort of, but he didn't have to like it. He turned on his heel to leave.

"The Briar King is waking," Cilth whispered.

Aspar paused, a bright tickle like a centipede crawling on his backbone. He turned very slowly to face the old woman again.

"What?"

"The Briar King. He wakes."

"That's sceat," Aspar said harshly, though a part of him felt as if the earth had opened beneath his feet. "I've traveled the King's Forest all my life. I've been in the deepest, black heart of it, and I've been places in the Mountains of the Hare that even the deer never saw. There is no Briar King. That's just more of your Sefry nonsense."

"You know better. He slept, and was unseen. Now he wakes. It is the first sign. Surely Jesp taught you."

"She taught me. She also taught me to cheat at dice, and to play the voice of a ghost for her seances."

The old woman's face went even harder than it had been. "Then you should know the difference," she hissed. "You should know the difference between the cold and the hot, between the breeze and the storm." She leaned even closer. "Look in my eyes. Look there."

Aspar didn't want to, but her eyes had already caught him, like a snake about to eat a mouse. The gold and copper of her orbs seemed to expand until they were all he could see, and then . . .

A forest turned into gallows, rotting corpses hung from every branch. The trees themselves gnarled and diseased, covered in black thorns, and instead of foliage they bore carrion birds, ravens and vultures, gorged and fat.

In the depths of the forest the shadows between the trees shifted, as if something large were moving there. Aspar searched, but the movement stayed at the corner of his eyes, always still when he stared full at it.

Then he noticed the nearest corpse. The rope that hung her was nearly rotted through, and mostly it was just bones and blackened flesh hanging there, but the eyes were still alive, alive and pale gold . . .

The same eyes he was looking into now. Mother Cilth's eyes.

With a harsh gasp, Aspar turned his gaze away. Mother Cilth grated out a laugh.

"You see," she murmured.

"Sceat," he managed, though his legs were trembling. "A trick."

Cilth drew back. "Enough. I thought you were the one foretold. Perhaps I was wrong. Perhaps you learned nothing after all."

"I can only hope."

"A shame. Truly. For if you are not the one foretold, he is not yet born. And if he is not yet born, your race—and mine—will be wiped from the earth, as if we had never been. *That* part of the telling cannot be doubted except by fools. But maybe you *are* a fool. My sister perished for nothing." She reached up and drew a veil over her face. "I dream," she said. "Leave me."

Aspar obeyed her, fighting an unaccustomed urge to run. Only when the Sefry camp was a league behind him did his breathing calm.

The Briar King.

What sceat, he thought.

But in the corner of his vision, something was still moving.

CHAPTER TWO

IN ANOTHER TAVERN

"THE QUEEN, OF COURSE, must die first. She is the greatest danger to our plans."

The man's voice was cultured and sibilant, speaking the king's tongue with a hint of some southern accent. His words sent a snake slithering up Lucoth's back, and he suddenly feared the sound of his heart was a drum for all to hear.

I am a mouse, he told himself. *A mouse.*

Which was what everyone called him. His real name was Dunhalth MaypHinthgal, but only his mother had ever called him Dunhalth. To everyone else in the small town of Odhfath, he was Lucoth, "the mouse."

A dry silence followed the man's pronouncement. From his vantage in the rafters, Lucoth could not see any of their faces, only that there were three of them, and from their voices, all men. He knew they'd paid hostler MaypCorgh for the use of the back room of the Black Rooster Inn, which in Lucoth's experience meant that they probably had some secret business to discuss.

Lucoth had eavesdropped on such meetings before. He had an arrangement with hostler MaypCorgh, who let him know when the room was in use. In the past, he'd mostly overheard smugglers and brigands, and often learned things that MaypCorgh could use to turn a profit, part of which he would pass on to Lucoth.

But these weren't smugglers or highwaymen. Lucoth had heard

murders plotted before, but never that of a queen. Excitement replacing fear, he listened as another of the men spoke.

"The queen," he sighed. This one had a deeper voice, with some gravel in it. "Is the prophecy so clear?"

"In all ways," the first man replied. "When *he* comes, there can be no queen of the blood in Eslen."

"What of the daughters?" the final man asked. His accent was strange even to Lucoth, who had heard many odd ones. The town of Odhfath was at a crossroads: Take the eastern way, and you came in time to Virgenya. West lay the port at Paldh. North brought you to Eslen and finally Hansa. The south road met the Great Vitellian Way, with its colorful merchant caravans.

"The daughters may not succeed to the throne," the second man said.

"There is movement afoot to legitimize their succession," the first man replied. "So they must all die, of course. The king, the queen, their female issue. Only then will our plans be assured."

"It is an important step," the third man said reluctantly. "A step that cannot be taken back."

The first man's voice dropped low and soft. "The Briar King wakes. The age of man is ended. If we do not step now, we will perish with the rest. That will not happen."

"Agreed," the second man said.

"I'm with you," the third said. "But care must be taken. Great care. The time is coming, but it is not yet here."

"Of course," the first man said.

Lucoth licked his lips, wondering what reward might come from saving a queen. Or a whole royal family.

He had always dreamed of seeing the wide world and seeking his fortune in it. But he was wise enough to know that a fourteen-year-old boy who went on the road with no coin in his pocket would meet a bad end, and likely sooner than later. He had saved over the years—almost enough, he reckoned, to make a start of it.

But this—he almost saw the gold before his eyes, heaps of it. Or a barony, or the hand of a princess. All of that.

Hostler MaypCorgh wouldn't know about this, oh no. Odds were too great he'd try to blackmail the men below. That wasn't the way to do it. The way to do it was to lightfoot out of the loft, wait till tomorrow, and get a good look at the men so he could describe them. Then he'd take his earnings, buy a donkey, and set out for Eslen. There he would find an audience with Emperor William and tell him of what he had heard.

He suddenly realized the men below had gone silent, and left his imaginings to focus on them.

The first man's head moved, and though Lucoth saw no eyes through the shadows, he felt a gaze burning on him.

Which was impossible. He held his breath, waiting for the illusion to fade.

"You have a loud heart, boy," the man said. His voice was like velvet.

Lucoth jerked into motion, but it was the motion of nightmare. He knew the rafters of the inn like he knew the inside of his palm, but somehow it seemed all alien to him now, the few yards he had to cross to find safety a distance of leagues. Still, the thinking part of his mind told him, *cross the wall, drop down. They'll have to go around, by the door; that will put them long moments behind, plenty of time for a mouse to find a hiding place in the town of his birth.*

Something smacked him on the side of the face, not too hard. He wondered what they had thrown at him, but was relieved it wasn't something more deadly.

Then he understood that whatever it was, was still there, resting against his cheek. He didn't have time for that, though. He went over the wall—it did not extend into the rafters—and dropped down into the next room. The open window was there, waiting for him. He felt dizzy and tasted something strange. For some reason he wanted to gag.

Only when he had reached the street did he feel to see what was stuck to him, and then he didn't quite understand it, because it was the hilt of a dagger, which made no sense at all . . .

Then he realized that it *did* make sense if the blade was in his throat. Which it was. He could feel the tip of it inside his windpipe.

Don't take it out, he thought. *Take it out, it'll bleed . . .*

He started running down the street, but he couldn't take his hand away from the thing in his neck, any more than he could wrap his mind around what had really happened to him.

I'll be fine, he thought. *It must have missed my veins. I'll be fine. I'll just get old Horsecutter to take it out. He'll sew the wound. I'll be fine.*

Something thumped onto the street behind him. He turned to see a man-shaped shadow.

It started toward him.

He ran.

He could feel the pulse in his neck now and something clotting in his throat. He vomited, and that brought agony that sheeted down the whole left side of his body. He stumbled a few more steps.

Saints, please, leave me be, I'll never talk, he tried to say, but his voice was pinned inside of him by the dagger.

Then something cold punched into his back. He thought it was three times, but maybe it was four. The final touch was faint, like a kiss, and right at the base of his skull.

"Sleep tight, boy," he heard someone say. It sounded like a saint, which made him feel a little better.

CHAPTER THREE

THE SQUIRE

NIGHT-WINGED CLOUDS RUBBED AWAY the moon, and a freezing sea wind bittered the darkness. Neil had almost no feeling in his toes or fingers. He could smell nothing but brine and hear nothing but the wind and waves savaging the shore. But he could imagine much more: the breath of the foe, somewhere out there in the night. The clash of steel that would greet the dawn. The droning dirge of the cold, restless *draugs* beneath the waves, dead yet alive, shark-toothed mouths gaping in anticipation of the meat of the living. Of Neil MeqVren's meat.

"Dawn's almost here," his father murmured, lowering himself to lie next to Neil on the sand. "Be ready."

"They might be anywhere," someone else said. Neil thought it was probably Uncle Odcher.

"No. There are only two places they could have put their ships in. Here, or on the Milkstrand. We're here. They must be there."

"They say the Weihands can march at night. That they can see in the dark, like the trolls they worship."

"They can't march at night any better than we can," Neil's father said. "If they aren't on their ships, they're doing exactly what we're doing— waiting for the sun."

"I don't care what they can do," another voice muttered. "They never reckoned on meeting the men of clan MeqVren."

What's left of us, Neil thought. He had counted twelve, last time the sun went down. Twelve. The morning before, they had been thirty.

He was rubbing his hands to try to warm them when a fist closed over his fingers. "You ready, son?" his father whispered.

"Yeah, Fah." He couldn't see his face, but what he heard in the voice made his scalp prickle.

"I shouldn't have brought you on this one."

"I been to war before, Fah."

"Yes. And proud I've been of you. No MeqVren—nor no man of no clan I've ever heard tell of—ever killed his first foe when he had only eleven winters, and that's been a year gone for you, now. But this—"

"We going to lose, Fah? We going to die?"

"If that's the way the saints want it, damn them." He cleared his throat and sang, very softly,

"To fight and die is why we're born
Croak, ye ravens, I'll feed ye soon."

Neil shivered, for that was part of the MeqVren death-chant.

But his father clapped him on the arm. "I don't intend for us to die, lad. We'll catch 'em off guard."

"Then the lord baron will pay us a pretty penny, eh, Fah?"

"It's his war. He's a man of his word. Now let's be still, for here comes the dawn."

The sky lightened. The twelve men of the MeqVren clan crouched behind the dune, motionless. Neil wondered what the baron or the Weihands might want with this wretched island anyway, with it so rocky and hard it wouldn't support even sheep. He turned to look back at the sea. The sky had lightened enough so he could make out the prow of their longship, a horse-head silhouette.

And down the beach, another. And another.

But the MeqVrens had only one ship.

He tugged at his father's sleeve.

"Fah—"

That's when something hissed along and thumped into his father's back, and his father sighed strangely. That's when the shouting started, and the MeqVrens rose to their feet in a shower of arrows, to face three times their number coming up the strand. Neil closed his eyes, then jumped up with the rest of them, his hands too cold to feel his spear, but he could see it, clutched in his hands.

Then an arrow hit him. It made the same sound as the one that had hit his father, just a little higher in pitch.

Neil jerked awake and found himself clutching his chest, two fingers below his heart, breathing as if he had just run a league. He felt like he was falling.

Where am I?

The confusion lasted only a few heartbeats, as he recognized the rocking of a ship, the furnishings of his cabin. His breathing slowed, and he felt the small puckered scar.

Eight years, but in his dreams it hadn't faded at all.

Eight years.

He sat there a few more minutes, listening to the sailors on the deck above. Rather than trust himself to sleep again, he rose to shave. He wanted to look his best today.

He stropped his razor and brought its keen edge to his cheek, then down the square lines of his chin, whisking off the stubble with sure, steady motions. He finished without a single scratch, and with the same blade he trimmed his wheat-colored hair well away from his eyes.

The Black Mary of that day on the beach faded, and his excitement grew. Today! Today he would see Thornrath!

He splashed water on his face, blinked it from his blue eyes, and went above decks.

They reached the Cape of Rovy by midafternoon and sailed with the alabaster cliffs on their left hand for another bell. There, clearing the headland, they turned into Foambreaker Bay, a wide haven in the shape of a moon two-thirds full, circumscribed on the north by the Cape of Rovy and on the south by the Craigs-Above-Ale. West was the open sea, and east, where *Saltspear*'s prow now pointed, stood a marvel so awesome

Neil thought his heart would crack. He almost welcomed it, if he could die with this much wonder on him.

"Saints of Sea and Thunder," he managed weakly.

His earnest thanksgiving was all but swept off by the wind buffeting the deck of the *Saltspear*, but the old man who stood beside him, Fail de Liery, heard and bit a fierce grin into the westerly. Hair streaming behind him like a banner of smoke, Fail glanced over at Neil, and though his face was pitted, scarred, and wrinkled by threescore years of life, he still seemed somehow youthful when he chuckled.

"There she is, lad," the elder said. "That's Thornrath. Does she measure up?"

Neil nodded his head dumbly as the cape dropped farther behind them. The eastern sky behind Thornrath was as black as coal smut, and above that darkest lens piled curtains of spume-gray clouds that broke at the meridian. But from the clear western sky, the sinking sun slanted golden light to blaze the bay and the mightiest fortress in the world against that storm-painted canvas.

"Thornrath," he repeated. "I mean I'd heard—you'd told me—" He paused to try to understand what he was actually seeing, to understand the size.

If Foambreaker Bay was a moon two-thirds full, the entire eastern third of it—perhaps four leagues—was a wall the hue of ivory. Seven great towers of the same stone jabbed at the sky, the centermost rising to such a high sharp point it was dizzying.

As Neil watched, a man-o'-war sailed through one of six arched openings in the wall. He reckoned its masts at more than twenty yards high, and they were in no danger of touching the top of the arch. And the arch was only half as high as the wall.

"Saints!" Neil breathed. "Men built that? Not the *Echesl*?" He crooked his finger and touched his forehead, a sign against the evil of that name.

"Men built it, yes. They quarried the stone in the Eng Fear mountains, two hundred leagues upriver. It was sixty years in building they say, but now no one can come against Crotheny by sea."

"It is a wonder," Neil said. "Proud am I to serve that."

"No, lad," Fail said gently. "You don't serve a thing of stone, no matter how grand. Never that. You'll serve Crotheny, and her king, and the royal line of Dare."

"That's what I meant, *Chever* Fail."

"They call a knight *sir*, in the king's tongue, lad."

"*Sir* Fail." The word sounded awkward, as did every word in the king's tongue. It lacked music, somehow. But it was the language of his lord, and he had learned it. Practiced at it as hard as he had the sword, the lance, and the mace.

Well, almost as hard.

"*Sir* Fail," he said again.

"And soon Sir Neil."

"I can't believe that. How can the king knight me? It's no matter, I'll be proud to serve him, even as a footman. Just so long as I can serve him."

"Lad, I tilted at Sir Seimon af Harudrohsn when I was only in my eighteenth winter. I fought beside all five Cresson brothers at the battle of Ravenmarh Wold, and I sent Sir Duvgal MaypAvagh—who himself slew more than twenty knights—to the shadowcity, along with his second, before the gates of Cath Valk. I have *known* knights, lad, and I tell you that in my fifty-six years, I've never seen a lad more deserving of the rose than you."

Neil's throat tightened further with love and gratefulness to the tough old man. "Thank you, Sir Fail. Thank you for—for everything."

"That better be the wind in your eyes, son. I don't go for all this courtly weeping, as well you know."

"It's the wind, chev—sir."

"Good. And keep it that way. And don't let any of these fops at the court steer you a different course. You're a warrior of the marches, raised by a good father and then by my hand. Just remember that, and you'll keep who you are. It's the steel in the marches that keeps safe the soft gold here in the center. Gold's pretty, but it'll scarce cut butter. Don't worry about pretty, lad. Worry about your edge. The court's more dangerous to a real warrior than a thousand Weihand raiders are."

"I'll remember that, sir." He tried to stand taller. "I will make you proud of me."

"Come below. I have something to give you."

*   *   *

"I was going to save this until after the king knighted you, but your armor took a hard beating at Darkling Mere. And it is, after all, a lord's duty to keep his warriors looking warlike, eh?"

Neil couldn't answer. As when he had first seen Thornrath, he was struck speechless as his master unrolled the sealskin bundle to reveal the gleam of oiled steel.

Neil had worn armor since he was ten. First toughened leather, as he had been wearing that ill-fated dawn his father died, then a steel cap and byrnie with greaves, and finally the hauberk of chain he wore now, with its battered but serviceable breastplate.

But he had only dreamed of what Fail de Liery presented him—a suit of lord's plate, articulated by lobstered joints. It was good, plain work, with no frills or elaborations.

It must have cost a small fortune.

"Sir Fail, this is more than I could ever dream of. How can I ever— I could never take that. Not on top of everything else."

"It's fitted for you," the old man said. "I had the measurements taken when your last suit of clothes was made. No one else could wear it. And as you know, I am much insulted when my gifts are refused."

"I—" Neil grinned. "I'd never insult you, Sir Fail."

"Do you want to try it on?"

"Saints, yes!"

Thus it was, when they passed beneath the great arch of Thornrath, Neil MeqVren stood proudly on the deck of the *Saltspear*, his house de Liery tabard cinched around the most perfect suit of armor ever made. He felt bright and deadly, a sword made human.

The wonders piled up. Passing through the great arch, the waters before them were parted by a high, hilly land.

"Two rivers meet here," Fail told him. "The bloody-minded Warlock from the southeast and the Dew tumbling out of the Barghs in the north."

"And so this island is royal Ynis itself?"

"It is. The rivers meet five leagues ahead of us, on the other side of the island, split again, and come back together here."

"Ynis! Then where is Eslen? Where are the rivers that flow above the land?"

"Patience, lad. It's farther east. We'll be there near sundown. But as to the rivers—you'll see."

Ynis rose from a flat plain, a series of hills spotted with delicate, spired castles, red-shingled hamlets, fields and forest. The plain around the island was mostly fields of grain, very green. Cottages were there, and men working the fields, and strange towers with great wheels turning on them. Canals ran off from the river, some so long they vanished in the hazy distance.

And indeed, Neil realized with a growing sense of excitement that he was looking *down* upon the landscape. Embankments had been raised along the riverside, forcing it to flow higher than the country around.

"When our ancestors fought here against the last stronghold of the Echesl, this was a plain, or so the legends say," Sir Fail said. "Ynis was the mount they raised for their castle. But after their defeat, and the castle Eslen was founded in its place, it all sank into quagmire, marsh, all the way to the horizon. The Echesl had used some sort of sorcery to keep the water back, and with their passing, it passed, too. The people living here could have abandoned it then, found better land in the east, but they wouldn't do it. They swore to take the land back from the waters instead."

"They found the secret of the Echesl sorcery?"

"No. They worked hard. They built dikes. They made these pumps you see, pushed by the winds, to drain away the water. Two thousand years of slow, hard battle with the waves, but you see the result." He laid a hand on Neil's shoulder.

"So, you see, men did this, too."

And finally, sailing above the land like characters in a phay story, they hove in sight of Eslen of the three walls.

On the highest hill stood the castle, with its eight towers of chalk-white stone bloodied by twilight, long pennants fluttering black against the rosy clouds. From there, the city spilled down like water poured from the top of a hill, dammed briefly by each of the concentric walls surrounding the castle but never quite contained, slate-topped waves of buildings flowing over the smaller hills until they reached the waterfront and piled against stone-faced quays and stout wooden piers. Shrouds of mist and woodsmoke lay in the low places between the hills, and candle-light already made windows into eyes here and there.

"It's all so grand," Neil murmured. "Like an enchanted city of the Queryen, from the old tales. I'm afraid to look away, for fear it will vanish."

"Eslen is no city of moonbeams and spider silk," the old knight assured him. "It's real enough, you'll see. And if you think this so grand, wait until you see the court."

"I can hardly wait."

"Oh—you'll learn about waiting, son, never doubt that."

The *Saltspear* came to a quay, a sort of watery plaza surrounded with docks replete with colorful boats of every size. One stood out above the rest, a five-masted battle-queen that dwarfed the *Saltspear* and every other ship anchored there. Neil was admiring her when he suddenly recognized the flag she flew and instinctively reached for his sword.

Fail touched his arm. "Ney, lad. There's no call for that."

"That's a Hanzish warship."

"So it is. That's nothing unusual. Remember, we're at peace with Hansa and the Reiksbaurgs."

Neil's mouth dropped open, closed, then opened again. "Peace? When they pay Weihand raiders hard silver for Liery scalps and ears, and their privateers sink our merchantmen?"

"There's the real world," Fail said, "and there's the court. The court says we're at peace with them. So don't you go pulling steel if you see a Reiksbaurg, and keep your tongue still, you hear?"

Neil felt as if he'd swallowed something unpleasant. "I hear, sir."

Even as they docked, darkness dropped like an ax. Neil set his foot upon the cobbles of Eslen in a most unfamiliar night.

The docks bustled with men and women half seen by lamplight. Faces came and went—beautiful, sinister, innocent, brutal—all mere impressions, appearing and vanishing like ghosts, going to and from ships, greeting and parting, slinking and carrying burdens. Gutted fish, hot tar, burning kerosene, and ripe sewage perfumed the air.

"The upper gates of the city are closed by now, so we'll be rooming at an inn," Fail told him, as they pressed through the dockside crowd and crossed a long plaza where young girls and hard-looking women cast provocative glances at them, where blind or legless beggars crouched in shadows and wailed for assistance and children skirmished in mock combat between the legs of pedestrians and the wheels of carts.

Buildings three and four stories tall crowded at the edges of the plaza like giants crouched shoulder to shoulder, playing at knuckle-bones, spilling cheery light, woodsmoke, and the scent of roasting meat into the cool night air.

It was to one of these giants they made their way, proclaimed the Moonfish Inn by a gilded sign that hung over the doorway.

"Be a good lad," Fail said, "and see our horses are stabled here. Give the hand a copper miser, no more or less, for each horse. Then change from your armor and meet me in the common room."

"On my word, Sir Fail," Neil told him.

The ale-and-cod pie was good—much better than the shipboard fare—but Neil hardly noticed it. He was too busy *watching*. Never had he seen so many strange faces and clothes or heard such a confusion of tongues. Two tables away, a group of dark-skinned men in colorful robes spoke guttural nonsense. When the serving girl brought their food, their mustached lips curled in what seemed like disgust, and they made strange signs at her back with their fingers before taking their food. Beyond them, two tables of men similar in complexion seemed to be taking turns making flamboyant speeches to one another and drinking wine in un-wise haste. They wore somber doublets and bloodred høse and long, silly-looking swords.

There were peoples he recognized, too—blond-shocked Schildings, with their rough fisherman's hands and quick laughter; sea rovers from the isles of Ter-na-Fath; a knight from Hornladh and his retainers, wear-ing the yellow stag and five chevrons of the house MaypHal. Neil asked about that one.

"Sir Ferghus Lonceth," Sir Fail told him.

"And him?" Neil pointed at a large man with dark red hair cut short, a neatly trimmed beard, and a sable tabard. His device was quartered—a golden lion rampant, three roses, a sword, and helm. Six men sat at his table, all with the northern look about them. Some might have passed for Weihands, and Neil took an almost instant dislike to them.

"I don't know him," Fail admitted. "He's too young. But his device is that of the Wishilms of Gothfera."

"Hanzish, then. From the ship."

"Yes. Remember what I said," the older man cautioned.

"Yes, sir."

About that moment, one of the men from the Hornladh knight's table arrived.

"Chever Fail de Liery, my master, Sir Ferghus Lonceth, begs the quality of your company."

"I would cherish his company," Fail said. "We shall join you, yes?"

"Is it not more meet that my master joins you? After all, in seniority and fame, you are most certainly first, and entitled to the board of your choosing."

"That may be so, lad," Fail replied. "But there's only two of us and eight of you, and you have the more room at your table. Seniority is all well and good, but in the inn, let us be practical, yes?" He rose, then turned to Neil. "Neil, be a good lad and invite the Wishilm knight to join us."

"Sir," the Hornladh squire said, "I invited him on behalf of my own master, and he did disdain the invitation."

"And he may disdain mine. But it shall not be said that I lacked the hospitality to invite him," Fail replied.

Neil nodded, and walked to the Hanzish knights' table.

When he arrived, he stood there politely for a moment or two, but they all ignored him, laughing and joking in their own language. Finally, Neil cleared his throat.

"Pardon me," he said, in Hanzish.

"By Tyw! It can speak!" one of the squires said, a giant of a fellow with a broken nose. He turned devil-filled blue eyes toward Neil. "I'll have another pint of ale, wench, and be quick!"

They all laughed at that.

Neil breathed slowly and smiled. "My master, Sir Fail de Liery, requests the quality of your presence."

"Fail de Liery," the Hanzish knight suddenly mused. "I don't know any such knight. There is a doddering old man by that name, but I'm quite sure he was never a knight. You, boy. What do you do for him?"

"I'm his squire," Neil said evenly. "And if you have not heard the fame of Sir Fail de Liery, you have no ears for the hearing, or wits to hold what you hear."

"Master! That sounded like an insult," one of the Hanzish squires exclaimed.

"Did it?" Wishilm said. "It sounded to me like the fart of a cock-a-roach."

Blue-eyes wagged a finger at him. "My master will not dirty his hands with you, I assure you. He fights only worthy knights, which it is plain you are not. Your insults are meaningless to him."

"But not to *us*," another of the Hansans put in.

"I have promised my master I shall not draw steel, nor disrupt the hospitality of this house," Neil told him.

"This man is a coward!" the fellow bellowed, loudly enough to stop conversation all around the common room of the inn.

Neil felt a sort of trembling in his hands. "I have made you an invitation, and you have not accepted it. Our conversation is done." He turned and walked toward where his master and the Hornladh knight sat.

"Don't walk away from me, you!"

Neil ignored him.

"Well done, lad," Sir Fail told him, offering him a place on the bench next to him. "It would be shame on the both of us were you to brawl in a public house."

"I would never shame you, Sir Fail."

"Let me introduce you. Sir Ferghus Lonceth, this is my protégé, Neil MeqVren."

Lonceth clasped his hand. "I took him for your son, sir! Is he not?"

"He is like a son to me, but no, I cannot claim that honor. His father was a warrior in my service."

"It's good t'meet you," Sir Ferghus said, still gripping Neil's hand. "MeqVren. I'm afraid I don't know that house. Are they allied with the clan Fienjeln?"

"No, sir. My clan has no house."

An instant of silence followed that, as they politely struggled with the concept of a squire with no birth claim to knighthood.

"Well," Sir Ferghus said, breaking the silence. "You are most welcome in our company. The recommendation of Sir Fail de Liery is better than the blood of ten noble houses."

As they drank, Neil thought that perhaps some of Lonceth's squires did not agree but were too polite to say anything.

"Tell me, Sir Ferghus," Sir Fail said, once the toast had gone around. "I've heard little of your illustrious uncle. How does he find Paldh?"

The two knights talked for some time after that, and the squires, as was meet, stayed quiet. Most of Lonceth's men drank heavily. Neil, as was his custom, did not.

When a lull came in the conversation, Neil tapped his master on the shoulder.

"I would check on the horses, Sir Fail," he said. "Hurricane and Sunstamper both were having trouble with their land legs."

Fail looked at him with a slightly suspicious smile. "See to it, then. But hurry back."

The two horses were fine, as Neil knew they would be. And the massive, blue-eyed Hansan and two of the other Hanzish squires were waiting for him in the street—also as he knew they would be.

CHAPTER FOUR

THE NOVICE

A SPAR AWOKE IN THE SURE GRASP of a tyrant, and to music. The music was a wild one—drumming of a woodpecker, the lark's trilling melody rising above, the drifting, whirring chords of cicadas beneath. He rubbed dream grit from his eyes, braced his hands on the narrow wooden platform, and sat up carefully to greet the quick of dawn.

A wind soughed through the tyrants as they stretched their ancient, creaking limbs to the morning, clucked their smaller branches, bruised a few leaves into giving up their green, peppery scent.

Below, Ogre whickered. Aspar leaned from his perch to gaze at the faraway ground, to see that both his mounts were where he'd left them the evening before. From his prospect they seemed no larger than dogs.

The woodpecker drummed again as Aspar loosened his joints for the climb down. He had overslept on purpose this time. He liked to be in the branches when the first bronze of the sun came slanting through and the forest hummed and grumbled to life. This ancient stand he called the tyrants was one of the few places he could do that. In other places, centuries of fire, logging, and disease left at best one or two of the ancient ironoaks towering over lesser trees. Here they stood proud and unchallenged for leagues, ancient, titanic wrestlers, their muscular arms intertwined, gripping and pulling at each other, holding up a world in itself. A man could be born, live, and die up here, drinking the dew that gathered in mossy recesses, eating shelf fungus and squirrel or the flightless branch quail that ran peeping along the great boughs.

The world below—the world of Man and Sefry—did not matter up here.

Or so he had believed when he was a boy, when he discovered this place and built his first platforms. He'd imagined then that he *would* live here.

But even the tyrants could be chopped down or burned. Even the eternal could be killed by a hungry charcoal burner or for a nobleman's whim. He had seen it, the boy Aspar had been. It was one of the few times in his life he had cried. That was when he knew he wanted to be a holter.

The King's Forest, bah. The boy back at the inn was right about that at least. The king came here once or twice a year to hunt. This was Aspar's forest. His to protect.

And *something* was happening out here. The Sefry were liars, yes, and not to be trusted. But if they really were fleeing the forest, with its deep sunless shadows and myriad caves, there had to be a reason for it. The Sefry did not step into the sun lightly.

So, reluctantly he made sure he had everything and started back down, limb to limb, to where the lowest branches, too heavy to keep themselves up, slopped in mazy, ropy paths to earth, there to put down new roots.

That was why Aspar called them tyrants; beneath their shading, creeping branches, no other green thing could live, save moss and a few ferns.

But deer and elk could survive, on the ankle-deep acorns, and the dappled cats that hunted them, like the lithe specimen he saw giving him a wary look from a few branches over. This one was small, just triple the size of a village tabby. In the Mountains of the Hare there were still lions, and here a few panthers worthy of note. But they wouldn't bother him.

Ogre gave him a cross look as he stepped onto the black leaf mold. Angel tossed her head in greeting.

"Don't look at me like that, you nag," Aspar grunted at Ogre. "You've had the night to roam. You want me to start tethering you or keeping you hobbled?"

Ogre continued to glare, but he let Aspar mount, and picking their way through roots that sometimes mounded as high as the horses' shoulders, they walked leisurely back to the Old King's Road, a wide track that ran along a series of low ridges. In places it had been built up with stone and embanked, so it stood above the roots. Low branches had been cut away, allowing wagons to pass. To Aspar, the Old King's Road was an affront, a leagues-long gash in the living forest. Still, it seemed unlikely that the tyrants would notice such a minor injury.

Midday he grew thirsty. He dismounted and made his way down a slope to where he knew a spring was—no point in wasting what he had bottled. Besides, springborn water was clean and cold, better than the flat rain-gathered stuff from the village. He found the stream bubbling from a sandy dish below a low cleft of crumbling rock, from whence it ran for a few large man's jumps into Edwin's Brooh. He knelt at the spring pan, cupping his hands, and then stopped still as a statue, trying to understand what he saw.

The natural basin was about as wide as his forearm, and water trickled cheerfully into it, as usual. But the pan seethed with black-peeping frogs scrambling away from his approach. A half dozen of them lay belly-up in the pool.

Nor were they alone. A yard-long creek-eel lay putrefying, its eyes filmed blue. Several large croaker-frogs sat there, too. All of them were alive, but they didn't look healthy, nor did they even try to flee.

Aspar backed away from the spring, his stomach feeling funny. In all his years, he had never seen such a sight.

After a moment, he walked the rivulet's length, down to where it met the brooh. All the way down it was clogged with dead frogs and, in its lower reaches, fish.

There were dead fish in the brooh, too, big ones, fetched up against the ferny banks or caught in natural weirs of sticks and roots.

The chill in his bones deepening, he unlimbered his bow and strung it, then started upstream. Something had poisoned the brooh, somehow, and its creatures had sought up to the springhead for cleaner water. There were folk who used the root of the sawbriar to stun fish to make them easy for the catching, but that worked only in a small, still pool. To kill a whole brooh would take more sawbriar than there was in the world.

The dead fish continued for a hundred paces, then a hundred more, and he was just about to return for his horses when he noticed that the stream had become clear again. He went a bit farther, to make sure, then backtracked, and on this pass noticed something else. A clump of ferns on the side of the stream had a distinct yellow cast to them. As if they, like the fish and frogs, were dying.

It was next to the ferns that he found the print.

Prints didn't take well in the dense leaf mold of the forest floor, but on the muddy verge of the stream he found the impression of a paw. Though water had filled it and softened its outlines, it looked essentially like a cat track. But no dappled cat paw made this, nor even a panther. Aspar's hand would just barely cover it. Even the lions of the Mountains of the Hare didn't get that big. If this track belonged to a cat, it was bigger than a horse.

He traced the outline with his finger, and the instant he touched it he tasted metal on his tongue, and his belly spasmed, trying to give up his lunch. Almost without thought he scrambled back from the brooh and stood fifteen paces away, shivering as if he had a fever.

He might have stood there longer, save that he heard voices in the distance. On the road.

Where his horses were.

He ran back that way, as quickly and quietly as he could, the sick feeling melting as swiftly as it had come.

There were four of them, and they had already found Ogre and Angel when he got there.

"Got the king's mark on 'em, they have," one of them was saying, a tall, gangly young man with a missing front tooth.

"Ought to leave 'em, then. No good will come of taking 'em." That was an older fellow, short, tending toward fat, with a big nose. The third man, a thickly built redhead, seemed to have no opinion. The fourth clearly had one, but he couldn't express it, bound and gagged as he was.

This last fellow appeared to be no more than sixteen and had the look of a townsman about him in his impractical doublet and hose. His wrists were tied in front of him and then tethered to an old yellow mare. They had two other horses, a bay gelding and a sorrel mare.

The redhead was watching the woods. He had looked twice at Aspar where he crouched in a brake of ferns, but gave no indication of having seen him.

"A kingsman wouldn't just abandon his horses," Gangly argued. "He's either dead or these have run away. See? They izn' tethered."

"You don't have to tether horses like that," Big Nose replied. "He's probably just off taking a piss."

"He went a long way, then," the redhead grunted. "He did'n want his horses to see 'im piss?"

Aspar had never seen these fellows, but he was pretty certain he knew who they were; the three fit the description of some bandits lately come down from Wisgarth to worry at the occasional traders on the King's Road. He'd planned to hunt them down in the summer, when he had enough men.

He waited to see what they would do. If they didn't take his horses, he'd just follow them for a while. In fact, maybe he had already found his killers; Gangly wore a bloodred cloak trimmed in umber. Those were close to the king's crimson and gold.

"We take 'em," Gangly said. "I say we take 'em. Even if he's here someplace, we can put a day between us easy with all of this horseflesh and him afoot." He started forward, toward Ogre. "Easy, you nag."

Aspar sighed, and fitted an arrow to his string. He couldn't afford to be generous with these three.

Ogre did the first part of his work for him, of course. As soon as Gangly was close, the great beast reared and dealt him a thunderous blow in the chest with his hooves. By the time Gangly hit the ground, Big Nose was staring at the arrow sprouting from his thigh.

Redhead was faster than Aspar anticipated, and keener of eye. Aspar got a shot off first, but he was still shaky from whatever had sickened him near the creek. He missed, and Redhead's bow sang out. The holter saw the arrow spinning toward him dead-on, deceptively slow, a trick of the mind. He could never move in time.

But the missile struck the tendril of a grapevine, glanced wide, and chuckled past his cheek.

"Raver!" Aspar swore. That had been close.

He bolted into motion, and so did Redhead, both fitting arrows to their bows, weaving through the trees. Redhead had the high ground. He was light of foot and a damned good shot. The two men ran parallel to each other, though their paths were gradually converging.

At fifteen yards Redhead took his second shot. It hit Aspar high in the chest and glanced from the leather cuirass beneath. Aspar missed his next shot, and then they were separated by a copse of new growth too dense to see through.

They came out six yards from each other, in a clearing. Aspar stopped, stood profile, and let his shaft fly.

Redhead's dart whirred by, missing by nearly a foot. Aspar's yard nailed through Redhead's right shoulder.

The man shrieked as if he had been disemboweled, and dropped his bow. Aspar reached him with five quick strides. The fellow was going for his dirk, but Aspar kicked his arm, hard, just at the elbow.

"Lie still and live," he grunted.

Redhead shrieked again when Aspar yanked both his injured and his good arm behind his back, cut the sinew cord from the discarded bow, and tied him up. With a long cord in his side bag he fashioned a noose to slip over Redhead's throat.

"Walk ahead," he commanded, still warily searching the surroundings for more enemies.

Gangly was still down when they reached the horses, and Ogre wasn't finished with him yet; the bay's foreparts rose and fell, and he was bloody to the withers. Big Nose was lying on the ground, staring at the scarlet pooling there.

About the time they reached them, Redhead's legs gave out and he collapsed, eyes closed and breath coming in harsh wheezes.

Aspar cut up the reins from the yellow mare and trussed Big Nose. Gangly he didn't bother with; his ribs had been splintered into his lungs and he'd choked on his own blood.

During all of this, the boy on the horse had been making all manner of gruntings and muffled squeals. It wasn't until he was sure the bandits were secure that Aspar turned his attention to him, pulling the gag down.

"*Ih thanka thuh, mean froa,*" the boy began, in breathless and somewhat clumsy Almannish. "*Mikel thanks. Ya Ih bida thuh, unbindan mih.*"

"I speak the king's tongue," Aspar grunted, though he understood the boy plainly enough.

"Oh," the fellow replied. "So do I. I just thought you must be from hereabouts."

"I am. And not being stupid, I learned the king's tongue, just like everyone in his service," Aspar replied, unaccountably annoyed. "Besides, Virgenya is just through the mountains, so Virgenyan is as common in these parts as anything else."

"My apologies. No offense intended. What I meant to say was thank you, thank you very much, and could you untie my hands, as well?"

Aspar glanced at the knot. It wasn't complicated. "Probably," he said.

"Well? Aren't you going to?"

"Why did they have you tied up?"

"So I wouldn't run away. They robbed me and took me prisoner. You probably saved my life."

"Probably."

"For which, as I said, I'm grateful."

"Why?"

The fellow blinked. "Well—ah—because I feel I have much left to do in my life, much of value—"

"No," Aspar said, talking slowly as if to a child. "Why did they take you prisoner after they robbed you?"

"I suppose they thought to ransom me."

"Why would they suppose that was worthwhile?"

"Because, I—" The boy stopped, suspicious. "You're like them, aren't you? You're just another bandit. That's why you won't cut me loose. You think you can get something from me, too."

"Boy," Aspar said, "don't you recognize by my colors and badges that I'm the king's holter? Yah, well, that's one sort of stupid. But insulting an armed man when you're tied up, that's another."

"You're the holter?"

"I'm not given to lying."

"But I don't *know* you. How do I know that? You could have killed the real holter and taken his things."

Aspar felt a smile try to quirk his lips. He resisted it. "Well, that's a point," he allowed. "But I'm the kingsman, and I'm not planning to sell you for your pelt or anything else. Who are you?"

The boy pulled himself straighter. "I'm Stephen Darige. Of the Cape Chavel Dariges."

"Indeed? I hayt Aspar White of the Aspar White Whites. What business have you in the King's Forest, Cape Chavel Darige? Lost your carriage?"

"Oh, very good," the lad said sarcastically. "A very clever rhyme. I'm traveling the King's Road, of course, which is free to all."

"Not if you're a merchant, it isn't. There's a toll."

"My father is a merchant, but I'm not. I'm on the way to the monastery d'Ef, or was when these ruffians took me. I'm to be a novice there."

Aspar regarded him for a moment, then pulled his dirk and cut the young man's bonds.

"Thank you," Stephen said, rubbing his wrists. "What changed your mind? Are you a devout man?"

"No." He gestured at the fallen men. "Priest, eh? You know any leeching?"

"I've been at the college in Ralegh. I can bind wounds and set bones."

"Show me, then. Get the arrows out of those two and make it so at least one of 'em doesn't bleed to death. I need to talk to 'em." He swept his hand around. "Are there any more of these fellows, or is this the whole gang-along?"

"That's all I ever saw."

"Good. I'll be back."

"Where are you going?" Darige asked.

"King's business. I'll be back."

Aspar scouted back down the road half a league, just to make certain there were no trailing bandits. Returning, he rode back up Edwin's Brooh, looking for more signs of whatever had made the print, but couldn't find anything. He suspected the creature must have walked in the stream itself. Given time, he could probably pick up the trail, but right now he didn't have the time. The boy seemed truthful enough, but you could never be certain. And he was starting to feel that it was very urgent indeed that he see exactly what sort of massacre had happened at Taff Creek.

When he rode back up, he found Stephen rising unsteadily; he'd been kneeling over what looked very much like a pool of vomit.

"Well, Cape Chavel Darige, how has it been?"

Stephen gestured at Gangly. "He's *dead*," he said weakly.

Aspar couldn't help it; a laugh burst entirely unbidden from his lips.

"What—what's so funny?"

"You. Of course he's dead. Grim's eye, look at him!"

"See here—" Stephen's eyes bulged and watered, and he spasmed, as if about to vomit again, but then he straightened. "I've never seen a dead man before. Not like that."

"Well, there's plenty more men dead than alive, you know," Aspar said. Then, remembering his first dead man, he softened his tone. "Never mind him. The other two? Did you leech them?"

"I—I started one . . ." Stephen looked sheepish.

"I shouldn't have left them to you. My mistake."

"I'm trying! It's just, well, the blood—"

"Like I said," Aspar said gruffly. "My fault. I should have reckoned you'd never actually done it before. I'm not blaming you."

"Oh," Stephen said. "Do you think they're dead, too?"

"I doubt it much. I shot 'em in muscle, see? Not in the organs."

"Why? You don't seem to care much about killing."

"I told you. I need to question 'em."

"Oh."

"Let's start again. Can you cut bandages? Can you do that?"

"I already did."

"Good. Let me see if I can't save these fellows from Mother Death, then, so as you can keep your next meal down, yah?"

"Yes," Stephen replied weakly.

Aspar knelt beside Redhead, who was dead to the world but still breathing. The arrow was lodged in his shoulder bone, so it would take a little cutting to get it out. Aspar started to it, and Redhead moaned.

"What did you want to question them about?" Stephen managed.

"I want to know where they were a few days ago," Aspar grunted, grasping the arrow shaft and working it back and forth.

"Kidnapping me."

"Where?"

"Two days back."

"Not when—*where*." The shaft came out, clean with the head. Aspar pressed the rag Stephen had cut into the wound. "Hold this here," he commanded.

Stephen made a gagging noise but did as he was told. Aspar found another bandage and began wrapping it.

"Where?" he repeated. "Press hard."

"Two days back along the King's Road," Stephen replied.

"That being where? Nearer Wexdal or Forst?"

"I don't really know."

"Well, had you crossed the Owl Tomb before they took you up?"

"That's a river? I'm not sure."

"*Yes*, the Owl Tomb is a *river*. You couldn't have missed it. It had an old stone causey over it. You can let go now."

Stephen lifted his hands, staring at the blood on them, his eyes a little unfocused. "*Oh*. You mean the *Pontro Oltiumo*."

"I mean what I say. What's that gibberish?"

"Old Vitellian," Stephen said. "The language of the Hegemony, who built that causeway a thousand years ago. They made this road, too. *Owl* must be a corruption of *Oltiumo*."

"What makes you think that?"

"I looked at maps before I came. Hegemony maps."

"How is it you thought that maps made a thousand years ago would do you any good at all?"

"The Hegemony made better maps than we do. More accurate. I have copies of them, if you want to see."

Aspar just stared at him for a second, then shook his head. "Priests," he muttered, making certain it sounded like a swear word. "Let's do this other."

Big Nose was easier. The shaft had gone straight through the muscle of the thigh without even grazing the bone.

If Gangly and his bunch had taken Darige east of the Owl, it was impossible for them to have been anywhere near Taff Creek. There went that possibility. So it was on to the Taff, after he figured out what to do with this bunch.

Whatever he decided, it would take him at least a day out of his way.

That couldn't be helped, he supposed, not unless he wanted to kill them all and set the priest a-wandering. It was a tempting thought.

"Help me get these men up on their horses," he grunted, when they were finished.

"Where are we going?"

"You'll see."

"I mean, I'll be late getting to the monastery."

"Will you? I'll try to hold my tears."

"Why—what are you so angry with *me* for, holter? I didn't do any-thing to you. It's not my fault!"

"Fault? What does that mean, or matter? You set out from Virgenya alone, didn't you? Just you and your maps, isn't that right?"

"Yes."

"Why? What book put that in your head?"

"Presson Manteo did it, almost a hundred years ago, when he wrote the *Amvionnom*. He said—"

"Doesn't matter what he said, does it? It didn't do you a damned bit of good."

"Well, I know it was stupid *now*," Stephen said. "It still doesn't ex-plain why you're mad at me."

It didn't, did it? Aspar took a deep breath. The boy didn't seem a bad sort, actually; he was just a burden Aspar didn't need at the mo-ment. And that superior tone and low-country accent didn't help make him more endearing.

"I see a few of your sort every year," he explained. "Little noblings off for a romp in the wild. Usually what I see are their corpses."

"You're saying I'm a burden to you?"

Aspar shrugged. "Come on. I'll take you someplace safe."

"Tell me the way. I'll go alone. You've saved my life. I don't want to trouble you anymore."

"I have to take the prisoners anyway," Aspar said. "Ride along with me."

He started to mount.

"Aren't we going to bury him?" Stephen asked, pointing at Gangly.

Aspar considered that, then walked over to the deceased bandit. He dragged the corpse about ten feet off the side of the trail, folded its arms across his breast.

"There we go," he said, with mock cheer. "A holter's funeral. Care to say any words?"

"Yes. There is a proper liturgy—"

"Say it as we travel, then. We have someplace to be before dark."

Like most priests—and boys—Darige couldn't seem to stop talking. Within a bell, he had quit moping from being chastised and begun chattering constantly about the most inane subjects—the relation of Almannish to Hanzish, the dialects of Virgenya, the virtues of certain stars. He gave trees and birds and hills names that were long, unpronounceable, and entirely wrong and thought himself clever. And he kept wanting to stop to look at things.

"There's another," he said, for the fifth time in two bells. "Can you wait just a moment?"

"No," Aspar told him.

"Really! Just a moment." Stephen dismounted, and from his refurbished pack drew a roll of paper and separated a leaf from it. From a pouch at his belt, he produced a chunk of charcoal. Then he hurried to a waist-high stone standing by the side of the road. There were many such, along Old King's way, all like this, squared columns two hands on a side. Most had been pushed out of the ground by roots growing up beneath them, expelled like infected teeth.

"This one still has writing on it!"

"So?"

Stephen pressed his sheet of paper against the stone and began blackening it with his charcoal.

"What in Grim's eye are you doing?"

"Taking a rubbing—I can study it later. See? The writing comes through." He held the sheet up, and Aspar saw, indeed, that in addition to the grain of the stone itself and the impressions of lichens, he could make out a number of angular marks.

"Ancient Vitellian," Stephen said triumphantly. "This marks the boundary of two meddixships, and tells the distance to the next and last guardtower." He squinted. "But here they call this road the Bloody Trace. I wonder what that means? The maps all mark it as the *Vio Caldatum*."

"Why is your head full of this?" Aspar asked.

"It's my calling—ancient languages, history."

"Sounds useful."

"If we have no past, we have no future," Stephen replied cheerfully.

"The past is dead, and the Bloody Trace is an old superstition."

"Aha! So you've heard the name. Local folklore? How does it go?"

"You wouldn't be interested."

"I just said I was."

"Then you shouldn't be. It's old pig-wife talk."

"Maybe. But sometimes the folk preserve a primitive sort of wisdom that scholarship has forgotten. Real bits of history, packaged up in simple conventions, made entertaining so common people can understand it, distorted here and there by misunderstandings, but still keeping some truth for those with the wits and education to riddle it out."

Aspar laughed. "Makes me proud to be 'folk,'" he said.

"I didn't mean to imply you were simple. Please, can't you tell me? About the Bloody Trace?"

"If you get back on your damned horse and start riding again."

"Oh—certainly, of course." He carefully rolled up his paper, placed it in a canvas sack, and remounted.

"Not much to tell, really," the holter said, as they started along once more. "It's spelt that long ago, when the demon Scaosen ruled the world, they used to keep humans like hounds, and race 'em up and down this road till their feet wore to the bone. They'd gamble on the outcome, keep 'em going until they all dropped dead. They say the road was ruddy from one end to the other, from the blood of their torn feet."

"Scaosen? You mean the Skasloi?"

"I'm just telling a story."

"Yes, but you see, with a bit of truth! You call them the Scaosen, while in the Lierish tongue they are known as *Echesl*. In Hornladh, *Shasl*. The ancient term was *Skasloi*, and they were quite real. History doesn't doubt them in the slightest. It was the first Virgenyans who led the slaughter of them, with the aid of the saints."

"Yah, I know the story. Me, I've never seen a Scaos."

"Well, they're all dead."

"Then it doesn't much matter whether I believe in them or not, does it?"

"Well, that's not a very enlightened attitude."

Aspar shrugged.

"I wonder," Stephen said, stroking his stubbly face. "Could this have really been a Skasloi road before it was Vitellian?"

"Why not? If you believe that sort of thing, the whole stretch of it's said to be haunted by alvs. The old people say the alvs come as white mists, or as apparitions, so terrible in beauty to see them is to die. The Sefry say they're the hungry ghosts of the Scaosen. People leave them things. Some ask them for favors. Most try to avoid them."

"What else do these alvs do?"

"Steal children. Bring sickness. Ruin crops. Make men do evil by whispering evil words in their ears. They can still your heart just by reaching their misty fingers into it. Of course, I've never seen one, so—"

"—you don't believe in them. Yes, holter, I think I'm starting to understand you and your philosophy."

"*Werlic*? Good. Now, if it please you, could you stop your nattering for a space? So if there be alvs or uttins or booghinns sneaking about us, I've me a chance to hear 'em?"

Miraculously, Stephen did quiet after that, studying his rubbing as they rode. After a moment, Aspar almost wished he would start up again, for the silence left him with the uneasy memory of the spring, the dead frogs, the print that had so bruised the earth. It reminded him that there were, indeed, things in the forest that he hadn't seen, even in all of his days roaming it.

And if some strange beast, why not the Briar King?

He remembered a song they had sung as children, when he lived with the Sefry. It went with a circle game and ended with all playing dead, but he couldn't remember the details. He remembered the song, though.

Nattering, nittering
Farthing go
The Briar King walks to and fro

Chittering, chattering
With him fly
Greffyns and manticores in the sky

Dillying, dallying
When you see
The Briar King he'll sure eat thee

Eftsoon, aftsoon
By-come-by
He'll spit you out and break the sky.

"What was that?" Stephen said.
"What?" Aspar grunted, starting from the membrance.
"You were singing."
"No, I wasn't."
"I thought you were."
"It was nothing. Forget it."
Stephen shrugged. "As you wish."
Aspar grunted and switched his reins to the other hand, wishing he could forget as easily. Instead, he remembered a verse from another song, one Jesp used to sing.

Blasts and blaws so loud and shrill
The bone-bright horn from o'er the hill
The Thorny Lord of holt and rill
Walks as when the world was still.

CHAPTER FIVE

THE PRINCESS

"THEY'VE SEEN US!" Austra gasped.

Anne leaned around the side of the oak, fingers gripping its rough skin. Behind her, her cream-colored mare stamped and whickered.

"Hush, Faster," she whispered.

The two girls stood in the shadows of the forest at the edge of the rolling meadow known as the Sleeve. As they watched, three horsemen made their way across the violet-spangled grass, heads turning this way and that. They wore the dark orange tabards of the Royal Light Horse, and the sun glinted from their mail. They were perhaps half a bowshot away.

"No," Anne said, turning to Austra. "They haven't. But they *are* looking for us. I think that's Captain Cathond in the lead."

"You really think they've been sent out to look for us?" Austra crouched even lower, pushing a lock of golden hair from her face.

"Absolutely."

"Let's go deeper in the woods, then. If they see us—"

"Yes, suppose they do?" Anne considered.

"That's what I just said. I—" Austra's blue eyes went as round as gold reytoirs. "No. Anne!"

Grinning, Anne drew her hood over her red-gold hair, then took Faster's reins, gripped the saddle, and flung herself up. "Wait until we're out of sight. Then meet me in Eslen-of-Shadows."

"I won't!" Austra declared, trying to keep her voice low. "You stay right here!"

Anne clapped her thighs against her horse's flanks. "Faster!" she commanded.

The mare broke from the woods in full gallop, a few leaves swirling in her wake. For perhaps ten heartbeats the only sound was the muffled thumping of hooves pounding damp soil. Then one of the mounted men started shouting. Anne glanced back over her shoulder and saw she had been right: Captain Cathond's red face was behind the shouting. They wheeled their white geldings to pursue her.

Anne shouted in joy at the rush of wind on her face. The Sleeve was perfect for racing, long and green and beautiful. To her right, the forest was dressed in spring leaves, dogwood and cherry blossoms. Left, the Sleeve dropped a steep shoulder down to the marshy rinns that surrounded the island of Ynis and bordered the broad river Warlock, which lapped honey-gold against his banks.

Faster was living thunder, and Anne was the bright eye of lightning. Let them try to catch her! Let them!

The Sleeve curved around the southern edge of the island, then turned right, climbing up to the twin hills of Tom Woth and Tom Cast. Anne didn't wait for the Sleeve to bend, however, but twitched the reins, commanding Faster into a sharp turn, sending clots of grass and black earth flying, veering them back into the woods. She ducked branches and held tight as the horse leapt a small stream. A quick look back showed the horsemen cutting into the woods earlier in hopes of heading her off. But the wood was thick with new growth through there and would slow them.

She had ridden, though, the tract that had been burned off a few years before. It was relatively clear, a favorite cutoff of hers, and Faster could whip around the great-girthed ash and oak. Anne crowed as they sped beneath one tree that had fallen aslant upon another, then up a hill, right, and back out onto the Sleeve, where it curved up to Tom Woth and Tom Cast. As she gained altitude, the topmost towers and turrets of Eslen castle appeared above the trees to her right, pennants streaming in the breeze.

When the men emerged from the wood again, they were twice as far behind her as they had been when they began the pursuit, and there were only two of them. Smugly, she started around the base of Tom Woth, headed back toward the south edge of the island. There was no challenge to it now; when she came to the Snake they wouldn't even see her performance. A shame, really.

"Good girl, Faster," she said, easing up the pace a little. "Just don't go skittish on me, you hear? You'll have to be brave, but then you can rest, and I'll find you something good to eat. I promise."

Then she caught motion from the corner of her eye and gasped. The third horseman, through some miracle, had just entered the Sleeve almost at her elbow. And worse, a new fellow on a dun wearing a red cape appeared just behind him. A hot flash of surprise burned across Anne's face.

"Hey, there! Stop!"

She recognized the voice of Captain Cathond. Her heart drummed, but she clapped Faster fiercely, circling the hill. Tom Woth and Tom Cast together looked like an ample woman's breasts. Anne rode right down the cleavage.

"You'd better slow up, you damned fool!" Cathond shouted. "There's nothing on the other side!"

He was wrong. There was plenty on the other side—a spectacular view of the verdant rinns, and far below, the river, the southern fens. Coming from between the hills, there was a terrible and wonderful moment when it seemed the whole world was spread before her.

"Here we go, Faster!" Anne cried, as they crossed the lip over nothing and all of Faster's feet were in the air. Now that it was too late, she felt a thrill of fear so sharp she could nearly taste it.

An instant stretched to eternity as Anne lay flat and knotted her hands in Faster's mane. The warm musk of horse, the oil and leather of the saddle, the rushing air were her whole universe. Her belly was stuffed with tickly feathers. She shrieked in delirious fear, and then her mount's hooves struck the Snake, a narrow gorge slithering down the steep side of the island.

Faster almost went end over end, and her hindquarters came around awkwardly. Then she caught a pace, bounding along the edge of the Snake, back and forth, now slipping out of control, then recovering and gathering her legs to spring. The world jumbled by, and Anne's fear was so mixed with giddy elation she couldn't tell the difference. Faster stumbled so hard she nearly plowed her head into the ground, and if that happened, there would be an end to both of them.

So be it then, she thought. *If I die, I die, and glorious!* Not like her grandmother, wasting like a sick dog in the bed, turning yellow and smelling bad. Not like her Aunt Fiene, bled dry in childbirth.

But then Anne knew she wouldn't die. Faster had her hooves on a gentler slope, and she became more surefooted. The giant willows at the base of the Snake beckoned her in, but before she entered their concealing shadows she cast a final glance up the way she had come and saw the silhouettes of her pursuers, still on the edge. They didn't dare follow her, of course.

She had escaped, for the moment. For the rest of the day, if she was lucky.

Faster's withers were trembling, so Anne got off to let her walk a bit. It would take the guards forever to get down here by any of the conventional routes, and then they had twenty paths to choose from. She smiled up at the gnarled roof of willow, got her bearings, and started back east, toward Eslen-of-Shadows.

"That was wonderful, Faster," she said. "They didn't even *think* about following us!" She brushed her hair from her face. "Now we'll just find Austra and hide out in the tombs the rest of the day. They won't look for us there."

Her blood and Faster's wheezing were so loud in her ears that Anne didn't hear the other rider until he had already turned the bend behind her. She spun and stopped still, staring at him.

It was the man on the dun, in the red cape—the latecomer. He was tall and fair, but dark-eyed, a young man, perhaps nineteen. His horse was blowing almost as hard as Faster.

"Saint Tarn, what a ride!" he exclaimed. "Quite mad! You, my lad, are—" He broke off, squinting at Anne.

"You're no lad," he said.

"Never have been," Anne replied coldly.

His gaze was fixed on her now, and his eyebrows went up. "You're Princess Anne!"

"Am I? And what is that to you?"

"Well, I'm not sure. I thought the Royal Horse was after a thief or a poacher. I thought I'd help 'em, for a lark. Now I'm confused."

"My mother sent them, I'm sure. I've probably forgotten some dull errand I was supposed to do." She put her foot in the stirrup and swung back into the saddle.

"What? So quickly?" the man said. "But I've just caught you. Don't I get something for that?"

"I can lose you again," Anne promised.

"You never lost me," he pointed out. "I came down on your heels."

"Not right on them. You were up there thinking about it for a while."

He shrugged. "You've ridden that before, I warrant. I've never ridden in Eslen before today."

"Well done, then." At that, she turned to leave.

"Wait. Don't you even want to know who I am?"

"Why should that matter to me?" she retorted.

"I don't know, but it certainly matters to me who *you* are."

"Oh, very well," she said. "What's your name?"

He dismounted and bowed. "Roderick of Dunmrogh," he said.

"Fine, Roderick of Dunmrogh. I am Anne Dare, and you have not seen me today."

"What a shame *that* would have been," he said.

"You're awfully bold, aren't you?"

"And you're awfully pretty, Princess Anne. Tarn's own horsewoman, I'm bound. But if you say I haven't seen you, I haven't seen you."

"Good."

"But . . . er . . . *why* haven't I seen you, if I may ask?"

"I told you. My mother—"

"The queen."

She glared at him. "Yes, the queen, saints save her. And me from her." She narrowed her eyes. "How do you know who I am?"

"I saw you. In court. I took the rose of knighthood only nineday ago."

"Oh! So it's *Sir* Roderick, then."

"Yes. But you were there, along with your sisters."

"Oh. Yes, I do suppose I stand out, the duck amongst the swans."

"It was your red hair that bought my attention," Roderick said, "not pinfeathers."

"Yes. And the freckles, and this boat keel of a nose."

"There's no need to bait a hook to catch my praise," he said. "I like your nose. I liked it right away, and I'm happy to say so."

Anne rolled her eyes. "You thought I was a *boy*."

"You're dressed like one! And you ride like one. It took only one glance up close to dispel that illusion." He wrinkled his brow. "Why *are* you wearing breeches?"

"Have you ever tried to ride in a dress?"

"Ladies ride in dresses all the time."

"Yes, of course—sidesaddle. How long do you think I would have stayed in my seat coming down the Snake sidesaddle?"

He chuckled. "I see your point."

"No one else does. They didn't care when I was little; the whole court thought it cute. 'Little Prince Anne' some called me. When I became marriageable everything changed, and now I must sneak about to ride like this. Mother says fifteen is far too old for childish habits. I—" She broke off, and a suddenly suspicious expression crossed her face. "You weren't sent to court me, were you?"

"What?" He seemed genuinely astonished.

"Mother would like nothing so well as to have me married off, preferably to someone dull, old, and fat." She looked at him. "But you are none of those."

For the first time, Roderick looked annoyed. "All I did, Princess, was to try to pay you a compliment. And I doubt very much that your mother would seek a husband for you from my house. We aren't grotesquely rich nor are we fawning sycophants, and so find no favor at your father's court."

"Well. You *are* plainspoken, aren't you? I apologize, Sir Roderick. When you've been at court a while, you'll find just how little honor and truth there is in it, and perhaps excuse me."

"Smile, and I'll forgive quite quickly."

To her dismay, she felt her lips bow of their own accord. For an instant her belly went light and weird, as if she were still plunging down the Snake.

"There. Better than a royal pardon." he said, and he started to re-mount. "Well. It was nice meeting you, Princess. I hope we can speak again."

"You're going?"

"That's what you wanted, isn't it? Besides, I just realized what sort of trouble could come, if we were found together, in the woods, unchaperoned."

"We've done nothing shameful," Anne said. "Nor will we. But if you're afraid—"

"I'm not afraid," Roderick said. "It was your reputation I was considering."

"That's very kind of you, but I can consider my own reputation, thank you."

"Meaning?"

"I don't trust you. You might tell someone you saw me. I think I must bind you into my service for the rest of the day, as my bodyguard."

"Now that's luck. I've been under the rose for only a week, and already I'm escorting a princess of the realm. I would be delighted, lady, though I cannot stay for the rest of the day. I have duties, you know."

"Do you always do what you ought?"

"Not always. But in this case, yes. I don't have the luxury of being a princess."

"It isn't a luxury," Anne said, spurring her horse forward. "Are you coming, or not?"

"Where are we going?"

"To Eslen-of-Shadows, where my grandfathers sleep."

They rode a few moments in silence, during which time Anne stole several glances at her new companion. He sat straight, easy, and proud in the saddle. His arms, bared almost to the shoulder by his riding vest, were lean and corded. His profile had a little hawk in it.

For the first time, she wondered if he was who he said he was. What if he was an assassin, a thief, a rogue—even a Hanzish spy? His accent was peculiar, and he did have the northern look to him.

"Dunmrogh," she said. "Where is that, exactly?"

"South. It's a greffy in the kingdom of Hornladh."

"Hornladh," she repeated, trying to remember the map in the Gallery of Empire. That *was* south, or so she seemed to remember.

They clopped across the stone bridge that crossed the Cer Canal, enduring the weathered gazes of the stone faces carved on the endposts. Silence settled around them again, and though Anne felt she ought to say something more, her head was quite empty of ideas for conversation.

"Eslen is larger than I thought," Roderick offered, at last.

"This isn't Eslen. Eslen is the castle and the city. The island is Ynis. Right now, we're in the rinns, the low ground between Ynis and the Warlock."

"And Eslen-of-Shadows?"

"Wait a moment—there." She pointed through a vaulted opening in the trees.

"Fist of Saint Tarn," Roderick gasped, gazing down at the city of the dead.

Its outskirts were modest, row on row of small wooden houses with thatched or shingle roofs facing out onto dirt streets. Some were in good repair, with neatly tended yards kept up by the families. More resembled the skeletons that lay within them, rickety frames pulled down beneath creepers, thorns, and years of falling leaves. Trees sprouted up through a few.

There were five circular canals within the borders of the necropolis, one within another. After they crossed the first the houses appeared more solid, built of dressed stone, with roofs of slate and fences of iron around them. The streets and avenues were cobbled there. From their vantage it was difficult for Anne and Roderick to make out more, save that the city rose in height and grandeur as it neared the center, where domes and towers stood.

"We have royal tombs in Dunmrogh," Roderick said, "but nothing like this! Who are buried in these smallest, poorest houses?"

Anne shrugged. "The poorest people. Every family in Eslen-on-the-Hill has a quarter here, in keeping with their means. What they build and how they keep it is up to them. If their fortunes change, they might move the remains of their ancestors inward. If someone beyond the third canal falls on hard times, they might have to move farther out."

"You mean to say that a man could be buried in a palace, and a century later find himself in a pauper's hovel?"

"Of course."

"That hardly seems fair."

"Neither is having worms eat your eyes, but that comes with being dead, too," Anne replied wryly.

Roderick laughed. "You have me there." He shifted in his saddle. "Well, I've seen it. And now I have to go."

"Already?"

"Will it take more than a bell to return to the keep?"

"Assuredly."

"Then I should have been on my way already. What's the quickest way?"

"I think you should find it on your own."

"Not if you want to see me again. My father will have me sent back to one of our lesser holdings a hundred leagues from here if I miss at my duties."

"What in the name of Saint Loy makes you think I'd want to see you again?"

For an answer he pranced his horse near, caught her eyes with his own steel blue ones. She felt a sudden surge of panic, but also a kind of paralyzation. When he leaned in and kissed her, she couldn't have stopped him if she wanted to.

And she didn't want to.

It didn't last long, just one brief, wonderful, confusing brush of lips. It wasn't what she had expected kissing would be like, not at all.

Her toes were tingling.

She blinked, and said softly, "Go along this canal until you reach a street paved in lead bricks. Turn left. It will take you up the hill."

He tossed his head at Eslen-of-Shadows. "I'd like to see the rest of this sometime."

"Come back in two days, around the noon bell. You might find me here."

He smiled, nodded, and without another word, rode off.

She sat, dazed, staring at the black water of the canal, recalling the feeling of his lips touching hers, trying not to let it escape, examining it, each nuance of his word and motion, striving to understand.

She didn't know him.

She heard hoofbeats approaching, and her heart quickened, both hoping and fearing that he had come back. But when she looked up, it was Austra she saw, her golden locks bouncing on her shoulders, her expression quite cross.

"Who was *that*?" Austra asked.

"A knight," Anne replied.

Austra seemed to consider that for a moment, then turned angry eyes back on Anne. "Why do you do these things? You came down the Snake, didn't you?"

"Did anyone see you?" Anne asked.

"No. But I'm your lady-in-waiting, Anne. And I'm lucky to be, since I've no noble blood in me. If something happens to you—"

"My father loved yours, Austra, noble blood or no. Do you think he would ever turn you out?"

Suddenly she realized that tears had started in Austra's eyes.

"Austra! What's wrong?" Anne asked.

"Your sister Fastia," Austra replied steadily, blinking through the tears. "You just don't understand, Anne."

"What don't I understand? We grew up together. We've shared the same bed since we were five, when your parents died and Father took you in as my maid. And we've been playing games like this with the guard since I can remember. Why are you crying now?"

"Because Fastia told me I wouldn't be permitted to be your maid any longer, if you couldn't be curbed! 'I'll set someone with more sense to her,' she said."

"My sister is just trying to scare you. Besides, we share the risk, Austra."

"You really *don't* understand. You're a princess. I'm a servant. Your family dresses me up and pretends to treat me as if I'm gentle, but the fact is, to everyone else I'm nothing."

"No," Anne replied. "That's not true. Because *I* would never let anything happen to you, Austra. We'll always be together, we two. I love you as much as any sister."

"Hush," Austra replied, snuffling. "Just hush."

"Come on. We'll go back, right now. Sneak in while they're still looking. We won't get caught this time, I promise."

"The knights—"

"They couldn't catch me. They won't say anything, from shame, unless Mother or Fastia asks 'em outright. And still, they never saw *you*."

"It doesn't matter to Fastia whether I'm an accomplice or if you duped me."

"Figs for Fastia. She hasn't as much power as you think. Now come along."

Austra nodded, wiping her eyes with her sleeve. "But what about the knight who *did* catch you?" Austra asked.

"He won't tell anyone, either," Anne said. "Not if he wants to keep his head."

Then she frowned. "How *dare* Fastia speak to you so? I should do something about this. Yes, and I think I know what."

"What?"

"I'll visit Virgenya. I'll tell *her*. She'll do something, I'm certain."

Austra's eyes widened again. "I . . . I thought you said we were going back up the hill."

"This won't take any time at all."

"But—"

"I'm doing this for you," Anne told her friend. "Come on. Be brave."

"Can we start back in a bell or so?"

"Of course."

Austra held her chin up. "Let's go ahead, then."

They continued across the inner canals, until they came to the royal quarter, where the streets were all paved with lead bricks, smoothed and slicked by shoes and the brooms of the caretakers, where the stone figures of saints supported roofs flat or slanted and everything was twined thick with pink-eyed primrose and ajister thorn and the doors of the buildings were sealed with sigils and good steel locks.

This last circle was walled in midnight and stars, a bastion of black granite, mica flecked, with spears of wrought iron. The gates were guarded by Saint Under, with his hammer and long, grim face, and Saint Dun with her tear-brimmed eyes and crown of roses.

It was also guarded by a tall fellow of middle years who wore the somber gray livery of the scathomen, the knight-priests who guard the dead.

"Good evening, Princess Anne," the man said.

"The best evening to you, Sir Len," Anne replied.

"Here without permission again, I take it." Sir Len removed his helm to reveal brown braids framing a face that might have been chiseled onto a brick, so stern and angular and flat it was.

"Why do you say that? Has Mother or Fastia been down here asking after me?"

The knight smiled briefly. "I can no more tell you of their comings or goings than I can tell them of yours. It is against my vow. Who comes here, what they do, of those things I cannot speak. As well you know, which is why you come here to do your mischief."

"Are you turning me away?"

"You know I cannot do that, either. Pass, Princess."

"Thank you, Sir Len."

As they proceeded through the gates, Sir Len rang the brass bell, to let the royal dead know visitors were coming. Anne felt a gentle fluttering in her belly, a sure sign the spirits had turned their eyes upon her.

We'll see, Fastia, she thought smugly. *We'll just see.*

Anne and Austra dismounted and tied their horses outside the small court-yard where the dead of house Dare made their homes. There stood a small altar, where lay fresh and withered flowers, candles—some half-burnt, some puddles—mazers that smelled of mead, wine, and oak beer. Anne lit one of the candles, and they both knelt for a moment, as Anne led them in the prayer. The lead was hard and cold beneath Anne's knees. Somewhere near, a jay scolded a raven, a sudden shrill cacophony. Anne chanted,

"Saints who keep my fathers and mothers,
Saint Under who defends, Saint Dun who tends,
Keep my footsteps light here
Let them sleep or wake as they please,
Bless them, keep them,

Let them know me, if only as a dream.

Sacaro, Sacaraum, Sacarafum."

She took Austra's hand. "Come on," she whispered.

They skirted the great house where the bones of her grandparents and great-grandparents lay, where her uncles and aunts held midnight courts and her youngest brother Avieyen played with the toys in his marble crib, around the red marble colonnaded pastato and wide-arched valve of bronze, past the lesser mansion, where her more distant cousins no doubt plotted, as they had in life, for a position amongst their more august relatives. On to the crumbling stone walls and wild, straggling trees of the horz.

Over the years, Anne and Austra had worn a regular path back to the tomb, enlarging the hidden way as their bodies grew—not by cutting, of course, just by pushing and prying their way along. The Wild Saints had made no complaint, stricken them with no fever or blemishes, and so they thought themselves safe in that small modification. Also in the steps they had taken to *hide* their secret—strategically placed mats of rudely woven grapevine, a rock moved here or there.

What really kept it hidden, Anne was sure, was Virgenya's will. She had hidden for over two thousand years from everyone but Anne and Austra. She seemed to want to keep it that way.

And so, after a few moments on hands and knees, Anne found herself once more before the sarcophagus.

They had never been able to move the lid any further, not even with a wooden lever, and after a time Anne had come to believe she was not *supposed* to look inside, and so she stopped trying.

But the little crack was still there.

"Now," she said. "Have you got the stylus and the foil?"

"Please, don't curse Fastia on my account," Austra pleaded.

"I'm not going to curse her," Anne said. "Not really. But she's become insufferable! *Threatening* you! She deserves punishment."

"She used to play with us," Austra reminded her. "She used to be our friend. She made us overdresses of braided nodding-heads and dandelions."

"That was a long time ago. She's different, now, since she married. Since she became our mistress."

"Then wish for her to be the way she was. Don't put any ill on her. Please."

"I just want to give her boils," Anne said. "Or a few pocks on her beautiful face. Oh, all right. Give those here."

Austra handed her a small, paper-thin sheet of lead and an iron scriber. Anne pressed the lead against the coffin lid and wrote.

Ancestress, please take this request to Saint Cer, petition her on my be-half. Ask her to dissuade my sister Fastia from threatening my maid, Austra, and to make Fastia nicer, as she was when she was younger.

Anne considered the sheet. There was still room at the bottom.

And fix the heart of Roderick of Dunmrogh on me. Let him not sleep without dreams of me.

"What? Who is Roderick of Dunmrogh?" Austra exclaimed.

"You were looking over my shoulder!"

"Of course. I was afraid you would ask for boils for Fastia!"

"Well, I didn't, you busybody," Anne said, waving her friend away.

"No, but you did ask for some boy to fall in love with you," Austra said.

"He's a knight."

"The one who chased you down the Snake? The one you just met? What, are you in love with *him*?"

"Of course not. How could I be? But what could it hurt for him to love me?"

"This sort of thing never turns out well in phay stories, Anne."

"Well, Cer likely won't pay attention to either of these. She likes *curses*."

"Falling in love with you could *easily* be a curse," Austra replied.

"Very funny. You should replace Hound Hat as court jester." She slipped the lead foil through the crack in the lid of the sarcophagus. "There. Done. And now we can go."

As she stood, a sudden dizziness struck her between the eyes, and for an instant, she couldn't remember where she was. Something rang brightly in her chest, like a golden bell, and the touch of her fingers against the stone seemed very far away.

"Anne?" Austra said, voice concerned.

"Nothing. I was dizzy for an instant. It's passed. Come on, we should get back to the castle."

CHAPTER SIX

THE KING

"Now, let me introduce myself," the big Hansan said to Neil. "I'm Everwulf af Gastenmarka, squire to Sir Alareik Wishilm, whom you've insulted."

"I'm Neil MeqVren, squire to Sir Fail de Liery, and I've promised him I will not draw steel against you."

"Convenient, but that's no matter. I'll tear your head off with my bare hands, no steel needed nor asked for."

Neil took a deep, slow breath and let his muscles relax.

Everwulf came like a bull, fast for all of his bulk. Neil was faster, spinning aside at the last instant and breaking the big man's nose again with the back of his fist. The Hansan pawed air and swayed back. Neil stepped in close, snapped his elbow into the squire's ribs and felt them crack, then finished with a vicious jab into the fellow's armpit. The breath blew out of Everwulf and he collapsed.

The rest of the squires weren't playing fair. From the corner of his eye, Neil saw something arcing down toward him. He ducked and kicked, struck feet. A man went down, dropping the wooden practice weapon he held in his hand. Neil scooped it up, rolled, and caught his next attacker across the shins. This one screamed like a horse being stabbed.

Neil bounced to his feet. The fellow he had tripped was scuttling away. Everwulf was panting in a heap on the ground, and Shin-struck was gurgling. Neil leaned on the wooden sword casually. "Are we done with this?" he asked.

"It's done," the one fellow still capable of talking said.

"A good night to you then," Neil said. "I look forward to meeting you fellows on the field of honor, once we've all taken the rose."

He dropped the wooden sword, brushed his hair back into place. High above, he could just make out the moonlit spires of the castle.

The court! Tomorrow he would see the court!

William II of Crotheny gripped the stone casement of the tall window, and for a moment felt so light that a rush of wind might pull him out of it. Alv-needles pricked at his scalp, and a terror seemed to burst behind his eyes so bright it nearly outshone the sun. It staggered him.

The dead are speaking my name, he thought, and then, *Am I dying?*

An uncle of his had died like this, one heartbeat standing and talking as if everything was fine, the next, cooling on the floor.

"What's the matter, dear brother?" Robert asked, from across the room. That was Robert, attracted to weakness like sharks to blood.

William set his jaw and took a deep, slow breath. No, his heart was still beating—furiously, in fact. Outside, the sky was clear. Beyond the spires and peaked roofs he could see the green ribbon of the Sleeve and the distant Breu-en-Trey. The wind was blowing from there, the west, and had the delicious taste of salt on it.

He wasn't dying, not on such a day. He couldn't be.

"William?"

He turned from the window. "A moment, brother, a moment. Wait for me outside, in the Hall of Doves."

"I'm to be ejected from my own brother's chambers?"

"Heed me, Robert."

A frown gashed Robert's forehead. "As you wish. But don't make me wait long, William."

When the door closed, William permitted himself to collapse into his armchair. He'd been afraid his knees would give out with Robert in the room, and that wouldn't do.

What was wrong with him?

He sat there for a moment, breathing deeply, fingering the ivory inlay on the oaken armrest, then stood on wobbly legs and went to the wash basin to splash water on his face. In the mirror, dripping features looked back at him. His neatly trimmed beard and curly auburn hair had only a little gray, but his eyes looked bruised, his skin sallow, the lines on his forehead deep as crevasses. *When did I get so old?* he wondered. He was only forty-five, but he had seen younger faces on men with another score of winters.

He brushed away the water with a linen rag and rang a small bell. A moment later his valet—a plump, balding man of sixty—appeared, clad in black stockings and scarlet-and-gold doublet. "Sire?"

"John, make sure my brother has some wine. You know what he likes. And send Pafel in to dress me."

"Yes, Sire. Sire—"

"Yes?"

"Are you feeling well?"

John's voice held genuine concern. He had been William's valet for almost thirty years. In all of the kingdom, he was one of the few men William trusted.

"Honestly, John? No. I just had some sort of . . . I don't know what. A terror, a waking Black Mary. I've never felt anything like it, not even in battle. And worse, Robert was here to see it. And now I have to go talk to him about something-or-other, who knows what. And then court. I wish sometimes—" He broke off and shook his head.

"I'm sorry, Sire. Is there anything I can do?"

"I doubt it, John, but thank you."

John nodded and started to leave but instead turned back. "There is a certain fear, Sire, that cannot be explained. It's like the panic one has when falling; it simply comes."

"Yes, it was much like that. But I wasn't falling."

"There are many ways to fall, Sire."

William stared at him for a moment, then chuckled. "Go on, John. Take my brother his wine."

"Saints keep you, Sire."

"And you, old friend."

Pafel, a ruddy-faced young man with a country accent, arrived a few moments later with his new assistant Kenth.

"Not the full court garb," William told them. "Not yet. Something comfortable." He opened his arms, so they could take his dressing gown.

"As you wish, Sire. If I may? Today is Tiffsday, so of course the colors of Saint Tiff are appropriate, but we are also in the season of equinox, which is ruled by Saint Fessa . . ."

They put him in raven hose with gold embroidered vines, a blood-red silk doublet with a standing collar and gold florets, and a robe of black ermine. The familiar routine of dressing—complete with Pafel's nonstop explanations—made William feel better. This was, after all, an ordinary day. He wasn't dying, and there was nothing to be afraid of. By the time he was dressed, his hands and legs had stopped shaking, and he felt only that distant foreboding he had carried for the past several months.

"Thank you, gentlemen," he told his dressers. When they were gone, he composed himself with a few deep breaths and went to the Hall of Doves.

The hall was as light and airy as a room all of stone could be, built of dressed alabaster and appointed with drapes and tapestries in pale greens and golds. The windows were broad and open; after all, if an army won past the floodlands, three city walls, and the outer fortress, all was lost anyway.

A faint rusty stain in the otherwise unblemished floor reminded William that it had happened once before. Thiuzwald Fram Reiksbaurg, the Wolf-Coat, had fallen here, struck through the liver by the first William Dare to reign in Eslen, just over a hundred years ago.

William stepped past the stain. Robert looked up from an armchair—*William's* armchair—where he pretended to study a prayerbook. "Well," he said. "There was no need to pretty yourself up on my account."

"What can I do for you, Robert?"

"Do for me?" Robert stood, stretching his long, lean body to its full height. He was only twenty, decades younger than William, and to emphasize the fact he wore the small mustache, goatee, and close-cropped hair that was currently in fashion among the more effete courtiers. His regular features were somewhat marred by a smirk. "It's what I can do for *you*, Wilm."

"And what might that be?"

"I went for a walk last night with Lord Reccard, our esteemed ambassador from Saltmark."

"A walk?"

"Yes. We walked first to the Boar's Beard, then to the Talking Bear, over the canal to the Miser's Daughter—"

"I see. The man isn't dead, is he? You haven't stirred us up a war with Saltmark, have you?"

"Dead? No. He's alive, if somewhat remorseful. War . . . well, just wait until I've finished."

"Go on," William said, trying to keep his face straight. He wished he trusted his brother more.

"You may remember Reccard's wife, a lovely creature by the name of Seglasha?"

"Of course. Originally from Herilanz, yes?"

"Yes, and a true daughter of that barbaric country. She cut her last husband into a gelding, you know, and the one before that was hacked to pieces by her brothers for slighting her in public. Reccard is quite terrified of her."

"Not without cause, it seems," William said.

Robert arched his brows. "You should talk, married to that de Liery woman! She's at least—"

"Speak no ill of my wife," William warned. "I won't hear it."

"No? Not even from your mistresses? I've heard a few choice complaints from Lady Berrye concerning your wife, in words I do not think she invented."

"Robert, I hope you didn't come to lecture *me* about proper behavior. That would be the goat calling the ram hairy."

Robert leaned against an alabaster pillar, folding his arms across his chest. "No, brother dear, I came to ask if you knew that Hansa had moved thirty war galleys and one thousand troops into Saltmark."

"What?"

"As I said, poor Reccard is quite terrified of his wife. I guessed correctly that he wouldn't want her to know about the games we played at the end of the night, with the ladies in the Lark's Palace. So I convinced him that he ought to be . . . *friendly* to me."

"Robert, what a schemer you are. It's not fitting for a Dare to act so."

Robert made a disgusted sound. "Now who is lecturing on morality? You *depend* on my 'unworthy' behavior, William. It allows you to keep the armor of your righteousness clean and polished, while at the same time retaining your kingdom. Will you ignore this information because I obtained it so?"

"You know I cannot. You *knew* I could not."

"Precisely. So do not lecture me, Wilm."

William sighed heavily and looked back out the window. "Who knows about this? About these Hanzish ships?"

"At this court? You and me, and the ambassador, of course."

"Why would Hansa invest Saltmark? Why would Saltmark allow it?"

"Don't be silly. What other reason could there be? They're preparing something, and Saltmark is with them."

"Preparing what?"

"Reccard doesn't know. If I had to guess, though, I'd say they have designs on the Sorrow Isles."

"The Sorrows? Why?"

"To provoke us, I wouldn't doubt. Hansa grows fat with men and ships, brother. The emperor of Hansa is an old man; he'll want to use them soon, while he still can. And there's nothing under the sun that he wants more than that crown you wear on your head."

Marcomir Fram Reiksbaurg isn't the only one who wants my crown, William thought sourly. *Or do you think me too thick to know that, dear brother?*

"I suppose you could simply ask the Hanzish emissary," Robert went on. "His ship anchored yesterday."

"Yes, that complicates things, doesn't it? Or simplifies them. Perhaps they've come to declare war in person." He sighed and ran his fingers through his hair. "In any event, I'm not scheduled to speak to that embassy until the day after tomorrow, after my daughter's birthday. I will not change that; it would seem suspicious." He paused, considering. "Where is Reccard now?"

"Sleeping it off."

"Put spies on him, and on the Hansans. If any correspondence passes, I want to know of it. If they meet, let them, but make certain they are overheard. Under no circumstances must either get a message out of the city." He knitted his fingers and looked at them. "And we'll send a few ships to the Sorrows. Quietly, a few at a time over the next week."

"Wise moves all," Robert said. "You want me to act as your sinescalh in this matter, then?"

"Yes. Until I tell you otherwise. I'll draft the formal writ of investment this afternoon."

"Thank you, William. I'll try to be worthy of you and our family name."

If there was sarcasm in that, it was too subtle to detect. Which meant nothing, actually. William had known his brother only since his birth. It wasn't long enough.

A bell jangled faintly, from the hallway.

"Enter!" William said.

The door creaked open, and John stepped in. "It's the *praifec*, Sire, just returned from Virginia. And he has a surprise with him."

The praifec. Grand.

"Of course. Show him in."

A moment later, the black-robed praifec Marché Hespero stepped into the chamber.

"Your Majesty," he said, bowing to William. He then bowed to Robert. "Archgreft."

"How good to see you, Praifec," Robert said. "You've made it back from Virginia in one piece."

"Indeed," the churchman replied.

"I trust you found our kinsmen as thickheaded as us?" Robert went on.

William wished, not for the first time, Robert would keep his mouth shut.

But Hespero smiled. "Let us say, they are as seemingly intractable in many ways, even in the matter of heretics, which is troubling. But the saints dispose, yes?"

"I trust they do," William said lightly.

Hespero's smile didn't falter. "The saints work in many ways, but their most cherished instrument is the church. And it is written that the kingdom should be the knight of the church, the champion of it. You would be distressed, King William, if your knights failed you?"

"They never have," William replied. "Praifec, what may I have brought for you? Wine and cheese? The jade pears came ripe while you were away, and they are excellent with the blue Tero Gallé cheese."

"A cup of wine would suit me well," Hespero replied.

John poured a goblet for Hespero, who frowned as he sipped at it.

"If it's not to your taste, Praifec, I can send for a different vintage," William said.

"The wine is excellent, Sire. That is not what troubles me."

"Please. Speak your mind, then, Your Grace."

Hespero paused, then rested his goblet on a pedestal. "I have not seen my peers on the Comven. Are the rumors true? Have you legitimized your daughters as heirs to the throne?"

"I did not," William said. "The Comven did."

"But it was your proposition, the one we discussed while you were drafting it?"

"I believe we did discuss it, Praifec."

"And you remember my opinion that making the throne heritable by women is forbidden by church doctrine?"

William smiled. "So thought one of the churchmen in the Comven. The other voted for the reform. It would seem the issue is not as clearly drawn as some believe, Eminence."

In fact, it had taken some doing to get even one of the priests to vote William's way—more of Robert's dirty but effective dealings.

At times like this, he had to admit that Robert indeed had his moments.

Anger gathered for an instant on the cleric's brow, then smoothed away. "I understand your concern over the need for an heir. Charles, while a wonderful son, has indeed been touched by the saints, and—"

"My son will not enter into this conversation, Praifec," William said mildly. "You stand in my house, and I forbid it."

Hespero's face grew more stern. "Very well. I will simply inform you then, reluctantly, that I must enjoin the high Senaz of the church to consider this matter."

"Yes, let them do that," William said. *And let them try to reverse a decision of the Comven,* he thought, behind his smile. *Let even the church convince that squabbling pack of lordlings they made a wrong decision. No. One of my daughters will rule, and my son, bless his soul, will continue playing with his toys and his Sefry jester until he is an old man.*

He won't be your lack-wit king, Hespero. If it came to that, I'd rather leave the throne to Robert, had he any legitimate heirs.

"Saints!" a female voice interrupted. "You three aren't going to argue politics all day, are you?"

Robert was the first to react to the newcomer.

"Lesbeth!" He bounded across the floor and swept her up in a hug. She giggled as he spun her around, her red hair losing a comb and fanning out behind her. When Robert put her down, she kissed his cheek, then disentangled herself and leapt ferociously into William's arms.

"Praifec!" Robert said. "He is a blessed man who returns my beloved twin from her rustic exile!"

William held his youngest sister back to look at her. "Saint Loy, but you've grown, girl!"

"The image of Mother," Robert added.

"You two!" Lesbeth said, taking their hands. "How I missed you both!"

"You should have sent word," William told her. "We would have had a grand celebration!"

"I wanted to surprise you. Besides, isn't Elseny's birthday tomorrow? I wouldn't want to cast a shadow on that."

"You could never cast a shadow, sweet sister," Robert told her. "Come here, sit down, tell us everything."

"We're being rude to the praifec," Lesbeth said. "And after he was gracious enough to escort me the whole, long way. And such delightful company! Praifec, I cannot express my thanks."

"Nor I," William added quickly. "Praifec, forgive me if my words were sharp. Though it is early, it's been a taxing day already. But now you've brought me joy, and I'm in your debt for seeing my sister home safe and sound. I am ever the friend of the church, and will certainly demonstrate it to you."

"It was my pleasure," the cleric said, bowing. "And now I hope I may excuse myself. My staff is somewhat helpless without me, and I fear it will take weeks to straighten out my office. Nevertheless, I would be honored to advise you when you hold court."

"I shall be honored to have you there. I've been too long without your wisdom, Praifec."

The churchman nodded and withdrew.

"We must have more wine!" Robert said. "And entertainment. I want to hear about everything." He spun on his heel. "I'll arrange it. Lesbeth, will you join me in my gallery, at half-bell?"

"Without doubt, dear brother," she replied.

"And you, brother?"

"I will stop by. Then I must hold court, you know."

"A pity." Robert wagged a finger at Lesbeth. "Half-bell. Don't be late."

"I wouldn't dream of it."

Robert hurried off.

When they were alone, Lesbeth took William's hand and squeezed it. "Are you well, Wilm? You look tired."

"I am, a bit. Nothing for you to worry about. And I'm much better, now." He squeezed her hand back. "It's good to see you. I missed you."

"And I missed you. How is Muriele? And the girls?"

"All well. You won't believe how Anne has grown. And Elseny, betrothed! But you'll see her at her birthday tomorrow."

"Yes." Her eyes flickered down, almost shyly. "Wilm, I have a secret to tell. And I must ask permission for something. But you must promise me that it won't interfere with Elseny's birthday. Will you promise?"

"Of course. Not something serious, I hope."

Her eyes sparkled strangely. "It is, I think. At least I hope so."

Muriele Dare, the queen of Crotheny, stepped back from the peephole. Whatever Lesbeth had to say to William, Muriele would let the siblings speak in private.

Quietly, she padded down the narrow passage, gliding on the smooth stone beneath her stockinged feet, through a secret red-oak panel and the small room beyond, down the stair behind the statue of Saint Brena, and finally to the locked and concealed door to her own chambers.

There, in near darkness, she took a moment for a few deep breaths.

"You've been in the walls again."

Muriele started at the female voice. Across the room, she made out a gowned shadow.

"Erren."

"Why have you started doing my job? I'm the spy. You're the queen."

"I was bored, you were elsewhere, and I knew the praifec had returned. I wanted to know what he would say."

"Well?"

"Nothing particularly interesting. He reacted as we expected to my daughters being named as heirs. On the other hand, have you heard anything about Hanzish troops in Saltmark?"

"Nothing so definite," Erren said. "But there is much happening in Hansa. They will take action soon."

"Action of what sort?"

"Crotheny will be at war within the year, I'm certain of it," Erren replied. "But there are nearer things I fear more. Rumors abound among the coven-trained."

Muriele paused at that. Erren was a very special sort of assassin, trained by the church to serve noble families.

"You fear for our lives?" she said. "Would Hansa be so bold as to use coven-trained to murder us?"

"No—and yes. No, they will not employ my sisters, for that would incur the wrath of the church. But there are others who will kill for kings, and the mood in Hansa is that there is in Crotheny a king needing killing. *That* I know." She paused. "But something else is in the wind. Talk of new kinds of murder, of encrotacnia and shinecraft unknown to the coven-trained. Some say perhaps assassins from Hadam or some other foreign place are responsible. Across the sea they may have unfamiliar skills."

"And you have cause to fear that these new killers will be turned against my family?"

"I fear it," Erren said. Her tone held no uncertainty.

Muriele crossed the room. "Then take whatever precautions you deem necessary, especially with the children," she said. "Is that all you can tell me now?"

"Yes."

"Then light some of the candles and send for mulled wine. The passages are chilly today."

"We could ascend to your sunroom. The sun is warm outside."

"I prefer to remain here, for the moment."

"As it pleases you."

Erren went into the antechamber, whispered to the serving girl there, and returned with a burning taper. Its light was kind to her face, painting away the years better than blush. She looked almost like a girl, her features delicate beneath the dark, straight hair. Only a few streaks of silver gave it the lie.

She lit the taper near the writing desk, and as the light in the room doubled, crow's feet appeared, spindling out from her eyes, and other lines of age reluctantly revealed themselves, beneath her chin, in the skin of her neck and forehead.

A corner of Muriele's room appeared, as well. The portrait of her father, on the wall, his eyes stern yet kind, flecked with gilt by the painter, not nearly as warm as they were in person.

Erren lit a third candle, and a red couch appeared from shadow, a table, a sewing kit, the corner of Muriele's bed—not the one she shared with the king, that was in their marriage room—but *her* bed, cut from the white cedar of the Lierish uplands and canopied with black cloth and silver stars, the bed of her childhood, where she had slipped each night into dream.

The fourth candle chased all of the shadows under things, where they belonged.

"How old are you, Erren?" Muriele asked. "Exactly?"

Erren cocked her head. "How nice of you to ask. Will you ask how many children I have, as well?"

"I've known you since you left the coven. I was eight. How old were you?"

"Twenty. Now do your sums."

"I'm thirty-eight," Muriele replied. "That makes you fifty."

"Fifty it is," Erren replied.

"You don't look it."

Erren shrugged. "Age has less to hold over one if one is never a great beauty to begin with."

Muriele frowned. "I never considered you plain."

"You are a poor authority in such matters. You often claim not to know *you* are beautiful, and yet your beauty has been famous since you were thirteen. How can one be surrounded by such admiration and not succumb?"

Muriele smiled wryly. "One cannot, as I'm sure you know, cousin. One can, however, cultivate the appearance of modesty. If the appearance is kept up long enough, who knows but that it might one day become true? And here age helps, for as you say, passing time steals beauty, and when one is sufficiently old, false modesty must become real modesty."

"Excuse me, Majesty, Lady Erren," a small voice said from the curtained doorway. It was Unna, her maid, a petite girl with honey-mud hair. "Your wine?"

"Bring it in, Unna."

"Yes, Majesty."

The girl placed the pitcher in the center of a small table, and a cup on either side. The scents of orange blossom and clove rose in steam.

"How old are you, Unna?" Muriele asked.

"Eleven, Your Majesty."

"A sweet age. Even my Anne was sweet at that age, in her way."

The maid bowed.

"You may go, Unna."

"Thank you, Majesty."

Erren poured some wine and tasted it. After a moment she nodded and poured some for Muriele.

"What is all of this about age?" Erren asked. "Have you been watching your husband and his mistresses again? I should never have shown you the passages to his room."

"I have *never* done such!"

"I have. Poor puffing, panting, pungent man. He cannot keep pace with the young Alis Berrye at all."

Muriele covered her ears. "I do not *hear* this!"

"And to make matters worse, Lady Gramme has begun to complain about his attentions to Alis."

Muriele dropped her hands. "What! The old whore complaining about the new one?"

"What do you expect?" Erren asked.

Muriele exhaled a shallow laugh. "My poor, philandering William. It's almost enough to make me feel sorry for him. Do you suppose I should start my own fuss again? About Gramme's bastards?"

"It might make things more interesting. Alis wears his body thin, Lady Gramme chews his ears off, and you do away with what remains. It shouldn't be difficult."

Muriele shrugged. "I could task him. But he seems . . . For a moment, watching him in the Hall of Doves today, I thought he might collapse. He looked more than weary, he looked as if he had seen death's shadow. And if a war really is coming with Hansa . . . No. Better I be the one that he can count on."

"You've always been that," Erren pointed out. "Ambria Gramme wants to be queen, and is spectacularly unsuited for it. Alis and the lesser young ones are hoping for a . . . shall we say, *pensioned*? . . . position such as Gramme enjoys. But you—you are queen. You aren't maneuvering for anything."

Muriele felt the humor rush from her face. She looked down at her wine, at the light of the nearest candle wriggling in it like a fish.

"Would it were true," she murmured. "But I do want something of him, the bastard."

"Love?" Erren scoffed. "At your age?"

"We had it once. Not when we married, no, but later. There was a time when we were madly in love, don't you think?"

Erren nodded reluctantly. "He still loves you," she admitted.

"More than he loves Gramme, you think?"

"More deeply."

"But less carnally."

"I think he feels guilty when he comes to you, and so does so less often."

Muriele plucked a small smile from somewhere. "I mean for him to feel guilty."

Erren arched her eyebrows. "Have you ever thought of taking a lover?"

"How do you know I haven't?"

Erren rolled her eyes. "Please. Don't insult me again. You have already made note of my advanced age. That's quite enough for one night."

"Oh, very well. Yes, I have considered it. I consider it still."

"But will not do it."

"Considering, I think, is more fun than doing, in such cases."

Erren took a sip of wine and leaned forward. "Who have you considered? Tell me. The young baron from Breu-n'Avele?"

"No. Enough of that," Muriele said, her cheeks warming. "You tell *me*. What mischief did my daughters find today?"

Erren sighed and squared her shoulders. "Fastia was a perfect princess. Elseny giggled a lot with her maids, and they made some rather improbable speculation as to what her wedding night will be like."

"Oh, dear. It's time to talk to her, I suppose."

"Fastia can do that."

"Fastia does too much of what I ought to do already. What else? Anne?"

"We . . . lost Anne again."

"Of course. What do you think she's up to? Is it a man?"

"A month ago, no. She was just sneaking off, as usual. Riding, getting drunk. Now, I'm not so sure. I think she may have met someone."

"I must speak to her, too, then." She sighed. "I should not have let things go this far. She will have a difficult time, when she is married."

"She need not marry," Erren said softly. "She is the youngest. You might send her to Sister Secula, at least for a few years. Soon, your house will need a new . . ." She trailed off.

"A new *you*? Do you plan to die?"

"No. But in a few years, my more . . . *difficult* tasks will be beyond me."

"But Anne, an assassin?"

"She already has many of the talents. After all, she can elude *me*. Even if she never takes the vow, the skills are always useful. The discipline will do her good, and Sister Secula will keep her well away from young men, of that I can assure you."

Muriele nodded. "I must think on it. I'm not convinced something so drastic is needed."

Erren nodded. "She has always been your favorite, Anne."

"Does it show?"

"To some. I know it. Fastia does. Anne certainly does not."

"Good. She *should* not." She paused. "She will hate me if I send her away."

"For a time. But not forever."

Muriele closed her eyes and rested her head on the back of the chair. "Ah. I hate these things," she whispered. "I will think on it, Erren. I will think on it close."

"And so now what? More wine?"

"No. You were right. Let's go to the sunroom and play nines." She smiled again. "Invite Alis Berrye. I want to watch her squirm a bit."

CHAPTER SEVEN

TOR SCATH

STEPHEN DARIGE COMPOSED A TREATISE in his head as he rode along, entitled *Observations on the Quaint and Vulgar Behaviors of the Common Holter-Beast.*

This pricker-backed woodland creature is foul in temper, mood, and odor, and on no account should it be approached by men of good or refined sensibility. Politeness angers it, civility enrages it, and reasonableness evokes furious behavior, like that of a bear that, while stealing honey, finds a bee lodged up his—

"Stop your horse a moment," the holter said gruffly.

It communicates mostly in grunts, growls, and trumpeting farts. Of these, the last are the most intelligible, though none could be confused with speech—

"I said, stop him." Aspar had halted his own mounts and those with the captives, as well.

"Why?"

Then Stephen could see why. The holter was clearly listening to something, or for something.

"What is it?"

"If you'll keep quiet, maybe I'll find out."

Stephen strained his own ears, but heard nothing but wind hissing through leaves and branches chattering together. "I don't hear anything."

"Me neither," Pol, one of the men who had kidnapped Stephen, grunted.

"Shut up, you," Aspar White said to Pol, kicking his own horse to a trot. "Come on. I want to make Tor Scath before sundown."

"Tor Scath? What's that?" Stephen asked.

"The place I want to reach before sundown," the holter replied.

"Someplace y'can bugger a bear?" Pol asked.

For that Pol got a cuff and after a brief stop a gag in his mouth.

Stephen liked horses, he really did. Some of his fondest memories were of the horse he'd had as a child, Finder, and of rides across his father's estates with his friends, pretending they were the knights of Virgenya, storming the fortresses of the Skasloi.

He liked horses when they ran, the rushing of it. He liked it when they walked sedately.

Trotting, he hated. It hurt.

They alternated between walk and trot for the next two bells. By that time, further inspired by the jolting ride, Stephen had added several pages to his treatise.

He'd also begun to hear something, as the holter predicted, and to wish he hadn't. The forest was growing dark, and he was already imagining movement in every shadow. Now the shadows had voices, hollow with distance, throaty ululations that worried at the edge of hearing and then vanished. He tried to ignore them, concentrating on the fourth chapter of his treatise, "The Very Annoying Personal Habits of the Holter-Beast," but the sounds crept deeper and deeper into his head, becoming a howling or baying that sounded unearthly.

"Holter—what *is* that?" he asked.

"Hounds," Aspar White told him, in his irritatingly brief manner. "Told you y'd hear them."

Stephen had heard hounds before. He didn't remember them sounding like *that*. "*Whose* hounds? This is the King's Forest! No one lives here! Or are they wild?"

"They aren't wild, not the way you mean."

"They sound vicious. And eerie." Stephen turned in his saddle, frowning. "What do you mean, 'not the way I mean'? Are they wild, or aren't they?"

The holter shrugged. At that moment, a particularly bloodcurdling note entered the baying, much nearer than before. Stephen's belly tightened. "Will they stop at dark? Should we climb a tree, or—"

"Pissing saints!" Aiken, the redheaded bandit, gasped. "It's Grim, id'n it? It's Grim and his hunt!"

"Quiet," Aspar said. "You'll scare the boy."

"What do you mean, Aiken?" Stephen asked.

The bandit's face had bleached itself so white even his freckles had disappeared. "One-eyed Grim! He hunts for the lost souls wandering the forest. Oh, saints, keep him off me! I never meant no harm to no one!"

Stephen wasn't sure who Grim was, but his grandfather had told stories of a host of nocturnal ghosts and demons led by a beast-man named Saint Horn the Damned. Stephen had never got around to checking whether or not Saint Horn was recognized by the church or was just a folk legend. He now sincerely wished he had.

"What's he talking about? Is he right?" Stephen asked the holter.

Aspar shrugged, looking almost nervous. "Could be," he replied.

"Pissing saints!" Aiken howled. "Cut me loose!"

"Do you want a gag, too?" the holter snapped.

"You don't believe in any such creature," Stephen accused, wagging his finger at Aspar. "I know you well enough by now."

"Werlic. Right. I don't. Ride faster."

For an instant, the holter almost looked frightened, and that put a chill deep in Stephen's bones. He had never met anyone so prosaic as Aspar White. If *he* thought there was something to fear . . .

Aspar was quiet for a moment, then said, in a low voice, "I've heard those dogs raging, but never seen 'em. Once, they came straight at me, and I thought to spy them at last. I nocked an arrow and waited. That's when I heard 'em—high above me, in the night air. I swear, it's the only place they *could* have been.

"Here, listen—they're coming at us. We'll see, yah? Be still."

"This is perfect nonsense," Stephen hissed. "I don't—"

"For pity, *let me down*!" Aiken moaned. "If it's the Raver, we have to lie flat in the road or be taken!"

"If it *is* him, I've a mind to make his work lighter," Aspar grunted, fingering the bone handle of his dirk. "It's the damned souls he likes best, after all, and those not all weighted down with skin and bone. Cover that cesshole with your teeth, or I'll cut you loose of your corpse!"

Aiken quieted to whimpering then, and they waited, and the hounds came closer and closer.

Stephen's fingers began to tremble on the reins. He willed them to stop, for his fear to blow away with the cool wind. Through the trees, the sky was dark lead, and the woods were so murky he could scarcely see ten yards.

Something huge and black exploded onto the road, and Stephen shrieked. His horse danced sideways and Stephen had a nightmare impression of gleaming eyes and twisted antlers. He screamed again, yanked at his reins, and his horse went widdershins like a puppy chasing its tail.

Then the hounds burst onto the road, huge mastiffs with glistening teeth, their howling so loud it actually hurt his ears. Most tore on, following their terrible quarry, but three or more began racing around the horses and men, yelping and slavering.

"Saints, keep us!" Stephen hollered, before losing his grip and thumping painfully onto the leaf-littered forest floor.

As he looked up, another horse and rider loped out from the trees. The rider was human in form, but with a face that was all beast, bright beady eyes and matted hair.

"Saints!" Stephen repeated, remembering Saint Horn the Damned.

"Grim!" Aiken screamed.

"Hello, Aspar," the beast-man said, in perfectly good king's tongue. "I hope you're happy. You probably cost me that stag."

"Well, you nearly cost the world a priest. Look at this boy; you nearly frightened him to death."

"Looks like. Who did you think I was, boy, Haergrim the Raver?"

"Gah?" Stephen choked. Now he knew what it meant to have his heart pounding in his throat, something he had always considered a fanciful literary expression. The rider was closer now, and Stephen realized that he had a human face after all, covered by a bushy, unkempt beard and long, ragged hair.

"Well, he's an educated fellow," Aspar went on. "His thousand-year-old maps say no one lives in the King's Forest, so who else could you be but the Raver, yah?"

The bearded figure bowed slightly, in the saddle.

"Symen Rookswald, at your service," he said.

"*Sir* Symen," Aspar amended.

"Once upon a time," Sir Symen said dolefully. "Once upon a time."

Tor Scath wasn't on Stephen's maps either, but it was as real as any black shadow in the night could be.

"It was built by King Gaut, more than five hundred years ago," Sir Symen explained in melancholy tones, as they wound up the path to the hilltop fortress. "They say Gaut was mad, fortifying his stronghold not against mortal enemies, but against the alvs and other dead things. Now it's a royal hunting lodge."

Stephen could make out only the outlines in the moonlight, but from what he could see, it certainly looked as if it had been built by a madman. It wasn't large, but weird spires and turrets jutted up with little rhyme or reason.

"I'm beginning to wonder if Gaut was sane after all," Rookswald added, his voice smaller.

"What do you mean?" Aspar White demanded.

"What needs to be done with these two?" Sir Symen asked, ignoring the question.

"A cell for them," the holter grunted, "to wait for the king's justice when he comes—what, next month?"

"We're innocent men!" Aiken asserted weakly.

Sir Symen snorted. "I have to *feed* them until then?"

"I don't much care. I might have left them to the wolves, but I suspect they might be persuaded to answer questions about a few other matters."

"Other matters?" Symen said. "Yes. I'm glad you came, Aspar. I'm glad my summons reached you."

"Your what?"

"Brian. I sent Brian to fetch you."

"Brian? I haven't seen him. How long ago did you send him?"

"Ten days ago. I sent him to Colbaely."

"Huh. He should have found me, then, or at least left word behind him."

They entered through a narrow tower, crossed a small, smelly courtyard, where Symen remanded the two prisoners and the horses to a hulking brute named Isarn. They proceeded into a dark hall, furnished in rustic fashion. Stephen noticed that only every fourth or fifth torch socket was plenished. A graying man in white and green livery greeted them.

"How was the hunting, sir?" he asked.

"Interrupted," Sir Symen said. "But by an old friend. Can Anfalthy find something to decorate this old board with?"

"I'm sure she can. Master White, it's good to see you again. And you, young sir, welcome to Tor Scath."

"The same, Wilhilm," Aspar replied.

"Thank you," Stephen managed.

"I'll fetch you some cheese, meantime."

"Thank you, Wil," Sir Symen said, and the old fellow left. He turned back to Stephen. "Welcome to King William's hunting lodge, and the most impoverished, thankless barony in the entire kingdom."

"Our host is somewhat out of favor at court," Aspar explained.

"And the sky is somewhat blue," the disheveled knight replied. In the light, he wasn't frightening at all; he looked gaunt, and sad, and old. "Aspar, I have things to tell you. The Sefry have left the forest."

"I saw Mother Cilth's bunch in Colbaely. They told me as much."

"No. Not just the caravaners. All of them. *All* of them."

"Even the Halafolk?"

"All."

"Well. I've been trying to get the Halafolk out of the forest for twenty years, and now they just up and leave? I don't believe it. How can you be sure?"

"They told me. They warned *me* to leave, too."

"Warned you about what?"

Suspicion flitted across Sir Symen's face. "If Brian didn't reach you, why did you come?"

"A boy came to Colbaely claiming his folk were killed by men in the king's colors, down by Taff Creek. I ran into the priestling and his captors on my way to investigate. I couldn't very well keep hauling them about, so I brought them here."

"Taff Creek. I didn't know about that one."

"What do you mean, 'that one'?"

"There was a woodcutting camp, two leagues south, killed to a man. We found them twenty days ago. Some tinkers on their way to Virgenya, likewise slaughtered. A half score of hunters."

"Did any of these hold patents from the king?" Aspar asked.

"Not a one. All were in the wood illegally."

"Then someone's doing my work for me."

Stephen couldn't stand it anymore. "So that's your work? Murdering woodcutters?"

"It's not my law, boy, but the king's. If the forest was open to anyone, how long do you think it would stand? Between trappers, charburners, woodcutters, and homesteaders, before long the royals wouldn't have any place to hunt."

"But murder?"

"I don't kill woodcutters, boy, not unless they try to kill me, and sometimes not even then. I arrest them. I lock them up someplace to await the king's justice. I scare them off, most of the time. What I meant just now was that whoever is behind this is killing those who ought not to be here in the first place. It doesn't gladden me; it makes me angry. This forest is *my* charge, *my* territory."

"But Brian is missing," Rookswald said. "And he was my man. Though I may be the least favorite of the king's knights, I still hold a patent to be here, and my household with me."

At that moment, Wilhilm reappeared, with a stoneware platter of cheese, a pitcher of mead, and mazers for each of them. It suddenly occurred to Stephen that he was hungry, and when he bit into the pungent, almost buttery cheese, he amended that to ravenous. The mead was sweet and tasted of cloves.

Aspar White ate, too. Only the bearded knight seemed not to notice the food.

"I don't think they were killed by men," Rookswald said softly.

"What then?" the holter asked, around a mouthful. "Bears? Wolves?"

"I think the Briar King killed them."

The holter stared at him for a moment, then snorted. "You've been listening to the Sefry, sure enough."

"Who is the Briar King?" Stephen asked.

"Another one of your folk stories," the holter scoffed.

"So I thought, once upon a time," Sir Symen said. "Now, I don't know. The dead we found—" He paused for an instant, then looked up. "They were of two sorts, the dead, the woodcutters. In the flat, where they were camped, they simply fell, no marks on them. No sword cut, no claw gashes, no arrow holes. Nor had they been gnawed or pecked at since death. There wasn't anything alive at the camp. Chickens, dogs, squirrels, the fish in the stream, all dead.

"But did you know that there's a *seoth* near there, a hill with an old fane? That's where we found the rest of them, or what was left of them. They had been most foully killed, by torture, and slowly."

Stephen noticed something cross the holter's face, something quickly hidden. "Tracks?" the woodsman asked. "Were there tracks?"

"There were tracks. Like those of a cat, but larger. And tracks of men, as well."

"Did you touch any of them? The tracks?"

A peculiar question, Stephen thought, but the old knight nodded. "I touched one of the bodies." He held out his hand. It was missing two fingers, and freshly bandaged. "I had to cut them off, before the rot spread to my arm." He scowled. "Aspar White, I know your look. You know something of this. What?"

"I came upon such a track," Aspar said. "That's all I know."

"The Sefry are old, Aspar, especially the Halafolk. They know a great deal. They say the greffyns have returned. And the lord of the greffyns, of all unholy things that slink in this wood, is the Briar King. If they are awake, he is awake, or soon to be. They do his bidding, the greffyns."

"Greffyns," Aspar White repeated. His tone somehow made the word mean *ludicrous*.

"Can't you tell me more of this?" Stephen asked. "I might be able to help."

"I don't need your help," the holter said bluntly. "Tomorrow, you continue to d'Ef. Play your games of maps and stories there, if you wish."

Stephen flushed, his tongue temporarily stilled by helpless anger. How could anyone be so arrogant?

"The Briar King has always been here," Sir Symen whispered. "Before the Hegemony, before the Warlock Wars, even before the mighty Scaosen themselves, he was here. Ages turn, and he sleeps. When his sleep is troubled enough, he wakes."

He turned rheumy eyes upon Stephen. "That's the real reason the King's Wood exists, though most have forgotten. Not to furnish a vast hunting park for whatever family rules in Eslen. No. It is so that when the Briar King rouses, he is not displeased." He grasped Aspar by the arm. "Don't you remember? The old tale? It was a bargain struck between the Briar King and Vlatimon the Handless, when the Scaosen were slaughtered and the kingdom of Crotheny established. The forest would be kept for him, from the Ef River to the sea, from the Mountains of the Hare to the Gray Warlock. The bargain was that if that were left untouched, Vlatimon and his descendants could have the rest.

"But if the bargain is broken, then every living thing shall perish, as it did before, and the Briar King will raise a new forest from our bones and ashes. When we say it's the *King's* Forest, you see, we don't mean the king of Crotheny. We mean the true lord of it, the undying one, the master of the greffyns."

"Symen—" Aspar began.

"We've broken Vlatimon's ancient vow. Everywhere, the borders are compromised. Everywhere, trees are cut. He wakes, and he is not pleased."

"Symen, the Sefry have muddled your brains. Those are old tales, no better than the stories about talking bears and magic ships that sail on land. Something strange is about, yes. Something dangerous. But I will find it, and I'll kill it, and that will be an end to it."

Symen didn't answer but just shook his head.

Anything further was interrupted by the arrival of the food, escorted out by a plain, cheerful woman of middle years and two young girls. They settled two steaming pies, a platter of roast pigeons, and blackbread trenchers on the table. The girls hurried off without speaking, but the woman put her hands to her hips and regarded the three of them.

"Well, hello there, Aspar, and hello, young sir, whoever you might be. My name's Anfalthy. We were ill prepared for guests, but I hope this will please you. If there's anything missing y'would like—anything at all—I'll see what I can do. I make no promise but that I'll try."

"Lady, anything you bring will please us, I'm sure," Stephen said, remembering his manners.

"Game has been scarce," Symen muttered.

"He hasn't been droning on about the end of days again, has he?" Anfalthy asked. "Look, Sir Symen, you've not even touched your wine. Drink it! I've mixed in herbs to cheer your mood."

"No doubt."

"Don't mind his dark mutterings, you two. He's been at that for months, now. A trip abroad is what he needs, but I can't convince him."

"I'm needed here," Symen insisted.

"Only to gloom up the place. Eat, you fellows, and call for more if you need it."

The pie, compounded of venison and boar and elderberries, was a little gamey to Stephen's taste, but the pigeon, stuffed with rosemary and marjoram and pork liver, was delicious.

"I'll go tomorrow to Taff Creek," Aspar promised. "Now do as Anfalthy said. Drink your wine."

"You'll see, when you go," the old knight said, but he did sip his wine, indifferently at first, but in ever larger gulps. As the evening wore on, the rest of the household joined them; it seemed there were about twenty people resident in the tower. Within a bell, the board was crowded, and pies, roast boar, partridge, and duck covered it from end to end, so that Stephen wondered how they ate when game *wasn't* scarce. The conversation grew boisterous, with children and dogs playing about their feet, and the force of the old knight's doomsaying faded.

Still, it nagged at Stephen, and more so, the holter's gruff dismissal of anything Stephen might have to add. So when the mead courage finally came on him, he leaned near Aspar White.

"You want to know what I think?" he asked.

The holter frowned, and for a moment Stephen thought that the older man would tell him, once again, to be silent. He decided not to give him the chance. "Listen," he rushed on. "I know you don't think much of me. I know you think I'm useless. But I'm not. I can help."

"Oh? Your thousand-year-old maps can help me with this?"

Stephen's lips tightened. "I understand. You're afraid I know more than you. That I might know some damned thing that might be of use."

Even as the words tumbled out of his mouth, Stephen knew the mead had brought him to a bad end. But the holter was just so damned smug, and Stephen was too drunk to feel fear as more than the distant whisper of a saint.

Then to his vast surprise, the older man laughed bitterly. "Plenty I don't know," he admitted. "Go ahead. Tell me what you make of all this."

Stephen blinked. "What?"

"I said, go on. What do you think of Sir Symen's story?"

"Oh." For a brief instant there were two Aspars, then one again. "I don't believe it," Stephen said, pronouncing each word very deliberately.

The holter raised an eyebrow. "Really."

"Really. First of all, too many of the details aren't right. Vlatimon, for instance. He didn't found Crotheny; he wasn't even of the Croatani, the tribe the country was named for. Vlatimon was Bolgoi, and he conquered a small kingdom in the Midenlands; and that lasted only a half century before it was gobbled up by the Black Jester in the first Warlock War.

"Shec . . . *sec*ondly, the whole notion of some old forest demon who has that sort of power—the power to punish the entire world—flies straight in the face of church doctrine. There are powers, yes, and the church tolerates that they be called saints, or angels, or gods as it might please local custom—but they're all shub . . . shubordin . . . they all serve the All-in-One. Not to get too technical, but—"

"And yet you were the one who said these tales carry some truth in them. Is that the case only when the truth doesn't clash with the teaching of your church?"

"It's your church, too." But of a sudden Stephen doubted that. Might the holter be heretic?

"*The* church, then?"

"The answer is yes and no. I recall now that in Virgenya we have phay stories about a character named Baron Greenleaf, who is also said to sleep in a hidden place and wake to avenge wrongs done the forest, very mush . . . *mush* . . . like this Briar King. Baron Greenleaf and the Briar King are probably both based on a real person—one of the early warlock kings, perhaps, or even a Skaslos who survived beyond the rest.

"Or perhaps he is a misunderstanding made manifest. After all, the church teaches that the Alwalder demands a balance between cultivated and wild ground. As each village must have a sacred horz, where things grow wild, so too must the world itself have wild places. In the imagination of the folk, perhaps this forest is the horz of the world, and the Briar King a personification of the punishment that comes from violating it."

"And these dead people? This talk of greffyns?"

Stephen shrugged. "Murderers who kill by poison? I don't know, but there could be many explanations."

"This from the fellow who only a few days ago argued for all manner of ghosts and ghoulies? Who flinched today when he thought Grim the Raver was come for him?"

"I argue from the knowledge of the church, from what the Alwalder allows as possible. The dead *do* have souls, and there are spirits in the world, creatures of light and darkness. All are accepted by the church, catalogued, named. Your Briar King is not.

"Greffyns—I can't say. Possibly. The Skasloi and the warlock lords after them created all sorts of fell, unnatural creatures to serve them. Some of those might still exist, in the corners of the world. It's not impossible."

"And this business Sir Symen spoke of, the sacrifices at the seoth? I know the church builds fanes on them."

"In the church we use the ancient term, *sedos*. They are the seats of the saints' power on earth. By visiting the sedoi, priests commune with the saints and gather holiness to themselves, and so, yes, we build fanes on them to mark them, and to insure that those whose visit them are in the proper frame of mind. But the church maintains fanes only on living sedoi, not on the dead ones."

"What do you mean, dead?"

"A sedos is a spot where a saint left some of his power, some virtue of his essence. Over time, that fades. Once the sacredness has faded, the church ceases maintaining the fanes. Most of those in the King's Forest are dead. But dead or alive, I've never heard of human sacrifice at a sedos—even among heretics. Not for centuries, anyway."

"Wait. Then you *have* heard of it."

"The blackest of the sorcerers in the Warlock Wars sacrificed victims to the nine Damned Saints. But this couldn't have anything to do with that."

Aspar stroked his chin. He glanced up. "Why not?"

"Because the end of the wars was the end of that. The church has kept careful watch for that sort of evil."

"Ah." Aspar took another swallow of mead and nodded. "Thank you, Cape Chavel Darige," he said. "For once you've given me something to think about."

"Really?"

"I've had a lot of mead."

"Still, thank you for listening."

The holter shrugged. "I've arranged for you to leave for d'Ef tomorrow."

"I could stay a bit longer, go with you to this creek—"

The holter shook his head. "So I can see this meal come back up out of you when we find the corpses? No thank you. I'll do well enough on my own."

"I suppose you *can*," Stephen flared, reaching for the mead jug. Somehow he miscalculated, however, and the next thing he knew it was spilling across the table, a honey flood.

"Anfalthy!" Aspar shouted. "Could you show this young fellow his bedchamber?"

"I'm not a *child*," Stephen muttered. But the room had begun to spin, and he suddenly didn't want to be anywhere near the arrogant holter, the morose knight, or any of the rest of these rustics.

"Come on, lad," Anfalthy said, taking his hand.

Mutely he nodded and followed, the light and noise fading behind him.

"He's right," Stephen heard himself say. His faraway voice sounded angry.

"Who's right?" Anfalthy asked.

"The holter. I'm no use wi' arms an' such. Blood makes me sick."

"Aspar is a fine man, good at what he does," Anfalthy said. "He is not a *patient* man."

"Just wanted to help."

Anfalthy led him into a room, where she used her candle to light another, already in a sconce on the wall. He sat heavily on the bed. Anfalthy stood over him for a moment, her broad, comforting face looking down at him.

"Aspar has too many ghosts following him already, lad. He wouldn't want to add you to them. I think he likes you."

"He *hates* me."

"I doubt that," she said softly. "There's only one person in the world Aspar White hates, and it's not you. Now go to sleep; tomorrow you're off, yah?"

"Yes," Stephen said.

"Then I'll see you for breakfast."

When Stephen rose the next morning, nursing a pounding head, Aspar White was already gone. Sir Symen supplied Stephen with two fresh horses and a young huntsman to be his guide, and wished him well. Anfalthy gave him a bundle of bread, cheese, and meat and kissed him on the cheek.

As his headache improved, so did Stephen's mood. After all, in two days, he realized, he would finally be at d'Ef, where his work would start. Where his knowledge would be appreciated, valued, rewarded. The *scriftorium* at d'Ef was one of the most complete in the world, and *he* would have access to it!

The eagerness he had felt when he started from Cape Chavel more than a month ago began to return. Bandits, kidnapping, and a crude holter had overshadowed it, but he figured he had had his run of trouble. What more could happen?

CHAPTER EIGHT

BLACK ROSES

A NNE FELT A FEATHERY TREMBLING in her belly and goose-bumps on her flesh, even though the night wind came from the sea—warm, heavy, wet, and salty. The air seemed to sag with the need to rain, and the moon came and went fitfully in the cloud-bruised sky. Around her, neat rows of apple trees swayed and rustled in the wind.

On the wall of the keep above, she could hear two guards talking, but couldn't make out what they were saying.

She felt faintly dizzy, a slight vertigo that had come and gone in the month since she had visited Eslen-of-Shadows. She stepped under one of the trees and leaned against the trunk, her head swimming with the scent of the blossoms. She lifted the scrap of paper that the stablehand had passed to her when she had put up Faster.

Meet me in the orchard by the west gate at tenth bell.
—R.

"You work fast, Virgenya," she whispered.
Though Fastia seemed unaffected by her request to Saint Cer.
It was surely tenth bell by now. Had they forgotten to ring it?
She shouldn't be doing this. What if he didn't come, anyway?
What if he came, and it was just a cruel joke, something to laugh

about with the other knights and the stablehands? Silly. What did she know about this fellow?

Nothing.

She brushed nervously at her dress of Vitellian brocade, feeling sillier by the instant.

The hairs on her neck suddenly pricked up. A shaft of the inconstant moonlight cast the silhouette of something big and dark moving through the branches of the apple tree nearest her.

"She is like a dream, like a mist, like the phay dancers seen only from the corner of the eye in the woodland glade," a voice whispered.

"Roderick?"

She jumped as the tenth bell began to chime, high up in the August Tower, and jumped again when the long shadow dropped from the tree and landed with a soft thump.

"At your service." The shadow bowed.

"You startled me," Anne said. "Were you a thief before you became a knight?" she asked. "Certainly you aren't a poet."

"That wounds, Princess."

"Go to a physician or a rinn witch, then. What do you want, Roderick?"

He moved into the moonlight. His eyes were shades in an ivory carving. "I wanted to see you in something other than riding dress."

"You said you had seen me in court."

"True. But you look lovelier now."

"Because it's darker?"

"No. Because I've met you now. It makes all the difference."

"I suppose you want to kiss me again."

"No, not at all. I want *you* to kiss me."

"But we just met!"

"Yes, and got off to a good start." He suddenly reached and took her hand. "You're the lady who rode down the Snake like a madman. There's nothing cautious about you, Princess. I kissed you, and I've kissed enough to know you liked it. If I'm wrong, tell me so, and off I'll go. If I'm right . . . why don't we try it again?"

She folded her arms and cocked her head, trying to think of a good response. He didn't give her time.

"I brought you this." He held something out to her. She reached for it and found herself clutching the stem of a flower.

"I cut off the thorns for you," he said. "It's a black rose."

She gasped, genuinely surprised. "Where did you find it?"

"I bought it from a sea captain, who got it in Liery."

Anne breathed in its strange scent of plum and anise. "They grow only in Liery," she told him. "My mother talks about them all the time. I've never seen one."

"Well," Roderick replied, moving a little closer. "I got it to please you, not to remind you of your mother."

"Shh. Not so loud."

"I'm not afraid," Roderick said.

"You should be. Do you know what will happen to you if we're caught here?"

"We won't be."

His hand found hers, and she suddenly felt her head go funny. She couldn't *think* anything. She felt frozen, almost uncomprehending, as he pulled her against him. His face was so near she could feel his breath on her lips.

"Kiss me," he whispered.

And she did. A sound like the sea rushed into her ears. She could feel the hard muscles of Roderick's back through his linen shirt, and a prickly, itchy sort of heat. He took her face in his hands and stroked lightly behind her ears as his lips pressed hers, now nibbling, now opening greedily.

He whispered things, but she hardly heard them. All sense of words dissolved when his lips crept down her neck, and she thought she was going to cry out, and then the guards would hear her, and then—well, who knew what would happen then. Something bad. She could almost hear her mother now . . .

"Anne. *Anne!*" Someone *was* calling her.

"Who's that? Who's there?" Roderick panted.

"It's my maid, Austra. I—"

He kissed her again. "Send her away." He said the words right into her earlobe. It tickled, and suddenly she giggled.

"Um. No, I can't. My sister Fastia will check my bed soon, and if I am not in it, she will raise the alarm. Austra is keeping watch of the time. If she's calling, I have to go."

"It cannot be, not yet!"

"It is. It is. But we can meet again."

"Not soon enough for me."

"My sister's birthday is tomorrow. I'll arrange something. Austra will carry the word."

"*Anne!*"

"I'm coming, Austra."

She turned to go, but he took her by the waist and spun her into the crook of his arm, like a dancer, and kissed her again. She laughed and gave it back. When she finally turned and left, she felt an ache beneath her breast.

"Hurry!" Austra took her hand and pulled her insistently. "Fastia may be there already!"

"Figs for Fastia. Fastia never comes until eleventh bell."

"It's nearly eleventh bell now, you ninny!" Austra practically dragged Anne up the staircase that wound to the top of the orchard wall. On the last step, Anne cast one more look down at the garden but saw only the inky shadow of the looming keep on the other side.

"Come on!" Austra commanded. "Through here."

Anne clutched the back of Austra's dress as they rushed through the dark. A few moments later they tripped up another staircase and emerged into a wider hall lit with long tapers. At a high, narrow door, Austra fumbled the key from her girdle and pushed it into the brass lock. Just as the door swung open, the sound of footsteps echoed up from the stairwell at the far end of the hall.

"Fastia!" Anne hissed.

They ducked through the door and into the anteroom of her chambers. Austra closed and locked the door, while Anne kicked off her damp slippers and dropped them into the empty vase on the table next to the divan. She fell back onto the little couch and yanked off both stockings at once, then ran barefoot through the curtained doorway to her bedchamber. She flung the stockings on the other side of the canopied bed and began trying to reach the fastenings of her gown. "Help me with this!"

"We haven't time," Austra said. "Just throw your nightdress over it."

"The train will show!"

"Not if you're in bed, under the covers!"

Austra, meanwhile, shucked her own dress right over her head. Anne stifled an amused shriek, for Austra wore no underskirt, no corset; she was naked as a clam in soup.

"Hush!" Austra said, wriggling into a nightgown and kicking her discarded dress under the bed. "Don't laugh at me!"

"You'd think *you* were the one out to meet someone."

"Hush! Don't be sick! It's just faster this way, and it's not like anyone was going to notice *I* was uncorseted. Get under the covers!"

A key scraped in the lock. Austra squeaked, pointing to Anne, and pantomimed letting down her hair.

Anne yanked the netting from her locks, threw it vaguely toward the wardrobe, and dived under the covers. Austra hit the mattress at almost the same instant, hairbrush in hand.

"Ouch!" Anne yelped, as the curtain parted and the brush caught in a tangle.

"Hello, you two."

Anne blinked. It wasn't Fastia.

"Lesbeth!" she exclaimed, leaping out of bed and rushing to embrace her aunt.

Lesbeth gathered her in, laughing. "Saint Loy, but we're almost the same height, now, aren't we? How could you grow this much in two years? How old are you now, fourteen?"

"Fifteen."

"Fifteen. And look at you—a Dare, through and through."

In fact, Anne realized she *did* look like Lesbeth. Which wasn't good, because while Lesbeth was very *pretty*, Elseny and Fastia and her mother were *beautiful*. She would take after the wrong side of the family.

"You're *warm*," Lesbeth said. "Your face is burning up! Do you have a fever?"

That drew a stifled giggle from Austra.

"What?" Lesbeth asked, her voice suddenly suspicious. She stepped back. "Is that a *dress* you have on under your nightgown? At this hour? You've been out!"

"Please don't tell Fastia. Or Mother. It was really all very innocent—"

"I won't have to tell them. Fastia is on the way up."

"Still?"

"Of course. You don't think she'd trust me with her duty?"

"How long do I have?"

"She's finishing her wine. She had half a glass when I left, and I asked for a moment alone with you."

"Thank the saints. Help me out of this dress!"

Lesbeth looked stern for a second, then laughed. "Very well. Austra, could you bring a damp cloth? We'll want to wipe her face."

"Yes, Duchess."

A few moments later they had the dress off, and Lesbeth was unlacing the corset. Anne groaned in relief as her ribs sighed out to where nature perversely reckoned they ought to be.

"Had that pretty tight, didn't you?" Lesbeth commented. "Who is he?"

Anne feared her cheeks would scorch. "I can't tell you that."

"Ah. Someone disreputable. A stablehand, perhaps?"

"No! No. He's gentle—just someone Mother wouldn't like."

"Disreputable, then, indeed. Come on—tell. You know I won't let on. Besides, I have a *big* secret to tell you. It's only fair."

"Well . . ." She chewed her lip. "His name is Roderick of Dunmrogh."

"Dunmrogh? Well, there's your problem."

"How so?" The corset fell away, and Anne realized her undershirt was plastered to her with sweat.

"It's political. The grefts of Dunmrogh have *Reiksbaurg* blood."

"So? Our war with the Reiksbaurgs was over a hundred years ago."

"Ah, to be young and naïve again. Turn, so I can get your face, dear. Enny, the war with the Reiksbaurgs will *never* be over. They covet the throne a thousand covetings for every year that has passed since they lost it."

"But Roderick isn't a Reiksbaurg."

"No, Enny," she went on, wiping the cool rag on Anne's face and neck, "but fifty years ago the Dunmroghs sided with a Reiksbaurg claimant to the throne. Not with arms, so they kept their lands when it was all over—but support him they did, in the Comven. They still have a bad name for that."

"It isn't fair."

"I know it's not, sweet, but we'd better talk about it later. Change that shirt and put on your gown."

Anne ran to her wardrobe and changed the sodden linen for a dry one. "When did you learn so much about politics?" she asked, shrugging back into her embroidered nightgown.

"I just spent two years in Virgenya. It's all they talk about, down there."

"It must have been terribly boring."

"Oh—you might be surprised."

Anne sat on the edge of her bed. "You won't tell anyone about Roderick? Even if it *is* political?"

Lesbeth laughed and kissed her on the forehead, then knelt and took her hand. "I doubt very much it's political for *him*. He's probably just young and foolish, like you."

"He's *your* age, nineteen."

"I'm twenty, meadowlark." She brushed a curly strand from out of Anne's face. "And when your sister comes in, try to keep the left side of your head away from her."

"Why?"

"You have a love bite, there, just below your ear. I think even Fastia will know what it is."

"Oh, mercifu—"

"I'll comb your hair, like I was doing when the duchess came in," Austra volunteered. "I can keep it pulled long over that spot."

"That's a good plan," Lesbeth approved. She chuckled again. "When did this happen to our little lark, Austra? When last I saw her she was still dressing up in the stablejack's clothes so she wouldn't have to ride sidesaddle. When did she become such a *lady*?"

"I still ride," Anne said defensively.

"That's true enough," Austra said. "That's how she met this fellow. He followed her down the Snake."

"Not fainthearted, then."

"Roderick is anything but fainthearted," Anne said. "So what's *your* big secret, Lez?"

Lesbeth smiled. "I've already asked your father's permission, so I suppose I'll tell you. I'm getting married."

"Married?" Anne and Austra said, in unison.

"Yes." Lesbeth frowned. "I didn't like the sound of that! You seem incredulous."

"It's just—at your age—"

"Oh, I see. You had me reckoned a spinster. Well, I had plenty of sisters, and they all married well. I was the youngest so I got to do something they didn't. I got to be choosy."

"So who is he?"

"A wonderful man, daring and kind. Like your Roderick, far from faint-hearted. He has the most elegant castle, and an estate that stretches—"

"Who?"

"Prince Cheiso of Safnia."

"Safnia?" Anne repeated.

"Where is Safnia?" Austra asked.

"On the shore of the southern sea," Lesbeth said dreamily. "Where oranges and lemons grow outdoors, and bright birds sing."

"I've never heard of it."

"Not surprising, if you pay no more attention to your tutors now than you did when I still lived here."

"You love him, don't you?" Anne asked.

"Indeed I do. With all of my heart."

"So it's not political?"

Lesbeth laughed again. "Everything is political, meadowlark. It's not like I could have married a cowherd, you know. Safnia, though you ladies have never heard of it, is a rather important place."

"But you're marrying for love!"

"Yes." She wiggled a finger at Anne. "But don't let that put foolish ideas in your head. Live in the kingdom that is, not the one that ought to be."

"Well," a somewhat frosty voice said, as the curtain to the ante-chamber parted again. "That's better advice than I expected *you* to be giving her, Lesbeth."

"Hello, Fastia."

Fastia was older than all of them, almost twenty-three. Her hair was umber silk, now bound up in a net, and her small features were perfect and demure. She was no taller than Anne or Austra, and a handswidth shorter than Lesbeth. But she commanded *presence*.

"Dear Fastia," Lesbeth said. "I was just telling darling Anne my news."

"About your betrothal, I suppose?"

"You already know? But I only just asked my brother William's permission a few bells ago."

"You forget how fast news travels in Eslen, I'm afraid. Congratulations. You'll find marriage a joy, I think."

Her tone said otherwise, somehow. Anne felt a faint pang of pity for her older sister.

"I think I shall," Lesbeth replied.

"Well," Fastia asked, "is all in order here? Have you girls said your prayers and washed your faces?"

"They were praying, I believe, even as I entered the room," Lesbeth said innocently.

Anne nodded. "We're all but asleep," she added.

"You don't look sleepy."

"It's the excitement of seeing Lesbeth. She was telling us all about Shanifar, where her betrothed rules. A delightful-sounding place—"

"Safnia," Fastia corrected. "One of the original five provinces of the Hegemony. That was over a thousand years ago, of course. A great place once, and still quaint from what I hear."

"Yes, that's right," Lesbeth said, as if she hadn't heard the condescension in Fastia's tone. "It's very quaint."

"I think it sounds wonderful and exotic," Anne put in.

"Most places do, until you've been to them," Fastia replied. "Now. I don't want to be the troll, but somehow the duty has fallen to me to make sure these girls get to bed. Lesbeth, may I entice you into taking a cordial?"

Hah, Anne thought. *You can't fool me. You* love *playing the troll. What happened to you?* "Surely we can stay up a bit. We haven't seen Lesbeth in two years."

"Plenty of time for that tomorrow, at Elseny's party. It's time for the women to chat."

"We *are* women," Anne retorted.

"When you are betrothed, then you'll be a woman," Fastia replied. "Now, good night. Or, as Lesbeth's Safnian prince might say, *dena nocha.* Austra, see that you are both asleep within the hour."

"Yes, Archgreffess."

"Night, loves," Lesbeth said, blowing them a kiss as the two passed through the curtain into the antechamber. After another moment, they heard the outer door close.

"Why does she have to be like that?" Anne muttered.

"If she weren't, your mother would find someone who was," Austra replied.

"I suppose. It just galls me."

"In fact," Austra said, "I'm something glad they're gone."

"Why is that?"

A pillow hit Anne in the face.

"Because you haven't told me what *happened* yet, you jade!"

"Oh! Austra, it was quite extraordinary. He was so—I mean, I thought I would catch afire! And he gave me a rose, a black rose—" She broke off abruptly. "Where's my rose?"

"You had it when we came in the room."

"Well, I don't have it now! I must press it, or whatever one does with roses . . ."

"I think one *finds* them first," Austra said.

But it wasn't in the receiving room, nor on the floor, nor under the bed. They couldn't find it anywhere.

"We'll see it in the morning, when the light is better," Austra said.

"Of course we will," Anne replied dubiously.

In her dream, Anne stood in a field of ebony roses, wearing a black satin dress set with pearls that gleamed dully in the bone light of the moon. The air was so thick with the scent of the blooms she thought she would choke.

There was no end to them; they stretched on to the horizon in a series of low rises, stems bent by a murmuring wind. She turned slowly to see if it was thus in all directions.

Behind her the field ended abruptly in a wall of trees, black-boled monsters covered with puckered thorns bigger than her hand, rising so high she couldn't see their tops in the dim light. Thorn vines as thick as her arm tangled between the trees and crept out along the ground. Through the trees and beyond the vines was only darkness. A greedy darkness, she felt, a darkness that watched her, hated her, wanted her. The more she stared at it, the more terrified she became of shapes that might or might not be moving, of slight sounds that might be footsteps or wings.

And then, when she thought her terror could be no greater, something pushed through the thorns coming toward her. Moonlight gleamed on a black-mailed arm and the fingers of a hand, uncurling.

And then the helmet came through, a tall, tapering helm, with black horns curving up, set on the shoulders of a giant. The visor was open, and there she saw something that wrenched from her own throat a keening sound somehow more alien than anything she had yet known. She turned and ran through the roses, and the small barbs caught at her dress, and now the moon looked like the rotted eye of a fish . . .

She awoke, thrashing with the motions of flight, not knowing where she was. Then she remembered, and sat up in her bed, arms wrapped about her middle.

"A dream," she told the dark room, rocking back and forth. "Just a dream."

But the air was still thick with anise and plum. In the pale moonlight streaming through her window she saw black petals scattered upon her coverlet. She felt them in her hair. Wet trickled down her face, and the bright taste of salt came to her lips.

Anne slept no more that night, but waited for the cockcrow and the sun.

CHAPTER NINE

ON THE SLEEVE

NEIL WOKE EARLY, inspected his new armor for any blemishing its single wearing might have left on it. He checked his spurs and tabard, and finally drew Crow, his broadsword, then made certain the hard, sharp length of her gleamed like water.

Moving quietly, he slipped on his buskins and padded from the room, down the stairs, and out of the inn. Outside, a morning fog was just starting to lift, and the docks were already alive with movement, fishing crews putting out for the middle shoals, seacharmers and salters and whores looking to be taken on, seagulls and fishravens fighting over scraps.

Neil had noticed the chapel of Saint Lier the day before, distinguished by its mast-shaped spire. It was a modest wooden building right at water's edge, built on a raised stone foundation. As he approached, several rough-looking sailors were on their way out. He greeted them by passing his hand over his face, the sign of Saint Lier. "His hand keep you," he told them.

"Thanks, lad," one of them said gruffly. "And you."

Within, the chapel was dark and plain, all wood, in the island style. The only ornament was a simple statuette of the saint himself above the altar; carved of walrus tusk, it depicted him standing in a coracle.

Neil carefully placed two silver coins in the box and knelt. He began to sing.

"Foam Father, Wave Strider
You feel our keels and hear our prayers
Grant us passage on your broad back
Bring us to shore when the storm's upon us
I beg you now
Grant passage to my song.

Windmaster, Seventh Wave
You know the line of my fathers
Held them curled in fingers of spray
Watched them fight and die on the wide sea roads
Neil, son of Fren
Asks you to heed his prayer."

He prayed for the souls of his father and mother, for Sir Fail and his lady Fiene, for the hungry ghosts of the sea. He prayed for King William and Queen Muriele, and for Crotheny. Most of all he prayed that he himself might be worthy. Then, after a time of silence, he rose to leave.

A lady in a deep green cloak stood behind him. He started, for in the intensity of his prayers, he hadn't heard her enter.

"I'm sorry, lady," he said softly. "I didn't mean to keep you from the altar."

"There's plenty of room," she answered. "You did not keep me from it. It just that it's been a long time since I heard anyone pray so beautifully. I wanted to listen, I'm afraid, and so it's to you I must apologize."

"Why?" Neil asked. "I've no shame for my prayers. It's an honor to me if you found something in them. I . . ."

Her eyes gripped him. Sea-green, they were. Curls of black hair cascaded from beneath her hood, and her lips were a ruby bow. He couldn't guess her age, though if pressed, he would put her in her thirties. She was too beautiful to be human, and with a sudden dizziness, it occurred to Neil that this was no earthly woman, but a vision, a saint or an angel, perhaps.

So strong and certain was the feeling that his tongue clove to the roof of his mouth, and he couldn't remember what else he had meant to say.

"The honor is mine, young man," she said. She cocked her head. "You have an island accent. Are you from Liery?"

"I was born on Skern, my lady," he managed. "But I am pledged to a lord of Liery, as was my father."

"Would that lord be the Baron Sir Fail de Liery?"

"Yes, my lady," he replied, feeling as if he were in a dream.

"A good and noble man. You do very well to serve him."

"Lady, how could you know—"

"You forget, I heard your prayers. Sir Fail is with you? He is near?"

"Yes, lady. In the inn, just up the way. We arrived yesterday; he intends to present me at court today, unworthy as I may be."

"If Sir Fail wishes to present you, the only thing unworthy about you is your doubt of him. He knows what he is about."

"Yes, lady. Of course."

She lowered her head. "You should know that the court will be on the hill of Tom Woth, today, to celebrate the birthday of the princess Elseny. Sir Fail may not know this, having just arrived. Take the northern gate and ride up the Sleeve. Sir Fail will know where. Tell him to go to the stone circle and wait."

"You command me, lady." His heart was thunder, and he could not say why. He wanted to ask her name, but he feared the answer.

"I wonder if you would excuse me now," the lady said. "My prayers are less elegant than yours. The saint will forgive my clumsiness, I know, but I would rather no one else heard. It's been long since I came here. Too long."

She sounded infinitely sad.

"Lady, if there is anything I can do for you, please name it."

Her eyes gleamed in the darkness. "Take care in the court," she said softly. "Stay true to yourself. Stay who you are. It is a . . . difficult thing."

"Yes, lady. If you ask it, it will be done."

So saying, he left her there, his feet feeling oddly heavy on the cobbles of the street.

"Quite a sight, isn't it?" Fail de Liery said.

Neil couldn't keep his head still. "I've never see anything like it. I've never seen clothes like this, so much color and silk."

Hundreds of courtiers were riding up the greensward, along with dwarves, giants, jesters, and footmen, all in fantastic costume.

"You'll see more. Come, those are the stones ahead."

They spurred their mounts to a gallop, toward the small circle of standing stones near the forest edge. A large group waited there, mounted and on foot. Neil noticed knights among them, all wearing livery of black and deep sea-green trimmed in bronze. He didn't know whose colors they were, and they bore no devices.

"Sir Fail!" a man called out, as they approached. Raising his hand in greeting, he rode out of the circle. He was unarmored, a man of middle years, his auburn hair held with a plain gold circlet, clearly a fellow of some importance. Sir Fail dismounted, and so Neil did, too, as the newcomer also swung down from his horse, a handsome white Galléan stallion with a peppering of dark spots on his withers and muzzle.

"You old de Liery warscow! How are you?"

"Right well, Your Majesty."

Neil's knees went suddenly weak.

Majesty?

"Well, I'm well pleased to see you here," the fellow went on easily. "Well pleased!"

"I'm glad I found you! I would've been going up to an empty palace, right now, if it weren't for my young squire, here. May I present him to you?"

The king's eyes turned on Neil, suddenly, lamps whose light seemed both intense and weary. "By all means."

"Your Majesty, this is Neil MeqVren, a young man of many talents and great deeds. Neil, this is His Majesty William II of Crotheny."

Neil remembered to drop to one knee and bowed so low his head nearly hit the ground. "Your Majesty," he managed to croak.

"Rise up, young man," the king said.

Neil came to his feet.

"He's a likely looking lad," the king said. "Squire, you say? This the fellow I've heard so much about, the lad from the battle of Darkling Mere?"

"It is, Sire."

"Well, Neil MeqVren. We'll have some talks about you, I expect."

"But not now," a prim-looking young woman said, sidling up on the back of a delicate-looking bay. She nodded to Neil, and he felt an odd sense that they had met before. Something about her hazel eyes was familiar, or *almost* so. She was a severe beauty, with high cheekbones and glossy hair several shades browner than chestnut.

"This day is for Elseny, and none other," the woman went on. "But I'll wish a good day to you—Neil MeqVren, is it?"

It took Neil an open-mouthed moment or two to realize she was presenting her hand. He took it, albeit belatedly, and kissed the royal signet ring.

"Your Majesty," he said. For this was surely the queen.

A laugh trickled through the group, at that, and Neil realized he had made a mistake.

"This is my daughter Fastia, now of the house Tighern," the king said.

"Hush your laughing, all of you," Fastia said sternly. "This man is our guest. Besides, it's clear he knows royal quality when he sees it, at least." Her smile was brief, more of a twitch, really.

At about that moment, another young woman came flying into Sir Fail's arms. He whirled her around and she shrieked delightedly.

"Elseny, what a sight you are!" the old man said, when he managed to step back from her.

Neil had to agree. She was younger than Fastia—seventeen, or thereabouts—and her hair was raven black, not brown. Where Fastia had a hardness to her beauty, this one had eyes as wide and guileless as a child.

"It's so perfect to see you today, Granuncle Fail! You came for my birthday!"

"That part was the work of the saints," Fail said. "Surely they smile on you."

"And who is this young fellow you've brought us?" Elseny asked. "Everyone has met him but me!"

"This is my charge, Neil MeqVren."

Neil's face grew warmer and warmer at all of the attention.

Elseny was clad outlandishly in a colorful silk gown elaborately embroidered with flowers and twining vines, and she wore what looked for all the world like insect wings sprouting from the back. Her hair was taken up in complicated tiers, and each level had a different sort of flower arranged in it: hundreds of tiny violets on the first, red clover next, pale green saflilies, to a crown of white lotus.

Like Fastia, she offered her hand. "Granuncle," she said, as Neil kissed her ring. "Really! Today I'm not Elseny, you should know! I am Meresven, the queen of the Phay."

"Oh my! I should have known. Of course you are."

"Have you come to be knighted?" Elseny asked Neil, quite suddenly.

"Ah—it is my greatest desire, Princess—I mean, Your Majesty."

"Well. Come to my court, and I will certainly make you a knight of Elphin." She fluttered her eyes and then, quite swiftly, seemed to forget him, turning back to Fail and taking his arm. "And now, Uncle," she said. "You must tell me how my cousins in Liery fare! Do they ask after me? Have you heard I am engaged?"

"And here is my son, Charles," the king said, once it was clear Neil's introduction to Elseny was done.

Neil had noticed Charles peripherally when they first rode up. He had seen such men before, grown adult in length and breadth but with the manner of a child. The eyes were the sign—roving, curious, oddly vacant.

At the moment, Charles was talking to a man clothed from neck to foot in garish robes that looked as if fifteen different garments had been torn, mixed, and patched back together. On his head sat an improbably broad-brimmed, floppy hat hung with silver bells that jangled as he walked along. It was so large, in fact, the fellow resembled a walking hat.

"Charles?" the king repeated.

Charles was a large man with curly red hair. Neil felt a little chill when the saint-touched stare found him.

"Hello," Charles said. "Who are you?" He sounded like a child.

"I'm Neil MeqVren, my lord," Neil said, bowing.

"I'm the prince," the young man said.

"That is clear, my lord."

"It's my sister's birthday, today."

"I've heard that."

"This is Hound Hat, my jester. He's Sefry."

A face peered up at him from beneath the hat, a face whiter than ivory with eyes of pale copper. Neil stared, amazed. He had never seen a Sefry before. It was said they would not venture upon the sea.

"Good day to you," Neil said, nodding to the Sefry, not knowing what else to say.

The Sefry put on a malicious little smile. He began to sing and caper a little, the huge hat wobbling.

"Good day to *you*, sir!
Or not-a-sir
For I can see
No rose on thee
Pray, in *your* land
Or far-off strand
Do you perhaps
Take knightly naps
In pens where pigs and horses craps?
Is that what marks the warrior there?
Tell us, traveler, ease our care!"

The jester's song brought howls of laughter from the crowd. The loudest was Charles, who slapped the Sefry on the back in his delight. That sent the jester flying. He tumbled crazily, grasping the corners of his huge hat and rolling into a ball. When he came near someone on foot, they kicked at him, and he tumbled off in another direction, hooting. Within instants, an impromptu game of football, led by the crown prince, had distracted everyone from Neil, but his ears still burned from their laughter. Even the king, Fastia, and Elseny had laughed at him, though thankfully Sir Fail had merely rolled his eyes.

Neil tightened his mouth, locking a reply to the jester inside of it. He didn't want to shame Sir Fail with the tongue that had brought him trouble more than once.

"Don't mind Hound Hat," Fastia told him. "He mocks everyone he can. It's his vocation, you understand. Here, walk alongside me. I will continue your education on the court. 'Tis plain you need one."

"Thank you, lady."

"We're missing a sister—my youngest, Anne. She's sulking down that way—see, that's her with the strawberry hair? And, look, here comes my mother, the queen."

Neil followed her gaze.

She no longer wore a cowl, but Neil knew her in an instant, by her eyes, and by her faint smile of recognition. And now he understood why Fastia and Elseny had seemed so familiar. They were their mother's daughters.

"So, you roused old Fail," the queen said.

"Majesty. Yes, Majesty." This time, he did knock his head against the grass.

"You've met already?" Fastia asked.

"I went to the chapel of Saint Lier," the queen said. "This young man was there, praying like a poet. They teach prayer like that only on the islands. I knew he must be with Fail."

"Your Majesty, please forgive any impertinence I might have—"

The king interrupted Neil. "You went without an escort? To the *docks*?"

"My guard was near, and Erren just outside, and I was hooded. Disguised, as it were."

"It was foolish, Muriele, especially in these times."

"I'm sorry if I worried you."

"Worried? I did not know. That's what worries, after the fact. From now on you will not go about without escort. Please." He seemed to realize that his voice had turned sharp, and calmed it. "We'll discuss it later," he said. "I don't want to welcome Fail and his young guest with a family quarrel."

"Speaking of quarrels," Queen Muriele said, "I hope you will all excuse me a moment. I see someone with whom I need to speak. Young MeqVren, I apologize for my deception, but it was worth it to see your face, just now." She looked over at her husband. "I'm going only so far as over there," she said, "if you wanted to know."

Neil was glad she had switched the object of her conversation so quickly, for he had nothing at all to reply. He felt guilty for something he could not name.

∘   ∘   ∘

"It had to be Fastia," Anne told Austra as the two girls walked their horses up the violet-spangled Sleeve. The air was thick with spring perfumes, but Anne was too agitated to enjoy them.

"Fastia is usually more direct," Austra disagreed. "She would have questioned you about the rose, not taunted you with it."

"Not if she already knew everything."

"She doesn't know everything," Austra said. "She can't."

"Who did it, then? Lesbeth?"

"She *has* changed," Austra pointed out. "Become more political. Maybe she's changed as much as Fastia has, but we just don't know it yet."

Anne considered that for a moment, shifting her seat a bit. She despised riding sidesaddle—or *slide*saddle, as it ought to be called. She always felt as if she was just about to slip off. If she and Austra were alone, she would switch in an instant to a more natural mode of riding, underskirts be damned.

But they weren't alone. Half the nobles in the kingdom were riding up the gently rising field.

"I can't believe that. Lesbeth wouldn't betray me any more than you would."

"You suspect *me*?" Austra asked indignantly.

"Hush, you stupid girl. Of course not. That's what I just said."

"Oh. Well, who, then? Who has a key to your rooms? Only Fastia."

"Maybe she forgot to lock the door."

"I doubt that," Austra said.

"I do, too. Still—"

"*Your mother.*"

"That's true. Mother certainly has a key. But—"

"No. Here comes your mother."

Anne looked up and, with a sudden dismayed prickling, realized it was true. Muriele Dare née de Liery, Queen of Crotheny, was trotting her black Vitellian mare away from her retinue and toward Anne and Austra.

"Good morning, Austra," Muriele said.

"Morning, Your Majesty."

"I wonder if I might ride with my daughter for a few moments. Alone."

"Of course, Your Majesty!" Austra immediately switched her reins and trotted off, leaving only an apologetic and worried glance. If Anne was in trouble, odds were good that Austra was, too.

"You girls seem agitated about something this morning," Muriele observed. "And you aren't riding with the royal party."

"I had a bad dream," Anne told her. It was part of the truth, at least. "And no one told us we had to ride with the royal party."

"That's a shame about the dream. I'll have Fastia bring you some fennage tea tonight. It's said to keep Black Mary away."

Anne shrugged.

"I think there's more to it than bad dreams, however. Fastia believes there is a deeper cause in your agitation."

"Fastia doesn't like me," Anne replied.

"On the contrary. Your sister loves you, as well you know. She just doesn't *approve* of you all of the time, as well she shouldn't."

"All sorts of people disapprove of me," Anne muttered.

Her mother searched her with her jade-green gaze. "You are a princess, Anne. You have yet to take that seriously. In childhood, it is forgiven—for a time. But you've entered into your marriageable years, and it is well past time for you to give up childish behavior. Your father and I were both terribly embarrassed by the incident with the greft of Austgarth—"

"He was a disgusting old man. You can't expect me—"

"He is a gentleman, and more, his allegiance is of the utmost importance to us. You find the well-being of your father's kingdom disgusting? Do you know how many of your ancestors have perished for this country?"

"That's not fair."

"Fair? We are not like normal people, Anne. Many of our choices are made for us by our birth."

"Lesbeth is marrying for love!"

Muriele shook her head. "Ah, this is what I feared, and what Fastia feared, as well. Hers is a fortunate match, but Lesbeth knows no more of love than you do."

"Oh, yes, Mother, as if you know the slightest thing about love!" Anne exploded. "All of Eslen knows Father spends more time with the lady Gramme than ever he did in your chambers."

Her mother could move quickly, at times. Anne never saw the slap coming until her face was already stinging from it.

"You have no idea what you're talking about," Muriele said, her voice low, flat, and as dangerous as Anne had ever heard it.

Tears welled in Anne's eyes and her throat swelled. *I will not cry,* she told herself.

"Now. Listen to me. There are three young men here today, all comely after a fashion. Are you listening? They are Wingaln Kathson of Avlham, William Fullham of the Winston Baronet, and Duncath MeqAvhan. Any of them would be a good match. None of them are disgusting old men. I expect you to entertain each, do you understand? They have come solely to meet you."

Anne rode in sullen silence.

"Do you understand?" Muriele repeated.

"Yes. How will I know them?"

"You will be introduced, never fear. It is arranged."

"Very well. I understand."

"Anne, this is all for your own good."

"How fortunate that someone should know what is good for me."

"Don't be a brat. This is your sister's birthday. Put on a happy face— if not for me, then for her. And for my sake, let us have an end to our arguments, please?" Muriele smiled the cold little smile that Anne never trusted.

"Yes, Mother."

But inside, despite the slap that still burned her face, Anne's heart felt lighter. Her mother didn't know about Roderick.

But someone knew, didn't they? Someone had found her rose.

For a moment, she wondered if it had to do with Roderick at all. He hadn't been in the dream.

"What's this?" a male voice piped in, from the side. "The two loveliest women in the kingdom, riding without escort?"

Anne and Muriele both turned to greet the newcomer.

"Hello, Robert," Muriele said.

"Good morning, dear sister-in-law. How lovely you are! The dawn was slow today, fearing to compare with you."

"How nice of you to say," Muriele replied.

Ignoring her cool tone, Robert switched his attentions to Anne. "And you, my dear niece. What a stunning creature you've become. I fear this birthday party might become a slaughterground of young knights jousting over you, if we don't provide restraint."

Anne almost blushed. Uncle Robert was a handsome man, fit, wide shouldered, slim waisted. He was dark, for a Dare, with black eyes and a small mustache and beard that perfectly fit his sardonic manner.

"Best worry about Elseny," Anne replied. "She's far the more beautiful, and it is, after all, her birthday."

Robert trotted his horse over and took Anne's hand. "Lady," he said, "my brother has three beautiful daughters, and you are in no way the least of them. If some man has said this, tell me his name and I shall see the ravens pecking at his eyes before nightfall."

"Robert," Muriele said, a hint of irritation in her voice, "do not flatter my daughter so unmercifully. It's not good for her."

"I speak only the truth, Muriele dear. If it sounds flattering, well, I hope I will be forgiven for it. But really, where is your bodyguard?"

"There," Muriele said, waving her hand to where the king and his retinue made their way along. "I wanted to speak to my daughter alone, but they are there, and quite alert, I assure you."

"I hope I haven't interrupted anything. You seemed serious."

"Actually," Anne replied—brightly, she hoped—"we were talking about Lesbeth's upcoming wedding. Isn't it exciting?" Too late, she saw the warning in her mother's eyes.

"What's that?" Robert's voice suddenly had a certain coldness to it.

"Lesbeth," Anne said, a little less certainly. "She asked Father's permission last night."

Robert smiled briefly, but his forehead was creased. "How odd that she didn't ask mine. Goodness! It seems the joke has been on me!"

"She was going to tell you today," Muriele said.

"Well. Perhaps I'd best go find her and give her the opportunity. If you will excuse me, ladies."

"Of course," Muriele said.

"Remind Lesbeth that she promised to see me today!" Anne shouted, as her uncle rode off.

They continued silently for a moment or two.

"You should perhaps be more careful about what you let drop," Muriele said. But somehow she didn't sound angry any longer.

"I—the whole castle knows by now. I thought she would have told her own brother."

"Robert has always been very protective of Lesbeth. They are, after all, twins."

"Yes. That's why I thought he would know."

"It doesn't always work like that."

"I see it doesn't. May I ride with Austra, now?"

"You should join the royal party. Your granuncle Fail is here— Oh, it looks like he's ridden off with your father. Very well, you may be standoffish if you wish. Tonight you must be sociable, however. And you must be agreeable at your sister's festival." She pulled her reins and started off. She cast back over her shoulder. "And stay proper on your horse, you hear me? Today of all days."

The Sleeve curved and rose gradually to the top of Tom Woth, a broad-topped hill that looked down on the reaches of the city east, and upon its twin, Tom Cast west. There was erected an open-sided pavilion of brilliant yellow silk, flying the banner of the bee and the thistle, the imaginary standard of Elphin.

An enormous floral maze surrounded the pavilion. Its walls consisted of close-planted sunflowers and pearly nodding-heads. Up and about those substantial stalks crept scarlet trumpet vines, morning glories, and blossoming sweet peas. Courtiers were already dismounting and making their way into the labyrinth, laughing and giggling. From someplace in the maze a delicate music played on hautboy, croth, great harp, and bells.

Austra clapped her hands. "It looks delightful, don't you think?"

Anne forced a smile, determined to enjoy herself. Things, after all, could be much worse, and the festival atmosphere was infectious.

"Very," she said. "Mother's outdone herself, this time. Elseny must be positively bursting."

"Are you well?" Austra asked, almost guiltily.

"Yes. I don't think Mother knows about Roderick, either. Maybe *I* tore up the flower, in my sleep."

Austra's eyes grew round. "You *have* done such things! You used to walk about, perfectly unaware of anyone trying to speak to you. And you mumble and mutter most constantly."

"That must be it, then. I think we are safe, my dear friend. And now I need only entertain three young fellows, and everyone will think well of me."

"Except Roderick."

"I shall make that up to him later in the day. You'll make the arrangements?"

"Of course I will."

"Well, then. Dare we enter Elphin?"

"I think we so dare!"

They dismounted and approached an archway that had been erected at the entrance of the maze. On either side stood two men wearing chain mail made of daisies. Anne recognized them as players from the household troop.

"Fair ladies," one said, in high manner. "What seek you, here?"

"Why, an audience with the queen of Elphin, I suppose," Anne said.

"Milady, betwixt you and that glorious queen lie the twisty courts of the phay, full of beauty and deadly danger. In all candor, I cannot admit you without you be accompanied by a true knight. I implore you, choose one."

Anne followed his pointing finger, to where a number of boys stood dressed as knights. They wore outlandish armor of paper, fabric, and flowers. Their helms formed into masks, so it was difficult to tell who they were.

Anne strode over to them, and they formed a line. It took only a few moments for her to be sure that Roderick wasn't among them.

"Which one?" she said aloud, tapping her chin. "What do you think, Austra?"

"They all look quite brave, to me."

"Not brave enough. I have another in mind. You, sir knight of the green lilies, lend me your sword."

Obediently, the young man handed her his weapon, which was, in fact, a willow wand painted in gilt and furnished with a guard of lacquered magnolia petals.

"Very good. And now your helm."

He hesitated there, but she was, after all, a princess. He removed the masked helm to reveal a young, somewhat homely face she didn't recognize. Anne leaned up and kissed his cheek. "I thank you, sir Elphin knight."

"Milady—"

"May I have your name?"

"Uh—William Fullham, milady."

"Sir Fullham, you will save a dance for me, when we reach the queen's court?"

"Of course, milady!"

"Wonderful." And with that, she donned his helm and marched back to the guards.

"I hayt Sir Anne," she proclaimed, "of the Bitter Bee clan, and I will escort the lady Austra to the queen."

"Very well, Sir Anne. But beware. The Briar King is said to be about."

When he said it, something went wrong in Anne's belly, as if she had stepped off of something higher than she thought it was, and the image of her dream flashed behind her eyes—the field of black roses, the thorny forest, the hand reaching for her.

She staggered for a moment.

"What's wrong?" Austra asked.

"Nothing," Anne replied. "It's just the sun."

With that, she entered the maze.

CHAPTER TEN

THE TAFF

ASPAR LEFT TOR SCATH before dawn, departing the King's Road and striking across the uplands of Brogh y Stradh, through meadows blazing with red clover, lavender weed, and pharigolds. He found the Taff near its headwaters, surprising a small herd of aurochs stamping the stream bank into a musky quagmire. They watched him with suspicious eyes as he, Ogre, and Angel picked their way through the twisty maze of ancient willows that surrounded and canopied their watering place. The wild cattle smell followed him downstream, long after the bellows of the bulls faded.

Everything seemed well, but it wasn't. He was more certain now than ever. It wasn't just the things Symen had told him.

Yes, he believed some of the old man's babblings. Ultimately, the knight was trustworthy when it came to reporting what he had seen. The dead bodies, the mutilations, the strange absence of wounds all were undoubtedly true, though Aspar wanted to see for himself.

The rest—greffyns, the Briar King, and the like—*that* part he didn't trust.

Though Symen's speculations were less than reliable, it was something in Aspar himself that worried him. The night before, on the road when he'd been trying to scare the young priest-to-be, he'd almost frightened himself, almost imagined that the wild soul-hunt had really fallen upon them—despite that he had always known, in his head, that it was merely Symen and his dogs.

Something was out there, and he didn't know what. For all his babbling about greffyns and Briar Kings, neither did Symen. And *that* was the worrisome thing, the not knowing.

Ogre was skittish, his ears pricking all of the time, and twice shying— Ogre, *shying*—at nothing at all.

And so, by degrees, Aspar prepared himself for what he would find on Taff Creek.

The bodies lay like a flight of birds broken by some strange wind, scattered around their unfinished nests. He tied his horses a safe distance away and went on foot among them.

They had been dead for days, of course. Their flesh had gone black and purple, and their staring eyes had sunk into their heads, as if they were really carved from pumpkins, then left too long in the sun. That shouldn't have been. The ravens should have picked their eyes long ago. There should be worms, and the stink of putrefaction.

Instead he smelled only autumn leaves.

It was as Symen had described; they had simply dropped dead. Which might mean . . .

He looked around.

Seothen—*sedoi*, the priestling had called them—were usually on high ground, but not always. If the church built fanes on them, there were paths, but as the boy said, few of the sedoi in the King's Forest were used by the church, though until last night Aspar had never thought to wonder why. He'd only known that the church didn't bother with most of them.

Somebody was bothering with them, though.

He found it on a little hillock, not far from the stream, aided by its smell of rotting flesh and the croaking of ravens. The fane itself was almost gone, a few rocks still holding the shape of an ancient wall and an altar stone. But on the trees encircling it, the bodies of men, women, and children had been nailed up by the hands and feet. They had been split open from sternum to crotch and their intestines pulled like ropes about the fane, forming a sort of enclosure. The big muscles of their arms and legs had been flayed open, too.

This near, the smell was almost enough to make him retch. Unlike those in the field, these corpses *were* rotting, and the trees were full of man-fatted corbies. A few bodies had already parted from their limbs, upsetting the unholy architecture of the murderers.

Down the hill, Ogre whinnied, then snorted. Aspar recognized the tone and, turning his back on the ghastly tableau, hurried back.

He stopped still as he neared the horses and saw, in the tangle by the stream, an eye the size of a saucer.

The rest of it was all guessing, lost in the mosaic shadows of the forest. But it was watching him, of that he was certain. And it was big, big enough to have made the print he had seen by Edwin's Brooh. Bigger than Ogre.

He exhaled softly, and as he inhaled again, he reached for the quiver on his back, pinched one of the black-fletched arrows in three callus-hardened fingers, and drew it out. He lay it on his bow.

The eye shifted, and a few leaves stirred. He saw a beak, black and curving and sharp, and wondered if he was dead already, just from having caught its gaze.

He couldn't remember that much about greffyns. They didn't exist, and Aspar White had never paid much attention to things that didn't exist. But there it was. And it had killed the squatters without touching them. Somehow.

Why was it still here? Or had it gone and returned?

He brought the weapon up, as the greffyn nosed into the clearing.

Its head was vaguely eaglelike, as the old stories told, though it was flatter than that. It had no feathers, but was scaled in black and dark, iridescent green. A mane of what looked like coarse hair began at its neck. Its foreparts were thickly muscled, ox-size but sinuous. It moved like a bird, jerky, but fast and sure. He would get one shot. He doubted very much that it would be enough.

He aimed for the eye.

The greffyn cocked its head, and he saw something in it then he had never seen in an animal. Consideration, calculation.

Disdain.

He drew the bow. "Come on, then, you mikel rooster," he growled. "Come or go, it makes me never mind to me, just do one or the other."

It crouched, like a cat preparing to spring. Everything went still. The bowstring cut into his fingers, and the scent of the resin on it tickled his nose. He smelled leaf mold and chestnut blossoms and woodsmoke—and *it*. Animal, yes, but also something like rain hitting the hot rocks around a campfire.

It uncoiled like a snake striking, bounding up and out, a blur. Despite its size, it was the fastest living thing he had ever seen. It tore across the meadow at a right angle to him, south. In two eye blinks it was gone.

He stood for a long moment, marveling, wondering if he could have hit it, glad enough that it hadn't come down to that.

Glad that its gaze wasn't enough to kill.

Then his feet wobbled out from under him. The forest floor came up to smack his face, and he thought he heard Dirty Jesp somewhere, laughing her silky, condescending laugh.

He awoke to fingers brushing his face and a soft murmuring. He reached for his dirk. Or tried to—his hand didn't move.

I'm tied up, he thought. *Or nailed to a tree.*

But then he opened his eyes and saw Winna, the hostler's daughter from back in Colbaely.

"What?" he mumbled. His lips felt thick.

"Did you touch one of them?" she asked. "I can't find any sign, but—"

"Where am I?"

"Where I found you, near the Taff, right by where all that poor boy's kin lie dead. Did you touch one of the bodies?"

"No."

"What's wrong with you, then?"

I saw a greffyn. "I don't know," he told her. He could move his hands now, a little. They were tingling.

"The boy died," she said. "That purple hand of his—his whole arm turned black. It wasn't a bruise. It started after he tried to shake his mother awake."

"I didn't touch any of them. Can you help me sit up?"

"Are you sure?"

"Yes."

She held up her own hands, showing angry red marks on the fingers and palms. "I got this from washing his wounds. It hurt that night, but I gave it no mind. By midday after you left, I was blistered."

Cold seeped up Aspar's back as he remembered Symen's missing fingers. "We'll need to find you a leic," he said.

Winna shook her head. "I saw Mother Cilth. She gave me an ointment and told me the poison was too weak to do me real harm." She paused. "She also told me you needed me."

He started to deny that last, but a wave of dizziness overcame him.

Winna got around behind him, reached her small arms up under his, and lifted. He felt weak, but between the two of them, they managed to get him scooted against a tree so he could stay up.

She felt soft, and she smelled good. Clean.

"I thought you were dead," she said, voice low.

"You followed me here?"

"No, you great fool, I conjured you back to Colbaely with my alvish broom-handle. Yes, of course I followed you. I was afraid you would touch the bodies, and catch whatever shinecraft killed them."

He looked up at her. "Sceat. You followed me here *alone*? Do you know how dangerous that was? Even on a good day, there's cutthroats and beasts, but now—wasn't it you warning *me* that the forest is different now?"

"And wasn't it you who scoffed at me for sayin' it? You're ready to admit I was right?"

"That's not the point," Aspar snapped. "The point is you could have been killed."

Winna's eyebrows lowered dangerously. "Aspar White, you're not the only one who knows a thing or two about the King's Forest, at least hereabouts. And *which* of us was almost killed? It might as easily have been a wolf or a bandit that found you as it was me, and then you would've slept through your own death."

"The same wolf could have found you."

She uttered a terse laugh. "Yes, and been too fat on holter-flesh to catch me. Aspar White, is this *you* wasting breath on something already done?"

He had a response to that, he was sure of it, but then another bout of sickness came over him, and it was all he could do not to vomit.

"You *did* touch one!" she said, her ire suddenly replaced by concern.

He shook his head. "I stopped by Tor Scath. Sir Symen found some dead like this, and lost two fingers for touching them. Why—why didn't y'send someone? You shouldn't have come yourself, Winn, whatever that old witch Cilth told you."

She regarded him for a long moment.

"You're a fool, Aspar White," she said.

And then she kissed him.

"That's enough firewood, I think," Winna said, when Aspar returned with his fourth armload.

"I suppose it is," he said. He stood there awkwardly for a moment, then nodded to the rabbits roasting on spits over a small fire. "Those smell good."

"They do."

"Well. I should—"

"You should sit there and tell me what happened. I've never seen you like this, Asp. You seem . . . well, not frightened, but as close to it as I've known you to come. First I find you laid out like a dead man, then you want to ride at neck-breaking speed until it's almost dark. What killed those people, Aspar? Do you think it's after us?"

You left something out, there, Aspar thought to himself, remembering the touch of her breath on his. *Something that's muddying my thoughts considerably.* He stood for a heartbeat longer, then took a seat across the fire from her. "I saw something."

"Something? Some kind of animal?"

"Something that ought not to be."

She spread her hands and shrugged, a silent *go on?*

"The Sefry had children's stories about them. Maybe you heard them, too. About greffyns."

"Greffyns? You think you saw a greffyn? A lion, with an eagle's head and wings, and all?"

"Not exactly like that. I didn't see any wings, or feathers. But someone as saw this might describe it that way. It was like a big cat, and it had a beak. It acted something like a bird."

"Well, they're supposed to hate horses. And lay golden eggs, I think. And wasn't there a story about a knight who tamed one to ride?"

"Do you remember anything about poison?"

"Poison? No, I don't." She brightened. "Could it have been a basil-nix? *They* were supposed to be poison, remember? So poison they could hide in a tree and the fruit of the tree would kill whoever ate it."

"That's it. That's what I was trying to remember. Winna, whatever I saw—what it touches, dies."

"And what touches whatever it touches, too, it would seem." Suddenly her face scrunched in horror. "It didn't touch *you*, did it?"

"No. It looked at me, that's all. But even that took its toll. Or it might have been poison vapor, in the air. I wat not. That's why I was in such a hurry to leave, to get you away from there."

"Where do you think it came from?"

"I don't know. From the mountains, maybe." He shrugged. "How did they kill them, in the stories?"

"Aspar. *No.*"

"I have to find it, Winn. You know that. I'm the holter. Maunt it."

"Maunt it yourself. How can you kill something you can't even look at? How do you know it *can* be killed?"

"Anything can be killed."

"That's just like you. Three days ago you didn't even believe such a creature existed. Now you know for certain you can kill it."

"I have to try," he said stubbornly.

"Of course you do," she said disgustedly. She turned the rabbits a bit.

"Are you sorry I kissed you?" she asked suddenly. Her face flushed red when she said it, but her voice was strong.

"Ah . . . no. I just—" He remembered how her lips had felt, the warm taste of them, the brush of her cheek against his, her eyes so close.

"I won't do it again," she went on.

"No, I wouldn't expect you to."

"No, next time you have to kiss *me*, Aspar White, if there's going to be any kissing. Is that clear to you?"

Clear? No, not one damned bit! he thought.

"Werlic, it's clear," he lied. Did that mean she wanted him to come kiss her *now*, or that she thought it was a mistake?

One thing certain—in the soft light of the fire she looked very kissable.

"The rabbits are ready," she said.

"Good. I'm hungry."

"Come on then." She handed him one of the spits. The coney was still sizzling when he bit into it. For a while he had the perfect excuse not to talk, or kiss, or do anything with his mouth but chew. But when he was down to greasy bones, the silence started becoming uncomfortable again.

"Winna, do you know the way to Tor Scath? It's less than a day east of here."

"I know where it is."

"Could you make it there on your own? I don't like asking it, but if I take you all the way there and then come back, I'm afraid I might lose the greffyn's trail."

"I'm not going to Tor Scath."

"It's too far back to Colbaely with things like that roaming the woods. In fact—" He broke off. The greffyn hadn't had hands, had it? How would it nail people to trees and make a corral from their intestines?

"In fact, I'm not thinking clear. *I'll* take you to Tor Scath. The greffyn's trail will keep."

"Aspar, if you take me to Tor Scath, I'll slip off first chance I get, and I'll follow *you* again. If you take me all the way back to Colbaely, I'll do the same. If you don't want me wandering the woods alone, you'll take me with you, and that's that."

"Take you *with* me?"

"If you're fool enough to hunt this thing, I won't let you hunt it alone."

"Winna—"

"It's not an argument," she said. "It's fact."

"Sceat! Winna, this monster is the most dangerous thing I've ever heard of, much less seen. If I have to worry about you as well as me—"

"Then you'll be that much more careful, won't you? You'll think more carefully before doing something foolish."

"I said no."

"And I said it's not an argument," Winna finished. "Now—we can talk about something else, something more pleasant, or we can get some sleep and an early start. Which will it be?"

Aspar stirred the fire with the tip of the greasy skewer. Nearby, Ogre grumbled something.

"Do you want the first watch, or the morning?" he asked finally.

"Morning," she said immediately. "Throw me that blanket. And don't fail to wake me."

Minutes later she was asleep. Aspar shouldered his bow and walked out of the circle of light. He had taken them back into the Brogh y Stradh, and a short distance away one of the many upland meadows showed through the trees. He stepped to the edge of it and regarded the rising moon. It was huge and orange, three-quarters full. A nightbird called to it, and Aspar shivered.

He had loved the forest at night, found leaves the most restful bed in the world. Now the dark felt like a cave full of vipers. He remembered the greffyn's eye, its awful disdain. How did you kill something like that? Would the young priest have known? Probably not, and even if he did, it was too late. He'd be a day's travel toward d'Ef by now.

Would that Winna were that far away.

Would that she had never found him.

No matter how earnestly he told himself that, it still felt like a lie. Disgusted, he turned his back to the evil-looking moon and returned to the edge of the firelight and Winna's slow, regular breathing.

CHAPTER ELEVEN

WIDDERSHINS

B Y THE TIME THEY HAD REACHED the festival grounds, Fastia had filled Neil's head with the names of so many lords, ladies, retainers, grefts, archgrefts, margrefts, marascalhs, sinescalhs, earls, counts, landfroas, andvats, barons, and knights he feared it would burst. He spent most of his time nodding and making noises to let her know he was listening. Meanwhile, Sir Fail, still speaking with the king, drew farther and farther away. The rest of the royal party outpaced them until only he and Fastia and a few of the deviceless knights were left.

When they reached the hilltop, with its gaudy and bewildering collection of tents, plant growth, and costumed servants Fastia, too, excused herself. "I need to speak to my mother," she explained. "Details about the celebration. Do try to enjoy yourself."

"I will, Archgreffess. My deepest thanks for your conversation."

"It is little enough," Fastia said stiffly. "It's rare we get a breath of fresh air in this court, and well worth breathing it when it comes along." She began to ride away, then paused, turned her horse back, and brought her head quite near his, so that he could smell the cinnamon perfume she wore. "There are others in the court you haven't met. I pointed out my uncle, Robert? My father's brother? My father has two sisters, as well. Lesbeth, the duchess of Andemeur, and Elyoner, the duchess of Loiyes. You'll find the first sweet-tempered and pleasant in conversation. Elyoner

I advise you to avoid, at least until you are wiser. She can be dangerous for young men like you."

Neil bowed in the saddle. "Thank you again, Princess Fastia, for your company and your advice."

"Again you are welcome." This time she rode off without looking back.

That left him alone, which gave him time to let it all sink in, to try to understand the seeming chaos around him.

And to struggle with the fact that he had actually met a king. No, not just *a* king, but *the* king, the *Amrath*, the *Ardrey*—the emperor of Crotheny and the kingdoms that served it, the greatest nation in the world.

He began a brief prayer of thanks to Saint Lier.

"Look how Sir Bumpkin sits his horse," someone said, behind him. "Praying to stay in the saddle, Sir Bumpkin?" Another man guffawed in response. Neil finished his prayer, then looked about to see who "Sir Bumpkin" might be, and found two of the sable-and-green-clad knights regarding him. The one who had spoken had a hawkish nose and a small black beard. His companion was pox-scarred, with chipped teeth and eyes like blue ice. Nearby, another of the knights started drifting toward them.

"You are wrong on at least one count," Neil replied. "I am not titled, and thus no 'sir' of any sort."

"It's just plain Bumpkin, then? A pity," the knight said, pulling thoughtfully at his goatee. "Seeing how poorly you sit a horse, I had a mind to see how you fall off of one. But I suspect if I watch long enough, that will happen of its own accord."

"Have I given you offense, sir?"

"*Offense* is too strong a word. You amuse."

"Well, I'm happy, I suppose, if I can give such a great lord as yourself amusement," Neil replied evenly.

"You *suppose*? You don't even know who I *am*, do you?"

"No, sir. You wear no device."

"This braying island ass doesn't know who I am, fellows."

The third knight arrived, a huge, bearlike man with a bristly blond beard. "Sometimes your own mother pretends she don't know you either, Jemmy," he ground out in bass tones. "Leave the lad be."

The man Neil gathered to be Jemmy pursed his lips as if to make retort, then laughed. "I suppose I must," he said. "And he is, after all, too far beneath me to muck about with. Go along, Bumpkin." He kneed his mount, turning dismissively away.

"I pray, sir, that you *do* tell me your name," Neil called after him.

The fellow turned slowly back. "And why is that, Bumpkin?"

"So when I take the rose and don my spurs I can call on you."

The knight laughed, and his companions with him. "Very well," he allowed. "I am Sir James Cathmayl. I will be happy to kill you, just as soon as you wear the rose. But rumor has it that you're merely a lost puppy, nipping about the heels of Sir Fail, with no house, lands, title, or good name. Is it true?"

Neil drew himself straighter. "All but the last. My father gave me this name, and his father before him, and we have faithfully served the Toute de Liery for three generations. MeqVren is a good name, and he who disputes that is a liar." He cocked his head. "And if I'm of so little count, why are there rumors about me already?"

Sir James tweaked his mustache. "Because Sir Fail, however eccentric, is one of the most important men in the kingdom. Because you spoke to both His and Her Majesty."

"And because it's said you made three squires of that oaf Alareik Fram Wishilm shit themselves," the blond-bearded giant added.

"That, too," Sir James admitted. "You're a curiosity, is what you are."

"And who are you fellows? What lord do you serve?"

Blond-beard chuckled good-naturedly; the other two sneered. "He *is* a babe, isn't he?" Sir James grunted, rolling his eyes. "Who do you *think* we are, boy?" He didn't wait for an answer, but turned and rode away. Poxy-face went with him.

Neil blushed, but stood his ground.

"We're the Craftsmen, lad," Blond-beard said. "The royal bodyguard."

"Oh." Of course, he had heard of the most famous guard in the land. How stupid that he hadn't known their colors. "My apologies. I should have known, by your very presence around the king."

The blond man shrugged. "Never mind Jemmy. He's not a bad sort, when you get to know him."

"And may I ask your name, sir?"

"Why? So you can call me out, too?"

"Not at all. I'd like to know the name of the man who showed me kindness."

"Well. Vargus Farre, at your service. I'm pleased to meet you, and I wish you luck. It's only honest to tell you this, though: I've never heard of an ungentle man being knighted, and if by some miracle you are, you'll know little peace. You'll be seen as an affront, and every knight in the country will bring challenge against you. Take my advice—stay with Sir Fail as his man-at-arms. It will be a good thing for you."

"I'll take what the king gives me, and desire no more," Neil replied. "My only wish is to serve His Majesty as best I can."

Sir Vargus smiled. "Those are words I've heard often enough to render 'em as meaningless as geese honking. And yet I think you mean them, don't you?"

"I mean them."

"Well, then. Saints smile on you. And now I must attend to my duties."

Neil watched him go, still feeling stupid. He noticed them, now, watching from afar. Even though the king and Sir Fail looked as if they were alone, in fact there was a circle of Craftsmen around them—at a distance, yes, looking almost uninterested. But when someone moved toward the king, so did they.

He looked for the queen and found her near the edge of the hill, talking to two ladies. There, too, vigilant Craftsmen kept both their range and their guard.

It was said these men renounced all lands and property upon entering the royal bodyguard. It was also said that they felt neither pain nor desire, that none could stand against them, that their weapons had been forged by giants.

Perhaps that's why he hadn't recognized them right away. To Neil, they seemed like any other men.

Alone again, Neil had the leisure to reflect on just how out of place he felt. In Liery, he had known who he was. He was Neil, son of Fren, and since the destruction of his clan, the fosterling of Fail de Liery. More than that, he had been a warrior, and a good one. Even the knights of Liery had recognized that, and complimented him on it. He had been one of them in all but title. None had successfully stood against him in single combat since he was fourteen. No enemy of the de Lierys had ever stood against him at all, not since that day on the beach.

But what use was he here, in this place of frilly tents and costumes? Where even the most civil of the royal bodyguard spoke to him with such condescension? What could he do here?

Better that he serve the empire as he always had, as a warrior of the marches, where it mattered little whether or not one wore a rose, and mattered much how one wielded a sword.

He would find Fail de Liery and ask him not to recommend him. It was the only sensible course of action.

He looked about and saw Sir Fail break away from the king.

"Come, Hurricane," he told his mount, "let's tell him, and hope it's not too late."

But as he turned, he caught a glimpse of the queen. The sight of her held him momentarily.

She was still mounted, silhouetted against the blue sky. Beyond her, the land dropped away to a distant green, still misty with morning. A breeze ruffled her hair.

He realized he had stared too long, and began to turn, when a motion caught his eye. It was one of the Craftsmen, his mount at full gallop, careening across the green toward her, a long silver flash of steel in his hand.

Neil didn't think but kicked Hurricane into motion. Clearly the knight was rushing to meet some threat. Frantically, Neil searched with his eyes as he galloped forward, but saw nothing the warrior might be responding to.

And then he understood. He drew Crow, flourishing her and uttering the piercing war cry of the MeqVrens.

Austra giggled as Anne shooed away some great lout dressed as an ogre, brandishing her willow-wand sword.

"This is fun," the maid said.

"It's good of you tell me," Anne replied. "Else I might never have known."

"Oh, foo. You're having fun."

"Maybe a little. But it's time we part company, fair lady."

"What do you mean?" Austra said. "You are my knight. Who else shall escort me to the center of the maze and the Elphin queen's court?"

"That isn't your charge, as well you know. You must find Roderick and direct him to meet me at the fane of Saint Under."

"In Eslen-of-Shadows? That's—"

"The last place anyone will look for us. And it's not far from here. He is to meet me there at dusk. Go find him, tell him, then find me again in the maze. We shall then proceed to my sister's birthday court, and none will be the wiser."

"I don't know. Fastia and your mother must be watching us."

"Amidst all this? That would be difficult."

"As difficult as *me* finding Roderick."

"I have confidence in you, Austra. Now hurry."

Austra rustled off, and Anne continued through the labyrinth on her own.

She knew how to work mazes, of course. Some of her earliest memories were of her aunt Elyoner's estate of Glenchest, in Loiyes, and the vast hedge labyrinth there. She had feared it until her aunt explained the secret. You simply trailed a hand on one wall and walked, always keeping contact. In that way you would work through the entire thing. Slow it might be, but not as slow as bumbling confusedly around in the same corner for four bells.

She was in no hurry, but from habit, she trailed her left hand along the floral wall.

Meanwhile, children and court dwarves dressed as boghshins and kovalds ran by, squealing and making fierce faces. Many of the court giants were dressed as pig-headed uttins with tusks and green-skinned trolls with bulging eyes. Hound Hat, her father's Sefry jester, tipped his huge brim to her as she went by, his shadowed face the only flesh visible, the rest of him clad in voluminous robes that swallowed even his hands.

She hoped Austra would find Roderick. The kiss in the orchard had been far different from that first peck in the city of the dead. Or rather, the *kisses* in the orchard, for she seemed to have lost more than half a bell, when she was with him. It wasn't just the lips, with kissing, as she had always imagined. It was the face, so close, the eyes so near they could hide nothing if you caught them open.

And the warmth of bodies—that was a little frightening. Confusing. She wanted more.

Anne paused, her hand still on the wall.

Something was different. She seemed to have entered a corner of the maze no one else had found, not even the "monsters" who were supposed to inhabit it. She had been so deep in thought that she had failed to take notice. Now, straining her ears, she couldn't even *hear* anyone else.

Just how big could this maze be?

The flowers had changed, too. The walls here were made of scarlet and white primrose—and they were denser. She couldn't see through them at all. In fact, at their bases the stems were quite thick, as if they had been growing for a very long time. But she had been on Tom Woth in midwinter, and there had been no trace of a maze. Sunflowers could grow more than head high in a few months, but a thick stand of primrose? That seemed unlikely.

Her breathing quickened.

"Hello?" she called.

No one answered.

Frowning, Anne turned around, so that her right hand was touching the wall she had been following. Walking quickly, she retraced her steps.

After a hundred paces or so, she lifted her skirts and broke into a run. The maze was still primroses, now sunset red, then sky blue or snow white, pink and lavender. No sunflowers or twining peas, no jesters or goblin-dressed children, no giggling courtiers. Nothing but endless corridors of flowers, and her own sharp breathing.

Finally she stopped, trying to stay calm.

Obviously she wasn't on Tom Woth anymore. Where was she, then?

The sky looked the same, but something *was* different. Something other than the maze.

She couldn't place it at first, but when she understood, she gasped and, despite herself, began to tremble.

She couldn't see the sun, which meant it must be low in the sky. Yet there were no shadows. Not from the maze, not from her. She lifted her skirt. Even directly underneath her, the grass was lit as uniformly as everything else.

She slapped herself. She pinched herself, but nothing changed.

Until behind her she heard a faint, throaty chuckle.

Time slowed, as it often did for Neil in such moments. The Craftsman's horse seemed almost to drift toward the queen, its great shanks rippling and glistening like black waters beneath the moon.

The queen hadn't yet noticed anything unusual, for the black-and-green-clad knight was approaching from behind her, but Fastia was facing the oncoming rider, and her face was slowly transforming from puzzlement to horror.

For the Craftsman's target was the queen herself. His sword was drawn back, level with his waist and parallel to the ground, in preparation for the strike known as *reaper*, aimed at kissing Her Majesty's neck and making a fountain of her lovely white throat.

In that long, slow moment of calculation, Neil was suspended between possibilities. If the Craftsman didn't flinch, Neil would never stop him.

The Craftsman didn't flinch, but his horse did, seeing Hurricane bearing down so fast. A single hesitation, less than a heartbeat, but it was enough.

Hurricane crashed into the other horse's hindquarters, striking from the side with such force that it spun the Craftsman clean around. For this, Neil's own decapitating blow went high, but Neil managed to get his left arm around, and the two steel-clad men hit with a noise like a ton of chain being dropped from a watchtower onto cobblestones.

Then there was a tangle of limbs and no weight, and Neil discovered that there was, indeed, an edge to the hill. A very steep slope, and he and the knight were flying out over it like the clumsiest, most improbable birds in the world.

Thunder smote repeatedly as they hit the grass-dressed hill and bounced, bounced again, and rolled. He lost his hold and they came apart. Crow wasn't in his hands anymore. He finally fetched to a stop against a rock, flashes like anvil sparks filling his vision.

He didn't know how long he lay there, but it couldn't have been long, because he and the royal guardsman were still alone, though the distant hilltop bristled with figures.

Neil got to his feet a few breaths before the Craftsman, who lay some ten paces away. Crow, by good chance, rested halfway between them. Less fortunately, the knight still held his blade.

Neil didn't get Crow up in time, and he had to take that first blow on his forearm. Sheathed in steel as it was, the heavy blade would still have shattered the bone, but Neil angled it so the blade skidded aside. The force struck like lightning all the way to his hip, and for an instant time paused again.

Then Neil lifted Crow, his bird of slaughter, and brought her straight up from the ground, one-handed, a weak blow, but it struck directly beneath the knight's chin. The helm caught it, but his head snapped back, and now Neil had two hands on his weapon.

He hammered in right, hit the helm again, this time just about where the man's ear should be.

The knight fell.

Neil waited for him to get up.

He did, but his helm was deeply dented, and he limped a little. He was a big man, and by the way he set his middle guard, Neil could tell he knew how to fight without a shield.

The Craftsman struck, coming straight on, feinting a head cut, dropping to strike under the arm instead. It was well done, but Neil saw it coming and took a fast, long step to his right, and the other blade bit only air. Crow, on the other hand, lifted as if to block the feint, then came back and once again struck the conical helm, in the same place it had before.

This time, blood spurted from the visor. His foe tottered and fell, trying to curl around his head.

Neil sighed, walked a few steps, and sat down, badly in need of a few deep breaths. It wasn't easy. His beautiful new armor was stove deeply in from below his left arm all the way to his hip, and he was pretty sure the ribs underneath were cracked, too.

He heard shouts above him. Too steep for horses. Five Craftsmen were clanging down the slope as best they could in their armor. Neil lifted Crow again, ready to meet them.

Her gown was of a red so dark it seemed nearly black, and it was hemmed with strange scrolling needlework that glinted ruby. Over it she wore a black robe, embroidered in pale gold with stars, dragons, salamanders, and greffyns. Amber hair fell in a hundred braids to her waist. She wore a mask of red gold, delicately wrought; one eyebrow was lifted, as if in amusement, and the lips carried a quirk that was almost a sneer.

"Who are you?" Anne asked. Her voice sounded ridiculous to her ears, quivering like a baby bird.

"You walked widdershins," the woman said softly. "You have to be careful when you do that. It puts your shadow behind you, where you can't look after it. Someone can snatch it—like *that*." She snapped her fingers.

"Where are my friends? The court?"

"Where they always were. It's we who are elsewhere. We shadows."

"Put me back. Put me back right now. Or . . ."

"Or what? Do you think you are a princess here?"

"Put me back. Please?"

"I will. But you must listen to me first. It is my one condition. We have only a short time."

This is a dream, Anne thought. *Just like the other night.*

She drew a deep breath. "Very well."

"Crotheny must not fall," the woman said.

"Of course it shan't. What do you mean?"

"Crotheny must not fall. And there must be a queen in Crotheny when *he* comes."

"When who comes?"

"I cannot name him. Not here, not now. Nor would his name help you."

"There *is* a queen in Crotheny. My mother is queen."

"And so it must remain."

"Is something going to happen to Mother?"

"I don't see the future, Anne. I see *need*. And your kingdom will need you. That is blazed on earth and stone. I cannot say when, or why, but it has to do with the queen. Your mother, or one of your sisters—or you."

"But that's stupid. If something happens to my mother, there will be no queen, unless father remarries. And he cannot marry one of his daughters. And if something happens to Father, my brother Charles will be king, and whoever he chooses for wife will be queen."

"Nevertheless. If there is no queen in Crotheny when *he* comes, all is lost. And I mean all. I charge you with this."

"Why me? Why not Fastia? She's the one—"

"You are the youngest. There is power in that. It is your trust. Your responsibility. If you fail, it means the ruin of your kingdom, and of all other kingdoms. Do you understand?"

"All other kingdoms?"

"Do you understand?"

"No."

"Then remember. Remembering will do, for now."

"But I—"

"If you want to know more, seek with your ancestors. They might help you when I cannot. Now go."

"No, wait. *You*—" Something startled her, and she blinked. When her eyes fluttered open again, Austra was standing in front of her, shaking her.

"—nne! What's wrong?" Austra sounded hysterical.

"Stop that!" Anne demanded. "Where did she go? Where is she?"

"Anne! You were just standing there. Staring no matter how hard I've been shaking you!"

"Where did she go? The woman in the gold mask?"

But the masked woman was gone. Looking down, Anne saw that she had a shadow again.

PART II

DEMESNES OF NIGHT AND FOREST

The Year 2,223 of Everon

The Month of Truthmen

As the armies of man defeated the Skasloi, the saints defeated the old gods. With their defeat, the ancient sorceries of the Skasloi were greatly diminished, but not destroyed. It was the Sacaratum—that most holy crusade that brought the blessings and wisdom of the church to all the kingdoms of Everon—that finally purified the world of that evil. The only lingering of it are phantasms that exist in the minds of the ignorant and heretical.

—FROM THE *Naration Lisum Saahtum: The Proclamation of Holy Law*, REVISED IN 1,407 E. BY THE SENAZ MAIMS OF THE CHURCH.

Niwhan scalth gadauthath sa ovil
Sleapath at in werlic
Falhath thae skauden in thae raznes
Af sa naht ya sa holt.

Evil never dies
It merely sleeps
Shadows hide in the demesnes
Of night and forest.

—INGORN PROVERB

CHAPTER ONE

THE HALAFOLK

LIGHTNING SHATTERED A TREE, so near that Aspar felt the tingle in the damp soil and smelled the metallic scent of scorched air. Ogre shivered and Angel shrieked, prancing madly. So did Pie Pony, Winna's horse, so that she had to knot her free hand in her mane.

Wind rushed through the forest like an army of ghosts on the run, and the ancient trees rattled and groaned like doomed titans facing the Stormlord. Low thunder rumbled distant, bright coppery claps nearer. Chariot wheels and whipcracks, his father had once called them, when Aspar was very young. He couldn't remember his father's face, his name, or almost anything else, except for that phrase and the smoky smell of tanned buckskin.

"Shouldn't we get out from under this?" Winna asked, raising her voice above the approaching storm.

"Yah," Aspar agreed. "The question is where? And the answer is, I don't know. Unless there's squatters hereabout I don't know of, there's no place to go."

A chattering swarm of swallows blew overhead, almost indistinguishable from the leaves caught up in the furious air. A raindrop the size of a quail's egg spattered against the ground.

Aspar searched the landscape. Two weeks on the greffyn's trail had taken them deep into the low-lying fens surrounding the Slaghish River. The Slaghish had its headwaters to the south, in the Mountains of the

Hare, which was where the storm was coming from. If they didn't find high ground, they would soon have flood to add to the worry of lightning.

It had been a long time since he had been here, and even then he'd just been passing through. Which side of the valley rose most quickly? In his recollection, there was a ridge pretty near in one direction, but leagues away in the other. And he suddenly remembered something else, too. Something Jesp had told him, many, many years ago.

"Let's try this way," he shouted.

"The river?"

"It looks like we can ford it, here."

"If you say so."

The water was already muddy and rough. They dismounted and felt their way across, Aspar first. At midstream the water came to his chest and nearly to Winna's neck. The current quickened noticeably in the crossing; they wouldn't be going back over anytime soon.

Across the river they remounted and rode east across the low ground.

A short time later, the rain arrived in earnest. Dry ground became scarce as the streams feeding the Slaghish rose, and Aspar feared he had made a mistake. He worried that they would have to clamber up a tree and cut the horses loose to fend for themselves.

But then, at last, the land began to rise, and they started climbing out of the valley. The rain was pounding now, a relentless curtain of gray. Aspar was soaked to the bone, and Winna looked miserable. The storm grew more violent, and limbs and whole trees shattered by lightning or wind fell all around them.

If what Jesp told him was true—and if the years hadn't dimmed his own memory too much—the ridge ought to be stony, full of caves and shelters. Even a small overhang would be welcome.

It was with some relief that he found the rocky back of the ridge. Jesp might have told him honest, then, which was always a pleasant surprise. He had loved the old witch, after all, and after her fashion she had loved him.

They followed along the ridge, as overhead the sky went one shade of storm gray to the next darker. Night was falling, and still the tempest gathered strength.

His reckoning was good, though. While there was still just enough light to see, he found a jutting ledge that overhung a shelter comfortably large for the two travelers and their mounts.

"Thank the saints," Winna said. "I don't think I could have taken another moment of that."

She looked pale and chill. It wasn't so cold outside, but it was cooler than a human body, and rain washed away all warmth. Aspar unwrapped a tarp proofed against water with resin, and drew out a dry blanket.

"Take off your wet things and wrap in this," he said. "I'll be back."

"Where are you going?"

"For firewood."

"You think you'll find something in *that* that will burn?" Her teeth were chattering.

"Yah. Change."

"Well, turn your back."

"I'm going."

It took a while to find what he was looking for—pine lighter knot, dry wood in the rainshadow of the rocks, other stuff that would fume but eventually light. When he had a good armload, and a haversack full of tinder, he returned to the cave.

By then it was near dark. The worst of the thunder had moved off, but the wind was still snapping trees. Winna watched him silently, tightly wrapped in her blanket, as he nursed flame from the damp wood. He noticed she had unsaddled the horses and brushed them down.

"Thanks for taking care of Ogre and Angel," he said.

She nodded thoughtfully. "Will we lose the trail?" she asked.

He shook his head. "The thing about the greffyn's trail is it gets easier to follow the farther we fall behind it. Gives things more time to die."

"What about the men?"

He hesitated. "You noticed that, did you?"

"Asp, I'm no tracker, never even hunted, but I'm not a fool either. The horse tracks are plain enough, and I see there's more than one. And boots, now and then."

"Yah."

"You think someone else is following the greffyn?"

"No. I think someone is traveling with it." He reluctantly explained his theory about the bodies at the sedos, the ones clearly killed by men, adding Sir Symen's stories of similar murders, as well.

"Fifteen days it takes you to tell me this?" she said.

"I wasn't sure they were *with* it, at first. The paths cross, part, then come back together."

"Anything else you aren't telling me?"

"The Sefry think this is the work of the Briar King."

She paled further. "Do you believe that?" she asked.

"I didn't at first."

"But now you do?"

He hesitated an instant too long. "No."

"But that's just you, isn't it, Asp? That would make you gullible, wouldn't it, to admit they might be right."

"Maybe I should have told you this from the start," he replied. "Maybe then I could have talked you out of coming."

"No. There you're wrong." Her face was set bravely, but he noticed her chin was quivering. He suddenly had a nearly overpowering urge to go fold her into his arms, keep her warm, tell her he was sorry to be such a closemouthed bastard, tell her everything would be fine.

"How can you hate the Sefry so, Aspar? When they raised you? When you *loved* one."

That broke something cold in him, spilled something harsh. "That's none of your damned business, Winna," he rasped out.

When he saw the hurt on her face, he couldn't look at her anymore. He was almost relieved when she silently stood and moved to where the horses were. He thought at first she might be crying, but discounted that. She was tough, Winna, not weepy like some women. Nosy, yes, but not weepy.

He wished he hadn't snapped, but it was too late now, and apologizing wouldn't make it better, would it?

The sky was still leaden the next day, but the rain was gone, leaving only a fog in the valley below. As Aspar had expected, the lowlands were flooded and would take several days to drain. He decided to continue south along the ridge; the greffyn's path had been going roughly in that direction anyway.

They came across the telltale trail of dead and dying vegetation before midday. Any trace of the monster's human escorts was gone, but he had expected no less.

As usual, they followed alongside the poison trail, rather than on it.

"The Briar King," Winna said, for the first time breaking the frosty silence. "When I lived in Glangaf, we used to have a Briar King every year—you know, for the spring festival. He broke open the beer casks and led the dance. He gave us kids sugar candy and presents. When Father moved us to Colbaely to take my uncle's business, they didn't do that. The old women build wickermen and burn chickens up inside of them. They make the sign of evil if anyone says his name."

"Yah. Colbaely's closer to the forest, and its folk are mostly from the old stock. Not Virgenyans from over the mountains or steaders from the west. For the old folk, the Briar King is no laughing matter."

"What do the Sefry say about him?"

Aspar cleared his throat with some reluctance. "That he was once a prince among the old gods, the ones who made the world. That while they all died, he was cursed to live. That his only wish is to die, but the only way for him to die is to destroy the world itself. The Scaosen, who killed the old gods, managed to bind him to sleep, but every age or so he wakes . . ." He frowned. "There is a woman, I kann, and a thief who tried to steal from him who is now part of the curse. And a doomed knight of some sort. The usual silliness. I never paid much attention."

"I remember hearing that he wakes only when the land is ill," Winna said.

"In Dolham town they spell he wakes every year," Aspar grunted. "That he begins to toss and turn in autumn, cracks his eye in the dead of winter, then rolls over and falls asleep again by spring. All of the stories tell a different tale. It's why I don't trust 'em. If they were true, they ought to say the same thing."

"Not completely different," Winna said. "They all seem to think it's a very bad thing for him to be awake."

"Except for your beer-pouring fellow in Glangaf."

"Even he did some hard things. I remember one fellow who had been judged an adulterer by the town Comven. The Briar King dumped hog sceat on him, right in the middle of the town square, and then rooted up half his potato crop. Anything the Briar King did to you, you had to bear. After the spring festival, no one wanted to see him, because that usually meant he was coming to punish someone. And he had to do it, you see? It was part of the geas laid on him by being chosen."

"Odd town, Glangaf. After his year was up, what happened to the fellow who was made king?"

"Everyone pretended to forgive him. Usually they didn't."

"How did they decide who the king was each year?"

"The men drew lots. The loser had to be king."

"Where did the trail go?" Winna asked.

Aspar was asking himself the same question, and he didn't like the answer that was suggesting itself. They stood facing a cliff of the same crumbling yellow rock that had sheltered them the night before. Behind it the foothills rose precipitously. A stream drizzled from the top of it, pattering into a pool some twenty paces in diameter. A stream from the pool continued downhill to the Slaghish lowlands. To the south, the vague blue outline of the Mountains of the Hare reared up into untroubled clouds.

The trail led into the water.

"Don't touch it," Aspar warned.

"I know better," Winna replied, as Aspar dismounted and began an examination.

No tracks, no dead fish. Probably the storm had flushed the pool out pretty well. In fact, since by his calculations they were at least three days behind the beast, he doubted that any of this water had been here when the greffyn was; it was all down in the Slaghish now, on its way to the Warlock and eventually the Lier Sea.

Still, he wanted to be sure. He found a talus slope that let him ascend to the top of the cliff. There was no sign of the greffyn's passage on top.

He went back down.

"It's in the water?" Winna asked.

"It went into it. I don't think it came out." He started stringing his bow.

"You mean you think it drowned?"

"No."

"Then—" She started backing up.

"Look," he said, pointing.

On the surface of the pool, water-skaters wove ripple-webs, and small fish chased away from the edge.

"If it was still in there, these wouldn't be alive, I don't believe."

"Unless it can choose when to kill and when not to. In that case it might be hiding, waiting for you."

"I don't think so. I don't think the pool is that deep."

"What then?"

"Jesp—the Sefry woman who raised me. She used to talk about this place. She claimed there was a Halafolk *rewn* in these hills."

"A what?"

"The Halafolk live in hidden caves. They call 'em rewns."

"I thought that was just phay-story dust."

Aspar shook his head. "If I remember right, this one is named Rewn Aluth. I'm guessing Jesp was telling the truth."

"The Halafolk," Winna repeated. "Down there."

"Yah. I'll bet there's an entrance below the water, there. Typical."

"You—you've been in one of these rewns before?"

He nodded. "Most people think the Sefry and the Halafolk are two different people. They aren't. The caravaners are the wanderers, the restless ones. But they return home, now and then. When I was a boy, they took me with them." He sat on a rock and started unlacing his cuirass.

"What are you doing?" Winna asked.

"Those tracks we've been following—the ones with the greffyn— they could just as easily be Sefry as human."

"You mean you think the two are connected? That the Halafolk are responsible for the killings?"

"All of the dead I've seen have been human. We've been trying to clear the Sefry out of the royal forest for decades. Maybe they got tired of it."

"If that's so, you can't just go in there yourself. Even if the greffyn doesn't kill you, the Halafolk will. You need an army or something."

"If the king is to send an army, he needs reason. I don't have anything to give him but guesses, yet." His shirt was off. "Wait here," he said.

The pool was just deeper than he was tall, and clear enough that he had little problem finding what he was looking for—a rectangular opening in the rock face that led into the hill and slightly down.

He came back up.

"There's a tunnel," he said. "I'm going to see where it goes."

"Be careful."

"I will."

He unstrung and recased his bow and placed it back on Ogre's saddle along with his armor. He made sure he had his dirk and ax, took several deep, even breaths, then a deeper one, and dived.

The tunnel was roomy enough, and smoothed, but he had no trouble pushing himself along. What he did have trouble with was the darkness. Daylight faded quite quickly behind him, as his lungs started to ache. He remembered, too late, that the Halafolk were known for making false entrances into their havens. Traps designed to kill the unwary.

And it occurred to him that tunnel was too narrow to turn around in easily. Could he back out quickly enough to save his life?

No, he couldn't.

He swam harder. Colored spots danced before his eyes.

And then air. Damp and gritty-smelling, but air, and total darkness. He took a few moments to breathe before exploring further.

He was in another small pool, not much larger than the one he had entered. Aspar determined by feel that it was surrounded by a stonewalled chamber, rough and natural, which seemed to go on in one direction.

Good enough. He would return the way he had come, get all of his weapons and some torches, come back and find out where the passage went. And somehow convince Winna to stay behind. That was going to be the hard part.

He was just thinking that when he heard a splash and a gasp of breath behind him. He yanked out his dirk, holding it between himself and the unknown.

"Aspar? Aspar, are you there?"

"Winna—I told you not to follow me. And keep your voice down!"

"Aspar!" She did lower her voice, but he caught the frantic, panicky quality.

"Just after you went in—some men came up, on horses. Three, maybe four. They started shooting arrows at me. I didn't know what to do, I—"

He had been feeling for her the whole time. Now he had her, and at his touch she stumbled through the water into his arms, gripping him with more strength than he knew she had. In the dark, it was easy to grip her back.

"Three or four, you say? Could it have been more?"

"Maybe. It happened fast, Aspar. Ogre and Angel are still loose—"

"That's best. You did right, Winna. You think fast, girl!"

"What now, though? What if they follow me?"

"Were they human or Sefry?"

"I couldn't see their faces very well. They wore cowls."

"Probably Sefry, then."

"Saints! That means they'll come after us! We're already in their haven!"

"Probably. Well. We'd better not be here when they come through. Take my hand. Feel with your other, and with your feet. Try to stay quiet. We'll get through this, Winna. Trust me."

"I trust you, Aspar."

"Good."

Now, he thought, *if I only trusted myself. What a hell of a situation.*

CHAPTER TWO

D'EF

"WELL, THAT'S IT THEN," Henne said, turning his sun-browned face toward Stephen and flashing him a chip-toothed grin.

"What is it?" Stephen asked. He didn't see anything unusual—just the King's Road, the straight, pale-barked columns of river birch all around, the green riot of cane that marked the edge of the river Ef, off to their right.

Henne pointed to a clump of ferns, and after a moment of incomprehension, Stephen realized they hid a stone boundary marker. From that point on the King's Road, a track that might have been worn by deer wandered off through the forest.

"Past that is monastery grounds. The main road comes in from the south, but this'll get you there quicker."

"I don't see the monastery."

"Yah. It's around the base of the hill, I reckon another league. I'll ride on with you, if you wish."

Stephen bit his lip. He had become more cautious about being alone in the forest, lately.

"They'll probably feed you at the very least, for bringing me all this way," he told the hunter.

"They would at that," Henne said. "But then I'd have to stay and make pleasant with 'em for a while. Nothing wrong with that as it goes, but Whitraff village is three leagues downstream, and I fancy faren there in time for Evenbell. They have those pretty sort of people in Whitraff, the sort you won't find in a monastery, no offense to you, lad."

"Oh," Stephen said. "Ah, none taken. And I'll manage the last league by myself. Thank you much for your company on the journey."

"Nothing to it," Henne replied. "I'll probably see you from time to time. Sir Symen sends someone down here every now and then to buy cheese and wine, and to make sure all is well. I may even stop on my way back. Maybe you can put in a word for a good price."

"I'll certainly tell the fratrex of the hospitality I received from the folk of Tor Scath," Stephen promised.

"Good. *Farst-thu goth,* then," Henne said, turning his mount back toward the King's Road.

"Saints keep you," Stephen replied.

A few moments later, for the first time since his kidnapping, Stephen found himself alone. To his surprise it felt good. He sat his horse for a moment, savoring the stillness of the forest. He wondered, suddenly, what it might be like to be Aspar White, alone and at home in this great land. Free, not bound to anyone or anything, able to come and go like the wind.

Stephen had never known that. He likely never would. He'd never even thought about it, until this moment. His road was set; the youngest son, he had been his father's tithe to the church since birth.

And Stephen wanted to serve, especially to study. He really did.

But sometimes . . .

Frowning at his foolishness, he kneed the horse into motion.

The forest began to open up. Stumps became as common as trees, and then even more so. The clearings were thick with blackberry and red-ticking, wild plum, horseteeth, and huckleberry. The drone of insects rose and fell around him, and for the first time in days the hot sun fell on him unhindered. It cheered him, and he began whistling a hornpipe.

A crash and a curse in the underbrush interrupted him and brought a rush of blood to his head. For a terrible moment, he was again being dragged from his mount, bound and gagged by men who might kill him at any moment. For a few drums of his heart the memory was more vivid than reality.

He calmed when he saw an old man in the habit of a fratir of the Decmanusian order.

"Can I help you, there?" Stephen called.

"Eh?" The old fellow's bushy gray eyebrows rose skyward. "Who are you?"

"I'm Stephen Darige, of the Cape . . . Ah, Stephen Darige, at your service."

"Well. Good, good. Going to buy cheese, then?"

"No, actually, I—"

"Yes, yes. Our cheese is noted far and wide. They come all the way from Fenburh for it. Well, since you're going to d'Ef, the saints would smile kindly if you would help an old man."

"As I said, I am in your service. What seems to be the trouble?"

"There is no trouble where saints prevail, young man, only challenge." He grinned sheepishly. "But to be wise, it's best to know when a challenge ought to be shared. I've a bundle of firewood here that I've, er . . . , *bundled* a bit too large. I would be much grateful for some aid with it. It's here, caught up in these blackberry vines." To emphasize that, he kicked at something Stephen couldn't quite see.

"No trouble," Stephen replied, dismounting. "No trouble for a fratir. Are you a novice or a first initiate? I can't tell the habits apart."

"I am what you see," the fellow said, looking a bit crestfallen. He brightened suddenly. "I am Brother Pell."

"From Hornladh?"

"Yes, yes. Of course." He suddenly looked suspicious. "How would you know?"

"You're named for Saint Queislas," Stephen said, a little smugly. "His name has many forms—Ceasel, here in Crotheny—but it's only in the rural parts of Hornladh where they call him Saint Pell."

"Not so. He is called the same in Tero Gallé."

"With respect, good brother, there he is known as Pelle."

"It's nearly the same."

"Quite so. But distinct, nonetheless."

Brother Pell blinked at him a few times, then shrugged. "Here is the firewood, then." He smiled vaguely.

Stephen looked down. The bundle was huge. It probably weighed more than the old man did.

"It's a good thing I came along, then," Stephen said. "How far is the monastery?"

"Half a league. The saints dispose. You'll give me a hand?"

"Rest a moment, Brother. I'll get this."

"Many thanks, young sir, so knowledgeable about the names of saints."

"It's no trouble," Stephen said, heaving at the heavy cords that bound the sticks. With a great deal of tugging, pulling, and lifting, he managed to get it onto his back. It was amazingly heavy and unwieldy. His knees were almost shaking. Half a league! He'd be lucky to make it as far as his horse. Let the beast drag it.

But when he started laying the bundle down behind the horse, the old man said, "What are you doing, young sir?"

"I'm going to harness my mount to your firewood."

"No, no, Master Darige. That won't do. Saint Decmanus, the patron of our sanctuary, is quite clear on that point. Limbs must be gathered with limbs and carried with limbs. We may not bring the wood back with the aid of your horse."

"Oh." Stephen shifted the weight on his back a bit. He had never heard that. "Well then, could you take her reins?"

"Assuredly, Master Darige."

They continued on down the path, Stephen grunting beneath the load, Brother Pell whistling a slip-reel.

The forest ended soon after that, and from his hunched position, Stephen had a good view of green grass and cowcakes. When he troubled his head to lift itself, he saw pleasant pastures cropped by slow-moving rust-and-white cattle.

"The source of our vaunted cheese, yes," Brother Pell said. "Good stock these, but the secret is the grass. Dew-drenched—you've never smelled anything sweeter. Almost you'd rather eat the grass, eh!" The brother waved at a pair of cowherds, and they waved back from their shaded resting spot near a willow-bordered creek.

"Nice bream in that brooh," Brother Pell remarked. "A good place to meditate." He chuckled. "Bream in the brooh. Almost a verse, that."

"I think I need to meditate *now*," Stephen said through gritted teeth. The shaded stream looked a paradise.

"Oh, it's not so much further," Brother Pell assured him. "Look, we're coming up on the orchard."

Stephen was beginning another treatise.

My Travels with the Damned, Part the Second: The odd affair of the monk with the brain of a cow.

If at first this human-seeming creature appears intelligent, the illusion quickly vanishes when it attempts conversation . . .

As Stephen composed, he staggered through long, beautiful rows of sweet spring apple blossoms, a kingdom of butterflies and bees. His legs begged him for rest, for just a moment leaned back against one of those perfumed trunks. He thought of apples, of crunching into one, and the juice flowing down his chin. Of cold cider wetting his parchment-dry throat.

The language of his treatise became harsher.

"See here, how much further is it, Brother?"

"No distance to speak of. Tell me, Master Stephen. How is it you know such lore about the names of saints?"

"I went to the college at Ralegh. I've come here to fill the novice position in the scriftorium."

"Saint Lujé! You're the lad who was coming from Virgenya! We had lost hope! Three searches went out and found no sign of you."

"I was kidnapped," Stephen said, between deep gasps. "Holter saved me. Took me . . . Tor Scath."

"Your patron must have been watching you. But—why did you tell me you were come here to buy cheese?"

Stephen managed to lift his eye enough to stare at the monk.

. . . any thought that enters its head flits about within the hollow like an aimless insect, causing endless perplexion . . .

"I didn't," Stephen said, exasperated. "I—"

"There, there. I'm sure your adventures have made you cautious. But you're safe now—you're with us. And see, that's where we live."

He pointed, but all Stephen could see was the ground. Until he raised his head, further, further. The path wound up the steep flanks of a conical hill, and there, perched on the very top of it, stood the walls and towers of the monastery d'Ef.

"Come on!" Brother Pell said. "Step lively, and we may be in time for the praicersnu. I think it's ham and cherries, today."

Stephen had reached the end of his strength, however.

"I'll rest before climbing that," he said, perhaps a little sharply.

"Oh, lad—no! You can't do that. You've set your foot on holy soil. Remember your Saint Decmanus! *The burden is a blessing, on the road of the righteous. Do not set it aside until journey's end, where it will be lifted from you.*"

"I'm not certain he meant a literal burden," Stephen protested.

"By the saints, you aren't one of *those*, are you? Endlessly making excuses that the saints never really said what they said, or if they said it, did not mean it? That won't go well, here. Besides, you're in full sight of our reverend fratrex, and you should make a good impression on him."

"You really think the *fratrex* is watching?"

"No doubt. I wouldn't chance it if I were you."

"I would think a fratrex would have better things to do than gaze out a window all day," Stephen complained.

"Come on, boy-o."

With yet another sigh of resignation, Stephen started up the path.

He folded at the very gates of d'Ef, to the grins and chuckles of several men in habit coming back from the fields.

"Brother Lewes," Brother Pell said to a hulking sandy-haired fellow, "could you take our new brother's burden?"

The monk nodded, came forward, and lifted the bundle as if it was a pile of twigs.

"Come around the side," Brother Pell said. "I've a feeling you can use some water."

"I'd be very thankful," Stephen said.

Without the crushing weight of the firewood, Stephen had a better look at the monastery. It was built in the high style of the early de Loy period, when regents from Liery sat upon the throne in Eslen and brought architects from Safnia and Vitellio to marry their talents with the local craftsmen. Here the result was exuberant, strong, and practical, constructed of a pale rose granite. The chapel was marked by a double arched bell tower above a long, narrow, steepled nave. The doors were set in high arches. Two wings extended from the center of the chapel, traveled some thirty yards, then took right-angle turns back toward Stephen, terminating in smaller versions of the chapel doors. In the two three-sided yards thus enclosed were herb gardens, small vineyards, chickens, outdoor hearths, a few lazy dogs, and a number of monks working at various tasks.

Brother Pell led him into the yard on the right, through an open arch in that wing, and Stephen saw that the back of the structure mirrored the front. This yard, however, was more serene, planted with rose gardens and adorned by statues and shrines to various saints. Against the chapel wall was built an arbor, covered in grapevines, and beneath were wooden benches and boards for dining. Brother Pell motioned Stephen to a bench. The board was set with a pitcher, two mazers, and several plates of food.

"Sit, sit," Brother Pell said. He took up the stoneware pitcher and poured them each a mazer of water. It was cold and clean-tasting, and it felt like the laugh of an angel going down his throat. Stephen finished it greedily, then poured himself another.

Brother Pell had turned his attention to the cloth-covered plates. "What have we?" he wondered, lifting the linen.

The answer set Stephen's mouth watering. Crusty bread, a round of soft, pungent cheese, slices of brick-red ham so salty he could already taste it on his tongue, and yellow and red spackled cherries.

"May I?" Stephen asked.

"The bread only," Brother Pell replied. "Novices are not allowed meat, cheese, or fruit their first month here."

"Not—" He closed his mouth. He had heard about this sort of thing. He should have been prepared for it.

Brother Pell laughed gently and clapped his hands thrice. "My apologies, yes? That was me having fun with you. Please, eat of anything before you. There is no hardship concerning food here, save on fast days or when contemplation is assigned. Eat frugally, but well. That's our motto, here."

"Then—"

"Tuck in," Pell said.

Stephen did. He forced himself to eat slowly, but it was difficult. His stomach wanted it all, immediately.

"What brought you here, Brother Darige?" Brother Pell asked.

"To the church or to d'Ef?"

"D'Ef. I heard you requested this monastery, specifically."

"I did indeed. For its scriftorium. There is only one more comprehensive—the one in the sacarasio of the Caillo Vallaimo in z'Irbina."

"Oh, yes. Your interest in names and such. But why not there, then? Why d'Ef?"

"The Caillo Vallaimo has more scrifti. D'Ef has better ones, at least by my interests."

"How so?"

"D'Ef has the best collection of texts from the early days of the Hegemony in this region."

"And why does that excite you?"

"It's the chronicle of the spread of the faith, its battles with heresy and black warlockery. I am also much interested in the early languages of these regions, spoken before Vitellian was imposed."

"I see. Then you are conversant with Allotersian dialects and script?"

Stephen nodded excitedly. "It was my major course of study."

"And Vadhiian?"

"That's more difficult. There are only three lines written in that tongue, though it's much like Old Plath, from what I can see. I—"

"We have ten scrifti in Vadhiian here. None are completely deciphered."

"What!" In his excitement, Stephen upset his mazer. It flew from the table and broke into pieces at the brother's feet.

"Oh!" Stephen said, as Brother Pell bent to gather the shards. "Oh, I'm sorry, Brother Pell. I was just so—"

"It's no matter, Brother Darige. You see?"

Stephen *did* see, and his mouth dropped wide. Brother Pell had gathered pieces, but what he set on the table was a whole mazer. A faint steam rose from it.

"You—" Stephen looked back and forth between the old man and the mended cup and felt his face pricked from within by a thousand needles.

"Y-you did a sacaum of mending. Only a—" The implications crystallized. "You must be the r-reverend fratrex," he stammered.

"Indeed, yes. You see? I *do* have better things to do than to stare out of a window all day." His thick brows lowered dangerously. "And now, we must consider what to do with such a prideful young man. Indeed, we must."

CHAPTER THREE

RUMORS OF WAR

"WE ARE NOT AT WAR WITH YOU," The archgreft Valamhar af Aradal explained to William II and his court, stroking his yellow mustache. "Indeed, Hansa is not at war with anyone."

William counted slowly to seven, a trick his father had taught him.

A king should not answer too quickly. A king should appear calm.

The old man had been full of advice, most of which, William had discovered later, came from a book written centuries ago by the prime minister of Ter Eslief—a country that no longer even existed.

He shifted on the simple throne of white Hadam ash and gazed around the lesser throne chamber. It was "lesser" only in that it wasn't as ornate as the room where coronations and high court were held. In size, it was just as grand, its ceiling rising high in a series of vaults, its ruddy marble floor expansive enough to make even a fat, haughty fool like Aradal look small. Which was quite the point.

Aradal's guards stood well behind him, armored but unweaponed, wearing garish black-and-sanguine surcoats. Ten Craftsmen more than doubled their four. On William's right hand stood Praifec Marché Hespero, in somber black robes and square hat. On his left, where a prime minister ought to stand, stood Robert, clad in bright yellow and green velvets. The only other persons in the room were Baron Sir Fail de Liery, in his dun-colored surcoat, and his young charge Neil MeqVren.

Seven.

And now he could speak mildly, rather than in a burst of fury. "Those weren't Hanzish troops on those Hanzish ships that sacked four towns in the Sorrow Isles? That seems dangerously close to war, so far as I am concerned."

"The war," Aradal said, "if you can call this sort of minor skirmishing that, is between the Sorrows and Saltmark. Saltmark, I'm sure you know, is a longtime ally of Hansa. They asked for our help, and we gave them what we could spare; our ships and troops are under their command. The Sorrows, after all, were the aggressors. And may I further point out, Your Majesty, that the Sorrow Isles are not part of the Crothanic empire."

William leaned his elbow on the armrest of his throne and propped his chin on his fist, regarding the Hanzish ambassador. Aradal had a fat, pink face above a corpulent body overdressed in a black sealskin doublet trimmed in martin and red kidskin buskins glittering with diamonds— hardly a sterling example of Hanzish manhood. Yet that was deceptive, as William knew from bitter experience. The man was as clever as a raven.

"The Sorrows are under our protection," William said, "as Saltmark is under yours, as well you know. What evidence have you that King Donech was the aggressor in this matter?"

Aradal smiled. "It began as a conflict over fishing grounds, Majesty. The west shoals are rich and, by treaty, neutral territory. In the last year, ten defenseless fishing ships from Saltmark have gone down to the draugs, sent there by Sorrovian privateers. Three more were sunk in Saltmark's own waters. Who could tolerate such a breach of treaty? And what sort of protector would Hansa be, to rest and watch while our ally faced the Sorrovian navy? A navy, I might add, equipped and supplemented by both Liery and Crothany."

"I asked for evidence, not sailor's stories," William exploded, forgetting to count this time. "What evidence have I that any of Saltmark's ships were ever sunk? And if they were, that they were sunk by any ship from the Sorrows?"

Aradal fiddled with his mustache. Were his lips moving? Was *he* counting? Damned book.

"The evidence can be presented," the ambassador finally said. "We have witnesses in plenty. But the real proof is that Your Majesty has doubled the number of his ships in the Sorrows."

"As you've more than doubled your own in Saltmark."

"Ah, yes, but it appears you sent *your* ships before we sent ours," Aradal replied. "Doesn't that suggest Your Majesty was well aware of a conflict developing between the Sorrows and our protectorate? And before you would take such action, would you not be aware of the cause of the conflict?"

William kept his face impassive. He'd moved the ships in secret, at night, to hidden harbors. How had Hansa learned of it?

"What are you saying?" he asked. "That *we* sank your fishing ships?"

"No, Sire. Only that you knew the Sorrows were due a just revenge. That the Sorrows are like your children, and even when they go astray you would protect them." His eyes hardened. "That such would be a mistake, just as it would be a mistake to commit a single knight, soldier, or sea captain from the army of Crotheny to join in this conflict."

"Is that a threat?"

"It is a simple statement. If you go to war with Saltmark, you must go to war with Hansa. And that, Majesty, would benefit no one."

Sir Fail de Liery, up until now sitting quietly, suddenly pounced up from his bench.

"You *fop*! Do you think Liery will stand by while you conquer our cousins on this ridiculous pretext?"

"If Liery joins with the Sorrows, we will have no choice but to assume that we are at war with you," the ambassador replied.

"And, no doubt," William said softly, waving de Liery back to his seat, "you will counsel me to not join with Liery? And when both the Sorrows and Liery are in your hands, and some excuse allows you to turn your attention to Andemeur, you will still insist that it isn't my affair? What, then, when you've camped on the Sleeve? Or in my own sitting room?"

"That is not the situation we are discussing, Majesty," Aradal said smoothly. "When Saltmark has a new treaty with the Sorrows, this sad little affair will be at an end. We have had thirty years of peace, Majesty. Do not risk that, I beg you."

"I'll show you risk, you damned popinjay—" Fail began, but William cut him off.

"This is our court, Sir Fail. We will consider what Liery has to say, but later. Lord Aradal is here to treat with Crotheny."

The old knight glared but took his seat. William sat back, then glanced to Marché Hespero.

"Praifec, do you have anything to add to this . . . discussion?"

Hespero pursed his lips, pausing a few breaths before speaking.

"I am grieved," he said, "that the church was not entrusted with our traditional role as peacekeepers. I fail to understand why I've had no word from my counterpart in Hansa, though I'm certain any delay was unintentional. Nevertheless, it seems that the church is consulted on fewer decisions of note with each passing day, and that is, as I said, a grievous thing."

His black-eyed gaze wandered over each man in the room. He clasped his hands behind his back.

"The church Senaz and His Holiness the Fratrex Prismo have been quite outspoken about their desire for peace, particularly between Hansa and Crotheny. War between them could lay waste the world. I urge both of you to set aside any further hostilities until I've had a chance to speak with Praifec Topan and to consult with the Senaz."

Neil watched the Hanzish ambassador as he left the chamber. He didn't like the man's smile.

"You see what I mean?" Fail grunted. "We've been fighting a slow war with Hansa for years. Your father was a casualty of it. But when it comes here, it's suddenly all talk of fishing rights and who should have been consulted."

"You disapprove of our governance, Sir Fail?" William asked mildly.

"I disapprove of catfooting around what all of us know," Sir Fail replied. "But I think Your Majesty was forceful, today. Still, what does it mean? That's what I want to know. Will you help us drive them from the Sorrows?"

"I would rather they retired," William replied. "And I will certainly wait until the praifec has made his inquiries."

"You'd rather they retired? As well await a she-wolf to suckle a fawn!"

"Enough, Sir Fail. We will discuss this matter at length, I assure you. I did not send for you so that we might argue today."

"Why then?"

"Two reasons. The one, so you would hear Ambassador Aradal and know, from his own lips, what he told me and what I said to him, so you can take it back to Liery when you go. The second—I wanted to see your young apprentice. It's been ten days since he saved my queen's life, and I have not properly thanked him."

Neil dropped to his knee. "Your Majesty, I require no thanks."

"I think you do, especially after the beating you took at the hands of my Craftsmen. You understand, of course, that they did not at first understand why you attacked Sir Argom."

Neil glanced briefly at Vargus Farre, one of the knights who stood in the room. He owed Vargus a cracked rib.

"I understand, Your Majesty. Had I been in their place, and known only what they knew, I would have done the same."

William leaned forward intently. "How *did* you know? That Argom was attacking the queen?"

"I didn't, at first. I thought he had seen some danger to her and was rushing to intercept it. But there was no one threatening the queen, and Sir Argom was preparing the reaper—that's what we call a low, flat stroke of the blade. It's for dealing with unarmed rabble, and well-bred knights do not care for it. If the queen were threatened by someone nearby her, he wouldn't have dared used *that* stroke. The chance of hurting her in the bargain would be too great. So I reckoned that he wasn't truly a Craftsman, rather some pretender who had donned the livery."

"All that, and in only a few heartbeats."

"He's very quick about such things," Sir Fail put in.

William leaned back on his throne. "Here is my problem, Neil, son of Fren. There was a day when your reward for saving the queen of Crotheny might well have been a small barony. Unfortunately, with things as they are, I shall require the good will of all my nobles, and to be frank, I cannot afford to anger any of them by giving lands to a man of mean birth."

"I understand, Majesty," Neil said. He had been preparing for this, but it still hurt an amazing amount. Much more so than the beating.

"Understand? *I* don't understand!" Fail bellowed.

"Come, Sir Fail," Robert, the king's brother, said. "I know you are fond of theatrics, but allow the king to finish, will you?"

William himself remained unperturbed. His lips seemed to be moving slightly. Was he praying?

"On the other hand, we were all greatly impressed by you. My wife in particular, as might be expected. You are from her homeland, you have Sir Fail's trust and good word, which means oceans in itself, and you proved better at keeping her from harm than her own bodyguard. Indeed, since we do not yet know why such a seemingly loyal knight as the late Sir Argom would so violently go renegade, all of our Craftsmen are suspect.

"And so here is what we will do. We will give you the rose, and you will become the captain of the queen's personal guard, which will henceforth be named the Lier Guard. Like the Craftsmen, you must renounce your lands and possessions. Since you have none to renounce, the matter is already settled. This will make the queen happy, it will make me happy, and will only slightly annoy my more extreme nobles.

"The question is, will it make you happy?"

"Your Majesty?" Neil's head seemed full of a white-hot light.

"Come here, and kneel."

Dumbly, Neil did so.

"Praifec, do you bless this young man to be a knight in my service?"

"I do," the cleric said, "and bless him to the service of the saints. By Saint Michael, Saint Mamres, Saint Anne, and Saint Nod."

"Very well." William drew his broadsword, and two of the Craftsmen brought a large wooden block.

"Place your right hand on the block."

Neil put his palm on the wood, noticing as he did so the deep cuts there.

William lowered his sword until the edge was resting on the bare flesh of Neil's wrist.

"Do you swear yourself to the kingdom of Crotheny?"

"I do, Your Majesty."

"And to the protection of its king and castle?"

"I do."

"Most especially, and above all, to the protection of the queen, Muriele Dare née de Liery?"

"I do, Majesty."

"Do you swear yourself to obedience and to poverty?"

"I do, Sire."

"Saint Nod gave his hand in sacrifice, so his people might live. Will you do the same?"

"My hand, my head, my life," Neil answered. "It is all the same to me."

William nodded and pulled the sword quickly along Neil's flesh. Blood started; Neil did not wince.

"Keep your hand for now, Sir Neil," the king told him. "You will have need of it."

A servant approached with a pillow. On it lay a red rose.

"You may add the rose to your standard, as ornament to your armor, sword, and shield. Rise up."

Neil did so. His knees were trembling, but his heart was a war drum, loud, fierce, and proud.

He almost didn't notice when Sir Fail came up and clapped him on the arm.

"That was well done, son. Shall we find a bandage for your wrist?"

"To keep the blood from the floor," Neil murmured. "But I shall not wrap it. Let it bleed as it wants. Am I really a knight?"

Sir Fail laughed. "You are indeed," he said, "and in deed."

A cough from behind summoned their attention. Neil turned to see Vargus Farre towering over him.

"Sir Neil," Vargus said, bending slightly at the waist. "Let me be the first of the Craftsmen to congratulate you. You are deserving. When we were asleep, you were awake."

Neil returned the bow. "Thank you, Sir Vargus. I much appreciate it." From the corner of his eye, Neil saw Sir James Cathmayl approaching.

"So it really *is* Sir Bumpkin now," he said. His voice sounded a bit forced.

"By Lier, man!" Fail snapped. "What cause have you to insult my charge? I'll have you on the field, for this."

Sir James shrugged. "That's fine, sir. But I've a date with your charge first. He swore that when he took the rose, he would put on spurs and kill me."

"And I am your charge no longer, Sir Fail," Neil reminded him. "I can fight my own battles."

"James, stop this nonsense," Vargus snapped. "The lad—er, Sir Neil doesn't know you're joking. He's sworn now to protect the queen; would you put your pride against that? You're a Craftsman! The household guards do not fight in their own ranks."

"It was his challenge," Sir James said. "If he wishes to withdraw it, I would not be opposed."

"I do withdraw it, if you will withdraw your insults, sir," Neil replied.

For a long, icy moment, Sir James regarded him. "Some insults come from haste and poor judgment," he said at last. "Some come from knowledge and consideration. Mine were spurious, and I apologize. Still, let me state my position. I remain disapproving of your promotion. Knighthood should be reserved for the gentle of birth. But my king is spoken, and my queen has a protector, and I find that I am unable to lay the blame at your feet—Sir Neil."

He made a face. "Sir Neil. It gripes my tongue to say that. But I shall." He looked levelly at Neil. "Do we still have cause to fight, sir?"

"No, Sir James, we do not. And I'm glad. My duty is to the queen now, and it would be frivolous to engage in combat that would lessen the royal guard by one—however the contest went—especially when nothing more important than my own honor is at stake. You've been truthful in stating your objections, and I find no fault in you."

Sir James gave a small, stiff bow. "Very well," he said. "Another time, then."

As he left, Vargus winked at Neil. "You'll be fast friends in no time," he said. "And now, if you would care, I'll show you where our armory and provisions are. Whilst you're a guard of one, you shall need to share ours, I think."

"That is very kind of you, Sir Vargus. Very kind indeed."

°　°　°

"Well, that was awfully touching, brother," Robert said, once they had removed themselves to William's outer chambers.

"I think it will work well."

Robert shrugged. "Some will be incensed, I'm sure. But you keep Fail's good will—the old fart—and anyway, the boy is very popular with the common folk. Never hurts to let 'em know one of their own can occasionally make good, does it? Any more than it hurts to remind the nobles who their king is."

"Not at all," William agreed. He waved the whole matter away with the back of his hand. "This situation with Hansa, though," he said. "Do you think the praifec will take our side?"

"Why should he?" Robert said, holding his nails up for his own inspection. "You've spent the last five years making it infinitely clear that you want no interference by him and his church in domestic affairs. Now you want him to commit himself to your cause? No, he will wait, and make you sweat. Withhold his endorsement until you *really* need it. Then he'll ask you for something. Perhaps he'll ask you to name a male heir."

"You'd like that, wouldn't you? Because I would have to name you."

"Nonsense. That would suit the praifec no better than having you remain on the throne. But your son could rule, with the proper guidance—if you know what I mean."

"Ah. Holy guidance, you're suggesting."

"Indeed."

"How do you know Hespero will ask for this?"

"I don't. It's just a guess. But I believe Hespero always imagined that one day he would rule this empire in all but name. You've spoiled his plans by naming your daughters as heirs. Fastia is too strong willed, and would besides have her husband to come between. Elseny, while a little less forceful, will soon be enspoused, as well. Anne—well, who can tell Anne what to do?"

William furrowed his brow. "Enough of Hespero and what he wants. Have you learned anything of the attempt on my wife? My spies tell me nothing."

"There is talk of shinecraft and encrotacnia," Robert replied. "Sir Argom served us loyally for ten years. I can trace no allegiance to our enemies, nor can I imagine anything for which he might have been blackmailed or bribed." He shrugged. "Then again, blackmail works only *because* a certain thing is secret. No, I cannot tell you any more than you already know, brother."

"Well." William ticked his fingers against the wall. "It tasks me. Why Muriele? If a Craftsman can be turned, then he could as easily have killed me. Or you. Or one of the children."

"A grieving king can be of more use than a dead one. Or perhaps it was Liery they were striking at, not you."

"*Who* was striking at?"

Robert laughed. "Brother! We cannot be *that* different. We don't know *how* Sir Argom was turned from protector to assassin, nor precisely *why*, but we assuredly know *who* accomplished it."

"Hansa?"

"They mean to take your throne, that much must be clear, even to you. They'll nibble at first, but soon their appetite will lead to larger bites. Small wars on our frontiers, assassinations and sabotage here in the capital. It's the way Marcomir *thinks*."

"How are you so certain?"

"Because I understand him. Marcomir is a practical man, undeterred by notions of honor or scruple. He is an able ruler, and a most dangerous enemy."

"He is, in other words, like you."

"Precisely, brother."

"Then what would *you* have me do?"

"Have Marcomir killed," Robert said promptly. "As soon as possible. His heir, Berimund, may not prove as able."

"Have Marcomir killed," William repeated incredulously.

Robert rolled his eyes. "For the teats of Saint Anne, brother! He tried to have your *wife* murdered. At your daughter's *birthday* party."

"I do not *know* that," William said.

"Of course you do. And even if I'm wrong, how can a dead Marcomir be *bad* for Crotheny?"

"If an assassin should be traced to me, that will bring war for certain."

"Yes. It will bring war with Berimund, a war we can *win*. Brother, in this room, let's you and I be honest. Hansa is too strong. If they are willing to pay a high enough cost, they will take Tier Eslen, your crown, and our heads. Marcomir is willing to pay that cost, and has the strength of will to force it upon his nobles. Berimund does not have that potence."

"If we have the support of the church—"

"If. Maybe. How long has it been since holy troops have been used in war between two kingdoms of the church? They are not heretics in Hansa, at least not to appearances. Brother, nip this candle at the quick. Have Marcomir killed."

"No."

"William—"

"No. That is an end of it. Not because I am prudish, as I'm sure you suspect, but because I am prudent. Marcomir is well protected, and not just by swords. Who could we send who would certainly succeed?"

"Lady Erren."

"She serves my wife, and would never be parted from her."

"Another coven-trained, then."

"Again, the risk. The coven-trained report to the church."

"I could find you one who would not."

"Stop this, Robert. If you wish to help, think of ways to win Hespero, instead of ways to anger the church toward us."

Robert sighed. "As you say. But at least do this—send Muriele and your children to Cal Azroth."

"Cal Azroth? Why?"

"They'll be easier to protect there. It's our most perfect fastness, without a city full of murderers and witches on its doorstep. No one can come or go there without being seen. Our sister Elyoner controls the countryside, and of all of us she is the one who has no political aspirations whatsoever.

"There is much moving here, William, much that even I cannot discern. Someone has chosen to strike at you through your family. You will make better decisions if they are safe."

William nodded reluctantly. "I will consider it."

"Good."

"Robert?"

"Yes, brother dear?"

"Don't be upset with Lesbeth because she did not come to you first for permission."

"She did not ask me at all," Robert said, in a strange, small voice.

"She feared you would not approve it."

"Of course. Why should I give my twin sister in marriage to that Safnian oaf? After the slight he paid me?"

"You see?"

Robert exhaled. "No. If she had asked, I would have protested, cajoled, extorted, but had she held firm, I would have assented." He looked up at William, and like his voice, his eyes had gone strange. "None of you think the least good resides in me," he murmured. "None of you can think even one generous thought on my behalf. I thought *she* of all people—" He broke off, his face pale. "Are we done, brother?"

"Yes. Except to say that I am pleased with your performance as my sinescalh. Lord Hynde has gone too long without a successor. I should like to appoint you prime minister."

"Do as you please," Robert said. "But mark—I know the difference between words and thoughts."

With that he left the room, glancing neither to the left nor to the right.

Anne looked up from where she knelt in the penitent box in time to see Praifec Hespero notice her and raise his eyebrows. Anne attempted a small smile.

"Who is this stranger?" the clergyman asked gently.

Anne dropped her head. "I suppose it's been some time since I came here," she murmured.

"Without an escort, yes. I can only assume something is troubling you deeply. Or did you merely come for lustration?"

Anne shook her head. "I didn't know who else to talk to, who could tell me if I—if I'm losing my sanity or not."

Hespero nodded. "I'm always here, child." He settled onto a stool, dipped his fingers in the dish of fragrant oil and touched a bit to her forehead. *"Piesum deicus, tacez,"* he murmured. Then he leaned forward, hands on his knees. "Now, what is it that troubles you?"

"I've been having dreams. Very strange dreams."

"Tell me."

"I dreamed I stood outside of a dark forest, a forest of thorns.

Around me were black roses, like those that grow in Liery. There was something terrible in the forest, watching me, and it started to come out, and then I woke."

She felt suddenly foolish, so attentively was Hespero listening to her nightmare. She almost told him about her disappearing rose, but held back. There was no need for Hespero to know about Roderick.

The praifec rubbed his jaw. "I take it you've had more than one troubling dream."

"The other wasn't a dream exactly. It happened at Elseny's party, at the same time as the attempt on my mother's life." She related the incident as best she could remember. Again, Hespero listened in silence. That silence stretched when she was done.

"You're certain you had not fainted?" Hespero finally asked. "Your maid found you, did she not, in an oblivious state?"

"Yes, Praifec."

"And when you thought you were lost in the maze, you were in a panic."

"But it *wasn't* the maze, Praifec. It was someplace else, and I had no shadow, and—"

"It may seem that way to you," Hespero said, in a calming voice. "This is not uncommon for girls your age. There are diverse vapors in the world, and in these first years of womanhood, you will be particularly susceptible to them. That is most likely what you suffered.

"It is remotely possible that you were the victim of shinecraft, and that would be much more serious. If it was witching, the things you were told were lies. Prophecy flows only from the saints, and only through the true church. To believe anything else is heresy."

"Then you don't think Crotheny is really in danger? Or my mother?"

"They are both in danger, my dear. An attempt was made on your mother's life. Rumors of war are on wing. But your father will deal with those dangers, with the help of the church. You aren't to worry your pretty head about this, Princess. It would be a needless brutality to yourself, and exactly what the enemies of this country would want." He held up a finger. "Wait a moment."

He vanished into a room behind the altar and returned a few moments later, carrying something small in his hand.

"This is a token of your namesake, Saint Anne. If you suffer from shinecrafting, it should protect you." He handed the object to her. It was a small wooden tablet, carved with the saint's name.

"It was made from a tree that grows on the sedos of Saint Anne, in Andemeur," he said. "You may wear it on a necklace, or keep it in a pocket in your dress."

Anne bowed. "Thank you, Praifec. I—" She broke off, unsure. She wanted to tell him about the tomb of Genya Dare, of the curse she had made there. But if he knew about that, he might see things differently. As she struggled to find the words, she changed her mind. Virgenya was her secret, hers and Austra's. She couldn't betray it, even to the most holy man in the kingdom.

Besides, he was doubtless right. Her dreams were nothing more than vapor phantasms, or witchwork.

"There was something else?" he asked mildly.

"No, Praifec. I'm sure you're right. About everything."

"Trust me. But if you have more bouts like this, let me know. As I said, I'm always here. This kingdom and the family that rules it are my holy trust, even if your father doesn't always see it that way."

Anne smiled, thanked him again, and left with a lighter heart.

CHAPTER FOUR

REWN ALUTH

THE PASSAGEWAY BECAME STAIRS, carved in the living rock. Aspar counted steps as they went.

After counting thirty, he heard voices rising from below. Winna heard them, too, and her grip tightened on his hand. He glanced at her, reflexively, and realized he could just make out her face.

Winna noticed the faint illumination, too. "It must be a way out!" she whispered hopefully as the silvery light grew brighter.

"Shh." Aspar looked up and saw the source of the light, moving languidly down the stairs. His hand went to his dirk, but then stopped.

"Witchlight," he said.

It was a pale sphere of luminescent vapor the size of a man's fist moving toward them.

"Is it dangerous?"

"No."

Winna reached to touch it, and her fingers passed into the glow.

"Saints!"

"Later," Aspar said. "Come on."

Thirty more steps brought them to the top of the curving stairs. For an instant the only sound was Winna's breathless gasp of wonderment and the distant plinking of water.

A thousand witchlights drifted among spires and columns of glassy stone, touching flashes of color here and there but only hinting at the vastness of the cavern that stretched out before them. Just beyond their feet, the ledge on which they stood dropped down to a vast obsidian mirror.

"It's beautiful," Winna breathed. "Is that . . . water? An underground lake?"

"Yah." Aspar had little time for wonder. He was peering into the gloom. If this ledge didn't go anywhere, he would make a stand and try to kill their pursuers one at a time as they came up the stairs. He might be able to do it, even if they had swords.

Odds were he couldn't.

But the ledge continued on and even widened to their left.

"This way," he said, tugging her hand.

Several of the witchlights began following them. He remembered how that had delighted him as a child, how he had named them as if they were pets. Now, however, he wished they would go away; clustered around, they would reveal Winna and him to their enemies.

Of course, that worked both ways. Their pursuers would soon acquire an entourage of helpful lights, too.

The path took them down, switchbacking along the cliffside. Aspar reckoned they descended ten yards before they came to a quay a few feet above the dark waters. There they had some good fortune, for two narrow boats were tied there. They got into one, and Aspar hulled the other with his ax.

As they rowed across the still water, Aspar noticed a clump of witchlights above, where the stairs debauched into the cavern. But the fickle illumination offered him only the occasional flitting silhouette. He couldn't tell how many they were.

Soon they were lost to sight, and there was only the water and a clean, wet, mineral smell.

"I never even dreamed of a place like this," Winna whispered. "How wonderful it is."

"I thought so, too, when I was little. But it closes in on you, after a while. The dark. Even among the Sefry not all can live with it. It's why they go out and brave the sun."

"Where are they? The Halafolk?"

"I don't know. I thought to see them by now."

Winna smiled. "You look funny, with those little lights following you around. Younger, like a boy."

He didn't have anything to say to that, so he just grunted. Then her face changed. "What's that?" she asked, pointing behind him.

He turned to see what she meant. A large, shadowy something loomed up out of the lake. An island, he figured, for the lake had seemed much larger from above.

"I'm guessing this is where we'll find the Halafolk," he murmured.

What they found was a city of the dead.

The houses were narrow and tall, almost whimsically so, making tight corridors of the streets that were beveled into the floor of the cave. The buildings themselves were built of carefully fitted stone, with high-pitched slate roofs designed to shed the constant dripping from above. On some, little fingers of stone had sprouted, growing toward the unseen ceiling of the cavern. Aspar had been told once that it was by this that the oldest dwellings could be known; stone did not grow quickly.

The houses were all quite empty. Aspar's and Winna's footsteps clattered like the echoes of a small army.

"Sir Symen said that all of the Sefry were leaving the forest, even the Halafolk," Aspar mused. "I didn't believe him. Why should they?"

"To leave all of this, they must have good reason."

"It's unimaginable," he murmured. He pointed to a shingle that hung above the door of one house. Silver inlaid in slate depicted a six-fingered hand, three of the fingers with little candle flames. "That's the standard of the house Sern. No one from that clan has gone aboveground for five generations, or so they say. Some of these houses I don't even know."

"Should we search the buildings?"

"Why? What we need is to find a way out."

"Do you think the greffyn is still here?"

"I don't know what to think. Let's keep going this way; I want to find the town center."

The island wasn't wide, but it was long. They crossed parks planted with pale fernlike trees and black rushes. Spidery bridges took them over canals where slender black gondolas still were moored, waiting for passengers that would never come.

In time they reached a broad plaza, and the largest building they had yet seen. It resembled a castle—or a parody of a castle, built for elegance rather than utility, with its spires of glassy stone and translucent domes glowing with natural luminescence.

"The palace?"

"It's where their prince would live and where their councils meet. If anyone is still here, that's where they'll be."

"If anyone is still here, do we really want to find them?"

Aspar nodded grimly. "Yah. We have to find out what has happened here."

"What about the men following us? Won't they come here, just as we did?"

"Yah." He considered for a moment. "Werlic, that's a good point. We'll stay in one of these other buildings by the square, and watch. With luck, there will be too few of them to search every building in town."

"Good. I'm tired. I'd like to rest."

Aspar chose an unremarkable four-story house with a good view of the plaza. The door was unlocked. Nine witchlights followed them in and up the spiral stair. They didn't stop until they reached the top floor.

It was a narrow bedroom the width of the house faced in mooncolored chalcedony, with a low sleeping couch and a larger, canopied bed. Crystal knobs on the bedposts glowed a faint white, so that even without the witchlights, there would be some illumination. Besides the staircase, a single arched doorway led to a small balcony facing away from the plaza. The view there was mostly darkness, of course, but in witchlight Aspar could just make out another four-story structure just across the way, and another balcony, a bit lower than the one on which he stood.

Back in the room, he dragged the couch over to a broad window that overlooked the plaza. He drew the heavy shades until only a crack remained to peer through. It wouldn't do for someone to notice that this upper story was illuminated.

"Keep watch here," he said. "I'll see if I can find something to eat."

"Don't be gone long."

"I won't."

The pantry was below street level, carved into the stone foundation of the island.

Most of the bread had gone to mold, which was just as well, but he found some salted fish, venison, wild boar, a wheel of yellow cheese, and several racks of wine.

He cut a hunk of cheese and a slab of the ham and tucked two bottles of wine under his arm. Then he returned to the top floor.

"Is it safe to eat?" Winna asked. "They warn against breaking bread with the Halafolk."

Aspar chuckled. "The cheese is from someplace in Holtmarh. The wine is from the Midenlands, and the meat was poached from the King's Forest. The only food they actually grow down here is hrew, a sort of nut that lives in the water. They make bread out of it. It tastes bad, but it's safe enough. If the lake has fish, they eat that, too." He nodded at the window. "Anything?"

"No. But I may have missed them." She looked up at Aspar, a very young expression on her face. "I'm not afraid," she said.

"You're a brave girl."

"No, I mean it. I ought to be afraid. I was, earlier, at the pool. I was even when I told you I was coming with you. Now—it's all gone out of me."

"It'll come back," Aspar said. "Take my word for it."

"I never thought of you as someone who could be afraid. As long as I can remember, you've always been there, Aspar. When I was a little girl, you would just appear, from out of the forest, like some ancient hero from the legends." She looked away.

"What you must think of me," she said.

Aspar poured her a mazer of wine, then one for himself. It was thick, a little bitter. He hadn't realized how thirsty he was.

"I've been afraid," he said.

"I know that, now," she replied.

He moved to the window, so he could see out. The square below was still and quiet. Winna stayed where she was, almost within touching distance.

"Where do you think they went? The Halafolk?"

Aspar shrugged. "The mountains, maybe. Across the eastern sea, for all I know." He took another drink. The wine was starting a small fire in his belly. "I was too rough last night," he murmured. "I didn't mean to grumble."

Her gaze fastened on his. "Well. You *do* know how to apologize," she said. "I would never have guessed that either, and no one will believe me if I speak of it."

"I'm not good at this," Aspar grunted.

"No, you're not. But I forgive you."

He took another drink of wine, and was searching for something to say, when Winna suddenly gasped.

"What's that?" Suddenly she was against him, gripping him, eyes wide.

"What? Do you hear something?"

Her face was inches from his, and smiling. "You really aren't good at this."

"That's not what I meant, Winna, I—" She felt good, in his arms, and he suddenly realized how long it had been since he *touched* anyone. Except for the kiss from a few weeks ago. The kiss.

He never decided to do it. He knew he didn't. But suddenly his face was against hers, his lips greedy on hers, and he felt stupid and awkward, like a boy with his first woman.

Their clothes came off, piece by piece, and fingers and lips traced the freshly exposed skin. Part of him sounded a little alarm; they had enemies outside.

Too much of him didn't care.

When they came together, and her ankles locked behind his knees, for a long, unblinking moment he looked into her eyes. What he saw there amazed him. She looked back, and laid her hand on his cheek.

Much later, as they lay tangled and sated, he stroked the skin over her ribs and wondered if he could believe what *he* was feeling.

He sat up to look out the window.

"Is the Sefry army out there yet?" Winna asked languidly.

"They might have marched around the square ten times, and I wouldn't know," he replied.

"I suppose that wasn't so smart just now."

He lifted his shoulders helplessly. "May have been the smartest thing I've done in years."

She chuckled and kissed him. "That was good. Now, don't say another word about it. You're sure to find some way to spoil it if you keep talking, and I want to be happy for a while."

"Very well." He looked back out the window.

"But talk about something, or I'll fall asleep."

"That's not a bad idea. I can keep watch."

"No, not yet. Who do you think they are? The men following us."

"From what you said, they were dressed like Sefry."

"Yah. I remembered something else. One of them had an eye patch."

"What?" He took her by the shoulders.

"Aspar! That hurts!"

"An eye patch! Which eye?"

"I don't know. Aspar, what's wrong with you? You know him?"

He dropped his hands away. "Maybe. I don't know."

"Saints! Aspar, your face—" She stopped. "This has to do with *her*, doesn't it?"

"Winna, I need to think."

"Think, then." He could hear the hurt in her voice, even through his anger.

"See?" he told her. "No matter what, I'll find a way to spoil it."

She got up and went over to the bed, wrapped herself in one of the sheets.

"I understand if you don't want to talk about her," she said. "But this man. He tried to kill *me*, Aspar."

"Come here," he said.

She hesitated a moment, then came into his arms.

"Her name was Qerla, my wife," he said softly. "She was of the Nere clan. We met—well, never mind. We were young, and we thought it didn't matter."

"What didn't matter?"

"That Human and Sefry can't make children together. That her clan would disown her, withdraw their protection. That we would be alone, just the two of us."

"It sounds romantic."

"It was, for a while. After that it was just hard. Harder on her than on me. I never really had a clan, just old mother Jesp. Qerla was the first person I ever really—who was ever *mine*, in any sense."

"You loved her."

"I loved her."

"And the man with the eye patch. He's the one who—" She stopped.

"He killed her," Aspar confirmed. "If it's the same man. He was an outlaw Sefry, a man named Fend. He was setting a trap for me, but he caught them instead."

"*Them?* I thought—"

"An old Sefry lover of hers, a Jasper clan man. A poet. Fend found them in bed and killed them there. And then I found him." He pursed his lips. "He put a sword through my belly, and I put a dirk in his eye. We both fell, and when I came around he was gone."

"She betrayed you."

"I think I must have betrayed her first, somehow," Aspar said.

"I doubt that," she whispered. "I doubt it much. Everyone gets weak. She got weak. It doesn't mean she didn't love you." When he didn't say anything, she took his hand. "You really think the man I saw was Fend?"

"I thought he was dead. But who knows? Maybe."

In his heart, there was no doubt. If his father's gods existed, this was just the sort of thing that would amuse them.

They didn't talk, for a while, and Winna drowsed against him. Looking at her face, he felt briefly guilty. She was so young! When Qerla had been alive, Winna hadn't even been born.

The guilt passed. In all of the important ways, Winna was older than he was.

One day she might realize that she had no interest in a scarred old holter. Until then he would just count himself lucky, and let it go at that.

And get her through this alive.

And kill Fend, if it was Fend. He couldn't imagine what the outlaw might have to do with Briar Kings and greffyns. But he would find out, and he would kill him, this time.

He was near drowsing himself when he heard the clatter of hooves on stone. He peered out the window and saw clumps of witchlights moving across the square. He jerked his head back in—for he had witchlights around his own head, of course. He thought he'd done it in time.

"Horses," he whispered. "They've found another way in."

"Maybe it's not the same bunch that tried to kill me."

"Maybe," he said dubiously.

From below he heard the high, shrill call of a horn, and the witchlights suddenly drifted out of the window, as if answering the call.

"Get dressed," he told Winna. "Fast."

CHAPTER FIVE

BROTHERHOOD

THE FRATREX MARCHED STEPHEN across the yard and through a small arched doorway. Stephen held his tongue, afraid that anything he might say at this point would simply dig a deeper grave for his self-respect. Instead, he tried to remember what he had heard about Decmanusian penance. What did it involve? Whippings? Confinement?

"Come, come, hurry up!" Fratrex Pell said. "Through here." He pointed to a very low doorway; the lintel was only as high as Stephen's waist. "Yes, yes—on your knees."

Stephen sank down contritely, crawling through the opening, steeling himself for whatever was to come. He said a small prayer and raised his head.

Then he uttered a loud gasp.

"We come to the saints on our knees," Fratrex Pell said, behind him. "And so we come to knowledge—humbly."

"It's wonderful," Stephen said. Tears stung his eyes. "It's like a hundred thousand presents, all waiting to be opened."

"Move through, son, that I may follow."

Stephen did so, mute with awe.

The scriftorium rose around him, a tower with walls of tomes, scrolls, tablets, parchment cases, maps. Nowhere could he see bare stone; the whole structure might have been held together by the insectile scaffolding of ladders that spindled up from the floor to the next level. There he saw no more than a narrow walkspace that ran around the base of yet another level of shelves and provided a footing for the ladders that climbed up to the third level. Four levels in all, then a dome set with crystal panes, so the sun's light fell in to illuminate it all.

Tables at ground level overflowed with scrifti, and studious monks remained absorbed in their studies and copywork as Stephen and the fratrex entered. Others worked at tables set precariously on balconies jutting at strange intervals up and down the wall. Ropes and pulleys were working everywhere, as monks lowered and raised baskets of manuscrifts from level to level or sent them hurtling horizontally across the room.

And the smell! Ink and vellum, paper and chalk and melted wax. Stephen realized he was beaming like a fool.

"Here is your punishment," Fratrex Pell said quietly.

"How do you mean?" Stephen asked. "The sight of this room brings me nothing but joy."

"Your sin was pride; you think you are knowledgeable, and indeed you are. But when you stand here, you must be reminded of how very much you do *not* know. Can never know. Be humble, Stephen. You will be a better man, and a better member of this order."

"Thank you, Reverend Fratrex. I'm so . . ." He shook his head. "So grateful. And eager! When may I begin? What should I do?"

"Today? Anything you want. Familiarize yourself with the scriftorium. Browse. Tomorrow we'll see how you are with Vadhiian. We have a pressing obligation to translate those texts; it's one of the reasons I pushed to have you appointed here."

"You mean you—"

"Go to it, son. I'll see you at vespers."

"Well. You must be the new fellow."

Stephen glanced up from the text he was hunched over and found a pleasant-faced man with cropped brown hair regarding him.

"Ah—yes, Brother." He carefully put the scrift aside and stood, finding himself a head shorter than the stranger. "My name is Stephen Darige."

"Desmond Spendlove."

"You're a Virgenyan!"

"Indeed I am," Spendlove replied.

"What part?"

"Just south of Quick, on the Nerih River."

"I know the place!" Stephen said. "We used to take the boat down to Cheter-by-Sea. We'd stop there in the little town—the one with the statue of the pig—"

"Wildeaston. Yes, that's just a furlong from where I grew up."

"Well. I'm pleased to meet you," Stephen told him.

"Finding your way around the scriftorium, are you?"

Stephen chuckled. "I haven't got very far. I ran across this right away. It's an original text of the *Amena Tirson*, a sort of geography of this region from—"

"—pre-Hegemonic times," Spendlove finished. "Yes, I'm quite familiar with the *Amena Tirson*. It was my project in the college at Pennwys."

"Really? Sorry, I've just got a lesson in humility, and here I am condescending to you."

"It's no matter. The old man got you with the wood-carrying trick, yes?"

"Trick?"

"No one can approach d'Ef without his knowledge. He greets most of the novices, in some similar fashion."

"Oh."

Spendlove gestured at the scrift. "But you were going to say something about the *Amena Tirson*," he reminded.

"Yes. This version is different from the ones I've seen."

"It's a little different. The chapter on trees goes on longer."

"That's not what I meant. There's a list of fane names and other locations I've never heard of, and talk of walking them."

"Well, there is the faneway here, the way of Saint Decmanus."

"Yes, of course. But these others—"

Desmond shrugged. "Are surely dead now, or so faint with the sainted presence as to be unwalkable."

"I know," Stephen replied. "It's just odd. There were murders—" He broke off. "Saints! How could I have forgotten that? I was just so overwhelmed, I mean, first carrying the wood, and then discovering he was the fratrex, and then all of *this*!"

"What are you going on about?" Desmond inquired mildly.

"There have been murders in the King's Forest."

"That's hardly new. The place is swarming with bandits."

"Yes, I know. But this is different, I think. Blood rituals on the old sedoi, and some sort of monster involved."

"Monster? Does this have to do with old Symen up at Tor Scath?"

"Yes, yes. That's where I heard about it."

"Then I have to warn you, the old knight is well known for his exaggerations. He sent a man down here a fortnight ago, to warn us of some evil in the forest. We set extra watches, just in case, and the fratrex made a report to the praifec in Eslen. Yet the search parties we sent out for you didn't find anything strange."

"Oh, I'd had my doubts about his story, too, but—" But Sir Symen had seen *something*. Of that Stephen was certain.

But the holter had gone to find the truth, and he hadn't wanted Stephen along. Whatever it was, Aspar White would surely kill it. Stephen would write a report for the fratrex, but there his obligations ceased. Then he could throw himself head-to-toe into his studies.

"Come on," Desmond said, clapping him on the shoulder. "It's just a bit before vespers and evening meal. Let's go for a walk. There are things about life at d'Ef that the fratrex wouldn't have told you."

Stephen glanced reluctantly at the *Amena Tirson*, then nodded. He recased the thin sheets of vellum in their cedar box and replaced it on the shelf.

"Ready!" he said.

Evening calm had settled outside. In the distance, cows lowed, the crickets had begun their nightly stridulations, and the frogs in the Ef lowlands warbled throaty tunes. The evening star was a jewel on velvet in the eastern sky, while the west was still a bed of fading embers. The forest was distant and green across acres of rolling pasture and vineyard. Stephen and Desmond stood upslope of the monastery, where soft candlelight was beginning to glow in windows.

"The faneway starts in the chapel," Desmond said, "and finishes out there. It takes about two days to walk."

"You've walked it, then?"

"Yes. You will, too, soon enough. You aren't a normal novice, from what I hear. The mysteries will be unfolded to you more quickly, I think."

"I hardly deserve it."

"No. You don't."

Something in Desmond's voice didn't sound right. Stephen looked at his companion and saw a hardness set on his face.

"There is an order to things," Desmond explained. "Or ought to be. I'm here to see that order is kept, do you understand?"

Stephen took a few steps back from the monk. "What do you mean?"

Desmond smiled. It wasn't a very comforting smile. Stephen backed up further, wondering if he should run. He backed right into another monk. It was Brother Lewes, the giant who had lifted the firewood like a willow wand. Stephen tried to jump away from him, but the monk grabbed him by the arm.

Stephen started to shout, but a meaty hand clamped over his mouth. It smelled like hay and cow manure.

"You're new," Desmond explained. "As I said, there are some things you ought to know. It starts with this: I don't care who you are, or who your family was. Here, you start over. Here, your life begins again. And here, I am your father, your brother, your best friend. I will help you through everything, but you have to trust me. You have to believe me.

"The fratrex thinks you're special. That means nothing to the rest of us. To us, you have to prove yourself. It won't matter what the fratrex thinks of you if you slip and hit your head on a rock, or fall on a pitchfork, or eat the wrong mushroom. It's only the rest of us that can keep you safe from things like that. Do you see what I'm saying?"

There were other monks gathered around now, at least ten of them. They had their cowls up, and Stephen couldn't see their faces. He was beyond panic; he knew he shouldn't struggle, but he couldn't stop. Since being kidnapped, the very thought of being restrained was intolerable. Now, caught in this steel grip, it was reality, and still intolerable. He could barely think, he was so frightened and angry. Tears started in his eyes.

"Brother, release Brother Stephen's tongue, so he can tell me he understands."

The hand came away.

"I understand! Of course I understand! Whatever you say."

Desmond nodded approvingly. "That sounded sincere. But I don't know you, Brother Stephen. I can't be sure. And you can't be sure of me. So let's have a lesson, shall we?" He jerked his head, and the other monks converged. Stephen tried to scream, but a cloth was forced into his mouth. His arms were pulled up straight and then his shift was yanked off. He was shoved to earth, facedown, and held spread-eagle.

"Here is your lesson," Desmond's voice said, from somewhere far away and much too close. "The seven virtues. The first is solidarity."

A streak of the most intense pain Stephen had ever felt cut his back in two. He screamed into his gag, a shrill hysterical shriek of pure animal terror.

"The second virtue is chastity."

Another stroke of fire fell, and droplets spattered across Stephen's cheek.

He lost track of the virtues after number three. He might have fainted. The next thing he was aware of was Desmond's voice very near his ear.

"I'm leaving you new robes and a rag. There's a well just down the hill. Clean yourself up and come to dinner. Sit at my table. Speak to no one of this—no one. There are, as you know, more than seven virtues. There are seven times seven."

The gag came out, and he was released. He lay there, unable to move, to even think of moving, as full night fell.

CHAPTER SIX

MOTHER GASTYA

"THEY'VE SEEN US?" Winna whispered.

"I think so," Aspar said, pulling on his breeks. "You saw what the witchlights did? Someone called them. They'll know where we are, since witchlights gather around people."

"Maybe the lights just flew down because there are more people there."

"Maybe. I doubt it, the way they went of a sudden. And then that burst on the horn. If the man with one eye *was* Fend—he has some shinecrafting. I don't doubt that he could call witchlights. So hurry, dress. We might not have long."

He cursed silently as he finished yanking on his breeches. Moments ago, their dalliance had seemed worth the risk. Now—how old did he think he was, anyway? He knew better. If he'd known one of their pursuers was Fend . . .

"Ready," Winna breathed. She didn't sound frightened.

"Here," Aspar said. He wrenched two of the glowing crystal globes from the bedposts and handed one to Winna. "It's not much," he said, "but with the witchlights gone, it's the best we have. Now, this way."

He went through the arched door onto the balcony. Without the witchlights, there was only a void, and the pale light of the crystals wasn't enough to fill it. Aspar weighed the crystal in his hand, trying to remember where the other balcony was. Then he tossed the sphere.

It struck with a silvery tinkling, and a sudden vague light bloomed, a glowing cloud. The balcony appeared, a low construct railed in iron wrought to resemble snakes with crowns and feathered tails.

"Can you jump to that?" Aspar asked Winna.

She cut her eyes. "Yes."

"Do it, then. Hurry, for in a few moments the light will dissipate. When you get there, go in, hunt up all of the ways off of that floor—up, down, out windows. I'll be right there."

"What are you going to do?"

"Wedge the door to the stairwells. Maybe they'll think we're trying to barricade ourselves in."

She nodded, braced herself, and jumped. The instant she did, Aspar knew he'd made a mistake. Winna didn't have any idea whether she could jump that far; she'd just said she could do it to sound confident for him. She almost made it clear anyway, but clipped the low railing going in, lost her balance, her arms windmilling, her back to a long drop and stone streets, and the balcony only to the back of her knees. Aspar held his breath, trying not to call out, all his blood racing into his head, his fingers itching to grab her. He bent to jump, in the dim hope he might somehow reach her before she fell, but by then she had recovered—by sitting down, hard.

Winna turned, flashed him an uncertain grin, then tried the casement. It swung open. She turned again, mouthed *hurry*, then slipped through.

Aspar let out the breath he had been holding, drew his ax and his dirk, and slipped back into the room. He crept down the stairwell they had ascended, hours earlier, willing his muscles to relax and his breath to stay even.

Without witchlights or globes it was pitch dark. He smelled dead leaves.

He came to the first landing and listened. Hearing nothing, he wondered if he had been wrong. Maybe no one knew they were here. He kept moving down, silent as a fog in the night.

He stopped on the next landing and crouched to listen.

He heard his own breathing—and something else.

Aspar closed his eyes—unnecessary, since he couldn't see anything, anyway, but it helped him concentrate. He drew a long, slow breath, tasting the air, smelling nothing but dust. He held the air in his lungs.

There was no sound at all, then, but still he didn't move. He kept crouched, waiting.

And then there was a breath, not his own. He didn't hear it; he felt it on his face.

Aspar struck upward with his dirk, hard, and felt it catch against chain mail. That brought a grunt and a rush of something going by Aspar's face. Aspar reached around, grappling for upper arms; something smacked against his back. His invisible foe shouted then, which helped Aspar find his opponent's face. A helmet belled under the edge of his ax, and he slipped his dirk into something soft where the throat ought to be. He'd guessed right; the scream gurgled off.

Then something kicked him in the chest with the force of a mule, a finger or two to the right of his sternum. Flashes of gold exploded inside of his eyes as he chopped down, found a solid wooden shaft there, and realized a spear was standing out of him, and someone was still pushing on it. He couldn't tell how deep it had gone.

He turned away from the force of the push and lashed out with his ax. It hit something meaty, and someone howled. The spear in Aspar's chest hung free, and then its own weight wrenched it out. That hurt, too, so much that Aspar's knees buckled. That may have saved him from whatever hissed over his head and struck yellow sparks from the wall.

In the brief light a shadow congealed, and Aspar uncoiled from his involuntary crouch, driving his dirk through a bottom jaw and up into brain. He pushed the jerking body back, roughly, and heard someone below grunt as if struck.

"Fools!" another voice shouted, from further down the stairwell. "I told you to wait until—there!" Suddenly the staircase was alive with color, as a swarm of witchlights flew around the curve of the next landing to surround Aspar like hungry blood flies. In the light, he saw three

Sefry in a pile, two probably dead, a third farther down, trying to put his half-severed hand back on.

Turning the corner behind the lights were at least four more. One had an eye patch, but Aspar already knew it was Fend; he'd recognized the voice.

Aspar almost leapt down the shaft at them anyway. He might be able to kill Fend before he died.

But if he didn't, Fend would catch Winna. If Aspar did manage to kill the Sefry bastard, Fend's men would probably kill him anyway, and then *they* would catch Winna.

So Aspar grabbed the spear up from the floor and ran back up the stairs, cloaked in witchlights. At the top, he slammed the door, dropped the bar on it, and wedged the blade of the polearm beneath it.

He touched his chest, and his fingers came away sticky. There wasn't enough light to see how far the blade had gone in. He could stick a finger in, to see how deep it was, but he was already queasy, and that might make him sick. Right now, he couldn't afford it.

So he ignored the wound and followed after Winna, dropping to the balcony and into the next building where Winna stood waiting.

"Where *were* you?" she asked.

"I killed a few. They'll be coming. We have to hurry. You found our next path?"

"Wait," Winna said. She lifted and upended a large basket onto the balcony. Broken glass poured out with a musical tinkling.

"I found some vases and broke them. Let them land on that, when they jump after us."

"Good thinking," Aspar said, feeling a burst of pride. "Now let's go."

"Out here, then," she said. "We don't want to go down yet. I think I found a better way. I couldn't see far, but now that we have the witch-lights back, we can be sure."

He followed her to the next window, one at right angles to the one they had just come through. Beyond were roofs, peaked and scaled and close.

They jumped out, Winna leading, and scrambled on polished slate, around the bottom of a steep-pitched spire, trying to hide their glowing escort from any line of sight their pursuers might be able to establish. Aspar cast his gaze back often. On the other side of the spire was another jump, though it was barely more than a long step. The steep angle of the other roof made the landing less than certain, however.

They went on like that, roof to roof.

Unfortunately, Aspar felt his strength ebbing, and he was getting a bit dizzy. As they came to the edge of the fourth roof, his footing betrayed him and he slipped. Clawing at the slate proved no good, and he went over, but the railing of the balcony below caught his body, hard, held him there long enough for him to get a grip on the iron rails.

By the time he pulled himself onto the balcony and got his breath, Winna had dropped down to join him.

"Are you all right? Did they—" Her eyes widened. "You're *bleeding*."

"I think we're done with rooftops," he muttered. "Let's get down to the street."

"But you're bleeding," she repeated.

"I'm fine. We can't stop to talk about this, Winna. We have to keep moving, and hiding. Eventually we'll find a way out, or they'll give up." *Unless Fend knows who he's chasing. He won't give up if he knows it's me.* "This time we'll find a place with no windows."

In the distance, he heard the horn again, and cursed as the witchlights that hovered around them suddenly flew up, like a colored fountain. They shot up toward the cave roof, then dropped like angry bees back toward Aspar and Winna.

Aspar didn't say anything. He didn't have to; Winna understood what had just happened.

"Down," she said.

Hoof-clacks on cobbles greeted them as they came onto the street, though Aspar couldn't ascertain exactly where they were coming from. The vast hollow of the cavern and the close walls of the city played slingstones with noise. He and Winna ducked in and out of alleys more or less at random. Aspar's feet seemed very distant from him, and he began to wonder if the spear might have been poisoned. Surely he hadn't lost *that* much blood.

"Which way?" Winna whispered, as they came to a cross intersection. A post in the center of it bore a carved head with four faces, all with bulging, fishlike eyes.

"Grim!" he muttered. "You choose."

"Aspar, how badly are you hurt?"

"I don't know. Choose a direction." The witchlights had left them again, and they had only the sphere to show the way.

She chose, and chose again. Aspar seemed to lose track of things for a moment, and the next he knew he was lying flat on the cobbles. If he raised his head a little, he could see the ragged edges of Winna's skirt, and he heard the lapping of water. He was lying at the edge of the canal.

Their witchlights were back.

". . . up, you damned fool," Winna was saying. Her voice sounded more than a little panicked.

He helped her wrestle him to a sitting position.

"You're going to have to go without me, Winn," he managed.

"Egg in a snake's den chance of that," Winna said.

"Do it for me. They'll find us, and soon. I can't have Fend— I can't have him kill another—" He stopped, and gripped her arm, as something big stepped from the alley. "Turn your head," Aspar gasped. "Don't look at it." He drew out his ax, holding up the flat for a dull mirror. It was spattered in gore, however, and all he could see was the faint yellow glow.

But the greffyn was there, at the end of the alley, bigger than a horse. He could feel the sick light of it against his face.

"The greffyn?" she asked, voice quaking. She'd done as he told her, thank Grim, and was averting her eyes.

"Yah. Into the canal with you. Don't look back."

"Into the canal with *both* of you. Or my boat, if you prefer." The voice was throaty, hoarse even, as from speaking too much or not enough. Aspar peered into the darkness and barely discerned a cowled figure in a slender gondola, just against the edge of the canal.

Then he found he didn't have much to say about it. Winna, grunting, rolled him from the canal edge over into the boat, then followed him in.

As the gondola began to move, a sort of burring sound, beginning below the edge of hearing and rising to sudden, intolerable shrillness exploded behind them, and Aspar felt his stomach heave.

Winna began to sob, then choke, then she vomited into the water.

They passed beneath an arch Aspar thought was a bridge, but it just went on, and on, a hole within a hole, the entrance to hell, probably, to the realm of dust and lead. But Winna's hand found his, and he didn't care, and yet another sort of nightfall took him away.

He awoke to the familiar scent of spider lily tea and ovenstone, to fingers on his face, and a dull fever in his chest. He tried to push his eyelids open, but they wouldn't move. They felt as if they had been sewn shut.

"He will be well," a voice said. It was the same throaty old voice from the boat.

"He's strong," Winna's voice replied.

"So are you."

"Who are you?" Aspar rasped.

"Ah. Hello, foundling. My name—I don't remember my real name. Just call me—call me Mother Gastya."

"Mother Gastya. Why did you save us?"

A long silence. Then a cough. "I don't know. I think I have something to tell you. I'm forgetting, you see."

"Forgetting what?"

"Everything."

"Do you remember where everyone went? The Sefry from the city?"

"They went away," Mother Gastya grated. "Of course they went away. Only I remained."

"But the men chasing us were Sefry," Winna said.

"Not of these houses. I do not know them. And they came with the sedhmhar. They came to kill me."

"Sedhmhar. The greffyn?"

"As you call it."

"What is it, Gastya?" Aspar asked. "The greffyn?"

"It is the forest dreaming of death. The shocked gaze before the eyes roll up. The maggot wriggling from the wound."

"What does that mean?" Winna asked.

Irritation finally gave Aspar the strength to open his eyes, though they were ponderous as iron valves.

He was in a small cavern or room, roughly furnished. By witchlight he made out Winna's face, lovely and young. Facing her was the most ancient Sefry Aspar had ever seen. She made Mother Cilth seem a child.

"Sefry can't talk straight, Winna," Aspar grunted. "Even when they want to. They lie so much and so often, it just isn't possible for them."

"You find the strength to insult me," the old woman said. Her silvery-blue gaze fastened on him, and he felt a vague shock at the contact. Her face was beyond reading; it looked as if it had been flayed, cured, and placed back on her skull. A mask. "That's good."

"Where are we?"

"In the ancient Hisli shrine. The outcasts will not find us here, at least not for a while."

"How confident you make me feel," Aspar said.

"She saved our lives, Aspar," Winna reminded him.

"That remains to be seen," Aspar grunted. "How bad'm I hurt?"

"The chest wound is not deep," Gastya replied. "But it was poisoned with the smell of the sedhmhari."

"Then I shall die."

"No. Not today. The poison has been drawn out. You will live, and your hatred with you." She cocked her head. "Your hatred. Such a waste. Jesperedh did her best."

"How do you . . . Have we met?"

"I was born here in Rewn Aluth. I've never left it."

"And I've never been here before. So how did you know?"

"I know Jesperedh. Jesperedh knows you."

"Jesp is dead."

The ancient woman blinked and smiled, then lifted her shoulders in a polite shrug. "As you wish. But as for your hatred—caring for humans is no easy task, you know. In most clans it is forbidden. Jesperedh might have left you to die."

"She might have," Aspar said. "I'm grateful to her. Just not to the rest of you."

"Fair enough," Gastya allowed.

"Why did the other Sefry leave Rewn Aluth?"

Mother Gastya clucked her tongue disapprovingly. "You *know*," she said. "The Briar King awakes, and the sedhmhar roams. Our ancient places are no longer safe. We knew they would not be, when the time came. We made our plans. All of the great rewns of the forest stand empty, now."

"But *why*? Surely all of you together could defeat the greffyn."

"Hmm? Perhaps. But the greffyn is only a harbinger. Sword and spear and shinecraft will never defeat what follows. When the water rises, we do not wait for the flood, we Sefry. Our boats have long been built."

"But the greffyn can be killed," Aspar persisted.

"Possibly. What of it?"

"Give me a straight answer, damn you. Mother Cilth wanted me to do something. What is it?"

"I . . ." She paused. "I'm remembering, yes. She wanted you to find me. To find me, and the Briar King. Beyond that, I do not know."

"And the greffyn will lead me to the Briar King?"

"It would be better if you reached him before the greffyn does," Mother Gastya murmured.

"Why? And how will I do that?"

"As to the first, it's just a tingle in my mind. As to the second—follow the Slaghish into the Mountains of the Hare, always taking the southern and westernmost forks. Between that headwater and the Cockspurs is a high valley."

"No, there isn't," Aspar said. "I've been there."

"There is."

"Sceat."

The crone shook her head. "There always has been, but behind a wall, of sorts. A breach has formed in it. Follow the valley down, through the thorn hollows. You'll find him there."

"There is no such valley," Aspar said stubbornly. "You can't hide such a thing. But suppose there was. Suppose pigs are rutting geese, and everything you say is true. Supposing all of that—why should I do what Mother Cilth wants me to accomplish? What good will it do?"

Mother Gastya's eyes seemed to shiver like distant lightning. "Because then you will *believe*, Aspar White. Only seeing him will do that. And to do what you must, you must first believe, in the deepest cistern of your blood."

Aspar rubbed his forehead with his hand. "I hate Sefry," he murmured. "I hate you all. Why me? Why do *I* have to do this?"

She shrugged. "You see with eyes both Sefry and Human."

"Why should that make a difference?"

"It will make a difference. *Human breath he shall draw, and Human soul charge him; but his gaze shall have Sefry quick and see the colors of night.* So the prophecy goes."

"Prophecy? Grim damn you, I—" He stopped short at the echo of a voice. "What's that?"

"The outcasts. They're coming for you."

"I thought you said they couldn't find us."

"No. I said they would, at the proper time. That time is near. But they will not find you. Only me. Take my boat, and let the current carry you downstream. In time, you will see light, and steer toward it."

"Why can't you go?"

"The light will end me, and there are things I must do first."

"Fend will kill you."

Gastya croaked softly at that and placed her hand briefly on Aspar's. With a terrible chill, he neither saw nor felt flesh on her fingers, only cold, gray bone. "Go on," Mother Gastya said. "But take this." The bones of her hand opened and dropped a small, waxy sphere into his palm. "This draws the poison out. You may not be well yet. If you sicken again, clutch it to the wound."

Aspar took the sphere, staring at the hand. "Come on, Winna," he murmured.

"Y-yes."

"The boat is there," Gastya said, lifting her chin to point. "Do not dally. Find him."

Aspar didn't answer. A shiver kept scurrying up and down his back like a mouse in a pipe. He was afraid his voice would quiver if he spoke. He took Winna's hand, and they went to find the boat.

But once the water had taken the gondola past the carved stone posts that marked the Hisli shrine, and into a low-roofed tunnel, away from Mother Gastya and her hollow, pitted voice, Winna squeezed his fingers.

"Was she, Aspar? Was she dead?"

"I don't know," he murmured. "The Sefry claim—they say their shinecrafting can do such things. I've never believed it. Never."

"But you do now."

"It could have been a glamour. Probably it was a glamour."

A long time later, it seemed, strange sounds came down the tunnel. It might have been screams, but whose Aspar could not say.

CHAPTER SEVEN

PLANS FOR AN OUTING

"MAJESTY!" THE GUARD PROTESTED. "You cannot—I mean, it's—"

Muriele glared up at the tall, weak-chinned fellow. He had a carefully trimmed mustache and was immaculate in the pale-and-blue livery of the house Gramme. Muriele couldn't remember his name, nor did she really try.

"Cannot *what*?" she snapped. "Am I your queen or not?"

The man flinched, bowed, and bowed again, as he had been doing from their first encounter. "Yes, Majesty, of course, but—"

"And is not the lady Gramme my subject, and a guest in my husband's house?"

"Yes, Majesty, quite, but—"

"But what? These are my rooms, sir, despite that your mistress lives in them. Out of my way, that I may enter. Unless you know some reason I should not."

"Please, Majesty. The widow Gramme is . . . entertaining."

"Entertaining? Surely she would have to be entertaining the king himself, if you are to put aside my wishes. Are you, sir, prepared to tell me that the lady Gramme is entertaining my husband?"

For a long moment, the young knight stood there, trying out various movements of his lips but never quite making a sound. He looked from Muriele, to Erren, to the young knight Neil MeqVren, who stood with hand on the hilt of his weapon. Then he sighed. "No, Majesty. *I* am not prepared to tell you that."

"Very well, then. Open that door."

A moment later she was striding into the suite. Adlainn Selgrene— Gramme's lady-in-waiting—dropped her needlework and gave a little shriek as Muriele marched toward the bedchamber, but at a hard glance from Erren, the small blonde fell quite silent.

Muriele paused at the double doors and spoke to Neil and Erren without looking at them.

"Stay outside for a moment," she said. "Give them time to get proper." Then she took the handle and shoved the doors open.

The lady Gramme and William II were a pink tangle of limbs on her enormous bed. *People look rather stupid in the act of sex,* Muriele thought, oddly detached. *Helpless and stupid, like babies without the charm.*

"By the saints!" Muriele said, deadpan. "Whatever are you doing with my husband, Lady Gramme?"

Gramme shrieked in an outrage altogether free of fear, and the king gave a kind of bullish bellow, but they both scrambled under cover in short order.

"Muriele, what in the name of the saints—" William shouted, his face ruddy.

"How *dare* you break into my rooms—" Gramme howled, pushing at her tangled ash-blonde curls with one hand and drawing the coverlet up with the other.

"Shut up, the both of you," Muriele shouted. "You especially, Lady Gramme. That everyone knows about . . . *this* . . . does not make it legal to the church. My husband may be above holy sanction, but I assure you, *you* are not, nor will he—in these times—stand in my way if I wish to press for it."

"Muriele—"

"No, hush, William. War is afoot, yes? With whose family would you rather risk a rift? Mine, with its matchless fleet and its legions of knights? Or this whore's, whose father commands forty skinny nags mounted by oafs wearing pots for helms?"

Gramme understood the threat more quickly than William. Her mouth clamped shut very quickly indeed, though she was near tears with anger.

William, biting his lip, also relented. "What do you want, Muriele?" he asked tiredly.

"Your attention, husband. I'm told I'm to be escorted by barge to Cal Azroth. I don't remember deciding that I wanted to go there. And I don't remember being *asked*."

"I am still your husband. I am still king. Need I ask permission to make my wife safe? You were nearly killed!"

"Your concern is noted. Is that what you came to Lady Gramme to discuss? Your deep worry and concern for my welfare?"

William ignored the dig. "It's not safe for you in Eslen, Muriele. That much is plain. It will be much easier to guard you at Cal Azroth. It's what the place was built for."

"Move the whole court, there, then, not just me."

"Impractical. I must be here, near the fleet. But Fastia, Anne, Elseny, and Charles will accompany you. I will not risk my children, either, with assassins abroad."

"I refuse this protection. Send the children if you will."

William's face tightened. "Erren, speak to your mistress."

From the corner of her eye Muriele noticed that Erren and Sir Neil had taken the moment she asked of them and finally entered the chamber.

"She already knows my mind, Majesty," Erren replied.

"Lady Erren, you, at least, must have the sense to know this is for the best."

Erren bowed politely. "Yes, Majesty. If you say so, Majesty."

"Well, I *do* say so!" William suddenly leapt out of the bed and dragged a robe up from the floor. He threw it over his shoulders.

"Muriele," he grated, "join me in Lady Gramme's sunroom. Immediately. The rest of you remain here. I am your king, damn you all, and never forget it!"

William leaned on the casement of the window and regarded the sunset. He did not look at Muriele when he spoke.

"That was childish, Muriele, childish and destructive. What sort of word might spread in the court now? Did you really want Lady Gramme to think I tell you *nothing*? Do you want her to spread that around?"

Muriele choked back tears. "You *do* tell me nothing, damn you. If I don't have your ear, why should anyone think I do? I'd rather be thought of as spurned than stupid, husband."

William turned a shockingly weary gaze on her. "This is not the usual course of our lives," he protested. "When all is normal, I do confide in you and seek your opinion. I kept this quiet because I knew you would not want to go, and I *need* you to go. You are correct, war looms everywhere, and they have already tried to kill you once. I don't even know how they *did* it. I'll wager hard that your deadly old Erren doesn't know, either."

"Then what makes you think Cal Azroth will be safer for me?"

"Because of all our manses, it is best built for defending against assassins, against craft and art and the winged, evil dead or whatever else might come along. It has a full garrison, so even if they send an army after you, you may be safe. You know the place, Muriele. Won't you see reason?"

"It's easier to see something in the plain light, than when it creeps behind you in the dark. I don't like hearing my fate through rumor. Even four years ago, you would not have treated me so. Now it is commonplace. Are Gramme's whispers growing strong in your skull? Do you really conceive of replacing me as queen?"

Something came over William's face, then, something she had not seen for some time. He turned away again, unable to meet her gaze.

"All kings have mistresses, Muriele. Your own father did."

"That never answers my question."

He turned back to her. "You are my queen, my wife, and I think my friend."

"We once were friends," she said, more softly, a little confused.

"I can't let you be killed. It's as simple as that. I can live without Ambria, or Alis, or any of those others. Without you . . ." His hands dropped helplessly at his sides. "Being king is hard enough, without you asking me to be better as a man. You've never asked that of me. You've never even mentioned my mistresses. Why now, of all times, when things are worst and weakest, do you choose to . . . to . . . *erupt* in this manner?"

She lifted her chin defiantly. "I don't know. I suppose because this is the first time I've felt truly unwanted. After I was nearly murdered, you came to me. You were tender, as you were of old. And then, poof! Nothing. As if in that one night you could take my terror away. And now to send me off, like a child, without even talking to me? Intolerable."

He cast his head down. "Tonight. Can't we talk tonight, when we have cooled a bit?"

"You want me to come to our bed when you still have her stink on you? When I know for certain? What do you think of me? That I have no pride at all? I'm a de Liery, damn you, Wilm!"

She knew she was going to cry, then, if she didn't leave quickly. "I'll go. Not for myself, but if my children will be safer at Cal Azroth, I'll take them there. Never mind your ridic—" She couldn't finish. She turned and walked swiftly down the stairs, through the bedchamber.

"Erren. Sir Neil. To me, now."

Her shoulders were shaking by the time she reached the hall. By the time they came to the Depren Stairs, the tears had started.

Neil paced slowly in the anteroom, wondering what he ought to do. Only a few hours ago, he had begun his service as the sole member of the Lier Guard. The queen had hardly said two words to him, and before he knew it he was off to confront his sovereign lord—the same king who had just given him the rose!—in a state of undress with his mistress.

Now the queen had shut herself in her bedroom, and the lady Erren with her.

The other knights assigned to the queen were confined to the halls. Only Neil was allowed in the apartment. He supposed he might stick his head out and ask them what he ought to do, but Vargus wasn't there, or even Sir James, and he did not know the rest.

A door creaked, and he turned, hand on the pommel of Crow.

It was the lady Erren.

"Take ease, young chever," she said, in Lierish. "The queen sends her apologies. She's been—as you've seen, I think—too distracted to properly welcome you to her staff."

"That's no matter," Neil replied. "This is so great an honor for me, I cannot even begin to say. But . . ."

"But you have questions, yes? Ask them of me."

"Thank you, Lady. Mostly, it's this—what exactly are my duties?"

Erren smiled sternly. "That's simple enough. You protect the queen. Not me, not her daughters, not her husband, not the crown prince—but the queen. Always and only, your eye is to her safety. If you can save the king's life by allowing the queen to be stung by a bee, you are to let the king perish. Is that simple enough?"

"It is. Quite simple."

"You have command of yourself, in that case. No order will you be given, no task or errand can keep you from her side. It matters not who gives it. Act always as you think best."

"And the other knights? The Craftsmen?"

"They are not under your command, if that is what you mean. Nor are you under theirs. The queen commands this household, and I am the chief of her staff. You obey the queen's command, then mine, then the king's, in that order. If at any time you feel any command jeopardizes the queen, you shall ignore it." She paused. "But be *certain*. I'll have no cocksure young man second-guessing every order I give. You are not the strategist, here. You are the watchdog. You are the sword. Do you understand the difference?"

"I do, Lady."

"Very well, then. In time, we will assemble a real Lier Guard, and you will be its captain. Until then, things stand as I've put them before you. Do you have other questions? About what just happened, for instance?"

"No question that is meet, I think."

"What do you mean?"

"I mean it is a question I would put to the king, if it were not impertinent," Neil said softly.

A mixed look of alarm and approval flashed across the lady Erren's face. She placed a hand on his shoulder.

"Love her," she said, "but do not fall *in* love with her. She counts on you for her life, and I would not want you to be dispassionate about that. But fall in love with her, and she is as good as dead. You might as well thrust the knife in yourself. You understand?"

Neil stiffened. "I know my place, Lady."

"I'm sure you do. That's not what I'm talking about."

"I know what you're talking about, Lady Erren. I may be young, but I'm not a fool."

"If I thought you were, you would not be here," Erren said softly. "And if I ever think you are, you will vanish quite quickly, be assured." She leaned in and kissed him on the cheek. "There. Welcome to the staff. I must go out for a time."

"In that case, Lady, shouldn't I be in her room? That is, if she is not in your sight, shouldn't she be in mine?"

"An excellent point," Erren replied. "Let me prepare her. I will return shortly enough. I have news to deliver to the archgreffess Fastia. Let her have the unpleasant task of carrying it further."

"Cal Azroth?" Anne blurted. "I can't go to Cal Azroth! Not now!"

Fastia gave Anne a peculiar look. "Whatever do you mean by that, Anne? What *particular* thing keeps you here at this *particular* moment?"

Anne felt something in her belly drop away. "That's not what I meant," she said quickly. "I just don't want to go, that's all. Cal Azroth is a boring place."

Fastia's suspicious gaze lingered for a moment. Then she shrugged. "Anne, let me explain the facts to you. Fact the first: our mother was nearly murdered. Fact the second: Father and Erren and everyone else who ought to know fear that you, or I, or any of us might be next. We're all going where we can be protected. Fact the third: you *are* going to Cal Azroth. This is not an evening chapel or a sewing lesson you can skip by dressing as a boy and leading the Royal Horse on a merry chase. If need be, you will be tied hand and foot until the barge is well under way."

Anne opened her mouth to begin an angry protest, but Fastia held her finger to her lips. "A moment," the older woman said. "Let me say more. Mother needs us, Anne. Do you think she wants to go into exile any more than we do? When she heard, she stormed to Father and railed against it. But Father needs to know we are safe, and Mother needs her children. Needs *you*, Anne."

Anne closed her mouth. Fastia had a way of making everything sound true. And if *Erren* was involved—well, Erren had a way of finding things out, if she put effort into it. And Erren most certainly should not find out about Roderick.

"Very well," Anne replied. "I see this is important. When do we leave?"

"On the morrow. And tell no one, you understand? Too many people already know where we're bound."

Anne nodded. "Austra will go, of course?"

"Of course."

Fastia took Anne's chin in her hand. "You look tired, Anne. Have you been sleeping well?"

"I've had Black Marys," Anne admitted. "I—" She had a sudden, powerful urge to tell Fastia about her experience in the maze. But if the praifec himself told her not to worry, there was no point in it. It would only be one more thing Fastia would think was wrong with her.

"Yes?" Fastia prompted. "What sort of Black Marys?"

"Silly things," Anne lied.

"If they keep up, you must tell me about them. Dreams can be important, you know."

"I know. But these are just . . . silly."

"Not if they make you unwell."

Anne forced a smile. "Well, there will be plenty of time to discuss this at Cal Azroth, I should think. There's nothing *else* to do there."

"Well, there's always Elyoner. I'm sure she'll pay us a visit. And I'll see about having your horse Faster brought along. How would you like that?"

"Oh, Fastia, would you?"

"I'll do my best."

"Thank you."

"Now, pack. I'll see you soon."

"Very well."

"And, Anne?"

"Yes, Fastia?"

"I do love you, you know. You are my little sister. I know sometimes you think—" She frowned, and reddened slightly. "Anyway." Her hands fluttered briefly, then settled. "Pack," she said.

•   •   •

When Fastia was gone, Austra came padding into the room.

"You heard?" Anne asked.

"Yes."

"What a nuisance. I'm supposed to meet Roderick tomorrow."

"Do you want me to get word to him?" Austra asked, a little trepidantly.

"Yes," Anne murmured. "Yes. Tell him I'll meet him tonight, instead. At the midnight bell, in the crypt of my ancestors."

"Anne, that's a very bad idea."

"I may not see him for months. I *will* see him before I go."

CHAPTER EIGHT

SCRIFTI

THE STING OF A SLAP brought Stephen out of his dream.
He was actually grateful to the pain, for it released him from terror, a phantasmic netherworld of horned beastmen, eviscerated women and children, feathered beasts, and leering faces that formed and dissipated like clouds, variously his kidnappers, Aspar White, and Brother Desmond.

He wasn't grateful for long. In his sleep, blood had glued his shift to his back, and in places to the wooden bench he slept on. The movements of waking pulled ropes of pain tight about his back and limbs.

"There's a good lad," the brother bending over him said as Stephen sat up. "Up with you." He slapped Stephen on the back, inciting a gasp of shock and tears of pain.

"Leave him be," a softer voice said. "Desmond and his bunch aren't around now."

"I don't know that," the first fellow muttered. He was a short man, barrel-chested with skinny arms, red-haired and copiously freckled. "For all I know, *you're* in with 'em. All I know is, it never hurts to treat the new ones rough. It *can* hurt to go soft on 'em." He thumped Stephen's back again, though not as hard this time.

But it was too much. Stephen bounced up from the sleeping board, towering a good head over his antagonist. "Stay back from me," he warned. "Don't touch me again."

The redhead gave two steps, but he didn't look terribly concerned.

"What's your name, fellow?" That was the other man, a gangly young fellow with big ears and an easy smile.

"Stephen Darige."

"I'm Brother Alprin, and the little one there is Brother Ehan."

"Don't call me the 'little one,' " the redhead warned.

"Gozh margens ezwes, mehelz brodar Ehan," Stephen said.

"Eh?" Brother Ehan exclaimed. "That's Herilanzer! How is it you speak my language?"

"I don't. Only a few words."

"How did you guess he was Herilanzer?" Brother Alprin asked.

"His name. His accent. I'm good at that sort of thing." *And it's been getting me in trouble, up until now. I should have kept my mouth shut.*

But Ehan grinned. "Well, that beats anything I've heard lately. Generally speaking, no one understands Herilanzer but Herilanzers. No one even tries. What's the point?"

Stephen shrugged. "Maybe someday I'll go to Herilanz."

"That's even funnier," Ehan said. "You'd last about half a bell in my homeland. If the frost didn't kill you, the first child to come along would."

Stephen mused that if Brother Ehan was a typical Herilanzer adult, the children must be knee-high at best, but decided against saying any such thing. He already hurt too much. He nodded instead. "Maybe," he conceded.

He glanced around the dormitory—a large room illuminated by high window slits. It was very spare—fifty wooden benches each just wide enough to sleep on, and a small open box at the end of each bench for possessions. He noticed his was empty.

"My things! My books, my charcoal—my rubbings! Where are they?"

"One of Desmond's boys took them. If you're lucky, and behave well, you'll get them back."

"Does—I mean, the fratrex—"

"Don't even start thinking that way," Alprin cautioned. "The only way around Desmond and his lot is to cooperate, thank them, and hope they eventually move on to someone else. Whether the fratrex knows about all of this, I can't say. That's a moot point. If you go to him—or to anyone—that's a very bad mistake."

"But how can he—how can *they* just—just *do* these things?"

Brother Ehan slapped him on the back again, and Stephen nearly bit his own tongue in half.

"You idiot!" Ehan hissed. "Do you know me? Or Brother Alprin? You just met us! We could be the worst of the lot! And if we were, right now you would, by the saints of storm and blood, be regretting it, oh, terribly you would. You want to survive here? Listen, learn—don't talk until you *know* the other fellow."

"Aren't you breaking your own rule? You don't know me either."

"I know you're new. That's enough."

"He's right," Alprin said. "And don't expect any kindness from us—or anyone—if there's the least chance anyone is watching. There are rules concerning new people. Even I won't break them, often."

"So you've been warned," Ehan grunted. "That's more than I meant to do, and it's the last you'll get. Trust no one." He scratched his chin. "Oh, and the fratrex wanted you in the scriftorium a quarter bell ago. Something about 'important translations.' "

"Saints!" Stephen said. "But my things—"

"Forget them," Alprin said. "Really. You're sworn to poverty anyway."

"But my things weren't riches. They were things I need for my work."

"You have the whole scriftorium," Ehan said. "What else could you need?"

"My notes."

"Too bad." Brother Ehan turned to Brother Alprin. "It's time we left. We've risked our necks enough for one day, and I've got work to do."

"Thank you," Stephen said. *"Eh Danka 'zwes."*

Ehan laughed as he left. "Speaking Herilanzer," he exclaimed. "What next?"

What indeed? Stephen thought. Back at Tor Scath, he thought things had gotten as bad as they could. Now he found he was already nostalgic for those days.

But the scriftorium awaited, and that thought still brought excitement, though a much warier excitement than he had known the day before.

"Stiff from carrying that wood, eh?" the fratrex asked, peering down his nose.

"Very stiff, Reverend," Stephen replied. He wasn't fooling himself. Despite choosing his words carefully, he'd just told his superior a lie. He didn't like it, but until he understood more about the monastery and its inhabitants, he was determined to take the ominous advice of Brothers Alprin and Ehan.

The fratrex looked sympathetic. "Well, this evening you can take the meal out to the watchposts. The walk will loosen you up."

"Thank you, Fratrex."

"No need for that. Now, my boy, did you find anything of interest yesterday? I'm sure you did."

I found rotten apples in the church bin, Stephen thought sourly.

"I found an early copy of the *Amena Tirson*," he said.

The fratrex nodded approvingly. "Ah, yes, the old geography. We have the original."

"I think that must have been what I found. Were—were the copies made here?"

The fratrex scratched his chin and cocked his head. "It's been here for the last two centuries, so I would guess that any copy you've seen elsewhere came from here. Why? Did you find an error?"

"Not exactly. What I—"

"Well then! Of course not. We have the best copyists in the world." He winked at Stephen. "And the most competent translators, eh? Now, do you want to see what I brought you here to show you?"

"Very much, Fratrex Pell," Stephen said.

The old man thumped a cedar box. "It's right here."

The box was much like the one that had held the *Amena Tirson*, but larger. This box looked new—but when the old man slid off the lid, what was inside did not.

"Lead sheets," Stephen murmured, almost to himself. "A holy text."

"So one would think. But see the date? This predates the Hegemony— and the spread of the church in this area—by two hundred years."

"True," Stephen agreed. "But scriving on lead was known to have significance even before the church codified its use. Messages to the dead, for instance, were written that way, in archaic Vitellian, before the Sacaratum and the first church."

"Messages to the dead, yes," the fratrex acknowledged. "According to our earliest doctrines, the spirits of the departed are best able to read from lead. But before the church, those messages were small things—curses and other requests, just as some still write today. It was only after the second reform that texts dedicated to the saints were written in this fashion, since the saints are served by the departed.

"But here, long before the second reform—well, see for yourself."

Stephen moved closer, for a better look, and his heart thumped faster. The pain in his back didn't go away, but for an instant he nearly forgot about it. "It's an entire text," he said. "A book, just like the sacred writings of the church."

"And do you know the language?"

"May I hold it?"

"Of course."

Stephen lifted out the first heavy leaf. When his fingers touched it, it almost seemed as if he could taste the lead in his mouth, and his fingers trembled slightly.

Who had scrived this? What had the author been feeling, when he set down this first page? The immensity of time swept over Stephen like a wave tumbling him in the ocean—delightful and a little frightening. He squinted at the small figures.

"There is a great deal of patination," he murmured, brushing at the white film that coated it. "Where was this found?"

"In the old chapel of Saint Donwys, in the Marches of Hume, or so I'm told."

"They didn't take very good care of it," Stephen noticed. "It's been kept damp." He frowned. "And it almost looks—could it have ever been buried?"

"I doubt *that*," the fratrex said. "In any case, we have it now, and will take proper care of it. Indeed, that's another reason we requested a brother of your qualifications. To be honest, I would have preferred someone higher in the order than a novice, but I'm sure you'll prove yourself worthy of the church's trust."

"I will strive to, Reverend."

"Now. What can you tell me of it? It's Vadhiian, that much even I can discern, but—"

"With greatest respect, Reverend," Stephen said, very cautiously, remembering his earlier lesson in humility. "At first glance, I'm not altogether certain that's the case."

"Oh?"

"It's similar, to be sure, but . . ." He stared at the first line, frowning.

"It's the Vadhiian characters, yes?" the fratrex asked.

"Yes. But look at this line. It looks like *Dhyvhubh khamy*, 'this addressed to the gods.' In Vadhiian, that ought to be *Kanmi udhe dhivhi*. You see? Vadhiian had lost the case endings from ancient Croatani. I think this is an unknown dialect—perhaps a very old form of Vadhiian."

"Indeed? How old? The date tells us it was written during the reign of the Black Jester. The language of his empire was Vadhiian."

"The text may have been copied. See here, below the date?"

"I see the letter *Q*, at least if I understand the scrift."

"It is *Q*," Stephen affirmed. "The Black Jester reigned for the most part of a century. During the early years of his rule, it became customary for a scrive or translator to put his mark below the date." He smiled grimly. "The Jester wanted to know who to punish if anything was copied incorrectly. After his defeat, of course, the Hegemony established itself, and the church along with it, and practices were brought into line with church procedure."

"You think this is a copy of something earlier, then?"

"Possibly. Or perhaps this was some sort of literary dialect—much as we use Vitellian and Croatani for our sacred texts."

The fratrex nodded. "Here I acknowledge my limits. It may be as you say."

"Or it may not," Stephen said hastily. "After all, I based that on just a few words. But with some study, I can develop a more confident opinion."

"And how long until you've translated the whole thing?"

"I can't say with certainty, Reverend. If it is an unknown dialect, it could be troublesome."

"Yes. Could you do it in a nineday?"

"Reverend?" Dismayed, Stephen tried to keep the strain from his voice. "I can try. Is it that important?"

The reverend frowned. "To me? No. But consider it a test, a first devotion. Do this in the time I've allotted, and you may well walk the fanes earlier than any other novice."

Mention of the fanes brought Stephen's pain back to mind. What would Brother Desmond say to that?

"Reverend, I desire no special treatment. Of course I will translate with alacrity. It's what you brought me here for, and I will not disappoint you."

"I don't expect you to." Then Fratrex Pell's voice sharpened. "Nor do I expect you to question my judgment. If I declare you are ready to walk the fanes, it will be because you *are*. Do you understand, yes? Special treatment does not enter into it.

"We've been banging our heads against this scrift for months, and in a count of one hundred you've already unraveled one of its mysteries. That is a clear sign from the saints. Your success or failure in the next nineday will also be a clear sign, one way or another. You see?"

"One way or another, Reverend?"

"Exactly." The fratrex patted him firmly on the shoulder, sending darts of agony shooting through Stephen's body. "My, you *are* tender," he said. "Well, I'll leave you to it. Saints be with you."

"And with you, Reverend," Stephen replied.

When the fratrex was gone, his words still hung in the air, as certain in form as if scrived in lead, and as uncertain as the content of the manuscrift.

One way or another. If Stephen succeeded, he would walk the fanes and become an initiate, something that might otherwise take a year or more. Of course, then Desmond Spendlove would probably beat him to death.

But what if he failed? What would the saints be telling the fratrex then?

But no, one thing was certain—no one had read these ancient words in more than a thousand years. Whatever might come, whatever he was risking, he would do it.

He found paper and charcoal for tracing, a brush for cleaning the characters, and mixed some ink.

A bell later he had forgotten the fratrex, Desmond Spendlove, and all threats of punishment and pain, as ancient thoughts slowly, tentatively revealed themselves.

The dialect was, indeed, unknown. The form of the words was much like Vadhiian, but the way those words were put together, and the grammar that gave them sense, were older, more akin to the tongues of the elder Cavarum.

The vespers bell found him still hunched over the manuscript, with translated lines scribbled on the paper next to it. As he progressed, he had crossed out preliminary guesses and replaced them with more certain ones. Sitting straight up, he cracked his neck and rubbed his eyes, then went back through his notes.

He had begun to gather the pieces of the puzzle—the conjugation of this and that verb, the relation of subject to object—but hadn't tried to put it all together. So, on a clean sheet, he began a running translation. It read:

This addressed to the gods.
In the thirty-eighth year of the reign of *Ukel Kradh dhe'Uvh* (a title of the Black Jester, meaning "Proud Heart of Fear," written in the Vadhiian dialect, unlike the rest of the document—S.D.) these words were scrived. Behold them, for they are terrible. They are for your eyes, Great Lord, and for none other. Lord of the Sedoi, here is told of the (*noybhubh*: fanes? altars? temples?) belonging to the (*zhedunmara*: damned gods? unsacred demons?). Here is told of the (*vath thadhathun*: sedos-paths? faneways?) of the Mother-Devouring, of the Sacred Desire, of the Madman Lord, of the Lightning-Twisted-Inside, of their kith and clan. Here is told how to entertain them. (*Uwdathez*: Cursed?) is any other who gazes upon these words. And (cursed?) is he who writes this.

A frost touched Stephen's spine. What in the name of the saints did he have here? He had never seen an ancient text even remotely like this.

Of course, little had survived from the era of the Warlock Wars. Much of what had been written then was profane and evil, and had been destroyed by the church.

If this was such a text, how had it slipped by? Simply because no one could read it? That was stupid. When the Hegemony brought peace to the north, they had with them some of the greatest scholars in the ancient world. Besides, this language would have been close enough to dialects of the time that any scholar back then should have been able to accomplish with ease what Stephen was now doing with difficulty—translate it by reference to sister languages.

Maybe this one had been hidden or, as Stephen suspected, buried. Maybe some peasant had dug it up in his field and brought it to the brothers at Saint Donwys, who assumed it was a sacred church text, and put it in their scriftorium.

Wherever it had come from, Stephen was virtually certain that it ought not to exist. Just as certainly, when the church learned what it was, it would be destroyed.

He should tell Fratrex Pell all this now. He should go no further.

"Brother?"

Stephen nearly jumped out of his skin. A monk he did not know was standing only a few feet away.

"I'm sorry?" Stephen said.

"Fratrex Pell asked you to deliver the evening meal to the watchtowers."

"Oh! Of course."

"Shall I replace that?" The brother waved at the scrift.

"Oh—no. It's something I'm translating for the fratrex. Could we leave it here, so I can take it up more easily tomorrow?"

"Of course," the fellow said.

"I'm Stephen Darige," he offered.

"Brother Sangen, at your service. I keep things on the shelves, here. That's one of the new Vadhiian scrifts?"

"There are more?"

"Oh, yes. They've been trickling in for the past few years."

"Really? All from Saint Donwys?"

"Heavens, no. From all over." He frowned slightly, as if suddenly concerned. "You'd better get going. Fratrex Pell is mostly patient, but if he asks that something be done, he means it."

"Of course." Stephen picked up his free translation and notes. "I'm going to keep these with me, so I can mull them over before sleep. Is that permitted?"

"Of course. Good evening to you, Brother Stephen." His voice dropped. "Keep you well on the path to the watchtowers. 'Tis said the south path, down by the woods, is longer but more . . . pleasant. I can explain the way to you, if you would like."

"I would," Stephen said. "Very much."

In the gloaming, with fireflies rising like ghosts departing the world, Stephen felt the chill return. He fought the urge to go straight to the fratrex and reveal what he had discovered.

He didn't fear the curse, of course. Whatever pagan god had been invoked was long dead, or a captive of the saints. The Black Jester had been defeated and lay dead for more than a millennium. The curse was no longer of any matter.

But any scrift that began with such a strong curse was likely to contain things no man ought to see, ought to have ever seen.

Yet he couldn't be sure. It might prove to be nothing more than a catalogue of dead fiends. And it might contain information useful to the church.

Until he was certain it was irredeemable, he couldn't give it up to be destroyed.

He would read further. If he came across something clearly unholy and dangerous, he would take it straight to the fratrex.

Right now he had other worries. Brother Sangen was either helping Stephen avoid Brother Desmond and his thugs or sending him into their arms. There was no way of knowing which, and nothing he could do about it but prepare himself.

He had the sudden, strange thought that it would be nice to have Aspar White with him right now. The holter was gruff, but he also seemed to know clearly what was right and wrong.

Not to mention the fact that Desmond Spendlove and his bullies wouldn't last a twenty count against Aspar. That was a fight Stephen would love to see.

Then again, Aspar White would scoff at Stephen for being a weak, pampered child. He straightened his back. He couldn't defeat his enemies, but he could make certain that they did not defeat him, even if they beat him to the ground. They would not beat his spirit.

It was the best he could do. It would have to be enough; he only hoped it didn't kill him.

On the heels of that thought, a voice spoke from the forest, soft but carrying.

"Well. What are you about, little one?"

Stephen took a deep breath, for courage, as Desmond Spendlove stepped onto the grass, a wicked gleam just barely visible in his eyes.

It took Stephen a moment to understand that Brother Desmond wasn't talking to him. In fact, he hadn't even seen Stephen. Quickly, Stephen ducked behind a hummock of hay, peering around the edge of it.

The prey Spendlove and his wolves were gathering around was Brother Ehan.

"Don't call me that," Ehan cautioned.

"I'll call you whatever I want. What did you tell the new fellow, Brother Ehan? Nothing disparaging, I hope."

"Nothing he didn't already know," Ehan replied.

"How do *you* know what he does or doesn't know? Are you that friendly with him already?"

Brother Ehan's chin lifted defiantly. "Come on, Spendlove. Just you and me. Without your dogs."

"Hear what he called you, fellows?" Brother Desmond said.

"Dogs," Ehan repeated. "Little bitches following a big one."

The circle closed in. Ehan suddenly leapt into motion, straight toward Brother Desmond.

He never got there. One of the other cowled figures swung a stiff arm so that Ehan caught it under his chin. His feet flew up in the air, and he landed with a pronounced *whoosh* of air, audible even from Stephen's hiding place.

Stephen felt a knot in his throat. He shouldn't interfere with this; every instinct warned him not to. And yet, from far away, he still somehow felt the holter's eyes on him. Aspar White, however crude he might be, whatever his faults, would never stand by and merely watch this.

"Damned cowards!" Stephen shouted. Or his throat did, anyway. He couldn't remember giving it the go-ahead.

But it got their attention. Brother Desmond and four others started toward him, at a run. Three made a beeline, and the other two circled around the other side of the haystack.

Stephen ducked behind the mound of fragrant straw. He could run, of course, but they were moving *fast*, much faster than he could. They would catch him.

So instead, he dug his fingers into the plaited grass and climbed as swiftly as he could. When he had nearly reached the top he stayed very still and watched his pursuers meet and mill below.

"He must have run on to the tree line, under cover of the haystack," one of them said.

"Find him." That was Brother Desmond, whose face Stephen could suddenly see quite clearly, for a torus of light had appeared around him, a sort of glowing mist.

Saint Tyw, don't let them look up, Stephen prayed silently.

Whether by the grace of the saint, or because it simply did not occur to them, they didn't but instead spread out and ran for the trees.

That wouldn't distract them long. Beyond the stream and its willow border lay nothing but open pasture, and they would quickly discover that he wasn't there.

Stephen scrambled on over the haystack and slid down the other side.

The two remaining men were still with Ehan; one was holding the little fellow down while the other produced what looked like a heavy bag.

They saw Stephen at the last second, as he kicked the fellow on top of Ehan under the chin. He felt teeth clack together, as the other man bellowed like a bull and swung the bag at him.

It hit hard, low in his back, and it *hurt*. It felt like a sack full of pears, and probably was. Stephen dropped to his knees, tasting blood in his mouth.

The next thing he knew, Ehan was tugging at him.

"Get up, you idiot! They'll be here any second!"

Stephen came woozily to his feet. The fellow he had kicked was lying still, and the other was on the ground, too. Moaning.

"Come on!" Ehan repeated. Then he ran.

Stephen followed, inspired because he could suddenly hear Desmond and the others, calling for them to stop, threatening dire things if they didn't.

He followed Ehan to the forest edge, and then it was all branches scratching at him, sudden outcroppings of unseen rock, and finally a trail that twisted its way uphill.

His lungs felt like a pair of hot lanterns, and the ache in his kidneys where the bag had hit him turned into a matching fire.

Finally, they dodged back into a clearing. It was now full pitch night, but Ehan seemed to know where he was going.

Just when Stephen thought he couldn't go another step, his companion grasped his arm and pulled him down.

"I don't think they're following anymore," he panted. "We'll wait here, and see. But they can find us anytime; they probably won't waste the effort."

"Why—did—we—run—then?" Stephen managed, between savage, painful breaths.

"I wouldn't have, if you hadn't done what you did," Ehan replied. "But they might have killed us, just then. Next time Desmond catches us alone, it'll be bad, but he'll have calmed them down."

"They can't just kill us!" Stephen protested.

"Oh, can't they, fellow-boy?" Ehan said. "They killed a novice just two months ago. Broke his neck and dumped him down a well, so it would look accidental. These fellows aren't playing. That was an ogre-stupid thing you did. We're just lucky they left Inest and Dyonis with me; they don't have any saint gifts yet. If it had been any of the others, we *would* be dead."

Ehan paused. "But—*Eh Danka 'zwes,* yah? Thanks. You didn't know any better. You're a better fellow than I reckoned you for. Stupid, but a good fellow."

"I couldn't just watch," Stephen explained.

"You'd better learn," Ehan said seriously. "You'd really better."

"Surely if we all got together—"

"Forget that. Listen, they really will leave you alone, eventually. That's the first time they've come after me in a year."

"Because you talked to me."

"Yah, I guess."

Stephen nodded at the darkness, and they both sat until the tempests in them had calmed to a normal-breathing zephyr.

"All right," Ehan said. "This way back to the dormitory."

Stephen felt the provision bag, still tied to his belt.

"I have to take this to the watchmen."

"They'll be waiting for you to do that, like as not."

"The fratrex told me to do it."

"The brothers on watch will understand."

"The fratrex told me to do it," Stephen said again, "and I will."

Ehan mumbled something in his own language, too low and quickly for Stephen to understand.

"Very well," he said finally. "If you insist on being a fool. But let me show you a back way."

CHAPTER NINE

EXILE

Breath caught in Anne's throat as Roderick's fingers brushed lightly over her breast. Had it been an accident? He had never done that before. But it had never been like this before, either, their kisses grown so urgent, demanding of something more.

No, here his hand came back to her breast, clever thing. The first brush had been a foray, to see what her reaction would be. But now he was there with confidence, tracing over the thin fabric of her gown, raising her nipple into a little fortress tower.

And his mouth nibbled and bit and licked its way around her throat, till he was standing behind her, panting into the nape of her neck, one hand still on her breast, one tickling over her belly, lower and lower, exploring her like an adventurer in an unknown land.

When she could stand it no longer, she turned in his grip and kissed him fiercely, beginning an exploration of her own around the base of his throat, to his chest where his shirt opened. When their lips met again it was with a furious, passionate tangle as something other than her brain took control, and Anne was pushing and pulling her body against his with all of her strength.

They came apart, both gasping like animals, and for an instant Anne felt ashamed and frightened. But then Roderick's hand came to her cheek, very gently, and his dark eyes held her, promising nothing but happiness and devotion.

Around them, the tomb was utterly silent, little revealed by the single taper burning in a wall sconce. They were in the center room, where bodies lay in state and the family gathered for the rites of the dead. No one had died recently; her ancestors were elsewhere, in their own rooms, in the vaults that made up the rooms of the great house. Before Roderick arrived she had said a prayer to keep them quiet.

"You are more beautiful than anyone I have ever laid eyes on," Roderick whispered. "When I first met you, it was not so. You were beautiful, yes, but now—" He struggled for words. "It's as if each time I see you, you glow with a greater light."

She couldn't think of anything to say, and she could hardly stand the intensity of his eyes, so she leaned in and tucked her head under his chin and laid her cheek against his chest.

"It must be that love brings greater beauty," he said, into her hair.

"What?" She drew back, to see if he was joking.

"I know, it's doomed, but there it is. I love you, Anne."

This time she didn't turn from his gaze but watched as his face dropped nearer, his lips parted, and he gave her a long, sweet kiss.

But then she pushed away from him.

"I have to leave tomorrow," she said roughly. She felt sudden tears clotting her head, trying to get out.

"What do you mean?"

"Father is sending us away, to Cal Azroth. My mother, my sisters, my brother—me. He thinks we're in danger. It's stupid. How could we be safer *there*?"

"Tomorrow?" Roderick sounded as if he was in pain. "For how long?"

"I don't know. Months, probably, until this stupid thing with Saltmark is over."

"That's terrible," he whispered.

"I don't want to go." Now it was her turn to stroke his cheek. "We still have time," she said. "Kiss me again, Roderick. Let's worry about tomorrow when it arrives."

He did kiss her slowly at first, but within moments he had reclaimed all of the ground he had conquered earlier, and pushed forward. When he took her nipple between thumb and forefinger, she laughed in delight: who would think of something like that? It was all so surprising!

He unlaced her bodice and kissed the long border of fabric and flesh, so each touch of his lips was wet and vivid, yet somehow far away, and all the more exciting for it.

The bodice slipped farther.

When his hand worked past her stockings, to the bare flesh of her upper thigh, her whole body went stiff. She moaned, and for the first time felt real fear. It was a strange fear, however, a mixed one. And Roderick seemed so certain of what he was doing, so confident.

And he loved her, didn't he?

He stopped, and caught her with those great eyes again. "Shall I stop? If you have any doubt, Anne, say it."

"Would you stop if I asked?" she panted.

"Yes."

"Because I'm not sure—but I don't want you to stop *yet*."

He grinned. "I love you, Anne Dare."

"I love you, too," she said, and just as she was realizing what she had said, he came back to her. And a sort of helplessness swallowed her, as if nothing could happen anyone would blame her for. Nothing.

And she was fifteen! Who remained virgin at that age?

Just then Roderick stiffened and leapt up, whirling, reaching for his sword.

"Young man," a familiar voice said, "do not be more foolish than you already have been."

Anne sat up, gathering her gown against her bosom. "Who is that? Erren?"

Erren stepped through the doorway, and behind, saints help her, came Fastia.

"We were—" Roderick began.

"About to hump like wild goats? Yes, I saw that," Erren said dryly.

"Anne, fasten your clothes," Fastia snapped. "Now. By all the saints, in the house of our ancestors?" Something strange quivered in her voice, something more than outrage, but Anne could not identify it.

"Anne is blameless," Roderick began.

But Anne had found her own voice. "How dare you!" she snapped. "How dare you follow me down here? This is my affair, and mine alone! It's no one's business who I love!"

"Perhaps not," Erren replied. "But it is very much the business of the kingdom with whom you *rut*, I'm afraid."

"Indeed? Really? What of my father, who lies with every slut who—"

"Hush, Anne!" Fastia shouted.

"—walks into the palace, *no,* I will not hush, Fastia. I cannot help that my blood does not run like ice, as it does in both of you."

"You *will* be silent," Fastia said. "And you, Roderick of Dunmrogh, you'd best begone. Now, before this turns into an incident that must come before the court."

Roderick lifted his chin. "I do not care about that. We have done nothing shameful, Anne and I, and we have only followed our hearts."

"When hearts swing between thighs, that will undoubtedly be true," Erren said.

"Don't go, Roderick," Anne said. It was more a command than a plea.

He took her hand. "I will go. But this is not done. You will hear from me."

He gave Erren and Fastia one arch glance, then left without looking back.

Anne glared at the other women, as well, marshaling her arguments even as the sound of Roderick's horse's hooves on lead cobbles faded. Fastia's face, meanwhile, was working through some frightful contortions.

And suddenly, Anne's older sister burst out laughing. Erren joined in by grinning and shaking her head.

"Heavenly saints!" Fastia managed. "Where did you find *that* one?"

"It's not *funny!* Why are you laughing?"

"Because it's so laughable! Do you think you're the first to come to the tombs for this sort of thing? Did you think you were being clever? And Roderick. 'Shall I stop?' Oh, dear. And you, thinking he would, that you would even want him to!"

"You were watching the whole time?"

Fastia calmed, but she was still chuckling. "No, not the whole time. Only as it was starting to get interesting."

"You had no right, you cold-blooded bitch!"

That stopped Fastia's laughter, and Anne was suddenly sorry. How long had it been since her sister had laughed? Even if it had to be at Anne's expense. Her self-righteousness faltered.

Fastia nodded, as if to herself. "Walk with me a moment, Anne. Erren, if you could stay here?"

"Certainly."

Outside, there was a faint chill in the air. The necropolis lay under silver light. Fastia took a few steps into the courtyard, then looked up at the half-empty moon. Her eyes were wide and glistening. Anne wasn't certain if there were tears there or not.

"You think I begrudge you this, Anne?" she asked softly. "You think I don't understand exactly how you feel?"

"No one knows how I feel."

Fastia sighed. "That's just part of it, Anne. The first time you hear a new song, you think you're the first to ever hear it, no matter how many lips it's been on. You think I never trysted, Anne? You think I never felt passion or thought I was in love?"

"You don't act like it."

"I suppose I don't. Anne, I do remember what you feel now. It was the most exciting time of my life."

"And then you married."

To Anne's surprise, Fastia chopped her head in agreement. "Yes. Ossel is a strong lord, a good ally. He is a good man, all in all."

"He is not good to you," Anne said.

"That's neither here nor there. Here is the point, Anne: Every passion I knew when I was your age, every pleasure, every desire—they are like thorns in me now, twisting. I regret ever—" She fluttered her hands helplessly. "I don't know how to say this."

"I do," Anne said. "If you had never known how good loving could be, you would not hate it so much with your husband."

Fastia's lips tightened. "That's crude, but that's it in a walnut."

"But if you had married for love—"

Fastia's voice grew harsher. "Anne, we do not marry for love. Nor may we, like our men, seek love after marriage. That sword does not swing both ways. We can find other pleasures—in our children, in our books and needlework and duties. But we may not—" Her hands darted about like confused birds, and she finally settled them by crossing her arms over her chest.

"Anne, I so envy you, and so pity you at the same time. You are just like me, and when reality falls upon your dreams, you will become just as bitter. I know what you think of me, you see. I have known it for years, since you cut me out of your heart."

"Me? I was a girl! You cut me out of yours, when you married that oaf."

Fastia clasped her hands together. "Perhaps I did not want to. But those first few years were the hardest, and after—" She shrugged. "After, it seemed best. You will marry, one day, and go off, and I will not see you anyway."

Anne stared at Fastia for a long moment. "If this is all true, I mean . . ."

"Why did I follow you down here?"

"Yes. Why didn't you leave well enough alone?"

"Weren't you listening? I told you *my* reasons. But there are other reasons. This Roderick—he is a schemer from a family of schemers, Anne. If he were to get you with child, there would be no end of it."

"That's not true! Roderick is—no, he's not like that. You don't know him, and I don't care about his family."

"You don't. I wish I didn't have to, but Mother and Father do. Absolutely. Anne, I have nothing if not my duty, do you understand? I could not willingly stand back and let this happen. As much as this may hurt now, it would have hurt much, much more later. And it would have hurt the kingdom, something I know you don't consider yet, but it is true."

"Oh, *figs!*" Anne exploded. "What nonsense. And besides, he and I—we never—I mean, he *couldn't* have got me with child, because we never—"

"You were going to, Anne. You may think you weren't, but you were."

"You can't know that."

"Anne, please. You know it's true. Without my interference, you would not have left the tomb a virgin."

Anne straightened her shoulders. "Will you tell Mother?"

"Erren already has. She's waiting for us now."

Anne felt a sudden tremor of fear. "What?"

"Mother *sent* us for you."

"What will she do? What can she do? I'm already exiled. I won't see him in Cal Azroth."

"I can't say, Anne. Believe it or not, I *did* speak for you. So did Lesbeth, for that matter."

"Lesbeth? She told? She betrayed me?"

Fastia's eyebrows went up. "Oh. So Lesbeth already knew? How interesting." Anne thought there was hurt in her voice. "And predictable, I suppose. No, Mother asked her opinion in the matter, as she did mine."

"Oh."

Fastia brushed Anne's hair from her face. "Come. Make yourself presentable. The longer we make Mother wait, the angrier she will be."

Numbly, Anne nodded.

Up the hill, through the gates into the castle—from Eslen-of-Shadows to her mother's chambers—Anne prepared her arguments. She nursed her outrage, reassured herself of the unfairness of it all.

When she entered her mother's chambers, however, and found the queen sitting in an armchair as if on a throne, her mouth went dry.

"Sit," Muriele said.

Anne did so.

"This is most disappointing," her mother began. "I thought, of all my daughters, in your own way, you had the most sense. I was fooling myself, I suppose."

"Mother, I—"

"Just keep your tongue, Anne. What can you say that would sway me?"

"He loves me! I love him!"

Her mother snorted. "Of course. Of course he does."

"He does!"

"Listen to me, Anne," her mother said softly, leaning forward. "*I. Don't. Care.*" She measured each word for fullest effect.

Then she leaned back in her chair and continued. "Most people in this kingdom would kill to live your life, to enjoy the privilege you hold. You will never know hunger, or thirst, or lack for clothing and shelter. You will never suffer the slightest tiny boil without that the finest physician in the land spends his hours easing the pain and healing you. You are indulged, spoiled, and pampered. And you do not appreciate it in the least. And here, Anne, here is the price you pay for your privilege: it is *responsibility*."

"The cost is my happiness, you mean."

Muriele blinked slowly. "You see? You haven't the slightest idea what I mean. But you will, Anne. You will."

The certainty of that clutched at Anne's heart. "What do you mean, Mother?"

"The lady Erren has written a letter for me. I have arranged for a coach, a driver, and an escort. You will leave in the morning."

"For Cal Azroth, you mean? I thought we were going by barge."

"We are. *You* are not going to Cal Azroth."

"Where am I going?"

"You are going to study, as Erren did. You will learn the most useful arts a lady may know."

"Erren?" Anne blurted. "You—you're sending me to a *coven*?"

"Of a very special sort."

"Mother, no!" Tendrils of panic seized her.

"What else can I do with you? You leave me at a loss."

"Please. Don't send me away."

"It won't be forever. Just until you've learned a few lessons, until you appreciate what you have, understand that you serve more in this world than your own desires. You need not take vows, though you may choose to do so, of course, in your fourth year."

"Fourth year! By all the merciful saints, Mother!"

"Anne, don't carry on. You've already embarrassed yourself aplenty for one night."

"But this isn't fair!" Anne felt the blood rushing to her cheeks.

"Life seldom is."

"I *hate* you!"

Muriele sighed. "I hope that is not true."

"It is. I *hate* you."

"Very well," her mother said. "Then that is the price *I* must pay. Go now, and pack. But don't bother with any of your better gowns."

CHAPTER TEN

INTO THE TANGLE

"I'VE NEVER SEEN ANYTHING SO BEAUTIFUL," Winna said, her voice hushed with awe. She stood on a stony ridge, profiled against the monstrous peak of Slé Eru, where glaciers threw the sun back at itself and eagles glided in lazy spirals. On either side the ridge— really a saddle between Slé Eru and the lesser but still dazzling peak of Slé Cray—dropped into breathtaking glens, deep and forested. They had just come up from Glen Ferth, where the headwaters of the Slaghish had their start in the ice melt of the two mountains. That was a very deep drop, a great green bowl whose other rim was hazed blue with distance, and the Slaghish was a tiny silver rill in its bosom. The other side of the ridge did not drop so far, but it was no less breathtaking, a highland valley of meadows and birch, and behind it another line of modest mountains, the footstool of the immense range whose pinnacles faded from sight, even in a clear blue sky.

"It's true," Aspar replied. But he wasn't looking at the landscape; he was looking at Winna standing against the backdrop of the high snowfields of Slé Eru. She wore a wide grin and her cheeks were pink with exertion and excitement, eyes all wonder-jeweled.

Winna caught that and gave him a sly, sidewise glance. "Why, Aspar White! Was that honey talk?"

"The best I can do," he replied.

"You do well enough," she assured him. She pointed at the highest peaks on the horizon. "What mountains are those?"

"*Sa'Ceth ag sa'Nem*—the Shoulders of Heaven," he said.

"Have you been there?"

"Yah."

"Did you climb them?"

"No man has ever climbed the Shoulders," he replied. "Not even the tribesmen who live on them. Those mountains have barely gotten started when the snowline starts."

"They're wondrous."

"That they are," he agreed.

"And this valley below us? What's it called?"

"Anything you like. I've never seen it before, nor heard it named. Those are the Cockspurs beyond."

"Then Mother Gastya was right. There *is* a hidden valley here."

"Looks like it," Aspar agreed. He wanted to be annoyed about that, but found he couldn't. Instead he wondered how powerful the magic must be to hide a whole valley—and what such power might mean if it was turned against two small people.

"Let's go, then!" Winna exclaimed.

"Give the horses a few moments," Aspar replied. "They aren't used to the heights, and they had a hard climb up. After all they've been through, I don't want to risk a bad step now."

When they'd come out of the waterway that led from Rewn Aluth, Ogre, Angel, and Pie Pony had been waiting for them. How they knew where to be would always remain a mystery; Ogre was a smart horse, but not *that* smart. Mother Gastya had to have had a part in such things, and Aspar didn't like that, much—the thought that his horses could be shinecrafted.

Though he was damned grateful to have them.

"How long should we let them rest?" Winna asked.

"A bell or so. Let them forage downslope a bit."

"Yah. And what might we do meantime?"

"Rest ourselves, I suppose," Aspar said.

"Indeed?" Winna replied. "With a bedroom view like this? I had other in mind." And she smiled, in a way he had come to like quite well.

*   *   *

"What are you looking at now?" Winna asked, a bell later. They were still on the ridge, Winna doing up the fastenings of her dress, Aspar pulling on his buskins. Aspar was gazing back toward the Slaghish, and the way they had come.

"Well?" Winna persisted. "Do you see them?"

"Not a sign. That's what worries me. Twenty-five days since we left Rewn Aluth, and no hint of either Fend or the greffyn."

"Are you disappointed?"

"No. But where are they? If the greffyn is coming here, as Mother Gastya said, and if Fend and his bunch are with it, or following it—" He shook his head. "What *are* they doing?"

"Don't you reckon they're the ones making the sacrifices at the old—how did you say it?—sedos fanes? The ones cutting up those poor people?"

"There were men with the greffyn at Taff Creek," Aspar said, lacing his buskin. "Some of them stayed with it all the way to Rewn Aluth, I think, but some went back west. I couldn't follow 'em both, of course. So, yah, I think Fend is mixed up in that, though it wasn't him alone. There's another bunch out there somewhere."

"So they killed squatters in the forest, and went after the Halafolk at Rewn Aluth," she said. "They're chasing folk out of the King's Forest."

"Yah."

"So maybe they aren't done yet. Maybe they went after more squatters, or another Halafolk rewn before coming back to the Briar King."

"That sounds sensible," Aspar agreed.

"But I don't understand the sacrifices. The greffyn kills just by a touch. So the men are the ones doing the awful things, yah? Not that any death isn't awful, but you know what I mean."

"I do. And, yah, men did what I saw on the Taff."

"Then why? What has it to do with the greffyn?"

Aspar examined the back of his hands, noticing as if for the first time how wrinkled they had become. "That priestish fellow I told you about, the Virgenyan—he said the warlocks used to do things like that, ages ago. Sacrifices to the Damned Saints, he said. My father's folk—"

He gestured vaguely northeast. "—they still hang criminals as sacrifice to the Raver."

Winna's eyes widened. "That's the first you've ever said of your parents."

"My father was an Ingorn, my mother a Watau. My mother died when I was born, but my father took a second wife, and we lived with my father's people, in the mountains. The Ingorns keep to the old ways, but I don't remember much about living there. There was a feud, of sorts, and my father was outlawed. He moved down a few leagues from Walker's Bailey, and we lived in the woods there till I was seven or thereabouts, I guess. Then the feud caught up with us. They killed my father and stepmother. I ran like a rabbit, but an arrow caught me. They reckoned me for dead, and I would have been, but Jesp found me."

"And raised you up."

"Yah."

"I'm sorry about your parents. I guess I reckoned they were dead, but nobody ever knew."

"I haven't told that story in a long time."

"Aspar?"

"Hmm?"

She kissed his cheek. "Thank you for telling me."

He nodded. "It's getting awful easy, telling you things." *Too easy, maybe.*

They followed the glen down, as Mother Gastya had instructed, camping that evening at the edge of a meadow, and waking to the low calls of aurochs. The forest cattle were rooting in the edge of the woods, and a few of the males cast uneasy glances in Aspar and Winna's direction. Ogre stamped and whinnied a challenge.

"Calves," Aspar whispered, nodding toward the smallest of the beasts. "Best we back away from here, slow."

So they broke camp and retreated into the woods, making a wide circle around the meadow and its touchy occupants.

For most of the day they continued down the gently sloping valley, through fields of brilliant green, or flaming with red clover. Deer, elk, and one pride of spotted lions that Aspar noticed watched them go, with mostly lazy eyes. It was as if the reputation of man had never reached this place.

Late in the day, the land fell more steeply, and they found themselves following the stony course of a stream bordered with head-high horsetails and ferns. The valley walls rose steeply on each side, closing them in, unscalable without rope and spike.

Night came swiftly in the narrow valley, and Aspar and Winna bathed in a shockingly cold pool, embracing first for warmth and then for more. Winna tasted like the water, almost metallic with youth and life. After, they curled in their blankets beneath the ferns. When Winna was asleep, Aspar lay listening to the warbling of frogs and nightbirds, and the trickle of water over stone. Somewhere near, that trickling became a rushing hiss as the stream dropped for some unknown depth. It was that sound that had stopped Aspar a little shy of true dark. If they were to negotiate a cliff, let them do it in morning's light.

As he lay there, he was amazed at how good he felt. There was something in the forest here, some almost sensual vitality, that he hadn't noticed since he was a boy. It was the force that had first made him fall in love with the woods, a force that was wonder and beauty and awe forged together.

He hadn't realized how much the hard years had stripped from him until now, when he suddenly had it back. Was it really this place that was different, somehow more alive than the rest of the world, or was it a change in Aspar White, brought on by—well, Grim, he could admit it to himself, however foolish it might sound aloud—love?

He didn't know and hardly cared. For the first time since he was a boy, he felt perfectly at one with the world.

There was indeed a cliff, as sheer as ever one could be, and it seemed to drop forever. That was difficult to tell, of course, for the canyon—it was certainly that now, with walls scarcely a stone's throw apart—was filled with trees. Not tall, slender boles, but a writhing, twisting, twining maze of thick branches, black-skinned and armed with thorns bigger than his hand. They rose from the unseen bottom in a heady tangle that reminded him of nothing so much as the tyrants. You couldn't fall far, in there. Of course, if you fell at all, you were likely to be impaled by the dagger-size thorns.

"What sort of tree is that?" Winna asked.

"I've never seen its like."

Winna waved at the glossy green leaves, shaped like long, narrow hearts. "Briar trees, maybe? For a Briar King?"

"Why not?" Aspar wondered.

"We have to climb down through that, though, don't we?"

"It's that or go back," Aspar replied.

"What about the horses?"

Aspar nodded reluctantly. "We'll have to leave 'em. I suspect we'll be back this way anyhow. I've a feeling this valley boxes, somewhere up ahead."

He turned and patted Ogre's cheek. "Take care of these two, as you did before, yah? I'll be back for you."

Ogre looked at him darkly, then tossed his head and stamped.

They kept close to the solid comfort of the granite wall, descending down the snaky branches from one to another. So tightly did they coil and twine, rarely was there room for Aspar to straighten. The thorns, at least, were spaced wide enough to avoid with relative ease, and in fact made good handholds.

The sky above became a mosaic, stained glass, a memory. At noon they were in twilight, and the leaves were going thin and yellow, starved for sunlight. A little lower, there were no leaves at all. Instead, the limbs were home to pale shelf fungi and yellow slime mold, white mushroom-like spheroids, and vaguely obscene crimson pipes.

Dragonflies the size of small birds wove in and out of the briars, and pale, squirrellike beasts scampered away from Aspar and Winna as they climbed farther and farther from the sun.

Winna, ever delighted, and getting comfortable with their descent, moved ahead of Aspar by a stone's throw. He didn't like that, and said so, but she replied with lighthearted taunts about his age and encouraged him to greater speed.

When first she shrieked, he thought it was another joke, so unreal did her scream sound. But when she repeated herself, he understood the terror in it.

"Winna!" He dropped his own height, hit a branch slick with fungus and nearly fell. He caught himself, though, and went down the next branch as dexterously as a squirrel. He could see her, but he couldn't see what threatened her.

He swung under the next branch, and something hit him in the face, something that gripped him like a giant, hairy hand. He gave a hoarse cry and clawed at it, pulling off a spider bigger than his head. He was mired in a web, too. It ripped easily enough, but it was sticky and disgusting. He hurled the spider away, hoping it hadn't bitten, not feeling a bite.

A moment later he was just above Winna. She, too, was veiled in the sticky white spider-weave, crying and shaking. One of the eight-legged creatures was advancing toward her along the limb.

He pinned it there with his throwing ax. Its legs flailed wildly, but it was stuck fast.

"Were you bit?" he asked, as he reached her at last. "Did one of those things bite you?"

She shook her head, but waved a trembling hand around them.

They were everywhere, the spiders, spread between nearly every limb. Some were the size of fists, some as large as a cat. They were thick-legged, hairy, with yellow striping. An arm's length from Winna, one of the squirrels struggled in a web, as its weaver moved toward it, mandibles working eagerly.

"Are they poisonous?" Winna rasped faintly.

"We aren't going to find out," Aspar said. "We're moving back up. We'll travel in the higher branches."

"But don't we have to go down?"

"Not yet. Not now. Maybe this is just a local nest of 'em."

Aspar retrieved his ax, and they climbed back up, weaving carefully between the webs. A spider dropped from a branch, straight toward Aspar's head, but he batted it away with a disgusted growl.

Finally, when they were well above the level where the spiders dwelt, they stopped and cleaned off as many of the webs as they could.

Then they examined one another for wounds and spent a few moments nestled together.

"We'll want to be out of these trees by nightfall," Aspar said.

"Why? You think the spiders will come up?"

"No. But what else lives in here? What lives even farther down, where it must always be dark? I don't *know* what might come up at sunfall, and that's the problem. As well, we won't sleep well in these branches, and we can't start a fire."

"We should go, then." She sounded shaky.

"Can you?"

"Yah. I can."

He had the sudden urge to kiss her, and he did.

"What was that for?" she asked.

"You're a brave lass, Winna. The bravest."

She uttered a staccato laugh. "I don't feel brave. Screaming at spiders."

Aspar rolled his eyes. "Come on, you."

They went on, keeping to the middle heights. The rift walls came nearly together and then began to widen again, and as they got wider, the thorn forest dropped lower and lower; without the narrow walls to crowd them up toward the sun, the branches wandered in a more leisurely fashion.

Now and then, Aspar could actually see the ground, covered with what resembled white ferns.

But the great, dark, unknown cavern behind them troubled him more and more as the day waned. He could almost smell the presence of something large and mirksome, caged by the sun but free to walk when the Shining King slept.

And he would sleep soon.

"Let's go down," Aspar said, "and hope for no more surprises."

The spiders were there, but in much fewer numbers and spread much more thinly. They were also generally smaller, and so Aspar and Winna made their way down through them with relatively few anxious moments. Finally, reluctantly, Aspar dropped around twice his height from the last branch onto the leaf mold that covered the ground, avoiding the patches of white, whisklike growth that might hide more many-legged predators.

A moment later, he caught Winna as she followed him down.

More than ever it seemed like a cave. The trunks of the thorn trees were massive in girth, but spaced wide apart. The result was like a gigantic, low-roofed hall with many pillars. A very dark hall, and from the way they had come, from the heart of that darkness, Aspar smelled something fetid.

"Come on," he said. "Let's hurry."

They more or less ran. Aspar strung his bow, brandishing it in front in case of spiderwebs they might not see. The ground was level and flat and deep with mold. It smelled like centipede, like the underside of a piece of rotting bark.

As the light faded, the tree trunks grew taller, but Aspar still saw no end to them. Finally, desperate, his back itching and the smell of autumn leaves filling his nostrils, he noticed one tree with a large hollow in it.

"If this forest has an end, we won't find it before nightfall," he told Winna. "This is the best we can do."

Striking tinder, he held it inside and made certain the space was empty, then the two of them crouched within.

The forest faded and vanished, and Aspar placed himself between Winna and the outside, gripping his bow.

Behind him, after a bell or so, Winna's breath starting coming slow and regular.

A little after that, the nightbirds stopped singing, and the dark grew very quiet indeed. And then—there was still no sound, but Aspar felt it, like a blind man feels the heat of the sun on his face. The earth trembled faintly, and then a stench thickened the air.

Aspar squinted at the darkness, and waited.

CHAPTER ELEVEN

DEPARTURES

"I KNOW IT ISN'T FAIR, DOVE," Lesbeth said, drawing Anne's hair back for the pin. "But your mother feels it's best for you."

"Roderick will forget about me."

"If that happens, then he never loved you," Lesbeth said. "Besides— Anne, I tried to warn you of this."

"But *you're* marrying for love!" Anne said. "You're the youngest, and so am I."

"I was patient," Lesbeth said. "And most of all, I was fortunate."

"*I* wish to be so fortunate," Anne said.

Lesbeth came around so she could look Anne in the eye. "Then do as your mother says. You may not understand, Anne, but she is giving you a chance for true love better than ever you had before."

"By sending me away? To a *coven*? That makes no sense."

"Oh, but it does," Lesbeth assured her. "It will keep marriage off you for a time, for one thing, and even after you leave the coven you will have a grace period wherein you might claim to be considering vows. You will have a way of delaying suitors, and thus opportunity to be courted by more of them. The more you have, the better your chance of finding one who pleases you. And if worse comes to worst—why, you *can* take the vows."

"Never." Anne tossed her head. "Besides, I've already found the suitor I want."

"Well, him you can't have, and that's that, Anne. Not now, anyway. Maybe in a few years—maybe Roderick will prove himself in service, or in some other way to redeem his family. More likely, you'll realize that what you two share is a young passion, a teakettle love, done once the steam boils out. More men are like that than you might think." Lesbeth took Anne's fingers in her own. "A merchant knows, never buy the first ware you see. It may appear all very well, but until you have some basis for judgment, how can you know?"

"Well, I'll get no better basis for comparison in the coven, and that's assured!" Anne replied bitterly.

"Patience," Lesbeth replied. "And you'll have Austra with you, yes?"

"Yes," Anne agreed reluctantly, "but it shall still be awful. Learn to be like Erren? What exactly does Erren do, besides sneak about and pry into things?"

Lesbeth made a funny little frown. "Surely you know what Erren does."

"She's Mother's spy."

"Yes, she's that. But she also—Anne, Erren *kills* people."

Anne started to laugh at that, but then she saw Lesbeth wasn't joking. "Kills who? How?" she asked.

"People. People who are dangerous to the kingdom, and to your mother."

"But who? Who has she killed?"

Lesbeth's voice dropped very low. "It's secret, mostly. That's the thing about Erren, she's very . . . quiet. But—do you remember that fat lord from Wys-on-Sea? Hemming?"

"Yes. I thought he was a sort of clown, always joking."

"He was a spy for the Reiksbaurgs. He was part of a plot to kidnap Fastia."

"But I remember—he died in his chambers. They said it was his heart."

"Maybe. But it was Erren who stopped his heart, whether by poison or needle or sacaum of death it cannot be said. But it was Erren. I heard your mother speak of it, once."

"That's . . ." Anne didn't know what it was. Erren had always been spooky, but . . . "*I'm* to learn such things?" Anne asked. "Why?"

"Great houses must have women like Erren. She is your mother's first cousin, you know, of gentle birth. But your mother has this in mind: If you will not serve your house in marriage, you will serve it in some other way. She's giving you a choice."

"I don't believe it. Mother hates me."

"How absurd. She loves you. She may love you best, of all her children."

"How can you say that?"

"You cannot see yourself, can you, Anne? Except in a mirror, and there everything is backwards. Believe me. Your mother loves you. I, too, wish she would not send you off, but I understand why she does. You will, too, one day, even if you never agree. That's what growing up ought to be, you know, or bring with it anyhow—the vision to understand something even when you're dead set against it."

Anne felt tears start. "I'll miss you, Lesbeth. Just as I get you back, now I have to go."

"I'll miss you, Anne," Lesbeth said, giving her a long hug. "And now I must go. I cannot bear to see you off."

"Neither can Mother, it seems. Or Fastia."

"They are already gone, Anne. Didn't you know? They left on the barge, before dawn. And everyone thinks you are with them."

Including Roderick, Anne thought, as she watched her aunt vanish through the arch in the stable yard. *He still thinks I'm going to Cal Azroth.* She and Austra had been watched like prisoners, and she had found neither the time nor the opportunity to send him a message.

Besides, she didn't know where she was going.

I'll take my first chance, she thought. *They can't do this to me. Even Lesbeth, though I love her dearly, doesn't understand me. I can't be trapped in a coven. I can't. If I have to live like a bandit, or dress as a man and fight as a soldier of fortune, I will do it.*

She was still thinking in that vein when the coach came, and Austra and some bearers with their luggage.

"Where do you think we're going?" Austra whispered, as the shades were drawn on the coach, and it began rumbling forward.

"It doesn't matter," Anne said, with false brightness. "It doesn't matter one bit."

∘   ∘   ∘

Muriele watched the elms go by. They lined the canal like a colonnade; elms had deep, straight roots that would never undermine the dikes they were planted on, only strengthen them.

Beyond the elms, the fields of Newland went flat and green to the horizons. Only the now distant bump that was the island of Ynis marred that flatness, for even the south hills were obscured by a noon haze.

"Did I do the right thing?" she murmured. Anne's face was vivid in her mind. *I hate you.* What mother could bear to hear that from her child?

Some things had to be borne.

"My queen?"

Muriele turned to find the young knight, Neil MeqVren, almost at her elbow. "Yes?" she said.

"I'm sorry, Your Majesty," he said, bowing hastily. "I thought you spoke to me."

"No," she said. "Only to myself, or to the saints."

"I'm sorry to bother you, then."

"It's no bother. You said your farewells to Sir Fail, I hope."

"I had little time, and we spoke only a few words," Neil replied.

"He's bursting with pride of you. If you were his own son, I think he could never be prouder."

"If he were my own father, I could never be gladder of it."

"I'm sure that's so," Muriele replied.

She let silence rest between them for a moment. "What do you think of all this, Neil?"

"Newland, you mean?"

"No, that's not what I meant, but since you bring it up, you must have some opinion."

Neil grinned a little sheepishly and looked very, very young. "I guess, Majesty, that it makes me nervous. You're from Liery, so you understand; we would never put chains on our lord the sea. We would never dream to tell him where he can and cannot go. Yet here—well, it *is* grand, I have to say, and astonishing—that land can be taken from the waves. And I suppose Saint Lier has raised no objection, but it seems . . . impertinent."

"Even for the emperor of Crotheny?"

"Begging your pardon, Your Majesty, but even an emperor is simply a man. I serve that man, and all he represents, and if you should ask me to throw my body into a hole in one of these dikes to plug it and keep the sea out, I'd do it, then let the saints judge me as they might. But still, in all—I love the sealord, but I do not trust him over my head, if you know what I mean."

"I do," Muriele said quietly. "The Reiksbaurgs began this, and my husband's people finished it. Beneath these waters, they found the most fertile soil in all the world. But don't allow yourself to be fooled; we pay a tithe to the saints of the waves, of marsh, and river. And sometimes they *take* their own tithe. It is, as you say, an uneasy arrangement."

Neil nodded. "And so what did you mean, Majesty, when you asked me what I thought?"

"Do you agree with my husband? Is going to Cal Azroth what we ought to do?"

Neil considered his words carefully before answering. "The lords of Hansa are a treacherous lot," he finally said. "They fight from the smoke, always behind masks. They pay Weihand raiders for Lierish scalps, and do not call that war. They are dabblers in shinecraft, despite all their pretense to be a holy, churchish nation. That man I fought was your man, through and through, I do believe it. And yet he would have killed you."

"These are all statements of fact, more or less," Muriele noted. "What do you *think*?"

"I think if Hansa believed that by striking at the king's family they could weaken the kingdom, they would do it. But, to be honest, this retreat to the countryside makes me uneasy."

"Why?"

"I am not altogether certain. It feels . . . wrong. Why try to slay *you*, rather than the king himself? And how can you be safe in any place when we don't even know how your man was turned against you? If 'twere shinecraft, *I* might be turned against you just as easily. I would throw myself on my sword before doing you harm, but I'll wager that knight I slew would have sworn the same thing."

"Perhaps. Sir Neil, in some things you are wise beyond your years, but in the ways of the court you are yet naïve. It takes no shinecraft to corrupt a man, not even a Craftsman. The magicks of greed, fear, and envy are quite enough to work most of the evil you will ever see at court.

"As to why me, rather than the king, I admit to puzzlement there, as well."

"Maybe   ." Neil frowned to himself a moment. "What if all your enemy desired was to *separate* you from the king? To divide your family?"

Something about what the knight was saying seemed very right. "Go on," she said.

"If I were the king, suddenly deprived of children and—wife—I would feel the weaker. Like a wagon missing a wheel."

"My husband still has his mistresses. And his brother."

"Yes, Your Majesty. But—what if it were *they* who wanted you out of the way?"

Muriele stared at the young man, suddenly realizing she did not have a measure of him at all. "By the saints, Sir Neil," she murmured. "It was purest libel for me to call you naïve. Accept my apologies, I beg you."

"I know nothing, Your Majesty," Neil said slowly, "but I follow the lady Erren's advice to the end of the path. In my mind, I must think everyone in the world your enemy. The lady Erren included. Myself included. And if I think like that, everything seems suspicious. And if I think like that, saints willing, I will not long stand surprised when your true foes raise their hands again. Instead, I will slaughter them where they stand."

The passion in his voice sent a shiver through her. Sometimes, at court, one forgot that there were real people in the world, genuine people. This young man was such a one, still. He was genuine, he was dangerous, and, saints willing, he was hers.

"Thank you, Sir Neil, for your opinion. I find it worth considering."

"Thank you, Your Majesty, for listening to my concerns."

Lesbeth tossed back her auburn hair and stared off across the western bay, and the great white teeth of Thornrath that marked it from the periwinkle sea beyond. She could just make out the white sails of a merchantman, near the horizon. A gull wheeled overhead, no doubt eyeing the remains of the baked hen, Donchest cheese, and honey cakes still spread on the picnic cloth.

"A beautiful day," her brother Robert said, sipping from the last half of their second bottle of wine. They sat together on the westernmost prominence of Ynis, a grassy spur littered with the crumbled ruins of an old tower.

"It is," Lesbeth replied, flashing him a smile she didn't quite feel. Robert had been . . . *brittle* since he learned of her betrothal. She'd accepted his invitation to picnic, in hopes of healing that. But she hadn't dreamed he would bring her *here* of all places. Robert was spiteful, yes, but usually not to her.

Just concentrate on the sea and sky, she told herself. *Concentrate on the beauty.*

But Robert seemed determined not to let her.

"Do you remember how we came up here as children?" he asked. "We used to pretend the tower there was our own castle."

"Those were excellent days," Lesbeth said, around the lump in her throat.

"I knew you, then," Robert said. "Or thought I did. I always fancied I knew your least thought, and you mine." He swallowed another mouthful of wine. *"Then."*

Lesbeth reached for his hand and took his fingers in hers. "Robert, I *am* sorry. I should have asked your permission to marry. I know that. And I'm asking now."

An odd look crossed Robert's face, but he shook his head. "You asked Wilm's. He's the eldest."

Lesbeth squeezed his hand. "I know I caused you pain, Robert. It's only that I didn't know *how* to tell you."

"How can that be?" he asked.

She drew a deep breath. "It is as you say. Once we were so close, one of us could not blink without the other knowing. And now, somehow—"

"You don't know me anymore," he finished for her. "We have grown separate. Every since that day when Rose—"

"Please, stop!" Lesbeth closed her eyes against the terrible memory, willing it away.

"As you wish," he said. "But we never spoke of—"

"Nor shall we. I *cannot*."

He nodded, and a look of resignation crossed his face.

"Besides," she went on. "I know you believe my prince Cheiso insulted you—"

"I do not *believe* he did," Robert said. "I am *certain* of it."

"Please, Robert. He did not mean to give offense."

Robert smiled and held his hands up. "Perhaps he didn't," he allowed. "And so where is he now? I should think *he* would have come to ask permission—if not from me, then at least from Wilm. Why did he leave you to do it?"

"He will arrive within a nineday or two," Lesbeth replied. "He had matters pressing him. He asked me to wait, so we might travel together, but I was impatient. I wanted to share my news." She turned her head to the side. "Please, Robert. Be happy for me. You are my brother, and I do love you, but after—"

"After we killed Rose?" he said bluntly.

Lesbeth nodded silently, unable to go on.

"It was an accident," he reminded her.

Lesbeth didn't remember it that way. She remembered a cruel game, played with a servant, a game that went further than it ever should have. And she remembered knowing that Robert meant for it to go that far, from the very start. After that, she hadn't wanted to know what Robert was thinking anymore.

But she nodded again, as if agreeing with him. "I cannot speak of this," she said again.

"I'm sorry," he murmured. "I've spoiled our outing. That was not my intention. There are years between us we cannot repair, I know. Silence has worked on us like poison. But we are twins, Lesbeth." He stood suddenly. "May I show you something?"

"What is it?"

He smiled and for a moment looked like the boy she remembered. "A wedding gift," he replied.

"Up here?"

"Yes." He looked a little embarrassed. "It's something I worked on with my own hands. It isn't far."

Lesbeth smiled tentatively. There was so much hurt in Robert, so much broken. She did love him, though. She took his hand and let him pull her up, and followed as he led her into the mostly wild gardens around them. When they had been young, these had been well-tended, but over the years this spot had fallen out of fashion, and the roses and hedges allowed their own way. Now, in places, it was as dense as a true forest.

Robert did not lead her far. "Here it is."

Lesbeth could only stare in dull shock. The sun was shining, flowers were blooming. She was going to be married. He could he do this?

He had dug up Rose. Her little bones—she had been ten—lay in the bottom of a yawning hole in the earth. Her clothes had gone to rotten rags, but Lesbeth recognized what remained of the blue dress she had last worn.

"By all the saints, Robert—" The horror choked off anything else she might have said. She wanted to run and scream, and bawl her eyes out. Instead she could only gaze into that hole, into that terrible crime of her past. She had never known what Robert did with the body. They had told everyone Rose had run away.

I'm sorry, Rose, she thought. *Saints of grief, but I'm sorry.*

"I love you, Lesbeth," Robert said softly. "You should have asked my permission. Mine, not Wilm's. Mine."

And as she turned to face him, he struck her in the breast, so hard she staggered back and sat down, her skirts billowing around her. She stared up at him, more perplexed than hurt. Robert had never hit her before, ever.

"Robert, what—" As soon as she tried to speak, she knew something was very, very wrong. Something inside her was all twisted, and her breath hurt like fire. And Robert, standing over her—his hand was still a fist, but there was a knife in it, the narrow bodkin he always wore at his belt, the one Grandpa had given him when he was eleven. It was red to the hilt.

Then she looked down at the front of her dress and saw the wet redness over her heart. Her hand was sanguine, too, where she had pressed it without thinking against the wound. As she watched, blood actually spurted between her fingers, like a spring bubbling from the earth.

"Robert, no," she sighed, her voice high and strange. "Robert, do not kill me."

He bent over her, his dark eyes glistening with tears. "I already have, Lesbeth," he said, very softly. "I already have." And he kissed her on the forehead.

Shaking her head, she crawled away, trying to get to her feet, failing. "I'm going to be married," she told him, trying to make him understand. "To a Safnian prince. He's coming for me." She could almost see Cheiso, standing before her. "I'll give him children. I'll name one for you. Robert, don't—"

Sheer panic swept through her. She had to get away. Robert had gone mad. He meant to hurt her.

But there was no strength in her arms, and something closed around her ankle, and the grass was sliding beneath her, and she was leaving a broad trail across it, like a giant snail, except that the trail was red.

And then a moment like floating, and Robert's face before her again.

"Sleep, sister," he said. "Dream of when we were young, and all was well. Dream of when you loved me best."

"Don't kill me, Robert," she begged, sobbing now. "Help me."

"You'll have Rose," he said. "And soon enough—soon enough, you'll have company aplenty. Aplenty."

And he smiled, but his face seemed very far away, retreating. She hadn't felt the fall, but the empty sockets of Rose's little white skull were right next to her.

Lesbeth heard the music of birds, and a whispering she ought to recognize, words she half understood. They seemed very important.

And then, suddenly, that was all.

CHAPTER TWELVE

SPENDLOVE

WHEN STEPHEN DARIGE AWOKE from the grips of Black Mary for the fourth time in one night, he cursed sleep, rose, and crept from the dormitory. Outside, the night was clear and moonless, with a feel like early autumn in the air. He walked a small distance, to where the hillside started its roll down to the pastures, and there sat gazing up at the stars.

The stars eternal, his grandfather had called them.

But his grandfather was wrong; nothing was eternal. Not stars, not mountains. Not the saints, nor love, nor truth.

"Saint Michael," he murmured. "Tell me what truth is. I don't know anymore."

He felt as if there was something spoiled in him, something he badly needed to vomit up. But he feared if it came out, it would take a life and form of its own, and devour him.

He should have told the fratrex what the scroll was as soon as he understood. He shouldn't have translated it. By the saints, he shouldn't have.

Now it was too late. Now he had those evil words in him. Now he couldn't get them out.

A faint brush of shoes on grass told him someone was behind him. He was sure he knew who it was, and didn't care.

"Hello, Brother Desmond."

"Good morning, Brother Stephen. Taking some air?"

Stephen turned enough to see the shadow of the man standing against the stars. "Leave me alone or kill me. I don't care which."

"Don't you?" It sounded strange, the way he said it, almost like a lullaby. Then a fist knotted in Stephen's hair and yanked him down flat. Desmond dragged him a few feet and then crouched, brought the edge of a broad-bladed knife against Stephen's throat.

"Don't you?" he whispered again, almost in Stephen's ear.

"Why?" Stephen managed. "Why are you doing this to me?"

"Because. I don't like you. You're going to walk the fanes next month. Did you know that?"

"What?"

"Yes. You're done with your translation, aren't you?"

"What? How did you know that?"

"I know everything that goes on around here, you little pissant. Why wouldn't I know that?"

"I haven't told anyone."

"Don't worry. I took your notes to the fratrex for you, after I read them."

The knife came away, and Brother Desmond stood. Stephen expected a vicious kick, but instead, to his surprise, Desmond sighed and sat next to him on the grass.

"Wicked stuff," Spendlove said, almost whispering. "Spells to turn men to jelly, prayers to the Damned Saints. Blood rites, deformation of children. First-rate wicked. Is that why you can't sleep?"

"You read it," Stephen said dully. "Can *you* sleep?"

Desmond growled up something like a laugh. "I never could," he replied.

"Why did you steal my work?"

"Why not?"

"But you gave it to the fratrex."

"Yes. Believe what you might about me, Brother Stephen, but I do serve my order." His voice dropped even lower. "Very well I serve it."

Stephen nodded. "Well, you've done me a favor. I didn't know if I would have the courage."

"What do you mean?"

Stephen suddenly wished he could see Brother Desmond's eyes. For the first time since they had met, the other man sounded puzzled.

"You know," Stephen said. "You know very well I won't be walking any fanes after the fratrex reads what I wrote and realizes what I've done."

"You did what he told you to do," Spendlove replied, and this time there could be no doubt about it, the monk was puzzled, or doing a blessed good imitation.

"Brother Desmond, the work of the church has always been to destroy such foul texts. The moment I knew what it was, I should have consulted with the fratrex. Instead, I barreled ahead and translated a forbidden scrift. I've probably damned myself, and I will certainly lose my position here."

That got a wry chuckle from Spendlove.

"Brother Stephen, you may think I'm your worst enemy in this place. I'm not. You're your own worst enemy. I wouldn't wish that on anyone." With that, Brother Desmond stood. "Good luck walking the fanes," he said. He almost sounded as if he meant it.

A moment later Stephen was alone again, with the stars.

The fratrex looked up from a desk cluttered with books, paper, and several inkwells.

"Eh? Good morning, Brother Stephen." He tapped some sheets of paper on his desk. "Excellent work, this. Are you quite sure of it all?"

"Reverend? As sure as I can be."

"Well. I am not disappointed in you, I can tell you that."

"But, Reverend—" He felt as he had in the woods, when the hounds were coming, and for an instant he really had believed Aspar White's Grim Raver was stooping on him. He had felt the same way when he was halfway through the manuscrift and really understood what he had.

It was that spinning sensation that came of suddenly realizing he truly didn't understand the world. Of having too many secure assumptions upset at once.

The fratrex sat waiting for him to continue, one eyebrow cocked.

"The nature of the scrift," Stephen explained. "I should have told you as soon as I knew. I should have stopped before I finished it. I'm sorry. I'll understand if you ask for my resignation."

"You don't have to tell me that," the fratrex said. "If I ask for your resignation, I shall get it, and whether you *understand* or not is entirely beside the point. But why should I ask for it? You did exactly what I requested, and splendidly."

"I don't understand, Reverend. Church policy—"

"Is much better understood by me than by you," the fratrex finished dryly. "The church has concerns you cannot begin to understand, and which I cannot, at this time, explain to you. Suffice to say that there is evil in the world, yes? And that evil may remain silent for many years, but when it speaks, we should at least know the language. If we do not, it may well talk us all into its spell."

The implications of that walked through Stephen like a ghost, leaving chill footprints on his heart.

"Reverend, may I confide in you?"

"As in no other."

"I heard . . . things on the way here. On the road. At Tor Scath."

"Go on. Please, sit. You look as if your legs are ready to give way."

"Thank you, Reverend." He settled onto a small, hard stool.

"So tell me these things."

Stephen told him the rumors of the greffyn, and the terrible rites on the abandoned sedos fanes. When he was done, the fratrex leaned forward.

"Such rumors are not unknown to us," he said, in a low voice. "Nor should they be spread any further. Keep them to yourself, and be assured that the church is not complacent in these matters."

"Yes, Reverend. It's just that—the sacrifices at the fanes. They resemble certain rites described in the scrift."

"I have seen that. What reason do you think I had for wanting this translated?"

"But—I think whoever is doing these things only half understands what they are about."

"What do you suppose they are about?"

"I'm not sure, but I think they are trying to revive an ancient faneway, one of the forbidden ones. Perhaps the very one that the Black Jester walked to gain his unholy powers. The rites are a sort of test, to help them learn which of the thousand fanes in the forest still have power, and to determine the order in which they ought to be walked."

"But they aren't doing the rites correctly, so we have nothing to fear—yet," the fratrex reasoned.

"Yet my work would help them," Stephen said softly. "Some of the missing pieces to their puzzle may lie in what you have before you."

The fratrex nodded solemnly. "Of course, we are aware of that. But we cannot risk fighting this enemy in the dark. They have some of the secrets. They got them somewhere. We cannot oppose them when we know nothing."

"But, Reverend—" The image of Desmond Spendlove flashed through his mind. "—what if our enemies are in our midst already? In the church itself?"

The fratrex smiled grimly. "The surest way to catch a weasel is to set a trap," he said. "And for a trap, bait is needed."

He stood. "I thought I taught you a lesson in humility, Brother Stephen. I wonder now if I succeeded. I am no doddering fool, and the church is too canny to be cuckolded by evil. But your loose tongue and your questions could do a great deal of damage, do you understand? Perform the tasks I set before you. Do not speak of them to anyone but me. Do your best to keep anyone else from seeing your work."

"But my work has already been seen."

"By Brother Desmond, yes. That was not unforeseen. But do better in the future. Hide your progress. Write faulty translations as well as sound ones."

"Reverend? The translation is done."

For answer, the fratrex stooped, and from beneath his desk he brought up a large cedar box.

"There are more," he said. "I expect the same alacrity that you have already shown." He smiled thinly. "And now, I suggest you meditate and prepare. Soon you will walk the faneway of Saint Decmanus, and you must be in the proper state of mind."

Stephen knelt and bowed. "Thank you, Reverend. And I apologize for any impertinence. I assure you it comes entirely from concern for the welfare of the church."

"In this place, that is my concern," the fratrex reminded him. He waved the back of his hand. "Go on," he said. "Put away your worries, and prepare for revelations."

But Stephen left feeling that he had already had one revelation too many. He feared another might break him.

CHAPTER THIRTEEN

THE BRIAR KING

MORNING'S SOFT STIRRING found Aspar still awake, legs cramping beneath him, bow still strung.

Whatever had come in the night had gone with it, leaving only the memory of its stink. And when Winna began to wake, Aspar stepped cautiously into the light and gazed around him.

Sun maidens were kissing the leaves high above, and though shadows lay long on the earth, they all pointed back toward the way from which Aspar and Winna had come. Before them, the forest grew thinner, and not far away, Aspar could reckon the end of it, by the open look of the treetops.

He inspected the damp leaf litter for some sign of what had come stalking the night before, but found no track or spoor, no broken branches, fur or feathers. This left him wondering if his senses hadn't betrayed him, somehow. He was, after all, on a Sefry errand, where truth and lies mixed in the same muddy water.

"Good morning to you, Aspar," Winna said. "Didn't you sleep at all?"

He grinned wryly. "Not likely."

"We agreed that we would share the watches," she reminded him, exasperation in her voice. "You should have waked me."

"You can have tomorrow night, then, the whole thing," he promised.

"Anyhow, look, I think we're nearly out of the forest." He nodded in the direction where the trees thinned.

Winna stretched and yawned. "Looks the same to me, but I'll take your word for it. Did we have any visitors in the night?"

"Something came out, but it made no sound and left no prints. It went away before the dawn."

Winna frowned. "I dreamed of something that smelled foul."

"The foul smell wasn't a dream," Aspar said. "That's for certain."

"Could it—could it have been the Briar King himself?" she wondered.

"Grim, I hope not," Aspar swore. "Whatever was out in the dark, I never want to see it."

Winna looked unsettled at that, but she didn't say anything.

"What now?" she asked instead.

"I suppose we go on, and see what there is to see. Do you need food?"

"Not yet. We can eat in a while. If there are more of those spiders overhead, I'd like to be out from under 'em. Saints, yes! They crawled all through my dreams, too."

As the space widened between the trunks of the trees the white, straw-like ground cover gave way to ferns and horsetails, then to bushier growth—rambling mounds of blackberry bushes, knee-high catgrass and broomsedge, grapevines groping over all. For Aspar, it was a relief to see plants he knew, by Grim's bloody eye!

At last, just short of midday, they left the forest behind them. The trees ended rather abruptly, giving way to a gently rolling valley floor. Mountains framed every direction, adding force to Aspar's guess that the only way in and out of the valley—short of crawling across the icy glaciers—was probably the way they had come.

The fields were brushy with grass and thistle and wild primrose, but riddled with enough animal trails to make the going easy most of the time.

If they had anywhere to go, which they didn't.

They struck on toward the far valley wall, but slowly. Aspar wondered just what in the name of the Sarnwood witch he was looking for.

It was a bell later when Winna pointed off to their right. "What's that?" she asked.

Aspar had already noticed what she was gesturing at—a line of small trees, not much taller than the grass, marching toward the valley wall, not quite paralleling their own path.

"A stream, most likely," he grunted.

"Most likely," Winna conceded. "But it seems odd to me."

"Nothing odd about it," Aspar argued.

"What would it hurt to have a look?" Winna asked. "I don't see anything else even a little strange."

"You've a point," he allowed. They turned their steps that direction.

After a few hundred paces, Winna asked, "Aspar, what do the Sefry expect us to do here?"

"Find the Briar King, I reckon."

"Just find him?"

"That's what Mother Gastya said," Aspar replied.

Winna nodded. "Yah. But aren't you the one who says the Sefry always lie?"

"I am," Aspar admitted. "But that doesn't matter. Whatever they want of me, I would have come here eventually. I've lived in this forest all of my life, Winn. Something's wrong with it. Very wrong." He chewed his lip, then cleared his throat. "I think it's dying. I think the greffyn has something to do with it, and if there *is* a Briar King, and he's at the bottom of this rot—I need to know."

"But suppose Mother Gastya lied. Suppose this isn't where the Briar King is. What if she sent you as far from him as she could?"

"I thought of that. I took the chance." He glanced at her. "But that's not what you're worried about, is it? You're worried that he *is* here."

For a few moments the swishing of Winna's tattered skirts against the grass was the only sound. "I *know* he's here," she said finally. "But what if the Sefry sent you to him so he could kill you?"

"If Mother Gastya wanted me dead, she needed only to have kept silent for another few heartbeats, back in Rewn Aluth," Aspar pointed out. "Whatever the Sefry want, it's not just my death."

"I guess not," Winna conceded. Then she stopped.

They had reached the line of small trees. "I don't see a stream."

"No," Aspar said slowly.

The trees were very small versions of the briar trees. They stood just over waist high.

"Look how regular they're spaced," Winna said. "Like somebody planted them."

"There's something else," Aspar said, crouching. "Something . . ." It reminded him of tracking, somehow. But it took him another twenty heartbeats to understand why.

"They're planted like a man's footsteps," he said. "A big man. But see? It's as if at every stride, a tree sprang up." He glanced back over his shoulder. The trail of trees led back into the forest—and it led ahead, to the valley wall.

"What's that up there?"

Aspar followed the imaginary line her finger traced in the air. Far off—half a league, maybe—the row of trees led to some sort of dome. It looked man-made.

"A building?" he speculated. "It looks a little like a Watau longhouse."

It wasn't a longhouse. His mother's people built their lodgings of freshly cut young trees, bending them into arches and then covering all with shingles of bark. The structure he and Winna beheld was likewise made of trees—but they were still alive, thrusting strong roots into the soil and lacing their branches tightly together. It was shaped like a giant bird's nest, turned upside down. It stood perhaps twenty yards high at its apex.

So tight and dense were the trees woven that nothing could be seen within, even when they drew near enough to touch it.

A circuit of the weird, living structure led them to an opening, of sorts—a twisting path between the trunks and branches just large enough for Aspar to squeeze through. No sound came from within.

"You'll stay here," Aspar told Winna.

Winna frowned at him. "Aspar White, I've climbed mountains, swum in freezing water, and endured thunderstorms with you. I've saved your life twice now, by my count—"

"Winna, do this for me."

"Give me a reason to. One that makes sense."

He stared at her, then took a step and put his palm to her cheek. "Because this is all different," he said. "There's nothing canny, here. Who knows which stories are true, and which are lies? Who knows but that if the gaze of the greffyn brings faintness, the eyes of the Briar King might not slay in a single blink?" He kissed her. "Because I love you, Winna, and would protect you, whether you want me to or not. And finally, if something happens to me, *someone* must get word to the king, and the other holters. Someone has to save my forest."

She closed her eyes for a long time, and when she opened them, they were smiling and moist. "I love you, too, you great lout. Just come out alive, will you? And then take me out of this place. I couldn't find my way back alone anyhow."

"I'll do that," he said.

A moment later, he stepped into the trees.

Immediately, something went strange. He felt a sort of shock, like he might feel if he had nodded off, then jerked his head up suddenly. A bumblebee seemed to be buzzing someplace inside his chest, accompanied by a rhythmic humming from his lungs.

He continued on, following the winding path, and felt deepness, as if he were far beneath the earth.

There was a scent, too, powerful and changeable, never the same from one breath to the next, and yet somehow consistent. It was pine sap, bear fur, snake musk, burning hickory, sour sweat, week-old carcass, rotting fruit, horse piss, roses. It grew stronger as he approached, and seemed to settle, to become less varied, until the smell of death and flowers filled his head.

Thus Aspar turned the last corner of the maze and beheld the Briar King.

He was shadow-shape, caught in the thousand tiny needles of light piercing the gaps in the roof of the living hall. He was thorns and primrose, root and branch and knotted vines, tendril-fingered. His beard and hair were of trailing gray and green moss, and hornlike limbs twisted up from his head.

But his face—his face was mottled lichen papered on human skull, black flowers blooming from his eye sockets. And as Aspar watched, the king turned slowly to face him, and the roses opened wider, still blooming.

Aspar opened his mouth, but he didn't say anything. He couldn't look away from those widening eyes, the ebony stamens that seemed to grow larger until they were the only things in the world. The stench of death and perfume choked him, and his limbs began to twitch, his body felt violent, itchy, and suddenly, without warning, his vision cracked like a mirror and from behind it he saw . . . things.

He saw the ironoaks—*his* ironoaks, the tyrants—rotting, limbs snapping, plagues of worms and flies bursting from beneath their putrefying bark like maggots from a corpse. He saw the Warlock River running black, deer falling in their tracks, green things shriveling and melting into a viscous pus. He smelled the putrefaction. The sickness he had felt on touching the greffyn's spoor hit him again, a hundred times stronger, and he doubled to vomit, and then—

—then he went mad.

The next time he knew anything clearly, it was agony. His shoulder was on fire.

"Aspar?"

He looked up through a film of pain to see Winna, staring frantically down at him. They were in a stand of trees, someplace. Poplars. He had something gripped in his hand.

"Aspar, is that you? Are you sensible?"

"I—wha's happening?"

"You were gone—" Her head suddenly jerked up, and when she started again, her voice was much lower. "You were in there for three days! The tree house closed up, and I couldn't go in after you. Then when you came out, you ran like a wild man. I chased you."

He clawed at his shoulder and found a crude bandage, soaked in blood.

"The one-eyed man and his band are here. You attacked them, and they shot you. They're hunting for us, now."

"Fend? He's here?"

"Shhh. I think they're close."

"Three days?" Aspar grunted. "How can that be?" He looked around. "My bow? Where is it?" He looked dully at what he held in his hand. It was a horn, a white bone horn, incised with weird figures. Where had he gotten that?

"Still with the Briar King, I guess. When you came out, you didn't—" Her head jerked up again, and she raised a dirk. It was Aspar's dirk.

"Give me that," he grunted. "I can still fight." He put the horn in his haversack and reached for the weapon.

"But I wouldn't advise it," a familiar voice said.

A circle of bows appeared around them, and there, in Aspar's pain-reddened vision, stood a Sefry in a broad-brimmed hat, bundled against the pale amber evening that suffused the scene. He wore a jerkin and cloak of umber felt, the same color as his hat. He had one eye of pale green, and where the other eye ought to be was a yellow patch.

"Fend," Aspar snarled. "Come and die."

Fend laughed. "No, thank you," he said.

"Stay back," Winna said. "I'll cut the first to come near."

"We won't come near, then," Fend said reasonably. "We'll fill you both with shafts from a distance. Aspar, tell your little girl to put down her knife and come here."

Aspar chewed that for less than a heartbeat. "Do it, Winna," Aspar said.

"Asp—"

"He'll kill you if you don't."

"What about you?"

"Girl," Fend said, "I've nothing against you, really. I can't allow Aspar to live, of course. He knows it, and so do I. But he also knows that if you behave, I might let *you* live."

"And leave her alone," Aspar said. "Promise to do her no harm."

"Why should I?" Fend asked. "After all, there are so many kinds of harm. She might even come to like some of them."

Winna reversed the knife and placed it against her breast. "You can forget that," she said.

But in the next eye blink, the dirk was on the ground, and Winna was screaming and staring wide-eyed at an arrow shaft neatly piercing her palm.

"Winna!" Aspar shrieked. And then, "Fend!" An impossible energy lurched into Aspar's limbs, and he picked up the knife, hurling himself forward.

A second shaft struck him in the thigh, a third in his arm. Even as he staggered, he knew they were missing his vitals on purpose, and he remembered the bodies around the old sedos shrine on the Taff, tortured and bled while they were still alive.

He got back up, grimacing, and heard Fend's laughter.

"Oh, Aspar. I *so* admire your tenacity."

"I'll kill you, Fend," Aspar said quietly. "Believe it, you bitchson." He twisted the shaft in his thigh until it snapped. He went light-headed from the pain, but then took another step toward the one-eyed Sefry. The point hadn't cut any tendons.

Suddenly, Fend's men gave ground, and Fend himself stepped back, eyes widening. Aspar felt an instant's savage satisfaction before he realized it wasn't him they feared.

It was the greffyn. It had stepped from the wood very, very quietly. With silent purpose it padded toward Aspar.

"Well," Fend said. "It's chosen you. I would have preferred to kill you myself, but I imagine this will do. Good-bye, Aspar."

Aspar blinked once at the greffyn, less than a kingsyard away. Then he turned and ran. Fend laughed again.

The greffyn seemed in no hurry to finish him. Aspar ran as if in a nightmare, his feet cloying to the ground. If he could only escape the greffyn and find his bow, he might have a chance to save Winna.

He clung to that thought, to keep him going, to keep his heart pumping blood and his legs moving. He didn't look back, but he could hear the greffyn behind him now, hissing along through the grass. Enjoying the chase, perhaps, like the cat it resembled.

He knew where he was, now, anyway. In his madness, he had gone farther along the canyon wall. Ahead he could see the Briar King's weird, living barrow. If he could reach it, the greffyn might not be able to squeeze through the narrow opening. And his bow was in there.

He ran on, but his legs called a halt, and his body left his feet behind. With dull surprise, he found his face pressed into the earth.

He managed to roll over, with the dirk held up.

The greffyn was there, looking down at him with saucer-size eyes.

Aspar's other hand strayed to his belt, and found his ax.

The greffyn came a step closer and lowered its head. It sniffed at him. It clacked its jaws, then came even closer and sniffed again.

"Just a little closer," Aspar said, gripping his ax. "Come on, what are you waiting for?"

But it sniffed once more, and then drew back.

Aspar didn't know what that meant, but he took the opportunity to regain his feet. He turned and continued on, staggering often, but the greffyn didn't follow.

Its gaze did, however, the sweet, hot sickness that he had known three times already. It wasn't as bad, this time. Maybe the medicine Mother Gastya had done to cure him back in Rewn Aluth was still working. Maybe that was why the greffyn hadn't wanted to touch him.

Whatever the case, two arrow wounds and the greffyn's deadly gaze proved finally too much. He fell into the tall grass and slept, and dreamt foul Black Marys.

He awoke smeared with his own vomit. His wounds were no longer bleeding, but they were throbbing and red, and felt hellishly hot.

He got up anyway, thinking of Winna in Fend's hands. He started a small fire and plucked out the remaining arrow, then seared out the wounds with a glowing coal. He pressed the paste Mother Gastya had given him into the cauterized holes and bound them with scraps of his shirt.

The night came and went before he could manage to stagger more than a few yards at a time, but the sun seemed to bring him new strength, and he grimly rose to search for Fend, and his men, and Winna. Most of all, Winna.

He found only their trail, leading back into the briar tree forest.

Implacably, wishing his head would clear, wishing the pain would ease off instead of getting worse with each step, he set off after them.

"I will kill you, Fend," he murmured. "By Grim, I will. I will."

He repeated it until it made no sense, until long after he was capable of rational thought.

But even then, he didn't stop moving. Only death could stop him.

PART III

THE RECONDITE STIRS

The Year 2,223 of Everon
The Month of Ponthmen

When wakes the recondite world, the sword shall appear as a feather, the wolf as a mouse, the legion as a carnival. I shall laugh from my grave, and it shall sound as a lute.

—From the confession of the shinecrafter Emme Viccars, at the pronouncement of her sentence of execution

CHAPTER ONE

IN THE WARHEARTH

WILLIAM POURED ANOTHER GOBLET of his favorite Virgenyan wine and paced across the red marble floor of Warhearth Hall. He took a healthy swallow of the amethyst-colored vintage, then set the goblet down on the broad black table in the center of the room.

The paintings were looking at him again. Rebelliously, he returned their scrutiny.

They were everywhere; whole floor-to-ceiling panels of the wall were bracketed in gilded oak-leaf molding and painted in dense and murky colors, as if rendered with mud and soot and blood. In a sense they were, for each was a depiction of some part of the long history of his family's wars.

"Would you rather look at those old pictures or me?" Alis Berrye inquired sulkily. She was draped upon an armchair, bodice unlaced so as to reveal her firm, rose-tipped breasts. She rolled off her stockings and threw one bare leg over the arm of the chair. It was a pretty leg, slender, white as milk. Her chestnut hair was mildly tousled, sapphire eyes languid, despite her vexed tone. She was nearly as full of wine as he, and totally unlike the paintings in character.

Well, not entirely true. She wasn't murky, but she was a bit dense.

"I am sorry, my dear," William murmured. "The mood is no longer on me."

"I can put it on you, my lord, I assure you."

"Yes," he sighed. "I'm certain you could. But I do not wish it."

"Do you tire of me, Your Majesty?" Alis asked, unable to hide a bit of panic in her voice.

He regarded her for a moment, taking the question seriously. She was an exuberant, enthusiastic lover, if one without the skills of an older woman. Her political designs were charmingly transparent and naïve. She got drunk well, and when her guard was down she was unselfconsciously sweet, and her mind went down tracks strange to his, which he enjoyed on the pillows.

She was a welcome change from Gramme, whose mind had turned almost obsessively to her bastards these last few years. They were provided for, of course, and he liked them, especially little Mery, but Gramme wanted them to have the Dare name and said so far too often. Alis was less ambitious, and perhaps didn't even have the intelligence for such ambition.

That was fine. Two intelligent women in his life were more than enough.

"No, not at all," he told her. "You are a delight to me."

"Then shall we to bed? It's something past midnight. I can soothe you to sleep, if you don't desire loving."

"You go to bed, lady," he said gently. "I shall join you presently."

"In your chambers, Majesty?"

William turned an irritated frown on her. "You know better than that. That is my marriage bed, and I share it only with my wife. Do not presume, Alis, merely because she is away."

Her face fell as she realized her mistake. "I'm sorry, Sire. You'll come to my chambers, then?"

"I said I would."

She swayed to her feet and picked up the stockings, then came over, stood on tiptoe, and gave him a little kiss on the lips. Then she smiled, almost furtively, and cut her eyes down, and for a moment he felt himself stir, but he was too drunk and too sad, and he knew it.

"Good night, Sire," she murmured.

"Good night, Alis."

He didn't watch her go, examining instead the largest painting in the room. It depicted Genya Dare, burning like a saint, leading a great army. Before her towered the vague but threatening shadow of the Skasloi fortress that had once stood on the very spot where Eslen castle now stood. Against that dark red citadel, giant formless shapes of black were barely discernible.

"What shall I do?" he murmured. "What is right?" He took his gaze round the other paintings—the battle of Minster-on-Sea, with its rolling thunderheads, the fight at the Ford of Woorm, the siege of Carwen. In each, a Dare stood at the head of an army, resolute and steadfast.

A hundred years ago, these same walls had depicted scenes of Reiksbaurg victory. They had been stripped and painted over.

It could happen again.

He shivered at the thought, and wondered if it wasn't time to go see *him*. The thing in the dungeon, the thing his father had shown him, so long ago. He found that thought nearly as troubling as a Reiksbaurg victory, however, and dismissed it.

Instead, William moved back to the table and unscrolled a map, weighting its corners with brass counters made to resemble ram-headed vipers, coiled to strike.

"Still up? Still brooding?" a faintly mocking voice asked.

"Robert?" William swung around, nearly lost his balance, and cursed. "What's the matter?"

"Nothing. I can hardly drink at all, these days. It takes no more than a bottle to give me clumsy legs. Where the saints have you been this past nineday?"

Robert smiled thinly. "Saltmark, actually."

"What? Without my leave? For what?"

"It were better not to have your leave for this," Robert said darkly. "It was more of my—I think you would say *inappropriate*—dealings." He put on a grim smile. "You did make me your prime minister, remember?"

"Had this to do with Lesbeth?"

Robert fingered his mustache. "In part."

William paused for courage before he asked the next question. "Is she murdered?"

"No. She is alive. I was even allowed to see her."

William took a deep draught of the wine. "Thank Saint Anne," he muttered. "What sort of ransom do they want?"

"May I have some wine?" Robert asked mildly.

"Help yourself."

Robert glanced at the carafe on the table and made a disgusted noise. "Do you have anything else? Something from a little farther south? I don't see how you stomach that sour stuff."

William waved at the cabinet. "There is a freshly decanted bottle of that red from Tero Gallé you're so fond of."

"Vin Crové?"

"That's the one."

He watched impatiently as Robert produced and poured some of the sanguine liquid and tasted it.

"Ah! That's better. At least your vintners have good taste."

"How you can be so calm, when our sister has been kidnapped?"

"Don't *ever* doubt my concern for Lesbeth," Robert said sharply.

"I'm sorry—I was wrong to remark so. But please, give me the news."

"As I said, she is well, and I was allowed to see her. She sends her love."

"From where? Where is she?"

"She is a captive of the duke of Austrobaurg."

"How? In the name of the saints, *how*? She was last seen on her horse, riding east from the Sleeve. How did they abduct her from this island?"

"That, Austrobaurg would not tell me."

"Her fiancé from Safnia arrived, you know. A day ago. He is beside himself."

"Indeed?" Robert's eyes gleamed strangely.

"Well, come. What does the duke want?"

"What do you suppose? He wants a ransom."

"What ransom is that?"

"He wants a ransom of ships. Twenty, to be precise."

"Twenty sailing ships? We cannot spare them, not if we go to war with Saltmark. Or Hansa, saints-me-to-bed."

"Oh, he doesn't want twenty of *our* ships. He wants twenty Sorrovian ships. Sunken. To the bottom of the sea."

"What?" William thundered. He hurled the goblet against the wall and watched it shatter into a thousand purple-drenched shards. "He dares? By Saint Rooster's balls, he *dares*?"

"He is an ambitious man, Sire. Twenty ships to his credit will take him far with the court at Hansa."

"To *his* credit? My ships must appear to be from Saltmark? You mean he expects *my* ships, my crews, to sail under *his* flag?"

"That is his demand, Your Majesty," Robert said. His voice took on an angry edge. "Else, as he put it, he will rut with our sister to his heart's desire, then give her to his men with orders to ride her until her back is broken."

"Saint Michael," William swore, taking his seat. "What has the world come to? Is there no honor in it?"

"Honor?" Robert bittered a humorless laugh. "Listen, William—"

"You know I cannot do it."

"You—" Robert actually lost his tongue, for a moment. "You pompous ass!" he finally got out. "This is Lesbeth!"

"And I am emperor. I cannot sell the honor of my throne for one sister, no matter how well I love her."

"No," Robert said, voice very low, finger pointing like a dagger. "*No.* William, I will sink those ships myself, do you hear me? With my bare hands, if need be. You should have sent Lesbeth off with the rest, but you heeded her whim and let her stay here to meet her Safnian prince. The same Safnian prince, I might add, who sold her to Austrobaurg."

"What?" William stared at his brother, wondering if he had somehow misunderstood the words.

"I said Austrobaurg would not tell me how he kidnapped her. But I did discover it through my spies, one murder and torture I'm sure you don't want to hear about. Austrobaurg has enemies, some very near him, though not near enough to open his throat, more's the pity. Not yet. But I discovered what I wanted to know. Lesbeth's Safnian prince has called in Hansa many times. He is well known there, and he is in their pay. He sent a letter, telling Lesbeth to meet him on the Cape of Rovy, that his ship was damaged and he'd made camp there. She went to him, only to find a Hanzish corvette."

"Prince Cheiso did this? You have proof?"

"I have the proof of my ears. I trust my sources. Oh, and there is this."

He pulled something from the pouch at his belt and tossed it to William, who caught it. It was a slim metal box, with a catch fastening it.

"What is this?"

Robert made a peculiar sound, and William was stricken to see tears start in his brother's eyes.

"It's her finger, damn you." He spread his right hand and wiggled the index finger. "This one, with the twin of this ring. We put them on when we were eight, and have not, either of us, been able to remove them since we were fifteen."

William opened the catch. Inside, indeed, was a slim finger, nearly black. On it was a gold band with a scroll of oak leaves about it.

"Ah, saints of mercy!" He snapped the box shut with shaking hands. Who could do this to Lesbeth? Lesbeth the ever smiling, the best, the most compassionate of them all?

"Robert, I did not know, I—" He fought back tears.

"Do not console me, Wilm. Get her back. Or I will."

William found another goblet. He needed more wine for this, to pacify the blood thundering in his ears, the blind rage he felt building again.

"How, Robert?" he snapped. "If we do this thing, it could cost us every alliance. Even Liery might break with us. It's impossible."

"No," Robert said, his voice still quavering. "It isn't. We have already sent ships in secret to the Saurga Sea, haven't we?"

"It's not much of a secret."

"But the ships have not been counted or accounted for. Only the two of us know how many have been sent. Crews can be found; I know where to find them. Crews that will ask no questions and tell no stories, if they are paid well enough."

William stared at Robert for a long moment. "Is this true?"

"It is. Austrobaurg will get all the credit, as he desires—and he will get all of the blame. The sea lords of Liery will be none the wiser of our part and will remain our friends. I will oversee this personally, William.

You know my love for Lesbeth; I would risk nothing, here, that might mean her life. But I would never risk our kingdom, either."

William drank more wine. Soon it would be too much; already the world was flat, like the paintings on the wall. This was a poor time for judgment. Or perhaps, in such matters, the best.

"Do it," he whispered. "Only do not give me details."

"It is done," Robert replied.

"And Prince Cheiso. Have him arrested and put in Spinster Tower. Him I'll deal with in the morning."

CHAPTER TWO

THE PRINCE OF SHADE

THE AIR ABOVE the ochre brick of the Piato da Fiussa shimmered like the top of a stove. It was so hot that even the pigeons and grackles—which normally covered the square, scavenging for bits of bread or cheese—would not light upon it for fear of roasting themselves.

Cazio, similarly concerned, exerted himself just enough to scoot an armspan, following the shadow of the marble fountain his back rested against as he gazed laconically around the square. There he found few people with any more ambition of mobility. Earlier, the little market town of Avella had been a bustling place. Now, with the sun at noon, people had more sense.

Buildings of the same yellow brick up to three stories high walled the piato, but only on the south side did they cast a meager shadow. In that welcome umbra, the shopowners, bricklayers, vendors, street officers, and children of Avella, sat, lay, or otherwise lolled, sipping the brash young wines of the Tero Mefio, nibbling cellar-cooled figs, or dabbing their brows with wet rags.

Smaller gatherings under awnings, next to stairways—wherever the sun was thwarted—made plain why the hours between noon and three bells were named *z'onfros caros*—the treasured shadows. And, in a city where noon shadows had value—indeed, were sometimes bought and sold—the shade of Fiussa's fountain was one of the dearest.

That was where Cazio rested, with the nude, flower-adorned goddess watching over him. The three nymphs at her feet disgorged tall plumes of water, so that a gentle damp mist settled on his darkly handsome face and broad shoulders. The marble basin was cool, and no matter which hour of the sessa it might be, there was ample shade—for perhaps four people.

Cazio lazily examined the upper-floor windows across the piato. This time of day the rust or sienna framed windows were all thrown open, and sometimes pretty girls could be seen, leaning on the casements to catch a breeze.

His laconic search was rewarded.

"Look there," he said to his friend Alo, who reclined nearby. "It's Braza daca Feiossa." He nodded his head toward a dark-haired beauty looking out over the square. She wore only a cotton undershift, which left much of her neck and shoulders bare.

"I see her," Alo said.

"She's trying to catch my attention," Cazio said.

"Of course she is. The sun came up just for you today, too, I'm sure."

"I wish he hadn't bothered," Cazio murmured, wiping a bead of sweat from his forehead and pushing back his thick mop of black hair. "What was I thinking, getting up so early?"

Alo started at that. "Early? You've just now risen!" A sallow-faced boy with caramel-colored hair, at sixteen Alo was a year younger than Cazio.

"Yes, and see, it's too hot to work. Everyone agrees."

"Work? What would you know of work?" Alo grunted. *"They've* been working all morning. *I've* been up since dawn, unloading bushels of grain."

Cazio regarded Alo and shook his head sadly. "Unloading grain—that isn't work. It's *labor*."

"There's a difference?"

Cazio patted the gleaming pommel of his sword. "Of course. A gentleman may work. He may do deeds. He may not *labor*."

"A gentleman may starve, then," Alo replied. "Since I labored for the food in this basket I doubt that you want any."

Cazio considered the hard ewe's cheese, the flat brown round of bread, the stoneware carafe of wine. "On the contrary," he told Alo. "A gentleman has no objection to living off the labor of *others*. It's the nature of the arrangement between master and servant."

"Yes, but I'm not your servant," Alo observed. "And if I were, I don't see what I would get out of the arrangement."

"Why, the honor of serving a gentleman. And the privilege of resting here, in my palace of shade. And the protection of my sword."

"I have my own blade."

Cazio eyed his friend's rusty weapon. "Of course you do," he said, with as much condescension as he could put in his voice.

"I *do*."

"And much good may it do you," Cazio replied. "And see, look, you may soon have a chance to use it."

Alo turned to follow his gaze. Two men had just ridden into the square from the Vio aza Vera. One was trimmed out in red velvet doublet, black hose, and broad-brimmed hat jaunted with a plume. His beard was neatly trimmed and his mustache delicately curled. His companion was attired more modestly in a plain brown suit. They were headed directly for the well.

Cazio put his head back and closed his eyes, listening to the sound of hooves approaching. When they were quite near, he heard a squeak of leather and then boots scuffing on brick as the two dismounted.

"You don't mind if I get a drink from the fountain, do you?" an amused voice asked.

"Not at all, *casnar*," Cazio replied. "The fountain is a public work, and its water free to all."

"Very true. Tefio, fetch me a drink."

"Yes, master," the fellow's lackey said.

"That looks a comfortable spot you're sitting in," the man said, after a moment. "I think I shall have that, too."

"Well, now there you are mistaken, casnar," Cazio said, in an amiable tone, his eyes still closed. "The shade, you see, is *not* a public work, but is cast by the goddess Fiussa, as you can see. And she—as you can also see—favors me."

"I see only a pair of boys who do not know their station."

Alo made to move, but Cazio restrained him with a hand on his arm. "I know only what I have been taught, casnar," he answered softly.

"Are you begging me for a lesson?"

Cazio sat up a little straighter. "Beg, did you say? I don't know the meaning of that word. Since *you* seem so well acquainted with it, am I to understand that you are offering me instruction in grammar?"

"Ah," the fellow said. "I understand now. You are the village fool."

Cazio laughed. "I am not, but if I were, my position would have changed the moment you rode through the gate."

"That is quite enough of that," the man said. "Relinquish your spot or my lackey will beat you."

"Set him on me and you shall be lackless. And do I understand you now, casnar? Do you feel unqualified to instruct me? Please, tell me more of this 'begging' of which you speak."

"You mark yourself when you speak so and wear a sword," the man said, his voice suddenly low and dangerous.

"Mark myself? What, with this?" Cazio asked, pointing to his weapon. "This is for marking, yes. It's a right good pen, if I dip it in the proper inkwell—but I've never marked *myself* with it. Or do you mean you see the marks of *dessrata* on me, and wish to trade in proficiencies? What a wonderful idea. You will teach me about begging, and I will teach you about swordplay."

"I will teach you to beg, yes. By Mamres, I will."

"Very good," Cazio replied, slowly levering himself to his feet. "But how is this: Let us make an agreement that whoever learns the best lesson shall pay the going rate for it. Now, I've no idea what they charge for lessons in begging, but at Mestro Estenio's school of fencing, I hear the rate is a gold *regatur*."

The man looked over Cazio's faded leather jerkin and threadbare velvet breeches. "You don't have a regatur to your name," he sneered.

Cazio sighed, reached under the collar of his white shirt, and drew forth a medallion. It was gold, with a rampant boar embossed on it. It was nearly all that remained of his father's fortune, and worth at least three regaturs.

The man shrugged his shoulders. "Who shall hold our money?" the man asked.

Cazio pulled off the medallion and tossed it to the man. "You seem an honest sort," he said. "Or at least you will be, as a corpse, for all the dead are stiffly honest. They lie, but they cannot lie, if you understand me." He drew his sword. "Meet Caspator," he said. "Between us, we are happy to teach you the art of dessrata."

The man drew his own weapon. Like Caspator, it was a rapier, with a light, narrow blade and half-basket hilt. "I do not bother to name my swords," he said. "My own name is Minato Sepios daz'Afinio, and that is quite enough."

"Yes, what need have you of a sword, with a name like that? Repeat it often enough—say, twice—and your opponent will fall straight to sleep."

"To guard, you," daz'Afinio said, taking a stance.

Cazio frowned and waggled a reproving finger. "No, no. Lesson one: stance is everything. See? Yours is too narrow, and too forward facing, unless you plan to use an off-hand bodkin. Point your front toe like so—"

Daz'Afinio roared and lunged.

Cazio danced to the side. "Ah," he said. "The lunge. The lunge is properly executed *thus*." He feinted with his shoulders, hopped to his left, and when daz'Afinio jerked his blade up to parry the nonexistent attack, flicked his blade out and kicked his front foot forward. The tip of Caspator pricked lightly into daz'Afinio's arm, not deeply enough to bring blood.

"You see? You prepare the ground with some other movement, then—"

Daz'Afinio just set his mouth grimly and came forward with a flurry of hard blows, shallow thrusts, and poor attempts to bind. Cazio laughed delightedly, parrying each or sidestepping, dancing clockwise around his opponent. Suddenly daz'Afinio lunged deep, his point aimed straight at Cazio's heart. Cazio ducked, so the steel went right over his head, extending his own blade as he did so. Daz'Afinio, still moving forward with the momentum of his attack, impaled his shoulder on Cazio's point— again, not deeply, but this time the tip of Caspator had a bit of red on it that wasn't velvet.

"The *pertumum perum praisef*," Cazio informed his foe.

Daz'Afinio threw a draw cut to Cazio's hand. Cazio caught the blade with his own, captured the fellow's weapon with a quick rotation, and then drove through. Daz'Afinio had to scramble backwards quickly to avoid another cut.

"The *aflukam en truz*."

Daz'Afinio beat his blade and lunged again.

Cazio parried, paused, and skewered him through the thigh.

"Parry *prismo*," Cazio said, "*com postro en utave*. A difficult riposte, but it pleases."

He watched as daz'Afinio dropped his weapon and crumpled to his knees, clutching his freely bleeding leg.

Cazio took a moment to bow toward the applause from the shaded spectators around the piato, noticing with interest that one of them was Braza daca Feiossa. He winked at her and blew her a kiss, then turned back to his fallen opponent.

"I believe, sir," he said, "that my lesson is concluded. Would you care to teach yours now? The one about begging?"

The door shuddered, uttered a rusty protest, and sagged on its hinges as Cazio tugged it open. Something—a rat, most likely—scurried along the cracked pavement in the darkened portico beyond.

Ignoring both, Cazio strode through the covered way to the inner courtyard of his villa.

Like the rest of the place, it was a mess. The garden had gone to weeds, and grapevines crept out of control on casement and wall. The copper basin and sundial that had once marked the center of the yard was lying on its side, as it had been for two years. The only orderly element of the house, in fact, was the small area set aside for the practice of dessrata—a cleared place on the flagstones, with a small ball dangling from a string, a battered practice mannequin with the various humors and crucial points of the body marked in faded ink. Near that, stretched out on a marble bench, a man snored fitfully.

He was perhaps fifty, his face covered in coarse black and gray stubble, save for a long white scar that marred one cheek. His long hair was an unruly mess. He wore a tattered brown jerkin stained copiously with red wine, and no pants at all. An empty carafe of wine lay near his half-opened hand, which rested on the floor.

"Z'Acatto."

The man snuffled.

"Z'Acatto!"

"Go, or I kill you," the man snarled, without opening his eyes.

"I have food."

He cracked his lids, then. The eyes within were red and watery. Cazio passed him a hempen bag. "There is cheese, and bread, and cloved sausage."

"And what to wash it down with, then?" z'Acatto asked, a murky spark appearing in his gaze.

"Here." Cazio handed him a ceramic carafe.

Z'Acatto immediately took a deep drink. An instant later he spat, howled like a damned soul, and hurled the container against the wall, where it burst into a hundred pieces.

"Poison!" he shrieked.

"Water," Cazio corrected. "That substance that falls from the sky. The grass finds it most nourishing."

"Water is what they drink in *hell*," z'Acatto groaned.

"Well, then you should begin building up a tolerance now, for there is no doubt that you will be the guest of Lord Ontro and Lady Mefita in the next life. Besides, I had no coin for wine."

"Ungrateful wretch! You think only of filling your own belly."

"And yours," Cazio corrected. "Eat."

"Bah," he groaned, levering himself slowly into a sitting position. "I—" His nose suddenly twitched, and suspicion knotted his forehead. "Step closer!"

"I don't think I will," Cazio told him. "Water can also be used on the outside of the body, you know," he added.

But z'Acatto stood and advanced on him. "I smell wine on your breath," he accused. "Last year's *vino dac'arva*, from Troscia."

"Nonsense," Cazio replied. "It was from Escarra."

"Hah! It's the same grape!" z'Acatto shouted, waving his arms like a madman. "The blight destroyed the Escarran vines ten years ago, and they had to beg their cuttings from Troscia."

"Interesting. I'll try to remember that. In any event, the wine was not mine; it was Alo's, and it is gone, now. Eat something."

"Eat." He frowned again. "Why not?" He returned to his bench, fumbled in the bag until he brought out the bread. He tore a hunk and began chewing it. Speaking through the paste thus formed, he asked, "How many fights did you get into today?"

"Duels, I take you to mean? Only one, that being the problem. It was too hot, I think, and there weren't enough strangers. So not enough coin."

"You do not duel," z'Acatto grumbled. "You brawl. It is a foolish waste of the art I teach you. A prostitution."

"Is it?" Cazio said. "And tell me, how should we live, if not like this? You scorn the food I bring, and yet it's the only food you are likely to see. And where does your wine come from, when you get it? You buy it with the coin you filch from me!"

"Your father never stooped so low."

"My father had estates, you fool. He had vineyards and orchards and fields of cattle, and he saw fit to get himself killed in one of your duels of honor, and thus pass his property to his killer instead of to me. Besides his title, the only thing my father left me was *you*—"

"And this house."

"Yes, and look at it."

"You could make income from it," z'Acatto replied. "It could be rented—"

"It is *my* house!" Cazio shouted. "I will live here. And I will make my money as I please."

Z'Acatto wagged a finger at him. "You will get killed, too."

"Who here can best me at swordplay? No one. No one has even come near in nigh on two years. There is no danger in this, no gambling. It is pure science."

"*I* am still your better," z'Acatto replied. "And though I am perhaps the greatest master of dessrata in the world, there are those who approach me in skill. One day, you will meet one of them."

Cazio looked unblinkingly at the old man. "Then it is your duty to make certain I am ready when they arrive. Or you will have failed me as you failed my father."

The old man's head dropped then, and his face pinched ever more sullen. "Your brothers have put it behind them," he said.

"I suppose they have. They would let our good name blow away in the sea wind to which they've fled. Not me, not Cazio. I am a da Chio-vattio, by Diuvo!"

"I do not know the face of the man who killed your father," z'Acatto said softly.

"I care little about that. My father dueled the wrong man, for the wrong reasons. I will not make that mistake, and I will not mourn him. But neither will I pretend to come from common birth. I was born to fight and to win, to reclaim what my father lost. And I will."

Z'Acatto grabbed him by the sleeve. "You think you are wise. You think you know something of the world. Boy, Avella is not the world, and you know *nothing*. You would rebuild your father's estates? Start with this house. Start with what you have."

Cazio brushed the hand from his sleeve. "I have nothing," he said, rising.

Z'Acatto did not reply as Cazio went back outside.

Once back on the street, Cazio felt a pang of regret. Z'Acatto wasn't much, but he *had* raised Cazio from the age of five. They had had their share of good times.

Just not lately.

Avella at night was darker than a cave, but Cazio knew his way around it well. He found the north wall as easily as a blind man feeling about his own house, and after ascending the stairs stood in the night wind look-ing out over the moonlit vineyards and olive groves, the gently rolling hills of the Tero Mefio, the heartland of Vitellio. He stood thus for more than a bell, trying to clear his head.

I'll apologize to him, he thought to himself. *After all, there are se-crets of the dessrata he still holds to himself.*

Returning to his house, Cazio felt an odd prickling at the back of his neck, and his hand strayed to Caspator.

"Who's there?" he asked.

All around him he heard the soft kissing of leather on brick. Four, maybe five of them.

"Cowards," he said, more softly. "Lord Mamres spit on you all." Caspator made no sound as he slid from his sheath. Cazio waited for the first rush.

CHAPTER THREE

FLIGHT AND FANCY

A NNE PUSHED OPEN the wooden shutters, wincing as they squeaked faintly. Outside, the night air was warm and strong with the scent of woodfire and the stink of horse manure. The moon wore her scantiest gown and fretted the slate rooftops of the hamlet with dull pearl light.

Anne couldn't see the ground—the street below was sooted with shadow—but she knew from earlier that it was only a single story down, that just beneath her window a narrow eave jutted, and under that was the front door of the small inn. She had jumped from higher places, in her life.

Twenty long days had come and gone since they left Eslen—Austra, five Craftsmen, and she. Anne didn't know where they were or how far they had to go, but she knew her best chance to escape when she saw it. She had been able to lay aside enough hard cheese and bread to last for a few days. If she could but find a bow and a knife, she was certain she could live off the land.

If only she had better clothes for riding—but she could find those, too. Saint Erenda would surely smile on her and bring her fortune.

Anne cast a glance in the direction of Austra's regular breathing, and repressed a pang of regret. But she couldn't tell her best friend what she planned; it would be better for Austra if she knew nothing of this, if she was just as surprised in the morning as Captain Marl and the rest of her escort.

Taking a deep breath, Anne sat up on the windowsill and felt for the eave below with her stocking feet. She found it—farther down than she had hoped, and more sloping than she remembered it. Fear of falling held her for a moment, but then she eased her weight on down.

And promptly slipped. Her hands scrabbled wildly as she slid forward. At the last moment she caught something—and held it, breath coming in gasps, her feet dangling over the unseen ground.

By its feel, she had grabbed the wooden gamecock that peered from over the doorway of the inn.

Nearby, harsh laughter suddenly cut through the darkness. At first she thought someone had seen her, then two men started talking in some language she didn't understand. Their voices passed under her as she held her breath, and continued on.

Her arms began shaking with the effort of holding herself up. She had to either drop or climb back up to her window.

She looked down, though she couldn't see even her feet, and after another quick prayer, she let go. Air seemed to rush by for much longer than it ought to, then she found the ground. Her knees buckled, and she fell face first. One of her hands went into a pile of something that gushed, and she recognized the smell of a fresh horsecake.

Trembling, but with a growing feeling of triumph, she came to her feet, shaking the wet dung from her hand.

"Anne!" A desperate voice from above, cracking with the attempt to whisper as loudly as possible.

"Hush, Austra!" Anne hissed back.

"Where are you going?"

"I don't know. Go back to sleep."

"Anne! You'll get killed. You don't even know where we are!"

"I don't care! I'm not going to any coven! Farewell, Austra—I love you."

"This will be the end of me!" Austra gasped. "If I let you go—"

"I slipped off while you were asleep. They can't blame you for that."

Austra didn't answer, but Anne heard a scrabbling from above.

"What are you doing?"

"Coming with you, of course. I'm not going to let you die alone."

"Austra, no!"

But it was too late. Austra gave the briefest of shrieks. Her passing made a slight breeze before she hit the ground with a pronounced thud.

"Her arm is badly bruised, but not broken," Captain Marl told her, very matter-of-factly. He was that sort of man, taciturn and plainspoken. His manner went well with his pitted, homely face.

"I want to see her," Anne demanded.

"Not just yet, Princess. There is the matter of what you two were doing."

"We were being silly. Wrestling near the window, and lost our balance."

"And how is it you aren't even bruised, when she was hurt?"

"I was lucky. But I did soil my gown, as you can see."

"There's that, too. Why were you fully dressed?"

"I wasn't. I didn't have my shoes on."

"Your maid was in a nightgown—as you should have been."

"Captain, who are you to presume how a princess of Crotheny ought to be dressed? You treat me as if I'm a captive of war!"

"I treat you as what you are, Princess—my charge. I know my duty, and I take it seriously. Your father trusts me. He has reason to." He sighed and folded his hands behind his back. "I dislike this. Young women should have their privacy, away from the company of men. I thought I could afford to give you that. Now I see I was foolish."

"You aren't suggesting that I share my room with one of your men?"

"No, Princess. None of my men will do." His face pinkened. "But when I cannot find lodging that precludes escape, I must stand watch in your room myself."

"My mother will have your head!" Anne shouted.

"If that's so, that's so," Marl replied obligingly.

She had learned not to argue with him when he adopted that tone. He had made up his mind and really would take a beheading before changing it.

"May I see Austra, now?" she asked, instead.

"Yes, Princess."

Austra's face was white, and her arm bound in a sling. She lay on her back and wouldn't meet Anne's gaze when she entered.

"I'm sorry," Austra said, voice curiously flat.

"You ought to be," Anne replied. "You should have done what I told you. Now Marl will never let me out of his sight."

"I said I was sorry." Tears were streaming down Austra's face, but she made none of the sounds of crying.

Anne sighed and gripped her friend's hand. "Never mind," she said. "How's your arm?"

Austra set her mouth stubbornly and didn't reply.

"It's all right," Anne said, more softly. "I'll find another chance."

Austra turned to her then, red eyes glaring and angry. "How could you?" she said. "After all the times I've watched out for you, *lied* for you, helped you play your stupid games. Your mother could have sent me to work with the scouring maids! Saints, she could have had me beheaded, but I always did what you said anyway! And for what? So you could leave me without a second thought?"

For a moment, Anne was so shocked she couldn't say anything.

"I would have sent for you," she finally managed. "When I was safe, and—"

"*Sent* for me? Do you have any idea what you're planning?"

"To run away. Seek my love and destiny."

"The destiny of a woman, alone, in a strange country where you don't even speak the language? What did you think you would do for food?"

"Live off the land."

"Anne, someone *owns* the land. People are hanged for poaching, do you know that? Or rot in prison, or serve as slaves until their debt is done. That's what happens to them who 'live off the land' in your father's kingdom."

"No one would hang *me*," Anne replied. "Not once they knew who I was."

"Oh, yes. So once caught, you would explain that you are a very important princess, and then they would—what? Let you go? Give you a small estate? Or call you a liar and hang you. Of course, since you're a woman, and pretty, they wouldn't hang you right at first. They'd have their pleasure from you.

"Or suppose you *could* somehow convince them of who you are. In the best case they would send you home, and this would all start again—except for me, for I'll be carrying charcoal on my back up from the barges, or something worse. Worst case, they would hold you for ransom, maybe send your fingers to your father one at a time, to prove they really have you."

"I plan to dress as a man," Anne said. "And I won't get caught."

Austra rolled her eyes. "Oh, dress as a man. *That* will work."

"It's better than going into a coven."

Austra's eyes hardened further. "That's stupid. And it's selfish." She balled her unbound fist and banged it against the bedpost. "*I* was stupid—to ever think you were my friend. To think you gave a single piss about me!"

"Austra!"

"Leave me alone."

Anne started to say something else, but Austra's eyes went wild. "Leave me *alone*!"

Anne stood up. "We'll talk later."

"*Away!*" Austra shrieked, dissolving into tears.

On the verge of bawling herself, Anne left.

Anne watched Austra's face, limned against a landscape of rolling pasture broken by copses of straight-standing cedar and elegant cottonwood. Her head eclipsed a distant hill where a small castle lorded over a scattering of red-roofed cottages. A herd of horses stared curiously at the carriage as it rattled by.

"Won't you talk to me *yet*?" Anne pleaded. "It's been three days."

Austra frowned and continued to look out the window.

"Fine," Anne snapped. "I've apologized to you until my tongue is green. I don't know what else you want me to do."

Austra murmured something, but it went out the window like a bird.

"What was that?"

"I said you could *promise*," Austra said, still not looking at her. "Promise not to try to run away again."

"I can't escape. Captain Marl is much too watchful, now."

"When we get to the coven, there will be no Captain Marl," Austra said slowly, as if speaking to a child. "I want you to promise not to try to escape from there."

"You don't understand, Austra."

Silence.

Anne opened her mouth to say something else, but it fell short of her teeth. Instead she closed her eyes, let her body fall into the restless shuddering of the coach, and tried to pretend she was far away.

She put on dreams like clothes. She tried on Roderick, to start with, the memory of that first, sweet kiss on horseback, their steadily more intimate trysts. In the end, however, that brought her only to that night in the tomb and the humiliation that followed. Her whole memory of that night was tainted, but she wanted to remember, to feel again those last exciting, frightening caresses.

She changed the scene, pretending that she and Roderick had met instead in her chambers at Eslen, but that went no better. When she tried to imagine what *his* chambers in Dunmrogh were like, she failed utterly.

At last, with a burst of inspiration that stretched a little smile on her face, she imagined the small castle on the hill she had seen a few moments before. She stood at its gates, in a green gown, and Roderick rode across the fields, brightly caparisoned. When he came near her he dismounted, bowed low, and kissed her hand. Then, with a fire in his eyes, pulled her close against the steel he wore and kissed her on the mouth.

Inside, the castle was light and airy, draped in silken tapestries and brilliant with sunlight through tens of crystal windows. Roderick entered again, clad in a handsome doublet, and now, finally she could conjure the feeling of his hand on her flesh, and imagine more, that he went farther, that they were both, finally, unclad. She multiplied the remembrance of the touch of his palm on her thigh, imagining the whole length of him against her. There was just one part she couldn't picture, exactly, though she had felt it against her, through his breeches. But she had never seen the privates of a man, though she had seen stallions aplenty. They must be shaped the same, at least.

But the image that conjured was so ridiculous she felt suddenly uncertain, and so she adjusted her imagination again, to his eyes staring into hers.

Something didn't fit there, either, and in swift horror, she understood what it was.

She couldn't remember Roderick's face!

She could still have described it, but she could not *see* it, in the shadows of her mind. Determined, she shifted scenes again, to their first meeting, to their last—

But it was no good. It was like trying to catch a fish with her hands.

She opened her eyes and found Austra asleep. Frustrated, Anne watched the scenery go by and now tried to imagine what sort of people lived out there, in that country so unknown to her.

But in the vain search for Roderick's face, she had somehow awoken something else and found a different face.

The masked woman with amber hair. For almost two months, Anne had pushed that phantasm away, encrypted it as she had the dream of the black roses. Now both came back, joined, nagging for her attention, despite Praifec Hespero's assurances. Having endured three days of silence and Austra's sulking, and with nothing else to distract her, thoughts of that day on Tom Woth nagged at Anne like an itch, and the only scratch for it was thinking.

What had happened? Had she fainted, as the praifec believed? That seemed most likely, and it was what she most often told herself. And yet, in the middle of her heart, she knew somehow it wasn't the truth.

Something real had happened to her; she had seen a saint, or a demon, and it had spoken to her.

She could almost feel the voice in her head, a sort of remonstration, a scolding. How could she be thinking of herself and Roderick when so much was happening? Her mother and father were in danger, maybe the whole kingdom, and only she knew it. Yet despite that, she had done nothing, told no one, pursued this hopeless, selfish love. The praifec's word had only given her the excuse.

"No," Anne said, under her breath. "That isn't me talking. That's Fastia. That's Mother."

But it was neither, and she knew it. It was Genya Dare, her voice whispering across the leagues from that crack in her tomb. Genya Dare, the first queen, her most ancient ancestress.

Would Genya Dare have ignored her responsibilities for the selfish pleasure of youth?

Anne gave a start. That hadn't been her own thought; that had been a voice, spoken into her ear. Not a whisper, either, but a confident tone. A woman's voice.

The voice of the masked woman, she was nearly certain.

Anne tossed her head back and forth, searching for the speaker, but there was only Austra, sleeping.

Anne settled back in her seat, breathing hard.

"Are you there?" she whispered. "Who speaks?"

But the voice didn't return, and Anne began to wonder if she had dropped into sleep for a moment, long enough for the Black Mary to whisper in her ear.

"You are not Genya Dare," she murmured. "You are not."

She was going crazy, talking to herself. That was certainly it. She had read of such things, of prisoners in towers who spoke at length to no one, whose minds were shaved of reason.

She shook Austra's knee. "Austra. Wake up."

"Hmm?" Austra opened her eyes. "Oh," she said. "It's you."

"I promise, Austra."

"What?"

"I promise. I won't try to run away."

"Truly?"

"Yes. I have to . . ." She frowned, embarrassed. "Everyone is trying to tell me the same thing. Mother, Fastia, you. I've been selfish. But I think—I'm needed for something."

"What are you talking about?"

"I don't know. Nothing probably. But I'm going to do my best. To do what I'm supposed to."

"Does that mean you're giving up Roderick?"

"No. Some things are meant to be, and the two of us are fated to be together. I asked Genya to make him fall in love with me, remember? This is my fault, and I can't just abandon his love."

"You asked Genya to make Fastia nicer, too," Austra reminded her.

"But she *was*," Anne replied, remembering their last two meetings. "She was. She was almost like the Fastia I loved, when I was a girl. She and Mother did this thing to me—but they think what they are doing is for the best. Lesbeth explained it, but I didn't want to listen, at the time."

"What convinced you?"

"A dream, I think. Or a memory. Mostly *you*. If even my dearest friend thinks I'm a selfish brat, how can I not wonder?"

"Now you're starting to worry me. Did you bump your head, going out the window?"

"Don't make fun of me," Anne said. "You wanted me to be better. I'm trying."

Austra nodded gravely. "I'm sorry. You're right."

"I was lonely, without you to talk to."

Austra's eyes watered up. "I was lonely, too, Anne. And I'm afraid. Of where we're going, of what it will be like."

"We're in this together, then, from now on. Yes?"

"By Genya?"

"By her grave. If I had lead to write it on, I would. I swear I will make no attempt to escape from whatever awful place my mother has sent us. And I will be your companion in this, and no matter what, I will never, ever leave you."

Finally, fitfully, Austra smiled. "Thank you," she said. She reached across the space, and they briefly squeezed hands.

"Where do you suppose we are, anyway?" Anne remarked, to change the course of the conversation. "I gather we've been traveling south."

Austra dimpled a little.

"I know that look!" Anne said. "You know something."

"I've been keeping directions," Austra said. "The names of towns, rivers, and all. So we might find our route, if ever we see a map."

Anne gaped in astonishment. "Austra! Clever girl. Why didn't I think of that? I'm so stupid!"

"No," Austra said. "You've just never been out in the world. You probably figured if you ran away the road would just take you where you wanted to go, like in the phay stories. But in the real world, you have to have directions."

"Your journal, then! May I see it?"

Austra reached into her purse and withdrew a small book.

"I didn't get every town," she said. "Only when I heard one of the guards mention it, or sometimes I would see a sign. The writing looks almost the same here, though with some odd flourishes. Here, I'll read it to you; you could have trouble with my scribbling, and I can sum up for you."

"Go on," Anne replied.

"We first crossed over the Warlock on the raised road. The sun set on our right, so we were going south. Then we went up into some hills, still south."

"We were in Hornladh, then!" Anne said. "Roderick is from Hornladh! I found it on the map, after meeting him."

"In the hills we stayed in a place called Carec, a very small town. The next few nights I didn't catch any names, but we went through a forest I think was named Duv Caldh, or something like that. At the edge of it we stayed in a little place named Prentreff."

"Oh, yes. The inn with the dreadful lute player."

"Exactly. From there, I think we went still south but more west, but then the next day it rained, so I couldn't tell. Then we spent two nights in Paldh."

"I remember Paldh from the map! It's a port, so we were on the sea! I thought I smelled the sea that night."

"After that we crossed a river. I think it was called the Teremené, and so was the town there. That's when we started seeing more fields than woods, and the houses with red or pale roofs. And vineyards—remember those endless vineyards? Then we slept in a little town named Pacre, then Alfohes, Avalé, and Vio Toto. Most of that time, I think we were going south and west. We crossed another river; I don't know its name, but the town on the other side was Chesladia. I missed some towns, after that, but the place where you tried to run away was named Trivo Rufo. Since then I haven't written anything. I was too angry."

"It's enough!" Anne said. "But I don't understand. If you didn't want me to run away, why do this? Why map me a way home?"

"I wasn't going to tell you about it until you promised not to run away. But I thought—it's always better to know where you are. Suppose something awful happens? Suppose we're attacked by bandits, our escort is killed, and we *have* to run? It's better to know." She shook a finger at Anne. "But a promise is still a promise, yes?"

"Of course," Anne replied. "But you're right. From now on, I'll keep a journal, too."

"What country do you think we're in, now?" Austra asked.

"I have no idea. I never paid attention in the tutorials, and I looked at the map only to find where Roderick was from. Perhaps we're in Safnia, where Lesbeth's fiancé lives."

"Perhaps," Austra said. "But I don't think so. I think it's Vitellio."

"Vitellio!" Anne peered out the window again. The road arrowed through a vast field of some sort of grain. It had cut steep banks, and the soil was a vivid white.

"I thought Vitellio was all yellow and red, and covered up with great cities and fanes! And the people are supposed to dress all in silk of fantastic colors, and quarrel most constantly."

"I could be wrong," Austra allowed.

"Wherever it is, the countryside is quite beautiful," Anne remarked. "I would love to run Faster through those fields. I wonder how far we have to go?"

"Who can say?" Austra replied. "This coven must be on the very edge of the earth."

"Maybe this will be an adventure after all!" Anne said, feeling her spirits rise.

But she did have one quick, guilty thought.

Roderick would walk off the end of the earth to find me, Anne told herself. *And if I can send him one letter, he'll know where that is.*

She tried to brush that away, stay firm to her new convictions, and a few moments later, as the girls chattered about what Vitellio might be like, she almost forgot that it had even occurred to her.

And eight days later, by the tattered light of sunset, in a countryside empty of houses but replete with gently swaying trees and pasture, she and Austra stepped from the carriage for the last time.

CHAPTER FOUR

THE FANEWAY

BROTHER EHAN STOOD ARMS AKIMBO, a worried expression on his face, watching Stephen prepare.

"Look out for Brother Desmond and his bunch," the little man said. "They're none too happy with you taking the walk this soon."

"I know." Stephen shrugged. "What can I do? If they follow me, they follow me. If they catch me alone in the woods, there won't be much I can do, whether I see them coming or not."

"You could run."

"They would just wait for me at the next fane. I still wouldn't be able to finish the walk."

"But you would be alive."

"That's true," Stephen allowed.

"You don't sound as happy about that as you might."

"Something's troubling him," Brother Alprin said. He'd just walked in from the vineyards, still wearing a broad-brimmed hat to protect him from the sun. "And it isn't Brother Desmond."

"Homesick?" Ehan said, a little tauntingly.

"No," Stephen replied. Except that he was. Homesick not for a place, but for a world that still made sense.

"What is it, then?" Ehan persisted. But Stephen remained silent.

"He'll tell us when he's ready," Alprin said. "Won't you, Brother? In any event, don't worry about Brother Desmond. The fratrex sent him off yesterday."

"Off?" Stephen said. "You mean away?"

"No such luck. Just off to do some sort of church business."

Stephen had a sudden memory of Brother Desmond that night on the hillside, when he had gone quiet and strange.

"After supplies or something?"

"Hah," Brother Ehan grunted. "No. He sends 'em to take care of things. Brother Desmond walked the fanes of Saint Mamres. He's one promotion short of being a knight of the church. Why do you think he's so strong and fast? That's the blessing of Mamres. A few ninedays before you got here, some bandits were raiding the temple at Baymdal, in the Midenlands. The fratrex sent Brother Desmond and his cohort."

"Desmond put a stop to the bandits, all right. A very decisive stop, as I hear it."

Ehan's brow pinched up. "This might be worse. What if they hung around, out in the woods for a day? If you're found with a broken neck, they'll have an alibi."

"Wait," Stephen said. "I didn't think a fratrex had that authority. He can dispose men only for the defense of his monastery. An order to send them someplace has to come from a praifec."

"A messenger from Praifec Hespero in Eslen came yesterday," Brother Alprin said.

"Oh."

"I shouldn't worry about Brother Desmond too much," Brother Alprin said. "He enjoys these trips he goes on. He can kill you anytime he wants."

"Very comforting," Stephen said.

Alprin smiled. "Besides, you must cultivate a meditative state to walk the fanes properly."

"I'm trying," Stephen said. "Can you tell me what to expect, what it feels like?"

"No," Brother Ehan and Brother Alprin said together.

"But you'll be different, after," Brother Ehan added. "After, nothing will be the same."

Ehan probably meant that to sound encouraging, but instead it opened another pit in Stephen's belly. Since leaving home, he had received one surprise after another, each ruder than the last. His whole world had already been turned upside down, and he had a sinking feeling that whatever he had thought walking his first faneway would be like, the reality would be completely different. And if it followed suit with everything else he had experienced, unpleasant.

And so, though he tried his best to contemplate the saints and begin his first step toward priesthood in a meditative mood, it was with trepidation that he set his foot on the path and approached the first of the twelve fanes of Saint Decmanus.

To Stephen, his own footsteps somehow sounded like intruders in the great nave of the monastery. He had never seen it this empty and still. He wished for ordinary sounds, for another person to talk to. But from this moment until he finished his circuit of the fanes, he would be alone.

He stood for a moment, examining the great buttresses that supported the ceiling, amazed that frail and imperfect human beings could make such beauty. Was that what the saints saw in them, that potential? Was the creation of a few beautiful things worth the price of the evil men could do?

He wouldn't get an answer to that question. Perhaps there wasn't one.

Mouthing prayers, he stopped at the stations, twelve small alcoves that held statues and bas-reliefs of the various guises of holy Decmanus. There was no power in them beyond the power inherent in any image, but they reminded him of what he would soon undertake, for the faneway was akin to these small stations, written large.

When he had lit a candle in each, he finally turned to the first fane. It lay behind a small door, in the rear of the nave. The stone around the door looked much older than the stone of the rest of the monastery, and almost certainly it was. The saint had left his mark here before the church ever found its way to these lands, before even the dread Skasloi were defeated.

Once there had been nothing here but a hill. Having a fane or even a monastery did nothing to enhance the power of the sedos itself; it could serve only to prepare those who were about to walk the way, to partake of the saint, for what was to come.

When he reached for the handle of the door, he felt a sudden prickling in his belly and knew that if he hadn't been fasting for three days he might have lost whatever was in it.

He stood, staring, unwilling to begin.

He wasn't *ready* to begin; his mind wasn't on his goal, on the sanctification of his flesh and soul. There was too much else in there that was decidedly unsacred.

So, sighing, he knelt on the stone before the door and tried to meditate.

Sometimes, when he couldn't sleep, it was because the events of the day kept scurrying around in his skull, like rats chasing their tails. What he should have said, should have done, shouldn't have said and done—playing over and over again. Trying to meditate now was like that. He tried to will the thoughts away, dissolve them like salt in boiling water, but each time they re-formed, more insistent than ever.

And chief among those thoughts was a simple question: After doing what he had done, how could he deserve the blessing of the saint?

After perhaps half a bell, Stephen knew the meditation of emptiness would never work, so he changed his tactics. Rather than trying to empty his head, he would try the meditation of memory. If in remembrance he could find a few moments of peace, he might achieve the state of calm acceptance needed for entering the fane.

So he closed his eyes and opened the gallery of memory, glanced down it at the images there, frozen like paintings.

There hung Brother Geffry in the oratory hall of Lord's College, straight and tall in the murky light filtered through narrow windows. Brother Geffry, explaining the mysteries of sacarization in language so eloquent it sounded like song.

His father, Rothering Darige, kneeling on the bluff of Cape Chavel, white-toothed sea behind and blue sky above. His father, giving him his first instruction in how to behave in the temple. Stephen was eight, and in awe both of his father's knowledge and the fact that he would soon see the altar chambers.

His sister Kay, holding his hand during the festival of Saint Temnos, where everyone wore masks like skulls and carried censers of smoking liquidamber. Watchfires in the shapes of burning men stood along the coast like immolated titans. Sefry musicians and acrobats, painted like skeletons, capered madly through the crowd once the sun was down. The Sverrun priests, all in black, singing dirges and dragging chains behind them. Kay, telling him that the Sefry took little boys away and they were never seen again. It was one of the most powerful experiences in his life, for it was the first time he had ever really felt the presence of the saints and ghosts that walked among humanity, felt them as surely as flesh and bone.

Yet of all these paintings of his memory, it was old Sacritor Burden, the elder priest of Stephen's attish, that brought him closest to what he needed. On that canvas, Stephen could see the old man's sallow face, his quick but somehow sad smile, his brows, almost lizardlike with age—as if time were making of him something quite different from human.

But his voice was human, and it had been soft that day he had taken Stephen into the small scriftorium in the rooms behind the altar.

Stephen concentrated, then relaxed, until the frozen painting began to move, until he saw again through eyes twelve summers old, heard the voice of his past.

He was gazing around the room at the boxes and rolls of scrifti. He had seen his father write, seen the book of prayer his mother kept at her belt, but these he had trouble comprehending. What could all of this writing be about?

"The greatest gift of the saints is knowledge," Sacritor Burden told him, pulling down a faded vellum scroll and unrolling it. "The most refined form of worship is in learning that knowledge, coaxing it like a little flame in the wind, keeping it alive for the next generation."

"What does this say?" Stephen asked, pointing to the scroll.

"This? I chose it at random." The priest gazed over the contents. "Aha. See, it's a list of all of the names of Saint Michael."

Stephen didn't see at all.

"Saint Michael has more than one name?"

Burden nodded. "It would be better to say that Saint Michael is one of many names for a power that is actually nameless—the true essence of the saint, what we call the *sahto*."

"I don't understand."

"How many saints are there, Stephen?"

"I don't know. Hundreds."

"If we go by their names," the sacritor mused, "I should say thousands. Saint Michael, for instance—he is also known as Saint Tyw, Nod, Mamres, Tirving—and that names only four of forty. Likewise, Saint Thunder is also called Diuvo, Fargun, Tarn, and so forth."

"Oh!" Stephen replied. "You mean they're called that in other languages, like Lierish or Crothanic." He smiled and looked up at the priest. "I learned some Lierish from a sea captain. Would you like to hear?"

The priest grinned. "You're a bright boy, Stephen. I've noticed your quickness with language. It recommends you to the priesthood."

"That's what Father said."

"You don't sound very enthusiastic."

Stephen looked down at the floor and tried not to squirm. His father didn't like it when he squirmed. "I—I don't think I want to be a priest," he admitted. "I'd rather be the captain of a ship that sails everywhere, sees everything. Or a mapmaker, maybe."

"Well," Sacritor Burden said, "that's something for later. Just now you made a keen observation; some of the names for the saints are just what other people call them in other languages. But it's more complicated than that. The very true essence of a saint—the sahto—is without name or form. It is only the varying *aspects* of the sahto we experience and name, and each sahto possesses many aspects. To each of these many aspects we attribute the name of a saint, in the king's tongue. In Hansa, they call them *ansi*, or gods, and in Vitellio they call them lords. The Herilanzers call the aspects *angilu*. That doesn't matter; the church allows local custom to call aspects whatever they wish."

"So, Saint Michael and Saint Nod are the same saint?"

"No. They are both aspects of the same sahto, but they are different saints."

He chuckled at the confused look on Stephen's face.

"Come here," he said.

Then Sacritor Burden led Stephen to a small, rickety table, and from a small wooden coffer lying on it he withdrew a peculiar piece of crystal, cut to have three long sides of equal width and two triangular ends. It rested easily in the sacritor's palm.

"This is a prism," Burden said. "A simple piece of glass, hmm? And yet see what happens when I place it in the light." He moved the prism into a shaft of sunlight coming through a small, paneless window and shining on the desk. At first Stephen didn't notice anything unusual— but then he understood. It wasn't the crystal that had changed but the desk. A small rainbow spread upon it.

"What's doing that?" Stephen asked.

"The white light actually contains all of these colors," the priest explained. "Passing through the crystal, they become divided so that we can see them individually. A sahto is like a light, and the saints like all of these colors. Distinct, and yet a part of the same thing. Do you understand?"

"I'm not sure," Stephen replied. But then he did, or thought he did, and felt a sudden giddy excitement seize him.

"Ordinarily," Sacritor Burden went on, "we can never experience the truth of any sahto. We know only their aspects, their various names, and what their nature is in each form. But if we take care, and understand the colors, and put them back together, we can briefly experience the white light—the real sahto. And in so doing, we can become, in a way, a minor aspect of the holy force ourselves."

"How? By reading these books?"

"We can understand them here, using the books," Burden replied, tapping his wisp-locked skull. "But to understand them here—" He motioned toward his heart. "—to put on even the feeblest of their raiment, we must walk the fanes."

"I've heard of that. It's what priests do."

"Yes. It is how we become sanctified. It is how we know them."

"Where do the fanes come from?"

"There are places where the saints rested or dwelt, or where parts of them are buried. We call these places *sedoi—sedos* in the singular. Little hills, usually. The church is blessed with the knowledge to find these sedoi and identify the saint whose power lingers there. Then we build fanes, to identify them, so those who visit them know to whom they pray and offer."

"And so if I go to a fane, I'll be blessed?"

"In some small way, if the saint chooses. But walking a faneway is something different. To do that, one must walk many fanes, each left by a different aspect of the same sahto. They must be walked in a prescribed order, with certain ablutions made along the way."

"And the saints—er, the sahto—gives you his powers?"

"They give us gifts, yes, to use in their service—if we are worthy."

"Could I—could *I* walk a faneway? Could I learn from these books?"

"If you want," Sacritor Burden said softly. "You have the potential. If you study, and devote yourself to the church, I believe you could do well, bring much good to the world."

"I don't know," Stephen said.

"As I said, your father is in favor of it."

"I know."

And yet, for the first time, it didn't sound so bad. The mystery of the words all around him pulled at his imagination. The prism and its patterns of colored light enthralled him. In a few words, Sacritor Burden had shown Stephen an unknown country, as strange and distant as rumored Hadam, and yet as near as any beam of light.

Burden must have seen something in his face. "It's not the easiest path," he murmured. "Few walk it of their own free will. But it can be a joyous one."

And in that instant, Stephen had believed the old man. It was a relief, really. He didn't know if he could have stood up to his father even if he wanted to. And now wonder had a grip on him, and he remembered how Sacritor Burden could bring light from the air, coax music from stones, summon fish from the shoals when the catch was poor. Little miracles, the sort that were so everyday no one even thought about them.

But there must be bigger miracles in such a wide, complex world. How many faneways were there? Had they all been discovered?

Maybe being a priest wouldn't be so bad after all.

He bowed his head. "Reverend, I would like to try. I would like to learn."

The sacritor nodded solemnly. "It's a joy to an old man to hear that," he said. "A joy. Would you like to begin now?"

"Now?"

"Yes. We start with the first gift of Saint Decmanus. With the alphabet."

Stephen came back from remembrance to the sound of a jay chasing some other bird in the high reaches of the nave, complaining loudly. He managed a troubled smile. Sacritor Burden had been a man of faith and principle, a good man. Fratrex Pell seemed like a good man, too, if a bit severe at times. The fratrex knew exactly what Stephen had done, and still thought him fit to walk the faneway. If there was any lesson that the past few months had taught him, it was that taking his own thoughts too seriously led only to trouble. What was he, anyway? Only a novice. No— he had trusted Sacritor Burden, and he would trust Fratrex Pell.

That sounded good, but he wondered if Sacritor Burden could have imagined that, hidden in the bright colors of the rainbow, there was a streak of purest darkness. That wonder held in its embrace more than its share of terror.

Fratrex Pell knew. And if that wasn't enough, the ineffable something that some called Saint Decmanus could judge whether Stephen was still worthy.

He pulled himself up by the door handle, tried once again to settle his thoughts, and opened the wooden portal. He hesitated briefly at the entrance, his hand on the weathered stone, then, murmuring a prayer, he stepped in and closed the door behind him. Darkness swallowed him.

Once inside, he produced his tinderbox and a single white candle. He struck fire to tinder and touched it to the wick, and watched the flame climb its ladder of smoke.

The fane was small enough that he could almost touch both walls by stretching his arms wide. It was spare, as well; a stone kneeling bench and the altar were its only furniture. Behind the altar, on the wall, was a small bas-relief of Saint Decmanus, a weathered figure crouched over an open scroll, a lantern held up in one hand and pen in the other.

"*Decmanus ezum aittis sahto faamo tangineis. Vos Dadom,*" Stephen said. *Decmanus, aspect of the Sahto of Commanding Knowledge. I surrender to you.*

"You embody the power of the written word," Stephen continued, in the liturgical language. "You *gave* us ink and paper and the letters we make from them. Yours is the mystery and the power and the revelation of recorded knowledge. You move us from past to future with the memories of our fathers. You keep our faith clean. I surrender to you."

In the inconstant light, the statue of the saint seemed to be laughing at Stephen, a gentle but mocking laugh.

"I surrender," Stephen repeated, very faintly this time.

When the candle was half-gone, and his vigil was complete, nothing had changed; he felt no different. With a sigh he reached to snuff the flame with the thumb and forefinger of his right hand.

The flame hissed out, and for a heartbeat Stephen understood something was wrong, but couldn't place what. Then he realized that he hadn't felt the flame at all. Or the wick.

He rubbed his fingers together, and again felt nothing. From the tips of his fingers to his wrist, his hand was that of a ghost. He pinched it until the blood welled red, but he might as well have been pinching a piece of roast.

Stephen's astonishment turned quickly to horror and then to brittle panic. He bolted from the fane, out into the empty chapel, where he fell to his knees and heaved dry, croaking sobs from an empty belly trying to be emptier. The dead thing that had been his hand disgusted him, and he suddenly found himself tearing into his pack, looking for the little woodchopping ax.

By the time he found it, he had gotten around to asking himself what he wanted it for. He sat there, wild eyed, switching his gaze from the ax to his unfeeling hand. He felt like a beaver with its foot in a trap, preparing to gnaw it off.

"Oh, saints, what have I done?" he groaned. But he knew; he had put himself in their hands, the saints' hands, and they had found him wanting.

Trembling, he put the ax away. He couldn't chop it off, now that the moment of madness was passing. Instead, still shaking and occasionally retching, he lay on the stone, staring up at the light coming through the stained glass, and wept until he was almost sane again. Then he rose shakily, retrieved his candle, and said another prayer to Saint Decmanus. Then, without looking back, he went through another door—a small one, which led outside to where the trail began.

Bleakly, he looked at the trail. From this point it went in only one direction. He could stop now, admit failure, and be done with it. His father would despise him, but that would hardly be anything new. If he quit now, he could escape it all—Brother Desmond, the awful texts, Fratrex Pell's demands, this cursing by the saints. He could be free.

But a hard resolve came after his panic. He would see this through. If the saints hated him, his life was done anyway. Perhaps, when they had punished him enough, they would offer him absolution. If they didn't—well, he would find out about that. But he wouldn't turn around.

The path went in only one direction.

He reached the fane of Saint Ciesel a few bells after noon, under a sky already dimmed by clouds, in a grove of ashes. It was fitting, for the story of Saint Ciesel was a dark one.

Once he been a man, the fratrex of a monastery on the then-heathen Lierish Isles. A barbarian king burned Ciesel's monastery and all of his scrifts, many of which were irreplaceable, then threw Ciesel in a dungeon. There, in the dark, the saint had written the destroyed scrifts again, from memory—carved them into his own flesh with his fingernails, sharpened by filing them against the stone of his cell, using the oily filth from the floor to darken the scars. When he died, his captors threw his body into the sea, but Saint Lier, lord of the sea, delivered the corpse to the shore of Hornladh, near a monastery of Ciesel's own order, where the monks found him. Ciesel's skin had been preserved and copied through the ages. The original skin was said to be preserved in salt in the Caillo Vallaimo, the mother temple of the church in z'Irbina.

Stephen burned his candle and made his ablutions. He left the fane without feeling in the skin of his chest.

Two bells later, Saint Mefitis, patroness and inventor of writing to the dead, took the sensation from his right leg. He camped a little later, and while building a fire to keep the beasts at bay, he was surprised to discover blood on his breeches. He had hit his leg a glancing blow with his ax and not noticed. The wound was minor, but he could have chopped the foot off and it would be no different.

He did not sleep, but dreamed of terror anyway. It hovered beyond the light of his fire; it had invaded his body. If he finished the fanewalk, he would surely die.

The first triad of fanes had been aspects of knowing connected with the written word; the next three were wilder, as reflected by the cruder, more primitive carvings. Saint Rosmerta, the patroness of memory and poetry, was picked out in almost savage simplicity, barely recognizable as human. She took the use of his tongue. Saint Eugmie took his hearing, and from then on Stephen stumbled through the forest in eerie silence. Saint Woth took the sight in his left eye.

When he woke to all of this on the third day, he wondered if he was already dead. He remembered his grandfather talking about how death prepares the old by taking their senses one at a time. How old did that make Stephen now, a hundred? He was crippled, deaf, and half blind.

The next day seemed better; the fanes were to Coem, Huyan, and Veiza—aspects of wisdom, cogitation, and deduction. So far as he could tell, they took nothing from him at all, and by now he was getting used to walking on an insensible leg.

He was settling into the silence, too. Without birdsong or creaking branches or the sound of his own feet, the forest became a dream, so unreal that Stephen could not longer imagine danger in it. It was like his memory paintings, an image or series of images to which he was only distantly connected, that seemed to have very little to do with the here and now.

But when he started to build his fire that night, he didn't know how to do it. He rummaged through his possessions, knowing that he had the tools he needed. He could not recognize them. He tried to picture the process, and failed in that, as well.

He couldn't even remember the word *fire*, he realized, with swelling dismay. Or his mother's name, when he tried, or his father's.

Or his own.

But he remembered fear perfectly, if not what it was called, and spent the night huddled over his knees, praying for the sun, praying for an end to everything.

Dawn peeked over the trees, and he wondered who he was. The only answer he got was *I am walking this path*. He stopped in the various buildings he encountered. He couldn't remember why he was doing it and he didn't care. When he reached the last—somehow he knew that it was the last, and he was nearly finished—he was a cloud with a single eye, moving through a jumble of unfamiliar colors and shapes, many alike, all different. He passed like less than a wind, and the only sensation that remained was a rhythmic beating that the Stephen of a few days before might have recognized as his heart.

When he walked into the last fane, that beating stopped, too.

CHAPTER FIVE

DUEL IN THE DARK

AN EYE OF FIRE BLINKED OPEN in the darkness, just to Cazio's right, and Cazio found himself leafed in lamplight. Another lantern was unshuttered near his right hand. Both were Aenan lamps, which directed their light strictly in one direction by means of a mirror of polished brass enclosed in a tin hood.

Now Cazio's enemies could see him quite well, but he could see only vague shapes and the occasional gleam of steel.

He turned slowly, relaxing his shoulders and thighs, holding Caspator almost languidly in his fingers. He hoped fervently his attackers had only swords. Bows were forbidden inside the city gates to all but the guard, but in Cazio's experience, murderers didn't care whether they broke the law or not.

One of the men grew bold, and the long tip of a sword cut into the light, in a slice aimed at Cazio's hand. Cazio laughed, stepping away easily. He let the tip of his weapon drop to touch the ground.

"Come, you brave fellows," he said. "You have me outnumbered and nearly blinded. And still you begin with this timid bit of poking?"

"Keep it shut, lad, and you may still have a heart beating when we leave you," someone said. His voice sounded vaguely familiar.

"Ah!" Cazio said. "It speaks, and sounds like a man, yet demonstrates none of the equipage. Do you keep a bag of marbles tied between your legs, so none will know in daylight how fainthearted you are beneath the moon?"

"I warned you."

A blade slashed into the light, swinging up for a cut from overhead. This wasn't a rapier, but a heavier sword suited for cleaving arms and heads from shoulders. In that instant, as the fellow cocked back for the cut, Cazio saw his forearm, limned by the lamplight. He hit it with a stop thrust, skewering through the meat and into the elbow joint. The man never completed his swing. The weapon clattered to the ground, as its owner shrieked.

"You *do* sing soprano," Cazio said. "That's the voice I imagined for you."

The next instant, Cazio found himself defending against three blades— two light rapiers and another butcher's chopper—and now he knew where his opponents were, sort of; attacking him, they entered the beams of light. He parried, ducked, lunged from the duck and very nearly pricked a surprised face. Then, very quickly, he spun and bounced toward one of the lanterns. A quick double lunge, and his point went right into the flame and on through. The startled bearer let go as oil spurted, caught fire, and turned the lantern into a torch.

Cazio spun again. Burning oil rushed along the length of his blade. Lifting his boot, he kicked the flaming mass that was clinging to the end of it, sending it flying toward his antagonists. They appeared in the sudden burst of light, and with a shout Cazio leapt toward them. He push-cut one along the top of his wrist, leaving a second man who couldn't hold a sword, then he bounced after another, rapier still flaming. He recognized the face—one of the household guards of the z'Irbono family, a fellow named Laro-something.

Laro looked as he might if Lord Ontro were come to take him to hell, which cheered Cazio considerably.

Then something struck him in the back of the head, hard, and pale lilies bloomed behind his eyes. He swiped with his weapon, but the blow was repeated, this time to his knee, and he toppled with a groan. A boot caught him under the chin, and he bit his tongue.

And then, suddenly, he was lying in the street, and the attack upon him had ceased. He tried to rise on his elbow, but couldn't find the needle of strength in the haystack of pain.

"This is no concern of yours, drunkard," he heard Laro say. "Move along."

Cazio finally managed to lift his head. The burning lamp lit the alley fully, now. Z'Acatto stood at the edge of the light, a carafe of wine in one hand.

"You've done wha' y'came for," z'Acatto slurred. "Now leave 'im alone."

"We're done when we say so."

Behind Laro, holding the other lantern, was daz'Afinio, the man Cazio had dueled earlier that day. One of the men nursing his hand was Tefio, daz'Afinio's lackey.

"This man took me unawares and robbed me," daz'Afinio asserted. "I merely return the favor."

"I'll fix him, my lord," Laro said, lifting his foot to stamp on Cazio's outstretched hand. "He won't play his sword games after this."

But Laro didn't stamp down. Instead, he pitched over backward as z'Acatto's wine carafe shattered on his face and broke his nose.

And, somehow in the same instant, z'Acatto had his blade out. He stumbled forward unsteadily. One of the other men made the mistake of engaging z'Acatto's blade. Cazio watched as the old man put it almost lazily into a bind in *perto*, then impaled the man in the shoulder.

Cazio wobbled to his feet, just as daz'Afinio drew his weapon and launched an attack—not on z'Acatto, but at Cazio. He managed to straighten his arm in time, and Caspator sank halfway to the hilt into daz'Afinio's belly. The nobleman's eyes went very round.

"I—" Cazio choked. "I didn't mean to—"

Daz'Afinio fell back, off of Caspator, clutching both hands to his gut.

"The next man to step forward dies," z'Acatto said. He didn't sound drunk.

Only one of the men was left unwounded, now, and they all backed away with the exception of daz'Afinio, who was clutched into a ball.

"You're both fools," another fellow said. Cazio recognized him from the z'Irbono guard—Mareo something-or-other. "Do you have any idea who you just ran through?"

"A skulk and a murderer," z'Acatto said. "If you get him to the chir-geon at the sign of the needle, he might yet live. It's more than he de-serves. Than any of you deserve. Now, go."

"There'll be more to this," Mareo said. "You should have just taken your beating, Cazio. Now they'll hang you in the square."

"Hurry," z'Acatto urged. "See? He's spitting out blood now, never a good sign."

Without another word, the men gathered up daz'Afinio and carried him off.

"Come," z'Acatto said. "Let's get you to the house and have a look at you. Were you stabbed?"

"No. Just beaten."

"Did you fight that man today? Daz'Afinio?"

"You know him?"

"I know him. Lord Diuvo help you if that man dies."

"I didn't mean to—"

"No, of course not. It's all just a game to you. Prick on the arm, cut on the thigh, and collect your money. Come."

Limping, Cazio did as his swordmaster bade.

"You're lucky," z'Acatto said. "It's just bruising, for you."

Cazio winced at the old man's touch. "Yes. Just as I said." He reached for his shirt. "How did you happen to be following me?"

"I wasn't. I went to find some wine and heard you shouting. Lucky for you."

"Lucky for me," Cazio repeated. "How do you know daz'Afinio?"

"Anyone with sense would. He's the brother-in-law of Velo z'Irbono."

"What? That lout married Setera?"

"That lout owns a thousand versos of vineyards in the Tero Vaillamo, three estates, and his brother is the aidil of Ceresa. Of all of the people to pick a brawl with—"

"It was a duel. And he started it."

"After sufficient insult from you, I'm sure."

"There were insults to go around."

"Well, whatever. Now you've insulted him with a hole from back to front."

"Will he die?" Cazio asked.

"You worry about that *now*?" The swordsmaster cast about for something. "Where's my wine?"

"You broke it on Laro Vintallio's face."

"Right. Damn."

"Will daz'Afinio die?" Cazio repeated.

"He might!" z'Acatto snapped. "What a stupid question! Such a wound isn't always lethal, but who can know?"

"I can't be blamed," Cazio said. "They came at me, like thieves in the dark. They were in the wrong, not me. The court will stand with me."

"Velo z'Irbono *is* the court, you young fool."

"Oh. True."

"No, we must away."

"I won't run, like a coward!"

"You can't use dessrata against the hangman's noose, boy. Or against the bows of the city guard."

"No!"

"Just for a time. Someplace where we can hear the news. If daz'Afinio lives, things will cool."

"And if he doesn't?"

Z'Acatto shrugged. "As in swordsmanship, deal with each attack as it comes."

Cazio wagged a finger at the old man. "You taught me to look ahead, to understand what the opponent's next *five* moves will be."

"Yes, of course," z'Acatto replied. "But if you *rely* on your prediction, you may die if you are wrong about his intentions. Sometimes your opponent isn't smart enough or skilled enough to *have* intentions, and then where are you? I had a friend in the school of Mestro Acameno; he had studied since childhood, for fourteen years. Even the mestro couldn't best him in a match. He was killed by a rank amateur. Why? Because the amateur didn't know what he was doing. He didn't react as my friend assumed he would. And so my friend died."

Cazio sighed. "I cannot leave the house. Suppose they take it as lien on my return?"

"They will. But we can see that it is purchased by someone we trust."

"Who would that be?" Cazio murmured. "I trust only you, and even you not so much."

"Think, boy! *Orchaevia*. The countess Orchaevia loved your family well, and you especial. She will take us in. No one will think to look for us there, so far in the country. And the countess can arrange that your house falls into the right hands."

"The countess," Cazio mused. "I haven't seen her since I was a boy. Would she really take us in?"

"She owes your father many favors, and the countess isn't the sort to let her obligations go unattended."

"Still," Cazio grumbled.

At that moment a fist thundered against the door.

"Cazio Pachiomadio da Chiovattio!" a voice cried, carrying faintly through the portal.

"You cannot duel a rope," the old man said, for the second time.

"That's true. If I die, I die by the sword," Cazio swore.

"Not here, you won't. You'll take a few, and then they'll bear you down by weight, just as they did in the alley." Z'Acatto shrugged. "You'll remember I said this, when you feel the noose tighten."

"Very well!" Cazio snapped. "I do not like it, but I concede your point. We'll gather our things and leave by the cistern."

"You know about the tunnel from the cistern?"

"Since I was eight," Cazio replied. "How do you think I got out, all of those nights, even when you sealed my window?"

"Damn. I should have known. Well, let's go, then."

CHAPTER SIX

THE ABODE OF GRACES

A PRIM WOMAN IN AN OCHRE HABIT with black wimple and gloves greeted Anne and Austra as they stepped down from the carriage. Her gray eyes surveyed the two girls rather clinically from above a sharp and upturned nose. She was perhaps thirty years of age, with a wide, thin mouth plainly accustomed to the shape of disapproval.

Anne drew herself straight, as behind her the knights began taking down her things from the roof of the carriage. "I am the princess Anne of the house of Dare, daughter of the emperor of Crotheny," she informed the woman. "This is my lady-in-waiting, Austra Laesdauter. Whom do I have the honor of addressing?"

The nun's lips twitched as if at a private joke.

"I am called Sister Casita," she said, in heavily accented Virgenyan. "Welcome to the Abode of Graces."

Sister Casita didn't bow or even nod as she said this, so that Anne wondered if she were perhaps hard of hearing. Could Vitellio be so different that they did not acknowledge the daughter of a king here? What sort of place had she come to?

I've made my decision, she thought, fighting down the sudden bad taste in her mouth. *I'll make the best of it.*

The Abode of Graces wasn't an unpleasant-looking place. Indeed, it was rather exotic, rising from the spare, rustic landscape as if it had grown there. The stones it was built from were of the same color as those they had seen exposed in seams along the road, a yellowish red. The coven itself sat on a ridgetop encircled by a crenulated wall longer than it was wide and enclosing an area the size of a small village. Square towers with sharply steepled roofs of rust-colored tile rambled up at odd intervals and inconsistent altitudes around the wall, while through the arched gate Anne could make out the large but oddly low-built manses across a flagstoned courtyard. The only height within the wall was a single ribbed dome that Anne assumed to be the nave of the chapel.

Grapevine and primrose crawled up the walls and towers, and olive trees twisted through cracked cobblestones, giving the place a look that was somehow both untidy and immaculate.

The only discordant note was provided by the ten persons with carts and mules who seemed to be camped outside of the gates. They were swaddled head to toe in patchwork linens and gauzy veils and sat or squatted beneath temporary awnings of light cotton fabric.

"Sefry," Austra whispered.

"What was that?" Sister Casita asked sharply.

"If it please you, Sister," Austra said, "I was just noticing the Sefry encampment." She gave a small curtsey.

"Be wary," the sister said. "If you keep your voice low, it will be assumed you mean mischief."

"Thank you, Sister," Austra replied, more loudly.

Irritated, Anne cleared her throat. "Where shall I have my men carry our things?" she asked.

"Men are not allowed within the Abode of Graces, of course," Sister Casita replied. "What you want, you will carry yourself."

"What?"

"Choose what you want and can carry in a single trip. The rest remains outside of the gates."

"But the Sefry—"

"Will take it, yes. It is why they are here."

"But that's insane," Anne said. "These things are *mine*."

The sister shrugged. "Then carry them."

"Of all—"

"Anne Dare," the sister said, "you are a very great distance from Crotheny."

Anne did not miss the lack of any title or honorific.

"Crotheny travels with me," she said, nodding at Captain Marl and the rest of her guard.

"They will not interfere," Sister Casita assured her.

Anne turned to glare at Captain Marl. "You're going to let her treat me this way?"

"My orders preclude interfering with the will of the sisters," Captain Marl replied. "I was to deliver you here, safe and whole, and place you in the care of the Coven Saint Cer, also known as the Abode of Graces. I have done so."

Anne switched her gaze from the captain to the sister, then looked back down at her things. There were two trunks, both too large and unwieldy for her to lift.

"Very well," she said at last. "Do your orders preclude giving me a horse, Captain Marl?"

"They do, Princess."

"A rope?"

He hesitated. "I see no reason not to supply you with a rope," he said at last.

"Give me one, then."

Anne grunted, straining her back and legs at the earth, and her trunks dragged reluctantly forward another handspan or so. She shifted her footing.

"I can assure you," Sister Casita said, "whatever you have there will not be worth the effort. Little is needed within these walls—habit, nourishment, water, tools. And all of those will be provided. If you are vain, rescue your comb. You will not be allowed to wear jewelry or fine gowns."

"It's *mine*," Anne said, through gritted teeth.

"Let me help her," Austra asked, for the sixth time.

"They aren't your things, my dear," the sister replied. "You may carry only your own things."

Anne looked up wearily. After an hour of dragging, she had nearly made it to the gate. She had attracted an audience, some twenty girls of various ages but tending toward her own. They wore simple brown habits with wimples of the same color. Most of them were laughing and jeering at her, but she ignored them.

She strained again, feeling the rope she had strapped across her chest cut into her bodice. Her foot sought purchase on the first of the flagstones and failed.

The Sefry seemed to be enjoying the spectacle as much as everyone else. One had produced a tambour and another a small five-stringed croth, which he played with a little bow.

"Give it up, Princess Mule!" one of the girls shouted. "You'll never bring them in, no matter how stubborn a jackass you be! And why would you?"

The japing girl got a good chorus of laughter for that. Anne marked her, with her long, slender neck and dark eyes. Her hair was hidden by her wimple.

Anne did not, however, reply but set herself grimly and pulled some more. She had to go back and work each trunk onto the flagstones individually, but after that they went a bit smoother. Unfortunately she was wearing out.

At first she didn't notice the sudden silence that fell across the other girls, and when she did she thought it was because she had stumbled. Then she looked up and saw what had really silenced them.

First she noticed the eyes, fierce and piercing and bright, like the eyes of Saint Fendve, the patroness of war madness, in the painting in her father's battle chapel. So striking were they that it took moments for her to understand their color—or rather that they had almost none, so black were they.

Her face was harsh and old and very, very dark, the color of cherry wood. Her habit was black, wimpled in storm gray, and the moment Anne laid her gaze on her she was afraid of her, of what damage crouched behind those eyes and the rough seams of that face.

"Who are you," the old woman said, "and what do you think you're doing?"

Anne set her jaw. Whoever this was, she was just a woman. She couldn't be any worse than Mother or Erren.

"I am Anne of the house of Dare, princess of Crotheny. I am told I may have only those things that I can carry to my room, so I am carrying them there. And may I ask your name, Sister?"

A collective gasp went up from the assembled women, and even Casita raised an eyebrow.

The old woman blinked, but her expression did not change. "My name is not spoken, nor is the name of any sister here. But you may call me Sister Secula. I am the mestra of this coven."

"Very well," Anne said, trying to remain brave, "where shall I put my things?"

Sister Secula looked at her for another dispassionate moment, then lifted her finger. Anne thought at first she was pointing to the sky.

"The top room on the left," she said softly. It was then Anne realized she was pointing at the tallest of the towers on the wall.

Midnight found Anne collapsed at the base of the narrow spiral stairs that led to the tower heights. Sister Casita had been replaced by another observer, an older member of the order who identified herself as Salaus. Austra was still there, of course, but otherwise the courtyard was empty.

"Why persist in this, Anne?" Austra whispered. "You would have left all this behind had you succeeded in fleeing. Why do you care so much for it now?"

Anne regarded her friend wearily. "Because that would have been my choice, Austra. All of my other choices have been made for me. To keep my things is the only choice it is still in my power to make."

"I have been up the stairs. You cannot do it, and they will not let you separate yourself from them. Leave one of the trunks behind."

"No."

"Anne . . ."

"What if I give one to you?" Anne asked Austra.

"I'm not allowed to help you."

"No. I mean I will give one of the trunks to you, and all of its contents."

"I see," Austra said. "And then I would give it back, later."

"No. It would be yours, Austra. Forever."

Austra's hand flew to her mouth. "I've never owned anything, Anne. I don't think I'm allowed to."

"Absurd," Anne said. She raised her voice.

"Sister Salaus. I'm giving one of my chests to my friend Austra. Is that permitted?"

"If it is a true gift."

"It is," Anne replied. She tapped the smaller of the chests. "Take this one. It has two fine gowns, stockings, a mirror and combs—"

"The mirror set with opal?" Austra gasped.

"Yes, that one."

"You can't give me that."

"I already have. Now. You can choose to carry your things to our rooms, or you can leave them for the Sefry. I've made my choice. Now you make yours."

They crossed the threshold into their room an hour or so before dawn, dragging the trunks behind them. Sister Salaus presented them with a lit taper and a pair of dun habits.

"The morning meal is at seven bells," she said. "You should not miss it." She paused, and her frown deepened. "I've never quite seen the like of that," she said. "I do not know if it bodes ill or well for you as a beginning here, but it certainly sets you apart."

And with that, she left. Anne and Austra looked at each other for a few moments, then both burst out in a fit of laughter.

"It certainly sets you apart," Austra said, imitating the sister's thick Vitellian accent.

"There's something to be said for that, I suppose," Anne replied. She cast her gaze around the room. "Saint Loy, is this really where we're to stay?"

The room was a quarter of the tower, about five paces on a side. The roof was mere beams, and above that was the deep darkness of the conical roof. The girls could hear doves cooing, and feathers and bird droppings decorated the floor and the two wooden beds that were the only furnishings. There was a small window.

"It's hardly better than a dungeon cell," Austra said.

"Well," Anne sighed. "It's a good thing I'm a princess and not a gref-fess, I suppose."

"It's not so bad," Austra supposed dubiously. "Anyhow, now you're a princess in a tower, just as in the story of Rafquin."

"Yes, I'll begin knitting a ladder from spider silk right away, so when Roderick comes—"

Austra's face went serious. "Anne!"

"I'm joking, dove," Anne said. Nevertheless, she went to the window and peered out. "Look," she said. "The sun is rising."

The pale horizon became a golden seam and eventually the sun himself peeked up to reveal the leagues of gently rolling pasture, sprinkled with gnarled olive trees and slender cedars. In the middle distance, a gently meandering river clothed itself more verdantly in cypress and willow, and beyond that, the scenery faded into pale green, yellow, and finally sky.

"This place will do," Anne said softly. "If I can see the horizon, I can bear anything."

"We'll test that now," Austra said, holding one of the habits toward Anne.

"Well, there's Princess Mule," the girl with the long neck said as Anne and Austra entered the refectory.

Anne's ears burned as the girls within earshot laughed, and a chatter went up in Vitellian.

"I seem to have earned a nickname," she noticed.

The refectory was an airy place, its flat roof supported by slim, open arches on all sides. The tables were long, common, and rustic, and few empty seats greeted them. Anne chose the least populated bench and sat at an end across from a thickset young woman with a large jaw and close-set eyes. As Austra settled beside her, Anne noticed that the other girls had already been served bowls of porridge dressed with some sort of curd or fresh cheese.

The girls at the table glanced at her from the corners of their eyes, but no one spoke until several uncomfortable moments had passed, when the thickset girl, without looking up from her meal, said, speaking Virgenyan, "You have to serve yourself, you know. From the cauldron on the hearth." She gestured, and Anne saw a cauldron tended by a pair of the dun-dressed girls.

"I'll fetch ours, Anne," Austra said quickly.

"They won't allow that," the girl said.

"Doesn't she know *anything*?" another of the girls wondered aloud.

"*You* didn't know when you arrived, Tursas," the thick girl pointed out. Then, to Anne, she said, "You'd best hurry. Soon they'll take the food to the goats."

"What kind of place is this?" Anne whispered. "My father—"

"You'd best forget your station here," the girl said. "Forget it, and quickly, or Mestra Secula will teach you to regret your stubbornness. You've already been foolish enough. Take my advice."

"Rehta should know," the other girl said. "Sister Mestra put her—"

"Hush, Tursas," Rehta said sharply.

Anne considered ignoring the advice, but her belly added the final weight to the argument. Cheeks burning, feeling all of their eyes upon her, she went and fetched the porridge, ladling it into a stoneware bowl and procuring a spoon to eat it with. Austra joined her. Despite its consistency, the mush was surprisingly good. Anne washed it down with cold water and wished for bread. Halfway through her meal, she glanced back up at the girl identified as Rehta.

"Thanks for the advice," she said.

"And so what happens now, I wonder?" Austra asked. "What do you do all day?"

"You'll interview with the mestra," Tursas said. "You'll get your names, then you'll be assigned studies and tasks."

"That sounds wonderful," Anne said sarcastically.

The other girls didn't answer.

They met the mestra in a small, dark room with no windows and lit by a single oil lamp. The ancient sister regarded the girls from behind a small writing desk for a very long space before speaking. Then she looked down at the ledger before her.

"Austra Laesdauter. Henceforth, in this place, you shall be known as Sister Persondra. You, Anne Dare, shall be Sister Ivexa."

"But that means—"

"In the language of the church it signifies a female calf, and denotes the behavior I desire from you—obedient and passive."

"Stupid, you mean."

The mestra focused her frightening gaze on Anne again. "Don't think to make trouble here, Sister Ivexa," she said quietly. "An education in the Abode of Graces is a rare privilege and a priceless opportunity. The lady Erren recommended you, and she is well thought of by me. When you disappoint me, I am disappointed in her, and to feel disappointment toward her is upsetting."

"I endeavor to do my best," Anne replied rigidly.

"You do nothing of the kind. You began your tenure here with an unseemly tantrum. I wish it to be your last. It may be that you will return to the world one day. If you do, your behavior must reflect well your time here or I and every other sister of this order and the very Lady of Darkness herself will bear your shame. If, after a time, I'm not assured that you will represent us well, I promise you—you shall not leave at all."

Anne's scalp prickled at that, and a sudden panic caught at the base of her throat. She suddenly felt very uncertain and very far from home, as she considered just how many ways Mestra Secula could make good on that promise. Already she could think of two, and neither seemed very promising.

CHAPTER SEVEN

GIFTS

STEPHEN AWOKE TO HIS BREATH, and agony that shot like flames from his lungs out to his fingers and toes, burning holes where his eyes ought to be and scorching hair from his head. His eyes flickered open to a terrifying light that poured nightmare colors into his skull and left them there to clot into shapes so terrible and fantastic that he shrieked at their very existence. He lay on the ground wailing, covering his eyes, until gradually the pain subsided, until he realized that it wasn't pain at all, but a return from nothingness to normal sensation.

Nothingness. He had been nothing at all. He hadn't even been dead. He'd been less and less and then—nothing.

Now he was back, and as he gradually grew more accustomed to feeling again, he saw that the terrible shapes were only the trees of the forest and the blue sky above it. The rasping across his skin was a gentle breeze swaying the fern fronds.

"My name," he said shakily, "is Stephen Darige." He sat up and brought his hands to his face, felt the shape of his bone beneath the skin, the stubble of beard on his chin, and began to weep. He drew breath and worshipped it.

A long time later he pulled himself to his feet with the aid of a nearby sapling. The bark was a luxury against his raw fingers, and he coughed out a laugh that sounded strange to his ears.

He was filthy, covered in mud and blood from shallow scratches. He smelled like he hadn't bathed in weeks, and it smelled wonderful.

As reason reasserted itself, he began to try to work out where he was. He had collapsed—who knew how long ago—on the gently sloping hill of a sedos, bare of trees but covered in bracken fern. At its summit was a small fane, and by the characters graved on its face he recognized it as dedicated to Saint Dryth, the final incarnation of Decmanus on the faneway.

Which meant he had finished the walk. The saints had not destroyed him.

He found a pool fed by the clear waters of a spring, stripped off his rank clothing, and bathed beneath the overhanging branches of an ancient weeping willow. His stomach was as flat and hollow as a tambour, but he felt incredibly good despite his hunger. He scrubbed his clothes, hung them out to dry, and lazed on the mossy bank, drinking in the sounds around him, so happy to be alive and sensible that he didn't want to miss anything.

Some sort of bird trilled a complex bramble of notes and was answered by another with a slightly different song. Bronze and metal-green dragonflies danced over the water, and water-skitters dimpled along the transparent surface of another world where silver minnows darted and crayfish lurked in search of prey. All was fascinating, all was wonder, and for the first time in a long time it seemed, he remembered why he had wanted to be a priest: to *know* the world, in all its glory. To make its secrets a part of him, not for gain, but for the simple pleasure of knowing them.

The sun climbed to noon, and when his clothes were reasonably dry he donned them and set his feet back on the path toward the monastery, whistling, wondering how long he had been gone. Trying to understand what had happened to him. He spoke aloud, to hear his own voice.

"Each saint took a sense from me," he told the forest. "In the end they gave them back. But did they fashion them? Did they change them, as a blacksmith takes rough metal and makes something better? Nothing feels the same!"

Moreover, he felt that nothing ever would be the same again.

He started whistling again.

He stopped still when his whistling was answered in kind, and with a start he realized that it was the birdsong he had heard earlier. Every note, every variation of it was still in his head, clear and delicate. He laughed again. Could he have done that before, or was it a gift from walking the fanes? The gifts were different for each faneway and for each person who walked them, so there was no way of knowing what he had gained. At the moment, he felt that if this one thing—the power to imitate the birds—was all he had received, it would be enough.

At night the songs changed, and as he sat beside his fire, Stephen delighted in learning them as he had those of the day. It seemed he could forget nothing, now. With no effort at all he could recall to the least detail the appearance of the pool he had bathed in. He could feel the patterns in the night as if he had always understood them.

The sahto of Decmanus was that of knowledge, understanding in all of its forms. It seemed he had indeed been . . . improved.

The next day he further tested his abilities by reciting ballads as he traveled. The *Gorgoriad*, the *Fetteringsaga*, the *Tale of Findomere*. He never stumbled on a word or phrase, though he had heard the last only once, ten years earlier, and its recitation took almost two bells.

He sacrificed near each shrine and thanked the saints but did not mount their sedoi. Who knew what walking the fanes backwards would do?

His second night, something in the nightsong changed. There was a tremor in it, an echo of a thing he knew, as if the forest were gossiping about something dark and terrible that Stephen had once met. The more Stephen listened, the more convinced he became that it had to do with him. The conviction grew as sleep eluded him, but he tried to ignore it. He was expected back at the monastery. He had work to do, and the fratrex probably would be unhappy if he dallied. He had walked the fanes early so as to better perform his tasks, after all.

But morning found the waking forest with the same terrible undertone, and whenever Stephen turned his face east he felt a chill and a vague sickness. He remembered the dark tales at Tor Scath, the old knight's conviction that something evil was abroad. When he thought of the Briar King, he felt a terror that nearly scalded him.

At the fane of Saint Ciesel, the feeling began to fade, and with each step nearer the monastery it faded more. Soon he began whistling again, singing other songs and ballads he knew, but even so his joy was diminishing, replaced by a nagging in his bones. Something out there was wrong, something needed him, and his back was to it.

He came to a stream, one he remembered crossing early in his journey. He was nearly there, would probably be at the monastery by sundown. By morning he would be testing his new gifts on the things he loved best, the ancient scrifts and tomes of the church. Surely that was what Saint Decmanus wanted of him, not to go chasing a bad dream through the wilderness.

He stared at the stream for a while, dithering, but in the end he let his newly minted heart turn him east. He struck from the path, out to the wilderness.

Hunger was a living thing in him now. He must have lost the food he'd brought early in his journey; he didn't think he had eaten for three or four days. The forest provided little; nothing edible grew beneath the great trees, and he knew nothing of hunting or snaring. He managed to spear a few fish with a stick he sharpened using his finger knife, and he discovered that open places, burned off by lightning in years past, were veritable oases; in those places not shadowed by branches he found understories of hard apples and persimmons, tiny cherries and grapes. By seeking these he managed to sustain himself, but his hunger continued to grow.

For the rest of the day he traveled east and camped in a high place where stone had cut up through the earth and dressed itself in lichen. He built a small fire and listened to the night grow frantic.

For whatever worried the forest was near. His ears were sharper than they had been; he could hear labored footsteps in the darkness, the snapping of limbs and scraping of something against bark. Now and then a coughing growl wended through the columns of the trees.

What am I doing here? he wondered, as the snapping became a crashing through the forest. *Whatever that is, what can I do about it?* He wasn't Aspar White. If it was the greffyn, he was surely dead. If it was the Briar King . . .

The crashing was very close, now. In a sudden panic, Stephen felt hideously exposed in the firelight. With his sharpened fish spear, he moved out of the circle of light, wondering belatedly if he should climb a tree, if he could find one with branches low enough.

Instead he crouched near a large bole, trying to still the echo of his heart beating in his ears.

Then the sounds ceased. *All* sounds had ceased. The nighthawks and whippoorwills, the frogs and the crickets. The night was an empty box. Stephen waited, and prayed, and tried to keep his fear from clawing out of his head and into his legs. He'd seen a cat, once, stalking a field rat. The cat had toyed with the smaller creature, never striking until the mouse's fear made it bolt. Not because the cat couldn't see its prey, but because the cat, like all of its kind, had a cruel streak. Stephen felt very much like the mouse now, but he wasn't one. He had reason. He could fight his instincts.

But maybe in this case, after all, it would be better to run . . .

The old Stephen would never have heard the sound in time to move, the faint whisper of leather against damp leaves. He threw himself forward, away from the sound, but something struck him hard across the back of his legs, and he lost his stride and fell. A dark thing clawed at his feet, and Stephen turned on his back and kicked at it, pushing away from it with the palms of his hands. The creature came on, rearing up and revealing itself in the firelight. It had the frame of a man, and a visage so terrible and so well known at the same time.

"Aspar!" Stephen shrieked, even then not absolutely certain.

But it was the holter, his face blackened and bruised, his eyes bereft of human knowing. He lurched forward at his name, gasping.

"Aspar, it's me, Stephen Darige!"

"Ste—?" The holter's face softened to a sort of insane puzzlement, and then he collapsed at Stephen's feet. Stephen opened his mouth and took a step toward the holter, then held himself very still as he saw what was behind his erstwhile companion, what his body had hidden when he was standing.

Behind the holter, a pair of glowing yellow eyes stared at Stephen through the darkness. They shifted noiselessly closer, and the wavering firelight limned something huge with a beak like a bird. It sniffed at him, and the eyes blinked slowly. Then the head raised, and it uttered a sound like a butcher sawing the long bone of a cow.

It took another step toward Stephen, then nodded its beaked head angrily at him. The eyes blinked once more, and in a silent rushing it was gone, off through the trees, running faster than anything could run, leaving only the silence, and Stephen, and the dead or unconscious Aspar White.

CHAPTER EIGHT

COURSE OF STUDY

ANNE FELT A BRIEF TASTE of bile in her throat as the flesh of the man's chest opened in two great flaps like floppy cupboard doors. Within was a wormy mess such as she had never imagined could be found in a human being. She supposed she had always imagined the inside of a person much like the outside, perhaps redder for the blood, but relatively featureless. What she saw now seemed senseless and bizarre.

The girl on her right dropped to her knees, retching, which began a trend that left all but two of the eight girls in the chamber relinquishing their morning meal. Anne did not join them, and neither did Serevkis, the long-necked young woman who had nicknamed her "Princess Mule." From the corner of her eye, Anne caught a glance from Serevkis and was surprised when the girl sent her a brief, sardonic smile.

Sister Casita, who had made the incisions on the corpse, waited patiently for the involuntary purging to end. Anne absently maneuvered to keep her shoes clean, but focused her attention on the cadaver.

"That's a natural reaction," Casita said, when the round of sickness seemed to be over. "Be assured that this man was a criminal of the worst sort. Serving the church and our order in death is the only virtuous thing he has ever accomplished, and it will earn his remains decent internment."

"Why isn't he bleeding?" Anne asked.

Casita regarded her with a lifted eyebrow. "Sister Ivexa asks an interesting question," she said. "Out of turn, but interesting." She gestured at something fist-size and bluish gray in the center right of the chest. "Here is the heart. An ugly thing, is it not? In appearance hardly worthy of the praise heaped on it in poetry and metaphor. But it is indeed an organ of importance. In life it contracts and expands, which makes the beating you feel in your own breasts. In so doing, it sends blood racing around the body within tubular canals. You see four of these here." She indicated four large pipes stuck fast to the heart. "In death, the heart ceases its activity and the blood ceases to move. It pools and congeals in the body, so as Sister Ivexa notices, even the most grievous cut draws little blood."

"Permission, Sister?" Serevkis murmured.

"Granted."

"If you were to cut a live man, we would see his heart beating, and the blood would flow?"

"Until he died, yes."

Anne placed her hand over her sternum and felt the heart beneath. Did hers really look like that?

"And whence comes the blood?"

"Ah. It is generated by a confluence of humors in the body. All of this you will learn in due time. Today we will learn the names of certain parts, and later the humors that control them. Eventually we will discuss how each organ can be made to sicken and die, whether by insult from a wound, from physic, or from holy sacaum. But today, I want you to be most clear on this." She swept her eyes about the chamber. "Sister Facifela, Sister Aferum—are you paying attention?" she snapped.

Facifela, a gangly girl with a weak chin, looked up meekly. "It is hard to look at, Sister Casita."

"At first," Casita said. "But you *will* look. By the end of the day, you must name all of these organs to me. But the first lesson is this, so all of you listen carefully." She reached into the body cavity and pushed things around, making a wet sucking sound.

"You, your father, your mother. The greatest warrior of your kingdom, the highest fratrex of the church, kings, scoundrels, murderers, stainless knights—inside, all of us are this. To be sure, there is variation in strength and health and internal fortitude, but in the end it matters little. Beneath armor and clothing and skin, there is always this soft, wet, infinitely vulnerable interior. Here is where life resides in our bodies; here is where death hides, like a maggot waiting to be born. Men fight from the outside, with clumsy swords and arrows, trying to pierce the layers of protection we bundle in. They are of the outside. We are of the inside. We can reach there in a thousand ways, slipping through the cracks of eye and ear, nostril and lip, through the very pores of the flesh. Here is your frontier, Sisters, and eventually your domain. Here is where your touch will bring the rise and fall of kingdoms."

Anne felt a little trembling in her and for an instant thought she smelled the dry decay of the crypt she and Austra had found long ago. The feeling wasn't one of fear but of excitement. It felt, suddenly, as if she sat in a tiny boat on a vast sea and had for the first time been explained the meaning of water.

Walking into the hall, she nearly bumped nose to nose with Sister Serevkis and found herself staring into the girl's cool gray eyes.

"You weren't repelled?" Serevkis asked.

"A little," Anne admitted. "But it was interesting. I notice you didn't get sick either."

"No. But my mother was the undertaker for the meddix of Formesso. I've seen the insides of bodies all of my life. This was your first time, yes?"

"Yes."

Serevkis looked off somewhere behind Anne. "Your Vitellian has improved," she noticed.

"Thank you. I'm working hard on it."

"A good idea," Serevkis replied. She smiled and her gaze met Anne's again. "I must go to my cyphers tutorial. Perhaps I'll see you at the evening meal, Sister Ivexa."

The rest of Anne's classes were less intriguing, and numbers least of all, but she did her best to pay attention and do her sums. After numbers came greencraft, which she thought at first would be better. Even Anne knew that the weeds from beneath a hanging tree and the dark purple blossoms of the benabell were used as poisons. They did not discuss any such thing, however, but instead doted on the care of roses, as if they were training to be gardeners instead of assassins. At the end of greencraft, Sister Casita came in and called three names. One of them was Anne's. The other two girls Anne did not know. They went, of all places, to the yard out back of the coven, where sheep were brought in from the fields to be milked and fleeced. Anne stared at the dumb creatures as they wandered aimlessly, while Sister Casita explained something to the other girls in their own language, which Anne thought might be Safnian. She turned her attention back to the older woman when she switched to Vitellian.

"My apologies," the sister said. "These two haven't made the progress in Vitellian you have. I must say, you've done very well in a short time."

"Brazi, Sor Casita," Anne said. "I studied the church Vitellian at home. I suppose more of it stuck than I thought, and many of the words are similar." She nodded at the animals. "Why are we here with the sheep, Sister?" she asked.

"Ah. You're going to learn to milk them."

"Is sheep's milk of some use in physic?"

"No. At the end of the first month, each sister is assigned a duty. This is to be your job, milking and making cheese."

Anne stared at her, then laughed aloud.

Tears stung Anne's eyes as the switch laid a bright strip across her bare shoulders, but she did not cry out. Instead, she fixed her tormentor with a glare that would have sent any courtier scurrying.

Sister Secula was no courtier, and she did not so much as flinch at Anne's expression.

Another lash came down, and this time a little gasp escaped Anne's lips.

"So," Sister Secula exclaimed. "Only three for you to find your breath? You don't have the bravery to suit your attitude, little Ivexa."

"Switch me all you want," Anne said. "When my father finds out—"

"He'll do nothing. He sent you here, my dear. Your royal parents have already agreed to any medicine I administer—and that is the last time I shall remind you of that. But I won't switch you again, not just now. I've already learned what I wanted. Next time, you may expect more than three strikes of the switch. Now—back to the task set for you.".

"No, I will not go," Anne told her.

"What? What did you say?"

Anne straightened her back. "I won't milk sheep, Sister Secula. I was born a princess of the house Dare and a duchess of the house de Liery. I will die as such, and I will be those things all the years between. However long you keep me in this place, and however you choose to treat me, I remain who I am, and I will not be lowered to menial tasks."

Sister Secula nodded thoughtfully. "I see. You're protecting the dignity of your titles."

"Yes."

"As you protected them when you ignored your mother's wishes and rode like a wild goat all over Eslen? As when you were busy spreading your legs for the first buck to spout poetry at you? It seems you've discovered the dignity becoming your station right quickly and conveniently when asked to do something you find distasteful."

Anne laid her head back down on the chastising table. "Strike me more if you wish. I do not care."

Sister Secula laughed. "That is another thing you will learn, little Ivexa. You will learn to care. But perhaps it is not whipping that will make you do so. Who do you think the ladies of this coven are, lowborn peasants? They are from the best families in all the known lands. If they choose to return to the world, they will find their titles waiting. Here, they are members of this order, nothing more and nothing less. And you, my dear, are the very least of them."

"I am not the least," Anne replied. "I will never be the least of anything."

"Absurd. You are the least learned in every subject. You are the least disciplined. You are the least worthy of even that novice robe you wear. Listen to you! What have you ever done? You have nothing that was not given to you by your birth."

"It is enough."

"It is if your only ambition is to be the brood mare for some highborn fool, for brood mares neither need nor have brains enough to want more than they were born with. Yet my understanding is that the very reason you were sent to me is that even that lowest of ambitions escapes your thick head."

"I have talents. I have a destiny."

"You have inclinations. You have desires. A plow-ass has those."

"No. I have more." *My dreams. My visions.* But she didn't mention those aloud.

"Well, we shall see, shan't we?"

"What do you mean?"

"You think yourself a creature apart, better than every other girl here. Very well—we shall give you the chance to prove that is so. Yes, we will. Come with me."

Anne gazed down into the utter blackness and tried not to tremble. Behind her, three sisters tightened a series of ropes supporting the leather harness they had strapped on her.

"Don't do this," Anne said, trying to keep her voice low.

None of the sisters answered, and Sister Secula was already gone.

The air wafting out of the hole was cold and metallic.

"What is it?" Anne asked. "Where are you putting me?"

"It is called the womb of Lady Mefitis," one of the initiates answered. "Mefita is, as you know, an aspect of Cer."

"The aspect that tortures damned souls."

"Not at all. That's a common misconception. She is the aspect of motion in rest, of pregnancy without birth, of time without day or night."

"How long am I to be down there?"

"A nineday. It is the usual penance associated with humility. But I urge you to use your time in meditation, and in perceiving the glory of our lady. After all, her fane is there."

"A nineday? I'll starve!"

"We're going to lower food and drink sufficient for that time."

"And a lamp?"

"Light is not permitted in the womb."

"I'll go mad!"

"You won't. But you'll learn humility." Her smile hid an uncertain emotion. Triumph? Grief? Anne thought it could be either. "You must learn it some time, you know. Now, in you go."

"No!"

Anne kicked and screamed, but for naught. They had her strapped well, and in no time the initiates had her out over the black well and descending into it.

The opening was as wide as she was tall. By the time her descent ended and her feet touched stone, it seemed no larger than a bright star.

"Keep near, where the stone is flat and level," a voice floated down. "Do not go beyond the wall we have built, or you will find danger. The caves are empty of beasts, but full of cracks and chasms. Stay in the wall, and you will be safe."

Then the circle vanished, and the only light remaining was the illusion of it painted on her eyelids, a single spot fading quickly from green, to pink, to deep red—gone.

And Anne screamed until her throat felt torn.

CHAPTER NINE

THE KEPT

PRINCE CHEISO OF SAFNIA spasmed and coughed flecks of blood onto the stone floor as his torturer drew a score across his back with a red-hot iron, but he did not scream. William could see the scream anyway, buried in the Safnian's face, digging to get out like the larvae of an earth wasp struggling to emerge from a paralyzed spider. But it stayed prisoned in that proud, dark face.

William could not help but admire Cheiso's bravery. The man had been whipped and burned, the flesh of his back sanded raw and rubbed with salt. Four of his fingers were broken, and he had been dunked repeatedly in a vat of urine and offal. Still he did not beg, or cry out, or confess. They were made of sterner stuff than William had known, these Safnians. He doubted that he would have held up so well.

"Will you speak now?" Robert asked gently. He stood behind the prince and stroked his brow with a damp rag. "You have sisters yourself, Prince Cheiso. Try to imagine how we feel. We degrade ourselves when we treat you thus, but we will know why you betrayed her."

Lying there on a table turned upright, Cheiso lifted his eyes then, but he did not look at Robert. Instead, his black eyes focused steadfastly on William. He licked his lips and spoke.

"Your Majesty," he said, in that faraway accent of his kind, "I am Prince Cheiso of Safnia, son of Amfile, grandson of Verfunio, who turned away the Harshem fleet at Bidhala with two ships and a word. I do not lie. I do not betray my honor. Lesbeth your sister is my dearest love, and if any evil has come to her, I will live to find who did it and make him pay. But you, Emperor of Crotheny, are a fool. You have supped on lies, and they have fattened your wits. You may dig with your prick of iron down to my very bones and carpet your floor with my blood, but there is nothing I can tell you save that I am innocent."

Robert gestured, and the torturer took the Safnian's ear in a grip of red-hot tongs. The prince's lean body arched, as if trying to break his own back and bend double, and this time a ragged sigh escaped him, but nothing more.

" 'Twill take but a little time," the torturer told Robert. "He will confess to us."

William clasped his hands behind his back, trying not to fidget.

"Robert," he grunted. "A word."

"Of course, dear brother." He nodded to the torturer. "Continue," he said.

"No," William said. "Respite, until we've spoken."

"But brother dear—"

"Respite," William said firmly.

Robert lifted his hands. "Oh, very well. But this is an art, Wilm. If you ask the painter to lift his brush in midstroke—" But he saw William meant it, and broke off. They moved away, into the dank and vaulted hall of the dungeons below Eslen, where they could speak unheard.

"What troubles you, brother?"

"I am altogether unconvinced that this man is dishonest."

Robert folded his arms. "The birds that twitter in my ear say otherwise," he said.

"Your birds have been magpies before," William said, "leading us astray. Now is such a time."

"You cannot be certain. Let us continue until all doubt is cleared away."

"And if we find him innocent after all? They have ships in Safnia, you know. They might lend those ships to our enemies, and in a time when war approaches, that is no small thing."

Robert's eyebrows arched. "Are you joking with me, Wilm?"

"What joke can you possibly hear in that?"

"I have already given it out that the prince and all of his retainers were killed by Rovish pirates in the Sea of Ale. Word of what we do here will not travel."

"You don't expect me to have this man murdered," William said incredulously.

"What sort of king are you? What sort of brother?"

"If he is innocent—"

"He is *not*," Robert exploded. "He is Safnian, born of a thousand years of oily southern lies. Of course he seems convincing. But he will confess, and he will die, and Lesbeth's betrayal will be avenged. My sources are not mistaken, Wilm."

"And how does this bring our sister back to us, Robert? Revenge is a sad feast next to a loved one restored."

"We will have both, I promise you, Wilm. You have met Austrobaurg's conditions; twenty ships have been sent to the basin of the Saurga Sea already."

"And you trust Austrobaurg to keep his word?"

"He is an ambitious coward; there is no more trustworthy sort of man, so long as you understand them. He will do as he says."

"Austrobaurg maimed Lesbeth, Robert. How can he hope to stay our revenge if he returns her to us?"

"Because if you try to take revenge, he will send word to the lords of Liery that you have been aiding his cause against their allies. Certainly he can produce proof."

"And you did not foresee this?"

"Indeed I did," Robert said. "And I saw it as the only guarantee of Lesbeth's safe homecoming."

"You should have been clear about that, then."

Robert lifted his nose a fraction. "You are emperor. If you cannot see the consequences . . . I am not your only councilor, brother."

"Liery must never know what we have done."

"Agreed. For that matter, it must never be known abroad that Lesbeth was ever taken captive. It would make us seem weak, which we can ill afford even in the best of times. No, this entire business must be erased. Austrobaurg will not talk. Lesbeth is our sister."

"And that leaves Cheiso," William grunted. "Very well."

Robert bowed his head, then lifted his eyes. "You need not witness the rest. It may take some time."

William frowned, but nodded. "If he confesses, I'll want to hear it. Do not kill him too quickly."

Robert smiled grimly. "The man who betrayed Lesbeth shall not die easily."

William's steps through the dungeon were slow ones. The vague fear that had lived in him for months was deepening, and at last it was beginning to take sharper form.

His reign had known border squabbles and provincial uprisings, but it had escaped real war. On the surface, this affair with Saltmark seemed another such petty dispute, yet William felt as if he and the empire were balanced on the tip of a needle. His enemies were striking somehow into his very house—first Muriele and then Lesbeth. They were laughing at him, the impotent king of the most powerful empire in the world.

And while Robert spun dark webs to snare their troubles, William did nothing. Maybe Robert *ought* to be king.

William paused, suddenly realizing that his steps had not taken him nearer the stairway that led to the palace, but rather, deeper into the dungeons. Torches still flickered here, clouding the dank air with scorched oil, but the passage faded into darkness. He stood there a moment, peering into it. How many years since he had been that way? Twenty?

Yes, since the day his father first showed him what lay in the deepest dungeon of Eslen castle. He had never returned.

He knew a moment of panic, and checked himself from fleeing back up into the light. Then, with something at least pretending to be resolve, he continued on a bit, until he came to a small chamber that was not a cell, but that did have a small wooden door. Through it, William heard a faint, sweet music, a not-quite-familiar tune played on the strings of a theorbo. The key was minor and sad, with small trills like birdsong and full chords that reminded of the sea.

Hesitating, he waited for a break in the music, but the melody never quite seemed to find its end, teasing the ear with promise of closure but then wafting on like a capricious zephyr.

Finally, remembering who was king, he rapped on the wooden surface.

For long moments, nothing happened, but then the music stopped in midphrase, and the door swung inward, silently, on well-oiled hinges, and in the orange light a narrow wedge of ghost-pale face appeared. Eyes of milky white looked upon no world William knew, but the ancient Sefry smiled as if at a secret joke.

"Your Majesty," he murmured, in a slight voice. "It has been many years."

"How—?" William faltered again. How could those unsighted eyes know him?

"I know it is you," the Sefry said, "because the Kept has been whispering for you. You were bound to come."

Corpse fingers tickled William's spine. *The dead are speaking my name.* He remembered that day in his chambers, the day Lesbeth returned. The day he'd first learned about Saltmark from Robert.

"You will want to speak to him," the old one said.

"I don't remember your name, sir," William said.

The Sefry smiled, to reveal teeth still white but worn nearly to the gums. "I was never named, my liege. Those marked to keep the key are never named. You may call me Keeper." He turned, and his silk robe shifted and pulled over what might have been a frame of bone. "I will fetch my key."

He vanished into the darkness of his abode, and reappeared a moment later with an iron key gripped in his white fingers. In the other hand he carried a lantern.

"If you would but light this, Your Majesty," he said. "Fire and I are not friendly."

William took a torch from the wall and got the wick going.

"How long have you been down here?" William asked. "My father said you were the Keeper in his father's time." *How long do Sefry live?*

"I came with the first of the Dares," the withered creature said, starting down the hall. "Your ancestors did not trust my predecessor, since he was a servant of the Reiksbaurgs." He hissed a small laugh. "A wasted fear."

"What do you mean?"

"That Keeper no more served the Reiksbaurgs than I serve you, my liege. My task is older by far than any line that ever sat this throne."

"You serve the throne itself, then, without regard for who sits it?"

The Sefry's soft footsteps scraped ten times on stone before he softly answered. "I serve this place and this land, without regard for thrones at all."

They continued in silence, down a narrow stair that cut through stone in which the black bones of unknown beasts could be seen now and then—here a rib cage, there the empty eyes of a flat and alien skull. It was as if the stone had melted and flowed around them.

"These bones in the rock," William asked. "Are they monsters imprisoned by my ancestress, or some older Skasloi sorcery?"

"There are sorceries more ancient than the Skasloi," the Keeper murmured. "The world is very old."

William imagined his own skull, gazing emptily from the stone across unimaginable gulfs of time. He felt suddenly dizzy, as if suspended over a great pit.

"We are below Eslen, now," the Sefry informed him. "We are in all that remains of Ulheqelesh."

"Do not speak that name," William said, trying to control his breathing. Despite the narrowness of the stair, his strange vertigo persisted.

The Sefry shook his head. "Of all names that might be spoken here, that is the least powerful. Your ancestress destroyed not only the form of the citadel, but the very soul of it. The name is only a sound."

"A dread sound."

"I will not speak it again, if it bothers you," the Sefry promised diffidently.

They continued without speaking, but the way was no longer silent. Along with the scraping of their shoes on the stone there was a hissing, a whispering. William could not make out the words, if indeed there were words, if it were not some movement of air or water in the deeps of the place. And as he drew nearer their destination, it began to sound familiar.

Was the old man right? Was the Kept calling his name? The words lisped, as if from some creature with no lips, *Hriiyah. Hriiyah Darrrr* . . .

"Why are his guardians never named?" William asked, to shut the voice from his head.

"You feel why, I think. Names give him a little power. Never fear. He is feeble, and what strength he has I will check."

"You're certain?"

"It is my only duty, Sire. Your grandfather did come here often, your father, as well. They trusted me."

"Very well." He stopped, staring at the door that appeared before them. It was iron, but despite the damp no rust marred its surface. In the lamplight it was black, and the curling characters that grooved its surface were blacker still. A faint smell hung in the air, a bit like burning resin.

The keeper approached the door and placed his key in one of two locks. But he paused.

"You need not do this, Sire," the Sefry said. "You may always turn back."

He thinks me weaker than my father and grandfather, William thought, ashamed. *He senses a lack of will.*

"I think I must continue," he said.

"Then it needs the other key."

William nodded and reached beneath his doublet to the chain that hung there, and extracted the key he had worn since taking the throne, the key that every king of Crotheny had worn since the days of the elder Cavarum. William himself normally didn't wear it; its weight felt cold against his breast, and most days it remained in a coffer near his bed. He had put it on that morning before descending to the dungeons.

Like the door it fitted, the key was black metal, and like the door, it seemed impervious to rust and all other marks of time's scythe.

He placed the key in the lock and turned it. There was hardly any sound, just the faintest of *snicks* from somewhere within the great portal.

I am king, William thought. *This is my prerogative. I am not afraid.*

He grasped the handle of the door and tugged, and felt the amazing mass of it. Yet despite its inertia, it moved, almost as if it was the touch of his hand rather than the strength of his arm that moved it.

The voice grew louder and broke into a weird, low sound that was perhaps a laugh.

"And now, Sire, you must extinguish the lantern," the keeper said, "before we open the inner door. Light has no place there."

"I remember. You can guide me?"

"That is my task, Sire. I am not yet too infirm for it."

William snuffed the lantern, and black welled up from the dark heart of the world. He felt the press of ancient bones all around him, as if in the darkness the stone were flowing, creeping closer to take him in.

A moment later, he heard the sound of metal sliding, and the odor strengthened and bittered. He had smelled something like it once in his own sweat, just after an unexpected bee-sting.

"*Qexqaneh*," the Sefry said, in the loudest voice William had yet heard him use. "*Qexqanehilhidhitholuh, uleqedhinikhu.*"

"Of course," a voice burred, so close and familiar it made William jump. "Of course. There you are, Emperor of Crotheny. There you are, my sweet lord."

The tone was not mocking, nor were the words, quite. Nevertheless, William felt mocked.

"I am emperor," he said, with forced confidence. "Speak to me accordingly."

"A mayfly emperor, who will live hardly more than two beats of my heart," the Kept replied.

"Not if I have your heart stopped," William said.

Motion then, a sound like scales scraping against stone, and more airy laughter. "Can you, could you? I would weep black garnet tears for you, Prince of Least. I would bleed white gold and shit you diamonds." A rasping cough followed. "No, little king," the Kept continued. "No, no. Those are not the rules of our game. Your bitch ancestress saw to that. Go back to your sunlit halls and cuddle 'round your fear. Forget me and dream away your life."

"Qexqaneh," the Keeper said firmly. "You are commanded."

The Kept snarled, and sultry rage infused his voice. "My name. Older than your race, my name, and you use it like a rag to wipe up the run from your bowels."

William tightened his lips. "Qexqaneh," he said. "By your name, answer me."

The Kept's anger vanished as quickly as it came, and now he whispered. "Oh, little king, gladly. The answers shall give me joy," he said.

"And answer truthfully."

"I must, ever since that red-tressed whore that began your line shackled me. Surely you know that."

"It is so, Sire," the Keeper agreed. "But he may answer elusively. You must sift his words."

William nodded. "Qexqaneh, can you see the future?"

"Could I see the future, I would not be in this place, foolish manling. But I can see the inevitable, which is something else again."

"Is my kingdom bound for war?"

"Hmm? A tide of blood is coming. A thousand seasons of woe. Swords will lap their fill and more."

Dread gripped William, but not surprise.

"Can I prevent it?" he asked, not really hoping. "Can it be stopped?"

"You can own death or it can own you," the Kept said. "There are no other choices."

"Do you mean by that that I should prosecute this war? Attack Saltmark, or Hansa itself?"

"Little does that matter. Would you own death, little king? Would you keep it near your heart and be its friend? Will you feed it your family, your nation, your pitiful human soul? I can tell you how. You can be immortal, King. You can be like me, the last of your kind. Eternal. But unlike me, there will be none to prison you."

"The last of my kind?" This was confusing talk. "The last Dare?"

"Oh, yes. And the last Reiksbaurg, and the last de Liery—the last of your pitiful race, manling. Your first queen killed you all. It has been a slow death, a sleepy death, but it is awake now. You cannot stop it. But you can *be* it."

"I don't understand. No war can kill everyone. That's what you are saying, is it, Qexqaneh? That only one man will survive the slaughter? What nonsense is this?" He looked at the Keeper. "You are certain he cannot lie?"

"He cannot knowingly lie, no. But he can twist the truth into rings," the Keeper replied.

"I can tell you," Qexqaneh murmured silkily. "You can be the one. You can put out the lights of this world and start a new one."

"You're mad."

"Someone will do it, little king. The Nettle-man is already arising, you know. The rot has spread deep, and maggots crawl up. Even here I smell the putrescence. You can be the one. You can wear the night raiment and wave the scepter of corruption."

"Be clear. Do you really imply the end of the world is at hand?"

"Of course not. But the end of your house, your kingdom, your foul little race and all its issue—that is indeed on time's nearest horizon."

"And one man shall cause this?"

"No, no. What are those things on the side of your head? Does nothing you hear reach your brain? One shall *benefit* from it."

"At what cost?" William asked skeptically. "Other than the cost of being like you?"

"The cost is light. Your wife. Your daughters."

"What?"

"They will die anyway. You might as well profit from their slaughter."

"Enough!" William roared. He turned to leave, then suddenly spun on his heel.

"Someone attempted to murder my wife. Was this why? This tainted prophecy of a future even you admit you cannot truly see?"

"Did I admit that?"

"You did. Answer me, Qexqaneh. This prophecy of yours. Do others know it?"

The Kept panted for a few moments, and the air seemed to warm. "When you wretched slave beasts stood on the bones of my kin," he grated at last, "when you burned every beautiful thing and believed that you—you lowly worms—finally owned the world, I told you then what would happen. My words began the new era, this age you name Everon. They are remembered in many places."

"So the attempt on my wife?"

"I do not know. Coincidences happen, and your race is fond of murder. It's what made you such entertaining slaves. But she will die, and your daughters, too."

"You do not know that," William said. "You cannot. You speak only to deceive me."

"As you wish it, so it is," Qexqaneh said.

"Enough of this. I was mistaken to come here."

"Yes," Qexqaneh agreed. "Yes, you were. You do not have the iron in you that your ancestors did. They would not have hesitated. Good-bye, mayfly."

William left then, returning to the halls above, but laughter walked behind him like a thousand-legged worm. He did not sleep that night, but went to Alis Berrye.

He had her room lit with tapers, and she played on the lute and sang lighthearted songs until the sun rose.

CHAPTER TEN

LOST

ASPAR WHITE OPENED HIS EYES to a vaulted stone ceiling and a distant, singsong litany. Fever crawled like centipedes beneath his skin, and when he tried to move, his limbs felt like rotting fern fronds.

He lay still, listening to the strange song and to his old-man breath, rasping, puzzling at the air above him, interrogating his mute memories.

He was better than he had been, he remembered that. He'd been fevered, his mind fettered with pain.

What had happened? Where was he now?

With an effort, he turned his head from side to side. He lay on a hard wooden bed with stone walls around him on three sides, a low curved ceiling above. It was almost like a tomb, except a slit of a window in the wall above his head let in air from the outside. It smelled like late spring. Looking over his feet, he saw the niche opened into a much larger space—the hall of a castle or, judging by the weird language of the singing, a church.

By inches he tried to sit up. His legs throbbed with agony, but an inspection showed them both still there, to his relief. But by the time he had lifted his head halfway to sitting, it was spinning so badly he surrendered to a supine position. He fought down his gorge, and sweat broke out thickly on his brow.

It was a while before he could continue his inspection. When he did, he found that beneath the sheet he was naked except for bandages. His weapons, armor, and clothes were nowhere to be seen. The bandages suggested someone was well disposed toward him, but that was anything but certain.

Where was he? He tracked along his memory like a hound on a faint trail, pausing at landmarks. He'd come down from the mountains that he knew, clinging to Ogre's back. He remembered half falling his way down a talus slope and a plummet into a ravine. At some point, he'd fallen off the beast and couldn't find him again. He had flashes of days clinging to a tree trunk floating down a river, then endless stumbling through hill country that grew steadily flatter. And he remembered something following him, always just behind, making a game of it.

After that, memory failed completely.

He walked backwards up the trail in his mind, back into the mountains, climbing a black tangle of boughs, a song repeating endlessly in his head.

Nittering, nattering

Farthing go . . .

The Briar King. He remembered with sickening suddenness the thing in the living barrow. *He* is *waking. It's all true.*

"Winna!" he croaked. The Briar King be damned. The world be damned. Fend had Winna. First Qerla, now Winna.

He heaved his legs over the side of the cot, ignoring the great waves of agony. Something in his head whirled like a child's top, but he nevertheless managed to stand. Two steps brought him to the upward-curving wall, and he used it for support to make his way out of the niche.

A black flash passed behind his eyes, and then he was in the larger space, an enormous cave, like a Sefry rewn, but regular, curving high, high above.

No, not a cave. That was stupid. He was inside a building . . .

His legs weren't under him anymore. The stone floor abruptly explained to him how foolish he had been to try to walk. Cursing it, he settled for crawling.

A bell tolled somewhere, and the singing stopped. A few moments later, he heard a gasp nearby.

"Gentle saints!" a man's voice exclaimed. "Sir, you should still be abed."

Aspar squinted up to see a man in the black habit of a churchman.

"Winna," Aspar explained, through gritted teeth. Then he fainted.

When he came around the next time, it was to a familiar face.

"Huh," Aspar grunted.

"I spent a lot of time and effort dragging you here," Stephen Darige said. The young man was sitting on a stool a few feet away. "I'd appreciate it if you'd not make that labor wasted by killing yourself now."

"Where am I?" Aspar asked.

"The monastery d'Ef, of course."

"D'Ef?" Aspar grunted. "More than sixty leagues?"

"Sixty leagues from where? What happened to you, Holter White?"

"And you found me?" Aspar grunted skeptically.

"Yes."

He tried to sit up again. "Darige," he said, "I have to go."

"You can't," Stephen said, placing a hand on his arm. "You're better than you were, but you're still badly wounded. You'll die before you get half a league, and whatever it is you need so badly to do will no more get done than if you rest here a while."

"That's sceat. I'm hurt, but not that bad."

"Holter, if I hadn't found you, you would be dead, right now. If I hadn't found you near a monastery where the healing sacaum are known, you would still be dead or at the very least you would have lost your legs. There are three sorts of poison still trying to kill you, and the only thing keeping them down are the treatments you get here."

Aspar stared into the young man's eyes, considering. "How long, then," he snarled, "before I can leave?"

"Fifteen, twenty days."

"That's too long."

Stephen's face went grim and he leaned forward. "What did you find out there?" he asked in a low voice. "What did this to you?" He paused. "When I discovered you, there was some sort of beast with glowing eyes following you."

It's not what I found, Aspar thought bleakly. *It's what I lost.* But he looked Stephen in the eye again. He had to tell someone, didn't he?

"That was the greffyn," he grunted. "It was as Sir Symon told us. I saw it all. The dead, the sacrifices at the sedos. The greffyn. The Briar King. I saw it all."

"The Briar King?"

"I saw him. I don't think he's fully awake yet, but he was stirring. I felt that."

"But who . . . what is he?"

"I don't know," Aspar said. "Grim take me, I don't know. But I wish I had never seen him."

"But he did this to you?"

"A man named Fend did some of it. His men shot me up with arrows. The greffyn did more." He rubbed his head. "Darige, at the very least I must get word to the other holters, as soon as possible. And to the king. Can you arrange that?"

"Yes," Stephen said, but Aspar thought he detected a hesitation.

"This man that wounded me—Fend. He took captive a friend of mine. I need to find Fend."

"You will," Stephen said softly. "But not now. Even if you found him—in this state, could you fight him?"

"No," Aspar said reluctantly. If Fend was going to kill Winna, she was dead. If he had some reason to keep her alive, she was likely to remain that way for a while. He winced at an image of her, spiked to a tree, her entrails pulled out and—

No. She's still alive. She must be.

The boy was right. He was letting his feelings get in the way of his sense.

Suddenly, something occurred to him.

"You saw the greffyn," Aspar said. "Up close."

Stephen nodded. "If that's what it was. It was dark, but it had luminescent eyes and a beak like a bird's."

"Werlic. Yah. But you didn't get sick? It didn't attack you?"

"No, that was strange. It acted cross, sort of, and then left. I don't know why. It could have killed me with a single blow, I'm sure."

"It could have killed you with its *breath*," Aspar corrected. "I fell down from merely meeting its gaze. I know one boy died just of touching a corpse that died of touching the monster. And yet you never even got a stomachache?"

Stephen frowned. "I'd just walked the faneway of Decmanus. Perhaps the saint protected me."

Aspar nodded. There was more than one thing he didn't understand about the greffyn, anyway. It could have killed Aspar any number of times, but it hadn't. "Can you take that letter for me?"

"I can find someone to do it," Stephen said. "Right now I have duties."

"Take it when you can, then. I don't trust anyone else here."

"You trust me?"

"Yah. Don't take it too close to heart. I don't know anyone else here. You I know a little." He paused. "Don't take this for much either—but, ah . . . thanks."

The young priest tried not to smile. "I owed you that," he replied. His face grew more serious. "I've something else to ask you. When I found you, you had this."

Stephen reached into a leather pouch and produced the engraved horn. A shudder ran through Aspar's limbs when he saw it.

"Yah," he allowed.

"Where did you find it?"

"I don't know. There's a space I don't remember, after I saw the Briar King. After, I had it with me. You know what it is?"

"No. But the language on it is very old."

"What does it say?"

"I don't know." The priest sounded troubled. "But I intend to find out. My I borrow it for a while?"

"Yah. I've no use for the damned thing."

Stephen nodded and started to rise. "Oh, another thing," he said. "Your horses showed up a day after I brought you here. No one can get near them, of course, but they have plenty of pasture. They'll be left alone until you recover."

Aspar's throat caught, and for an instant he had a terrible fear he might cry in front of the boy. At least he hadn't lost Ogre and Angel. They'd followed him, the damned stupid, loyal beasts, even with a greffyn behind them.

"I'll be back when my duties are done," Stephen assured him.

"Don't trouble yourself," Aspar said gruffly. "I don't need a nursemaid."

"Actually, you do," Stephen replied.

Aspar grunted and closed his eyes. He heard Stephen's footsteps recede.

I'll find you, Winna. Or I'll avenge you, he promised.

Fratrex Pell smiled at Stephen as he entered his spare chamber.

"I am most pleased," he said, tapping the newest sheaf of translations. "No one else has managed even a phrase of this lamina. The saints must have blessed you well."

"They did, Fratrex," Stephen replied. "The language itself was not difficult—a dialect of the elder Cavarum."

"Then why the difficulty?"

"It was written backwards."

The fratrex blinked, then laughed. "Backwards?"

"Each word, front to back."

"What scribe would do such a thing?"

Stephen remembered the disturbing content of the lamina. "A scribe who did not want his work widely read, I should say." He struggled for his next words. "Fratrex, I know we've discussed this before, but I feel I must say again that my heart tells me these things are best left encrypted."

"Knowledge belongs to the church," the fratrex said gently. "All knowledge. Let's have an end to your questioning, Brother Stephen, once and for all. I admire your persistence, but it is ill placed."

Stephen nodded. "Yes, Fratrex."

"Now, this other thing." He held up a vellum scroll. "I'm puzzled. I didn't ask you to translate this."

"No, Fratrex, but in light of what the holter told us, I thought it pertinent to see what the scriftorium might hold concerning the Briar King and greffyns."

"I see. I assume you're doing this in spare time?"

"At night, Fratrex, in the meditation hour."

"The hour is called that for a reason, Brother Stephen. You should meditate."

"Yes, Fratrex. But I think this might be important."

The fratrex sighed and pushed the scrifti back. "The holter was mad with fever when you brought him here, at the quay awaiting Saint Farsinth's boat. Whatever hallucinations he may have had aren't likely to be relevant to anything."

"He was badly hurt," Stephen admitted. "And yet I know this man, somewhat. He is deeply pragmatic and not given to flights of fancy. When last I saw him, he thought greffyns and Briar Kings no more than children's fantasy. Now he is convinced he has seen them both."

"We often mock those things we believe most deeply," the fratrex said, "especially those things we do not *wish* to believe. There is much separation between the waking mind and the mind of madness."

"Yes, Fratrex. But as you see, in the *Tafles Taceis*, the *Book of Murmurs*, there is a passage copied from an unnamed source in old high Cavari. In it, mention is made of the *gorgos gripon*, the 'bent-nosed terror.' They are described as the 'hounds of the horned lord,' and it is further said that their glance is fatal."

"I can read, you know," the fratrex said. "The *Tafles Taceis* is an enumeration of pagan follies. It goes on to say in the annotation that this was most likely a term used to describe the personal guard of the witching-king Bhragnos, yes? Vicious killers known for their beaked helms?"

"It does say that," Stephen allowed. "And yet that annotation was written five hundred years after the original passage."

"By a learned member of the church."

"But, Fratrex, I *saw* the beast."

"You saw *a* beast, certainly. Lions have been known to come out of the hills, on occasion."

"I do not think this was a lion, Fratrex."

"Have you ever seen a lion, in the dead of night?"

"I have never seen a lion at all, Eminence."

"Just so. If what you saw was one of these beasts, why did it not slay you? Why were you not poisoned by its mere presence? You should have been, if we take the holter's ravings seriously."

"I cannot answer that, Fratrex."

"I feel this inquiry of yours is a waste of our time."

"Is it your wish I no longer pursue the matter?"

The fratrex shrugged. "So long as it does not interfere with the tasks expected of you, you may pursue whatever you wish. But to my mind, you're chasing phantasms."

"Thank you for your opinion, Fratrex," Stephen said, bowing.

Why didn't I mention the horn? Stephen wondered, as he left the fratrex's presence. The horn was something of a problem. The script on it was one he had seen only twice. It was a secret script used during the reign of the Black Jester. It was decipherable only because of a single scrift—written on human skin—which was accompanied by a parallel inscription in the Vadhiian script.

The letters were unlike any other writing known to the church, and heretofore Stephen had always assumed that it had been invented by the scribes who used it. And yet here it was again, this time recording something in a language so strange Stephen hadn't the faintest inkling what it might say. The language resembled no tongue he had ever seen or heard.

No human tongue, rather. But the way the words were formed resembled the tiny fragments of the Skasloi language he had seen glossed in elder Cavarum texts.

What had the holter found?

Pursing his lips, Stephen returned to the scriftorium.

A closer inspection of the *Book of Murmurs* proved frustrating. In the back of his mind, he'd thought that perhaps *horned lord* might be better translated as *lord with horns*, but the word in question quite plainly referred to something like antlers, not a sounding instrument made of horn. He sat for a while, staring glumly at the text, wishing he had the original sources the unknown author had drawn upon.

His mind whirred up various roads that went nowhere. He thumbed through the *Tome of Relics*, hoping to find some religious icon that matched the horn's description, though without much hope. If the language was really a Skasloi dialect, it probably predated the triumph of the saints over the old gods.

As he was putting the book away, memory intruded, of an evening not long past, when Aspar White had frightened him with the threat of

Haergrim the Raver. He remembered his own fanciful connection to his grandfather's mention of Saint Horn the Damned, and on impulse he tracked down a volume of obscure and false saints peculiar to eastern Crotheny. It didn't take him long to find it. Since walking the fanes, Stephen found that the scriftorium had become almost like an extension of his own mind and fingers; simply thinking of a subject led him quickly to the appropriate shelfs.

The book was a recent one, written by a scholar from the Midenlands, and though its organization was somewhat archaic, he soon found the reference he was seeking. He thumbed to the page and began to read.

The Oostish folk speak in whispers of Haergrim Raver, a bloodthirsty spirit of madness who rides in hunt of the dead. It cannot be doubted that this is none other than a manifestation of Saint Wrath, or as he is called in Hanzish, Ansi Woth, a saint with a strange history. Originally one of the old gods, he was of fickle nature, and at the beginning of the age of Everon did alter his allegiance and become a saint, though a dubious one. He presides over the hanging of criminals, and his blessing is to be avoided, for it unfailingly leads to madness and ruin. The sound of his horn, like that of the Wicker Lord, is said to awaken doom.

Stephen paused at that, but read on. What followed, however, was mostly a recitation of other names for the Raver, one of which was indeed Saint Horn the Damned, for it was said he had drawn the curse of the old gods upon himself by betraying them.

But Stephen kept returning to the reference to the Wicker Lord, and when he was done, searched for an entry concerning him. To his disappointment, the entry was slim.

The Wicker Lord is a false saint, doubtless an invention of the country folk, condensed from their fear of the dark and unfathomable forest that surrounds them. He is found most often in children's songs, where he is an object of terror. His awakening is said to break the sky and is connected with a horn that accompanies him in his thorny barrow. He is perhaps connected with the tales of Baron Greenleaf and may be a

confused version of Saint Selvans, for similar tales are told of them. In
some songs he is known as the Briar King.

Excited, Stephen pored through similar sources, and found some of
the children's songs mentioned, but nothing that cast more light on the
current situation.

The hour was late, and he alone remained in the scriftorium. Sleep
tugged at the corners of his eyes, and he was near concluding that he had
found all he was going to. One scrift remained, and it wasn't promising,
being little more than a book of children's tales, but as he wearily unscrolled it, a small illustration caught his eye. It was of a manlike creature made up of leaves and vines, with limbs spreading from his head
like antlers. In one hand, he gripped a small horn. It captioned a song
he had already seen twice, a circle dance for children.

As he was about to put it away, his fingers brushed the margins, and
he felt something—an imprint in the vellum. Intrigued, he examined it
more closely.

It looked as if someone had written a note on another vellum or
piece of paper, likely with a lead stylus, and the impression had gone
through. Eagerly, he found a piece of charcoal and lightly rubbed the
paper, as he had the stone markers on the Vio Caldatum, and faint characters emerged. When he was done, he sat staring at the results.

The characters were the same as those inscribed on Aspar's horn, to
the letter. Following it was a single word in the king's tongue.

Find.

"I'd stay away from her, if I were you," Brother Ehan remarked the next
day as Stephen sidled nearer Angel.

"I've ridden Angel before," Stephen said. "Haven't I, girl?"

The mare looked dubious.

"Well, she may not be as crazy as the other, but she's learned some
wildness."

"Shh. Angel." He proffered the mare an apple. She sniffed suspiciously and her eyes rolled, but she took a step or two closer.

"That's it, good girl. Come here."

"I don't see what the point is, anyway," Ehan said.

"The point is," Stephen said softly, "I want to ride her."

"Why?"

"Because it would take too long to walk where I want to go."

"What in Saint Rooster's name are you talking about?"

The mare was almost close enough to touch now. Her flanks were trembling as she took another step, ducked her head, pulled it back up, and gently took the apple.

"That's fine, girl," Stephen said. "Remember this?" He drew a bridle from behind his back.

Angel eyed the thing, but seemed almost calmed by its presence. Stephen lay it against the side of her head, letting her get a good whiff of him and it, then gently started putting it on her. She didn't object.

"That's my sweetheart," Stephen cooed.

"Tell me where you're going," Ehan demanded. "We're supposed to be tending the orchard after this."

"I know. If I'm missed, I don't expect you to lie for me. I'm not going to tell you where I'm going for the same reason."

Ehan chewed his lip and spat. "You'll be back by vespers?"

"Or not at all," Stephen assured him. "All right, girl, are you ready?"

Angel answered by not throwing him once he'd gingerly climbed on her back. She stamped a little skittishly, but then took the bridle. Stephen switched her into a brisk trot, which wasn't all that pleasant bareback, for either party.

"Sorry, girl," he said, "I couldn't have brought a saddle out here without being noticed."

It had taken him almost two days to drag Aspar White from where he had found him to the monastery, but in fact the distance was only about a league. Unencumbered and mounted, he covered the distance in under two bells. His memory was as perfect at mental mapmaking as in every other thing since his fanewalk, so he found the spot without much trouble.

He surveyed the scene, frowning, and dismounted. Dead leaves littered the ground, fallen from a tree that might have been lightning struck but there was no mark of lightning on it. Nevertheless it was dead, and so was a trail of ferns and undergrowth that wound into the clearing, stopped short of the remains of his fire, then continued off in a different direction. The point where the trail turned was exactly where he remembered the beaked creature standing.

"No lion did this, Angel," he murmured. Not that he had ever accepted the fratrex's rationalization.

He was still studying the unnatural trail when he heard voices in the distance.

Stephen had had plenty enough experience with strangers in the forest for one lifetime, so he began quietly leading Angel away. Remembering Aspar's story, he went up a ridge where a line of thicker growth hid him from the valley. He tethered the mare on the other side of the ridge, then crept down where he could have a view of the place he'd found Aspar White.

After perhaps half a bell, eight mounted men came into view. Stephen felt a cold shock when he saw who they were.

It was Desmond Spendlove and his men. They had their cowls down, and Stephen recognized several of them: the hulking Brother Lewes, Brothers Aligern, Topan, and Seigereik—the four nastiest of the bunch, according to Ehan. The others he had seen but couldn't name. They were eight in all.

They stopped and examined the campfire and dead vegetation.

"What is it up to?" Lewes grunted.

Spendlove shook his head. "I don't know. It was chasing someone. Maybe that holter Fend told us about."

"Right. Then where is he?"

"Someone dragged his body out," Seigereik said, examining the ground. "That way."

"D'Ef is a league that way," Spendlove mused. "How interesting."

"But the greffyn didn't follow," Seigereik said.

"It probably left after killing its prey."

"Are we to take up its trail again, then?"

Spendlove shook his head. "No. We've work to do in the west."

"Ah. The queen?"

"The changeling in her guard bungled her killing. Now it's our turn.

We're to meet with Fend in Loiyes." He looked again at the greffyn's trail. "But first I think we'd better stop in at d'Ef, to learn more about what happened here."

"With the allies Fend has, he should be able to handle this on his own," Topan said, his ice-blue gaze needling casually through the surrounding forest.

"Fend can fail, just like the changeling. They should have sent us to begin with, but ours isn't to question."

"Still, it could take us a month to get there," Topan argued. "What if we go all that way for nothing?"

"There are other matters to tidy," Spendlove assured him. "Besides, the country air will do you good."

"I've had too much of that lately."

"We do what we do," Spendlove replied. "If you don't want to do it anymore, you know the way out." He started for his horse.

As they rode off, Stephen didn't dare breathe. He lay there, teeth clenched, realizing that he had taken Aspar White to perhaps the most dangerous place imaginable.

CHAPTER ELEVEN

THE WOMB OF MEFITIS

ANNE DREAMED OF THE LIGHT of the sun on the grassy Sleeve, of the furnace of sunset on the rinns, of the simple dance of a candle flame. She wrapped herself in the memory of color and shadow and hoped she wouldn't forget the way the wind in the leaves of the tall elms along the canals shivered the light into pieces of phay gold. Not the way she had forgotten Roderick's face.

They won't let me go mad, she thought. *They won't leave me down here for a nineday.*

But maybe they already had. Maybe she had been here for a month. A year. Maybe her hair had turned gray and Roderick was married. A father dead of old age. Maybe her madness was in clinging to hope, in pretending she hadn't been here for very long at all.

She tried to re-create time by counting heartbeats or tapping her fingers. She tried to measure it by her periods of hunger, and how much food and water remained. She preferred to keep her eyes shut rather than open. With them shut, she could pretend things were as they ought to be, that she was in her bed, trying to sleep.

Of course, she had mostly lost the difference between waking and sleeping.

Her only consolation was that she had begun to hate the darkness. Not to fear it, as she first had, or capitulate to it as Sister Secula surely meant her to.

No, she loathed it. She plotted against it, imagining how she might strike a light in its ugly belly and kill it. She searched through the meager supplies, hoping to find some small piece of steel, something that would make a spark against stone, but there was nothing. Of course there wasn't. How many girls had they put down here, over the centuries? How many must have thought of the same thing?

"But I'm not another girl," Anne muttered, listening as the sound of her voice filled the place. "I'm a daughter of the house Dare."

And so, with great determination, she stared at nothingness and imagined a single point of light, banishing every other thought. If she couldn't break the darkness in reality, she could at least do so in her heart. She tried, and maybe she slept, and she tried again. She took the idea of light, her memories of it, and squeezed them together between her eyes, willing it to be real with every fiber of her being.

And suddenly it was there—a spark, the tiniest of points, no larger than a pinprick.

"Saints!" she gasped, and it vanished.

She wept for a little while, dried her eyes, and with greater determination than before, began again.

The next time the spark appeared, she held it, nurtured it, fed it all of the membrance of light she could find, and slowly, hesitantly, beautifully it grew. It grew to the size of an acorn, then as large as a hand, and it had color in it, and spread like a morning glory opening its petals. She could see things now, but not what she had expected. No walls and floor of stone, but instead the rough bark of an oak, twining vines, a spray of yellow flowers—as if the light was really a hole through the wall of a dark room, opening into a garden.

But it wasn't a hole; it was a sphere, and it pushed away the darkness until there was none left and she stood not in a cave, but in a brightly lit forest glade.

She looked down and could not see her shadow, and with a skip of her heart knew where she was. She also knew her madness must be complete.

"You've come without your shadow," a voice said.

It was a woman, but not the same one she had seen before, that day on Tom Woth. This one had unbound hair of fine chestnut and a mask carved of bone polished very smooth. Its features were fine and lifelike, and her mouth was not covered by it. She wore a dress of golden brown silk embroidered with interlaced braids and knots of ram-headed serpents and oak leaves.

"I didn't mean to come here at all," Anne told her.

"But you did. In Eslen you made a pact with Cer. It took you to the Coven Saint Cer and now it brings you here." She paused. "I wonder what that means?"

For some reason, that simple question frightened Anne more than the darkness had.

"Don't you know? Aren't you a saint? Who are you, and where is the other woman, the one with the golden hair?"

The woman smiled wistfully. "My sister? Near, I'm sure. As for me, I don't know who I am, anymore," she said. "I'm waiting to know. Like you."

"I know who I am. I'm Anne Dare."

"You know a name, that's all. Everything else is a guess or an illusion."

"I don't understand you."

The woman shrugged. "It's not important. What do you want?"

"What do I want?"

"You came here for something."

Anne hesitated. "I want out of the cave, out of the womb of Saint Mefitis."

"Easily done. Leave it."

"There's a way out?"

"Yes. You found one way already, but there is another. Is that all?"

Anne considered that carefully for a moment. She was probably mad, but if she wasn't . . .

If she wasn't, she would do better this time than she had the last.

"No," she said firmly. "When your sister abducted me she said some things. I thought they were nonsense, or that I was having a dream. Praifec Hespero thought so, too, when I told him."

"And now?"

"I think she was real, and I want to understand what she said."

The woman's lips curved in a smile. "She told you that there must be a queen in Eslen when he comes."

"Yes. But why, and who is 'he'? And why tell me?"

"I'm sure you asked those questions of my sister."

"Yes, and she answered with nonsense. I was scared then, too scared to demand better answers. Now I want them."

"You can't always have the things you want."

"But you—she—wants me to do something. Everyone wants me to do something. Act one way instead of another, go to a coven, promise this or that. Well, here I am! If you want something from me, explain it or stay out of my dreams!"

"You came here this time, Anne, of your own free will." The masked woman sighed. "Ask your questions. I'll try to be more helpful than my sister. But you must understand, Anne, that we are far less masters of ourselves than you are, however you might feel. A dog cannot speak like a man and a cloud may not sound like a lute. The dog can bark, the cloud can thunder. It is how they are made."

Anne pursed her lips. "Your sister said that Crotheny must not fall, and that there must be a queen in Eslen when your mysterious 'he' comes. At the very moment she told me that, my mother the queen was nearly killed. Did she know about that?"

"She knew."

"Why didn't she tell me?"

"What good would it have done? The attempt on your mother was over before you returned to Eslen. My sister told you what you needed to know."

"She didn't tell me anything. Who is this man who is coming? Why must there be a queen? And mostly—*mostly*—what must I do?"

"You'll know when the time comes, if you only remember what she said. There must be a queen. Not the wife of a king, you understand, but a queen paramount."

Anne's jaw dropped. "No. No, I didn't understand that at all. But still—"

"You must see that there is a queen, Anne."

"You mean become one?"

The woman shrugged. "That would be one way."

"Yes, an impossible one. My father and mother and brother and all of my sisters would have to be dead . . . before . . ."

For a moment she couldn't go on.

"Is that it?" she asked, feeling cold. "Is that what's going to happen?"

"I don't know."

"Don't tell me that! Tell me something *real*."

The woman cocked her head to the side. "We only see need, Anne. Like a good cook, I know when the roast needs more salt or a bay leaf, whether it needs to stay on the spit for another bell or not."

"Crotheny is not a roast."

"No. Nor is the world. Perhaps I am more like a chirgeon, then. I see a man so wounded and infected that parts of him have begun to rot, and the worms, growing bolder, begin to devour what is left. I feel his pain and disease, and know what salves he needs, where fire needs to be put to the wound, and when."

"Crotheny isn't rotting."

The woman shook her head. "It is very nearly dead."

Anne slashed the back of her hand in the woman's direction. "You're a cloud, you're a chirgeon. Crotheny is a roast, it's a wounded man. Speak plain words! You suggest that my country and family are in gravest danger, and that I must be queen or queen-maker, yet here I am in Vitellio, a thousand leagues away! Should I stay or leave? Tell me what to do, and no more nonsense about roasts and invalids."

"You're where you are supposed to be, Anne, and I've already told you what to do. The rest you must discern for yourself."

Anne rolled her eyes. "No better. No better. Then answer this straight, if you can. Why me? If you can't really see the future, why am I needed, and not Fastia, or Mother, for love of the saints?"

The woman turned her back on Anne and walked a few paces. Her back still turned, she sighed. "Because I feel the need for you," she said. "Because the oaks whisper it, even as the greffyn kills them. And because, of all living women, you are the only one who can come to me like this, unbidden."

"What?"

"My sister summoned you when you walked widdershins under the sun. I did not summon you—you summoned *me*."

"I . . . how?"

"I told you. You made a pact with Saint Cer. When you send prayers by the dead, there is always a cost, there is always consequence."

"But I didn't know."

The woman uttered a chilling little laugh. "If a blind man walks over the edge of a cliff, does the air ask if he knew what he was doing before it refuses to hold him up? Do the rocks below ask what he did or didn't know about them before they break his bones?"

"Then Cer has cursed me?"

"She has blessed you. You have walked her strangest faneway. You are touched by her as no other mortal."

"I never walked any faneway," Anne said. "Faneways are for priests, not for women."

A smile drew across the woman's thin and bloodless lips. "The tomb below Eslen-of-Shadows is a sedos," she said. "The womb of Saint Mefitis is another, its twin. They are two halves of the same thing. A very short faneway, I suppose, but very difficult to find. You are the only one to walk it in more than a thousand years. You will be the last to walk it for another thousand, perhaps."

"What does it mean?"

The woman laughed again. "If I knew, I would tell you. But I do know this: It needed to happen. Your prayer to Saint Cer brought you here and set in motion every consequence of that trip. Including this one. As I said, you are where you were meant to be."

"So I'm to stay in the coven, even if they throw me in the earth to rot? No, I see. They were *supposed* to throw me down here, because Saint Cer willed it." She snorted. "What if I choose not to believe you? What if I think you're some shinecrafting witch, trying to trick me? You come into my dreams and tell me lies and expect I will eat them like gingercake."

A sudden thought occurred that struck her straight to the middle. "What if you're a Hanzish shinecrafter? That you and your sister bewitched the knight into trying to murder my mother? Of course, you must be! How stupid of me!"

The implications made her knees buckle. Everyone in Eslen was looking for someone with the power to bewitch a Craftsman and at the very moment it happened Anne had been holding conversation with just such a person.

And she hadn't told anyone but the praifec, who hadn't believed her, and now here she was, caught in the grip of sadistic nuns a thousand leagues from anyone she trusted.

Even Austra had made her promise not to run away. Maybe Austra was bewitched, too.

"You're a liar," Anne said. "A liar and a witch."

The woman shook her head, but Anne couldn't tell if it was a denial. She started to walk off, into the woods.

"No! Come back here and answer me!"

The woman waved her hand, and all was darkness.

"No!" Anne wailed again. But she was back on the cold stone floor of the cave. She pounded the floor with her fists, tears of anger wincing from her eyes.

After calling herself stupid a few hundred times, Anne came to one very certain conclusion: She could not and would not trust Sister Secula to let her out of the caves. The masked woman had told her there was another way out. It was probably a lie, but she remembered now the stories in which caves figured, and indeed there usually was more than one exit.

And so, very carefully, moving very slowly and on all fours like a beast, she crossed the boundary the nuns had warned her not to cross, and passed onto the unknown, uneven floor of the cave.

It was easier than she expected it to be. Each dip and curve in the floor seemed to be somehow where it ought to be, and exploring quickly became more like remembering. It was both frightening and exciting. What if she really had somehow walked a faneway, like a priest? Like Genya Dare and her heroes? What if this strange new sense wasn't her imagination, but exactly what it seemed to be?

Imagination or not, she grew more and more confident of her way, and stood up. The echo of her footsteps told her when she was in a large gallery or small. A colder feel to the air warned her of a deep cleft in the rock, and the taste of the cave's breath suggested water. The taste grew stronger as she went along, until finally she could hear a merry trickling. And, after crawling up and down through passages—some almost too small to move through at all—she saw light.

Dim light.

Real light.

Soon the light was bright enough to be painful, and she had to stop to let her eyes regather their strength after so many days of darkness. But finally, when the sun's rays were no longer daggers, she advanced farther to the mouth of the cave, and for a while she did nothing more than luxuriate in the feel of the light and wind upon her skin. Then she began taking in her surroundings.

The cave opened from a hillside thick in olive, bay, and juniper. Anne reasoned it was the same long ridge that the coven stood upon, but a few careful glances showed the towers nowhere in sight, which meant she must be on the other end of it. She carefully picked her way toward the top until she finally could see the coven, and see as well that it was quite a distance away. Satisfied that she knew where she was, Anne made her way back down and began to explore, being careful to fix the landmarks near the cave firmly in her mind.

The flatter land below the cave was lightly forested, the lines of trees broken often by grassy clearings. It must once have been pasture— probably for the stupid sheep—but she saw no recent signs of grazing.

A little farther on she again heard the trickle of water, and to her delight found a spring-fed pool. A flight of birds darted up from the trees surrounding it, such a bright yellow in color that she exclaimed aloud.

Finishing her survey around the pool, she tested the water and found it cool. She looked around again, until she convinced herself she was quite alone, then stripped out of the smelly habit and eased into the water. It felt wonderful, and after a little swimming she was content to rest in the shallows, submerged to her chin, and close her eyes. The insides of her eyelids shone red, and she tried to forget about her experiences in the womb of Saint Mefitis—and to forget, too, that she had to go back there. Whether the woman of her vision was a liar or not, there was still her promise to Austra, and she would not break that.

She might have dozed, for she came awake certain she had heard something but wasn't at all sure what it was. Suddenly frightened, she looked quickly around the pool, realizing this wasn't Eslen, that there could be any number of wild beasts around that she knew nothing of.

But it wasn't a beast staring at her with wide, dark eyes. It was a man, a tall, young one, in black doublet with brown hose and large-brimmed hat. He had one hand draped on the pommel of a very long sword. He smiled a smile that Anne did not like at all.

CHAPTER TWELVE

A QUICK DECISION

W HEN BROTHER SPENDLOVE AND HIS MEN were out of sight, Stephen urged Angel into a walk that angled them away from the direct path that led back to d'Ef. Spendlove had walked the faneway of Mamres, but he had also walked the same faneway that Stephen had. Each person who walked a faneway received different gifts, but it was reasonable to suppose that Spendlove's senses had been heightened, as well—and prudent to suppose he could hear at least as well as Stephen.

Once Stephen couldn't make out their voices anymore, he turned Angel to a parallel path back to the monastery and urged her to a gallop.

Riding a running horse with a saddle on a trail was one thing; doing so bareback in the forest was another. Stephen gripped his knees against Angel's flanks, dug his fists into her mane, and kept his body low. Angel splashed through a stream, stumbled climbing the opposite bank, then recovered. Stephen prayed the mare wouldn't step into some leaf-hidden hole or den, but he couldn't afford to spare the poor beast; he knew to his marrow that if he didn't reach d'Ef before Desmond Spendlove, Aspar White was a dead man.

He swallowed his fear at the breakneck pace and did his best to hold on.

He and the mare broke from the woods into the lower pasture, where a handful of cows scattered from their path and the two brothers tending them gawked curiously. Once in the clearing, Angel's pace went from breathtaking to absolutely terrifying. The two of them pounded up the hill to where he had last seen Ogre.

The big stallion was still there, watching their approach with suspicious eyes. Stephen slowed as he neared, cleared his throat and shouted, "Follow, Ogre!" in the best approximation of Aspar White's voice he could manage. He was startled by how good the impersonation was. To his ears and memory, it sounded exactly right.

Ogre hesitated, stamping. Stephen repeated the command, and the beast tossed his head before—with a steely glint in his eye—he began trotting after Angel.

Together, they raced through the orchard, whipping past Brother Ehan. The short fellow shouted something Stephen couldn't hear. Stephen ignored him; he didn't have time to go back, and there was no need to involve the closest thing he had to a friend in this mess. He had to reach Aspar. With the possible exception of Brother Ehan, there was no one else at d'Ef he could count on. The holter would never survive alone in his condition, and anyway, Stephen himself would be in danger for helping White.

They would have to flee together, and though he felt shame and failure and all of those things his father would see in this flight, he also had to admit that he was damned well ready to leave the monastery d'Ef. There was too much wrong here, too much darkness, and he wasn't equipped to deal with it. Furthermore, if the queen of Crotheny was in danger, it was his duty to warn her.

He halted Angel at the very foyer of the nave and leapt down, then rushed into the cool dark, hoping he wasn't already too late. Aspar lay where he had been, eyes closed and pale, but before Stephen was within five strides the holter's eyes flicked open and he sat up.

"What?" Aspar grunted.

"You're in danger," Stephen said. "*We're* in danger. We have to go, and right away. Can you do it?"

Aspar's mouth pinched, probably around a caustic remark, but then he snapped his head in assent. "Yah. I'll need a horse."

Stephen drew a deep breath of relief, surprised and gratified that the holter took his word so readily. "Ogre is just outside," he said.

"You have weapons?"

"No. And there isn't time to find any."

"Will we be pursued?"

"I'm sure we will."

"I'll need weapons. A bow. Do you know where you can get one?"

"Maybe. But, Holter—"

"Go."

Exasperated, Stephen sprinted back outside, remembering that a bow used for shooting at deer in the orchard was kept in the garden shed. He had never seen any other weapon at d'Ef, unless the butcher's cleavers counted. There must be an armory somewhere, but he'd never thought to discover it.

He nearly bowled over Brother Recard on the way out.

"Brother!" the Hanzish monk asked. "What's the matter?"

"Bandits," Stephen improvised. "Maybe fifty of them, coming through the orchards! We'll need to defend against them. Ring the alarm."

The monk's eyes went wide. "But why did you come in here?"

"Because I know the bandits," Aspar grunted. "They may have followed me here. Outlawed cutthroats from beyond the Naksoks. Bloody-handed barbarians. They'll not respect your clericy. If you don't fight them, they take you alive and eat one eye while you watch with the other."

"I'll ring the bell!" Recard said, already racing to do so.

"I'll get your bow, now," Stephen said.

"Yah. The horses are outside? I'll meet you there."

Stephen reached the shed and took the bow down from its peg, checking quickly to make sure the sinew was there and grabbing the quiver of eight arrows hung next to it. On the way back out of the shed, he noticed a swingle-blade leaning against the wall, the kind used for clearing underbrush. He grabbed that, too, and hurried back to the nave. He found the holter outside, his face white and sweating as he tried to mount Ogre. Monks darted past him, going to the places assigned them in the event of an attack on the monastery, there to await orders from the fratrex.

The fratrex, who stood in the doorway of the nave, watched the holter mount with a frown.

Stephen approached warily. The fratrex shifted his gaze.

"Brother Stephen," he asked mildly. "Are you behind this commotion? Why are you armed?"

Stephen didn't answer but handed the holter the bow and climbed upon Angel, keeping the swingle-blade in his hand.

"Answer me," the fratrex said.

"Brother Spendlove is coming to kill this man," Stephen said. "I will not allow it."

"Brother Spendlove will do no such thing. Why should he?"

"Because he's the one murdering people in the forest, doing the blood rites on the sedoi. The same blood rites you've had me research."

"Spendlove?" the fratrex asked. "How do you know that?"

"I heard him say it," Stephen said. "And now he's going to murder the queen."

"One of our own order?" the fratrex asked. "That's not possible, unless—" His eyes went wide, and wider still. He gurgled, spit blood from his mouth, and collapsed. From the shadows of the nave behind him, Desmond Spendlove stepped into the light, his men just behind him.

"Congratulations, Brother Stephen," Spendlove said. "To spare this holter, you've killed the fratrex."

Once again, Stephen's orderly world of assumptions collapsed around his ears.

"But I thought . . ."

"I know. Very amusing, to think this doddering old fool was at the bottom of anything. Did you ever think him wise?" He looked up at Aspar. "And you. I have friends looking for you. I suspect they will be happy enough with some token of your death. Your head, perhaps. And stop trying to string that bow, or I'll have you cut down right now." He looked back at Stephen. "Brother, despite your trespasses, you can be forgiven. Well, perhaps not forgiven, but certainly spared. You can still be useful."

"I won't help you anymore," Stephen said. He swallowed a hard lump of fear, but to his surprise he felt in his chest something stronger forming. "I won't betray my vows or my church or the people of my country. You'll have to kill me, too." He raised his makeshift weapon. "I wonder if you have the courage to kill me yourself."

Spendlove shrugged. "Courage? Courage is nothing. You'll see what happens to your courage when we cut you open. Not to kill you, mind you. Just to convince you of your worth. I'm afraid I can't merely release you to Saint Dun."

Stephen tried to say something in return, but he faltered. Hands shaking, he raised the weapon.

"Ride away, Aspar White," he said. "I'll do my best to keep them back."

"I wouldn't get far," Aspar replied. "I might as well die here as anyplace."

"Then do me a favor," Stephen said. "Stick that arrow of yours in my heart if they take a step toward me."

"This is very touching," Spendlove said. He suddenly bared his teeth, and Stephen felt something like a hot wind pass him. Aspar White gasped in agony and the arrow he was holding dropped to the ground.

"There," Spendlove said. "And now . . ."

He looked down at a sudden movement near his feet. It was the fratrex, pushing himself up on his palms, reaching toward the wall of the monastery.

"Spendlove, betrayer, heretic," the old man murmured, just barely loud enough to hear.

Suddenly cracks spidered up the stone walls of the nave, multiplying, and in an instant, with a gritting roar, the entire face of the building collapsed. Spendlove and his men vanished behind the rubble and dust.

"Ride, damn you," Aspar shouted, even before the stones settled.

"But I—" Stephen started helplessly toward the collapsing building.

"Ride and we may live to fight later. Stay and today we'll die."

Stephen hesitated an instant longer, then spun on his toe and leapt up on Angel's back. Together, the two men rode as if all the dark saints were at their backs.

As perhaps they were.

CHAPTER THIRTEEN

A MEETING

CAZIO RESTED HIS HAND on the pommel of Caspator and leaned against a pomegranate tree. The girl in the pool saw him, and with an audible gasp sank suddenly to her chin, which was disappointing. Though he'd only been teased by the view of her slim white body in the water, her neck had been shapely enough, and now even that was hidden.

He smiled and picked at her pile of clothes with the tip of his sword.

"Thank you," he said, in a carrying voice, directing his face at the sky. "Thank you, Lady Erenda, patroness of lovers, for granting my wish."

"I am not your wish," the girl snapped angrily. "You must leave immediately, whoever you are." She spoke with a lilt as foreign and exotic as the color of her hair. This girl was growing more interesting all of the time. Of course, she was also the first girl he had seen in weeks, since he and z'Acatto had accepted the hospitality of the countess Orchaevia. The countess preferred male servants, and the nearest village was a full day's walk. But here, only a league's ramble from the mansion, he'd happened on a bit of luck.

"And I am not your slave, lady," Cazio replied. "I do not answer to your orders." He waggled a finger at her. "Anyway, who are you to know what I do or do not wish? As I was walking along, just now, I said to our lady Erenda, 'Lady, this world is full of ugliness and pain. It is a dismal domain of woe, and my trials have taught me to despise it. As a result, I, Cazio Pachiomadio da Chiovattio, who once loved life, now weary of it.

Lady Erenda—' I prayed this. '—if you could show me but one instant of the most perfect beauty imaginable, just a single glimpse, I could find the strength to forge on, to bear the burdens a man such as myself is fated to bear.' Only a moment later I heard the sound of this water, saw this pool, and in it the answer to my prayer."

That wasn't entirely a lie. He had been hoping steadily for female company, but hadn't actually addressed the lady of love, at least not formally.

The girl frowned a little deeper. "Are Vitellian girls more stupid than the usual sort? Or do you think me dense because I am from another land?"

"Stupid? Not at all. I can see the intelligence in your eyes. You have, perhaps, been careless, to bathe in a pool frequented by highwaymen and other scoundrels of low repute, but I'm certain it's only because you don't know the area."

"I'm learning it quickly enough," the girl replied. "I've been here only a few moments and already I've met someone of ill repute."

"Now you try to wound me," Cazio said mournfully.

"Leave, so I may dress."

"I cannot," Cazio said regretfully. "My heart will not let me. Not until I know your name."

"My name? My name is . . . Fiene."

"An intriguing name."

"Yes, and now you have it, so begone."

"A musical name. Already my heart is singing it. From what distant land comes that name, Lady?"

"Liery, you graceless oaf. Will you go now?"

Cazio blinked at her. "You're smiling at me, Fiena."

"Fiene. And I'm not. Or if I am, it's because you're so absurd. And it's pronounced Fee-en-uh."

"Don't you want to know my name?"

"You already said. Cashew, something like that."

"*Ca*-tsee-oh," he corrected.

"Cazio. Cazio, you must leave now."

Cazio nodded and sat down on the gnarled root of a willow. "Certainly I must," he agreed. It suddenly struck him that the pile of clothes was a habit. "Are you a nun?" he asked.

"No," the girl said. "I found one and killed her and took her clothes. What do you think, you lout, with the Abode of Graces right up the hill?"

Cazio looked up and around. "There's a coven nearby?"

"On the other side of the hill."

"A whole house full of women as lovely as you? Lady Erenda must indeed be pleased with me."

"Yes, you'd better hurry and court them," Fiene said. "They're all quite naked as I am."

"It would be a waste of time," Cazio said, trying to sound mournful. "I've already seen the loveliest of them. I'd have to go up around that hill just to come back here. Which raises a question—why *are* you here? Something tells me you aren't supposed to be."

"Are you a highwayman?" the girl demanded suddenly. "Are you a rogue?"

"I am at your command," Cazio answered. "If you want a rogue, I can certainly be that."

"I want a gentleman who will allow me to get dressed."

"This gentleman will allow that," Cazio replied, patting the clothes.

"Not while you're watching."

"But the sight of you was granted me by a goddess. Who am I to deny her will?"

"You didn't see me," Fiene corrected, though her tone betrayed some doubt. "I was submerged."

Cazio peered over his nose. "I admit, I've not viewed the undistorted image. The rippling of the water might mask defects in figure. I'm starting to wonder if you could actually be as beautiful as I imagine."

"Figs!" Fiene replied. "I don't have to take such a slight. Here, you judge whether there are any defects."

So saying she began to rise from the water—but when the water rested across her breastbone, she snorted derisively and sank back down. "I repeat," Fiene said, "why do you think I'm stupid?"

Cazio drooped his head. "I'm the stupid one. I already know that your beauty is perfect."

Fiene rolled her eyes, then settled them boldly on him. "I am betrothed, sir," she said. "I don't care whether you find me perfect or perfectly ugly."

"Ah. Then you are *not* a nun."

"I have been sent here for my education, that is all."

"Praised be every lord and lady in the night sky and under earth," Cazio said. "For now I have at least a slim hope."

"Hope? For you and me?" She laughed. "There's no hope of that, unless you intend to kill me and abominate my body. After that you can look forward to your own death at the hands of my betrothed, Roderick."

"Roderick? That is an unwholesome name. It sounds of pimples and deception."

"He is noble and good, and he would never take advantage of a lady's distress, as you do."

Despite himself, Cazio suddenly felt his ears burning. "Then he is hardly a man," he replied, "for no true man could ever unfasten his eyes from your face."

"Oh, it's my *face* you're interested in. Then you won't mind my dressing. My wimple will not hide my features."

"Not if you'll promise to stay here and speak with me a bit," Cazio relented. "I sense that you're in no great hurry."

The girl arched her brows. "You'll turn your back, at least?"

"Lady, I will." And he did so, despite the tantalizing sound as she emerged from the pool, and the rustle of her clothes as she retrieved them. For a moment she was so near he could have turned and touched her. But she was skittish, this one. She would take work.

He heard her carry her clothes back toward the pool.

"What day is it?" she asked.

"May I turn yet?"

"You may not."

"The day is Menzodi," he replied.

"Three more days," she murmured. "Good. Thank you."

"Three more days of what?" he asked.

"Do you have anything to eat?" Fiene asked, instead of answering him.

"Nothing, I'm afraid."

"Very well. No, keep your back turned. I'm not quite finished."

Cazio puffed his cheeks and tapped his foot.

"You never told me what you were doing out here," he said. "You're up to mischief, aren't you?"

She didn't answer. "May I turn yet?" he asked. "I've kept my bargain."

When she didn't answer again, he did turn—in time to see her vanish up the hillside.

"Faithless beauty!" he shouted after her.

She popped back into view briefly, waved, and blew him a kiss. Then she was gone. He thought about chasing her, but decided against it. If she wanted to play that sort of game, to Lord Ontro with her.

With a sigh, he turned and began walking back toward the mansion of the countess Orchaevia. But he took care to remember the landmarks of the place.

The sun was a perfectly golden coin and it was an hour before sunset when Cazio came back in sight of the manse. It lay below him, in the midst of a hundred versos of vineyards, a single narrow road wandering to and away from it. The house itself was splendidly huge, white-walled and red-roofed, with a spacious inner courtyard and a rustic-walled horz on its west wing. Behind that were stables, barnyard, and the must-house where wine was fermented and bottled.

Cazio descended between rows of grapevines, idly picking the amethyst fruits now and then, enjoying the sweet, winelike smell of those that had fallen to rot upon the ground.

He couldn't stop wondering about the girl. She said she'd come from Liery. What country was Liery? One of the northern ones, surely, where such pale skin and strangely colored hair were commonplace.

He found himself at the mansion gate almost before realizing it. A sharp-featured serving boy in yellow stockings and plum doublet recognized him and let him into the red-flagstoned courtyard.

A throaty female voice greeted him as he entered. "Cazio, my *dello*!" she said. "Where have you been? You've almost missed dinner."

Cazio bowed. "Good evening, *casnara* Countess Orchaevia. I was merely taking my leisure in the beautiful countryside around your estate."

The countess Orchaevia sat at a long table beneath the eaves of the courtyard wall. She was a woman in her middle years, enlarged and rounded by the copious foods that always graced her table. Her face was as round and shiny as a porcelain platter, with a little snubbed nose, emerald eyes, and pink cheeks. Cazio had rarely seen her without a smile on her face.

"Rambling again? I wish I could think of more to entertain you with here, so you needn't walk all over creation."

"I enjoy it," Cazio told her. "It keeps me fit."

"Well, a young man should be fit," she allowed. "Please, join me in repast." She nodded at the viands before her.

"I think I will," he said. "I've worked up a bit of an appetite." He pulled out a leather-bottomed chair, sat, and surveyed what was to be had. He settled on a fig, cut and opened to resemble a flower and garnished with the dry, salty ham of the region. A servant approached and poured him a goblet of dark red wine.

"Was z'Acatto with you?" the countess asked. "I haven't seen him today either."

"Have you checked your wine cellars?" Cazio asked. "He has a tendency to settle there."

"Well, let him stay there then," she pouted, spooning a cube of fresh cheese, drenched in olive oil and garlic, onto a slice of toasted bread. "He can't get to the choicest vintages, anyway. He thinks I don't know he's searching for them." She looked up at Cazio. "Which direction did you go today?"

Cazio gestured west with the half of the fig that remained.

"Oh! You paid a visit to the Abode of Graces."

"I don't know what you're talking about," Cazio replied innocently, taking a sip of the wine. "I saw only trees and sheep."

She looked at him suspiciously. "You're telling me a handsome young dello like you hasn't yet sniffed out a coven full of young ladies? I never thought it would take you this long."

Cazio shrugged and reached for a ripe black olive. "Perhaps I'll go there tomorrow."

The countess wagged a grilled partridge leg at him. "Don't go to cause trouble. Those are my neighbors, you know. Each year I throw a small fete for them. It's the only such luxury they are allowed."

"Do you indeed?" Cazio said, placing the olive pit in a small dish and turning his attention to a plate of sliced pears and hard ewe's cheese.

"Oh, Orchaevia has your attention now, doesn't she?"

"Nonsense," Cazio said, stretching his legs out and lazily crossing them at the ankle.

"Well, if you're not interested . . ." She shrugged and took a long draught of her wine.

"Oh, very well, let us assume I have some slight interest. When might this fete take place?"

The countess smiled. "On the eve of Fiussanal, the first day of Seftamenza."

"In three weeks' time."

"Of course, you aren't invited," she said slyly. "But I might be able to arrange something, if a matter of the heart is involved."

"No such matter exists. Besides, I may not be here in three weeks."

Orchaevia shook her head. "Oh, things haven't cooled in Avella yet. That will take more time."

"I had considered a trip to Furonesso," Cazio said.

The countess sputtered into her wine. "In this heat? Whatever for?"

"My sword is growing rusty."

"You practice every day with my guards!"

Cazio shrugged.

The countess narrowed her eyes, then suddenly laughed merrily. "You'll stay," she opined as she spread rabbit liver pâté on another toast. "You're only trying to convince yourself that someone hasn't got you by the nose."

Cazio stopped with a buttered quail egg halfway to his mouth. "Casnara, what under heaven are you talking about?"

She smiled. "I can see it in that distracted look on your face, the expression when I mentioned my fete. Never try to fool Orchaevia when it comes to matters of love. You *are* in love."

"And that is very ridiculous," Cazio said emphatically. He was becoming annoyed. "Even if I did meet someone today, you think my heart could be so quickly swayed? That's the stuff of your romances, Countess, not real life."

"That's what every young man thinks until it happens to him," the countess replied, with a wink. "Tomorrow you'll wander in the same direction you did today. Trust me."

Anne woke in darkness. From a vantage on the hill, she'd watched the strange man leave, but she didn't trust him not to return, so she'd slept in the cave. Of course, he seemed relatively harmless; he'd never threatened her, only swaggered and strutted like a rooster. But there was no sense in being stupid.

She rose, stretched, got her bearings, and began cautiously back toward the outside. Her stomach rumbled; all of the food that had been sent down with her was back in the fane of Mefitis, and Anne didn't want to go back there until she had to. She'd considered going all the way back there to sleep, on the off chance that the sisters might check on her, but if they hadn't in the six days that had already passed, she couldn't imagine they would today.

Still, she would have to do something about her hunger soon. Perhaps she could find apples or pomegranates.

She waited at the cave entrance for a while, watching and listening, then began climbing back down. She found the pool again, circled it several times, and found no one there. Then she went to look for food.

Around noon she was ready to give up and go back to the fane. She'd found some fruits, but either didn't know what they were or didn't find them ripe. She'd seen a rabbit and many squirrels, but knew nothing of hunting or how to build a fire if she did manage to get one. Austra had been right, of course; her fantasy of living free and off the land was just that, a fantasy. It was a good thing she hadn't managed to run away.

Disconsolate, she started back toward the cave.

Passing by the pool again, she caught a motion from the corner of her eye and ducked behind a bush. She winced at the stir of noises she made, then cautiously peered around the leaves.

Cazio was back. Today he wore a white shirt and dark red breeches. His sword was propped against a nearby olive tree and he sat on a blanket. He was busy removing items from a basket—pears, cheese, bread, a bottle of wine.

"I've brought food this time," he said, without turning.

Anne hesitated. He was far enough away that if she ran, he probably couldn't catch her. Still, what did she know of this fellow other than he was an arrogant ass?

That he'd kept his back turned when she was naked, as she'd asked him. After a moment's consideration, she emerged and walked toward him.

"You're persistent," she noticed.

"And you're hungry," the fellow replied. He stood and bowed. "There were no proper introductions, yesterday. I am Cazio Pachiamadio da Chiovattio. I will be in your debt if you will join me for a time."

Anne quirked her mouth. "As you say, I am hungry."

"Then, if you please, casnara Fiene, sit with me."

"And you'll be a gentleman?"

"In every way."

She settled warily on the other side of the blanket, with the food between them. She eyed the victuals hungrily.

"Please, eat," Cazio said.

She reached for a pear and bit into it. It was sweet and ripe, and the juice drizzled down her chin.

"Try the cheese with it," Cazio suggested, pouring her a goblet of red wine. "It's *caso dac'uva*, one of the best in the region."

Anne took of a wedge of the cheese. It was sharp, hard, and piquant, and went very well with the pear. She washed it all down with the wine. Cazio began eating, too, at a much more leisurely pace.

"Thank you," Anne said, when she had eaten some of the bread and had a little more wine, which was already warming her thoughts.

"Seeing you is thanks enough," Cazio replied.

"You aren't a rogue at all," Anne accused.

Cazio shrugged. "Some would argue with that, but I've never made the claim, only the offer."

"What are you, then? Not a shepherd, with that sword. A wanderer?"

"Of sorts," Cazio replied.

"So you aren't from these parts?"

"I'm from Avella."

Anne let that pass. She didn't know where Avella was, and didn't care. "You've taken a holiday?" she asked.

Cazio grinned. "Of sorts," he repeated. "Though it was never festive until now."

"I'm still betrothed, you know," Anne reminded him.

"Yes, so I've been told. A temporary situation, for once you've gotten to know me—"

"I will undoubtedly still think you an ass, if you keep talking that way," Anne replied.

Cazio clutched at his chest. "Now *that* was an arrow," he said, "striking right to my heart."

Anne laughed. "You have no heart, Cazio, or at least not a loud one. I think other parts of you are more outspoken."

"You think you know me well, so soon?" Cazio said. "This fiancé of yours—he is better spoken?"

"Infinitely so. He writes wonderful letters, he speaks poetry." She paused. "Or he did when he could still speak to me and write to me."

"Does he tell you how your hair is like the rarest red saffron of Shaum? Does he reflect on the myriad colors of your eyes? Does he know your breath as well as he knows his own?" Cazio's eyes were suddenly, uncomfortably focused on hers.

"You shouldn't say things like that," Anne mumbled, feeling a sudden empty pain. *I can't even remember his face.* Nonetheless she loved Roderick. She knew that.

"How long since you've seen him?" Cazio asked.

"Almost two months."

"Are you sure you're still betrothed?"

"What do you mean?"

"I mean a man who would let his love be carried off to a coven a thousand leagues away might be less sturdy in his affections than some."

"That . . . You take that back!" Anne rose to her feet in fury, almost forgetting that her "betrothal" was a lie. Roderick had mentioned nothing of marriage. She'd brought that up only to deflect Cazio's attentions.

"I did not mean to offend," Cazio said quickly. "If I've gone too far, I apologize. As you say, I can be an ass. Please, have some more wine."

The wine was already having considerable effect on Anne, but she nevertheless knelt back down and accepted the newly filled glass. Still, she regarded him with something resembling a cold stare.

"I have an idea," Cazio said, after a moment.

"What a lonely creature it must be."

"I *have* apologized," he reminded her.

"Very well. What is your idea?"

"I presume your lover has not written you because you are not allowed correspondence in the coven?"

"He doesn't know where I am. But even if he did, a letter of mine would never reach him, I fear."

"You know his hand?"

"Like my own."

"Very well," Cazio said, leaning back on one elbow and holding his wineglass up. "You write and seal a letter, and I shall see it delivered to this Roderick person. I shall receive any reply and bring it to you, at a place of your liking."

"You would do that? Why?"

"If he is, as you say, fond of you, he will write you back. If he is in love with you, he will ride here to see you. If he has forgotten you, he will do neither. In that case, I hope to gain."

Anne paused, stunned at the offer, though she quickly saw the flaw in it. "But if I trust *you* with his correspondence," she pointed out, "you might easily libel him as faithless by never sending the letter."

"And I give you my word I will deliver any letter he sends to you. I swear it on my father's name and on the blade of my good sword, Caspator."

"I could still never accept the absence of correspondence as proof."

"Nonetheless, my offer still stands," Cazio replied easily.

"Again, why?"

"If nothing more is to exist between us," Cazio said, "I want you to at least know I'm honest. Besides, it costs me little to do this. A trip to a nearby village, a handful of coins to a *cuveitur*. I need only know where your Roderick might be found."

"It might be difficult for us to meet after today," Anne said. "And I have nothing to write with."

"Surely we can think of something."

Anne considered that for a moment, and it struck her that she could send not only Roderick a message, but also one to her father, warning him of her visions and the threat they foretold to Crotheny. "You have seen the coven?" she asked.

"Not yet. It is around the hill, yes?"

"Yes. My room is in the highest room of the highest tower. I will write the letter, weight it with a stone, and drop it down. Perhaps we can contrive something with string for you to send his return letters up. Or perhaps I can meet you here again. If so, I will drop further notes to you." She looked up at him. "Does this require too much of you?"

"Not in the least," Cazio replied.

"You aren't going to wander on?"

"I am comfortable in this region for the moment," he said.

"Then I thank you again," Anne replied. "Your offer is more than I dreamed to hope for. I will find some way to reward you."

For an instant, it almost looked as if Cazio was blushing. Then he shrugged again. "It is nothing. If there is a reward, it shall be our friendship." He raised his glass. "To friendship."

Smiling, Anne matched the toast.

Cazio grinned wryly to himself as he crossed the fields toward Orchaevia's manse. He was well pleased with himself. It might be that there was no one in these parts worthy of his sword, but at least he had found a challenge. Love, no. Orchaevia was a foolish romantic. But the chase, yes, that was worthwhile. It would make the loving all the sweeter when Fiene submitted. She was a project worthy to occupy his time.

And if this Roderick should come looking? Well, then Caspator might teach him a lesson or two, and that would be even better.

CHAPTER FOURTEEN

PURSUIT

"I HEAR THEM," Stephen whispered in as low a voice as he could manage. "That way." He thrust his finger east, pointing through the trees.

"I don't hear anything," the holter said.

"Shh. If I can hear them, they may be able to hear us. The faneway blessed my senses, and some of them have marched the same fanes."

Aspar just nodded and laid his finger to his lip in a gesture of silence.

After a time, the sounds of horses and riders receded.

"They're out of earshot," Stephen told the holter, when he was sure.

"They took the false trail, then. Good." The holter stood. His face was still strained and pale, and he moved as if his limbs were half-severed.

"You need rest, and attention," Stephen said.

"Sceat. I'll live. I'm feeling better."

Stephen was dubious, but didn't argue. "What now?" he asked instead.

"Tell me exactly what you heard them say."

Stephen repeated the conversation as he'd heard it. When he came to the part about Fend, the holter stiffened.

"You're sure. You're sure they mentioned Fend?"

"Yes. My memory is better now, too."

"Fend and a bunch of monks, off to kill the queen. What in the Raver's eye is going on?"

"I wish I knew," Stephen said.

"Cal Azroth," Aspar mused. "It's in Loiyes. It's where the royals go when they need extraordinary protection. I don't see how a handful of assassins plan to get in there."

"They have the greffyn."

"I'm not so sure about that," Aspar said. "They were following it, yes, and it didn't attack them, but I don't think they control it."

"But the Briar King controls it," Stephen replied. "And the Briar King seems to be behind all this. And who knows what powers Spendlove has gained from the dark faneways?"

"Yah," Aspar grunted. "Doesn't matter. We'll follow 'em and kill 'em."

"You're not in any shape to kill anyone," Stephen said. "Can't we contact the king? Get him to send knights?"

"By the time we could do that, they'll be at Cal Azroth."

"What about Sir Symen?"

"Too far out of the way."

"So it's just us?"

"Yah."

Stephen took a deep breath. "Well, then. I guess we'll do that." He cast a glance at the holter. "Thank you, by the way."

"What for? Was you saved my hide. Again."

"For believing me. Trusting me. If you'd paused to question—"

"Listen," the holter said. "You're green and naïve and annoying, but you're not a liar, and if *you* see danger, it must be pretty damned obvious."

"I almost didn't see it in time," Stephen said.

"But you saw it. Must be those new eyes of yours."

"I didn't see it in time to save the fratrex," Stephen said, feeling the dig of that fact in his belly.

"Yes, well, the fratrex was there longer than you. He should have known, himself," Aspar said, moving toward Ogre. "Anyway, this is a waste of time, all this back-patting and bemoaning. Let's pick up their trail before it cools."

Stephen nodded, and they mounted and set out. Around them, the forest sang of death coming.

PART **IV**

THE BLOOD
OF REGALS
The Year 2,223 of Everon
The Month of Seftmen

O mother I am wounded sore
And I shall die today
But I must tell you what I've seen
Before I've gone away

A purple scythe shall reap the stars
An unknown horn shall blow
Where regal blood spills on the ground
The blackbriar vines shall grow

—FROM *Riciar ya sa Alvqin*, A FOLK BALLAD OF EASTERN CROTHENY.

CHAPTER ONE

AN EXCURSION

NEIL MEQVREN CAST HIS GAZE around the hillside, searching for murder. He clucked under his breath to Hurricane, urging him to catch up with the queen and Lady Erren, riding sidesaddle just ahead of him on the raised track of road.

"Majesty," he said, for the third time, "this is not a good idea."

"Agreed," Erren said.

"I'm aware of your opinions," the queen replied, waving off their protests. "Indeed, I have heard them at least two times too many."

"We came to Cal Azroth for its protection," Erren noted.

"So we did," the queen replied.

"But if we are not *in* Cal Azroth, what protection can it afford?" She motioned toward the keep, which was still visible behind them. It wasn't large, but it did have three defensive walls, a garrison, and a good position on the hill, further surrounded by broad canals. Ten men had once held Cal Azroth against two thousand.

"I am not convinced we are any safer in the fortress than out here," the queen replied. "It is protected against an army, I'll give you that. But do you think anyone will send an army to kill my daughters or me? I do not. More and more I come to share Sir Neil's opinion."

"What opinion is that, if I may ask?" Erren asked mildly, giving Neil a glance so sharp it could have cut steel.

"That William was maneuvered into sending us here by someone—

Robert or Lady Gramme perhaps—who wants us away from the court for a time."

Erren's eyes narrowed. "Not that I don't suspect that myself," she said, "but I would like to know why Sir Neil did not mention this opinion to me."

I am just the sword, remember? Neil thought. "I was certain my lady had a more informed opinion than mine."

"You were right in that, if nothing else," Erren replied. "But did it occur to you that if someone maneuvered Her Majesty and her children here, the goal might be more than to merely remove their influence from court? The intent to do them harm, as well?"

Before Neil could answer, the queen laughed. "If that's the case, then the *last* place we ought to be is in the fortress, where our hypothetical conspirators expect us to be gathered, like lambs awaiting the butcher's hammer."

"Unless they count on you doing something stupid, like riding out to Glenchest."

The queen rolled her eyes. "Erren, we've been prisoned in Cal Azroth for near two months. Elyoner's home is less than half a day's ride, and we have twelve armored knights and thirty footmen with us."

"Yes, we're eminently noticeable," Erren commented.

"Lady Erren, Sir Neil, surrender!" Fastia advised, riding up from behind. "Once mother has made up her mind, it is set, as at least *you* ought to know, Erren. We're going to see Aunt Elyoner, and that's that."

"Besides," Elseny chimed in, "I'm tired of that old castle. There's nothing to *do* there." She sighed. "I *so* miss the court. Prince Cheiso, Aunt Lesbeth's fiancé, was to have arrived by now, and I wanted to meet him."

"You'll meet him soon enough," the queen soothed.

Neil heard all of that with only one ear; the other he kept pricked for danger. The road they followed passed through mostly open country— pear and apple orchards, fields of wheat and millet. And yet even such terrain offered ample opportunity for ambush. A single well-placed arrow from someone hidden in the branches of a tree, and all was lost.

As Erren said, they made quite a procession. The queen, Erren, Fastia, Elseny, and himself rode in a close clump. Audra and Mere—the maids of Fastia and Elseny respectively—rode a few yards behind, chattering like magpies. Prince Charles trailed farther behind, singing a children's song as Hound Hat capered along beside him on foot. Today the jester's red cap was so large it covered him nearly to the knees, and though Neil was sure that the Sefry could by *some* artifice see, exactly how he couldn't say, for the hat had no holes in it.

Around the royal party, mounted Craftsmen and the Royal Footguard formed a loose hollow square, ready to tighten at any moment.

That didn't give Neil much comfort. For all he knew, any or all of those men might turn against him. Still, if that were the case, the queen was right: they could as easily do murder in a keep as in clear light.

"Why so glum, Sir Knight?"

Startled, Neil swung about in the saddle. Concentrating on the middle and far distance, he hadn't noticed Fastia dropping back to pace him.

"I'm not glum, Archgreffess. Just watchful."

"You look more than watchful; you look as nervous as a rabbit caught in a fox hunt. Do you really expect danger out here? We're in Loiyes, after all, not Hansa."

"And we were in Eslen when your mother was attacked."

"True. Still, it's as I said a moment ago—Mother won't be dissuaded, so you might as well make the best of it." She smiled, and it was so unexpected on her normally tightly composed face that he couldn't help but follow suit.

"That's better," she said, still smiling.

"I—" He suddenly worried that he had a bug in his teeth or something. "Is something funny, Archgreffess?"

"Turn and look behind you."

Neil did as he was told. There was Prince Charles and Hound Hat, the maids . . .

When his gaze touched Audra and Mere they both turned as red as ripe cherries and then burst into giggling. Mortified, Neil turned around quickly.

"They've been back there talking about you all morning," Fastia said. "They really can't seem to get enough of watching you."

Neil felt his own face burning and guessed it a good match for the girls. "I didn't—I mean I haven't . . ."

"So much as spoken to them? I know. If you *spoke* to them, I expect they would fall off of their horses."

"But why?"

"Sir Neil! Please. You're a handsome man, and you must know it. There were girls in Liery, weren't there?"

"Ah—well, there was one." He was uncomfortable with such talk, especially around the prim Fastia.

"One? In all of the islands?"

"I meant only one who I, ah . . ."

"You had only one sweetheart?"

"She was never my sweetheart," Neil said. "She was betrothed, soon after we met."

"How old were you?"

"Twelve."

"She was betrothed when you were twelve? And so after that, no young woman has ever pursued you?"

"Some did, I suppose. But my heart was given. I promised her, you see, that as long as she lived I would love no other."

"A promise given when you were twelve. And she never released you from your vow?"

"She died in childbirth, Princess, a year ago."

Fastia's eyes widened and went oddly soft. He had never seen them so soft. "Saint Anne bless her," she said. "I'm sorry to hear that."

Neil merely nodded.

"But—and forgive me if this sounds cruel—you are released from your vow now."

"That's true. But I've taken another—to protect your mother."

"Ah." Fastia nodded. "You will find, I think, that few men keep vows as you do." A note of bitterness crept into her voice. "Marriage vows in particular."

Neil could think of nothing tactful to say to that, and so remained silent.

Fastia brightened, after a moment. "What a bore I can be," she said. "Anne is right about me."

"I do not find you boring," Neil replied. "Of everyone I have met in this court, you have been the kindest and most helpful to me."

Fastia's cheeks pinkened. "How kind of *you*, sir. Your company these past months has been appreciated."

Neil suddenly feared he had crossed some threshold he should never have approached, and so he needled his gaze around the landscape again. Along the side of the road, stalks of spindly flowers like tiny spiral stairs caught his attention with their vivid orange blossoms.

"Do you know the name of that flower?" he asked, for want of anything better to say. "I have never seen it in Liery."

"Those are Jeremy towers," Fastia said. "You know, I once could name every kind of flower on this road."

"Would you entertain me by doing so, Princess? It would help me stay vigilant. I know it is impolite to look away while conversing, but . . ."

"I understand completely. I would be happy to entertain you thus, Sir Neil."

When they stopped to water the horses, Fastia braided necklaces of pharigolds—one for each girl and Charles, and one for Neil. He felt rather silly wearing it, but could think of no polite way of refusing it, either.

While the party reassembled itself, Neil rode to the top of the nearest hill, to get a better view.

The land was rolling and lovely, copsed with trees but mostly pasture dotted with brown-and-white cows. About a league away, he could make out the slender towers of a castle—presumably Glenchest, their destination.

Hoofbeats signaled the arrival of Sir James Cathmayl and Sir Vargus Farre.

"Well, if it isn't the captain of the queen's guard," Cathmayl said. "How do our chances look, Captain? Do you think you can take her?"

"Pardon?"

"You're a fine tactician, I'll tell you that. You've got the ice princess smiling, up top, which is a good first step to that smile down below."

"Sir James, I most honestly hope you are not implying what you seem to be."

"Let imps lie where they may," Sir James said.

"Crudeness aside," Vargus interposed, "you do seem to have a way with her."

"She's still a girl, under that dress," James said. "That fool Ossel barely touches her, they say. But I've never seen her show an itch till now."

Neil regarded Sir James seriously. "Princess Fastia, if that's who you mean, is a perfect and gentle lady," he said. "Any kindness she shows me is from politeness, I assure you."

"Well, let's hope she very politely licks your—"

"Sir, stop there, I warn you!" Neil shouted.

James did, and let a wicked grin spread across his face. Then he chuckled and rode off.

"Sir Neil," Vargus said, "you are far too easy a target for James to hit. He means no malice, but he loves to see your blood up."

"He should not talk that way about the archgreffess. It offends honor."

Vargus shook his head. "You were brought up by Sir Fail. I know for a fact that he taught you that honor has its place. But so does levity, and even a little crudeness." He swept his hand at the party down the hill. "We're ready to lay down our lives for any of them, anytime, and Sir James is not the slightest exception. Why begrudge us a little harmless fun? More to the point, the guard isn't going to like you, if you keep this stiff, standoffish mien. And you need the men to like you, Sir Neil. You are to assemble a staff for the queen's new bodyguard, yes, and captain it?"

"I am."

"Better to have men who like you."

"Most will not like me anyway, however I act. I am not of gentle birth, and many find that offensive."

"And many do not. There are ties that can bind warriors much more surely than any title or rank. But you have to be willing to make some of the rope."

Neil pursed his lips. "I was well liked in Liery, as you say. I fought alongside lords and called them brother. But this is not Liery."

"You earned your place there," Vargus told him. "Now earn it here."

"That's difficult, with no battles to fight."

"There are many kinds of battle, Sir Neil, especially at court."

"I know little of that sort of warcraft," Neil admitted.

"You're young. You can learn."

Neil nodded thoughtfully. "Thank you, Sir Vargus," he said sincerely. "I shall keep that in mind."

Glenchest, as it turned out, was not so much a castle as a walled amusement. Its towers were tapering, beautiful, and utterly impractical for defense. Its wall, while high enough to keep goats and peasants out, would do little more than make an army pause. The gate was a joke, an elaborate grill of wrought iron made to resemble singing birds and blooming vines, through which could be seen a vast park of trees, hedges, fountains, and pools. Besides the towers Neil could see the roof of the villa, bright copper, shaped very much like an upside-down boat.

The castle stood upon a low mount, and the town below was clean, trim, and very small, clearly grown up recently to service Glenchest. Its inhabitants watched the queen's party curiously as they approached.

When they drew nearer, four young girls broke from the rest, dancing excitedly up to the party. Neil's hand strayed to his sword.

"Sir Neil, stay your hand," Fastia whispered. "Village girls pose no danger."

For their part, the girls seemed oblivious to Neil's guarded attitude. They came right to Hurricane's withers, eyes bright and upturned. They giggled, much in the same manner as the maids had earlier.

"Sir Knight," the eldest-looking said, a brown-haired lass who might have been thirteen. "Couldn't you give us a favor?"

Neil stared at them, confused. "Favor?" he replied.

"For my wishing chest," the girl said demurely, casting her eyes down.

"Go ahead, Sir Neil," Vargus urged jovially. "Give the girl a little something."

Neil balked, feeling his face flush, but remembered the older knight's advice.

"I don't—" He broke off, befuddled. Elseny laughed.

"Here," Sir Vargus said. "I'm a knight, as well, ladies, though not so young and pretty as this one. Would a favor from me do?"

"Oh, for me!" one of the younger girls cried, changing her attentions in an instant to Vargus. The older knight smiled and produced a knife, cutting a lock of his curly hair.

"That's for you, miss," he said.

"Thank you, sir!" the girl said, and then ran off, holding up her prize.

"It's the custom, hereabouts," Fastia said. "They'll wish on it and pray to Saint Erren for a love as noble as you."

"Oh," Neil said. He looked down at the three still eagerly waiting. "I suppose it's no harm." He produced his little belt knife, sawed through a bit of his own hair, and handed it down to the girl. She beamed up at him, bowed, and ran off. The others followed, demanding a part of her prize. Elseny applauded. Audra and Mere looked sullen.

"As I said," Sir James drawled, "this one has a way with the ladies."

Neil caught movement from the corner of his eye, and to his chagrin realized he'd been distracted enough to miss the arrival of a sizable party.

It was a gaudy group emerging from the gate. There were pages dressed in yellow hose and orange frocks, footmen in silver mail—it looked like real silver, which was ridiculous—knights in baroque, flowery armor and red and blue surcoats trimmed in gold lace. In the center of all this, on a palanquin covered with a silk awning and sprouting pennants of cloth of gold and argent, reclined a woman in a voluminous gown of gold and forest green brocade, touched here and there with scarlet flowers. It spilled down the sides of the palanquin like a waterfall, in all directions, and was surely impossible to walk in. The bodice was cut precariously low and pushed dangerously high, and it seemed to Neil that any motion at all might send her breasts forth to reveal what little of them was hidden.

The face above all of this was, at first glance, almost plain. It was gently oval, with a tiny sharp nose and small lips. But the woman's eyes were cerulean and radiated an easy mischief, and her lips were painted red and bowed in a smile to match. All this somehow made her whimsically beautiful. Her hair was pale brown, caught up in a complex silver coronet.

"My aunt Elyoner, my father's sister and the duchess of Loiyes," Fastia whispered. She leaned away, and then back. "She is a widow and an enemy of virtue, my aunt. Watch yourself with her, especially if you are alone."

Neil nodded, thinking the duchess did not resemble her brother the king in the least.

"Muriele, my love!" the duchess said, when they were near. "What a disaster that you should come now! I'm barely fit to receive visitors. I just came out to the country a few days ago and haven't had time to properly put things in order. I hope you will forgive this drab reception! It was the best I could manage on such short notice, but I could not fail to welcome you!"

As she spoke, the pages scattered the road before them with lilies, while others offered goblets of wine and took the reins of the horses. The queen took one of the proffered cups.

"A gracious reception, as always," she said. "It pleases to see you, Elyoner."

The duchess coyly averted her eyes. "You are always so kind, Muriele. Please, all of you, come down off those sweaty things. I have chairs for most of you, and your guard will enjoy the walk." She gestured at four palanquins, each with two seats. They were somewhat smaller than her own.

"Elseny, what a beauty you've become!" she continued, as the party dismounted. "And Fastia! You have color back in your cheeks. Have you finally taken my advice and found a lover?"

Fastia made a sound like a hiccup, and suddenly, for some reason, the duchess focused her eyes on Neil. "Aha!" she said. "An excellent choice."

"I've done no such thing, Aunt Elyoner," Fastia said, "as you ought to know."

"Really? How sad. I take it, then, that this delicious young knight is free for sport?"

"He is Sir Neil MeqVren, captain of my Lier Guard," Muriele said.

"How odd. I could have sworn he was guarding Fastia. But that hardly answers my question."

With a guilty start, Neil realized that he was, indeed, nearer to Fastia than to her mother.

"Aunt Elyoner, you have no shame, truly," Fastia said.

"Why, I never claimed to, dear. Now, come give us a kiss, and let's get out of this dreadful sunlight!"

°   °   °

"Please accept my apologies, once again," the duchess said, that night at supper, gesturing at the table, an enormous affair the size of some galleries. "The cupboard was rather bare, and my best cook is too ill to be troubled."

Neil was starting to notice a pattern with the duchess. The polished oaken surface was filled from end to end with partridges in butter gravy, quail pie with currants and almonds, ten kinds of cheese, mixed herbs, steaming platters of eel stew, capons in crust of salt, three roasted suckling pigs, and a gilded bull's head. Wine had been flowing like water since they passed through the gates and fantastic gardens of Glenchest, and Elyoner herself had taken quite a bit of it, though to no obvious effect. Servants hurried everywhere, keeping glasses full, and Neil had to be careful to keep up with what he drank.

"Your hospitality, as usual, is far more than adequate," the queen assured her.

"Well, as long as I got you out of that dreary Cal Azroth. What a hole!"

"But a safe hole," Erren muttered.

"Oh, yes. The attempt on Muriele's life. I got that news only a little while ago. It must have been terrible, my dear."

"I hardly had time to notice it before Sir Neil removed the danger," the queen replied.

"Aha!" the duchess said, waving her cup at Neil. "This is the one? I knew this young man had a quality about him. I can spot that sort of thing right away."

"Those are kind words, Duchess," Neil said. "But I simply did what any man in the guard would have done. It's only that I was nearer."

"Oh, and modest, too," the duchess said.

"He is that, and truly," Fastia said, setting her goblet down and spilling a little wine in the process. "It's no courtly pretension, with him. Heezh—" Fastia looked surprised, and glanced at her wineglass with a bit of chagrin. Misunderstanding, a page hastened to fill it. By her slurred speech and pink cheeks, that was hardly what the usually sober Fastia needed.

Neil was the only one who seemed to notice her discomfort, perhaps because he shared it.

"Well, Sir Neil," the duchess said, with a sly smile, "we shall have to
think of some reward for you. Our sister-in-law is very dear to us, and
we thank you very much indeed for preserving her life."

Neil nodded politely.

"Now, dear Muriele, tell me every little thing about the court. Well,
no, not the boring things, you know, no politics or war or matters of that
sort. Just the interesting things—which cocks are in which henhouses,
you know. Page! Bring the brandy, will you?"

After dinner it was games in the garden—darts, tennis, hide-and-seek in
the hedge maze. The duchess sent more and stronger spirits to Neil,
which he sipped at and poured out when she wasn't looking. The queen
took part in the games, and even seemed to be enjoying herself. So did
Fastia, though she swayed unsteadily as she consumed more wine and
brandy.

The duchess had changed before dinner, and now wore a black
gown embroidered in silver and of more manageable length, though still
scandalously revealing. She presided over the play from a little throne
her servants carried from place to place.

As the sun set, she beckoned Neil over. When he drew near, her servant produced a small golden key.

"This is for you," she said, her gaze tracing his face languidly. "I do
hope you'll use it."

"I don't understand, Duchess."

"It is the key to a certain chamber, in the tallest tower, there. In it I
think you will find a reward you will quite enjoy."

"My lady, I must stay near the queen."

"Foo. I will protect her. I am the lady of this house, and I command it."

"Lady, with greatest respect, and with all of my apologies, I cannot
leave my queen's side."

"What? Will you sleep with her?"

"No, Lady. But near."

"She has Erren, when she sleeps."

"I am very sorry," Neil said again firmly. "But my first and only duty is to the queen."

The duchess studied his face in fascination. "You *are* the virtuous one, aren't you? I thought they threw all of your sort off of the cliffs long ago." She bit one side of her lower lip, then straightened her smile. "How exciting. It only makes the chase more worthwhile. I am young, I've plenty of time." She frowned a bit. "Agree with me, Sir Neil. Tell me I am young."

"You are, my lady. And beautiful."

"Not so beautiful as some, perhaps," she replied. "But I will tell you this, Sir Neil: I am very, very learned. I have read books—forbidden books—and I *do* so hate to read. But it was worth it." She stroked his cheek and parted his lips with her finger. "You would find my studies were not in vain, I assure you."

Neil's body was already convinced, and he had to swallow before answering. "Duty," he managed.

She laughed, a trilling, beautiful sound. "Yes, we shall see about that," she said. "You will take some breaking, but every horse can be ridden." She dimpled. "Suppose I told you I could have something put in your drink, something that would drive you mad with desire?"

"Then I should have to stop drinking," Neil said.

"Suppose I told you you already drank it?"

Neil's mouth dropped. He did feel flushed, and certain parts of him were very much attentive. He could smell the flowery fragrance on the duchess, and his eyes were drawn more and more to the precipitous cleavage she exposed.

"May I be excused, lady?" Neil said.

"Of course, my dear," she replied. She took his hand and stroked it, sending a jolt through his body. "A little jumpy, are you?" She released his hand. "I'll see you later, Sir Neil. Hopefully all of you."

Later that night, once he was certain the queen's suite was secure, Neil retired to a small chamber outside of her receiving room, and there removed his armor, gambeson, and underclothes. He splashed cold water from the basin on his face and then sat on the bed, trying to control his breathing, which was still a bit irregular. He was almost certain now that the duchess *had* somehow bewitched him. It was as if lightning were flashing in his head, and each bright eruption illuminating an imagined feminine limb or curve. He knew that in the next room the queen was undressing, and it disgusted him that he could not keep that fact from his mind. He lay on the bed, summoning memories of battle and death, of anything to divert his thoughts from lust. Failing, he rose and exercised, padding silently in his small chamber, working through the motions of sword practice with his open hands, as he had first learned them.

Finally, sweating and knowing he needed sleep to be alert, he sat back on the bed and put his head in his hands.

He almost missed the slight creak of the door under the pounding of his pulse, but his body was limbered and ready, and in a swift instant he had his sword in hand and at guard.

"Sir Neil, it is me," a woman's voice whispered.

Slowly he lowered the sword, trying to make out the vague shadow in the doorway. He knew it must be the duchess, and his blood roared even more loudly in his ears.

She stepped a little farther in, so that the moonlight through the window touched her face, and he beheld with a start that it was Fastia.

CHAPTER TWO

TRACKS

ASPAR KNELT BY THE STILL-SMOKING ASHES of the camp-fire and growled in the back of his throat.

"What's wrong?" Stephen asked.

The holter didn't look at the boy but stood and surveyed the clearing again. "They didn't try to hide their sign," he grunted. "They didn't even stop the embers smoking. They led us right here."

"Maybe they don't imagine we're following them. It's been nearly a month."

Indeed, they'd left d'Ef in the hottest days of Sestemen, but they were now well into the month of Seftmen. The leaves were already touched with autumn color, even here in the lowlands, where pasture and farmland cut up the King's Forest. Aspar simply hadn't been able to keep the pace needed to catch the monks early on. He was stronger now, though he still didn't feel quite himself.

"They know we're after them," he said. "Make no mistake." He fitted an arrow to his bow, one of the four that remained. The others had broken in hunting.

"You think—" Stephen began, but in that moment Aspar smelled the ambush. Two men were racing from the trees behind them. Stripped to the waist, they were heavily tattooed on their shoulders and chests, and they bore broadswords. They were running faster than men ought to be able to run.

"That's Desmond's men!" Stephen shouted. "Or two of them."

"Mount," Aspar shouted, leaping onto Ogre and digging in his heels. The big horse jolted into motion. The men split, one headed toward Stephen and one keeping a course toward Aspar.

Aspar stood in his stirrups and turned, sighting down a shaft at the one attacking Stephen. Ogre wasn't quite settled into a stride, but Aspar couldn't wait. He released the dart.

The arrow flew true, or almost so, striking the monk in the kidney. He fell, giving Stephen time to get up on Angel, but came back to his feet with absurd speed.

Meanwhile, incredibly, the other monk was gaining on Ogre. Grimacing, Aspar fitted another arrow to his bow and shot it, but just as he did so Ogre leapt a downed log and his shot went high and wide.

Now he was down to two arrows.

He yanked on his reins, spun the horse around, and aimed him right at his pursuer, staring down the shaft at him. He saw the man's face, set and determined, and as mad as one of the Raver's berserks. He aimed for the heart.

At the last instant, the monk threw himself aside, so the arrow buried itself in sod. He cut viciously at Ogre's legs as he tumbled past, but the horse avoided the blow by whiskers. They thundered by, back toward Stephen, whose wounded attacker was nearly on him. He was bleeding freely, but that seemed only to have slowed him a little. Fortunately, he was so intent on the boy that he didn't notice Ogre until it was too late, until the beast's forehooves had crushed his skull.

Aspar wheeled again, taking out his last arrow and leaping down from the beast.

"Ogre, *qalyast!*" he shouted.

Ogre immediately charged the monk, who set himself grimly to meet the horse. In that instant of relative stillness, Aspar shot him in the center of the chest.

The monk spun with the blow, avoiding Ogre as he did so, and ran past the horse toward Aspar. Cursing, Aspar turned and lifted the dead man's sword. It wasn't a weapon he knew a lot about—he wished he had his dirk and ax—but he held it at guard and waited. Behind him, he heard Stephen drop to the ground.

The monk was on him, then, cutting fast and hard toward Aspar's head. Aspar gave ground, but not enough, and had to bring the heavy weapon up to parry. His shoulder jarred as if he'd just stopped thirty stone falling from a tower. Stephen came in from the right, swinging his farm tool, but the swordsman turned and neatly hacked through the wooden shaft. Aspar swung clumsily, and the monk danced aside, feinted, and cut. Aspar leapt inside the swing, dropped his own weapon, grabbed the sword arm with his left hand, and punched the monk in the throat. He felt cartilage crush, but his opponent kneed him viciously in the chest, hurling him back and to the ground, empty of breath. The monk staggered forward, lifting his sword, just as Ogre hit him from behind. He fell, and Ogre kept stamping him until his hooves were red and the corpse wasn't twitching.

"They could have killed us if they'd been a little smarter," Aspar said, when he got his wind back. "They were overconfident. Should have ignored us and gone straight for Ogre."

"Contemptuous is more like it," Stephen replied. "Those were two of the pettiest of Spendlove's bunch—Topan and Aligern. Spendlove himself would never be so stupid."

"Yah. I maunt he sent the men he could most afford to lose. Even if they'd got only one of us, it would have been a bargain. He should've given 'em bows."

"Those who walk the faneway of Saint Mamres are forbidden to use bows," Stephen remembered.

"Well. Thank Saint Mamres in your prayers, then."

They stripped the corpses, and to Aspar's satisfaction found a fighting dirk not unlike his own lost one. They also found a few silver tierns and enough dried meat and bread for a day, all welcome additions to Aspar and Stephen's meager possessions.

"I reckon that leaves about six of them," he mused, "and however many Fend brings. Let's hope they keep sending them two at a time like this, so we can keep evening the odds."

"I doubt Spendlove will make the same mistake twice," Stephen said. "Next time, he'll be sure."

"Next time could be anytime. These two might have just been to lull us. We're riding out of here, right now, and not the way they'll expect. We know where they're going, so we don't need to trail them."

Once they were mounted, Aspar chuckled.

"What?" Stephen asked.

"I notice you aren't arguing we bury these, like you did those last."

"A holter's burial is good enough for them," Stephen said.

"Werlic," Aspar allowed, "at least you've learned *something*."

CHAPTER THREE

PLOTS

"WELL, SISTER MULE," Serevkis said. "The greencrafting has become much more interesting, hasn't it?"

Anne glanced up from her examination of the double boiler and the fermenting ewe's milk it contained. She loved the scent of it, still warm from the sheep, and even more the anticipation of the magic that was soon to occur.

"Why do you still call me that?" she asked absently.

"Wouldn't you rather be a mule than a little cow?"

Anne smiled. "There's that," she admitted. "Yes, greencraft is more interesting now. Everything is."

"Even numbers?" Serevkis sounded skeptical.

"Yes. If they'd told me from the start that we were studying numbers so we could manage the moneys of our households, I might have paid more attention in the beginning."

"But greencraft is the most interesting," Serevkis insisted. "Who knew how many poisons lie right beneath our feet or in garden walls, and requiring only a little alchemy to make them potent."

"It's like a lot of things," Anne said. "Even this cheese I'm making. To know we have the power to change things, to make one thing into another."

"You and your cheese. Is it doing anything yet?"

"Not yet," Anne said.

"But you're right," Serevkis went on. "To be able to make something harmless into something deadly—it's wonderful."

"You're a wicked girl, Sister Serevkis," Anne said.

"Who will you kill first, Sister Mule?"

"Hush!" Anne said. "If the mestra or one of the elders hears you talking like that . . ."

Serevkis yawned and stretched her long limbs. "They won't," she said. "The mestra and her favorites went off through the gates four bells ago, and the rest are teaching. No one ever comes to the creamery. Who will you murder in the night?"

"No one comes to mind, except a certain long-necked name-caller."

"I'm serious."

Anne met the girl's casually evil gaze. "Do you have someone in mind?"

"Oh, indeed. Several someones. There's Dechio—he'd be first. For him it will be the pollen of the witherweed, cooked into a gum with nightshade. I'll put it in the candles in his room."

"That's a slow, cruel death. What did this Dechio ever do to you?"

"He was my first lover."

"And jilted you?"

"I was ten. He was twenty. He pretended to be my friend and made me drink wine until I couldn't stand, and then he had his way with me."

"He raped you?" Anne asked, incredulous.

"There's the word," Serevkis said. Her mouth twitched, after.

"And your father? He did not avenge this?"

Serevkis laughed, a bit bitterly. "What use to a father a daughter so early despoiled? No, it would have been better to leap to my death from the moat tower than tell my father what Dechio did that day, and continued to do until I grew too old to attract him."

"I see." Anne didn't see, though. She couldn't imagine. "May I make a suggestion?"

"Certainly."

"Black widow spiders, fatted on corpse flies. Glue little threads to them and the other ends under the edge of the sitting-hole in his privy. When he dangles down . . ."

Serevkis clapped her hands. "Wonderful. It would rot like an old sausage, wouldn't it? But it might not kill him."

"True. But there are other ways to finish him off. After all, the candles might kill someone innocent—the girl who cleans his chambers, or another of his victims."

"Or I could leave him to live with a rotted poker," Serevkis said. "Clever, Sister Mule."

"Thank you." She glanced back at her boiler. "Look!" she exclaimed. "See! It curdles!"

Serevkis got up to see.

A solid white mass had formed in the pot, shrinking slightly as it did so, so that it pulled away from the edges of the container. It floated there like an island, surrounded by clear, yellowish liquid. Anne inserted a wooden skewer into the solid part, and when she withdrew it, the hole remained.

"The thick part is the curd," Anne explained. "The rest is whey."

"What worked this change?" Serevkis asked, suddenly interested. "What broke the milk in two?"

"Rennet, taken from a cow's belly."

"Appetizing. What else might it clot, I wonder? Blood? I suppose I see why you find this interesting."

"Of course. It once was one thing—milk—and now it is two."

"It still doesn't look much like cheese."

"True. There is more magic to be worked."

"You know," Serevkis mused, "when I was young, we had a servant from Herilanz. She had the pretense of religion, but in fact she was pagan. Once, she told me her god, Yemoz, created the world from milk."

"Separating curd from whey, sea from land," Anne mused. "It makes a sort of sense. After all, the saints did separate the world into its parts."

"Saint Mule, the woman who brought curd and whey from milk," Serevkis said, and laughed. "You are like a goddess now."

"You may laugh," Anne said, "but that's the point. When we learn to create these things—your poison candles, my cheese—we partake of creation. In a little way, we do become like the saints."

Serevkis pinched a skeptical frown. "You've been listening to Sister Secula too much," she said.

Anne shrugged. "Cruel she may be, but she knows everything."

"She put you in the cave!"

Anne smiled enigmatically. "It wasn't so bad."

Everyone had been surprised at Anne's composure when they brought her up from the shrine of Mefitis, and Sister Secula had given her more than one suspicious look and remarked on her color. The matter hadn't been pursued, though. Anne didn't expand now to Sister Serevkis. She hadn't even told Austra. She felt somehow that what happened in the cave and beyond were her secrets, and hers alone.

It certainly would not do for Austra to know that she'd sent a letter to Roderick; though it wasn't a violation of the oath, Anne still suspected Austra would be anything but pleased.

Cazio had been good to the first part of his word. When she cast the letters down from the window her first evening back in the coven, he'd appeared near sundown, waved to her, and taken the correspondence with him. Time would tell if he was truly honest.

Meanwhile, she was content. Everything was suddenly interesting to her, and she'd begun to understand what Sister Secula meant when she called Anne's presence at the Abode of Graces a privilege.

She still hated the mestra, but she'd begun to grudgingly admit that she was worth listening to.

"Now what?" Serevkis asked.

"Now we cut our new-made world into cubes," Anne replied, "to let the whey still within it seep out."

With a sharp ivory knife, she did just that, slicing it first lengthwise, then crossways, then at an angle toward the bottom of the crock. When she was done, and had stirred it once, a jumble of neat cubes floated in the yellowish whey.

"Now we cook it a little longer and put it in a mold and press. Six months from now, we eat it."

"Creation takes a long time," Serevkis said. "I'm hungry now."

"That's why saints are patient," Anne told her. "But there's plenty of food around—"

Austra, dashing into the creamery from the garden outside, interrupted her.

"Have you heard?" the blonde girl said excitedly.

"Hello, Sister Persondra," Anne said, rolling the *r*s comically.

"I have heard," Serevkis remarked. "I continue to."

"The news, I mean," Austra said. "The girls are all talking about it. We're going out."

"What do you mean?"

"To a grand *triva* in the country. The casnara there hosts an annual fete for the women in the coven, and it's happening in three days' time!"

"Really?" Anne said. "I can hardly see Sister Secula allowing that."

"No, it's true," Serevkis confirmed. "The older girls have spoken of it. It's said she throws a lovely ball, albeit one without men."

"It still sounds fun," Austra said, a bit defensively.

"If it's not," Serevkis replied, "we'll make it so."

"What sort of party can we have with everyone dressed in these habits?" Anne wondered.

"Well, you have your things, Sister Mule," Serevkis said. "But I've heard the countess keeps gowns enough for all of us."

"A borrowed gown?" Anne said distastefully.

"But not for us," Austra exclaimed. "As Sister Serevkis says, thanks to your stubbornness, we at least may wear our own things."

"You may," Anne replied. "I brought only one dress, and I gave that to you."

Austra's mouth hung open for a moment. "But your other chest. It's even heavier than mine."

"That's because my saddle is in it."

"Your saddle?" Austra said.

"Yes. The one Aunt Fiene gave me, the one I rode Faster with."

"You worked all night and earned the mestra's displeasure for a saddle?" Serevkis asked.

Anne merely nodded. She didn't feel like explaining.

But Austra, of course, would not let the matter rest.

"Why?" she demanded, that night in their room. "Why did you bring the saddle? So you could run away?"

"That was one reason," Anne allowed.

"But you dragged it up the stairs, after you promised me you wouldn't try to leave."

"I know."

Austra was silent for a moment, and when she spoke again it seemed almost as if her voice crept out of her reluctantly. "Anne, are you cross with me?"

Anne sat up in her sheets and looked at her friend's face in the faint moonlight. "Why would you think that?" she asked.

"Because you—you're different," Austra answered. "You spend so much time with Serevkis, these days."

"She's my friend. We're studying the same subjects."

"It's just—you never had any other friends in Eslen."

"You're still my favorite, Austra. I'm sorry if you feel neglected, but—"

"But I cannot discourse of the same things you and Serevkis do," Austra said flatly. "You learn sorcery while I scrub pots. And she is gentle born. Naturally you prefer her company."

"Austra, you silly *diumma*, I don't prefer her company to yours. Now go to sleep."

"I don't even know what you just called me," Austra murmured. "You see? I'm stupid."

"It's a sort of water spirit," Anne told her. "And you aren't stupid just because you don't know a particular word. If you were allowed to study what I do, you would know it. Enough of this! Austra, I will always love you best."

"I hope so," the younger girl said.

"Just think how you'll look at the ball. The only girl in her own gown."

"I'm not going to wear it."

"What? Why? It's yours."

"But you don't have one. It wouldn't be right."

Anne laughed. "As a lot of people—you included—have been fond of telling me, we are not in Crotheny anymore. I am not a princess here, and you are not a maid."

"No?" Austra said softly. "Then how is it you learn magic, and I beat rugs?"

For that, Anne didn't have a comfortable answer.

The blade darted toward Cazio, faster than he had imagined it could, cutting his cheek slightly. The pain brought everything into sharp focus, and with a shout he stamped, sidestepped, then ducked quickly back in the direction he had come from, and committed himself to a shallow fleché.

It proved an unwise commitment. Z'Acatto parried in prismo, deflecting Cazio's attack and stepping in close, his free hand clenching in the cloth of Cazio's tunic. In a continuation of the parry, the swordsmaster lifted the hilt of the weapon above his head, so the blade slanted down to rest its bright sharp tongue in Cazio's navel.

"What in Lord Fufio's name is wrong with you?" the old man barked in his face. "Where is your brain? You can't fence with just your hands and feet!"

Z'Acatto's breath was rancid with the wine of the night before. Cazio wrinkled his nose in disgust.

"Let go of me," Cazio demanded.

"Is that what you'll say to your next opponent when he has you in this position, or worse?"

"I would never allow that to happen in a real fight," Cazio asserted.

"Every time you pick up that sword it's a real fight," z'Acatto roared. He let go and stalked off. "You're hopeless! I give up!"

"You've been saying that for ten years," Cazio reminded him.

"And it's been true the entire time. You're hopeless as a dessrator."

"That's ridiculous. I've never been beaten, except by you."

Z'Acatto whirled to face him, eyes bulging. "*Now* you're going to tell me you know more about being a dessrator than *I* do?" He held his sword level to the ground, pointed at Cazio. "On your guard," he snarled.

"Z'Acatto—" Cazio began, but the older man launched himself forward, and Cazio was forced to bring his blade up. He gave ground, parried, and launched a riposte with a step-lunge, but his master caught the blade in a bind and pressed, then released in a lightning-fast disengage.

Cazio backpedaled and parried again, riposting desperately. Almost contemptuously, z'Acatto danced nimbly aside and counterattacked. Cazio avoided the deadly thrust only by hurling himself backwards, tripping as he did so, but not quite falling. Z'Acatto followed, a look in his eyes Cazio had never seen before, one that sent a sudden chill of panic down his spine.

No. I will not fear, Cazio thought, setting himself.

For a moment the two men circled each other warily, weaving into and out of striking distance. Cazio struck first, this time, a feint that turned into a draw cut aimed at his master's arm. Z'Acatto dropped his hand away from danger, then stabbed toward Cazio's throat. With sudden understanding Cazio realized that during his feint the older swordsman had drawn his back foot up and was lunging in much deeper than Cazio ever imagined he could.

He turned, so the point took him in his left shoulder. It sank in and hit bone, and with a cry he extended his sword arm. Z'Acatto yanked his weapon out with a twist, and in an instant the two men were touching each other on the chest with the tips of their blades.

"Shall we perform the parry of two widows?" z'Acatto growled.

"Neither of us is married," Cazio gasped, feeling blood soak his shirt. They continued to stand that way, and for a long terrible moment, Cazio thought he would have to thrust. He could almost feel the older man's steel in his own heart.

But z'Accato finally dropped his blade.

"Bah," he snarled, as it rang on the stone floor. In relief, Cazio sank into a chair, clutching his shoulder.

"I thought you were going to kill me," he said, as soon as he had caught his breath.

"I thought so, too," z'Acatto said, his eyes still flashing with anger. Then, softer, he murmured, "Boy, you're a fine swordsman. You're just not a dessrator. You don't have what it takes, in here." He tapped his chest over the heart.

"Then teach me."

"I've tried. I can't." He lowered his head. "Let's bind up that wound. I need a drink. So do you."

A short time later, they sat beneath the verandah in the courtyard, one bottle of wine already gone and another half-empty. It was almost enough for Cazio to ignore the pain in his shoulder. Around them, Orchaevia's servants were stringing up lanterns, banners, and chains of dried flowers.

Orchaevia herself bustled up, wearing a lime-green gown embroidered with golden roses.

"Well, you two are a sight," the countess remarked. "How do you like that year? I never considered it one of the best from the region."

"No," z'Acatto grumbled. "That would be the vintage from the year the baron Irpinichio became meddisso of the Seven Cities."

"Quite right," the countess said. "And perhaps one day your tour of my various cellars obvious and obscure will lead you to it. Though I don't think that likely." She turned to Cazio. "You, on the other hand, I might be able to help."

"Countess?"

"The young ladies from the coven will be here tomorrow night."

"What's this?" z'Acatto said. "The last thing the boy needs is to go solid over a band of nuns. He's already distracted enough."

"Yes, and what do you think has him so distracted?" Orchaevia asked.

"Ridiculous," Cazio said, waving her words away as he might a fly.

"That's it!" z'Acatto exploded. "I remember now. It's just like when you were chasing after that little da Brettii girl. The same stupid expression. No wonder you can't even hold your sword."

"There is no girl," Cazio insisted. This was too much. He was really starting to feel put upon.

"Of course not," Orchaevia said. "And if there were, you wouldn't see her at my party, for the mestra of the coven forbids her charges to see men. I've had to hire serving girls from Trevina and send my regular servants on holiday. But . . . it is *possible* that one of the young darlings might find herself alone, in the lavender garden, if I knew what she looked like."

Cazio nodded and drank more wine. His head was starting to swim, and he relented. "There is no girl," he said, "but as long as you're going to throw one my way, make her one with pale skin and red hair. A northern girl. I've always fancied one of those."

Orchaevia's smile broadened until Cazio thought it would split her head. "I shall see what can be done," she said.

Z'Acatto finished the bottle of wine in a single long draught. "No good will come of this," he predicted with a sigh.

CHAPTER FOUR

An Encounter

"Lady Fastia?" Neil gasped, in utter astonishment. She stood there in the moonlight, her long hair flowing unbound to her waist, shimmering like silk.

"I . . ." Fastia looked confused, then suddenly gaped and put her hand to her mouth. "Sir Neil, you're quite unclothed."

Realizing she was right, he grabbed a sheet from the bed and wrapped it around himself. He felt stupid for taking so long to react; what if Fastia had been an assassin, come to kill the queen?

What *had* she come for?

"Have you taken a wrong turn, lady? May I show you to your room?"

"No." Fastia looked down at the floor. He noticed then that she wore a dressing gown of silk brocade over a flimsy shift of cotton. "No," she said, "I came because . . . I . . . Elyoner gave me the key. And she— Sir Neil, I must be going mad."

Neil knew what she meant. His heart was pounding a warbeat. Fastia's face was perfect in the near dark, all jewels and precious ivory, a mystery of shadow that needed touching, needed more than touching. He felt a profound ache in his chest and an even more profound rush of blood throughout his body.

"The duchess, she gave us something, made a spell," Neil said.

"Yes," Fastia replied. "Yes." Then she looked up boldly. "And I am also quite drunk, though I do not care." Her brows scrunched. "Well, yes, I care, but I don't."

She moved toward him, then, or at least so it seemed, and he must have reciprocated, for in the next instant he was looking down into her face and her eyes were inches from his, her lips so near he could smell her breath. Much of *him* suddenly didn't care what happened, either. Her arms were wrapped firmly about his back, and her head tilted.

He felt Elyoner's spell overcoming him, and could think of no good reason not to surrender and kiss Fastia, feel those lips against his, and let the emotions coursing his blood have him.

But there *was* a reason. He knew it.

He pushed her gently back, and her eyes suddenly filled with hurt.

"You will not have me?" she asked.

"I . . . think I cannot," Neil replied. Speaking the words felt like eating shattered glass. Seeing her expression was worse.

"I am a young woman," Fastia told him softly. "I am a young woman married to an old man, an old man who does not care the least that I am a woman, much less young, though he finds his sport with those who are even younger. I am so unhappy, Sir Neil. The closest I have come to happiness has been in our conversations these last two months. I want more of it, now, while I don't care, while Elyoner's spell has me."

Then she began to weep, which was unfair. It meant he had to reach for her again, to try to brush away her tears.

"Archgreffess—" he began.

"My name is Fastia. Just Fastia. At least call me Fastia."

"Fastia, you are the daughter of my queen."

"I know who I am," she said, her voice suddenly angry. "Saints believe, I know who I am. Day in and day out I act my part and keep my place, like a vine trained to climb a trellis, like a dog taught to fetch slippers. I never forget myself, I never sin—" Her expression went suddenly ferocious, and she hurled herself at him. This time he was unable to resist. Her lips closed upon his. With her tears on them, they tasted like the sea. "Just this once," she said into his lips, as they kissed. "Just this once."

They fell fumbling to the bed, her dressing gown falling over him like wings as she kissed into his throat, and for a time there was no thought, only sensation and a crazy sort of happiness. But when much of her flesh was bare against his, and their lips had moved from neck and throat to other regions, his heart stopped him again—or at least the tiny bit he still owned.

"I cannot," he said. "Fastia—"

She pulled away from him, sitting up. The moonlight was stronger now, and she looked like a saint hovering above him.

"I do wish it," he said huskily. "But I cannot."

Fastia stared down at him unreadably for several moments, and then she smiled wanly. "I know," she said, patting his cheek. "I know. Neither can I." She swung her leg over and gathered her clothes back about her. But she did not leave.

"May I lie with you a moment?" she asked. "By your side?"

"That you may," he said. In truth he wished she would lie there all night.

She settled next to him and fastened her eyes on the ceiling. "I'm sorry," she said. "I'm terribly embarrassed. I'm really not like this. I'm never—"

"I'm the one to apologize," he said. "The duchess warned me about her drug. I thought I was prepared to fight its effects. But that's when I thought *she* was coming, and not you."

Her face tilted toward him. "Is this true? You have feelings for me?"

"I did not know it until tonight. Or admit it."

"Perhaps, then, it *is* just her spell."

Neil smiled faintly. "Do you really believe there was a spell?" he asked. "I have my doubts."

"So do I," Fastia admitted. "Tomorrow we shall know, each alone. But we will be ourselves again, either way. I do not think we will speak of it."

"Nor do I. But only know, if you were unmarried, and I of proper station—"

"Hush. If wishes were teardrops, the world would flood, Sir Neil." Her eyes did glisten with teardrops, and they spoke no more.

In time, when her breathing became regular and quiet with sleep, Neil rose, gathered her in his arms, and started toward her chambers.

When he opened the door, he saw a figure standing in the hall.

"Lady Erren," he said stiffly.

"Sir Neil," she replied. "Do you need help delivering that package?"

"Think no ill of the archgreffess, Lady Erren," Neil said. "She was not in possession of her senses. Any blame falls on me."

Erren shrugged. "Come. Let us put her in her right bed."

They took the sleeping Fastia down the hall and placed her there. Despite Erren, he paused to look at her dreaming face, so youthful in the light of the candle. Then the two of them quietly left.

Back in the hall, Erren examined him. "You did not do the deed," she said. "You walked that way, but did not open the door."

"How can you know that?" Neil asked, both astonished and somehow grateful that Erren knew the truth.

"I know," she said. "It's my art to know such things. Not that I would have disapproved of your bedding Fastia, Sir Neil, not as an act of itself. Saints know she needs that, needs someone like you. Maybe even needs you, specifically. I have watched this family's philandering for most of my life, and I no longer have a moral opinion on it. But, Sir Neil, you are sworn to the queen, do you understand? You cannot be distracted by love. If you need a body to press, one can be found, and discreetly, and I will think none the worse. But you cannot be in love." Her eyes narrowed. "Though it may be too late for that, saints pity you. But we will see. An enemy might have walked past you tonight. That mustn't happen again."

"I understand, Lady Erren."

"And, Sir Neil?"

"Lady."

"You are quite right. The only spell Elyoner used on you was suggestion, and the only physic was alcohol. In the future, remember the effects both can have, will you?"

"My lady, I will," Neil replied, deeply ashamed.

The next day, Neil donned his armor and went down with the queen to breakfast. Elyoner was already there, a little bleary-eyed but smiling, wearing a dressing gown of gold lamé trimmed in black mink. She greeted him with a little smile, which quickly turned to an exasperated frown.

"Oh, pish, Sir Neil," she sighed.

Neil felt naked beneath her gaze. How could she know? Did *everyone* know?

The queen didn't. "What have you done to my knight, Elyoner?" Muriele demanded mildly. "What mischief have you been up to?"

"Not enough, by the looks of him," Elyoner grumbled. Then she brightened. "Well, each day brings new hope."

As she spoke, her servants brought platters of boiled eggs, soft white cheese and fried apples, clotted cream, scones, and persimmon marmalade. Elseny came tripping excitedly down the stairs dressed in a vivid blue gown, followed by her flaxen-haired maid Mere.

"What entertainments have you planned for us today, Aunt Elyoner?" she asked.

"Boating on the Evermere, I think," the duchess replied, "and quoits in the orchard meadow."

"Out of the question," Erren said.

"Agreed," Neil said.

"Mother!" Elseny protested. "It sounds delightful."

Muriele sipped her tea and shook her head. "I think this time I shall defer to my keepers. I fear I have already strained them too much by bringing us here."

"Thank you, Majesty," Neil said.

"Yes, praise the saints," Erren grumbled.

"But my dear," Elyoner said, frowning. "It's all planned! I assure you, there is no danger, here on my lands."

"Nevertheless," Muriele replied, "I must think of my children."

"As you were thinking of Anne?" Elyoner asked, a hint of sarcasm in her voice.

"Anne is my affair, Elyoner. I did what was needed."

"You've sent a perfectly wonderful, spirited girl off to be broken into a nag," Elyoner retorted, "like that old killjoy jade Erren, there."

"I have protected her from herself," Muriele replied. "And we shall no longer talk of this."

As they spoke, Charles and Hound Hat had descended, the prince still in his nightclothes.

"Apples!" Charles exclaimed, sounding like a child. "Aunt Elyoner, my favorite!"

"That's right, child, I always remember," Elyoner said. "Have as many as you want. I fear it's the only entertainment you'll get today."

She sighed and fingered her chin. "I suppose I could have my players do something for us, if you don't consider *that* too threatening, Sir Neil. Elseny, you might do a scene with them, if you wish."

"Yes, I suppose that would be better than nothing," Elseny pouted. "Though the boat ride would be more dear by far."

Audra came down the stairs, alone.

"Where is the princess Fastia?" Elyoner asked the maid.

"She is feeling unwell, Duchess," Audra replied. "She's asked me to fetch something from the kitchen."

"I see. Well, the cook will make whatever she wants. And do take something for yourself, child."

"Thank you, Duchess," Audra replied. "It all looks wonderful."

Neil bit into a boiled egg, relieved that he didn't have to face Fastia yet, ashamed for feeling that way. She probably hated him for taking what advantage he had. He ate glumly as the family chattered around him and the house awoke.

A footman entered and interrupted his worries.

"There's a rider here, Duchess," he announced. "From Eslen."

"Indeed? What news does he bring?"

The footman bowed. "News of war, Duchess. Liery has declared war on Saltmark."

"It's beginning," Erren muttered. "Muriele—"

"Quite right," Muriele said. "Sir Neil, inform the guard. We are returning to the safety of Cal Azroth. We depart in one hour."

"That's ridiculous!" Elyoner said. "You are quite safe here, I tell you. It isn't as if Crotheny is at war."

"It took the rider at least five days to get here," Muriele reasoned. "This news is old. If Liery is at war, Crotheny cannot be far behind, and if we enter, so does Hansa. It is probably done as we speak. Children, have your things packed."

"But we just *got* here," Elseny protested. "Cal Azroth is so unutterably *dull*."

"Yes, it is," Muriele acknowledged. "Pack your things."

Despite himself, Neil felt only relief. War was less dangerous than Glenchest.

CHAPTER FIVE

MEETING ON THE HEADLAND

T HE SUN ROSE SMOTHERED IN FOG, paling the headland of Aenah with the color and feel of frost, so that William pulled his cloak tighter, though the sea breeze still had summer in it. His gaze searched restlessly down the cliffs to the shatter of rocks there, and beyond to the unsteady lines of water and sky. Around him, fifteen knights sat their horses silently. Robert, his face creased in unaccustomed severity, had dismounted. He, too, gazed out at the sea.

"Where are they?" William growled.

Robert shrugged. "You know as well as I that the sea roads are uncertain," he said. "Saint Lier cares little for the punctuality of mariners."

"And even less for that of pirates. You are certain this is arranged? Lesbeth will be returned to us?"

"We've kept up our bargain," Robert replied. "They will keep theirs. Austrobaurg knows he has extracted all he can from us by her captivity. That's been made clear."

"But why this clandestine meeting? Why insist that we two come along?"

Ananias Hargoln, captain of the lancers, spoke up. "My very thought, Sire. This seems most transparently a trap." His blue-steel eyes traveled the line of the coast suspiciously.

"We've covered this ground before. My spies have secured the region," Robert stated tersely. "Does Sir Ananias doubt his prime minister?"

Sir Ananias shook his graying head. "Not in the least, my prince. But I do doubt the duke of Austrobaurg. First he takes captive one of the royal family, and now he will exchange her only in the presence of the emperor himself on this saint's forsaken heath of a headland. Though we agreed to allow only fifteen men apiece, the emperor has it right. This is kingslaying begging to happen."

"Austrobaurg will have only fifteen men, as well," Robert pointed out.

"So he promised. That does not make it so."

Robert pointed to the winding cliffside path that led up from the sea. "We shall have ample time to notice if he brings more. No, Austrobaurg's motives are far less clandestine. He wants to throw his piss in our face and laugh when we can do nothing in response."

"Yes, that fits," William muttered. "I remember him all too well. A puffed-up fellow, a braggart." He leaned in close to Robert. "Let him enjoy his moment," he whispered. "But when this is done, and Lesbeth safe in Eslen—then, Robert, we shall discuss Austrobaurg again."

Robert arched his brows. "Indeed," he said. "Perhaps we'll make a politician of you after all, Wilm."

"Assuming he comes at all," William added.

But Robert was nodding at the waves and lifting a finger to point. "There," he said.

William's eyes weren't what they once had been, but only a few moments later he made out what Robert had seen—the long silhouette of a galley cutting through the whitecaps toward the stony shingle below. Over the crash of surf, he began to make out the pulling chant that went with the long, even strokes of the oars.

"How many men do you make?" William asked Sir Ananias.

The knight leaned his lanky frame forward in the saddle and studied the approaching ship.

"Narry more than fifteen, Sire," he said at last. "Same as promised."

"Might there be more belowdecks?"

"That there might be, Sire. I advise you stay here on the clifftop whilst I make certain there's no trickery. Let me keep you safe as I can."

"Sound advice, brother," Robert said.

"Very well. Meet them on the landing. Tell them you've come to insure that the terms of the meeting are kept—on both sides. Tell them they may send an emissary to verify our numbers, as well."

He watched as Ananias wound down the narrow trail cut into the white face of the cliffs, shrinking in perspective until he and his mount might have been a silver beetle. He reached the shore just as the ship was beaching, and a figure in gold-chased armor stood in the prow. They spoke, and few moments later, the knight boarded the galley. A horse was brought up from the hold, and soon a knight of Austrobaurg's was ascending the headland. As he did so, more horses were brought from the ship to the shore.

The Austrobaurg knight introduced himself in stilted king's tongue as Sir Wignhund Fram Hravenfera, and proceeded to search the headland for any troops William might have concealed there. It didn't take much of a search; the headland was where the plain of Maog Vaost stooped to the sea. It was sheepland, clear of trees and gently sloping, with no concealing ridges or crevasses in any direction.

Ananias returned presently.

"They are as agreed," Sir Ananias said. "Fifteen, no more and no less."

"And Lesbeth? She is well?"

The knight's long face pinched into a frown. "I did not see her, Sire."

William turned to his brother. "What's going on here, Robert?"

Robert shrugged. "I do not know. More posturing, no doubt."

"I don't like it, Sire," Sir Ananias said. "I suggest a withdrawal. Let the prime minister ask the questions."

"Indeed," Robert said. "Let someone with a full set of stones do the talking with this 'puffed-up' fellow."

"I am thinking only of the emperor and his safety, Prince Robert," the knight said stiffly.

"No one is withdrawing," William said. "I want to speak to Austrobaurg myself."

He sat impatiently as the opposing company drew nearer. They were caparisoned in high Hanzish fashion, silver and gold bells jangling on the manes and saddles of their horses, horsehair or feathered plumes streaming from their helms. William had kept his company plain, to avoid recognition on the ride to the cape. But Austrobaurg was shouting to the world who he was, knowing only William and his knights would see.

Robert was right—it was a boast, salt rubbed in the wound by the duke of a small province who had made the emperor bend to his will.

The humiliation of it tasted like rotten meat and sat sour in William's belly.

The duke of Austrobaurg was a thick, short man with a brushy mustache and eyes as green as a sea swell. His long black hair was streaked gray, and his expression was imperious as he drew rein a few yards away.

One of his knights raised a hand and spoke.

"The Duke Alfreix of Austrobaurg greets the empire of Crotheny and wishes well-meeting."

Robert cleared his throat. "The emperor—"

William cut him off, speaking in Hanzish. "What is this, Austrobaurg? Where is my sister? Where is Lesbeth?"

To his astonishment, the duke appeared puzzled.

"Lord Emperor?" he said. "I have no knowledge of Her Highness. Why should you ask me of her?"

William tried to count to seven. He made it only to five.

"I have no patience for this nonsense," he exploded. "You have what you wanted: twenty Sorrovian ships lie at the bottom of the sea. Now you will return my sister, or by Saint Fendve I will burn every one of your cities to the ground."

The duke shifted his gaze to Robert. "What is His Majesty talking about?" he demanded. "We had an agreement."

"You know very well what my royal brother speaks of," Robert snarled.

"Your Highness," Austrobaurg said, looking back to William, "I make nothing of this. I am here at your behest, to settle the matter between Saltmark and the Sorrows. This war benefits no one, as we agreed in our letters."

"Robert?" William asked, turning to his brother.

Robert cackled and kicked his horse to full gallop. William watched him go, his mouth gaping.

And as he stood confused, and his knights began to shout and reach for arms, the earth vomited up death.

At first William thought it a strange flock of darkling birds, winging up from some subterranean nest, for the air was full of black flight and fearsome humming. Then the part of him that had once—so long ago—been a warrior sorted it out, as an arrow pierced Sir Ananias through the eye and pushed its blood-head through the back of his skull.

Twenty yards away, a trench had appeared as the archers hidden there pushed up its coverings of cut sod. They were clad in raven black, like the arrows they shot.

"Treachery!" Austrobaurg cried, desperately trying to wheel his mount and find cover behind his men. "Crothanic treachery!"

"No!" William cried, but the Austrobaurg knights were already engaged with his own, and swords were spilling blood. Only he seemed to notice that both sides were falling from the deadly aim of the archers.

"There's our enemy!" he shouted, drawing his sword and waving it toward the trench. "The enemy of us both!" *Robert has betrayed me.* He tried to fight clear to charge the archers, gasping as a shaft glanced off his breastplate. He watched as Sir Tam Dare, his cousin, made for the murderers, and saw him fall, quilled like a hedgehog.

An Austrobaurg knight went down in the same fashion. The head flew from the shoulders of Sir Avieyen MaqFergoist, cut by the sword and arm of a knight wearing the crest of house Sigrohsn.

A horse screamed, his own, and William saw an arrow in its neck. It reared so as to take another in the belly, then crashed to earth, twisting as it went. William twisted himself, felt a brief, grinding snap of bone as the beast covered him. The horse writhed off, kicking. A hoof—maybe that of his own horse, maybe another—struck William in the head, and for a time he knew nothing.

He came back to the sea wind, and a view over the cliffs. He was propped sitting against a stone, feet facing the water, and his head hurt terribly. He tried to rise and found his legs wouldn't work.

"Welcome back to us, brother."

William turned his head, sending splinters of pain down his neck. Robert stood there beside him, looking—not at him—but out toward the horizon. The sun had clotted the mist into clouds, and the waves danced now in fitful sunlight.

"What has happened?" William asked. He wasn't dead yet. Perhaps if he pretended continued ignorance, Robert would choose another course. "The ambush—"

"They are all quite dead, save me."

"And me," William corrected.

Robert clucked his tongue. "No, Wilm, you're merely a ghost, a messenger to our ancestors."

William looked at his brother's face. It was quieter than he had ever seen it, almost serene.

"You're going to kill me, brother?" he asked.

Robert scratched his neck absently. "You're already dead, I told you. Your back broke when you fell from your horse. Have some dignity, Wilm."

Hot tears started in William's eyes, but he held them back. The very air seemed unreal, too yellow, like the colors in a dream.

He pushed down his fear and dread along with his tears. "Why, Robert? Why this slaughter? Why murder me?"

"Don't worry," Robert said. "You'll have plenty of company on your journey west," Robert told him. "Muriele dies today. And your daughters. Lesbeth is already there, awaiting you."

"All of them? All of them?" William could move his hands, he found, though they shook as if palsied. "You filthy beast. You're no Dare. You're no brother of mine."

A touch of anger at last entered Robert's voice. "But you'd already decided that, hadn't you, Wilm? If you thought me a brother, you would never have betrothed Lesbeth without asking me. I could never forgive you that."

"*You* killed her. You killed her and cut off her finger so I would think— Why? And my children? My wife? All for a single slight?" He had his hand on the hilt of his *echein doif*, now, the little knife every warrior kept concealed in a special place.

The knife of last resort.

"And for the combined thrones of Hansa and Crotheny, and one day Lier, as well," Robert said absently. "But the slight might have been enough. I have been too often neglected by this family. Too often betrayed."

"You are mad. Crotheny will not have you, not for long. And Hansa—"

"Is almost mine already." He smiled. "There is a secret I have. It will stay so, for now. There are ways of talking to the dead, and even though your spirit will wander far from the houses of our ancestors, I am not so foolish as to take that risk. But I will thank you for your help, brother."

"Help?"

"I could not have sent our ships against the Sorrows. You did that. Did you know that the lords of Liery have discovered the identity of those ships? Had you lived another few days, you would have had an earful, I'll tell you. You should thank me for sparing you the righteous pomposity of that old de Liery fool, Fail."

"I don't understand."

"Can't you just think for once, Wilm? The sea lords discovered that we've been aiding Saltmark against their allies. I let slip the hints that led them to know."

"But I agreed to that only because I thought Lesbeth—"

"Hush and listen. They'll never know that, of course. Everyone who believed the story of Lesbeth's kidnap is dead. The hue and cry over your policy is already begun, and now you and Austrobaurg, dead, in the midst of trying to conclude a lasting peace. Very suspicious. Especially since you were slain with Lierish arrows." His smile was ghastly.

"It'll be war," William groaned. "By the saints, it will be war with Liery."

"Yes, especially when Muriele's death is discovered. Her family will not take that lightly."

"Why Muriele? Why my girls?"

"You killed the girls when you legitimized them to replace you. Muriele had to die, of course. She is beautiful, and I would not mind making her my queen, but she is too strong in temper."

William understood suddenly. "Charles?"

"Exactly so. Your poor idiot son will be emperor, and I will be his prime minister. The girls—even Elseny—might have developed minds of their own. Too much of their mother in them. But Charles—never."

"I see," William murmured dully, willing Robert to draw nearer. "But if you plan to rule our country, why do you court war with Liery? It makes no sense. It will only weaken you."

Robert laughed. "Exactly so. Hansa could never have triumphed over a strong Crotheny that maintained Liery as an ally, not even with a bumbler like you on the throne. Your generals, after all, have great sense, some of them. But now—at the very least, this will drive the sea lords from our side, if not provoke them to war. Either way this gives Hansa the advantage in the coming war."

"The coming . . . You *want* Hansa to conquer Crotheny? Are you *completely* mad?"

"You see?" Robert whispered. "Even you can learn to reason, if only a little. Too late, I think. And now, dear brother, it's time to bid you farewell."

He walked to William's feet and bent to grasp them.

"Wait. How did you kill Muriele?"

"I didn't, obviously, since I'm here and she's at Cal Azroth. Indeed, it isn't even through my agency that she shall die. Others have seen to that."

"Who?"

Robert looked coy. "No, no. I can't tell. Just some people with whom I share common goals, for the time being. Only for the time being." He licked his lips. "They desired Muriele dead for . . . superstitious reasons. I made use of their credulity. Now, if you'll just bear up with a little of that famous Dare stoicism . . ."

William saw Robert grasp his ankles, but felt nothing. Robert tugged him a few inches toward the cliff's edge.

"Tell me where the key is, by the by," Robert said. "You aren't wearing it."

"What key?"

"William, please. Don't be petty, now of all times. The emperor must possess the key to the cell of the Kept."

A brief hope intruded on William. "I can show you where it is," he said. "But I will not tell you."

Robert stroked his beard thoughtfully, then shook his head. "I will find it. Likely it's in the coffer in your room."

He returned to his task.

Saint Fendve give me the strength, William prayed.

"Tell me one last thing, Robert," he asked. "What did you do with Lesbeth's corpse?"

"I buried it in the garden on the point."

William's feet were almost dangling over the cliff, now. Robert frowned, seeing that he couldn't drag his brother straight off. "I see how to do it," he muttered, more to himself than to William. "Less dignified, but that's how it is."

He pulled William's dead legs, changing his position so that he was parallel to the edge. William heard the gulls below. If Robert threw his legs over now, the weight would take the rest of him.

"I didn't mean where did you bury her, Robert," William said. "I meant what did you do with the body before you buried it, besides cut off the finger? A clever man like you, surely there must be some fun to be had with a sister's corpse, especially a sister you so unnaturally desired—"

He was cut off by a kick in the head, and the bloodred flash that blinded him.

"I never!" Robert shrieked, his calm shattered like brittle glass. "We *never*! My love for her was pure—"

"Pure rut-lust, you loathsome shit."

The foot came again, but this time William caught it and drove the sharp of his echein doif into his brother's calf. Robert shrieked at the unexpected pain and fell with his knee on William's chest. With an inarticulate cry, William rose up and drove the knife at Robert's heart.

It sunk in to the hilt.

Then Robert gave him a great shove, and he was in the air, without weight. He clawed for a handhold, almost found one . . . and then there were no more to be had.

The rocks caught him, but there was no pain. The spray of the sea, the salty blood of the world, spattered on his face.

Muriele, he thought. *Muriele.*

In the deeps he heard the draugs singing, mournful and greedy, coming for him.

At least he'd killed Robert.

His eyes closed, and the wind died, and then, like a figure in a shadow play, a shape appeared against a gray background. Tall, man-shaped and yet not, antlers like a stag's spreading from its head. The figure gestured, and William saw Eslen a smoking ruin, held in its palm. He saw the heartlands of Crotheny blasted and withered in the other outstretched hand. In its eyes, as in a fire-lit mirror, he saw war. Far, far away, William heard the keen bray of a horn.

The stag-crowned figure began to grow, not at all like a man now, but like a forest, his horns multiplying to make the branches, his body stretching and tearing into dark boughs and thorny, creeping vines. And as he grew, the dark thing spoke a single name.

Anne.

The name broke his soul from his body, and that was the end of William II, emperor of Crotheny.

Robert's mouth worked, trying to draw air. He stared at the hilt in his breast, feeling foolish.

"Good for you, Wilm," he muttered. "Good for you, saints damn you." It was a strange moment to feel pride for his brother, but there it was.

"My prince!"

Robert recognized the voice of the captain of his Nightstriders, but it sounded far away.

Robert didn't look back; he couldn't tear his gaze from the hilt of the knife. From his perspective, it stood like a tower against the sea.

Far away, he thought he heard the wild sounding of a trumpet, and then the sky fell on him.

CHAPTER SIX

THE EVE OF FIUSSANAL

ANNE, AUSTRA, AND SEREVKIS STROLLED in the gardens of the countess Orchaevia. Laughter and music suffused the twilight, blossoms of fantastic color and shape perfumed the air, and the mood was, overall, undeniably gay.

It made Anne intensely uncomfortable, and she didn't know why.

Part of it was surely the borrowed dress; it was a bit too tight and such a bright green it nearly hurt her eyes. But the most of her discomfort was lurking anonymously in the back of her mind until Austra put a light on it with a simple observation.

"This reminds me of Elseny's birthday," she said. "All these flowers."

"That's it," Anne muttered.

"What?"

"Nothing."

But that *was* it. It was the festival of Saint Fessa—or as they called her here, *Lady* Fiussa. Fiussa was the patroness of flowers and vegetation, and in the early days of autumn, when Fiussa departed for her long sleep, it was customary to wish her well and pray for her to return the next spring. Thus, as at Elseny's birthday, there were flowers everywhere, many dried in the spring to retain their color.

Austra noticed her discomfort, of course, and probed at it. "They make much of the Fiussanal here, don't they?" she said cautiously. "Much more so than in Eslen."

"Yes," Anne answered distractedly, not caring to put her mouth on the bait. She hadn't told Austra about her visions. She wasn't sure she intended to. She'd never kept secrets from her best friend, but now that she'd started down that road it would be difficult to turn back.

Serevkis rescued her without meaning to.

"Indeed?" the Vitellian girl remarked. "How is Fiussanal celebrated in Crotheny?"

"We exchange lockets with pressed flowers," Austra told her. "We build a feinglest in the sacred horz and drink the last of the new wine."

"What's a feinglest?" Serevkis asked.

"It's a sort of wickerwork, filled with flowers," Anne told her. "I think the custom came from Liery."

"Ah." Serevkis grinned. "We have that custom, I think, though we name it differently. Follow me. I think I saw the horz around here." They walked past a rambling stand of olive trees cheery with box-shaped paper lanterns, along a wing of the triva to a small walled garden.

There, beside a gnarled, ancient oak, stood a woman made of flowers. Her eyes were red poppies, her skirt of goldenrod and orange-damsel, her fingers purple asters.

The sight of her sent an awful, sick jolt through Anne, recalling vividly the women in her visions, the black roses, the horned thing in the woods.

"Like that?" Serevkis asked. "Is that a feinglest?"

"No," Anne said weakly. "I mean, yes, I guess it is, but in Crotheny we make cones, or tall baskets, or . . . never anything like that. Never anything that looks like a person."

But she remembered that *feinglest* was Leirish for *green woman*. A hollow of anxiety deepened in her.

"Let's leave this place," she said. In the lantern light, it looked as if the green woman was widening her smile, as if at any moment she would take a step toward them.

"I think she's pretty," Austra opined.

"I'm leaving." Anne turned and walked back toward the house and the sounds of celebration.

"Well, what's wrong with her?" Serevkis muttered, more puzzled than angry.

Anne quickened her pace. She wanted away from the garden, out from under the night sky, the fields and trees. She wanted lantern light and people and wine. Especially wine.

As they stepped back into the huge courtyard of the mansion, the countess herself came toward them, smiling. She wore a gown embroidered to the point of tastelessness with gold and silver flowering vines.

"My dear," she said to Anne. "That face! I hope you are enjoying yourself."

"I am, casnara," Anne lied. "Thank you so very much for your hospitality."

"It's nothing," the woman said, beaming. "And for you, my dear, I think I may have a special surprise."

Anne blinked. She had met the countess, of course, upon arrival when everyone else had, but couldn't imagine how she had drawn the woman's special attention.

"Here," the countess said, taking her aside and whispering in her ear. "Enter my house through the largest door, and you will find a staircase on your left. Follow it up, then down the hall, where it will open into my lavender garden. There you will find a young man who very much desires your company."

"I . . . a young man?"

The countess looked very pleased with herself. "By your face, you must be the one. I think you must know who I mean."

"Thank you, Countess," Anne said, trying to keep her expression neutral. But in her chest, her heart was doing strange things, and her mind was racing.

By now, Roderick would have received her letter. By now, he could be here. He might have heard of this fete, and impressed upon the countess his great love and need to see her, and of course this was the only time and place such a thing could happen. If he came to the coven, he would certainly be turned away. Perhaps he had already tried that, and no word had come to her.

"What was all that about?" Serevkis asked.

"Nothing," Anne replied. "She's asked Austra and me to do her a favor, that's all."

"I'll go along," Serevkis said.

"No!" Anne said, a bit too loudly. Several heads turned in her direction, including Sister Casita's. "No," she repeated more softly. "She asked that only Austra and I go."

"How mysterious," Serevkis said, a bit skeptically. "One would almost think something devious was going on."

"No, nothing of the sort," Anne insisted.

"Of what sort?" Serevkis asked, raising an eyebrow.

"I'll tell you about it later," Anne said. "Come on, Austra." She pulled her friend by the hand, toward the doorway the countess had indicated.

"What did the countess say to you?" Austra asked, after they had slipped through the portal and started up the stairs. "Wherever are we going?"

Anne turned and took Austra's hands in her own. "I think Roderick is here," she confided excitedly.

Austra's eyes went saucer-shaped. "How could that be?" she asked.

"I sent him a letter, and directions."

"What? How did you do that?"

"I'll explain in time. But it must be him."

They reached the end of the hall, which terminated in a wrought iron door. Beyond, leaves rustled softly in the breeze, and she could see the stars above a tiled wall. Anne felt herself nearly petrified with anticipation.

"He's supposed to be in there," Anne told her friend.

"Shall I wait here?" Austra asked. "To sound alarm if one of the sisters approaches?"

"No. Come in with me, until I am certain. I'll let you know if I want you to leave."

"Very well," Austra said. She didn't sound entirely happy.

Together the two girls stepped through the door. The garden was small, floored in red brick. Orange and lemon trees rose up from terracotta pots, and lavender grew in stone boxes making the air especially fragrant. A small fountain trickled water into a scalloped basin.

A man stood in the shadows. Anne could see his outline.

"Roderick?" she asked, almost breathless.

"I have no news from him, I'm afraid," the man said. She knew the voice at once, and her heart fell.

"You!" she said.

Cazio stepped into the moonlight and smiled, sweeping his hat from his head. "I told you I was guesting in the country," he said. "I must say, you look altogether different wearing clothes."

"Anne," Austra murmured, tugging at her sleeve. "Who is this? How do you know him?" She gave a sudden start. "And what does he mean about clothes?"

"I am Cazio Pachiomadio da Chiovattio," Cazio said, bowing again. "And you must be the lady Fiene's sister, so fair and graceful are you."

"Fiene?" Austra said, confused.

"Cazio knows me by my *real* name, not my coven name," Anne said, hoping Austra would catch on.

She did. "Oh," she said. "I see."

"Would you enchant me with your own name, lady?"

"It is Margry," Austra improvised.

Cazio reached out, took her hand, and raised it to his lips.

"Watch him," Anne warned her friend. "He uses honey where most use words."

"Better honey than lemon juice," Cazio said. He turned his head a little. "Can it be that you are annoyed with me, Lady Fiene?"

"No," Anne admitted, finding she wasn't. "It's just that I thought Roderick might have come."

"And you are disappointed. Rightly so. All went well with the dispatch of the letter, but perhaps the weather has been bad in the north. Any number of things might delay even a man who is deeply in love."

Anne thought she caught a subtle dig in that.

"Margry," Anne said, "could you wait in the hall and give alarm if anyone comes? I promise to explain this all to you later."

"As you wish," Austra said, a bit of rancor lurking in her voice.

When Austra had left the garden, Anne turned back to Cazio. "What did you want, then?" she asked bluntly.

To her surprise, he hesitated, as if searching for words, something she had not known him to do before.

"I don't know," he said at last. "The countess offered to arrange our meeting. I suppose I just wanted to know how you were doing."

Anne felt a bit of her guard drop away.

"I am well enough. What happened to your arm? It's bandaged."

"A scratch from swordplay. It was nothing."

"Swordplay? You were in a fight?"

His voice grew jauntier. "Not much of a fight. Five bandits. They didn't last long."

"Really?"

Again, he hesitated. "No," he admitted. "I got it in practice with my swordmaster. He was angry at me."

"For what reason?"

"He thinks I'm too distracted to fence. I think he's right."

Anne felt an odd little warmth in her belly. "What has distracted you?" she asked innocently.

"I think you know." His eyes were luminous in the dark, and for an instant . . .

"I told you, Cazio," she said.

"Told me what?" he asked mildly. "You haven't even told me your real name. And you complain of *my* honesty."

She was silent for a moment, then nodded. "I deserved that." She looked back up at him. "My name is Anne."

He took her hand. She meant to pull it away, but somehow failed. "I'm pleased to meet you, Anne." And he kissed the top of her hand.

"May I have that back now?" Anne asked.

"It was always yours."

"Did you send my letter at all?"

"Yes," he said. "I hoped he would come. I still hope so."

"Why?"

"Sometimes distance improves love. Sometimes it dissolves it. I think you deserve to know which has happened."

"Roderick loves me," Anne snapped.

"Let him prove it, then," Cazio replied.

"Do *you* love me then?" Anne asked, regretting the question in the same breath that asked it.

But Cazio didn't answer immediately. When he did, it was in that new, uncertain tone. "I do not think people fall in love so quickly."

That sounded honest, and somehow it upset Anne more than any declaration of love ever could have.

"In that case, what do you want from me?" she asked.

"To know you better," Cazio said softly.

Anne's throat felt thick. "And how will you do that?" she asked, trying to sound sarcastic. "Stare up at my tower all day?"

"I might," he replied. "If it is the only way to see you."

"This is ridiculous," Anne said. She glanced over her shoulder. "We'll be missed. We have to go."

"When can I see you again?"

"You can't," Anne replied, and with that she turned and went back out of the garden.

It was hard not to look back, but she managed it.

Cazio scuffed his foot in frustration and sighed. What was wrong with him? What did he care about this skinny, sickly pale, red-mopped witch anyway?

Nothing, that's what. This whole thing had been Orchaevia's scheme, not his.

A slight sound alerted him, and his hand flew to the hilt of Caspator, but it was only the other girl, the yellow-haired one.

"It was nice to meet you, Casnar Chiovattio," she said, and made a little curtsey.

Inspiration struck Cazio. "A moment, please," he said.

"I must follow my mistress."

"I implore you, casnara. Anne won't miss you for a moment or two." He paused. "Did you say mistress?"

"I'm her maid."

"And also in the coven?"

"I'm there, yes."

"And is your name really Margry?"

The girl looked behind her. "No, casnar, it isn't. My name is Austra."

Cazio put on what he considered to be his most effective smile.

"Now there is a proper name for a winsome creature like you," he purred.

"You shouldn't say things like that, casnar," the girl said, looking demurely down.

"Call me simply Cazio, if you please." He reached for her hair. "Was this spun from gold?"

She bridled at his touch. "Please, I must go." She started to withdraw.

"A moment." He stepped even closer. At first he thought she would flee, but she didn't. He drew very near and took her hand.

"This Roderick fellow, Anne's betrothed—is he so fine?"

"Betrothed?" Austra said, her eyes widening.

Aha! Cazio thought. *So not even really engaged!*

"I mean, yes, they are betrothed," Austra corrected.

Cazio let the falsehood pass. "But that wasn't my question. Answer me, pretty Austra."

"He is—" Her voice dropped. "I do not think him so fine. To be honest, I think you're much nicer, though I've just met you."

"Thank you, Austra. That's very kind of you."

"It's just that Anne can be . . . stubborn."

"Well, let her be, then," Cazio said. "I won't pursue someone who has no desire to be caught." He squeezed her hand. "Thank you for speaking to me," he said.

"It was my pleasure, Cazio."

He bowed, then wrinkled his brow in a show of consternation. "Oh, look," he told her, pointing to her mouth. "You've something on your lip."

"What?" She put her hand up, but he caught it, bent in quickly, and kissed her lips. She gave a little gasp and pulled back—not too violently.

"You see? There was a kiss there," he said. "But I got it."

He could see her white skin blush even in the faint light. Without another word she withdrew and fled down the hall after the vanished Anne.

Cazio watched her go, feeling pleased. Service hadn't done the trick. Maybe a little jealousy would, he thought. The hunter was back on the trail. Whistling, he went to gaze at the stars.

CHAPTER SEVEN

SACRIFICE

ASPAR KNELT TO EXAMINE the horse droppings on the trail and nodded to himself.

"We're close," he said gruffly. "Not even a day behind 'em. And they've been joined by more, maybe ten more."

Stephen watched what the holter was doing, trying to pick out the faint signs the older man was reading. "Do you think the newcomers are Sefry? This Fend fellow and his rogues?"

Aspar's expression darkened. "That's what your brother said, yah? That he was going to meet Fend at Cal Azroth?"

"I'm no brother of Desmond Spendlove's," Stephen replied, irritated by Aspar's tone. "Whatever he's about is nothing to do with the church."

"You seem mighty certain of that," Aspar said.

"Think, Holter," Stephen said. "The fratrex saved our lives. Would he have done that if the church was behind all this?"

Aspar straightened. "You tell me," he said seriously.

It still took Stephen aback when the holter really wanted his opinion. He recalled Desmond, that night at the monastery, talking about how he served the church. It had felt real, that conversation, like the one pure moment of honesty he had ever had from the murderous Spendlove.

"Brother Desmond answers to someone," Stephen allowed. "It might be someone in the church. It might not. He's not entirely sane, I think."

"You think he answers to Fend?" Aspar grunted.

Stephen examined that for a moment. "No," he said at last. "He spoke of Fend as a sort of coconspirator, and with a certain amount of distaste. I think Spendlove and your Sefry outlaw serve a higher master. I don't know who it could be."

"Well, the forest ends soon," Aspar said. "We're coming to the plain of Mey Ghorn, where Cal Azroth stands. They've met up, so whatever they're planning, it'll happen soon."

"Could we go around them? Reach the fortress before they do and warn the queen?"

"Maybe," Aspar mused. "Likely not."

"What then? Ten more makes sixteen men and Sefry. We can't fight them all."

Aspar arched one eyebrow. "We, Cape Chavel Darige? I could put what you know about fighting on the head of a beer and it would float."

"Yes, well, you could have taught me a little, Holter. I might have been some help."

"I could have taught you just enough to help you make a corpse of yourself," Aspar rebutted.

"So you'll kill them all yourself? How?"

Aspar grunted a laugh. "I never said I couldn't find a use for you. You could wave your arms and draw their arrows while I creep around behind."

"I'm willing to do that," Stephen said earnestly. "If it will work."

"That was a joke, boy."

"Oh," Stephen said, and his sarcasm got the better of his sense. "My mistake, but a natural one. A joke from you? Apologies, but the first time you see a fish fly, you're likely to think it's a bird." Then he sobered again. "Well, what, then?"

"I have no idea," the holter said. "I'll think of something before we catch up to them."

"Marvelous plan."

Aspar shrugged. "Do you have a better one? Something you read in a book, maybe?"

"Well," Stephen considered, "in the *Travels of Hinn*, when beset by brigands, Hinn and his companions made themselves seem more numerous by building figures of mud and straw."

"Yah. Were they able to make these figures walk?"

"Ah . . . no. But if we could lure Desmond and his men to come after us—"

"To fight our stick men?"

"Fine, maybe that wouldn't work. What if we set a trap? Dig a pit and put sharpened stakes in it, cover it over with leaves or something?"

Aspar nodded. "Fine idea. We'll dig this pit with our hands, shall we, before sunup? Maybe you can lead them in circles while the horses and I dig."

"I'm just trying to help," Stephen muttered. "And you asked."

"I did, didn't I?" Aspar sighed. "Next I'll ask for a clout on the head. It would be more useful." He remounted Ogre, then shot Stephen a more companionable glance. "Keep thinking," he said. "Who knows, maybe you'll actually come up with something helpful."

Stephen did prove himself useful a few bells later, when he waved for Aspar's attention. The holter caught the motion instantly and reined Ogre to a halt. Stephen tapped his ear, then pointed. He could hear men talking up ahead, and he was certain it was the rogue monks.

He had formed the opinion that none of the men they pursued had senses as well honed as his own, but there was still no point in taking chances. Thus far, remaining at the edge of his own hearing had kept them undetected. Stephen intended to treat it as a rule.

Aspar understood his signals and carefully dismounted. Stephen followed suit. The holter quietly commanded the horses to stay where they were, and the two men began creeping through the forest edge toward the source of the sound.

They stopped and crouched in a tangled mass of grapevines on the worn shoulders of a hill. Below, the forest broke into sparsely wooded fields, and beyond that a broad plain, green-gold in the afternoon sunlight.

Sixteen men were setting up camp around a small conical mound in the lightly wooded fringe. A couple of tents were already up. Ten of the figures wore broad-brimmed hats and their faces were wrapped in gauze; that would be the Sefry, Stephen mused. The rest were human, and their number included Desmond and his remaining monks. Stephen glanced over at Aspar, who wore a look he had come to recognize as quiet fury. Stephen raised an eyebrow, and the holter glanced back, mouthing a word.

Fend.

Doubtless the holter was already working out how to kill fifteen men so he could get to the one.

Aspar motioned for Stephen to remain where he was and prowled off so silently he might have been a forest cat. Stephen desperately wanted to ask him where he was going, but he didn't dare.

Once the holter had vanished from sight, Stephen lay there, watching, wondering what he was supposed to do.

Below, the monks and Sefry were soon done preparing their camp, but their activities didn't cease. In fact, the small mound became the focus of new activity. It was with foreboding that Stephen realized the hill must be a sedos.

It was cool, but sweat beaded on his brow as he crawled nearer, hiding at last behind the mounded roots of a huge oak on a lower part of the hill. His senses expanded, and the life of the forest pulsed through him in sound. The chattering of squirrels above him worried into his head, accompanied by the stridulations of crickets and cicadas anticipating the coming of dark, just a bell or so away. The clicking chorus of leaf-cutting ants going about their tasks tickled the drums of his ears. Finches twittered happily and jays protested the presence of Spendlove's party below.

He strengthened his concentration, and through the stir of forest heard his enemies talking.

Spendlove chanted in a language Stephen did not recognize, though every now and then he caught a word that sounded like Old Vadhiian. Two of the other monks—Seigereik and one Stephen didn't know—had been stripped to the waist, and one of the Sefry was painting strange glyphs or symbols on their chests. Yet another man—Stephen did not recognize him either, but did not think him a monk—had been stripped naked. He was taken to the top of the sedos and staked out spread-eagle. He had something stuffed in his mouth.

Where is Aspar? Stephen wondered desperately. Something very bad was about to happen, something that needed stopping. He searched the surroundings, but the holter could move so invisibly when he wanted to that even Stephen's saint-given senses couldn't always locate him.

Desmond switched languages, to Old Vadhiian, and Stephen was suddenly riveted. His mind translated so swiftly it was like hearing his native tongue.

One to open the way, dread power, and one to walk the way. A path of blood for the changeling, a soul to work the change.

Spendlove drew something from his robes, something that glittered so sharply it brought an ache to Stephen's eyes. Brother Desmond moved to the prone man, who tried to shriek but could not. Desmond knelt over the bound man, and Stephen realized with a dull shock that the terrible thing in his hand was some sort of knife, as the monk split the man open from sternum to groin and begin pulling out his innards. The struggling quickly diminished to twitching.

Stephen's morning meal rose to his throat, but he kept it there, tightening his will, concentrating on the details of what was happening, trying to abstract them, to pretend it wasn't the end of a human life he was watching, that those weren't intestines Spendlove and his men were spreading in strange patterns around the still-writhing figure.

After a time, seemingly satisfied, Spendlove beckoned one of the bare-chested monks—Seigereik—to step forward. Seigereik did so, face grim, straddling over the still-twitching, disemboweled figure.

"Are you ready, Brother?" Spendlove asked softly.

"I am, Brother Spendlove," Seigereik said, his voice tight with determination.

"Be strong," Spendlove bade him. "There will be a moment of disorientation. There will be pain, but you must bear it. And you *must* succeed. There can be no more failure."

"I will not fail, Brother Spendlove."

"I know you won't, Brother Seigereik, my warrior."

Seigereik lifted his arms and closed his eyes.

"A soul to work the change," Spendlove intoned, and struck Seigereik in the heart with the glittering knife. Stephen choked back a gasp as the monk's legs folded and he dropped lifeless. The air around the sedos seemed to darken, and something like a high keening of wind whipping black smoke soughed off through the treetops.

What have I just seen? Stephen wondered. Two sacrifices, one willing, one not. And Seigereik was supposed to complete a task after he was dead? It didn't make any sense. Unless . . .

Would the corpse rise again? Had Desmond done the unthinkable and broken the law of death?

But the monk's body remained where it had fallen. No, it was the soul that had been sent away, wrapped in dark magic.

He shook himself away from his suppositions. The Sefry and two of the remaining monks were mounting their horses.

"He'd better succeed," one of the Sefry—by his eye patch, probably Fend—remarked.

"Your way is prepared," Spendlove assured him. "It might even be over by the time you get there."

"I doubt that."

"One more will make it certain," Spendlove replied. He knelt over the disemboweled man on the ground. "There's still life in him. I can probably use him again. Brother Ashern, prepare yourself."

The other painted monk nodded.

"Why take chances?" Fend asked, waving at the disemboweled captive. "Use the girl."

"I thought you wanted to kill her in front of the holter," Spendlove said. "After all, you brought her all this way."

"I had that whim," Fend said. "It has passed. Just leave her where he'll find her."

Desmond glanced at the dying man.

"You may be right," he allowed. "If he pops off in the middle, Ashern's sending will go awry."

Fend and his Sefry rode off. A few moments later Spendlove chopped his head at one of the men, and said, "Bring her out." A struggling woman was led from one of the tents.

Holter, where are you? Stephen wondered frantically. Aspar White was nowhere to be seen.

If the holter noticed Fend riding off—and of course he would—he would probably follow in hopes of killing him. Stephen realized he could no longer count on Aspar White; the man's obsession with the one-eyed Sefry was obvious, though he had never deigned to explain why.

Stephen thought he knew what Spendlove was up to, now, though it seemed incredible. If he didn't act very soon, the young woman below was going to be murdered in a very unpleasant way.

He'd just seen one man die that way. He would die himself before he watched it happen again. Steeling himself, he began moving toward the camp as quickly as he could.

CHAPTER EIGHT

THE PLAIN OF TERROR

A SAINT'S BREATH OF WIND sighed along the battlements of Cal Azroth as Neil gazed past the queen to the sun melting on the distant green horizon. The plain of Mey Ghorn was open and still, the only motion in sight the occasional whirl of swallows overhead. The triple ring of canals around the fortress was already in shadow, and soon their waters would hold stars. Off to his right he heard soldiers talking in the garrison, connected to the inner keep by a causeway.

The queen often stood like this at evening, facing Eslen.

Laughter bubbled up from the gap between keep and garrison. Elseny, by the sound of it. Neil glanced behind and down and saw her there. From above, the circle of her yellow dress and her dark hair made her resemble a sunflower. She was in the citadel's narrow, high-walled horz, on the big flat rock that was at the center of it, putting flowers in the wickerwork feinglest two of the old serving women had built earlier that day. Neil had never seen one exactly like this, vaguely human in shape. In Liery it was considered ill luck to build one so, though he had never heard why.

A movement to the side caught his eye, and with a start he realized he could see the edge of a second dress, peeking from beneath the canopy of an ash tree, this one blue and less noticeable in the fading light. Then came the flash of a white face looking up, and Fastia's gaze touching his own. She quickly looked back down, while Neil bit his lip, a blush creeping up his face. Fastia often had avoided him in the two ninedays that had passed since that evening in Glenchest. He didn't know if she hated him or . . .

Nor does it matter, he told himself. *Remember what Erren said.* He couldn't control what he felt, but he could certainly control what he *did.* With one exception, that was what he had been doing all of his life.

Once was enough, though. The unfamiliar feel of failure rested heavy in his heart.

"Ten thousand men and women died on this plain," the queen said softly.

Neil started and turned his gaze guiltily from the horz, but the queen wasn't looking at him. He wasn't even sure she was talking to him.

"Is it so, Your Majesty?" he asked, not certain how to respond. "Was it in battle against Hansa?"

"Hansa?" the queen said. "No. Hansa wasn't even a dream in those days. Nor was Crotheny. In those days, the houses of men weren't divided. The ancestors of Marcomir fought beside the Dares."

"It was the war against the Skasloi, then?"

She nodded. "They had loosed their shackles and burned the citadels in the east, but that was nothing if they did not reach Ulheqelesh and win there." She turned to him, and with a shock he saw tears in her eyes. "Ulheqelesh was where Eslen now stands."

"I never knew its name in the demon's tongue," Neil replied. He felt profoundly ignorant.

"We don't speak it often. Most do not know it. It is one of the burdens of royalty that we must read the oldest histories."

"And the battle here, at Mey Ghorn?"

"The name has become corrupted over time. In the old tongue it was *Magos Gorgon*, the Plain of Terror."

"And the battle—it was a great one?"

"There was no battle," the queen said. "They marched and they died, their flesh stripped from their bones, their bones burned into dust. And yet they marched on."

"They never saw their enemy? There was never a foe to lift arms against?"

The queen shook her head. "They marched and they died," she

repeated. "Because they knew they must. Because the only other choice was to live as slaves."

Neil stared out at the darkening plain, a strange tickle of awe working in him.

"Every footstep on that plain must fall on the remains of those warriors."

The queen nodded.

"It is a terrible story," Neil offered. "Warriors should die in battle."

"Warriors should die in bed," the queen countered, her voice suddenly edged with anger. "Didn't you hear me? Ten thousand ghosts are bound in the soil of Mey Ghorn. Ten thousand brothers and sisters, the fathers and mothers of Hansa, Crotheny, Saltmark, Tero Gallé, Virgenya—every nation of Everon has bones in this dirt. They were noble, and they were proud, and their only real weapon was the hope that their sons and daughters would see a better day, know a better world.

"And see what we have done with it. What do we fight about now? Fishing disputes. Trade tariffs. Bickering over borders. Our whole race has become petty and vicious. We fight for nothing." She waved her hand to encompass the land around. "We denigrate their memory. How ashamed they must be of us."

Neil stood silent for a few moments, until the queen turned to face him.

"Sir Neil?" she said softly. "You have something to say?"

He kept his gaze on hers, on those eyes so like her daughter's.

"I know little of trade tariffs or politics," he admitted. "I know little of the deep histories."

"But you know something," she said.

"I knew my grandfather, Dovel MeqFinden. He was a good man. He made little ships of wood for me when I was a boy, and he trooped across the rocky fields of Skern with me on his shoulders. He showed me the sea, and told me of the beautiful Fier de Meur and the terrible draugs who dwell in its depths."

"Go on."

"Skern is a small place, Majesty. You may not know that in those days our overlord was a duke from Hansa, and it had been thus for six generations. Our own language was forbidden us, and one half of our crops and cattle were forfeit to that man and his house. When that brought us to starvation, we must needs borrow from the duke, and to pay him back we must go into his service. We are a proud people, Majesty, but not so proud as to let our children starve."

"Your grandfather?"

"A plague came and killed the most of his cattle, and he could not pay what he had borrowed. He was forced to work in the stables of our lord, the duke. One day a daughter of that lord sat a horse too wild for her. My grandfather warned her against it, but she ignored him. She was thrown."

"She was killed?"

"She was not. Ten men were present to bear witness. My grandfather reached her and pulled her from beneath the hooves of the horse, taking a hard blow. He saved her life. But in so doing, he touched her, the great lady of a Hanzish house. For that he was hanged."

Sympathy softened the queen's face. "I'm sorry," she said.

Neil shrugged. "It is one story of many," he said. "Many times we tried to rise against our Hanzish masters. Always we failed, until the day Fail de Liery came over the sea with his boats and brought us arms, and fought beside us, and drove the duke and all of his men back to their homeland. Perhaps Liery fought for Skern due to some petty dispute— I do not know. I only know that now my people can feed and clothe themselves and are not hanged for speaking their native tongue. I know we can live now like men and not like Hanzish lapdogs. This is a small thing, perhaps, compared to what happened on this plain. But in my heart, Majesty, I know tyranny did not end with the Skasloi, and the fight for what is right did not end with the men who marched across Mey Ghorn. I know my opinion lacks education—" He felt suddenly as if he had said far too much. Who was he to contradict the queen?

"No," she said, a small smile brightening her face. "The only thing your opinion lacks is the jaded view from the towers of the highborn. Thank the saints for you, Neil MeqVren. You put me in my place."

"Majesty, I never meant to—"

"Hush. I'm done brooding, thanks to you. Let's speak of this no more, but go down and make merry. It's the eve of Fiussanal, you know."

Memory flashed, of a blue dress and a face glancing up at him, and eagerness and trepidation exchanged blows on the battlefield of his heart.

But when they reached the horz, Fastia was nowhere to be seen.

Night gentled upon the fortress, and by the toll of the eighth bell the preparations for Fiussanal were done and even the excited Elseny was quiet in her chambers awaiting sleep.

Sleep eluded Neil, however. The memory of Fastia by moonlight haunted him, but something besides that nagged him. Perhaps it was the queen's talk of the host of ancient dead around Cal Azroth that drew him back outside, to the rampart of the tower in which she had her apartments. From there he would notice any who might come and go into the royal residence, and so prosecute his duty. But he could also gaze over the haunted, moonlit plain, studying it for any wisps of mist or light that might remark some sign of ghosts.

After the tenth bell tolled, his eyelids were finally drooping and the moon was setting on the horizon. Neil was considering a return to his quarters when, with a faint thrill, at the corner of his eye he detected motion.

Staring straight on, he saw nothing at first, but from the periphery of his vision he made out several figures moving swiftly toward the castle.

He did not think they were ghosts.

He descended the tower as far as the battlements, hoping for a better view and to alert the watch. What he had seen could have been anything—a pack of wild dogs, a Sefry band, messengers from the court—but his watchword was suspicion.

He saw no better from the battlements, but in the courtyard below them he noticed something that raised his hackles. Two human figures lay there unmoving. The moon was not yet risen, so he couldn't make out who they were, but the positions in which they lay made him doubt they were merely asleep from too much drink.

He hesitated only long enough to wonder if he should put on the rest of his armor. He wore his leather gambeson and a light chain hauberk, and donning the plate would take far too long. Grimly, heart pounding, he started toward the stair, keeping his steps light.

Down in the courtyard, he found his worst fears realized; the massive double gate stood open, and he could see stars beyond. Now, too, he could see the insignia of the Royal Footguard on the fallen men, and the pools of blood that pronounced them dead.

A man he hadn't seen from above lay crumpled against the base of the stairs. He was still alive, though his breath wheezed strangely. Neil approached carefully, gaze sweeping the compound. To the right of the open gate stood a second portal, still closed, beyond which lay the causeway leading to the garrison. To his left was the queen's tower. When he detected no one, and no movement in either direction, he turned his attention to the injured man.

With a start, he saw it was Sir James Cathmayl. His throat was cut, and he was trying futilely to stop the flow of his life's blood with his own two hands. His eyes fastened on Neil, and he tried to say something. No sound emerged, only more blood, but the downed knight gestured at something behind Neil, and his dying eyes glittered bright warning.

Neil flung himself to the right, and steel smote the cobbles where he'd knelt. He turned and brought Crow to guard.

A man stood there, a fully armored knight. "Death has found you," the knight told him.

"Death has found me many times," Neil replied. "I've always sent her away hungry." Then, raising his voice, he shouted, "Alarm! The gate is breached, and enemies are within!"

The knight laughed and stepped closer, but didn't raise his weapon, and with a thrill of astonishment, Neil saw it was Vargus Farre.

"Traitor," Neil rasped, leaping forward, scything Crow in a hard blow down.

The knight merely retreated, now bringing his weapon to guard.

"Don't you feel it, Sir Knight?" Vargus asked. There was something wrong with his accent, with the way he spoke, and despite the fact that the man wore Sir Vargus' face, Neil suddenly doubted it was really the man he knew at all.

"Don't you?" Sir Vargus repeated. "Death arriving in you?"

"What is this, Sir Vargus, or whatever you be? For whom have you opened the gate?"

"You'll feel it soon."

And suddenly, Neil did. Something struck him like flame between the eyes, but a flame that ate out from within. He heard a voice that wasn't his, inside his ears, felt a will not his own scratching within his skull. With a shriek he fell to his knees, Crow clattering beside him.

The knight who could not be Sir Vargus laughed again, and something behind Neil's lips bubbled a sardonic reply.

CHAPTER NINE

NIGHT VISITORS

"WELL, THAT WAS RATHER DULL," Anne muttered, lighting a taper to illuminate the tower room she shared with Austra.

"Really?" Austra said, her voice somehow faraway sounding. "I found it entertaining enough."

"I would go so far as to call it quaint," Anne replied.

"Quaint," Austra repeated, nodding. She went to the window and looked out at the night. Anne sighed and began changing out of her dress.

"It was nice to wear a gown again, at least," she said, "even one in such questionable taste." She held the empty dress up before her, then, shrugging, folded it carefully. She pulled her coarse sleeping shift over her head.

"It's back to lessons tomorrow," she said, trying to distract herself from the lingering disappointment that Cazio hadn't been Roderick, and the uneasy feelings the shameless Vitellian had stirred in her. "We're learning the uses of alvwort, I hear, which I'm much looking forward to."

"Uh-huh," Austra murmured.

Anne turned a suspicious glance on her friend.

"We're also having a lesson on changing babies into puppies, and the reverse."

"Good," Austra said, nodding. "That will be interesting."

"Saints, what's wrong with you?" Anne demanded of her friend. "You aren't even listening to me."

Austra turned guiltily from the window.

"Nothing," she said. "Nothing's wrong. I'm just sleepy."

"You don't *look* sleepy. You look positively excitable."

"Well, I'm not," Austra insisted. "I'm sleepy."

"Yes? Then what's got you so interested outside?"

"Nothing. It's just pretty, tonight."

"There's no moon. You can't see anything."

"I can see plenty," Austra replied. "Maybe I'll see Roderick riding up."

"Austra Laesdauter, are you making fun of me?"

"No, I'm not. I hope for your sake he does come. You still love him, don't you?"

"Yes."

"And this what's-his-name—"

"Cazio?"

"Yes, that's it. How did you meet him? You said you would tell me."

Anne considered that. "This is one of *those* secrets, Austra," she said finally. "One of our sacred ones."

Austra placed her hand on her heart. "By Genya Dare, I'll keep this secret."

Anne explained how she'd found her way out of the cave and met Cazio, still leaving out any mention of the mysterious woman and her newfound senses. She felt ashamed for that, but something still warned her it was prudent.

"So you see," Anne concluded, "whatever impression Cazio made tonight, at heart he is an ill-mannered rogue."

"A handsome one, though," Austra said.

Anne opened her mouth, closed it, and then laughed. "You're *taken* with him," she said.

"What?" Austra's face scrunched in dismay. "No, I'm not."

Anne folded her arms and looked skeptically down one shoulder. "You stayed behind me a bit," she said. "What happened? What did he say to you?"

Austra blushed deeply enough that it was visible even by candlelight. "It's as you say," she said, looking toward the corner of the room as if she had lost something there. "He is an errant rogue."

"Austra, tell me what happened."

"You'll be angry," Austra said.

"I'll be angry only if you keep so secretive and phayshot. Tell me!"

"Well—he gave me a bit of a kiss, I think."

"You think?" Anne asked. "What do you mean, you *think*? He either kissed you or he didn't."

"He kissed me then," Austra said, a bit defiantly.

"You *are* taken with him," Anne accused again.

"I don't even know him."

"The fickleness of the man!" Anne exploded. "First he's doting on me, then twelve heartbeats later he's slavering over you. What could you see in such a faithless heart?"

"Nothing!" Austra said. "Only . . ."

"Only what?"

"Well, it was nice. The kiss. He kisses well."

"I wouldn't know how he kisses. I wouldn't want to."

"You shouldn't. You have Roderick for that. Anyway, I'm sure neither of us will ever see Casnar da Chiovattio again."

"If the saints are kind."

Austra shrugged and turned back to the window. "Oh!" she said.

"What is it? Is he down there?" Anne said. "That would be typical of him, to follow us back here and bother us."

"No, no," Austra averred. "Not unless he brought friends. Look at all the torches."

"What? Let me see."

Anne shouldered her way into the window, and saw that Austra was right. A long glowworm of lights was approaching the coven. Anne heard the snorting of horses and the sound of hooves.

"Who could that be, at this hour?" Anne wondered.

"A Sefry caravan, perhaps," Austra offered. "They travel in darkness."

"Maybe," Anne replied dubiously.

At that moment, the coven bells began to peal the signal to gather.

"I suppose we're going to find out," Anne said.

o   o   o

Sister Casita met them in the courtyard at the foot of the stairs, where other sleepy girls were already beginning to converge, murmuring in irritation and confusion at being wakened so soon after bed.

"Go to the wine cellar," Casita said, gesturing in the general direction with a willow wand. "Remain there until you are told to return to your rooms."

"What's going on?" Anne asked. "We saw riders approaching from the tower."

"Hush, Sister Ivexa. Keep quiet and do as you're told. Go to the wine cellar."

"I'm going nowhere until I know what's wrong," Anne insisted.

Before Anne could dodge, Sister Casita switched her across the mouth with her wand. Anne tried to cry out, but found her lips frozen together.

"Obey me," Casita said, to all of the girls assembled there.

Seeing what had happened to Anne, no one else dared question her. Anne, furious and frightened, nevertheless went with the rest of the girls toward the cellar.

The sacaum Sister Casita had laid on Anne's lips wore off a few moments later, leaving only an odd tingling in her jaws. By then she and Austra had reached the head of the stairs that led below the coven, but rather than descending them with the rest of the girls, Anne pulled Austra into a side corridor.

"Come on," she said.

"Where?"

"Up on the wall. I'm going to find out what the matter is."

"Are you mad? Haven't you learned not to disobey yet?"

"We'll keep hidden. But I'm going to find out. Something is wrong. I think the coven is under attack."

"Why would anyone attack a coven?"

"I don't know. That's why I'm not going into the wine cellar."

"Anne—"

"Go with the rest if you like," Anne said. "I know what I'm doing."

She turned and walked off. After a moment she heard a sigh and the soft swish of Austra following her.

They wound past the kitchen and the herb garden beyond, to where the small arbor of grapevines sent tendrils out to climb the cracked stone. There, Anne remembered, was a narrow stair that led to the top of the wall that surrounded the coven. It was steep and crumbly, and she slipped twice, but soon enough they had reached the top and the walkway there. She began softly moving toward the front gate, Austra behind her. Once, they heard running feet and ducked into the shadows of a tower as a robed figure entered it. Anne listened to the muted sound of footsteps ascending its heights, then scurried past.

The large court inside the front gate was filled with dark-robed figures, the greatest part of the members of the Cerian order. Sister Secula wasn't with them; she stood on the wall above the gate, along with Sisters Savitor and Curnax, looking down at whoever was there. Anne could hear that she was talking, but couldn't make out the words. She crept ever nearer, Austra still following, and together they discovered an outjutting section of the bastion from which they could see both Sister Secula and the men who had arrived outside the gate.

"Saints!" Anne murmured.

In the torchlight she made out about thirty riders, handsomely mounted on warhorses and clad in full plate. None of them, however, bore standards—not even their leader, who wore armor gilded at the edges and sat his horse about two yards in front of the rest. He had his visor pushed up, but Anne couldn't discern his features at the distance. He was talking to Sister Secula—or, rather, she was talking to him.

". . . the matter," the mestra was saying. "We are under the protection of the church and the meddisso. If you do not heed me, the consequences will be dire. Now, go." Her voice was taut with command, and even though her words weren't directed at Anne, they made her wince. She wouldn't want to be that knight, whoever he was.

The knight, however, seemed unimpressed. "That I may not, lady," he shouted up. Behind him, spurs rattled and horses stamped. The smell of burning tar from torches wafted over the wall. The whole scene was unreal, dreamlike.

"I am sworn to this," the knight continued. "Send her out, and we can be done with this business. Make whatever complaints you wish."

"You think because you come as cowards, bearing no standard or emblem, we will not find who you are?" Sister Secula returned. "Go. You will get nothing here save the curses of the saints."

"The saints are with us, Sister," the knight replied matter-of-factly. "Our cause has no blemish, and I do not fear any shinecraft you may loose on me. I warn you once more. Send me down Anne Dare, or you will force me to incivility."

"Anne!" Austra gasped.

Anne took Austra's hand, her heart picking up a few beats. The world seemed to whirl as everything that was happening realigned itself.

This was about *her*.

"I warn *you* once more," Secula told the knight. "Trespass is beyond bearing. No man may set foot in this coven."

Anne couldn't see the mestra's face, but she could imagine it, and wondered if the nameless knight was actually meeting her gaze.

"I regret what I must do," the man said. "But you have forced me to it."

He gestured, and the ranks of his cavalry parted, and through it came ten archers and as many men bearing a wooden beam clad at one end in a head of steel. The archers trained their weapons on the sisters on the wall.

"Open the gate," the knight said. "For the love of the saints, open it and let us in."

For answer, Sister Secula spread her fingers, and Anne felt a sudden prickling across her skin, a sensation akin to and yet different from facing a fire. Something dark spun out from the mestra's fingertips, like a spiderweb but more gossamer and insubstantial. It drifted onto the men below. When it touched the tallest, they shrieked and threw hands up to their eyes. Anne saw blood spurting from between their fingers, and her belly tightened in horror. She had heard rumors of the encrotacnic sacaums, though she had never quite believed in them.

In response the knight lifted up his arms and shouted, and again Anne felt a surge of force, this one passing through her like a cold shock. The mestra's sacaum shredded, floated up on the night air, and vanished.

"So," Secula said. "Now you show your face, brother. Now I know the truth."

"A truth perhaps," the knight said. "This matter is beyond your understanding, Mestra."

"Enlighten me."

"I may not." He gestured, and his men surged forward; the ram crashed against the gate. At the same moment, the knight's hands flashed white, the air crackled with sudden thunder, and blue fire twisted in a helix from below the wall. Anne couldn't see the gate from the side that was struck, but she could see it from the courtyard side, and gasped as the fire crackled through its seams like the reaching tendrils of a vine.

On the second blow, the gate collapsed, and the knight rode through, his men behind him.

Anne couldn't feel her body anymore. She felt detached, outside, a presence as frail as a specter witnessing what followed.

The sisters tightened into a bunch and spoke dark words, and knights fell, tearing off their helms to reveal faces gone azure. They bit off their tongues and crushed their own teeth as their jaws spasmed, weeping green tears as they crossed the waters of death.

The leader strode unaffected through the unseen veil of slaughter. His heavy sword lifted, and in an instant one of the nuns was headless, her body sinking to its knees slowly as her neck seemed to stretch up and out, blooming like a red orchid. The bloody sword came back, and back, hewing into the sisters of Cer. At first the women held their line, and warriors continued to fall like ants marching into a fire, but suddenly the sisters broke before the murdering blade. Arrows whistled up into the battlements, where Sister Secula was raining black sleet that fell through armor as if it wasn't there. Savitor and Curnax collapsed, staring at the arrows standing in them. Sister Secula grimly clapped her hands and seemed to slip into a shadow that wasn't there. Then the shadow wasn't there, either.

"Oh, saints," Austra shrieked.

"This is because of me," Anne said numbly. The words didn't make sense, but there they were.

"We have to get to the wine cellar," Austra said. "We have to get somewhere safe. Anne, come on."

But Anne couldn't move. Blood was everywhere, now. She had never dreamed so much blood existed in the whole world, or that headless bodies could twitch so, or the eyes of the dead seem so like glass.

"Anne!" Austra screamed in her ear.

The leader of the knights heard and looked up. His visor was still open, but the only thing Anne noticed about his face were eyes so blue they seemed almost white.

"There!" he shouted, thrusting his mailed finger at her.

"Anne!" Austra was weeping uncontrollably with fear and grief, tugging at her arm.

Anne found her legs, or they found themselves, and in a rush she was running, tripping along the battlements, all of her senses gone to feed her fear. Austra was close behind, nearly pushing her. They found the stair they had ascended and stumbled down it. Anne slipped and her knees smacked hard into the stone but she scarcely noticed, for as they entered the courtyard there came another hoarse male shout.

"The wine cellar!" Austra cried, gesturing.

"And be trapped? No!" Anne turned into the refectory, not daring to face the sound of mailed feet slapping the stone behind them. As they rounded past the entrance to the larder, however, Austra shrieked again, and Anne was forced to turn.

Their pursuer—a man in half plate with long black hair gathered in a tail—had Austra by her hair and his sword leveled at Anne.

"Stop your running," he commanded. "Come with me."

Austra's eyes had lost all semblance of sanity, and Anne was suddenly more furious than terrified.

The nearest thing at hand was a hammer used for nailing up kegs. She snatched it up and threw it.

It wasn't a strong throw, but it was surprisingly true. She had a glimpse of the astonishment spreading on the knight's face, just before the mallet crushed his nose. He swore and stumbled back, and Austra was free.

The two girls started running again. Behind them, Anne heard the knight howl and stamp, and then something struck her hard on the head. She went light and then heavy, and her cheek crushed against the floor. She spit blood and tried to rise, but a boot came down on her back.

"Little bitch," the man said. "I'll teach you—*saints!*"

The last word rose into a scream so high pitched it sounded like a horse dying, and the pressure came off Anne's back. Confused, she came groggily to her hands and knees, turning to see that the knight lay dead, with vapor drifting from between his lips.

"Get up. Quickly."

Anne looked toward the new voice. Next to her, Austra was struggling up, as well. Sister Secula stood looking down at them.

"Come along," she said. "The sisterhood can't keep them back much longer."

Anne nodded mutely, rubbing her head, which was still ringing from the blow. She fastened her eyes on the back of the mestra's robe, wondering again if this was all actually happening.

Too fast. All too fast. Things blurred.

The next time she noticed where they were, they were standing before the pit that led down to the fane of Mefitis.

The mestra took her by the shoulders.

"I didn't expect this," she murmured, in a strangely soft voice. "I'm not done with you and you aren't ready, but what is, is."

"What do those men want with me?" Anne asked.

Sister Secula's dark eyes narrowed. "To take hope from the world," she said. "To take you from it." She gestured to the harness. "Get in, the both of you."

"Wait," Anne said. She felt there was something she ought to ask.

"No time," the older woman said. "Grasp the ropes firmly."

"What am I supposed to do?" Anne asked, as she and Austra arranged themselves in the twining cords. "I don't understand what I'm supposed to do."

"Stay alive," Sister Secula advised. "The rest will unfold as well as it can, saints willing. Leave here, and quickly, or they will find you. Keep moving, and do not trust any illusion of safety." She began letting off the winch, lowering them down, and her face receded above Anne. Something began thudding against the door above them.

"You know the way out," the mestra said. "Go, the moment you reach the bottom."

"You knew?" Anne blurted.

Sister Secula's only answer was a soft laugh.

She let them down quickly, and no sooner had they touched the stone floor than came from above a chorus of howls, like damned souls, and the faint smell of sulfur.

Then silence.

In the darkness, Anne suddenly felt stronger. "Austra, take my hand," she said.

"It's too dark," Austra protested. "We'll fall in a chasm, or trip."

"Just trust me and take my hand. You heard the mestra. I know the way."

Men's voices floated down from above.

"You hear that? They know we're here."

"Yes," Austra said. "Yes, let's go."

Fingers gripped together, the two girls started out into the dark.

CHAPTER TEN

THE SOUNDING

LONG BEFORE STEPHEN ENTERED THE CLEARING, Desmond saw him, of course. Stephen had known he would. The monk stopped his incantation, and a sardonic smile spread across his face.

"Lewes, Owlic," he said. "On your guard. The holter will be near. He's a dangerous man, if he killed Topan and Aligern." He smiled a little more broadly. "You couldn't have had much of a hand in killing them, could you, Brother Stephen?"

"No, you're right there," Stephen said cheerfully. He crossed his arms and tried to look nonchalant.

Desmond cocked his head at the tone, then shrugged. "You've gone mad, I take it. That's to your advantage, considering what I'm going to do to you."

"You're wrong about the holter, though," Stephen went on. "He killed Topan and Aligern, but Topan gave him a mortal wound. I'm going to have to kill you by myself."

"That's fine," Spendlove said. "You can do that in a moment. In the meantime, make yourself comfortable—sit if you wish. I've a small task to finish before I take up your case." He looked at Lewes and Owlic. "He's probably lying about the holter. Stay alert." He turned back to the girl.

"You don't have to repeat all of that rigmarole, you know," Stephen confided. "The sedos doesn't care if you say anything or not."

Desmond scowled. "Perhaps not. The dark saints, however, care a great deal."

"The dark saints are dead," Stephen said. "You're showing your ignorance, chanting like some Watau wonderman. The sedoi are the remains of their puissance, their old tracks of power. The potence is there, but it's insentient." He switched his tone to one he might use with a small child. "That means it can't hear you," he said.

Desmond tried on another smile, but it seemed strained. "You're talking about things of which you know nothing," he said.

Stephen laughed. "That's good, coming from a thickwit like you. What don't I understand? You're making changelings. You just sent Brother Seigeriek's soul off to steal a body, and now you're sending Ashern to do the same. Knights in the queen's guard, perhaps? Is that a lock of hair I see around Brother Ashern's neck? A personal item is needed to find the body, yes?"

"Lewes, shut him up until I'm done," Desmond grunted. He held up an admonishing finger. "Don't kill him, though."

The hulking monk started toward Stephen.

"You're the ones who don't understand what you're doing," Stephen said. "Your knowledge is less than complete, and more superstition than anything else. That's why you needed me. You still do."

"Oh, and you're ready to help us now?" Spendlove said. "I doubt that, somehow."

"Call off Lewes," Stephen said. "Call him off, or I'll use this." He brought the horn from his haversack, the one the holter had carried from the Mountains of the Hare to d'Ef.

Desmond's eyes pinched to slits.

"Hold off, Lewes," Spendlove said. He stepped a little away from the girl, holding his empty hands out so as to make clear he was not threatening her. "Where did you get that?"

"You should have spent a little more time in the scriftorium and a little less time buggering corpses," Stephen told him. "Do you know what this is? I think you do."

"Something you ought not to have. Something you won't have for long."

"I don't need it for long. Only for an instant."

Desmond shook his head. "You can't think I'm that stupid. The ritual involved—"

"Is as meaningless as the one you're gibbering now. Any sedos can unlock the power in the horn. Any lips can blow it. And look here, we have both."

"If you really know what you have, you know better than to use it," Desmond said. "Calling *him* won't help you."

"You're afraid to name him? I'm not. The Briar King. The horned lord. The Nettle-man. And the thing about calling him, you know, is that I really *don't* know what will happen, and neither do you. He might kill us all, though the *Codex Khwrn* claims that the holder of the horn won't be harmed. A chance I'm willing to take, that, considering how by your own admission, you've some nasty things planned for me." He raised the horn, wondering if there really was any such scrift as the *Codex Khwrn*.

"Stop," Desmond said, a note of desperation in his voice. "Wait a moment."

"You're so partial to the dark saints, yet you don't want to meet one?"

"Not *him*. Not yet." He cocked his head. "You don't know everything, Brother Stephen. Not by half. If you wake him now—if you call him out of his wood before we've finished the preparations—you'll have more blood on your hands than I ever dreamed of."

Stephen shrugged. "Let's not wake him, then."

Desmond's voice took on a bargaining tone. "What do you want?" he asked.

"The girl. Let her go."

"You know this slut?"

"I've never laid eyes on her before. But I won't watch you kill her. Let her go, and let the two of us walk away."

"Where's the holter?"

"I told you. He's dead."

Spendlove shook his head. "He probably went after Fend. They're old friends, those two."

Lewes was only a few yards away, tensing as if to spring. Stephen raised the horn almost to his lips and waggled a warning finger at the giant.

Brother Ashern, standing bare-chested on the sedos, cleared his throat.

"Seigereik has probably opened the gate by now," he said. "There may be no need for me to go."

Desmond laughed bitterly. "You always were a coward at heart, Brother Ashern. You've the most important task of all. You're to kill the queen, if the others fail. She'll trust you."

"If he blows that horn, I won't be killing any queen," Brother Ashern said defensively. "Seigereik has the gates open by now, and Fend and his men will be inside soon. It's a ride of less than half a bell, even in the dark. They'll get the queen, sure enough."

"We don't even know it's the real thing," Lewes growled. "It could be a cow horn he picked up someplace."

"Or it could be I've been traveling with the holter who saw the Briar King, who went into his very demesne. Surely Fend told you about that. That was what Fend was after in the first place—the horn. Do you think he found it?" This was all guesswork, of course, but Stephen saw from their faces he had caught the sparrow.

Lewes was edging closer.

"No, Lewes," Spendlove said. "He's right, and so is Brother Ashern. Soon the queen and all of her daughters will be dead; the holter can't kill Fend and all of his men by himself. The deed is accomplished. We've no need to kill this little whore." He produced a knife from his belt, one that glittered with actinic light. "I'm going to cut her loose."

Stephen pressed the horn to his lips, a tacit warning.

He hadn't counted on how fast Spendlove could move. The knife was suddenly a blur in the air, and then a shearing pain in Stephen's arm. He gasped.

He gasped, and the world filled with sound.

Stephen had never intended to blow the horn, of course, nor did he really believe it would do anything if he did. He'd been counting on Spendlove's superstitious belief in the dark saints.

He didn't even know *how* to blow a horn, though he had seen it done and knew that it wasn't like a hautboy or recorder; it involved buzzing the lips or somesuch. Just putting air in it shouldn't work.

But the clear note that soared into the dark air denied all that. And it wouldn't let him stop. Even as he sank to his knees, blood spraying from his arm, the horn blew louder, sucking the wind from him as the very rocks and trees seemed to take up the note, as the sky shivered from it. Even when Brother Lewes hit him and tore the instrument from his hands, the sound went on, gathering force like a thunderhead, building higher until it was deafening, until no other sound existed in the world.

Brother Lewes knocked Stephen roughly to the ground. Grinding his teeth, Stephen pulled the knife from his arm, nearly fainting from the redoubled pain that brought. He rolled onto his back, vaguely bringing the blade up in a gesture of defense.

But Brother Lewes was doing something odd. He seemed to have found a straight stick and driven it into his own right eye. Why would he do that?

When a second arrow struck the monk in the heart, it all suddenly made sense. He watched numbly as Lewes pawed at the shaft, gave a final mutter of consternation, and fell.

"Aspar," Stephen said. He couldn't hear his own words for the sound of the horn.

Clutching the knife, he stumbled to his feet. He willed away the pain in his arm, and it went, just as the feeling had gone out of his body on the faneway. Grimly he started toward Desmond.

The monk watched him come. Stephen was peripherally aware that Aspar was attacking Owlic, now.

In the air around them, the note from the horn was finally beginning to fade, but slowly.

"You're the greatest fool in the world," Spendlove screamed. "Idiot! What have you done?"

Stephen didn't answer. His first breath after blowing the horn felt like a winterful of icy draughts. He knew Spendlove would kill him. He didn't care. Raising the knife he began to run straight toward the other monk, his wounded arm forgotten.

Desmond glanced down at the bound woman and then, fast as a cat, he grabbed Brother Ashern, positioned over the first still slightly twitching victim. He stabbed Ashern in the heart. At nearly the same moment, an arrow struck Desmond near the center of his chest, and he grunted and fell back.

That gave Stephen an instant to choose, and in that instant he felt a bright certainty. He shifted his charge, putting his shoulder into the dying, goggle-eyed Brother Ashern and knocking him from the mound. Then he knelt by the other man, the one still gaping at his own bowels.

"Forgive me," he said, and drove the shining knife into one tortured blue eye, pushing it in as far as it would go.

"Once the blade is in," he remembered reading in the *Physiognomy of Ulh*, "wiggle well to scramble the brains. Quick death will follow."

He wiggled, and something in the earth beneath him seemed to groan.

He looked up just as Desmond hit him. He felt his nose collapse and tasted blood in the back of his throat, and when he bounced down the sedos, he barely felt anything. Desmond came grimly after him, snapping off the arrow in his chest. Stephen watched him sidestep another arrow, and then the monk had him by the collar, and Stephen was in the air again. He crashed to earth on the other side of the hill.

He'll have cover here, Stephen thought. *Aspar won't be able to shoot him without moving. I'll be dead by the time he gets here.*

Desmond came around the sedos and kicked him in the ribs. Stephen grunted; he couldn't breathe through his nose, and his mouth was full of blood.

"Enough of you, Stephen Darige," Desmond said. "That's very much enough of you."

Stephen felt something in his hand as he tried to flop back, and he realized he still had the knife. Not that he would ever have the chance to use it. Spendlove was too fast. He couldn't throw it, the way Spendlove had.

Or could he? He remembered Spendlove drawing his hand back and flipping it toward him. As lightning-quick as the throw had been, Stephen remembered it, every nuance of the motion. He thought of his own hand making the same motion.

Spendlove came, almost contemptuously. Stephen, not even half risen, cocked his hand and threw.

He was certain he had missed, until Spendlove, eyes wide and unbelieving, reached for his sternum, where the hilt stood, just below the arrow wound.

Stephen leapt up, fierce exultation finally moving his limbs. Spendlove hit him again, in the chest. It felt like a sledgehammer, but Stephen lurched forward, throwing his arms around the monk.

Spendlove put both of his hands around Stephen's neck and began to squeeze. The world went gray as the monk's fingers bit into his neck. Stephen, with winter in his belly, wondered how Spendlove could be so stupid. Was it a trick?

He decided it wasn't; Spendlove was just mad with rage. With both hands, Stephen grabbed the hilt of the knife and pulled down.

"Oh, shit me," Spendlove said, watching his guts spill to the ground. He let go of Stephen, took three steps back, and sat down heavily on the mound. He wrapped his arms around his yawning belly.

"I wondered why you didn't think of that," Stephen commented, dropping to his knees.

"Too mad. Saints, Darige, but you know how to make me mad." His eyes rolled back. "You've killed me. Me, killed by the likes of you."

"You shouldn't have betrayed the church," Stephen pointed out. "You shouldn't have killed Fratrex Pell."

"You're still a fool, Brother Stephen," Spendlove replied.

"I know others in the church must be involved," Stephen told him. "I know you took orders from someone. Tell me who. Make absolution to me, Brother Desmond. I know you must regret some of what you've done."

"I regret not killing you when I met you, yes," Brother Desmond allowed.

"No. That night on the hill."

Spendlove looked very weary. If it weren't for the sanguine river flowing through his crossed arms, he might have been preparing for a nap. He blinked.

"I never had a chance," he murmured. "I thought they would make something better of me. They made something worse." He looked up, as if he saw something. "There they are," he said. "Come to get me."

"Tell me who your superiors were," Stephen insisted.

"Come close, and I'll whisper," Spendlove said, his eyelids fluttering like broken moths.

"I think not. You've still the strength to kill me."

"Well, you've learned a little, then." He lay back. "It's better that you live to see the world you've made, in any case. I hope you enjoy it, Brother Stephen."

"What do you mean?"

"They're here." Spendlove sounded suddenly frightened. His head threw back and his back arched. "It's only ashes, now. I was a fool to think I could be more. Great lords!"

The last was a shriek, and then he lay still, his body as quiet as his face was tortured. Stephen sat watching him, chest heaving, slowly trying to become sane again.

Aspar finally hit the troublesome monk in the neck and, while he staggered, put the last shaft in his heart. That left only the leader, who had gone behind the mound with Stephen. Aspar sprinted from cover.

The fellow he'd just shot hadn't given up, though. They met halfway to the mound, and he cut at Aspar with a sword, the steel a gray blur. Aspar stopped short, hopped back, then leapt forward inside the length of the weapon, crossing his dirk and the hand ax he'd acquired in a village two days back. He forced the sword down, then brought the hand ax up, edge-first, under the monk's chin, splitting his lower jaw. In return he got a blow from the sword-pommel that sent him sprawling.

The swordsman came on, stabbing down, slower this time. Aspar batted the blade aside and sat up fast, punching his dirk into the man's groin. When he doubled, Aspar withdrew the blade and put it through his heart, which finally stopped him. Groaning, Aspar climbed painfully to his feet and resumed his run to the mound where Winna still lay bound.

"Winn!" Beyond her, he could see the last monk folded around his belly, with Stephen watching laconically from a few yards away. The boy was bleeding freely from his arm wound, but otherwise looked well enough.

Winna was looking up at him, her eyes strangely calm. Kneeling, he cut her bonds and with a muffled cry lifted her into his arms and yanked off her gag.

"Winna—" He wanted to say more, but he couldn't, for it felt as if he'd swallowed something big and got it stuck in his throat. And why was his face wet? Was his forehead cut?

Winna sobbed then and buried her face in his neck, and they stood that way for a long moment.

Finally, he pushed her back gently.

"Winna, did they hurt you? Did they . . ."

"They didn't touch my body," she whispered. "They talked of it often. He wouldn't let them, Fend. He wanted me pure, he said. He wanted to do things in front of you. Is he dead?"

"Fend, no. Not yet. Winna?"

"I knew you would find me."

"I love you, Winna. If you'd died . . ."

She wiped her eyes, and her voice was suddenly its old practical self. "I didn't die," she said, "and neither did you. So here we are, and I love you, too. But the queen *will* die if we don't do something."

"I've the only queen I care about," Aspar said gruffly. "I'll kill Fend, right enough. But first, by the Raver, I'll see you safe."

"Nothing of that. We started this together, Aspar. We'll stay in it together."

"She's right," Stephen said, rising behind them. "We've got to do what we can."

"That we've done, I think," Aspar said.

"No," Stephen said. "Not yet. We may not be able to help them at Cal Azroth, but we have to try."

"You made a damned good fight here, lad," Aspar said. "You did us all proud. But look at you. You've no fight left in you. If we don't bandage that arm, you'll bleed out."

"Bandage it, then," Stephen said. "And we'll go."

Aspar looked at the two determined young faces and sighed, feeling suddenly outnumbered.

"Winna, aren't you the one 'sposed to have sense?" he asked.

Winna lifted her chin toward Stephen. "My name is Winna Rufoote," she said.

"Stephen Darige, at your service." He shot Aspar a look that said, *you could have told me,* but didn't say anything. Aspar felt suddenly embarrassed and put upon.

"Has he been as stone-stubborn with you as with me?" Winna asked Stephen.

"I don't know. I don't know how he could be any more stubborn than I've known him to be," Stephen replied.

"Well, he can," Winna said. "But I'm his match." She went up on tiptoe and kissed him. "Aren't I, love?"

Aspar felt bloodfire in his cheeks. He pursed his lips.

"Sceat," he grunted. "We'll go, but we do it as I say. Yah?"

"Always," Winna agreed.

"And we get the horses. We'll need 'em."

CHAPTER ELEVEN

CHANGELING

NEIL FELL TO HIS KNEES, vomiting. He couldn't feel the stone beneath his hands, or even his hands, for that matter. Threads of darkness stitched across his vision.

"Welcome, Brother Ashern," the knight who was and was not Vargus Farre said. "You're late. Was there trouble?"

Neil couldn't compel his vocal cords to answer.

"What's wrong with him?" another voice asked. Neil closed his eyes and saw the voice as a fidgeting blue line, like lightning.

"I don't know," the false Vargus replied. "I was sick at first, but not like that."

"It's no matter," the new voice said. "We can do what needs doing, with or without him. But we cannot wait."

"Agreed," Vargus replied. "Brother Ashern, when you've recovered from your journey, find the queen. If she's not already disposed of, then do so. Remember, she thinks you are her personal guard. Your name is Neil. Do you remember that?"

His words made no sense. The black web spinning across Neil's vision was tightening its weave, wrapping around him, sinking toward his bones like a net cast into the sea. He briefly wondered what that net might bring up, and he remembered sunlight on whitecaps. He felt his father's hand in his own.

Then nothing.

.   .   .

He woke where he had fallen, face pressed into the stone. His mouth was dry, and his head ached as if from too much wine. Fighting the urge to retch again, he found Crow and clambered to his feet. He swayed there a moment, still dizzy, gaze exploring the shadows of the keep. It was still night, so he had not been unconscious too long, but the false Vargus and whoever he had been talking to were nowhere to be seen.

What happened to me? The two men had talked as if he was someone else.

But he still felt like Neil MeqVren.

Glancing down, he saw that Sir James Cathmayl was dead, his glassy eyes staring beyond the lands of fate. All about, Cal Azroth was absolutely still and quiet, and yet somehow Neil sensed a stir of motion, of sharp darkness waiting to close on him and prick his veins.

The queen.

He started up the stairs at a dead run. Vargus had let someone into Cal Azroth, someone with murder in them. He prayed to the saints there was still time to stop them.

The guardhouse on the wall contained only dead soldiers, slain where they had been sitting or lying. As he entered the tower, Neil found more dead there. The blood pooled on the floor was still warm.

He passed Elseny's room and saw the door standing open.

"Elseny?" he hissed. He could see her lying in her bed. He hesitated—his duty was to the queen first—but decided to wake her and keep her close.

But there was no waking Elseny. The sheets beneath her chin were dark, and a second mouth gaped in her thin white neck. Her eyes were stones, and her expression was one of puzzlement.

Fastia. Panic surged through Neil. Fastia's room was on the other side of the tower, in the opposite direction as the queen's.

He hesitated only an instant, then grimly continued toward the queen's apartments.

In the anteroom, he found carnage. Two men and a Sefry lay still on the floor. The inner door was sealed. He started toward it, but something sharp pricked into the base of his neck, and he froze where he was.

"Move not," Erren's voice rasped. "I can kill you before you draw another breath, long before you can turn."

"Lady Erren, it is I, Neil."

"I have seen Vargus Farre, too," Erren said. "But he was not Vargus Farre. Prove yourself, Sir Neil. Tell me something only Sir Neil might know."

"The queen is well?"

"Do as I say."

Neil bit his lip. "You knew I was with Fastia," he said, "that night in Glenchest. You told me not to fall in love with her."

The assassin was silent for a heartbeat. "Very well," she said. "Turn."

He did, and she moved so quickly he almost didn't see. Her hand cracked across his face. "Where were you? Damn you, where were you?" she demanded.

"I saw men coming across the plain. I tried to raise the alarm, but the gate was already open. Sir Vargus opened it. And then he did something to me, witched me. I was sick and fainted; I don't know for how long. Is the queen . . ."

"She is within, and well."

"Thank the saints." He lowered his voice. "Lady Erren, Elseny is dead. Fastia may be in danger, as well."

"Elseny?" Erren's face twisted in grief, but then her eyes narrowed and her features were again carved of marble. "You will stay here, Sir Neil," Erren hissed. "Your duty is to Muriele, and Muriele alone."

"Then you go, Lady Erren," Neil urged. "Bring Fastia back here, where we can protect her. And Charles. All of the children must be in danger."

Erren shook her head. "I cannot. I do not have the strength."

"What do you mean?"

"I am injured, Sir Neil. I will not last the night. I may not last the hour."

He stepped back, then, and saw how strangely she leaned against the wall. It was too dark to see exactly how she was hurt, but he smelled the blood.

"It cannot be so bad," he said.

"I know death, Sir Neil. She is like a mother to me. Trust what I say, and waste no time on grief—for me, for Elseny—and no time on fear for Fastia. Stay clear headed, and answer my questions. I have killed three. How many are there in sum?"

"I don't know," Neil admitted. "When the illness overcame me, I was not sensible. But they told me I was to kill the queen."

Erren's brow furrowed. "They thought you changeling, like Vargus. Yet you were not. Somehow the sorcery was interrupted."

"I don't understand."

"Darkest encrotacnia," Erren whispered. "A man is killed, and his enscorceled soul sent to take the body of another. The soul already in the body is ripped from it. You should not be alive, Sir Neil, and yet you are. But that may work to your advantage. If you pretend to be what they think you are, it might give you more space to strike."

"Yes, lady."

"The guards and servants are dead, you think?" Erren asked.

"Yes, lady."

"Then you must get the queen to the garrison," Erren told him. "They could not have killed all of the soldiers there. There are far too many."

A faint noise came from down the hall.

"Hsst." Erren stepped to the side of the door. Neil made out two pale figures moving toward them, and tightened his grip on Crow.

"That is you, Ashern?"

Neil seemed to remember that name from the courtyard.

"Aye."

"Have you done it? The queen is dead?"

They were closer, now, and Neil could see they were both Sefry. The speaker had an eye patch.

"Aye, it's done."

"Well, let's see. We should not tarry."

"You will not trust my word?" They were almost close enough, but the Sefry with the eye patch hesitated, just as Neil struck. Both men leapt back, but the one who had spoken was faster, so Crow took the other in the shoulder and opened him to the lungs. Something hard hit Neil's armor, just over his heart. The one-eyed Sefry was running backward, his hand cocking back . . .

Neil understood and threw himself aside as a second thrown knife whirred by his head and snapped against the stone. By the time he recovered, the Sefry was gone.

"That's the end of your advantage," Erren said. "Now you must go, and swift, before he returns with more."

"It may be that he has no more."

"The changeling Vargus still lives. That makes at least two, but we must assume more."

She rapped on the queen's door, three soft taps, a pause, then two harder ones. Neil heard a bolt draw, and then the door cracked inward. He saw the queen's eyes beyond.

"Sir Neil is here," Erren said. "He will stay with you."

"Erren, you're hurt," the queen noticed. "Come inside."

Erren smiled briefly. "We have more visitors for me to receive. Sir Neil will take you to the garrison. You'll be safe there."

"My daughters—"

"Your daughters are already safe," Erren replied, and Neil felt her hand touch his back in warning. "Now you must go with Sir Neil."

"I won't leave you."

"You will," Erren replied simply. "I will join you at the garrison."

A noise sounded near the end of the hall, and Erren spun in time to receive one of the three arrows that sped through the door. It hit her in the kidney. The other two thudded against the wall next to Neil.

"Erren!" the queen screamed.

"Sir Neil!" Erren reminded, in a tone of cold and absolute command.

Neil was through the door in an instant, shouldering the queen aside. He slammed the portal behind him, just as several more shafts thocked into the other side. He bolted it.

"Do not open it," Neil told the queen.

"Erren—"

"Erren is dead," Neil told her. "She died so you might live. Do not betray her."

The queen's face changed, then. The confusion and grief fled from it, replaced by regal determination.

"Very well," she said. "But whoever did this will have cause to regret it. Promise me that."

Neil thought of Elseny, dead in her bed, all her laughter and whimsy bled into her sheets. He thought of Fastia, and nursed a terrible hope that she still lived.

"They will," he said. "But we must survive the night."

He went to the window, sheathing Crow as he did so. He'd examined the room earlier, of course, and even without the moon he knew the tower wall dropped some five yards to the wall of the inner keep, where he had stood earlier that night watching for ghosts. A glance showed no one without. He returned to her bed and began knotting the sheets together, tying one end to the bedpost.

The door shuddered beneath repeated blows.

"Finish here," he told the queen. "Tie them well. When you've fixed two more together, start down. Do not wait for me."

The queen nodded and went to the task. Neil, meanwhile, pushed a heavy chest to add weight to the door.

He wasn't in time. The bolt suddenly snapped open, as if pulled by invisible fingers. Neil leapt to it, drew Crow, yanked it open, and slashed.

The pale face of a Sefry looked at him in surprise as Crow split collarbone, heart, and breastbone. Neil didn't let the malefactor drop, but with his other hand lifted him by the hair, using him as a shield against the inevitable darts that flew from the darkness. Then he shoved the body away and slammed the door again, drawing the bolt firmly into place.

A glance behind him showed that the queen had already begun her descent. He went to the window and watched until she reached the stone cobbles, and was turning to follow her when the door exploded inward.

Neil slashed the sheet at the bedpost and leapt to the windowsill, dropping to hang by his fingers as two arrows hummed by and a third glanced from his byrnie. Then he dropped.

A fall of three yards even in half armor was easily enough to snap bones. He hit the cobbles and collapsed his knees. The air blew out of him and glimmer-lights danced across his vision.

"Sir Neil." The queen was there. On the horizon a purple sickle was rising. For a moment, Neil did not recognize it as the moon.

"Away from the window," he gasped, reaching up to her.

She took his hand, and they ducked around the curve of the tower, away from any sharp-nosed arrows that might scent them from above.

"This way," Neil said. They started along the battlements toward the stair to the courtyard, glancing behind them often. Neil made out at least one slight figure dropping from the tower in the moonlight. He hoped it wasn't one of the archers.

They reached the steps without incident, however. Once down them, they needed only to cross the courtyard and open the gate that led through the old wall and across the canal to the garrison. Last Neil had seen, that yard was empty of the living, and he hoped it still was.

They had taken only a step down, however, when the queen suddenly jerked away from him and started back up.

"Your Majesty—" he began.

"Fastia!" the queen shouted.

Neil saw Fastia, turning the corner of the battlements perhaps twenty yards away, still wearing the same blue dress he had seen her in earlier. She looked up at the sound of her name.

"Mother? Sir Neil?"

"Fastia. Come to us. Quickly. There is danger." She started toward her daughter.

Neil swore and started after her, noting the three figures closing rapidly from the way they had come.

A fourth appeared silently from the shadows behind Fastia.

"Fastia!" he shouted. "Behind you! Run toward us!"

He passed the queen an instant later, his heart roaring, watching Fastia's face grow nearer, confusion mixing with fear as she turned to see what he was yelling about.

"Keep back from her!" Neil thundered. "By the saints, keep back from her!"

But the black-clad figure was there, moving terrifically fast, a sliver of moonlight in his hand, lifted and then buried in Fastia's breast, two heartbeats before Neil reached her. The man danced back and drew a sword as Neil howled and drove in, hammering Crow down with both hands. The man parried, and cut back, but Neil took the slash on his hauberk and crashed into him, bringing an elbow up into his chin with a hoarse shout. The man went down but was already bouncing back up when Crow split his skull.

The queen was kneeling with her daughter, and the men approaching from the tower were nearly upon them. They could never make it to the stairs and down before the men arrived.

Fastia looked up at him, blinking, hiccuping.

There was only one way, and Neil took it.

"Over the wall, into the canal, and swim to the causeway," he told the queen. "I have Fastia."

"Yes," the queen said. She never hesitated, but jumped.

Neil lifted Fastia in his arms.

"I love you," she gasped.

"And I you," he said, and leapt.

The wall here was seven yards high, and the water felt like stone when he hit it. His hauberk dragged him straight to the bottom, and he had to let loose of Fastia to shuck it off. For a panicked instant he couldn't find her again, but then felt her arm, got his grip, and brought her up. He found his bearings and struck toward the causeway that led to the garrison. It seemed impossibly far away. Ahead of him, the queen was already swimming. Fastia's eyes had closed, but her breath still whistled in his ear.

Two loud splashes sounded behind him. He struck harder, cursing.

He emerged onto the causeway at almost the same time as the queen. He lifted Fastia into a cradle-carry and they ran for the garrison gate, keenly aware that the gate to the other courtyard—and those who probably now occupied it—lay behind them.

The garrison gate was open, too, the bodies of perhaps ten soldiers crumpled beneath its arch.

In the darkness beyond, something growled, and Neil saw glowing eyes and a shadow the size of a horse, but shaped like no horse he had ever seen.

CHAPTER TWELVE

A LESSON IN THE SWORD

CAZIO WOKE, wondering where he was, chagrined that he had dozed. Without moving more than his eyes, he quietly took in his surroundings.

He lay in a small copse of olive trees, through which the stars twinkled pleasantly in a cloudless sky. Not far away reared the shadow of the Coven Saint Cer.

He sat up, rubbing his eyes, reaching instinctively to see if Caspator was there, and felt reassured to find the familiar hilt next to him.

What had wakened him? A familiar noise, it seemed. Or had it merely been a dream?

Memory came lazily, but there wasn't much to remember. When the girls left Orchaevia's fete, he'd taken a walk into the countryside. He'd never been afraid of the dark, and felt learning to move in it, to sense the unseen, could only improve his fencing skills.

Why and how exactly his footsteps had taken him to the coven, he couldn't say. He'd just looked up and there it was. Once there, he'd pondered what to do; it was too early and would have seemed far too eager on his part to try to get Anne and Austra's attention. So he just stared up at their tower for a while, finally rationalizing that the best hunter was the one who knew the habits of his prey. That being the case, he would observe and perhaps catch a glimpse of them. And after all, it was a pleasant night—not a bad one to spend beneath the stars. No doubt z'Acatto was wandering drunkenly around the triva, spoiling for an argument, and if Orchaevia found him, he would be forced to report on his success or failure with Anne. Avoiding that conversation was one of the reasons he'd gone on his nocturnal stroll in the first place.

With those thoughts in mind, he'd found the olive grove and waited. A lantern eventually brightened the tower, and he watched the shadow play of the two girls at the window—discussing him, no doubt.

Then the light had gone out, disappointingly soon, and he'd closed his eyes for a moment—

And slept, apparently.

He congratulated himself on avoiding a close call. How foolish he'd have seemed if he'd slept until morning. Anne might have seen him and thought him become what Orchaevia claimed he was, a lovesick fool.

Even thinking the word startled him. He, Cazio Pachiomadio da Chiovattio, lovesick.

Ridiculous.

He glanced back up at the tower. No light showed in the window, but then why should it? It must be well into the morning by now.

The noise that had awakened him repeated itself, a bell ringing, and with sudden interest Cazio realized that *something* was going on at the coven. He saw torches all along the battlements, most of them moving at what must be a frantic pace. He thought he heard horses, too, which was odd. And faintly, ever so faintly, shouting, and what might be the occasional sound of steel.

He sat up straighter. No, by Diuvo, he *did* hear steel. That wasn't a sound he was likely to misplace.

That took him straight from muddled to wide awake, and he sprang to his feet with such haste that he bumped his head on a low branch. Cursing, he found his hat and donned it, took the cloak he'd been using as a bed and pinned it back on.

Who was fighting in the coven? Had bandits attacked the place? Crazed rapist vagabonds from the Lemon Hills to the south?

He had to know. He began striding toward the left, where he supposed the gate was. If it was naught—some strange exercise to celebrate the Fiussanal—the worst they could do was turn him away.

He'd gone no more than fifty pereci when he heard the drumming of hooves in the night. He stopped, cupping his ear and turning this way and that until he determined that the noises came from the very direction he was going—and they were getting louder. He watched for torches—who would ride at night without torches—but he saw none. A slice of moon was half risen, the strangest color he had ever seen, almost purple. It seemed to him he'd heard that meant something, but he couldn't remember where. Was it a verse?

The shadows of two, perhaps three horses appeared against the paler walls of the coven. They rode at full gallop, and there was much metal in the sound, by which he reasoned whoever it was wore armor. They passed nearby but did not stop.

Rapist vagabonds from the yellow hills wouldn't wear armor. Only the knights of the meddisso were allowed armor.

Or knights from an invading army, who did not care what the meddisso allowed.

More intrigued than ever, Cazio changed his direction, setting off at an easy lope after the horsemen, Caspator slapping at his thigh.

"I've always wanted to try one of these vaunted knights with their great clumsy swords, Caspator," he confided to the rapier. "Perhaps tonight I'll find my chance."

The riders were easy enough to follow, for they soon entered the wilder growth around the hill, where he had first met Anne. There they were forced to slow their mounts, which fact Cazio could tell from the frequent crashing and breaking of limbs. Now and then he caught the sound of some outlandish tongue.

A new suspicion took root in him, an exciting one. Perhaps Anne's foreign lover had come for her after all. Cazio knew the girl must have some secret way in and out of the coven, near the pool where he had met her—and that was the logical place for a rendezvous. If such was the case, this might indeed prove amusing.

He checked himself, realizing that the horses had stopped, and that he had almost walked right into them. He could vaguely make them out—two of them—through the trees, the purple light of the moon reflecting from burnished armor.

"*Unnut,*" one of the men said, in a clear baritone. He sounded bored. "*Sa taujaza ni waiht,*" he added.

"Ney," the other replied, in the same ugly, incomprehensible jargon. *"Wakath! Jainar, inna baymes."* He pointed as he said this, and in the next instant they spurred the horses into motion again, but this time going in different directions. Furthermore, Cazio saw what the man had been pointing at—two slim figures in robes crossing a clearing in the moonlight.

The knights were trying to circle their quarry. With horses and armor, they had a harder time in the trees than those on foot, but it would be only a matter of time if the knights knew what they were doing.

Cazio heard one of the running figures gasp, a distinctly feminine sound.

He drew Caspator and ran, tearing a straighter line through the brush than the horsemen. In a flash of moonlight, he was certain he saw Anne's face.

One of the mounted men tore from the trees right on top of him. The smell of horse sweat filled the swordsman's lungs, and for the briefest instant the very size of the beast touched a tiny chord of fear in his heart. Incensed that he should be made to feel so—and angry that the knight didn't even seem to have noticed him—Cazio leapt up and struck the man high in the chest with Caspator's hilt, holding it two-fisted. It felt like slamming at a run into a stone wall, but the knight yelped and rolled back off the horse, falling with one foot still in the stirrup. His helm knocked hard against a rock, and the horse slowed to a stop. The man groped feebly.

Cazio reached down and yanked off the helmet, spilling out long hair the color of milk. The face seemed very young.

"My apologies, casnar," Cazio said. "If you wish, we may duel when I've finished with your friend. For the time being, though, I must assure honorable conditions rather than assume them." With that he struck the man a blow with his hilt, rendering him unconscious.

Pleased with himself now, Cazio continued after the girls.

He caught up with them as they hesitated at the edge of the trees, probably trying to decide between cover and a run across the open country.

"Anne! Austra!" he hissed.

The two spun, and he saw it was indeed them.

"Cazio?" Anne asked, sounding hopeful. Then her voice sharpened in pitch. "Stay away from me, you—what have you to do with all of this?"

That took him flat-footed. "What? Why, you—"

But in that moment the second knight broke from the trees. Cazio tossed Anne a contemptuous glance as he planted himself in front of the mounted man. He was emerging from between two trunks, so he would have to come through Cazio to reach Anne and Austra, or else back out and try another way.

"Will you fight me, casnar?" Cazio shouted at the knight. "Do they make men where you come from, or just rapists of helpless women?"

The knight's visor was up, but Cazio couldn't make out his features.

"I don't know who you are," the knight said in an accent that suggested he was trying to swallow something and speak at the same time, "but I advise you to stand aside."

"And I advise you to dismount, sir, or I shall impale your fine horse, something I do not wish to do. You may continue to wear your turtle shell, for I would not disadvantage you by asking you to fight fairly."

"This is not a game," the knight growled. "Do not waste my time, and I will let you live."

"A lesson in dessrata would not be a waste of your time," Cazio replied. "At least you will have something to mull over, whiling away the long hours in hell or curled weeping on your mother's couch—depending on how merciful I am."

The knight didn't say another word, but dismounted, taking a shield shaped like a curved triangle from the side of his horse and drawing an incredibly clumsy-looking broadsword with his free hand. He closed his visor and advanced toward Cazio at a walk. Cazio grinned and settled into a broad dessrata stance, making passes in the air with his blade, bouncing on his knees a little.

The knight didn't salute, or strike a stance, or anything of the sort. When he was within two pereci he simply charged with the shield held in front of him and the sword cocked back on his shoulder. That startled Cazio, but at the last instant he did a quick *ancio*, swinging his body out of the way and leaving his point in line for the knight to run into.

Caspator slid over the shield and arrested against the upper part of the breastplate, where the steel gorget stopped the point. The knight, unimpressed by this, swung the shield backhand, forcing the rapier up and slamming Cazio's forearm into his chest with such force that he left the ground. He landed on his feet but nearly didn't keep them under him, stumbling back as the knight quickly overtook him, sword still cocked. Cazio found his balance just in time to parry the overhand blow, which came with such force that he nearly lost Caspator, and his already abused arm went half numb with shock. Without thinking, he riposted to the thigh, but again all he got was the sound of steel on steel. It gave him time to recover, however, and he danced back out of range while the knight brought his sword back up.

Cazio recalled something z'Acatto had told him once, something he hadn't paid too much attention to at the time.

"Knights in armor don't fence, boy," the old man had said, after taking a drink of pale yellow Abrinian wine.

"Don't they?" Cazio had replied diffidently, whetting Caspator's long blade.

"No. Their swords weigh eight coinix or more. They just hit each other with them until they find out who has the better armor."

"Ah," Cazio had replied. "They would be slow and clumsy, I imagine."

"They have to hit you only once," z'Acatto had replied. "You don't duel knights. You run from them or you drop something very heavy on them from a castle wall. You do not fence them."

"As you say," Cazio had replied, but he hadn't been convinced. Any man with a sword could be beaten by a master of dessrata. Z'Acatto had said it himself, in his more sober moments.

The thing was, this knight wasn't nearly as slow or clumsy as he ought to be, and he did not fear being struck by Caspator in the least. Cazio kept dancing out of range, trying to think. He'd have to hit him in the slit of his mask, he decided, a challenging target indeed.

He tried that, feinting at the knee to draw the shield down. The armored man dropped the shield incrementally, but brought it back up when Cazio lunged, pushing the rapier high again. Then that huge cleaver of a sword came whistling around the side of the shield, a blow aimed to cut Cazio in half at the waist. It would have, too, but Cazio coolly parried in prismo, dropping the tip of his weapon perpendicular to the ground with the hilt on the left side of his head, guarding that entire flank.

Another rapier would have been deflected harmlessly, but not eight or nine coinix of broadsword. It beat Caspator into him, and all of the air out of him. Cazio felt and heard ribs crack, and then he was off his feet again, this time flopping painfully onto his back. He grabbed his side and it came away wet; some edge had gotten through. The cut felt shallow, but the broken ribs hurt so badly it was nearly paralyzing. The knight was coming toward him again, and he didn't think he could get up in time.

It occurred to Cazio that he might be in trouble.

CHAPTER THIRTEEN

THE RAVEN'S SONG

As Muriele stared at the thing from Black Marys and children's tales, darts of fever seemed to pierce her lungs. For an instant, they all stood like statues in some strange pantheon—Neil MeqVren with her dying daughter in his arms, the beaked monster, herself.

Wonder is a terrible thing, she thought. Her mind seemed to be drifting away from her.

Then she saw Neil reach for his sword.

"No!" she shouted. "Do not!" It felt like shouting in a dream, a sound no one could hear.

But the young knight hesitated.

"I am your queen," she cried. Terror was a tiny voice in her now, nearly silenced by madness. "I command it!"

That seemed to get through to the young knight. He turned on his heel and, still carrying Fastia, followed Muriele at a staggering run back toward the inner keep they had just abandoned. The gate was shut, however, and barred from the other side. There was no escape for them there.

Muriele glanced back. The monster was padding softly toward them, in no great hurry. Why should it be?

In sudden epiphany she understood that the entire world—Crotheny, her children, her husband, she herself—existed on the edge of a vast, invisible pit. They had trod its upper slopes, never recognizing that it was even there. Now they were all sliding into it, and the beast behind her was at the bottom, waiting for them.

Waiting for her.

Almost as unhurried as their pursuer, she looked around and saw there was only one place left to go.

"The horz!" she said, gesturing.

The horz occupied an area between the keep and the garrison. The doorway was only about ten yards away. Muriele ran toward it, and the greffyn followed, increasing its speed a little. She felt its eyes burning into her back, imagined its breath on her neck, knew by her renewed terror that she wasn't yet entirely mad. She ran toward the arched gate of the sacred garden. Perhaps the saints would protect them.

As they crossed the threshold into the horz, Sir Neil seemed to get his senses back. He quickly but gently placed Fastia on a bed of moss near the central stone, then drew his sword and turned quickly. The gateway to the horz had no door, but was open to all.

"Hide, Your Majesty," he said. "Find the thickest part of the garden and hide there."

But Muriele was staring past him. The greffyn, which had been just behind them, was nowhere to be seen.

Then Muriele doubled over, the muscles of her legs cramping and fever burning in her veins. She collapsed next to her daughter and reached to touch her, to comfort her, but Fastia's skin was cool and her heart beat no more.

Unable to do anything more, Muriele lay, and wept, and waited for death.

Neil swayed against the door frame, his vision blurring. Where had the monster gone? It had been only footsteps behind them. Now it had vanished as mysteriously as it had appeared.

Not for the first time that night, he began to wonder if he had lost his sanity. His legs were shaking, and a hot, sick feeling twisted in him.

"I've failed, Father," he whispered. "I should have heeded the warnings. I never belonged here."

In Liery he'd known who he was. In Liery he'd never failed in anything. Here, he'd made one misstep after another, each worse than the last. His feelings for Fastia—feelings no true knight ever would have had—had cauterized his conviction and drained his confidence. He flinched, he hesitated, and now that lack of surety had killed Sir James and Elseny. He had failed the queen, his sworn charge, and even now a part of him knew he would do it again if it would save Fastia. Despite his vow, despite the wrongness of it.

He didn't deserve the breath in his lungs.

An arrow chirruped against stone, and he realized he had all but forgotten his mortal antagonists. Yet another failure. Cursing, he took what cover he could behind the gate frame, trying to see who was without. He made out two, perhaps three of the Sefry archers on the causeway. Another had come through the gate from the inner keep and was under cover of the now open door.

Striding toward him was the armored figure of the man who had once been Vargus Farre. When he saw Sir Neil he bellowed and increased his pace, drawing the greatsword from his back.

Neil, barely able to stand, grimly summoned all of his strength and stepped out to meet him.

"You aren't Ashern," the false knight said, when he drew near.

"I don't know who Ashern is," Neil replied. "But know this: I am the hand of death."

"You are sickened from the gaze of the greffyn. You are weary from flight and battle. Lay down your arms and accept the inevitable."

To Neil's horror, it sounded tempting. Lay down his arms, let the enemy strike off his head. At least he'd make no more mistakes, then. At least he would be at peace.

But no. He should die like a man, however little that might mean. "When the sea falls into the sky, that will be," he said.

"That day may not be as far off as you might think," Farre replied. He lifted his sword and struck.

Neil parried the blow but staggered beneath it. He replied with a cut to the shoulder joint, but missed, his weapon clanging harmlessly on steel. Farre swung again, and this time Neil managed to duck. The blade missed, but he went dizzy, and before he could recover, a re-

versed blow caught him on the back. The chain mail hauberk took the
edge with a snapping of rings, but it absorbed none of the force of the
attack, which drove him down to his knees. Sir Vargus kicked him under
the chin, but Neil manage to wrap one arm around the armored leg and
stab upward with Crow.

It was not a strong jab, and again Crow screeched in frustration as it
scored across armor but did not harm the man.

The hilt came hammering down toward his head, but Neil twisted
so it took him in the shoulder instead. Agony ruptured along his clavicle,
which he distantly reckoned was probably shattered.

Farre kicked him again, and he went back like a rag doll into the
horz. The knight stepped through after him. The saints, it seemed, did
not care what might become of Neil MeqVren.

Spitting blood, Neil climbed slowly to his feet, watching the changeling come foward through a red fog of pain. He seemed to come very
slowly, as if each blink of the eye took days. In a strange rush, Neil heard
again the sound of the sea and tasted cold salt on his lips. For an instant,
he was there on the strand again with his father, the older man's hand
gripping his.

We goin' to lose, Fah? We goin' to die?

And then, so plain it might have been spoken in his ear, he heard a
voice.

You're a MeqVren, boy. Damn you, but don't lie down yet.

Neil straightened and took a breath. It felt like a burning wind.

Muriele managed to raise her head when she heard the song. It started
weakly, barely a whisper, but it was in the language of her childhood.

"Mi, Etier meuf, eyoiz'etiern rem
Crach-toi, frennz, mi viveut-toi dein."

It was Sir Neil, standing before Vargus Farre.

"Me, my father, my fathers before
Croak, ye ravens, I'll feed ye soon."

He sang, though it seemed impossible he could even stand. Sir Vargus swung a great two-handed blow at the smaller man. Almost laconically, Sir Neil parried the weapon, and his voice grew louder.

"We keep our honor on sea and shore
Croak, ye ravens, I'll feed ye soon."

Suddenly Sir Neil's sword lashed out, all out of keeping with his demeanor, and there came a din of metal. Vargus staggered back from the stroke, but Sir Neil followed it up with another that seemed to come from nowhere. He was shouting, now.

"With spear and sword and board of war,
Croak, ye ravens, I'll feed ye soon."

Sir Vargus rallied and cut hard into Neil's side. Chain mail snapped with bright ringing and blood spurted, but the young knight didn't seem to notice. He kept chanting, beating a rhythm of terrible blows that rang against plate mail.

"To fight and die is why we're born.
Croak, ye ravens, I'll feed ye soon."

Neil was shrieking now, and Muriele understood. He had a rage on him. Vargus Farre never got in another blow. He stumbled and fell beneath the onslaught, and Neil pounded him with his blade as if it were a club, shearing sparks from the armor. He chopped through the joint of Farre's arm at the elbow; he crushed in his helm. Long after there was no motion, he hacked into the steel-clad corpse, screaming the death song of his Skernish fathers. And when he finally stood and his eyes turned to her, she thought she had never seen a more terrifying sight.

"The gates are open," Stephen murmured, as they rode over the succession of drawbridges that led to Cal Azroth.

"I reckon I can see that," Aspar grunted. "Quiet a moment, and listen."

Stephen nodded, closing his eyes. The only sound Aspar could make out was his own breath and the labored panting of the horses. Winna was a welcome weight against his back, and a fear, as well. He had her back. He couldn't lose her again.

But Fend was here. He could smell him.

"I hear steel meeting steel," Stephen said, after a moment. "And someone singing, in Llerish, I think. That aside, it's quiet."

"Fend is quiet," Aspar murmured. A wind blew from Cal Azroth, and autumn was on it. "You'll both stay here and wait for me."

"We'll do nothing of the kind," Winna replied.

"There'll be fighting," Aspar said. "You'll hinder me."

"You need Stephen's ears and my sense," Winna replied evenly. "We've both saved your skin in the past, Aspar White. There's nothing to say it won't need doing again."

Aspar was figuring a reply to that when Stephen made an odd sound.

"What is it?" Aspar asked.

"You don't hear it?"

"Ney. I've only the ordinary sort of ears."

"The blasting of the horn. It's returning."

"Maybe another horn."

"No," Stephen said. "The same."

"An echo? That makes no sense," Aspar said.

"No," Stephen said. "It does. He's coming. The Briar King is answering the call, and it's coming back with him." Stephen's eyes held fear, but his voice was steady. "I think we'd best hurry, Holter. There's more at risk here than a queen."

"Wait and maunt a moment," Aspar protested. "Fend and his Sefry are in there, waiting to murder whoever comes through that gate. We'll go deliberately and cautious or not at all."

Stephen nodded as if he understood. The next instant he gave Angel a hard kick and the beast was flying toward the open gate.

"Grim eat you and sceat you out," Aspar snarled. But he gave Ogre the flank and followed.

He clattered into the corpse-strewn keep just behind Stephen. As he'd fully expected, he immediately heard the snap of bowstrings. He wheeled Ogre into cover behind the gate and leapt off the horse.

"Get down," he commanded Winna. "Ogre will fight best protecting you. Stay under cover here."

"Yah," Winna breathed. She squeezed his hand. "Watch my love for me," she said.

"Yah. I'll do that."

He took out his bow and darted from beneath the door, painfully aware that he'd recovered only five arrows intact from his last skirmish. He'd gone scarce ten yards when a shaft hissed down from above and cracked against the courtyard stone. Aspar turned coolly, saw the shadow on the wall above, and took a full breath to aim. His shaft leapt starward at the same moment a second dart skinned along his arm. He didn't wait to see what happened, for he knew he'd hit.

Instead he turned and ran after Stephen, who was already in considerable trouble. Angel had taken a shaft in the flank and thrown the boy. He was trying to get up, but it was a miracle he hadn't yet been skewered, for arrows were skittering on the stone around him. Aspar found the source of some of those and hit the archer with his next arrow. It was a hard shot, and he could tell he hadn't pierced anything vital, but the man stopped shooting for the time being.

The rest of the killers were taking cover behind a second gate. Aspar counted five or six, and he could hear someone fighting on the other side, as well.

"Get some cover!" he shouted to Stephen, sending the Sefry ducking with another dart. He had only three shafts remaining, so he needed to close the distance. He paced toward the door, another dart on his string. It was easier than he thought, for the archers were plainly distracted by the ruckus Aspar couldn't see.

One peeped out, though, and Aspar gave him cause to regret it. He noticed Stephen had done what he'd told him to do, and was flat against the same wall as the gate. He also noticed Stephen was pointing at something behind Aspar.

"Holter!" the boy shouted.

Aspar didn't question, he just swung and stepped hard to the right, finding himself nearly face to face with Fend. The Sefry had a knife in either hand, and an expression half-turned between glee and fury. Aspar raised the bow in defense, but he was far too close to shoot, and Fend's knives were lightning, flashing toward him.

Aspar blocked with the bow as best he could, but the Sefry's right-hand blade darted past the wood and drew blood on his forearm. Aspar managed a return blow with the bow; it didn't do Fend any harm, but it gave the holter space to draw out his dirk and ax.

Warier now, Fend circled, feinting with his shoulders. Aspar turned with him, weapons ready.

"You're getting old, Asp," Fend commented. "Slow. There's no challenge in this now."

"That why you came at me from behind?" Aspar asked.

"Oh, I would have let you see me before you died. So you'd know." He glanced toward Winna. "Pretty little piece of meat," he allowed. "Almost as sweet as Qerla. Probably as faithful, too."

Aspar grinned coldly. "I think I'll have your other eye, Fend."

"I doubt that, old man. But you're welcome to try for it."

Aspar's fury was so deep and complete that he felt glacially calm. He heard a little chuckle bubble from between his lips and was surprised.

"What's that?" Fend asked.

"You. Trying to provoke me, like a frightened little boy."

"I'm just enjoying myself," Fend said. "It's not so much—"

He didn't finish his sentence, but instead bounded forward. Aspar had noticed him drawing his rear leg up as they spoke. He caught the right-hand dagger with his own dirk and cut at the other wrist with his ax. He got a little of it and sent flecks of blood into the night, but Fend was nothing if not quick, and the cut wasn't deep.

The Sefry bounced fractionally out of range and then back in, slashing with his right and keeping the left back. Aspar let him come, fading from the blow and kicking sharply at Fend's forward ankle. He made solid contact, and his opponent lost balance. Aspar followed up, but rather than trying to recover, Fend went down tumbling. When he came back to his feet, he had only one knife.

Aspar thought that was good until he realized the hilt of the other was jutting out of his leg.

"Your aim is off," Aspar said, reaching down and yanking the weapon out. It hurt, that, but the muscle on the front of the thigh was pretty forgiving. It probably wouldn't even bleed much. He tucked the dagger in his belt and closed on Fend again.

Fend, still looking confident, began a light-footed dance around Aspar. The holter turned, using slower footwork. When Fend came again, his left hand caught at Aspar's ax wrist, and Aspar let him think he was slow enough to be caught. As soon as the finger touched him, however, he suddenly swung away, avoiding a thrust toward his heart, and lashed with the ax. He made it in deep, digging a gouge into Fend's shoulder and feeling bone crunch. The Sefry gasped and dropped back, his eye widening in amazement.

"Yah, I reckon I'll kill you today, Fend," Aspar said. "You had your chance when you threw your knife, and you missed it." He started forward, still cautious.

They closed again, but there was something desperate in the way the Sefry fought now, something worried. It was fast and close, and when they parted once more, each had several new wounds. Aspar's were all shallow, but Fend had a hole in his ribs. Not deep enough to kill him anytime soon, but it probably hurt.

"Why Qerla, Fend?" Aspar asked. "Why did you kill her? I've never known that."

Fend grinned, showing his teeth. "You don't know? That's delightful." He coughed. "You're a lucky old man, you know that? Always lucky."

"Yah. Very lucky. Are you going to tell me or not?"

"Not, I think."

Aspar shrugged. "That's the only thing I wanted from you besides your life. I suppose I'll settle."

"I have a little luck of my own," Fend said. "Look to your lady."

It was an old trick, and Aspar didn't fall for it until Winna screamed. Then Aspar wheeled and dropped, knowing no matter what was happening his enemy wouldn't miss the opportunity. Fend's second knife whispered over his head, but Aspar didn't care about him anymore. The greffyn had just entered through the gate. It was moving toward Winna, and Ogre was stamping, ready to meet it.

CHAPTER FOURTEEN

THE ARRIVAL

As Anne watched the knight advance on Cazio, something seemed to dim in her even as the purple moonlight seemed to brighten, as if the darkness the moon was displacing sought a hiding place in her soul.

"He's going to kill Cazio," Austra said. "Then he'll kill us."

"Yes," Anne said. She realized that they should have been running while Cazio fought, but something had stayed her feet. There might still be time; the Vitellian was certainly losing the battle, but he might last a little longer, long enough for them to escape.

But no, she was horsewoman enough to know how quickly she and Austra would be run down. Their first hope had been in an unnoticed escape, and their second had been Cazio. Neither had proved out. She eyed the knight's horse speculatively—but no, a warhorse would never let her mount. It would probably strike her dead if she drew near enough to try.

"Can't we help him?" Austra asked.

"Against a knight?" But even as she said it, Anne suddenly felt a strange dislocation, as if she were two people—the Anne who had fearlessly ridden down the Sleeve, and the Anne who was starting to understand the consequences of life, who had just watched knights like this slaughter women as if they were barnyard beasts.

Once, she had imagined adventures in which, dressed as a knight herself, she had triumphed over evil foes. Now all she could see was blood, and all she could imagine was her own head lifting from her shoulders in a spray of it.

A few months ago she would have rushed to Cazio's aid. Now her illusions were dying, and she was left with the world that was. And in that world, a woman did not stand against a knight.

Austra gave her an odd look, one Anne didn't recognize, as if her friend was a stranger she had only just met.

The knight, meanwhile, lifted his sword over the fallen Cazio, who put up his own slender weapon in frail defense.

"No!" Austra shrieked. Before Anne could think of stopping her, the younger girl ran forward, snatched up a stone, and threw it. It glanced from the knight's armor, distracting him for a second. Austra kept running toward him.

Anne grabbed a fallen branch, cursing. She couldn't just watch Austra die.

Austra tried to grab the warrior's sword arm, but he cuffed her hard on the side of the head with a mailed fist. Cazio wobbled back to his feet, a little out of range, as Anne drew up and stood over her friend, stick in hand. The knight's visor turned toward her.

"Do not be foolish," he said. Through the slits in his helm she saw contempt and moonlight reflected in his eyes, and a sudden dark fury raged through her. Her thoughts were whisper-winged owls, stooping on mice. How dare he, beneath the sickle moon? How dare he, in the very womb of night? He, who had violated the sacred soil of Cer and soaked it with the blood of her daughters? *How dare he look at her in such a way?*

"Man," Anne husked. "Man, do not look at me." She didn't recognize her own voice, so inert it seemed, so devoid of life, as if the dimness in her spilled out with her words.

The light in the knight's eyes vanished, though the moon was still there, though he had not turned his head. His breath caught, and rattled, and then he did turn his head, this way and that. He rubbed at those eyes, like two holes darker than moonshadow.

Men fight from the outside, with clumsy swords and arrows, Sister

Casita had said, *trying to pierce the layers of protections we bundle in. They are of the outside. We are of the inside. We can reach there in a thousand ways, slipping through the cracks of eye and ear, nostril and lip, through the very pores of the flesh. Here is your frontier, Sisters, and eventually your domain. Here is where your touch will bring the rise and fall of kingdoms.*

Anne, confused and suddenly frightened again, stumbled back, shaking.

What had she done? How?

"Casnar!" Cazio shouted. Anne noticed he'd managed to stand, though not firmly. "Leave off your brave battle against unarmed women and address me."

The knight ignored him, cutting wildly in the air.

"*Haliurun! Waizeza! Hundan!*" he shouted. "*Meina auyos! Hwa . . .* What have you done to my eyes?"

"Hanzish!" Anne said. "Austra, they're from Hansa!" She turned to Cazio. "Kill him! Now, while he's blind."

Cazio had begun advancing, but now he stopped, puzzled.

"He cannot see? I can't fight a man who cannot see."

The knight lurched toward Cazio, but even in his injured state the Vitellian easily avoided him.

"How did you do that, by the by?" Cazio asked, watching his erstwhile opponent crash into a tree. "I've heard a dust ground from the nut of Lady Una's frock—"

"He was going to kill *you*," Anne interrupted.

"He has no honor," Cazio said. "I do."

"Then let us flee!" Austra urged.

"Will honor allow that?" Anne asked sarcastically.

Cazio coughed and a look of pain wormed through his brow. "Honor discourages it," he said.

Anne shook a remonstrative finger at him. "Listen to me well, Cazio Pachiomadio da Chiovattio," she said, remembering how her mother sounded when she was giving orders. "There are many more knights than this one, and we are in danger from them. I require your protection for Austra and myself. I require your aid in removing us from harm's way. Will your honor deny me that?"

Cazio scratched his head, then grinned sheepishly. The blinded knight stood with his back against a tree, sword out, facing no one in particular. "No, casnara," he said. "I will accompany you."

"Then let us go, and *quickly*," Austra said.

"A moment," Anne told them. She raised her voice. "Knight of Hansa. Why have you and your companions sinned against Saint Cer? Why did you murder the sisters, and why do you pursue me? Answer me, or I shall wither the rest of you as I have darkened your eyes."

The knight turned at the sound of her voice.

"I do not know the answer to that, lady," he said. "I know only that what my prince tells me to do must be done."

At that he charged her. Almost casually, Cazio stuck out his foot, which the knight tripped over. He went sprawling to the ground.

"Have you more questions for him?" the Vitellian asked.

"Let me think," Anne replied.

"The night wanes, and she is our ally. The sun will not be as kind."

Anne nodded. She didn't think the Hanzish knight would tell her more even if he knew it. They would waste precious time.

"Very well," Cazio said. "Follow me, fair casnaras. I know the countryside. I will guide you through it." His brow wrinkled. "If you do not rob me of my sight, of course."

Cazio's ribs felt as if they were aflame, but his blood, at least, did not flow strongly. He was able to set a good pace but could not run for any length of time. That was just as well, he knew, for running would only wear them all out.

Of course, there was no reason to expect the knights attacking the coven would come after them. If it was women they wanted, they already had plenty.

Didn't they?

"How many of these beetle-backed ruffians are there?" he asked.

"I'm not certain," Anne answered. "Some thirty to begin with. Some were killed by the sisters of the coven."

That was impressive. "And you've no idea why?" he asked.

It seemed to Cazio that Anne hesitated too long before answering.

"I don't know," she said. "But I think they killed all of the sisters.

The novitiates were hiding. I don't know what happened to them. Austra and I fled through the fane of Saint Mefitis, a cave that emerges near where you found us. Where are we going?"

"Back to the triva of the countess Orchaevia."

"Can she protect us? I saw no soldiers there."

"True," Cazio replied. "She sent them away for the Fiussanal. But why should these knights pursue us?"

"Why shouldn't they?"

"Have they some especial grudge against you two? Did you endear them in some way?"

Again, Anne seemed to hesitate. "They will pursue us, Cazio."

"Why?"

"I cannot tell you that. I'm not sure I know why myself. But it is a fact."

She did know something then, but wasn't willing to tell it. He looked at her again. Who was this girl, really? The daughter of some northern warlord? What had he gotten himself into?

"Very well, then," he said. Whatever it was, he was deep in it now. He ought to see it through. Perhaps there would even be some reward in it for him.

Lady Ausa's robe lay coral on the eastern horizon and the stars were vanishing above. They were out in open countryside, easy prey for horsemen. He tried to quicken his pace. If Anne was right, and they were followed, returning to Orchaevia's triva would repay the countess in poor coin for the hospitality she had shown him. The place was defensible, but not by two swordsmen and a few serving women.

"There is an old estate nearby," he considered aloud. Z'Acatto had dragged him to it one day in hopes of finding an unplundered wine cellar. They had found the cellar, but all of the wine had gone to vinegar. "It will make a good hiding place," he decided. After all, if he couldn't defeat one of the knights in single combat, what chance did he have against ten, or twenty? His father had made the mistake of choosing to face the wrong enemy for the wrong reasons. He would not make the same blunder.

Anne didn't answer, but she was beginning to stumble. The sandals she and Austra wore were hardly fit for this sort of travel.

Lord Abullo's horses were well in the sky, pulling a burnt orange sun free of the horizon, before Cazio made out the crumbling walls of the ancient triva. He wondered if the well was still good, for he was terribly thirsty. The vinegar was all gone, smashed by z'Acatto in a fit of disappointment.

They had almost reached the walls when he thought he heard hooves, and a glance back showed two horsemen approaching. There was little need to wonder who they were, for the gleam of the now-golden sun on their armor was evident.

"They may not have seen us yet," Cazio hoped aloud, leading them behind a picket of cedars bordering the abandoned mansion. "Quickly." The gate had long since crumbled, leaving only the columns of the pastato, and walls that were sometimes knee high and sometimes higher than his head. Weeds and small olive trees had cracked the stone of the courtyard and pushed it up as Lord Selvans sought to reclaim the place for his own. In the distance, he heard the approaching percussion.

"Just where I left it," Cazio murmured, when they reached the vine-draped entrance to the cellar. The stairs still remained, albeit broken and covered in earth and moss. A cool breath seemed to sigh up from its depths.

"We'll be trapped down there," Anne protested.

"Better there than in the open," Cazio pointed out. "See how narrow the way down is? They won't get their horses in, and won't be able to swing those pig-slaughtering blades. It will give me an advantage."

"You can barely stand," Anne said.

"Yes, but a da Chiovattio who can barely stand is worth six men hale and healthy. And here there are only two."

"Don't lie to me, Cazio. If we go down in there, can you win?"

Cazio shrugged. "I cannot say. But out in the open, I cannot." The words sounded strange to him, though he had already thought them. He took Anne's hand, and she didn't protest. "On foot, outside, you will be run down before you can travel a cenpereci. We should not wish for choices we do not have."

Reluctantly, the two girls followed him down.

"It smells like vinegar in here," Austra observed.

"Indeed," Cazio remarked. "Now remain below."

For a moment the world seemed to turn strangely, and the next he was lying on the cold stone.

"Cazio!" Austra cried, coming to his side.

"It's nothing," Cazio murmured. "A dizziness. Perhaps another kiss might cure it."

"He can't fight them," Austra said. "He'll be killed."

"They still may not know we're here," Cazio pointed out.

But they heard hooves on stone, and nearby.

"I'll need that kiss," Cazio whispered.

He couldn't see her blush, but Austra leaned close and touched her lips to his. They tasted sweet, like wine and plums, and he lingered on it. It was likely the last kiss he would ever have. He thought of asking Anne for one, too, but she wouldn't give it and time was dear, now.

"That will be my token," Cazio said, clambering to his feet. "And now it will be my pleasure to defend you ladies."

His legs shaking, Cazio climbed back up toward the sun, where shadows were moving.

For some reason, he remembered where he had heard of a purple moon. It was in a song his father used to sing when he was a boy.

And when will the clouds come down from the sky?
When the fogs down in the valley lie.

And when will the mountaintops meet the sea?
When the hard rains come, then shall it be.

And when will the sky have purple horns?
When the old man walks who calls the thorns.

He remembered the line because, unlike the other verses, it never made any sense to him.

It still didn't.

In the distance, he thought he heard a cornet sounding.

To Muriele the world felt suddenly silent, as if all of the sounds of battle had retreated to an infinite distance. She looked at the dead face of her daughter, saw her as an infant, as a child of six spilling milk on the Galléan carpet in her sunroom, as a woman in a wedding gown. The silence gripped beneath her breast, waiting to become a scream.

Elseny must be dead, too. And Erren, and Charles . . .

But the silence was in her, not without. Steel still rang, and Neil's fierce battle cries proved him still alive. And over all that the sound of a horn, growing steadily louder.

It had sounded far off, at first, as if shrilled from the ends of the earth. Now it called from much nearer, but with a prickling she realized that it wasn't approaching, only growing louder. And the source of the sounding was quite close indeed.

But where? Muriele puzzled at it, used the mystery to cloak Fastia's dead face and her own imaginings. It didn't take her long to discover the sound came from the wickerwork feinglest Elseny had filled with flowers only the day before. And in her dazed sight, the feinglest was changing, as slowly and surely as the sunrise drowning the morning star in gray light.

Her gaze fastened and would not waver, and as the horn droned louder she saw the change quicken, the wickerwork drawing tighter and taller. The vague resemblance to human shape was more pronounced with each heartbeat. Muriele watched, unable to move or speak, her mind refusing the sight as anything more than a waking dream.

It grew on, and the wailing of the trumpet rose so loud that Muriele at last managed to pull her hands to her ears to try to stop the sound, but her palms held no power to diminish it. Nor could her brain arrest her eyes from seeing the feinglest shiver like a wasp-wing in flight, throw out arms and sprout proud antlers from its head, and open two almost-human eyes, leaf-green orbs in black almond slivers. A powerful animal musk penetrated her nostrils, overwhelming the sickly sweet scent of the flowers.

The Briar King towered the height of two men over her; his gaze connected with hers. He was naked, and his flesh was mottled bark. A beard of moss curled from his face, and long unshorn locks of the same dangled from his head. His eyes seemed to see nothing and everything, like those of a newborn. His nostrils quivered, and a sound came from his throat that carried no meaning for her, like the snuffling of a strange beast.

He leaned near her and sniffed again, and though his nose was of human shape, Muriele was reminded more of a horse or a stag than of a man. His breath was damp and cold, and smelled like a forest stream. Muriele's flesh crawled as if covered with ants.

The Briar King turned to Fastia and blinked, slowly, then shifted his strange eyes back to Muriele, narrowing them as they came mere fingers from her own.

Her vision dissolved in those eyes. She saw strange, deep woods full of trees like giant mosses and trunked ferns. She saw beasts with the eyes of owls and the shapes of mastiffs.

He blinked again, slowly, and she saw Eslen fallen into ruins and swallowed by vines of black thorn with blooms like purple spiders. She saw Newland beneath the stars, covered by dark waters, and then those waters dancing with pale flame. She saw a vast hall of shadow and a throne of sooty stone, and on it a figure whose face could not be seen but for eyes that burned like green flame. She heard laughter that sounded almost like a hound baying.

And then, as if in a mirror of polished jet, she saw her own dead face. Then it was again the face of the Briar King, and her fear was gone, as if she really were dead and moved beyond all mortal thoughts. As in a dream, she reached to touch his beard.

His face contorted in a sudden expression of pain and rage, and he howled, a sound with nothing human and everything wild in it.

Aspar was too far from his bow. The greffyn would reach Winna and Ogre long before he could fit an arrow to string. He did the only thing he could do; he threw his ax. It struck the greffyn in the back of the head and bounced, leaving a gash and drawing a thin train of ruby droplets.

"So you *can* bleed, you mikel rooster," Aspar snarled in perverse satisfaction.

The greffyn turned slowly to face him, and Aspar felt the fever from its eyes strike straight through to his bones. But it wasn't so bad as before;

his knees trembled but did not betray him. He gripped his dirk as it came, but he did not watch it. Instead he focused on Winna, on her face, for he wanted to remember it.

He couldn't quite remember Qerla's face.

It was luck to find love twice in one lifetime, he decided, and luck always came with a price. It was time to pay it, he supposed.

Give me strength, Raver, he thought. He'd never asked Haergrim for anything before. Perhaps the Raver would take that into account.

The greffyn came, then, almost faster than sight could follow. Aspar turned just slightly, striking the beast above and between the eyes with the iron hilt of his dirk. He felt a terrible shock in his arm and knew he was already dead.

He heard Winna scream.

Incredibly, the greffyn stumbled at the blow, and Aspar took the only chance he had. He threw himself upon the scaled back and wrapped one arm beneath the hooked jaw. The creature screamed then, a shrill cacophony that almost overshadowed the rising sound of the horn.

He guessed where the heart might be and drove his dirk there, once, twice, again. The greffyn crashed into the courtyard wall, trying to dislodge him, but for the moment his arm was a steel band. Aspar felt larger, like one of the great tyrants of the forest, his roots sinking deep, pulling strength from stone and soil and deep hidden springs, and when his heart beat again he knew he was the forest itself, seeking vengeance.

Motion blurred everything. He caught a brief glimpse of Winna's anguished face, of Ogre, proud and fearless, rushing to his aid. There was air, and then water, as they plunged into the canal beyond the gate.

Close the gate, Winna, he thought. *Be the bright girl.* He would have shouted it, but the water was wrapped too tightly about him.

All the while his dirk was cutting, as if the Grim had indeed taken Aspar's hand for his own. The water of the canal burned like lye.

Cazio stood unsteadily at the entrance to the wine cellar, but when he raised Caspator, the weapon did not waver.

"Hello, my fine casnars," he said to the two armored men. "Which of you do I have the honor of killing first?"

The knights had just dismounted. He noticed one of them had more ornate armor than the other, all gilded on the edges. That was the one who answered him.

"I know not who you are, sir," the fellow said. "But there is no need for you to die. Leave here and return to a life that might be long and prosperous."

Cazio looked down the length of Caspator. He wondered if his father had felt this way at the end. There was certainly no profit in this fight. No one would hear of it.

"I prefer to live an honorable life to a long one, casnar," he said. "Can the same be said of you?"

The knight regarded him enigmatically for a moment, and Cazio felt a brief hope. Then the man in gilded armor turned his head toward his companion.

"Kill this one for me," he said.

The other man nodded slightly and started forward.

He doesn't have a shield, at least, Cazio remarked to himself. *The eye slits. That's my target.*

The horn in the distance grew louder. More knights, probably.

The knight came hewing. Cazio calmly parried the blows, though Caspator shivered from them. He riposted at the steel visor, but the fellow stayed out of distance, and Cazio didn't have the footing needed to lunge. They fought for several long phrases before the heavy broadsword finally smashed down onto Caspator's hilt, shocking his already numbed arm enough that the weapon clattered to the ground.

It was then that a cascade of mortar and brick fell on the knight's head. Dust and grit followed, stinging Cazio's eyes. Masonry tumbled past him down the worn stairway, and he saw the knight collapse, his helm deeply dented.

The gilded knight—who hadn't been beneath the fall of rubble— looked up in time to receive a brick in the face, and then another. Stunned, Cazio bent to retrieve Caspator as z'Acatto dropped down from above the arch of the cellar door.

"I told you, boy," the swordmaster grunted. "You don't *fence* knights."

"Granted," Cazio said, noticing that the gilded knight was regaining his feet. With what little remained of his strength, Cazio leapt forward. The broadsword came up and down, but he turned and avoided it, and this time Caspator drove true, through the slit in the helm and further, stopped only by the steel on the other side of the skull, or the skull itself. He withdrew the bloody point and watched the knight sink first to his knees, and then to a prone position.

"I'll follow your advice more closely next time," he promised the older swordsman.

"What have you gotten yourself into, lad?" z'Acatto asked. He looked past Cazio, then, and shook his head.

"Ah," he said. "I see where the trouble is."

Anne and Austra had come to the top of the stair and were staring at the tableau.

"There will be more," Cazio said.

"More women?"

"More trouble."

"The same thing," z'Acatto remarked.

"More knights," Cazio clarified. "Maybe many more."

"I've two horses," z'Acatto said. "We can ride double."

Cazio crossed his arms and gave his swordmaster a dubious look. "It's fortunate you brought horses," he said. "Also very odd."

"Don't be an empty bottle, boy. The road to the coven goes near the well at the edge of Orchaevia's estates. I saw them arrive."

"What were you doing there?"

Z'Acatto grinned and drew a narrow bottle of green glass from beneath his doublet. He held it up to the light.

"I found it," he said triumphantly. "The very best year. I knew I would smell it out."

Cazio rolled his eyes. "At least we were saved by a good vintage," he said.

"The best," z'Acatto repeated happily.

Cazio made a weak bow to the two women.

"My casnaras Anne and Austra, I present to you my swordmaster, the learned z'Acatto." He hesitated and caught the old man's eyes. "My master and best friend."

Z'Acatto held his gaze for an instant, and something glimmered there Cazio did not quite understand. Then he looked to Anne and Austra.

"My great pleasure, casnaras," z'Acatto said. "I hope one of you will not mind my company on horse."

Anne bowed. "You've saved us, sir," she said. She looked at Cazio significantly. "The two of you. I'm in your debt."

It was then Austra shrieked at something behind Cazio. Cazio sighed and turned, ready for anything.

Anything except for what he saw. Slowly, tremulously, the gilded knight was trying to rise. Blood ran from his visor like water from a fountain. Cazio raised his sword.

"No," z'Acatto said. "No. He's not alive." Cazio couldn't tell if it was a statement or a question, but z'Acatto drew his own sword and jabbed it through the other eye. The knight fell back again, but this time started to get up immediately.

"Diuvo's wagging—" Z'Acatto didn't finish the curse, but instead picked up the knight's abandoned broadsword and hewed off the man's head.

The fingers continued to claw at the dirt.

Z'Acatto watched that for a moment. "I advise rapid flight," he told them. "And later, some wine."

"We're in agreement," Cazio husked.

The rage had almost left Neil when the horz exploded. The Sefry archer on the point of his sword was gaping at the otherworld, and with no other enemies at hand, the red cloud was lifting, allowing reason back into his head.

He had heard of the rage before; his uncle Odcher had had that gift. In all of his years of battle, Neil had never experienced it before.

Watching the Sefry slowly relinquish his life, he stared at the carnage around him, trying to remember what he'd been doing when the lightning had entered his soul.

The sound of shattering stone turned him, and he saw what appeared to be turbid coils of black smoke billowing through the rent walls of the garden. He staggered toward the horz, remembering that he had left the queen and Fastia within. It was only when he actually plunged into what he'd believed to be smoke that focus came, though not comprehension.

Black tendrils groped past him, gripping at his limbs, fastening to the stone of the walkway. He cut at them, and they fell writhing to the ground, but they were merely the vanguard of the thicker vines they sprang from, wide as a man's legs and growing larger with each moment. The sharp points of thorns tore at Neil's armor. The briars pushed him back to the edge of the causeway, though he hacked at them with Crow. It had been a long while since he'd understood much of anything, and he no longer cared. He'd left the queen in the horz; he had to return for her.

So he pitched himself forward, sweat and blood sheening his face and stinging his eyes, slowly fighting through the impossible foliage, until his sword hit something it would not cut. He looked up and green eyes stared back down at him.

It was far taller than a man, the thing, entirely wrapped about in the black vines. They tugged at him, as if trying to pull him into the earth from which they sprang, but he ignored their grasping just as he ignored Neil after a single glance.

Neil smelled spring rain mingled with rotting wood.

The green-eyed thing strode past the young warrior, snapping the vines and tearing them from the stone as he went, but wherever his feet trod new growth sprang up. Neil watched him, gape-mouthed, as he stepped into the canal, the deepest waters of which came only to his waist.

He'd never seen a monster before, and now he'd seen two. Neil wondered if the world was coming to an end.

The queen, you fool. The end of the world was not his concern. Muriele Dare was.

He turned to what was left of the horz, slashing at the thick vines with Crow, weeping, for what could tear apart stone must be able to do much more to human flesh.

But he found the queen untouched upon the stone from which the largest of the vines had emerged, staring at where the dark briars had crept over Fastia's form. Numb of all human feeling, Neil took the queen in his arms, stumbling through the path he had cut in the vines, through the courtyard full of corpses and out the front gates. He saw the thorn-giant again, striding up the canal where it bent around toward

the front gate of Cal Azroth, where others stood watching. Neil lay the
queen on the grass and fumbled for Crow; they were surely more of his
enemies—

But Saint Oblivion beckoned, and he had no power to resist her.

The greffyn rolled and pitched beneath the water, and Aspar's lungs
would stay shut no longer. His hold loosened, and he was flung away. He
struck toward the surface, the dirk still in his hand.

He came up near the edge of the canal and clambered at it, pulled
himself from the water with little more than strength of will. He fought
to stand, tremors running through his entire body, watching the roiling
water for a quicker doom he felt certain would emerge.

Everything in him felt broken. He vomited, and saw that it was
mostly blood. Far away he heard his name, but he hadn't time for that,
for the greffyn did come out of the water, sinuous and beautiful, like
something a poet might sing made flesh. He marveled that he hadn't
seen it that way from the start. That he'd wounded it seemed almost a
shame—except that of course it had to die.

"Come here," Aspar told it. "There's not much left of me, but come
get what's here, if you can."

It seemed to him that it moved a little slower, this time, when it
lashed at him with its great beak. It seemed he shouldn't have had time
to drive the dirk into its eye, but he did.

Just like Fend, he thought, wondering where the Sefry had gone.
Then the greffyn hit him with a weight like a horse in full barding.
Everything went white, but he kept hold of consciousness, flexing his
now empty hands, knowing they would do him no good at all, but happy
he could at least fight to the end.

But when he turned, he saw that the beast lay still. It had hit a stone
piling, and its neck was crooked at an implausible angle.

*Well. Easier than I thought. Grim, if that luck was sent by you, my
thanks. It's good to see your foe die before you. Now if Fend would be so
good as to drop dead nearby . . .*

Aspar lay there, coughing blood, the now familiar feel of poison
deepening. He hoped Stephen would keep Winna away, but then she
had enough sense not to touch his corpse anyway, didn't she?

He turned his head and saw her there, standing beside Stephen, on the other side of the canal. She was weeping. He raised his hand weakly but didn't have enough strength to call out. "Stay there, lass," he whispered. "By Grim, stay there." There must be poison every place the greffyn had spilled blood.

But now something else went across Winna's face, and Stephen's, as well.

A shadow fell over him, blocking the morning sun, and Aspar wearily raised his head to look once more upon the Briar King.

Stephen dropped Aspar's bow from trembling hands. He'd been trying to shoot the greffyn, but he'd feared hitting Aspar, and now, incredibly, the beast was dead.

Winna, by his side, started forward, but he held her back.

"There's nothing you can do for him," he said. "If you go near, you'll die, too."

"I don't care," she said huskily. "I don't care."

"But he would," Stephen told her. "I'll not let you."

She opened her mouth, probably to argue further, but then around the corner of the keep, wading up the canal, came what could only be the Briar King, dragging a train of thorns behind him. One great step brought him out of the water, and with large and purposeful strides he started toward the King's Forest.

But then he paused and lifted his nose as if scenting something, and his antlered head turned to regard the fallen figures of Aspar and the greffyn. It moved toward them purposefully.

"It's happened," Stephen whispered. "Saints, but it's happened." He saw in his mind's eye the scrifts and tomes he had pored over, the bits of time-shattered clues, the terrible prophecies. And he felt something, in the earth and sky, as if something were broken and sifting away, as if the world itself was bleeding.

As if the end had truly begun.

Which meant nothing much was worth doing, was it?

But he ought to try, he supposed.

He picked up the bow and shot the single remaining arrow. He didn't know if he actually hit the monster or not, but it certainly didn't notice.

It stooped first upon Aspar, and vines writhed all about him. Then it left him there and moved on to the greffyn. Stephen saw him lift the slain beast in his arms, cradling it like a child, and then walk away, leaving a trail of black springlings in his footsteps.

Behind them, the stones of Cal Azroth began to slowly shatter as the vines pulled it down.

CHAPTER FIFTEEN

OBSERVATIONS QUAINT
AND CURIOUS

"STEPHEN DARIGE?"

Stephen glanced up at the page, who wore orange stockings and a fur-trimmed coat of black. He supposed, from his brief acquaintance with her, that this was the best the duchess of Loiyes could do in the way of mourning clothes for her servants, at least on short notice.

Observations and Speculations on the Multicolored Popinjays, he began in his head. *Or, the Assorted Maladies of Royal Blood.*

"My lord," the servant repeated, "are you Stephen Darige?"

"That I am," Stephen allowed wearily, his gaze languidly tracing the carefully manicured lawns of Glenchest. In the distance he could see Crown Prince Charles, the poor saint-touched oaf, playing a game of jackpins with his Sefry jester. Stephen had met the prince four days earlier, on their arrival at Glenchest. Charles hardly seemed aware of the butchering of his family. He hadn't been in the keep at Cal Azroth when Fend and the changelings came, but was sleeping in the stables after a day of childlike play.

The small footguard assigned to him had much to be grateful for, for they were the only survivors of the household guard that had accompanied the royals to Cal Azroth. While the fortress was rent to pieces by the unnatural thorns of the Briar King, they had easily managed to get Charles out of danger, then sent to Glenchest for help.

"Her Majesty Muriele Dare requests your presence in the Chamber of Sparrows."

"At what bell?" Stephen asked.

"If you please, you are to follow me."

"Ah. This instant?"

"If it please you, lord."

"And if it doesn't?"

The page looked confused. "Lord?"

"Never mind. Show me the way, good fellow." He wished the page would stop calling him lord, but the duchess insisted all of her guests be treated as nobility, in address at least.

He followed the boy through the hedges and up a path overarched with twined willows. He mused that while he had once enjoyed such gardens, he found them somehow claustrophobic now. He remembered the great trees of the King's Forest and had a sudden, powerful urge to be among them, even if it meant enduring Aspar White's sarcasm and disdain.

What good did *I think thousand-year-old maps would be?* he wondered. Sometimes it was hard to comprehend that earlier Stephen Darige, so much of him was gone now.

Faint voices touched his saint-blessed ears, intruding on his thoughts.

". . . found the bodies. They were monks, as was said, but then so is this Stephen Darige. And of the same order, too." That was Humfry Thenroesn, councilor to the duchess of Loiyes, such as he was. Stephen could smell the sour brandy of the fellow's breath on the autumn breeze, though they still hadn't even entered the manse.

"Darige risked his life for my children. He took wounds for them." And that was the queen herself.

"So he says," Thenroesn replied. "We have only his word for that. Perhaps he was one of the invading force, and when he saw they were losing—"

The queen interrupted. "The holter with him slew half of the remaining assassins, and the greffyn, as well."

Thenroesn sniffed. "Again, Majesty, that is based on hearsay. It is a grave risk to trust this Darige."

Stephen passed into the arched foyer of the manse. He noticed the walls were patterned with gilded sea serpents.

Humfry's voice grew prouder. "I have sent a rider to his eminence, Praifec Hespero," he boasted, as if taking such initiative deserved high praise. "He will surely send someone to confirm Darige's story. Until such time, I recommend that he be incarcerated."

There was a pause in which Stephen heard only his own footsteps, and then the queen's voice came, so chill that even at this distance Stephen shivered.

"Am I to understand that you contacted the praifec without my knowledge?" she asked.

Stephen followed the page down a long hall as Thenroesn suddenly became defensive. "Your Majesty, it is within my prerogative to—"

"Am I to understand," the queen asked again, "that you contacted the praifec without my knowledge?"

"Yes, Majesty."

"Duchess, do you have a dungeon in this . . . this place?"

Stephen recognized the duchess of Loiyes answering. "Yes, dear Majesty."

"Have this man placed in it, please."

"But, Your Majesty," Humfry Thenroesn began, then the duchess cut him off, just as Stephen came to the entrance to the chamber.

"You really should be more careful not to offend my sister-in-law, dear Humfry," the duchess said. She turned to one of her guards. "Drey, please escort Lord Humfry to one of the danker cells."

The queen glanced at Stephen, as he stood in the doorway, waiting to be admitted. She was as beautiful as her reputation, but her features were tightly composed. She might have been in fury, or despair, or felt nothing at all, if one had only her expression to read. Yet to Stephen's senses her voice revealed a heart in turmoil and a soul in torment.

"Dispatch a rider to intercept Lord Humfry's courier," the queen told the duchess. "Do no harm unless needs be. Just return him here with his message."

The duchess signed, and another of the Loiyes guard bowed and rushed off on that errand.

The queen turned her attention back to Stephen.

"*Fraleth* Darige. Please join us," she said.

Stephen bowed. "Your Majesty."

The queen sat in a modest armchair and wore a gown of black brocade with a collar that stood stiffly up her neck. The duchess, seated in a chair next to her, was also clad in black, though her neckline was less modest.

"Fraleth Darige, two of my daughters are dead. Tell me why." To Stephen, her voice was a raw wound, despite its flat and measured tone.

"Your Majesty," he said, "I do not know. As I told the duchess and her councilor, I discovered the plot by chance at the monastery d'Ef, when Aspar White, your holter, came to us injured. We followed Desmond Spendlove and his men to near here, where they met with Sefry outlaws and performed forbidden encrotacnia. I believe that is how they had the gates of your keep opened from the inside."

"Explain."

Stephen explained the rite as best he could. He expected disbelief, but the queen nodded as if she understood. "My late handmaiden, Erren, suggested as much before she was taken from me," she said. "Is there any protection for us? Must we continually fear these changelings in our midst?"

"There are protections against encrotacnia," Stephen said. "If Your Majesty wishes, and can provide me with a scriftorium, I can discover them, I'm certain."

"You will have access to whatever this kingdom has," the queen assured him. "Now, tell me. Do you see anything of Hansa in all of this?"

"Hansa, my queen?" Stephen asked, confused. "Nothing. Desmond Spendlove was from Virgenya. The Sefry owe allegiance to no nation."

"You see no involvement of Liery, either?" she asked, very softly.

"No, Majesty."

"Did you know the king was dead, as well? Did they speak of him?"

Stephen found his mouth was open, with nothing coming out.

"Well?"

"No, Majesty," he managed. "No mention was ever made of the king."

"It must have happened on the same day," the queen said. "The rider just reached us with the news."

"I . . . my deepest condolences, Your Majesty."

"Thank you." Her brow wrinkled and smoothed. She seemed to start to say something, think better of it, and start again. "Much strange happened at Cal Azroth. Much out of the ordinary. Your account has been passed to me, but I would like to hear it again, and your thoughts on the matter."

Stephen told her what he could of the greffyn and the Briar King, of Aspar White's adventures and his own. He knew it all sounded incredible, but his saint-blessed memory was clear. He could not, like an ordinary person, retreat to a dreamworld where the events themselves had been a dream, where the Briar King and the greffyn had been born of terror and exhaustion, blood haze or wine.

"The accounts are mixed," he concluded. "The greffyn was in the habit of following the Sefry, I cannot say why. I don't think they commanded it, or it them, merely that they traveled untouched by it, as did the monks. The Briar King himself was wakened and summoned by the horn, I think, and it seems he has returned to the King's Forest."

"His trail is clear enough," the duchess remarked. "My riders found a path of dark thorns marching to the edge of the forest."

"The same thorns that destroyed Cal Azroth," the queen said. "You cannot say why he came?"

Stephen winced. "As you know, I returned yesterday to Cal Azroth with knights in the service of her ladyship the duchess. The growth of the vines, at least, has subsided; they creep still, but at slower pace. As for the Briar King—and I do believe that is who we saw—the Briar King is very ancient, perhaps one of the old gods the saints were said to have defeated. He came to Cal Azroth because I summoned him there with his horn. The sedos provided the summoning, and the feinglest sacred to Fiussa became the door of his manifestation.

"Whatever he was before, he is flesh now, and walks the world."

"You haven't answered my question," the queen replied.

"I do not know the answer, Majesty," Stephen said quietly. "But if the accounts we have are to be trusted, his waking forebodes evil times." He paused. "Very evil times. Perhaps the end of everything we know."

"So I have heard. And yet the world still exists."

"Your pardon, Majesty," Stephen replied. "That may be so, but I feel as if an hourglass has been turned, and when the sands run out . . ." He shook his head. He had nothing to finish the thought with.

The queen seemed somehow to understand, and did not press him. And yet her silence itself was a weight.

"Majesty," he began again, "I threatened blowing the horn only to stop Desmond Spendlove completing his sorcery." He paused, and guilt as keen as grief nearly stoppered his throat. "I did not intend to sound it, nor did I believe anything would result if I did so. I am to blame for whatever follows."

The queen shrugged. "If Sir Neil had turned changeling, I would now be dead. That threat is ended, thanks to you. I only wish you had acted earlier, for my daughters would also be alive. As to the apparition we all saw, despite your instincts, there seemed no malice in his actions. He spared me, certainly. He left as soon as he appeared, and the destruction of Cal Azroth, I think, was just a by-blow of his coming. Keep your guilt, Stephen Darige, for when it has proven itself justified."

Stephen bowed. "I will try to learn what I have done and right it, Majesty. I once thought I knew quite a lot. Now I think I know very little indeed." He looked the queen directly in the eye. "But I must repeat. I speak from something deeper than instinct. Our troubles are not ended. They have just begun. The world is changed. Can you not feel it, Majesty?"

"Two of my children are dead," the queen said, her eyes focused on some middle distance. "My husband, the emperor of Crotheny, is dead. My best friend is dead." Her gaze suddenly stabbed into Stephen's. "The world *I* knew is not changed. It is dead."

Stephen's audience was ended soon after that, and he took the opportunity to wander through the airy halls of Glenchest to the hospital that had been set up in one of the lesser-used chambers. A young knight from Liery lay there, one Neil MeqVren. His deep, regular breaths proved him asleep, taking the rest his body needed to recover from the insults dealt it.

Stephen's own bed had been empty for two days; the wound in his arm still ached and leaked frequently, but the fever in it had gone quickly.

The third bed—Aspar's—was empty, of course.

Outside he heard voices. He peeked through the door to the terrace beyond, where two figures shared a bench between a pair of potted orange trees, gazing on the rich, rolling hills of Loiyes.

He'd turned, deciding not to interrupt, when a gruff voice called his name.

"What are you skulking about for, Cape Chavel Darige? Join us in the sun."

"Yes, do," Winna—who sat next to Aspar—said. Stephen noticed the two were holding hands.

"You've told me often how poor my skulking is," Stephen replied. "I thought to improve it."

"By practice? Is there no book on the subject?"

"Indeed," Stephen said. "It's contained in a certain bestiary I know." *Observations on the Quaint and Vulgar Behaviors of the Common Holter-Beast.*

Stephen suppressed a smile. "But sometimes," he went on, "sometimes, I've learned, a bit of practice is necessary."

"Yah," Aspar allowed. "Sometimes, I suppose. And sometimes—not often, mind you—the learning of books may have its use."

Stephen ambled out onto the white stone of the terrace. The air was edged with a promise of autumn, and to prove it the apple trees out on the fields wore golden crowns.

Winna rose, patted Aspar's hand, and kissed him lightly on the lips. "I'll return," she said. "I'm off to see what I can garner from the kitchen. I'll bring us back a picnic."

"No pickled lark's tongue or gilded cockatrice balls," Aspar grunted. "Look in the servant's larder and see if you can find some honest cheese."

When she had gone, Aspar glowered at Stephen. "What are you grinning about?"

"You blushed. When she kissed you."

"Sceat. It's the sun, is all."

"She's good for you, I think. She improves your disposition considerably."

"It never needed improving."

"So the old rooster said before ending in the pot," Stephen replied.

"Huh," Aspar grunted, apparently at a loss for a protracted defense.

Stephen took a seat on another bench, and a quiet grew between them, until Aspar cleared his throat.

"Why am I alive?" he asked. "The medicine Mother Gastya gave me could never have been that potent, and it was gone, besides."

"True," Stephen replied. "I'd hoped you would remember. Don't you?"

Aspar looked off toward the King's Forest. "*He* did it, didn't he?"

"I think so. Don't ask me why."

"You've no fine, scholarly words to explain it, then? The Briar King was supposed to come and kill us all, yah?"

"He might yet. He left us because he had other things to do, and I suspect we will not like what those things are." He shrugged. "He took the poison from you. He did not close your wounds or stop your blood; that was for us to do, and still you nearly went to pale." Stephen lifted his hands. "Perhaps he thought you a creature of his kingdom. Perhaps you are—you certainly smell like one. A crippled boar, a mangy bear. You might be mistaken for such a thing."

Aspar stared at him for a long moment.

"I only remember that when he touched me I felt something, something I haven't known since I was a child. It was . . ." He frowned. "Sceat, I haven't the words." He waved his hands, dismissing the entire matter. He was silent for long time, and Stephen began to wish Winna would hurry her return. She had a way of easing things.

But Aspar spoke, without looking at him.

"I've a sense it's a lucky thing I met you, Cape Chavel Darige," he said.

Stephen blinked back an unexpected moistness in his eye.

On the Very Strange and Subtle Dispositions of the Holter-Beast, he composed, in his head. *Though irascible in the extreme, it must be admitted the beast has not only a talent for annoyance, but beneath its tough and leathersome skin, something that resembles, in many respects, a human heart.*

"*Now* what are you grinning at?" Aspar asked.

Stephen realized he *was* smiling. "Nothing," he replied. "Something I read, once."

∘　∘　∘

When Cazio stepped into the small circle of firelight, Anne flinched involuntarily.

Z'Acatto clucked his tongue. "No need to worry, young casnara," he said. "We're well away from those devils."

"At least for the time being," Cazio corrected. "If they are as persistent in the hunt as in leaving life, we shall see them again."

"Don't worry the ladies with such talk," z'Acatto growled. "We have eluded them for the time being, of that we can be sure. A hundred crooked leagues we have put between them and us, and never leaving any sign." He looked up significantly at the younger man. "Unless you did so tonight."

"I was a ghost," Cazio replied. "A shadow entered the Inn of the Lisping Boar, a shadow left it."

"Left it the heavier, I hope," z'Acatto said hopefully, eyeing the sack Cazio had slung casually over one shoulder.

"Heavier, yes. But this is your sort of work, old man. I'm no thief, by trade."

"You'll do as an amateur," the swordsmaster said. "What've you got there?"

Anne found her own stomach rumbling. The countryside offered little in the way of sustenance, and avoiding anyone who might describe them to pursuers meant they couldn't beg the hospitality of strangers, though z'Acatto had assured them that hospitality was lacking in the poor and rustic province of Curhavia. Whatever the truth, the four of them had eaten only moldy bread the day before, and not much of that.

"Tonight we feast," Cazio said. He proceeded to produce a joint of ham, a spit-roasted hen, a full loaf of crusty brown bread, a small amphora of olive oil, and two black bottles of wine. Anne watched this unloading hungrily, but when she glanced at Austra she saw something that more resembled worship, which was irritating. Cazio was made of better stuff than she had first supposed, true, and she and Austra doubtless owed him their lives, but there was no reason to be silly.

"This is the wrong year," z'Acatto complained.

"Ghosts drink what they can find," Cazio replied. "I'm sure this will do."

Z'Acatto snatched one of the bottles, took a swallow, and swirled it about in his mouth.

"Hardly better than vinegar," he said. Nevertheless, he took another long drink of it.

They ate with no thought to conversation. It was only later, when most of the wine was gone, that speech resumed.

"In three days we'll reach the coast," Cazio said. "I've no doubt we can find the two of you passage there to someplace safe. Your home, perhaps."

"You've been most kind," Anne said.

"You can't just put us on a ship, two women alone," Austra protested. "What if the Hanzish knights should find us at sea?"

"I'd be more worried about the sailors," z'Acatto said. "They're the more known and obvious danger."

"Well, go with them, then," Cazio said. "Me, I'm returning to my house in Avella and pretending I never saw a knight who wouldn't die."

"Anne's father will reward you," Austra blurted.

"Austra, hush," Anne said. "Casnars da Chiovattio and z'Acatto have done more than we could ever repay them for already."

"A gentleman does not require payment for saving young ladies in need," Cazio pointed out.

"But a gentleman without funds can't pay off the lien on his property," z'Acatto said, "even if certain legal complications have vanished, which cannot be taken for granted."

Cazio looked pained. "Must you trouble me with such mundane matters?" he asked. But he turned to Anne. "Who *is* your father, by the by?"

Anne hesitated. "A wealthy man," she said.

"From what country?"

"The empire of Crotheny."

"That's a long journey," Cazio noticed.

"Hah!" z'Acatto shouted. "You don't even know where it is! You've no idea! To you, z'Irbina is the end of the world."

"I am content in Vitellio, if that's what you mean," Cazio said. "I've my father's estates to win back."

"You'll pardon him, casnaras," z'Acatto said. "The experience with your Hanzish knights has taught Cazio here a certain reluctance when it comes to things foreign. You see, in Avella, he can fancy himself a great swordsmaster. In the wider world, he might find himself proven wrong."

Cazio looked stung. "That is purest slander," he said, "and you know it."

"I know what I see. Dessrata is deeds, not words."

"And you've told me on many occasions that I am no dessrator," Cazio replied.

"And, on occasion, I tend toward pessimism," z'Acatto murmured.

"Meaning?" Cazio's eyebrows leapt in surprise.

"Meaning there might be hope for you," z'Acatto said. He wagged the wine bottle at his student. "Might."

"So you admit—!"

"I admit nothing!"

"You drunken old fool, I—"

They argued on, but Anne knew the battle was won. She and Austra would have their escort back to Crotheny.

She thought again of her visions, of the thing she had done to the Hanzish knight, and wished everything in the world was as simple as Cazio. For her, the world would never be simple again.

CHAPTER SIXTEEN

THE EMPEROR SITS

THE EMPEROR OF CROTHENY counted to three and then clapped his hands in delight as Hound Hat produced a partridge from what appeared to be thin air.

"Most excellent, Sire!" the Sefry said. "And now I shall produce a fire, if to you I might implore, please this time to count to four."

Muriele glanced hard at the Sefry and then more gently at her son. "Charles," she said. "It is time to hold court."

Charles looked at her, his face working. "Mother," he whispered, "I can't count to four. What am I to do?"

"Charles," she said, her voice a bit more insistent. "It is time for court. You must concentrate and be king."

"But Father is king."

"Your father is away. In his place, you must be king. Do you understand?"

He must have heard the frustration in her voice, for his face fell. Charles didn't always understand words, but at times he could be surprisingly sensitive to mood.

"How do I do that, Mother? How do I be king?"

She patted his hand. "I will teach you. Some men are going to come in, in a moment. You will know some of them. Your uncle Fail de Liery, for instance."

"Uncle Fail?"

"Yes. I will talk to them, and you will remain silent. If you do this, then afterwards you can have fried apples and cream, and play games on the lawn."

"I don't know that I want to go to the lawn," Charles replied dubiously.

"Then you can do whatever you wish. But you must be silent while I talk to these men, unless I look at you. If I look at you, then you are to say, 'That is my command.' Only that, and nothing more. Can you do that?"

"That is how a king behaves?"

"It is *exactly* how a king behaves."

Charles nodded earnestly. "That is my command," he practiced.

Muriele flinched, for in that instant he sounded almost exactly like her dead William. Charles must have listened more than she'd thought, the few times he had been to court.

"Very well." She started to nod at the Royal Footguard, but paused, briefly, to glance at Sir Neil, who stood stiffly a few feet from her.

"Sir Neil?" she asked. "Are you fit for this?"

Sir Neil turned his dark, hollowed eyes to her. "I can serve, Your Majesty," he said.

She took a deep breath. "Come close, Sir Neil," she said.

He did so, kneeling before her.

"Rise, and sit with me."

The young knight with the old eyes did as he was told, taking a seat on the armless chair to the left of her own.

"Sir Neil," she said softly, "I need you with me. With Erren gone, I need all of you here. Are you here?"

"I am with you, Majesty," Neil replied. "I will not fail you again."

"You have never failed me, Sir Neil," she said. "How can you think you did? I owe you my life more than twice. No other man in the kingdom could have preserved me at Cal Azroth, and yet you did."

Neil did not answer, but his lips tightened, and she saw the doubt.

"I know you loved my daughter," she said softly. "And no, Erren never told me. I never saw it on your face, either, but I saw it in Fastia's.

"Sir Neil, we do not lead lives aimed toward happiness, here near the throne. We lead the lives we are given, and we do as best we can. My daughter had little happiness in her life. I watched her wither from a joyful maid to a bitter old woman in the space of a few years. You brought happiness and hope back to her, before her end. I could not have asked a better service of you."

"You could have asked me to save her," he said bitterly.

"That was not your charge," Muriele said. "Your duty was to me. That duty you discharged. Sir Neil, you are my one true knight."

"I do not feel worthy of that, Majesty."

"I do not care what you feel, Sir Neil," she said, letting anger creep into her voice. "When this court begins, look around you. You will see Praifec Hespero, a man of ambition and influence. You will see Lady Gramme, and next to her my husband's bastard, and you will notice a keen glint of avarice in her eyes. You will see twice five nobles who believe this is an opportune time to substitute their fat bottoms for my son's on the throne. You will see my own family and your old companions from Liery, spoiling for a war with us, wondering if perhaps it isn't time that Crotheny returned to a Lierish patrimony. And always there is Hansa, building her armies, weaving her plots against us.

"Who among them killed my husband? It could have been any of them. He was feathered with Lierish arrows, but that is a most transparent ploy. Someone here killed him, Sir Neil, and my daughters, and Prince Robert. Someone in this very court, but who? Here in Eslen you will see nothing but my enemies, Sir Neil, and all I have between them and me is you. So I do not care what you think your shortcomings are. I do not care how much you grieve, for I swear to you it is no tenth of what I feel. But I will command you, as your queen and the mother of your king, that you *will* protect me, keeping your senses sharp and your wits about you. With you, I may last a few months at this game. Without you, I will not survive the day."

He bowed his head, and then raised it, and at last she recognized something of the young man she had first seen praying in the chapel of Saint Lier.

"I am here, Majesty," he said, firmly this time. "I am with you."

"Good. That is fortunate."

"Majesty? May I ask a question?"

"Yes."

"Will it be war with Liery?"

She measured that a moment before answering. "If it is," she asked, "can you kill those you once fought beside?"

He frowned as if he did not understand the question. "Of course, Majesty. I will kill whoever needs killing, for you. I want to know only so I can better prepare the guard."

"The war with Liery is the least of my concerns," she said. "In me they see a way to eventually have this throne without a fight, and they have Saltmark and Hansa to concern them. I need only suggest that in me they have a powerful influence on the throne; let one of my cousins court me, perhaps. The facts surrounding my husband's death and the Sorrovian ships we sank can be quietly forgotten, and they will be. I do not know what William and Robert were about, and probably never will, but I can sweep up the mess. It is Hansa that concerns me, and daggers in my own house."

"Yes, Majesty," Neil said.

She inclined her head. "Now, as I said, you must watch what I cannot. Hespero will be admitted first, and I will make him my prime minister."

Sir Neil raised his brow. "I thought you did not trust him."

"Not in the least, but he must not know that. He must be lulled and coddled. He must be watched, and that were easiest if he is always at my right hand. After I have spoken to him, then the sea lords will come, and we will make our peace with them."

"Yes, Your Majesty."

"Yes." She drew a deep breath.

"That is my command!" Charles shouted experimentally.

Neil bowed to Charles. "Yes, Your Majesty," he told the emperor. "As in all things, I am your servant."

Charles grinned, a boyish, silly grin. "This will amuse," he said.

EPILOGUE

A FINAL CURSE

As THE LAST ECHOES of her footsteps were eaten by the hungry darkness, Muriele Dare perceived a low moan, like talons scratching across the skin of a kettle drum. Something unseen shifted, and though no light appeared in the darkness, she felt eyes like two hot coals pressed against her flesh.

"The stink of woman," a voice graveled. "Many long centuries since I have scented that." A soft clicking, then, and the voice continued thoughtfully. "You are not her. Like, but not."

Muriele's nose twitched at a resiny scent that censed the chamber.

"Are you what this man says you are?" she asked. "Are you a Skaslos?"

"Am I, was I, will I." The words seemed to creep through the air like centipedes. "How come you here if you do not know me?"

"I found a key in my husband's chambers. I inquired about it. Qex-qaneh, answer my question."

"My name," the Kept said. It sounded like an imprecation. "I have forgotten much of what I was. But yes, I was once called that."

"You've been here for two thousand years?"

"I remember years no more than I remember the moon." Another scraping in the darkness. "I mislike your scent."

"I care not what you like," Muriele told him.

"Then what care you for? Why do you disturb me?"

"Your race had knowledge of things mine does not."

"To make little of much, yes."

"Tell me—can you see things unseen? Do you know who killed my daughters and my husband? Can you tell me if my youngest daughter still lives?"

"I see," the Kept replied. "I see a smoke spreading in the wind. I see the cloak of death brushing the world. I see a sickle in you, eager to reap."

"Who murdered my daughters?" Muriele demanded.

"*Kissssss,*" he wheezed. "Their shapes are too vague. They stand behind the pall." He raised his voice to a shout. "Queen! You have a knife in you, eager for poking and twisting."

"Is he lying?" Muriele asked the Keeper.

"He cannot lie," the ancient Sefry told her.

"What did you tell my husband?" Muriele asked.

"To be death or die. I see which he chose. Would you be death, you who stink of motherhood?"

"I would see the murderers of my family dead."

"*Sssssssssssss!* That is a simpler matter than seeing who did the deed," the Kept said. "I can tell you a curse. It is a most terrible curse, the most terrible I remember."

"Majesty," the Keeper said. "Do not listen to him."

She ignored the old man. "I can curse those who took my children?"

"Oh, easily. Very easily."

"Tell me, then."

"Majesty—" the Keeper began again, but Muriele cut him off.

"You have warned me thrice, Keeper," she said. "Do not warn me again, or I shall have the drums of your ears broken. How then will you delight in your solitary music?"

The Sefry fell momentarily silent at the threat. "As you say, Majesty," he finally submitted.

"Await me where you cannot hear this conversation. I will call for you when I need guidance."

"Yes, Majesty."

She heard him shuffle away.

"A daughter of the queen are you," the Kept said, once the Sefry was gone.

"I *am* the queen," Muriele replied. "Tell me of this curse."

"I will tell you a thing to write, and you will scrive it on a lead tissue and place it in a certain sarcophagus you will find beneath the horz in the city of the dead. Who sleeps there will take your message to one who knows well how to curse."

Muriele considered that a moment, remembering the breath leaving Fastia.

"Tell me what to write," she said.

The candles in the chapel flickered as if some unseen wing beat above them. Sacritor Hohn looked around nervously, feeling as if he had just awoken from a night terror, though he hadn't been asleep.

Nothing seemed amiss. The chapel was quiet.

He had almost soothed himself when the screaming began. It came from the chamber of healing, where the stranger was. Hastily the sacritor made his way there, knowing what it must mean.

Hard men in dark clothing had brought the stranger weeks ago. Sacritor Hohn did not know who he was, but he was certainly a man of importance by his dress and the way he was attended. He'd been wounded near the heart, and his medicines and sacaums of healing had been able to do little but slow the rate of his demise. Only this morning, he had taken a turn for the worse. The only surprise was that he still had the strength to scream.

When the sacritor drew back the curtain, however, the stranger was not screaming, nor was he dead. He stood naked, staring at some unseen horizon of horror.

"My lord," the sacritor said. "You've woken."

"Indeed?" the man whispered. "I feel I dream. A dream most foul."

"The saint has blessed you," the sacritor said, making a sign. "I never thought to see you stand. Only this morning, your soul was slipping away."

The man looked at him, and something in his eyes sent worms up the sacritor's back. "Where am I?" he asked.

"The chapel of Saint Loy at Copenwis," the sacritor answered.

"Where are my men?"

"Quartered in the town, I think. One stands guard outside. Shall I fetch him?"

"In a moment. A moment. My brother is dead?"

"I do not know your brother, my lord."

"Do you know me?"

"I do not, my lord."

The stranger nodded and stroked his beard. "I think I do not, either," he said.

Sacritor Hohn wasn't sure he understood. "Have you lost your memory?" he asked. He'd heard of that. "Sometimes the shock of a wound—"

"No, I don't mean that. I remember all too well. Fetch my clothes."

"My lord, you cannot travel yet."

"I think that I can." Something in the man's eyes told Sacritor Hohn he ought not to argue. And after all, he had just seen a miracle. If the saints had saved a man from death, they could as easily restore him to perfect health.

Of course, the wound was still there . . .

"As you wish, my lord," he said, bowing. "But before you go, shall I shrive you? Shall I perform lustration?"

The man stared at him, and his lips parted. He made a sound as if he were choking, and another.

It was only after a third that the sacritor understood that he was hearing laughter more bitter than the harshest sea.

ACKNOWLEDGMENTS

Thanks to the following for reading and commenting on the manuscript at various stages of development: T. Karen Anderson, Kris Boldis, Ken Carelton, Veronica Chapman, Dave Gross, Professor Lanelle Keyes, Nancy Ridout Landrum, and Brian Smith.

A book is made by many hands. I often think they ought to include credits, like a movie.

At Del Rey, I have a lot of people to thank. Betsy Mitchell, the editor in chief and a real booster for *The Briar King* from the beginning of her tenure. Nancy Delia, the managing editor, who kept the trains on their tracks. Lisa Collins, the copy editor, who had to deal not only with my spelling mistakes in English, but in several imaginary languages. Denise Fitzer, the editorial assistant—without a competent editorial assistant, things can break down very quickly. Things did not break down. And of course, Steve Saffel, my editor, who has believed in this book and fought hard for it for years. Finally, thanks to Kuo-Yu Liang for years of support as publisher, friend, and drinking buddy.

I'd like to thank the production manager, Barbara Greenberg, Eric Peterson for the cover painting, David Stevenson for the cover design and a good deal of back-and-forth with me making certain the maps were right. Map artist Kirk Caldwell for what are truly works of art, publicity guru Colleen Lindsay, and online-marketing sorceress Christine Cabello.

A big thanks to Dana Hayward for expending her own time and effort to make a pre-proof proof, to get the word out as early as possible.

Beyond that I'd like to thank Elizabeth B. Vega for her help with the soundtrack (you'll see more what I mean in book two) and the Savannah Fencing Club for moral support. This book also seems to have supporters farther afield than my immediate circle of friends, for which I'm grateful—David Weller, Chuck Errig, Lisa Congelosi, Rebeccah Fitting, David Phethean, Ron Schoop, and David Underwood.

315973

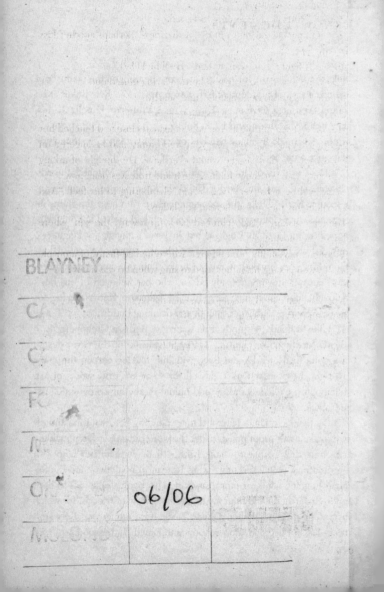

BLAYNEY		
C		
C		
FC		
I		
O	06/06	
MOLONG		